Edgar Allan Poe

TALES OF MYSTERY AND
IMAGINATION

TALES OF MYSTERY AND IMAGINATION

By

EDGAR ALLAN POE

ODHAMS PRESS LIMITED
LONG ACRE - LONDON, W.C.2

Printed in Great Britain

the editor of various periodicals and proceeded to publish his short stories and poems. He a poet he will be remembered for "The Raven," "To Helen," "Annabel Lee," and "The Bells." He died in 1849.

It is as the author of these "Tales of Mystery and Imagination" that Poe is most widely known, and it is a tribute to the mastery of the difficult medium of the short story that many of these tales, some of which are the best in the language, lose nothing on re-reading.

INTRODUCTION

WEIRD tales of the supernatural, of reincarnations and of ghostly manifestations have been the legacy of practically every nation's literature, and have been in fashion mostly when society reached its higher levels of advancement. Possibly it is because, as civilisation progresses, people have to content themselves more and more with make-believe thrills retailed at second hand to satisfy the perfectly natural and instinctive craving for excitement. It is in fact part of our nature to cultivate excitement, and there is much to be said for choosing arm-chair adventure in preference to the real article—to have our flesh creep and our hair stand on end, although realizing all the time that we are perfectly safe and out of danger.

As a generation we are particularly attracted to sensational literature. We revive Frankenstein, and Dracula, produce ghoulish films of mummies and relish the escapades of monster apes. And having "supp'd full with horrors" we have come to the conclusion that the days of red-ink melodrama, of murders in the Barn and of simple, undisguised blood and thunder are over; and that, as connoisseurs, we can only be satisfied with first-class artistry and technique.

That is why Edgar Allan Poe's "Tales of Mystery and Imagination" has achieved the status of a classic. Their artistry is unsurpassed. The feeling of mystery and suspense; the wild imagery; the weird unnatural beauty of dream visions; the anticipation and the reality of fear—all these have never been more finely expressed. Even in these days of enlightened experience, the B.B.C. uttered a word of warning when broadcasting "The Fall of the House of Usher," just in case listeners might find Poe's recipe for horror too strong meat late at night.

A deep-seated melancholy, extreme nervous tension, and a feverish morbidity were the key-notes to Poe's short and reckless career. Born at Boston, Mass., in 1809, he was educated in this country at Stoke Newington. Returning to America, he spent a short time at a university and then in the army as a cadet. Subsequently he became the editor of various periodicals and proceeded to publish his short stories and poems. As a poet he will be remembered for "The Raven," "To Helen," "Annabel Lee" and "The Bells." He died in 1849.

It is as the author of these "Tales of Mystery and Imagination" that Poe is most widely known, and it is a tribute to his mastery of the difficult medium of the short story that people have such different views on which are the best in this remarkable collection. Some readers prefer the pure and undiluted excitement of "The Pit and the Pendulum," others the unearthly horror of "The Fall of the House of Usher"; to some "The Murders in the Rue Morgue" is a first favourite; others again will vote for "The Gold Bug," or "The Black Cat," or the poetic parables, or even the stories of coffins and premature burials.

It may well be that Poe's greatest title to immortality is his invention of the detective story—a point which few critics have emphasized, but which considering the subsequent history and popularity of crime and mystery stories, cannot be disregarded by any student of literature. In "The Murders in the Rue Morgue," "The Purloined Letter" and "The Mystery of Marie Roget," we have the first examples ever penned of the pure detective story, containing the solution of a problem by an amateur expert who beats the police at their own game through his skill in sifting the evidence and his superior logic. Poe indeed set the fashion, introducing numerous "tricks of the trade" which have since been imitated and adapted by most writers of detective fiction. As Miss Dorothy Sayers has said, "taking it all round 'The Murders in the Rue Morgue' constitutes in itself almost a complete manual of detective theory and practice."

These three cases are narrated by a hero-worshipping Dr. Watson, and the detective Dupin is certainly the parent of Sherlock Holmes. Even in such details as personal mannerisms there is a close resemblance between Dupin and Conan Doyle's famous detective.

Particular interest attaches to "The Mystery of Marie Roget," as this story was based on the disappearance in New York of a Cecilia Rogers, and although the conclusions of Poe's arguments could not be published in the paper, the confession years later of the guilty parties proved that his reasoning was perfectly correct.

CONTENTS

CONTENTS

TALES OF MYSTERY AND
IMAGINATION

THE GOLD-BUG

What ho ! what ho ! this fellow is dancing mad !
He hath been bitten by the Tarantula.
—*All in the Wrong.*

MANY years ago I contracted an intimacy with a Mr.
William Legrand. He was of an ancient Huguenot family,
and had once been wealthy ; but a series of misfortunes
had reduced him to want. To avoid the mortification
consequent upon his disasters, he left New Orleans, the
city of his forefathers, and took up his residence at Sullivan's
Island, near Charleston, South Carolina.

This island is a very singular one. It consists of little
else than the sea sand, and is about three miles long. Its
breadth at no point exceeds a quarter of a mile. It is
separated from the mainland by a scarcely perceptible
creek, oozing its way through a wilderness of reeds and
slime, a favourite resort of the marsh-hen. The vegetation,
as might be supposed, is scant, or at least dwarfish. No
trees of magnitude are to be seen. Near the western
extremity, where Fort Moultrie stands, and where are
some miserable frame buildings, tenanted, during summer,
by the fugitives from Charleston dust and fever, may be
found, indeed, the bristly palmetto ; but the whole island,
with the exception of this western point, and a line of hard,
white beach on the sea-coast, is covered with a dense
undergrowth of the sweet myrtle, so much prized by the
horticulturists of England. The shrub here often attains
the height of fifteen or twenty feet, and forms an almost
impenetrable coppice, burdening the air with its fragrance.

In the inmost recesses of this coppice, not far from the
eastern or more remote end of the island, Legrand had

built himself a small hut, which he occupied when I first, by mere accident, made his acquaintance. This soon ripened into friendship—for there was much in the recluse to excite interest and esteem. I found him well educated, with unusual powers of mind, but infested with misanthropy, and subject to perverse moods of alternate enthusiasm and melancholy. He had with him many books, but rarely employed them. His chief amusements were gunning and fishing, or sauntering along the beach and through the myrtles, in quest of shells or entomological specimens ;—his collection of the latter might have been envied by a Swammerdamm. In these excursions he was usually accompanied by an old negro, called Jupiter, who had been manumitted before the reverses of the family, but who could be induced, neither by threats nor by promises, to abandon what he considered his right of attendance upon the footsteps of his young " Massa Will." It is not improbable that the relatives of Legrand, conceiving him to be somewhat unsettled in intellect, had contrived to instil this obstinacy into Jupiter, with a view to the supervision and guardianship of the wanderer.

The winters in the latitude of Sullivan's Island are seldom very severe, and in the fall of the year it is a rare event indeed when a fire is considered necessary. About the middle of October, 18—, there occurred, however, a day of remarkable chilliness. Just before sunset I scrambled my way through the evergreens to the hut of my friend, whom I had not visited for several weeks—my residence being, at that time, in Charleston, a distance of nine miles from the island, while the facilities of passage and re-passage were very far behind those of the present day. Upon reaching the hut I rapped, as was my custom, and getting no reply, sought for the key where I knew it was secreted, unlocked the door and went in. A fine fire was blazing upon the hearth. It was a novelty, and by no means an ungrateful one. I threw off an overcoat, took an arm-chair by the crackling logs, and awaited patiently the arrival of my hosts.

Soon after dark they arrived, and gave me a most cordial welcome. Jupiter, grinning from ear to ear, bustled about to prepare some marsh-hens for supper. Legrand was in one of his fits—how else shall I term them ?—of enthusiasm. He had found an unknown bivalve, forming a new genus, and, more than this, he had hunted down and secured, with Jupiter's assistance, a *scarabæus* which he believed to be totally new, but in respect to which he wished to have my opinion on the morrow.

" And why not to-night ? " I asked, rubbing my hands over the blaze, and wishing the whole tribe of *scarabæi* at the devil.

" Ah, if I had only known you were here ! " said Legrand, " but it's so long since I saw you ; and how could I foresee that you would pay me a visit this very night of all others ? As I was coming home I met Lieutenant G——, from the fort, and, very foolishly, I lent him the bug ; so it will be impossible for you to see it until the morning. Stay here to-night, and I will send Jup down for it at sunrise. It is the loveliest thing in creation ? "

" What ?—sunrise ? "

" Nonsense ! no !—the bug. It is of a brilliant gold colour—about the size of a large hickory-nut—with two jet-black spots near one extremity of the back, and another, somewhat longer, at the other. The *antennæ* are——"

" Dey aint *no* tin in him, Massa Will, I keep a-tellin on you," here interrupted Jupiter ; " de bug is a goole bug, solid, ebery bit of him, inside and all, sep him wing—neber feel half so hebby a bug in my life."

" Well, suppose it is, Jup," replied Legrand, somewhat more earnestly, it seemed to me, than the case demanded, " is that any reason for your letting the birds burn ? The colour "—here he turned to me—" is really almost enough to warrant Jupiter's idea. You never saw a more brilliant metallic lustre than the scales emit—but of this you cannot judge till to-morrow. In the meantime I can give you some idea of the shape." Saying this, he seated himself at a small table, on which were a pen and ink, but no paper. He looked for some in a drawer, but found none.

" Never mind," said he at length, " this will answer ; " and he drew from his waistcoat pocket a scrap of what I took to be very dirty foolscap, and made upon it a rough drawing with the pen. While he did this, I retained my seat by the fire, for I was still chilly. When the design was complete, he handed it to me without rising. As I received it, a loud growl was heard, succeeded by a scratch-ing at the door. Jupiter opened it, and a large Newfoundland, belonging to Legrand, rushed in, leaped upon my shoulders, and loaded me with caresses ; for I had shown him much attention during previous visits. When his gambols were over, I looked at the paper, and, to speak the truth, found myself not a little puzzled at what my friend had depicted.

" Well ! " I said, after contemplating it for some minutes, " this *is* a strange *scarabæus*, I must confess : new to me : never saw anything like it before—unless it was a skull, or a death's-head—which it more nearly resembles than anything else that has come under *my* observation."

" A death's-head ! " echoed Legrand. " Oh—yes— well, it has something of that appearance upon paper, no doubt. The two upper black spots look like eyes, eh ? and the longer one at the bottom like a mouth—and then the shape of the whole is oval."

" Perhaps so," said I ; " but, Legrand, I fear you are no artist. I must wait until I see the beetle itself, if I am to form any idea of its personal appearance."

" Well, I don't know," said he, a little nettled, " I draw tolerably—*should* do it at least—have had good masters, and flatter myself that I am not quite a blockhead."

" But, my dear fellow, you are joking then," said I, " this is a very passable *skull*—indeed, I may say that it is a very *excellent* skull, according to the vulgar notions about such specimens of physiology—and your *scarabæus* must be the queerest *scarabæus* in the world if it resembles it. Why, we may get up a very thrilling bit of superstition upon this hint. I presume you will call the bug *scarabæus caput hominis,* or something of that kind—there are many similar titles in the Natural Histories. But where are the *antennæ* you spoke of ? "

" The *antennæ* ! " said Legrand, who seemed to be getting unaccountably warm upon the subject ; " I am sure you must see the *antennæ*. I made them as distinct as they are in the original insect, and I presume that is sufficient."

" Well, well," I said, " perhaps you have—still I don't see them ; " and I handed him the paper without additional remark, not wishing to ruffle his temper ; but I was much surprised at the turn affairs had taken ; his ill humour puzzled me—and, as for the drawing of the beetle, there were positively *no antennæ* visible, and the whole *did* bear a very close resemblance to the ordinary cuts of a death's-head.

He received the paper very peevishly, and was about to crumple it, apparently to throw it in the fire, when a casual glance at the design seemed suddenly to rivet his attention. In an instant his face grew violently red—in another as excessively pale. For some minutes he continued to scrutinise the drawing minutely where he sat. At length he arose, took a candle from the table, and proceeded to seat himself upon a sea-chest in the farthest corner of the room. Here again he made an anxious examination of the paper, turning it in all directions. He said nothing, however, and his conduct greatly astonished me ; yet I thought it prudent not to exacerbate the growing moodiness of his temper by any comment. Presently he took from his coat pocket a wallet, placed the paper carefully in it, and deposited both in a writing-desk, which he locked. He now grew more composed in his demeanour ; but his original air of enthusiasm had quite disappeared. Yet he seemed not so much sulky as abstracted. As the evening wore away he became more and more absorbed in reverie, from which no sallies of mine could arouse him. It had been my intention to pass the night at the hut, as I had frequently done before, but, seeing my host in this mood, I deemed it proper to take leave. He did not press me to remain, but, as I departed, he shook my hand with even more than his usual cordiality.

It was about a month after this (and during the interval I had seen nothing of Legrand) when I received a visit, at Charleston, from his man, Jupiter. I had never seen the good old negro look so dispirited, and I feared that some serious disaster had befallen my friend.

" Well, Jup," said I, " what is the matter now ?—how is your master ? "

" Why, to speak de troof, massa, him not so berry well as mought be."

" Not well ! I am truly sorry to hear it. What does he complain of ? "

" Dar ! dat's it !—him neber plain of notin—but him bery sick for all dat."

" Very sick, Jupiter !—why didn't you say so at once ! Is he confined to bed ? "

" No, dat he aint !—he aint find nowhar—dat's just

whar de shoe pinch. My mind is got to be berry hebby bout poor Massa Will."

"Jupiter, I should like to understand what it is you are talking about. You say your master is sick. Hasn't he told you what ails him ? "

"Why, massa, taint worf while for to git mad about de matter—Massa Will say noffin at all aint de matter wid him—but den what make him go about looking dis here way, wid he head down and he soldiers up, and as white as a gose ? And den he keep a syphon all de time——"

"Keeps a what, Jupiter ? "

"Keeps a syphon wid de figgurs on de slate—de queerest figgurs I ebber did see. Ise gittin to be skeered, I tell you. Hab for to keep mighty tight eye pon him noovers. Todder day he gib me slip fore de sun up and was gone de whole ob de blessed day. I had a big stick ready cut for to gib him deuced good beating when he did come—but Ise sich a fool dat I hadn't de heart arter all—he look so berry poorly."

"Eh ?—what ?—ah yes !—upon the whole I think you had better not be too severe with the poor fellow—don't flog him, Jupiter—he can't very well stand it—but can you form no idea of what has occasioned this illness, or rather this change of conduct ? Has anything unpleasant happened since I saw you ? "

"No, massa, dey aint bin noffin onpleasant *since* den —'twas *fore* den I'm feared—'twas de berry day you was dare."

"How ? what do you mean ? "

"Why, massa, I mean de bug—dare now."

"The what ? "

"De bug—I'm berry sartain dat Massa Will bin bit somewhere bout de head by dat goole-bug."

"And what cause have you, Jupiter, for such a supposition ? "

"Claws enuff, massa, and mouff too. I nebber did see sich a deuced bug—he kick and he bite ebery ting what cum near him. Massa Will cotch him fuss, but had for to let him go gin mighty quick, I tell you—den was de time he must ha got de bite. I didn't like de look ob de bug mouff, myself, no how, so I wouldn't take hold ob him wid my finger, but I cotch him wid a piece ob paper dat I found. I wrap him up in de paper and stuff piece ob it in he mouff—das was de way."

"And you think, then, that your master was really bitten by the beetle, and that the bite made him sick ? "

"I don't tink noffin about it—I nose it. What make him dream bout de goole so much, if taint cause he bit by de goole-bug ? Ise heerd bout dem goole-bugs fore dis."

"But how do you know he dreams about gold ? "

"How I know ? why, cause he talk about it in he sleep —dat's how I nose."

"Well, Jup, perhaps you are right ; but to what fortunate circumstance am I to attribute the honour of a visit from you to-day ? "

"What de matter, massa ? "

"Did you bring any message from Mr. Legrand ? "

"No, massa, I bring dis here pissel ; " and here Jupiter handed me a note which ran thus :—

"MY DEAR ——, Why have I not seen you for so long a time ? I hope you have not been so foolish as to take offence at any little *brusquerie* of mine ; but no, that is improbable.

"Since I saw you I have had great cause for anxiety. I have something to tell you, yet scarcely know how to tell it, or whether I should tell it at all.

"I have not been quite well for some days past, and poor old Jup annoys me, almost beyond endurance, by his well-meant attentions. Would you believe it ?—he had prepared a huge stick, the other day, with which to chastise me for giving him the slip, and spending the day, *solus*, among the hills on the mainland. I verily believe that my ill looks alone saved me a flogging.

"I have made no addition to my cabinet since we met.

"If you can, in any way, make it convenient, come over with Jupiter. *Do* come. I wish to see you *to-night*, upon business of importance. I assure you that it is of the *highest* importance.—Ever yours,

"WILLIAM LEGRAND."

There was something in the tone of this note which gave me great uneasiness. Its whole style differed materially from that of Legrand. What could he be dreaming of ?

What new crotchet possessed his excitable brain ? What " business of the highest importance " could *he* possibly have to transact ? Jupiter's account of him boded no good. I dreaded lest the continued pressure of misfortune had, at length, fairly unsettled the reason of my friend. Without a moment's hesitation, therefore, I prepared to accompany the negro.

Upon reaching the wharf, I noticed a scythe and three spades, all apparently new, lying in the bottom of the boat in which we were to embark.

" What is the meaning of all this, Jup ? " I inquired.

" Him syfe, massa, and spade."

" Very true ; but what are they doing here ? "

" Him de syfe and de spade what Massa Will sis pon my buying for him in de town, and de debbil's own lot of money I had to gib for em."

" But what, in the name of all that is mysterious, is your ' Massa Will ' going to do with scythes and spades ? "

" Dat's more dan *I* know, and debbil take me if I don't believe 'tis more dan he know, too. But it's all cum ob de bug."

Finding that no satisfaction was to be obtained of Jupiter, whose whole intellect seemed to be absorbed by " de bug," I now stepped into the boat and made sail. With a fair and strong breeze we soon ran into the little cove to the northward of Fort Moultrie, and a walk of some two miles brought us to the hut. It was about three in the afternoon when we arrived. Legrand had been awaiting us in eager expectation. He grasped my hand with a nervous *empressement* which alarmed me and strengthened the suspicions already entertained. His countenance was pale even to ghastliness, and his deep-set eyes glared with unnatural lustre. After some inquiries respecting his health, I asked him, not knowing what better to say, if he had yet obtained the *scarabæus* from Lieutenant G——.

" Oh yes," he replied, colouring violently, " I got it from him the next morning. Nothing should tempt me to part with that *scarabæus*. Do you know that Jupiter is quite right about it ? "

" In what way ? " I asked, with a sad foreboding at heart.

" In supposing it to be a bug of *real gold* ! " He said

this with an air of profound seriousness, and I felt inexpressibly shocked.

" This bug is to make my fortune," he continued, with a triumphant smile, " to reinstate me in my family possessions. Is it any wonder, then, that I prize it ? Since Fortune has thought fit to bestow it upon me, I have only to use it properly and I shall arrive at the gold of which it is the index. Jupiter, bring me that *scarabæus* ! "

" What ! de bug, massa ? I'd rudder not go fer trubble dat bug—you mus git him for your own self." Hereupon Legrand arose, with a grave and stately air, and brought me the beetle from a glass case in which it was enclosed. It was a beautiful *scarabæus*, and, at that time, unknown to naturalists—of course a great prize in a scientific point of view. There were two round black spots near one extremity of the back, and a long one near the other. The scales were exceedingly hard and glossy, with all the appearance of burnished gold. The weight of the insect was very remarkable, and, taking all things into consideration, I could hardly blame Jupiter for his opinion respecting it ; but what to make of Legrand's concordance with that opinion, I could not, for the life of me, tell.

" I sent for you," said he, in a grandiloquent tone, when I had completed my examination of the beetle, " I sent for you, that I might have your counsel and assistance in furthering the views of Fate and of the bug——"

" My dear Legrand," I cried, interrupting him, " you are certainly unwell, and had better use some little precautions. You shall go to bed, and I will remain with you a few days, until you get over this. You are feverish and——"

" Feel my pulse," said he.

I felt it, and, to say the truth, found not the slightest indication of fever.

" But you may be ill and yet have no fever. Allow me this once to prescribe for you. In the first place, go to bed. In the next——"

" You are mistaken," he interposed, " I am as well as I can expect to be under the excitement which I suffer. If you really wish me well, you will relieve this excitement."

" And how is this to be done ? "

" Very easily. Jupiter and myself are going upon an expedition into the hills, upon the mainland, and, in this expedition, we shall need the aid of some person in whom we can confide. You are the only one we can trust. Whether we succeed or fail, the excitement which you now perceive in me will be equally allayed."

" I am anxious to oblige you in any way," I replied ; " but do you mean to say that this infernal beetle has any connection with your expedition into the hills ? "

" It has."

" Then, Legrand, I can become a party to no such absurd proceeding."

" I am sorry—very sorry—for we shall have to try it by ourselves."

" Try it by yourselves ! The man is surely mad !— but stay !—how long do you propose to be absent ? "

" Probably all night. We shall start immediately, and be back, at all events, by sunrise."

" And will you promise me, upon your honour, that when this freak of yours is over, and the bug business (good God !) settled to your satisfaction, you will then return home and follow my advice implicitly, as that of your physician ? "

" Yes ; I promise ; and now let us be off, for we have no time to lose."

With a heavy heart I accompanied my friend. We started about four o'clock—Legrand, Jupiter, the dog, and myself. Jupiter had with him the scythe and spades— the whole of which he insisted upon carrying—more through fear, it seemed to me, of trusting either of the implements within reach of his master, than from any excess of industry or complaisance. His demeanour was dogged in the extreme, and " dat deuced bug " were the sole words which escaped his lips during the journey. For my own part, I had charge of a couple of dark lanterns, while Legrand contented himself with the *scarabæus*, which he carried attached to the end of a bit of whip-cord ; twirling it to and fro, with the air of a conjuror, as he went. When I observed this last, plain evidence of my friend's aberration of mind, I could scarcely refrain from tears. I thought it best, however, to humour his fancy, at least for the present, or until I could adopt some more energetic measures with a chance of success. In the meantime I endeavoured, but all in vain, to sound him in regard to the object of the expedition. Having succeeded in inducing

me to accompany him, he seemed unwilling to hold conversation upon any topic of minor importance, and to all my
questions vouchsafed no other reply than " we shall see ! "

We crossed the creek at the head of the island by means
of a skiff, and, ascending the high grounds on the shore
of the mainland, proceeded in a north-westerly direction,
through a tract of country excessively wild and desolate,
where no trace of a human footstep was to be seen.   Legrand led the way with decision ; pausing only for an
instant, here and there, to consult what appeared to be
certain landmarks of his own contrivance upon a former
occasion.

In this manner we journeyed for about two hours, and
the sun was just setting when we entered a region infinitely
more dreary than any yet seen.   It was a species of table-
land, near the summit of an almost inaccessible hill, densely
wooded from base to pinnacle, and interspersed with huge
crags that appeared to lie loosely upon the soil, and in
many cases were prevented from precipitating themselves
into the valleys below, merely by the support of the trees
against which they reclined.   Deep ravines, in various
directions, gave an air of still sterner solemnity to the
scene.

The natural platform to which we had clambered was
thickly overgrown with brambles, through which we soon
discovered that it would have been impossible to force
our way but for the scythe ; and Jupiter, by direction of
his master, proceeded to clear for us a path to the foot of
an enormously tall tulip-tree, which stood, with some
eight or ten oaks, upon the level, and far surpassed them
all, and all other trees which I had then ever seen, in the
beauty of its foliage and form, in the wide spread of its
branches, and in the general majesty of its appearance.
When we reached this tree, Legrand turned to Jupiter,
and asked him if he thought he could climb it.   The old
man seemed a little staggered by the question, and for
some moments made no reply.   At length he approached
the huge trunk, walked slowly around it, and examined
it with minute attention.   When he had completed his
scrutiny, he merely said—

" Yes, massa, Jup climb any tree he ebber see in he life."

" Then up with you as soon as possible, for it will soon
be too dark to see what we are about."

"How far mus go up, massa ? " inquired Jupiter.

"Get up the main trunk first, and then I will tell you which way to go—and here—stop ! take this beetle with you."

"De bug, Massa Will !—de goole bug ! " cried the negro, drawing back in dismay—" what for mus tote de bug way up de tree ?—damn if I do ! "

"If you are afraid, Jup, a great big negro like you, to take hold of a harmless little dead beetle, why you can carry it up by this string—but, if you do not take it up with you in some way, I shall be under the necessity of breaking your head with this shovel."

"What de matter now, massa ? " said Jup, evidently shamed into compliance ; " always want for to raise fuss wid old nigger. Was only funnin anyhow. *Me* feered de bug ! what I keer for de bug ? " Here he took cautiously hold of the extreme end of the string, and, maintaining the insect as far from his person as circumstances would permit, prepared to ascend the tree.

In youth, the tulip-tree, or *Liriodendron Tulipiferum*, the most magnificent of American foresters, has a trunk peculiarly smooth, and often rises to a great height without lateral branches ; but, in its riper age, the bark becomes gnarled and uneven, while many short limbs make their appearance on the stem. Thus the difficulty of ascension, in the present case, lay more in semblance than in reality. Embracing the huge cylinder, as closely as possible, with his arms and knees, seizing with his hands some projections, and resting his naked toes upon others, Jupiter, after one or two narrow escapes from falling, at length wriggled himself into the first great fork, and seemed to consider the whole business as virtually accomplished. The *risk* of the achievement was, in fact, now over, although the climber was some sixty or seventy feet from the ground.

"Which way mus go now, Massa Will ? " he asked.

"Keep up the largest branch—the one on this side," said Legrand. The negro obeyed him promptly, and apparently with but little trouble ; ascending higher and higher, until no glimpse of his squat figure could be obtained through the dense foliage which enveloped it. Presently his voice was heard in a sort of halloo :

"How much fudder is got for go ? "

"How high up are you ? " asked Legrand.

" Ebber so fur," replied the negro ; " can see de sky fru de top ob de tree."

" Never mind the sky, but attend to what I say. Look down the trunk and count the limbs below you on this side. How many limbs have you passed ? "

" One, two, tree, four, fibe—I done pass fibe big limb, massa, pon dis side."

" Then go one limb higher."

In a few minutes the voice was heard again, announcing that the seventh limb was attained.

" Now, Jup," cried Legrand, evidently much excited, " I want you to work your way out upon that limb as far as you can. If you see anything strange, let me know."

By this time what little doubt I might have entertained of my poor friend's insanity was put finally at rest. I had no alternative but to conclude him stricken with lunacy, and I became seriously anxious about getting him home. While I was pondering upon what was best to be done, Jupiter's voice was again heard.

" Mos feerd for to ventur pon dis limb berry far—'tis dead limb putty much all de way."

" Did you say it was a *dead* limb, Jupiter ? " cried Legrand in a quavering voice.

" Yes, massa, him dead as de door-nail—done up for sartain—done departed dis here life."

" What in the name of heaven shall I do ? " asked Legrand, seemingly in the greatest distress.

" Do ! " said I, glad of an opportunity to interpose a word, " why, come home and go to bed. Come now ! that's a fine fellow. It's getting late, and besides, you remember your promise."

" Jupiter," cried he, without heeding me in the least, " do you hear me ? "

" Yes, Massa Will, hear you ebber so plain."

" Try the wood well, then, with your knife, and see if you think it *very* rotten."

" Him rotten, massa, sure nuff," replied the negro in a few moments, " but not so berry rotten as mought be. Mought ventur out leetle way pon de limb by myself, dat's true."

" By yourself !—what do you mean ? "

" Why, I mean de bug. 'Tis *berry* hebby bug. Spose
B*

I drop him down fuss, and den de limb won't break wid
just de weight ob one nigger."

" You infernal scoundrel ! " cried Legrand, apparently
much relieved, " what do you mean by telling me such
nonsense as that ? As sure as you drop that beetle I'll
break your neck. Look here, Jupiter, do you hear me ? "

" Yes, massa, needn't hollo at poor nigger dat style."

" Well ! now listen !—if you will venture out on the
limb as far as you think safe, and not let go the beetle,
I'll make you a present of a silver dollar as soon as you get
down."

" I'm gwine, Massa Will—deed I is," replied the negro
very promptly—" mos out to the eend now."

" Out to the end ! " here fairly screamed Legrand, " do
you say you are out to the end of that limb ? "

" Soon be to de eend, massa—o-o-o-o-oh ! Lor-gol-a-
marcy ! what is dis here pon de tree ? "

" Well ! " cried Legrand, highly delighted, " what is it ? "

" Why, taint nuffin but a skull—somebody bin lef him
head up de tree, and de crows done gobble ebery bit ob de
meat off."

" A skull, you say !—very well !—how is it fastened to
the limb ?—what holds it on ? "

" Sure nuff, massa ; mus look. Why, dis berry curous
sarcumstance, pon my word—dare's a great big nail in
de skull, what fastens ob it on to de tree."

" Well now, Jupiter, do exactly as I tell you—do you
hear ? "

" Yes, massa."

" Pay attention, then !—find the left eye of the skull.'

" Hum ! hoo ! dat's good ! why, dare aint no eye lef at
all."

" Curse your stupidity ! do you know your right hand
from your left ? "

" Yes, I nose dat—nose all bout dat—'tis my lef hand
what I chops de wood wid."

" To be sure ! you are left-handed ; and your left eye is
on the same side as your left hand. Now, I suppose, you
can find the left eye of the skull, or the place where the
left eye has been. Have you found it ? "

Here was a long pause. At length the negro asked—

" Is de lef eye of de skull pon de same side as de lef
hand of de skull, too ?—cause de skull aint got not a bit

ob a hand at all—nebber mind ! I got de lef eye now—
here de lef eye ! what mus do wid it ? "

" Let the beetle drop through it, as far as 'the string
will reach—but be careful and not let go your hold of the
string."

" All dat done, Massa Will ; mighty easy ting for to put
de bug fru de hole—look out for him dare below ! "

During this colloquy no portion of Jupiter's person
could be seen ; but the beetle, which he had suffered to
descend, was now visible at the end of the string, and
glistened like a globe of burnished gold, in the last rays of
the setting sun, some of which still faintly illumined the
eminence upon which we stood. The *scarabæus* hung
quite clear of any branches, and, if allowed to fall, would
have fallen at our feet. Legrand immediately took the
scythe, and cleared with it a circular space, three or four
yards in diameter, just beneath the insect, and, having
accomplished this, ordered Jupiter to let go the string
and come down from the tree.

Driving a peg, with great nicety, into the ground, at
the precise spot where the beetle fell, my friend now
produced from his pocket a tape-measure. Fastening
one end of this at that point of the trunk of the tree which
was nearest the peg, he unrolled it till it reached the peg,
and thence farther unrolled it, in the direction already
established by the two points of the tree and the peg, for
the distance of fifty feet—Jupiter clearing away the
brambles with the scythe. At the spot thus attained a
second peg was driven, and about this, as a centre, a rude
circle, about four feet in diameter, described. Taking
now a spade himself, and giving one to Jupiter and one
to me, Legrand begged us to set about digging as quickly
as possible.

To speak the truth, I had no especial relish for such
amusement at any time, and, at that particular moment,
would most willingly have declined it ; for the night was
coming on, and I felt much fatigued with the exercise
already taken ; but I saw no mode of escape, and was
fearful of disturbing my poor friend's equanimity by a
refusal. Could I have depended, indeed, upon Jupiter's
aid, I would have had no hesitation in attempting to get
the lunatic home by force ; but I was too well assured of
the old negro's disposition, to hope that he would assist

me, under any circumstances, in a personal contest with his master. I made no doubt that the latter had been infected with some of the innumerable Southern superstitions about money buried, and that his fantasy had received confirmation by the finding of the *scarabæus*, or, perhaps, by Jupiter's obstinacy in maintaining it to be " a bug of real gold." A mind disposed to lunacy would readily be led away by such suggestions—especially if chiming in with favourite preconceived ideas—and then I called to mind the poor fellow's speech about the beetle's being " the index of his fortune." Upon the whole, I was sadly vexed and puzzled, but, at length, I concluded to make a virtue of necessity—to dig with a good will, and thus the sooner to convince the visionary, by ocular demonstration, of the fallacy of the opinions he entertained.

The lanterns having been lit, we all fell to work with a zeal worthy a more rational cause ; and, as the glare fell upon our persons and implements, I could not help thinking how picturesque a group we composed, and how strange and suspicious our labours must have appeared to any interloper who, by chance, might have stumbled upon our whereabouts.

We dug very steadily for two hours. Little was said ; and our chief embarrassment lay in the yelpings of the dog, who took exceeding interest in our proceedings. He at length became so obstreperous that we grew fearful of his giving the alarm to some stragglers in the vicinity— or, rather, this was the apprehension of Legrand—for myself, I should have rejoiced at any interruption which might have enabled me to get the wanderer home. The noise was, at length, very effectually silenced by Jupiter, who, getting out of the hole with a dogged air of deliberation, tied the brute's mouth up with one of his suspenders, and then returned, with a grave chuckle, to his task.

When the time mentioned had expired, we had reached a depth of five feet, and yet no signs of any treasure became manifest. A general pause ensued, and I began to hope that the farce was at an end. Legrand, however, although evidently much disconcerted, wiped his brow thoughtfully and recommenced. We had excavated the entire circle of four feet diameter, and now we slightly enlarged the limit, and went to the farther depth of two feet. Still nothing appeared. The gold-seeker, whom I sincerely pitied, at length clambered from the pit, with the bitterest disappointment imprinted upon every feature, and proceeded, slowly and reluctantly, to put on his coat, which he had thrown off at the beginning of his labour. In the meantime I made no remark. Jupiter, at a signal from his master, began to gather up his tools. This done, and the dog having been unmuzzled, we turned in profound silence towards home.

We had taken, perhaps, a dozen steps in this direction, when, with a loud oath, Legrand strode up to Jupiter, and seized him by the collar. The astonished negro opened his eyes and mouth to the fullest extent, let fall the spades, and fell upon his knees.

" You scoundrel ! " said Legrand, hissing out the syllables from between his clenched teeth—" you infernal black villain !—speak, I tell you !—answer me this instant, without prevarication !—which—which is your left eye ? "

" Oh, my golly, Massa Will ! aint dis here my lef eye for sartain ? " roared the terrified Jupiter, placing his hand upon his *right* organ of vision, and holding it there with a desperate pertinacity, as if in immediate dread of his master's attempt at a gouge.

" I thought so !—I knew it ! hurrah ! " vociferated Legrand, letting the negro go, and executing a series of curvets and caracoles, much to the astonishment of his valet, who, arising from his knees, looked mutely from his master to myself, and then from myself to his master.

" Come ! we must go back," said the latter ; " the game's not up yet ; " and he again led the way to the tulip-tree.

" Jupiter," said he, when we reached its foot, " come here ! Was the skull nailed to the limb with the face outwards, or with the face to the limb ? "

" De face was out, massa, so dat de crows could get at de eyes good, widout any trouble."

" Well, then, was it this eye or that through which you dropped the beetle ? "—here Legrand touched each of Jupiter's eyes.

" Twas dis eye, massa—de lef eye—jis as you tell me," and here it was his right eye that the negro indicated.

" That will do—we must try it again."

Here my friend, about whose madness I now saw, or fancied that I saw, certain indications of method, removed the peg which marked the spot where the beetle fell, to a spot about three inches to the westward of its former position. Taking, now, the tape-measure from the nearest point of the trunk to the peg, as before, and continuing the extension in a straight line to the distance of fifty feet, a spot was indicated, removed, by several yards, from the point at which we had been digging.

Around the new position a circle, somewhat larger than in the former instance, was now described, and we again set to work with the spades. I was dreadfully weary, but, scarcely understanding what had occasioned the change in my thoughts, I felt no longer any great aversion from the labour imposed. I had become most unaccountably interested—nay, even excited. Perhaps there was something, amid all the extravagant demeanour of Legrand —some air of forethought, or of deliberation, which impressed me. I dug eagerly, and now and then caught myself actually looking, with something that very much resembled expectation, for the fancied treasure, the vision of which had demented my unfortunate companion. At a period when such vagaries of thought most fully possessed me, and when we had been at work perhaps an hour and a half, we were again interrupted by the violent howlings of the dog. His uneasiness in the first instance, had been, evidently, but the result of playfulness or caprice, but he now assumed a bitter and serious tone. Upon Jupiter's again attempting to muzzle him, he made furious resistance, and, leaping into the hole, tore up the mould frantically with his claws. In a few seconds he had uncovered a mass of human bones, forming two complete skeletons, intermingled with several buttons of metal, and what appeared to be the dust of decayed woollen. One or two strokes of a spade upturned the blade of a large Spanish knife, and, as we dug farther, three or four loose pieces of gold and silver coin came to light.

At sight of these the joy of Jupiter could scarcely be restrained, but the countenance of his master wore an air of extreme disappointment. He urged us, however, to continue our exertions, and the words were hardly uttered when I stumbled and fell forward, having caught the toe of my boot in a large ring of iron that lay half buried in the loose earth.

We now worked in earnest, and never did I pass ten minutes of more intense excitement. During this interval we had fairly unearthed an oblong chest of wood, which, from its perfect preservation and wonderful hardness, had plainly been subjected to some mineralising process—perhaps that of the bi-chloride of mercury. This box was three feet and a half long, three feet broad, and two and a half feet deep. It was firmly secured by bands of wrought iron, riveted, and forming a kind of open trellis-work over the whole. On each side of the chest, near the top, were three rings of iron—six in all—by means of which a firm hold could be obtained by six persons. Our utmost united endeavours served only to disturb the coffer very slightly in its bed. We at once saw the impossibility of removing so great a weight. Luckily, the sole fastenings of the lid consisted of two sliding bolts. These we drew back—trembling and panting with anxiety. In an instant a treasure of incalculable value lay gleaming before us. As the rays of the lanterns fell within the pit, there flashed upwards a glow and a glare, from a confused heap of gold and of jewels, that absolutely dazzled our eyes.

I shall not pretend to describe the feelings with which I gazed. Amazement was, of course, predominant. Legrand appeared exhausted with excitement, and spoke very few words. Jupiter's countenance wore, for some minutes, as deadly a pallor as it is possible, in the nature of things, for any negro's visage to assume. He seemed stupefied—thunderstricken. Presently he fell upon his knees in the pit, and, burying his naked arms up to the elbows in gold, let them there remain, as if enjoying the luxury of a bath. At length, with a deep sigh, he exclaimed, as if in a soliloquy—

" And dis all come ob de goole-bug ! de putty goole-bug ! de poor little goole-bug, what I boosed in dat sabage kind ob style ! Aint you shamed ob yourself, nigger ?—answer me dat ! "

It became necessary, at last, that I should arouse both master and valet to the expediency of removing the treasure. It was growing late, and it behoved us to make exertion, that we might get everything housed before daylight. It was difficult to say what should be done, and much time

was spent in deliberation—so confused were the ideas of
all. We, finally, lightened the box by removing two-thirds
of its contents, when we were enabled, with some trouble,
to raise it from the hole. The articles taken out were
deposited among the brambles, and the dog left to
guard them, with strict orders from Jupiter, neither,
upon any pretence, to stir from the spot, nor to open his
mouth until our return. We then hurriedly made for
home with the chest ; reaching the hut in safety, but
after excessive toil, at one o'clock in the morning. Worn
out as we were, it was not in human nature to do more
immediately. We rested until two, and had supper ;
starting for the hills immediately afterwards, armed with
three stout sacks, which, by good luck, were upon the
premises. A little before four we arrived at the pit, divided
the remainder of the booty, as equally as might be, among us,
and, leaving the holes unfilled, again set out for the hut, at
which, for the second time, we deposited our golden
burdens, just as the first faint streaks of the dawn gleamed
from over the tree-tops in the east.

We were now thoroughly broken down ; but the intense
excitement of the time denied us repose. After an unquiet
slumber of some three or four hours' duration, we arose,
as if by preconcert, to make examination of our treasure.

The chest had been full to the brim, and we spent the
whole day, and the greater part of the next night, in a
scrutiny of its contents. There had been nothing like
order or arrangement. Everything had been heaped in
promiscuously. Having assorted all with care, we found
ourselves possessed of even vaster wealth than we had at
first supposed. In coin there was rather more than four
hundred and fifty thousand dollars—estimating the value
of the pieces, as accurately as we could, by the tables of
the period. There was not a particle of silver. All was
gold of antique date and of great variety—French, Spanish,
and German money, with a few English guineas, and some
counters, of which we had never seen specimens before.
There were several very large and heavy coins, so worn
that we could make nothing of their inscriptions. There
was no American money. The value of the jewels we
found more difficulty in estimating. There were diamonds
—some of them exceedingly large and fine—a hundred
and ten in all, and not one of them small ; eighteen rubies

of remarkable brilliancy ; three hundred and ten emeralds, all very beautiful ; and twenty-one sapphires, with an opal. These stones had all been broken from their settings and thrown loose in the chest. The settings themselves, which we picked out from among the other gold, appeared to have been beaten up with hammers, as if to prevent identification. Besides all this, there was a vast quantity of solid gold ornaments—nearly two hundred massive finger- and ear-rings ; rich chains—thirty of these, if I remember ; eighty-three very large and heavy crucifixes ; five gold censers of great value ; a prodigious golden punch-bowl, ornamented with richly-chased vine-leaves and Bacchanalian figures ; with two sword handles exquisitely embossed, and many other smaller articles which I cannot recollect. The weight of these valuables exceeded three hundred and fifty pounds avoirdupois ; and in this estimate I have not included one hundred and ninety-seven superb gold watches ; three of the number being worth each five hundred dollars, if one. Many of them were very old, and as time-keepers valueless ; the works having suffered, more or less, from corrosion—but all were richly jewelled and in cases of great worth. We estimated the entire contents of the chest, that night, at a million and a half of dollars ; and upon the subsequent disposal of the trinkets and jewels (a few being retained for our own use), it was found that we had greatly under-valued the treasure.

When, at length, we had concluded our examination, and the intense excitement of the time had, in some measure, subsided, Legrand, who saw that I was dying with impatience for a solution of this most extraordinary riddle, entered into a full detail of all the circumstances connected with it.

" You remember," said he, " the night when I handed you the rough sketch I had made of the *scarabæus*. You recollect also, that I became quite vexed at you for insisting that my drawing resembled a death's-head. When you first made this assertion I thought you were jesting ; but afterwards I called to mind the peculiar spots on the back of the insect, and admitted to myself that your remark had some little foundation in fact. Still, the sneer at my graphic powers irritated me—for I am considered a good artist—and, therefore, when you handed me the scrap of

parchment, I was about to crumple it up and throw it
angrily into the fire."

" The scrap of paper, you mean," said I.

" No ; it had much of the appearance of paper, ana at
first I supposed it to be such, but when I came to draw
upon it, I discovered it, at once, to be a piece of very thin
parchment. It was quite dirty, you remember. Well, as
I was in the very act of crumpling it up, my glance fell
upon the sketch at which you had been looking, and you
may imagine my astonishment when I perceived in fact,
the figure of a death's-head just where, it seemed to me,
I had made the drawing of the beetle. For a moment I
was too much amazed to think with accuracy. I knew
that my design was very different in detail from this—
although there was a certain similarity in general outline.
Presently I took a candle, and seating myself at the other
end of the room, proceeded to scrutinise the parchment
more closely. Upon turning it over, I saw my own sketch
upon the reverse, just as I had made it. My first idea,
now, was mere surprise at the really remarkable similarity
of outline—at the singular coincidence involved in the fact,
that unknown to me, there should have been a skull upon
the other side of the parchment, immediately beneath my
figure of the *scarabæus*, and that this skull, not only in
outline, but in size, should so closely resemble my drawing.
I say the singularity of this coincidence absolutely stupefied
me for a time. This is the usual effect of such coincidences.
The mind struggles to establish a connection—a sequence
of cause and effect—and, being unable to do so, suffers a
species of temporary paralysis. But, when I recovered
from this stupor, there dawned upon me gradually a conviction which startled me even far more than the coincidence. I began distinctly, positively, to remember that
there had been *no* drawing upon the parchment when I
made my sketch of the *scarabæus*. I became perfectly
certain of this ; for I recollected turning up first one side
and then the other, in search of the cleanest spot. Had
the skull been then there, of course I could not have failed
to notice it. Here was indeed a mystery which I felt it
impossible to explain ; but even at that early moment,
there seemed to glimmer, faintly, within the most remote
and secret chambers of my intellect, a glow-worm-like
conception of that truth which last night's adventure

brought to so magnificent a demonstration. I arose at once, and putting the parchment securely away, dismissed all further reflection until I should be alone.

" When you had gone, and when Jupiter was fast asleep, I betook myself to a more methodical investigation of the affair. In the first place I considered the manner in which the parchment had come into my possession. The spot where we discovered the *scarabæus* was on the coast of the mainland, about a mile eastward of the island, and but a short distance above high-water mark. Upon my taking hold of it, it gave me a sharp bite, which caused me to let it drop. Jupiter, with his accustomed caution, before seizing the insect, which had flown towards him, looked about him for a leaf, or something of that nature, by which to take hold of it. It was at this moment that his eyes, and mine also, fell upon the scrap of parchment, which I then supposed to be paper. It was lying half buried in the sand, a corner sticking up. Near the spot where we found it, I observed the remnants of the hull of what appeared to have been a ship's long-boat. The wreck seemed to have been there for a very great while ; for the resemblance to boat timbers could scarcely be traced.

" Well, Jupiter picked up the parchment, wrapped the beetle in it, and gave it to me. Soon afterwards we turned to go home, and on the way met Lieutenant G——. I showed him the insect, and he begged me to let him take it to the fort. Upon my consenting, he thrust it forthwith into his waistcoat pocket, without the parchment in which it had been wrapped, and which I had continued to hold in my hand during his inspection. Perhaps he dreaded my changing my mind, and thought it best to make sure of the prize at once—you know how enthusiastic he is on all subjects connected with Natural History. At the same time, without being conscious of it, I must have deposited the parchment in my own pocket.

" You remember that when I went to the table, for the purpose of making a sketch of the beetle, I found no paper where it was usually kept. I looked in the drawer, and found none there. I searched my pockets, hoping to find an old letter, when my hand fell upon the parchment. I thus detail the precise mode in which it came into my possession ; for the circumstances impressed me with peculiar force.

" No doubt you will think me fanciful—but I had already established a kind of *connection*. I had put together two links of a great chain. There was a boat lying upon a sea-coast, and not far from the boat was a parchment—*not a paper*—with a skull depicted upon it. You will, of course, ask ' where is the connection ? ' I reply, that the skull, or death's-head, is the well-known emblem of the pirate. The flag of the death's-head is hoisted in all engagements.

" I have said that the scrap was parchment, and not paper. Parchment is durable — almost imperishable. Matters of little moment are rarely consigned to parchment ; since, for the mere ordinary purposes of drawing or writing, it is not nearly so well adapted as paper. This reflection suggested some meaning—some relevancy—in the death's-head. I did not fail to observe, also, the *form* of the parchment. Although one of its corners had been, by some accident, destroyed, it could be seen that the original form was oblong. It was just such a slip, indeed, as might have been chosen for a memorandum—for a record of something to be long remembered and carefully preserved."

" But," I interposed, " you say that the skull was *not* upon the parchment when you made the drawing of the beetle. How then do you trace any connection between the boat and the skull—since this latter, according to your own admission, must have been designed (God only know how or by whom) at some period subsequent to your sketching the *scarabæus* ? "

" Ah, hereupon turns the whole mystery ; although the secret, at this point, I had comparatively little difficulty in solving. My steps were sure, and could afford but a single result. I reasoned, for example, thus : When I drew the *scarabæus*, there was no skull apparent upon the parchment. When I had completed the drawing I gave it to you, and observed you narrowly until you returned it. *You*, therefore, did not design the skull, and no one else was present to do it. Then it was not done by human agency. And nevertheless it was done.

" At this stage of my reflections I endeavoured to remember, and *did* remember, with entire distinctness, every incident which occurred about the period in question. The weather was chilly (oh, rare and happy accident !)

and a fire was blazing upon the hearth. I was heated with exercise and sat near the table. You, however, had drawn a chair close to the chimney. Just as I placed the parchment in your hand, and as you were in the act of inspecting it, Wolf, the Newfoundland, entered, and leaped upon your shoulders. With your left hand you caressed him and kept him off, while your right, holding the parchment, was permitted to fall listlessly between your knees, and in close proximity to the fire. At one moment I thought the blaze had caught it, and was about to caution you, but before I could speak you had withdrawn it, and were engaged in its examination. When I considered all these particulars, I doubted not for a moment that *heat* had been the agent in bringing to light, upon the parchment, the skull which I saw designed upon it. You are well aware that chemical preparations exist, and have existed time out of mind, by means of which it is possible to write upon either paper or vellum, so that the characters shall become visible only when subjected to the action of fire. Zaffre, digested in *aqua regia*, and diluted with four times its weight of water, is sometimes employed ; a green tint results. The regulus of cobalt, dissolved in spirit of nitre, gives a red. These colours disappear at longer or shorter intervals after the material written upon cools, but again become apparent upon the reapplication of heat.

" I now scrutinised the death's-head with care. Its outer edges—the edges of the drawing nearest the edge of the vellum—were far more *distinct* than the others. It was clear that the action of the caloric had been imperfect or unequal. I immediately kindled a fire, and subjected every portion of the parchment to a glowing heat. At first, the only effect was the strengthening of the faint lines in the skull ; but, upon persevering in the experiment, there became visible, at the corner of the slip, diagonally opposite to the spot in which the death's-head was delineated, the figure of what I at first supposed to be a goat. A closer scrutiny, however, satisfied me that it was intended for a kid."

" Ha ! ha ! " said I, " to be sure I have no right to laugh at you—a million and a half of money is too serious a matter for mirth—but you are not about to establish a third link in your chain—you will not find any special connection between your pirates and a goat—pirates, you know, have nothing to do with goats ; they appertain to the farming interest."

" But I have just said that the figure was *not* that of a goat."

" Well, a kid, then—pretty much the same thing."

" Pretty much, but not altogether," said Legrand. " You may have heard of one *Captain* Kidd. I at once looked upon the figure of the animal as a kind of punning or hieroglyphical signature. I say signature ; because its position upon the vellum suggested this idea. The death's-head at the corner diagonally opposite, had, in the same manner, the air of a stamp, or seal. But I was sorely put out by the absence of all else—of the body to my imagined instrument—of the text for my context."

" I presume you expected to find a letter between the stamp and the signature."

" Something of that kind. The fact is, I felt irresistibly impressed with a presentiment of some vast good fortune impending. I can scarcely say why. Perhaps, after all, it was rather a desire than an actual belief ; but do you know that Jupiter's silly words, about the bug being of solid gold, had a remarkable effect upon my fancy ? And then the series of accidents and coincidences—these were so *very* extraordinary. Do you observe how mere an accident it was that these events should have occurred upon the *sole* day of all the year in which it has been, or may be, sufficiently cool for fire, and that without the fire, or without the intervention of the dog at the precise moment in which he appeared, I should never have become aware of the death's-head, and so never the possessor of the treasure ? "

" But proceed—I am all impatience."

" Well ; you have heard, of course, the many stories current—the thousand vague rumours afloat, about money buried, somewhere upon the Atlantic coast, by Kidd and his associates. These rumours must have had some foundation in fact. And that the rumours have existed so long and so continuous, could have resulted, it appeared to me, only from the circumstance of the buried treasure still *remaining* entombed. Had Kidd concealed his plunder for a time, and afterwards reclaimed it, the rumours would scarcely have reached us in their present unvarying form. You will observe that the stories told are all about money-seekers, not about money-finders. Had the pirate recovered his money, there the affair would have dropped. It seemed to me that some accident—say the loss of a memorandum indicating its locality—had deprived him of the means of recovering it, and that this accident had become known to his followers, who otherwise might never have heard that treasure had been concealed at all, and who, busying themselves in vain, because unguided attempts, to regain it, had given first birth, and then universal currency, to the reports which are now so common. Have you ever heard of any important treasure being unearthed along the coast ? "

" Never."

" But that Kidd's accumulations were immense, is well known. I took it for granted, therefore, that the earth still held them ; and you will scarcely be surprised when I tell you that I felt a hope, nearly amounting to certainty, that the parchment so strangely found, involved a lost record of the place of deposit."

" But how did you proceed ? "

" I held the vellum again to the fire, after increasing the heat ; but nothing appeared. I now thought it possible that the coating of dirt might have something to do with the failure ; so I carefully rinsed the parchment by pouring warm water over it, and, having done this, I placed it in a tin pan, with the skull downwards, and put the pan upon a furnace of lighted charcoal. In a few minutes, the pan having become thoroughly heated, I removed the slip, and, to my inexpressible joy, found it spotted, in several places, with what appeared to be figures arranged in lines. Again I placed it in the pan, and suffered it to remain another minute. Upon taking it off, the whole was just as you see it now."

Here Legrand, having reheated the parchment, submitted it to my inspection. The following characters were rudely traced, in a red tint, between the death's-head and the goat :—

53‡‡†305))6*;4826)4‡.)4‡);806*;48†8¶60))85;1‡(::‡*8†83(88)5*†;46(;88*96*?;8)*‡(;485);5*†2:*‡(;4956*2(5*—4)8¶8*;4069285);)6†8)4‡‡;1(‡9;48081;8:8‡1;48†85;4)485†528806*81(‡9;48;(88;4(‡?34;48)4‡;161;:188;‡?;

" But," said I, returning him the slip, " I am as much

in the dark as ever. Were all the jewels of Golconda awaiting me upon my solution of this enigma, I am quite sure that I should be unable to earn them."

"And yet," said Legrand, " the solution is by no means so difficult as you might be led to imagine from the first hasty inspection of the characters. These characters, as any one might readily guess, form a cipher—that is to say, they convey a meaning ; but then, from what is known of Kidd, I could not suppose him capable of constructing any of the more abstruse cryptographs. I made up my mind, at once, that this was of a simple species—such, however, as would appear, to the crude intellect of the sailor, absolutely insoluble without the key."

"And you really solved it ? "

"Readily ; I have solved others of an abstruseness ten thousand times greater. Circumstances, and a certain bias of mind, have led me to take interest in such riddles, and it may well be doubted whether human ingenuity can construct an enigma of the kind which human ingenuity may not, by proper application, resolve. In fact, having once established connected and legible characters, I scarcely gave a thought to the mere difficulty of developing their import.

"In the present case—indeed in all cases of secret writing—the first question regards the *language* of the cipher ; for the principles of solution, so far, especially, as the more simple ciphers are concerned, depend upon, and are varied by, the genius of the particular idiom. In general there is no alternative but experiment (directed by probabilities) of every tongue known to him who attempts the solution, until the true one be attained. But, with the cipher now before us, all difficulty was removed by the signature. The pun upon the word ' Kidd ' is appreciable in no other language than the English. But for this consideration I should have begun my attempts with the Spanish and French, as the tongues in which a secret of this kind would most naturally have been written by a pirate of the Spanish main. As it was, I assumed the cryptograph to be English.

"You observe there are no divisions between the words. Had there been divisions, the task would have been comparatively easy. In such case I should have commenced with a collation and analysis of the shorter words, and had a word of a single letter occurred, as is most likely (a or I for example), I should have considered the solution as assured. But, there being no division, my first step was to ascertain the predominant letters, as well as the least frequent. Counting all, I constructed a table, thus :—

" Of the character 8 there are 33.

;	„	26.
4	„	19.
‡)	„	16.
*	.,	13.
5	,,	12.
6	,,	11.
† 1	,,	8.
0	,,	6.
9 2	,,	5.
: 3	,,	4.
?	,,	3.
¶	„	2.
—.	„	1.

" Now, in English, the letter which most frequently occurs is e. Afterwards, the succession runs thus : a o i d h n r s t u y c f g l m w b k p q x z. E predominates so remarkably that an individual sentence of any length is rarely seen, in which it is not the prevailing character.

" Here, then, we have, in the very beginning, the ground-work for something more than a mere guess. The general use which may be made of the table is obvious—but in this particular cipher we shall only very partially require its aid. As our predominant character is 8, we will commence by assuming it as the e of the natural alphabet. To verify the supposition, let us observe if the 8 be seen often in couples—for e is doubled with great frequency in English—in such words, for example, as ' meet,' ' fleet,' ' speed,' ' seen,' ' been,' ' agree,' etc. In the present instance we see it doubled no less than five times, although the cryptograph is brief.

" Let us assume 8, then, as e. Now, of all words in the language ' the ' is the most usual ; let us see, therefore, whether there are not repetitions of any three characters, in the same order of collocation, the last of them being 8. If we discover repetitions of such letters, so arranged, they will most probably represent the word 'the.' Upon inspection, we find no less than seven such arrangements, the characters being ;48. We may therefore assume that ; represents *t*, 4 represents *h*, and 8 represents *e*— the last being now well confirmed. Thus a great step has been taken.

"But, having established a single word, we are enabled to establish a vastly important point; that is to say, several commencements and terminations of other words. Let us refer, for example, to the last instance but one, in which the combination ;48 occurs—not far from the end of the cipher. We know that the ; immediately ensuing is the commencement of a word, and of the six characters succeeding this 'the,' we are cognisant of no less than five. Let us set these characters down, thus, by the letters we know them to represent, leaving a space for the unknown—

t eeth.

"Here we are enabled, at once, to discard the '*th*,' as forming no portion of the word commencing with the first *t*; since, by experiment of the entire alphabet for a letter adapted to the vacancy, we perceive that no word can be formed of which this *th* can be a part. We are thus narrowed into

t ee,

and, going through the alphabet, if necessary, as before, we arrive at the word 'tree,' as the sole possible reading. We thus gain another letter, *r*, represented by (, with the words 'the tree' in juxtaposition.

"Looking beyond these words, for a short distance, we again see the combination ;48, and employ it by way of *termination* to what immediately precedes. We have thus this arrangement—

the tree ;4(‡?34 the,

or, substituting the natural letters, where known, it reads thus—

the tree thr‡?3h the.

"Now if, in place of the unknown characters, we leave blank spaces, or substitute dots, we read thus—

the tree thr...h the,

when the word '*through*' makes itself evident at once.

But this discovery gives us three new letters, *o*, *u*, and *g*, represented by ‡ ? and 3.

"Looking now, narrowly, through the cipher for combinations of known characters, we find, not very far from the beginning, this arrangement—

83(88, or egree,

which, plainly, is the conclusion of the word ' degree,' and gives us another letter, *d*, represented by †.

"Four letters beyond the word ' degree,' we perceive the combination

;(48;88.

"Translating the known characters, and representing the unknown by dots, as before, we read thus—

th rtee,

an arrangement immediately suggestive of the word ' thirteen,' and again furnishing us with two new characters, *i* and *n*, represented by 6 and *.

"Referring, now, to the beginning of the cryptograph, we find the combination

53‡‡†.

"Translating, as before, we obtain

. good,

which assures us that the first letter is *A*, and the first two words are ' A good.'

"It is now time that we arrange our key, as far as discovered, in a tabular form, to avoid confusion. It will stand thus—

5	represents	a
†	,,	d
8	,,	e
3	,,	g
4	,,	h
6	,,	i
*	,,	n
‡	,,	o
(	,,	r
;	,,	t
?	,,	u

"We have, therefore, no less than eleven of the most important letters represented, and it will be unnecessary to proceed with the details of the solution. I have said enough to convince you that ciphers of this nature are readily soluble, and to give you some insight into the *rationale* of their development. But be assured that the specimen before us appertains to the very simplest species of cryptograph. It now only remains to give you the full translation of the characters upon the parchment as unriddled. Here it is :—

" ' A good glass in the bishop's hostel in the devil's seat forty-one degrees and thirteen minutes north-east and by north main branch seventh limb east side shoot from the left eye of the death's-head a bee-line from the tree through the shot fifty feet out.' "

" But," said I, " the enigma seems still in as bad a condition as ever. How is it possible to extort a meaning from all this jargon about ' devil's seats,' ' death's-heads,' and ' bishop's hotels ' ? "

" I confess," replied Legrand, " that the matter still wears a serious aspect, when regarded with a casual glance. My first endeavour was to divide the sentence into the natural division intended by the cryptographist."

" You mean to punctuate it ? "

" Something of that kind."

" But how was it possible to effect this ? "

" I reflected that it had been a *point* with the writer to run his words together without division, so as to increase the difficulty of solution. Now, a not over-acute man, in pursuing such an object, would be nearly certain to overdo the matter. When, in the course of his composition, he arrived at a break in his subject which would naturally require a pause, or a point, he would be exceedingly apt to run his characters, at this place, more than usually close together. If you will observe the MS., in the present instance, you will easily detect five such cases of unusual crowding. Acting upon this hint, I made the division thus :—

" ' A good glass in the Bishop's hostel in the Devil's seat— forty-one degrees and thirteen minutes—north-east and by north—main branch seventh limb east side—shoot from the left eye of the death's-head—a bee-line from the tree through the shot fifty feet out.' "

" Even this division," said I, " leaves me still in the dark."

" It left me also in the dark," replied Legrand, " for a few days ; during which I made diligent inquiry, in the neighbourhood of Sullivan's Island, for any building which went by the name of the ' Bishop's Hotel ' ; for, of course, I dropped the obsolete word ' hostel.' Gaining no information on the subject, I was on the point of extending my sphere of search, and proceeding in a more systematic manner, when, one morning, it entered into my head, quite suddenly, that this ' Bishop's Hostel ' might have some reference to an old family, of the name of Bessop, which, time out of mind, had held possession of an ancient manor-house, about four miles to the northward of the island. I accordingly went over to the plantation, and re-instituted my inquiries among the older negroes of the place. At length one of the most aged of the women said that she had heard of such a place as *Bessop's Castle*, and thought that she could guide me to it, but that it was not a castle, nor a tavern, but a high rock.

" I offered to pay her well for her trouble, and after some demur, she consented to accompany me to the spot. We found it without much difficulty, when, dismissing her, I proceeded to examine the place. The ' castle ' consisted of an irregular assemblage of cliffs and rocks—one of the latter being quite remarkable for its height as well as for its insulated and artificial appearance. I clambered to its apex, and then felt much at a loss as to what should be next done.

" While I was busied in reflection, my eyes fell upon a narrow ledge in the eastern face of the rock, perhaps a yard below the summit upon which I stood. This ledge projected about eighteen inches, and was not more than a foot wide, while a niche in the cliff just above it, gave it a rude resemblance to one of the hollow-backed chairs used by our ancestors. I made no doubt that here was the ' devil's-seat ' alluded to in the MS., and now I seemed to grasp the full secret of the riddle.

" The ' good glass,' I knew, could have reference to nothing but a telescope ; for the word ' glass ' is rarely employed in any other sense by seamen. Now here, I at once saw, was a telescope to be used, and a definite point of view, *admitting no variation*, from which to use it.

Nor did I hesitate to believe that the phrases, ' forty-one degrees and thirteen minutes,' and ' north-east and by north,' were intended as directions for the levelling of the glass. Greatly excited by these discoveries, I hurried home, procured a telescope, and returned to the rock.

" I let myself down to the ledge, and found that it was impossible to retain a seat upon it except in one particular position. This fact confirmed my pre-conceived idea. I proceeded to use the glass. Of course, the ' forty-one degrees and thirteen minutes ' could allude to nothing but elevation above the visible horizon, since the horizontal direction was clearly indicated by the words, ' north-east and by north.' This latter direction I at once established by means of a pocket-compass ; then, pointing the glass as nearly at an angle of forty-one degrees of elevation as I could do it by guess, I moved it cautiously up or down, until my attention was arrested by a circular rift or opening in the foliage of a large tree that overtopped its fellows in the distance. In the centre of this rift I perceived a white spot, but could not, at first, distinguish what it was. Adjusting the focus of the telescope, I again looked, and now made it out to be a human skull.

" Upon this discovery I was so sanguine as to consider the enigma solved ; for the phrase ' main branch, seventh limb, east side,' could refer only to the position of the skull upon the tree, while ' shoot from the left eye of the death's-head ' admitted, also, of but one interpretation, in regard to a search for buried treasure. I perceived that the design was to drop a bullet from the left eye of the skull, and that a bee-line, or, in other words, a straight line, drawn from the nearest point of the trunk through ' the shot ' (or the spot where the bullet fell), and thence extended to a distance of fifty feet, would indicate a definite point—and beneath this point I thought it at least *possible* that a deposit of value lay concealed."

" All this," I said, " is exceedingly clear, and, although ingenious, still simple and explicit. When you left the Bishop's Hotel, what then ? "

" Why, having carefully taken the bearings of the tree, I turned homewards. The instant that I left ' the devil's seat,' however, the circular rift vanished ; nor could I get a glimpse of it afterwards, turn as I would. What seems to me the chief ingenuity in this whole business, is the fact

(for repeated experiment has convinced me it *is* a fact) that the circular opening in question is visible from no other attainable point of view than that afforded by the narrow ledge upon the face of the rock.

" In this expedition to the ' Bishop's Hotel ' I had been attended by Jupiter, who had, no doubt, observed, for some weeks past, the abstraction of my demeanour, and took especial care not to leave me alone. But, on the next day, getting up very early, I contrived to give him the slip, and went into the hills in search of the tree. After much toil I found it. When I came home at night my valet proposed to give me a flogging. With the rest of the adventure I believe you are as well acquainted as myself."

" I suppose," said I, " you missed the spot, in the first attempt at digging, through Jupiter's stupidity in letting the bug fall through the right instead of through the left eye of the skull."

" Precisely. This mistake made a difference of about two inches and a half in the ' shot '—that is to say, in the position of the peg nearest the tree ; and had the treasure been *beneath* the ' shot,' the error would have been of little moment ; but the ' shot,' together with the nearest point of the tree, were merely two points for the establishment of a line of direction ; of course the error, however trivial in the beginning, increased as we proceeded with the line, and by the time we had gone fifty feet, threw us quite off the scent. But for my deep-seated impressions that treasure was here somewhere actually buried, we might have had all our labour in vain."

" But your grandiloquence, and your conduct in swinging the beetle—how excessively odd ! I was sure you were mad. And why did you insist upon letting fall the bug, instead of a bullet from the skull ? "

" Why, to be frank, I felt somewhat annoyed by your evident suspicions touching my sanity, and so resolved to punish you quietly, in my own way, by a little bit of sober mystification. For this reason I swung the beetle, and for this reason I let it fall from the tree. An observation of yours about its great weight suggested the latter idea."

" Yes, I perceive ; and now there is only one point which puzzles me. What are we to make of the skeletons found in the hole ? "

" That is a question I am no more able to answer than

yourself.   There seems, however, only one plausible way
of accounting for them—and yet it is dreadful to believe
in such atrocity as my suggestion would imply.   It is clear
that Kidd—if Kidd indeed secreted this treasure, which
I doubt not—it is clear that he must have had assistance
in the labour.   But this labour concluded, he may have
thought it expedient to remove all participants in his
secret.   Perhaps a couple of blows with a mattock were
sufficient, while his coadjutors were busy in the pit ;
perhaps it required a dozen—who shall tell ? "

WILLIAM WILSON

" What say of it ? what says conscience grim,
That spectre in my path ? "
                    —W. Chamberlayne's " *Pharonnida.*"

Let me call myself, for the present, William Wilson.   The
fair page now lying before me need not be sullied with my
real appellation.   This has been already too much an object
for the scorn, for the horror, for the detestation of my race.
To the uttermost regions of the globe have not the indignant
winds bruited its unparalleled infamy ?   O outcast of all
outcasts most abandoned ! to the earth art thou not for
ever dead ? to its honours, to its flowers, to its golden
aspirations ?—and a cloud, dense, dismal, and limitless,
does it not hang eternally between thy hopes and heaven ?
    I would not, if I could, here or to-day, embody a record
of my later years of unspeakable misery and unpardonable
crime.   This epoch—these later years—took unto themselves a sudden elevation in turpitude, whose origin alone
it is my present purpose to assign.   Men usually grow base
by degrees.   From me in an instant all virtue dropped
bodily as a mantle.   From comparatively trivial wickedness
I passed, with the stride of a giant, into more than the
enormities of an Elagabalus.   What chance—what one
event brought this evil thing to pass, bear with me while
I relate.   Death approaches, and the shadow which fore-
runs him has thrown a softening influence over my spirit.

I long in passing through the dim valley for the sympathy, I had nearly said for the pity, of my fellow-men. I would fain have them believe that I have been in some measure the slave of circumstances beyond human control. I would wish them to seek out for me, in the details I am about to give, some little oasis of *fatality* amid a wilderness of error. I would have them allow, what they cannot refrain from allowing, that although temptation may have erewhile existed as great, man was never *thus* at least tempted before, certainly never *thus* fell. And is it therefore that he has never thus suffered ? Have I not indeed been living in a dream ? And am I not now dying a victim to the horror and the mystery of the wildest of all sublunary visions ?

I am the descendant of a race whose imaginative and easily excitable temperament has at all times rendered them remarkable ; and in my earliest infancy I gave evidence of having fully inherited the family character. As I advanced in years it was more strongly developed, becoming for many reasons a cause of serious disquietude to my friends, and of positive injury to myself. I grew self-willed, addicted to the wildest caprices, and a prey to the most ungovernable passions. Weak-minded, and beset with constitutional infirmities akin to my own, my parents could do but little to check the evil propensities which distinguished me. Some feeble and ill-directed efforts resulted in complete failure on their part, and of course in total triumph on mine. Thenceforward my voice was a household law, and at an age when few children have abandoned their leading-strings, I was left to the guidance of my own will, and became in all but name the master of my own actions.

My earliest recollections of a school-life are connected with a large rambling Elizabethan house, in a misty-looking village of England, where were a vast number of gigantic and gnarled trees, and where all the houses were excessively ancient. In truth, it was a dream-like and spirit-soothing place that venerable old town. At this moment, in fancy, I feel the refreshing chilliness of its deeply-shadowed avenues, inhale the fragrance of its thousand shrubberies, and thrill anew with indefinable delight at the deep hollow note of the church-bell, breaking each hour with sullen and sudden roar upon the stillness

C

of the dusky atmosphere in which the fretted Gothic steeple lay imbedded and asleep.

It gives me perhaps as much of pleasure as I can now in any manner experience to dwell upon minute recollections of the school and its concerns. Steeped in misery as I am—misery, alas! only too real—I shall be pardoned for seeking relief, however slight and temporary, in the weakness of a few rambling details. These, moreover, utterly trivial, and even ridiculous in themselves, assume to my fancy adventitious importance, as connected with a period and a locality when and where I recognise the first ambiguous monitions of the destiny which afterwards so fully overshadowed me. Let me then remember.

The house, I have said, was old and irregular. The grounds were extensive, and a high and solid brick wall, topped with a bed of mortar and broken glass, encompassed the whole. This prison-like rampart formed the limit of our domain : beyond it we saw but thrice-a-week, once every Saturday afternoon, when, attended by two ushers, we were permitted to take brief walks in a body through some of the neighbouring fields ; and twice during Sunday, when we paraded in the same formal manner to the morning and evening service in the one church of the village. Of this church the principal of our school was pastor. With how deep a spirit of wonder and perplexity was I wont to regard him from our remote pew in the gallery, as with step solemn and slow he ascended the pulpit ! This reverend man, with countenance so demurely benign, with robes so glossy and so clerically flowing, with wig so minutely powdered, so rigid and so vast—could this be he who, of late, with sour visage, and in snuffy habiliments, administered, ferule in hand, the Draconian laws of the academy ? O gigantic paradox, too utterly monstrous for solution !

At an angle of the ponderous wall frowned a more ponderous gate. It was riveted and studded with iron bolts, and surmounted with jagged iron spikes. What impressions of deep awe did it inspire ! It was never opened save for the three periodical egressions and ingressions already mentioned ; then in every creak of its mighty hinges we found a plenitude of mystery, a world of matter for solemn remark, or for more solemn meditation.

The extensive enclosure was irregular in form, having

many capacious recesses. Of these, three or four of the
largest constituted the playground. It was level, and
covered with fine hard gravel. I well remember it had no
trees nor benches, nor anything similar within it. Of
course it was in the rear of the house. In front lay a small
parterre, planted with box and other shrubs, but through
this sacred division we passed only upon rare occasions
indeed, such as a first advent to school or final departure
thence, or perhaps, when a parent or friend having called
for us, we joyfully took our way home for the Christmas
or Midsummer holidays.

But the house!—how quaint an old building was this!
to me how veritably a palace of enchantment! There
was really no end to its windings, to its incomprehensible
subdivisions. It was difficult, at any given time, to say
with certainty upon which of its two stories one happened
to be. From each room to every other there were sure to
be found three or four steps either in ascent or descent.
Then the lateral branches were innumerable, inconceivable,
and so returning in upon themselves that our most exact
ideas in regard to the whole mansion were not very far
different from those with which we pondered upon infinity.
During the five years of my residence here I was never
able to ascertain with precision in what remote locality
lay the little sleeping apartment assigned to myself and
some eighteen or twenty other scholars.

The school-room was the largest in the house, I could
not help thinking, in the world. It was very long, narrow,
and dismally low, with pointed Gothic windows and a
ceiling of oak. In a remote and terror-inspiring angle was
a square enclosure of eight or ten feet, comprising the
sanctum, " during hours," of our principal, the Reverend
Dr. Bransby. It was a solid structure, with massy door,
sooner than open which in the absence of the " dominie "
we would all have willingly perished by the *peine forte et
dure*. In other angles were two other similar boxes, far
less reverenced, indeed, but still greatly matters of awe.
One of these was the pulpit of the " classical " usher, one
of the " English and mathematical." Interspersed about
the room, crossing and recrossing in endless irregularity,
were innumerable benches and desks, black, ancient, and
time-worn, piled desperately with much-bethumbed books,
and so beseamed with initial letters, names at full length,

grotesque figures, and other multiplied efforts of the knife, as to have entirely lost what little of original form might have been their portion in days long departed. A huge bucket with water stood at one extremity of the room, and a clock of stupendous dimensions at the other.

Encompassed by the massy walls of this venerable academy, I passed, yet not in a tedium or disgust, the years of the third lustrum of my life. The teeming brain of childhood requires no external world of incident to occupy or amuse it ; and the apparently dismal monotony of a school was replete with more intense excitement than my riper youth has derived from luxury, or my full manhood from crime. Yet I must believe that my first mental develop ment had in it much of the uncommon—even much of the *outré*. Upon mankind at large the events of very early existence rarely leave in mature age any definite impression. All is grey shadow—a weak and irregular remembrance— an indistinct regathering of feeble pleasures and phantasmagoric pains. With me this is not so. In childhood I must have felt with the energy of a man what I now find stamped upon memory in lines as vivid, as deep, and as durable as the *exergues* of the Carthaginian medals.

Yet in fact—in the fact of the world's view—how little was there to remember ! The morning's awakening, the nightly summons to bed ; the connings, the recitations ; the periodical half-holidays, and perambulations ; the playground, with its broils, its pastimes, its intrigues ;— these, by a mental sorcery long forgotten, were made to involve a wilderness of sensation, a world of rich incident, a universe of varied emotion, of excitement the most passionate and spirit-stirring. " *Oh, le bon temps, que ce siècle de fer !* "

In truth, the ardour, the enthusiasm, and the imperiousness of my disposition, soon rendered me a marked character among my schoolmates, and by slow but natural gradations gave me an ascendency over all not greatly older than myself—over all with a single exception. This exception was found in the person of a scholar, who, although no relation, bore the same Christian and surname as myself, a circumstance, in fact, little remarkable ; for notwithstanding a noble descent, mine was one of those everyday appellations which seem, by prescriptive right, to have been, time out of mind, the common property of the mob. In

this narrative I have therefore designated myself as William Wilson—a fictitious title not very dissimilar to the real. My namesake alone, of those who in school phraseology constituted " our set," presumed to compete with me in the studies of the class—in the sports and broils of the playground—to refuse implicit belief in my assertions, and submission to my will—indeed, to interfere with my arbitrary dictation in any respect whatsoever. If there is on earth a supreme and unqualified despotism, it is the despotism of the master-mind in boyhood over the less energetic spirits of its companions.

Wilson's rebellion was to me a source of the greatest embarrassment : the more so as, in spite of the bravado with which in public I made a point of treating him and his pretensions, I secretly felt that I feared him, and could not help thinking the equality which he maintained so easily with myself a proof of his true superiority, since not to be overcome cost me a perpetual struggle. Yet this superiority—even this equality—was in truth acknowledged by no one but myself ; our associates, by some unaccountable blindness, seemed not even to suspect it. Indeed, his competition, his resistance, and especially his impertinent and dogged interference with my purposes, were not more pointed than private. He appeared to be destitute alike of the ambition which urged, and of the passionate energy of mind which enabled me to excel. In this rivalry he might have been supposed actuated solely by a whimsical desire to thwart, astonish, or mortify myself ; although there were times when I could not help observing, with a feeling made up of wonder, abasement, and pique, that he mingled with his injuries, his insults, or his contradictions, a certain most inappropriate, and assuredly most unwelcome *affectionateness* of manner. I could only conceive this singular behaviour to arise from a consummate self-conceit assuming the vulgar airs of patronage and protection.

Perhaps it was this latter trait in Wilson's conduct, conjoined with our identity of name, and the mere accident of our having entered the school upon the same day, which set afloat the notion that we were brothers among the senior classes in the academy. These do not usually inquire with much strictness into the affairs of their juniors. I have before said, or should have said, that Wilson was not,

in the most remote degree, connected with my family.
But assuredly if we *had* been brothers we must have been
twins ; for, after leaving Dr. Bransby's, I casually learned
that my namesake was born on the nineteenth of January
1813—and this is a somewhat remarkable coincidence,
for the day is precisely that of my own nativity.

It may seem strange that in spite of the continual anxiety
occasioned me by the rivalry of Wilson, and his intolerable
spirit of contradiction, I could not bring myself to hate
him altogether. We had, to be sure, nearly every day a
quarrel, in which, yielding me publicly the palm of victory,
he in some manner contrived to make me feel that it was
he who had deserved it, yet a sense of pride on my part and
a veritable dignity on his own, kept us always upon what
are called " speaking terms," while there were many points
of strong congeniality in our tempers, operating to awake
in me a sentiment which our position alone, perhaps,
prevented from ripening into friendship. It is difficult
indeed to define or even to describe my real feelings towards
him. They formed a motley and heterogeneous admixture ;
some petulant animosity, which was not yet hatred, some
esteem, more respect, much fear, with a world of uneasy
curiosity. To the moralist it will be unnecessary to say
in addition that Wilson and myself were the most inseparable of companions.

It was no doubt the anomalous state of affairs existing
between us which turned all my attacks upon him (and
they were many, either open or covert) into the channel of
banter or practical joke (giving pain while assuming the
aspect of mere fun), rather than into a more serious and
determined hostility. But my endeavours on this head
were by no means uniformly successful, even when my plans
were the most wittily concocted ; for my namesake had
much about him in character of that unassuming and
quiet austerity which, while enjoying the poignancy of
its own jokes, has no heel of Achilles in itself, and absolutely refuses to be laughed at. I could find indeed but
one vulnerable point, and that lying in a personal peculiarity, arising perhaps from constitutional disease, would
have been spared by any antagonist less at his wit's end
than myself ; my rival had a weakness in the faucial or
guttural organs which precluded him from raising his
voice at any time *above a very low whisper*. Of this defect

I did not fail to take what poor advantage lay in my power.

Wilson's retaliations in kind were many ; and there was one form of his practical wit that disturbed me beyond measure. How his sagacity first discovered at all that so petty a thing would vex me is a question I never could solve, but having discovered, he habitually practised the annoyance. I had always felt aversion to my uncourtly patronymic and its very common, if not plebeian prænomen. The words were venom in my ears ; and when, upon the day of my arrival, a second William Wilson came also to to the academy, I felt angry with him for bearing the name, and doubly disgusted with the name because a stranger bore it, who would be the cause of its twofold repetition, who would be constantly in my presence, and whose concerns, in the ordinary routine of the school business, must inevitably, on account of the detestable coincidence, be often confounded with my own.

The feeling of vexation thus engendered grew stronger with every circumstance tending to show resemblance, moral or physical, between my rival and myself. I had not then discovered the remarkable fact that we were of the same age ; but I saw that we were of the same height, and I perceived that we were even singularly alike in general contour of person and outline of feature. I was galled, too, by the rumour touching a relationship, which had grown current in the upper forms. In a word, nothing could more seriously disturb me (although I scrupulously concealed such disturbance), than any allusion to a similarity of mind, person, or condition existing between us. But, in truth, I had no reason to believe that (with the exception of the matter of relationship, and in the case of Wilson himself) this similarity had ever been made a subject of comment, or even observed at all, by our school-fellows. That *he* observed it in all its bearings, and as fixedly as I, was apparent ; but that he could discover in such circumstances so fruitful a field of annoyance can only be attributed, as I said before, to his more than ordinary penetration.

His cue, which was to perfect an imitation of myself, lay both in words and in actions, and most admirably did he play his part. My dress it was an easy matter to copy ; my gait and general manner were without difficulty appropriated ; in spite of his constitutional defect, even my voice did not escape him. My louder tones were of course unattempted, but then the key, it was identical ; *and his singular whisper, it grew the very echo of my own.*

How greatly this most exquisite portraiture harassed me (for it could not justly be termed a caricature), I will not now venture to describe. I had but one consolation —in the fact that the imitation, apparently, was noticed by myself alone, and that I had to endure only the knowing and strangely sarcastic smiles of my namesake himself. Satisfied with having produced in my bosom the intended effect, he seemed to chuckle in secret over the sting he had inflicted, and was characteristically disregardful of the public applause which the success of his witty endeavours might have so easily elicited. That the school, indeed, did not feel his design, perceive its accomplishment, and participate in his sneer, was for many anxious months a riddle I could not resolve. Perhaps the *gradation* of his copy rendered it not so readily perceptible, or more possibly I owed my security to the masterly air of the copyist, who, disdaining the letter (which in a painting is all the obtuse can see), gave but the full spirit of his original for my individual contemplation and chagrin.

I have already more than once spoken of the disgusting air of patronage which he assumed toward me, and of his frequent officious interference with my will. This interference often took the ungracious character of advice— advice not openly given, but hinted or insinuated. I received it with a repugnance which gained strength as I grew in years. Yet at this distant day, let me do him the simple justice to acknowledge that I can recall no occasion when the suggestions of my rival were on the side of those errors or follies so usual to his immature age and seeming inexperience ; that his moral sense, at least, if not his general talents and worldly wisdom, was far keener than my own ; and that I might to-day have been a better, and thus a happier man, had I less frequently rejected the counsels embodied in those meaning whispers which I then but too cordially hated and too bitterly despised.

As it was, I at length grew restive in the extreme under his distasteful supervision, and daily resented more and more openly what I considered his intolerable arrogance. I have said that in the first years of our connection as schoolmates, my feelings in regard to him might have been easily ripened into friendship ; but, in the latter months of my residence at the academy, although the intrusion of his ordinary manner had, beyond doubt, in some measure abated, my sentiments in nearly similar proportion partook very much of positive hatred. Upon one occasion he saw this, I think, and afterwards avoided, or made a show of avoiding me.

It was about the same period, if I remember aright, that, in an altercation of violence with him, in which he was more than usually thrown off his guard, and spoke and acted with an openness of demeanour rather foreign to his nature, I discovered, or fancied I discovered, in his accent, his air, and general appearance, a something which first startled, and then deeply interested me, by bringing to mind dim visions of my earliest infancy—wild, confused, and thronging memories of a time when memory herself was yet unborn. I cannot better describe the sensation which oppressed me than by saying that I could with diffi-culty shake off the belief of my having been acquainted with the being who stood before me at some epoch very long ago, some point of the past even infinitely remote. The delusion, however, faded rapidly as it came, and I mention it at all but to define the day of the last conversa-tion I there held with my singular namesake.

The huge old house, with its countless subdivisions, had several large chambers communicating with each other, where slept the greater number of the students. There were, however (as must necessarily happen in a building so awkwardly planned), many little nooks or recesses, the odds and ends of the structure, and these the economic ingenuity of Dr. Bransby had also fitted up as dormitories, although, being the merest closets, they were capable of accommodating but a single individual. One of these small apartments was occupied by Wilson.

One night, about the close of my fifth year at the school, and immediately after the altercation just mentioned, finding every one wrapped in sleep, I arose from bed, and, lamp in hand, stole through a wilderness of narrow passages from my own bedroom to that of my rival. I had long been plotting one of those ill-natured pieces of practical wit at his expense in which I had hitherto been so uniformly unsuc-cessful. It was my intention now to put my scheme in
c*

operation, and I resolved to make him feel the whole extent
of the malice with which I was imbued. Having reached
his closet, I noiselessly entered, leaving the lamp, with a
shade over it, on the outside. I advanced a step, and
listened to the sound of his tranquil breathing. Assured
of his being asleep, I returned, took the light, and with it
again approached the bed. Close curtains were around
it, which, in the prosecution of my plan, I slowly and quietly
withdrew, when the bright rays fell vividly upon the
sleeper, and my eyes, at the same moment, upon his
countenance. I looked, and a numbness, an iciness of
feeling, instantly pervaded my frame. My breast heaved,
my knees tottered, my whole spirit became possessed with
an objectless yet intolerable horror. Gasping for breath,
I lowered the lamp in still nearer proximity to the face.
Were these—*these* the lineaments of William Wilson ?
I saw, indeed, that they were his, but I shook as if with a
fit of the ague in fancying they were not. What *was* there
about them to confound me in this manner ? I gazed,
while my brain reeled with a multitude of incoherent
thoughts. Not thus he appeared, assuredly not *thus*, in
the vivacity of his waking hours. The same name, the
same contour of person, the same day of arrival at the
academy ; and then his dogged and meaningless imitation
of my gait, my voice, my habits, and my manner. Was
it, in truth, within the bounds of human possibility that
what I now saw was the result merely of the habitual
practice of this sarcastic imitation. Awe-stricken, and
with a creeping shudder, I extinguished the lamp, passed
silently from the chamber, and left at once the halls of
that old academy, never to enter them again.

After a lapse of some months, spent at home in mere
idleness, I found myself a student at Eton. The brief
interval had been sufficient to enfeeble my remembrance
of the events at Dr. Bransby's, or at least to effect a material
change in the nature of the feelings with which I remembered
them. The truth, the tragedy, of the drama was no more.
I could now find room to doubt the evidence of my senses,
and seldom called up the subject at all but with wonder at
the extent of human credulity, and a smile at the vivid
force of the imagination which I hereditarily possessed.
Neither was this species of scepticism likely to be diminished
by the character of the life I led at Eton. The vortex

of thoughtless folly into which I there so immediately and so recklessly plunged washed away all but the froth of my past hours, engulfed at once every solid or serious impression, and left to memory only the veriest levities of a former existence.

I do not wish, however, to trace the course of my miserable profligacy here—a profligacy which set at defiance the laws, while it eluded the vigilance of the institution. Three years of folly, passed without profit, had but given me rooted habits of vice, and added, in a somewhat unusual degree, to my bodily stature, when, after a week of soulless dissipation, I invited a small party of the most dissolute students to a secret carousal in my chambers. We met at a late hour of the night, for our debaucheries were to be faithfully protracted until morning. The wine flowed freely, and there were not wanting other and perhaps more dangerous seductions, so that the grey dawn had already faintly appeared in the east, while our delirious extravagance was at its height. Madly flushed with cards and intoxication, I was in the act of insisting upon a toast of more than wonted profanity, when my attention was suddenly diverted by the violent, although partial, unclosing of the door of the apartment, and by the eager voice of a servant from without. He said that some person, apparently in great haste, demanded to speak with me in the hall.

Wildly excited with wine, the unexpected interruption rather delighted than surprised me. I staggered forward at once, and a few steps brought me to the vestibule of the building. In this low and small room there hung no lamp, and now no light at all was admitted, save that of the exceedingly feeble dawn which made its way through the semi-circular window. As I put my foot over the threshold I became aware of the figure of a youth about my own height, and habited in a white kerseymere morning frock, cut in the novel fashion of the one I myself wore at the moment. This the faint light enabled me to perceive, but the features of his face I could not distinguish. Upon my entering he strode hurriedly up to me, and seizing me by the arm with a gesture of petulant impatience, whispered the words " William Wilson ! " in my ear.

I grew perfectly sober in an instant.

There was that in the manner of the stranger, and in the

tremulous shake of his uplifted finger, as he held it between my eyes and the light, which filled me with unqualified amazement ; but it was not this which had so violently moved me. It was the pregnancy of solemn admonition in the singular, low, hissing utterance, and, above all, it was the character, the tone, *the key*, of those few, simple, and familiar, yet *whispered* syllables, which came with a thousand thronging memories of by-gone days, and struck upon my soul with the shock of a galvanic battery. Ere I could recover the use of my senses he was gone.

Although this event failed not of a vivid effect upon my disordered imagination, yet was it evanescent as vivid. For some weeks, indeed, I busied myself in earnest inquiry, or was wrapped in a cloud of morbid speculation. I did not pretend to disguise from my perception the identity of the singular individual who thus perseveringly interfered with my affairs, and harassed me with his insinuated counsel. But who and what was this Wilson ?—and whence came he ?—and what were his purposes ? Upon neither of these points could I be satisfied—merely ascertaining in regard to him, that a sudden accident in his family had caused his removal from Dr. Bransby's academy on the afternoon of the day in which I myself had eloped. But in a brief period I ceased to think upon the subject, my attention being all absorbed in a contemplated departure for Oxford. Thither I soon went, the uncalculating vanity of my parents furnishing me with an outfit and annual establishment which would enable me to indulge at will in the luxury already so dear to my heart—to vie in profuseness of expenditure with the haughtiest heirs of the wealthiest earldoms in Great Britain.

Excited by such appliances to vice, my constitutional temperament broke forth with redoubled ardour, and I spurned even the common restraints of decency in the mad infatuation of my revels. But it were absurd to pause in the detail of my extravagance. Let it suffice, that among spendthrifts I out-Heroded Herod, and that giving name to a multitude of novel follies, I added no brief appendix to the long catalogue of vices then usual in the most dissolute university of Europe.

It could hardly be credited, however, that I had, even here, so utterly fallen from the gentlemanly estate as to seek acquaintance with the vilest arts of the gambler by profession, and having become an adept in his despicable science, to practise it habitually as a means of increasing my already enormous income at the expense of the weak-minded among my fellow-collegians. Such, nevertheless, was the fact ; and the very enormity of this offence against all manly and honourable sentiment proved, beyond doubt, the main, if not the sole reason of the impunity with which it was committed. Who, indeed, among my most aban-doned associates, would not rather have disputed the clearest evidence of his senses than have suspected of such courses the gay, the frank, the generous William Wilson—the noblest and most liberal commoner at Oxford—him whose follies (said his parasites) were but the follies of youth and unbridled fancy—whose errors but inimitable whim—whose darkest vice but a careless and dashing extravagance ?

I had been now two years successfully busied in this way when there came to the university a young *parvenu* noble-man, Glendinning—rich, said report, as Herodes Atticus—his riches, too, as easily acquired. I soon found him of weak intellect, and of course marked him as a fitting subject for my skill. I frequently engaged him in play, and con-trived with the gambler's usual art to let him win consider-able sums, the more effectually to entangle him in my snares. At length, my schemes being ripe, I met him (with the full intention that this meeting should be final and decisive) at the chambers of a fellow-commoner (Mr. Preston) equally intimate with both, but who, to do him justice, entertained not even a remote suspicion of my design. To give to this a better colouring I had contrived to have assembled a party of some eight or ten, and was solicitously careful that the introduction of cards should appear accidental, and originate in the proposal of my contemplated dupe himself. To be brief upon a vile topic, none of the low finesse was omitted, so customary upon similar occasions, that it is a just matter for wonder how any are still found so besotted as to fall its victim.

We had protracted our sitting far into the night, and I had at length effected the manœuvre of getting Glendinning as my sole antagonist. The game, too, was my favourite *écarté*. The rest of the company, interested in the extent of our play, had abandoned their own cards, and were standing around us as spectators. The *parvenu*, who had been induced by my artifices in the early part of the evening to drink deeply, now shuffled, dealt, or played with a wild nervousness of manner for which his intoxication, I thought, might partially but could not altogether account. In a very short period he had become my debtor to a large amount, when, having taken a long draught of port, he did precisely what I had been coolly anticipating—he proposed to double our already extravagant stakes. With a well-feigned show of reluctance, and not until after my repeated refusal had seduced him into some angry words which gave a colour of *pique* to my compliance, did I finally comply. The result of course did but prove how entirely the prey was in my toils : in less than an hour he had quadrupled his debt. For some time his countenance had been losing the florid tinge lent it by the wine, but now, to my astonishment, I perceived that it had grown to a pallor truly fearful. I say to my astonishment. Glendinning had been represented to my eager inquiries as immeasurably wealthy ; and the sums which he had as yet lost, although in themselves vast, could not, I supposed, very seriously annoy, much less so violently affect him. That he was overcome by the wine just swallowed was the idea which most readily presented itself ; and, rather with a view to the preservation of my own character in the eyes of my associates, than from any less interested motive, I was about to insist peremptorily upon a discontinuance of the play, when some expressions at my elbow from among the company, and an ejaculation evincing utter despair on the part of Glendinning, gave me to understand that I had effected his total ruin under circumstances which, rendering him an object for the pity of all, should have protected him from the ill offices even of a fiend.

What now might have been my conduct it is difficult to say. The pitiable condition of my dupe had thrown an air of embarrassed gloom over all, and for some moments a profound silence was maintained, during which I could not help feeling my cheeks tingle with the many burning glances of scorn or reproach cast upon me by the less abandoned of the party. I will even own that an intolerable weight of anxiety was a brief instant lifted from my bosom by the sudden and extraordinary interruption which ensued. The wide heavy folding-doors of the apartment were all at once thrown open to their full extent, with a vigorous and rushing impetuosity that extinguished, as if by magic, every candle in the room. Their light, in dying, enabled us just to perceive that a stranger had entered, about my own height, and closely muffled in a cloak. The darkness, however, was now total, and we could only *feel* that he was standing in our midst. Before any one of us could recover from the extreme astonishment into which this rudeness had thrown all, we heard the voice of the intruder.

" Gentlemen," he said, in a low, distinct, and never-to-be-forgotten *whisper* which thrilled to the very marrow of my bones, " Gentlemen, I make no apology for this behaviour, because in thus behaving, I am but fulfilling my duty. You are, beyond doubt, uninformed of the true character of the person who has to-night won at *écarté* a large sum of money from Lord Glendinning. I will therefore put you upon an expeditious and decisive plan of obtaining this very necessary information. Please to examine at your leisure the inner linings of the cuff of his left sleeve, and the several little packages which may be found in the somewhat capacious pockets of his embroidered morning wrapper."

While he spoke, so profound was the stillness that one might have heard a pin drop upon the floor. In ceasing, he departed at once, and as abruptly as he had entered. Can I—shall I describe my sensations ? Must I say that I felt all the horrors of the damned ? Most assuredly I had little time for reflection. Many hands roughly seized me upon the spot, and lights were immediately reprocured. A search ensued. In the lining of my sleeve were found all the court cards essential in *écarté*, and in the pockets of my wrapper a number of packs, fac-similes of those used at our sittings, with the single exception that mine were of the species called, technically, *arrondées* ; the honours being slightly convex at the ends, the lower cards slightly convex at the sides. In this disposition, the dupe who cuts, as customary, at the length of the pack, will invariably find that he cuts his antagonist an honour ; while the gambler, cutting at the breadth, will as certainly cut nothing for his victim which may count in the records of the game.

Any burst of indignation upon this discovery would have

affected me less than the silent contempt, or the sarcastic
composure, with which it was received.

" Mr. Wilson," said our host, stooping to remove from
beneath his feet an exceedingly luxurious cloak of rare
furs, " Mr. Wilson, this is your property." (The weather
was cold ; and, upon quitting my own room, I had thrown
a cloak over my dressing wrapper, putting it off upon
reaching the scene of play.)   " I presume it is supereroga-
tory to seek here (eyeing the folds of the garment with a
bitter smile) for any further evidence of your skill.   Indeed,
we have had enough.   You will see the necessity, I hope,
of quitting Oxford—at all events, of quitting instantly my
chambers."

Abased, humbled to the dust as I then was, it is probable
that I should have resented this galling language by
immediate personal violence, had not my whole attention
been at the moment arrested by a fact of the most startling
character.   The cloak which I had worn was of a rare
description of fur ; how rare, how extravagantly costly,
I shall not venture to say.   Its fashion, too, was of my
own fantastic invention, for I was fastidious to an absurd
degree of coxcombry in matters of this frivolous nature.
When, therefore, Mr. Preston reached me that which he
had picked up upon the floor, and near the folding-doors
of the apartment, it was with an astonishment nearly
bordering upon terror that I perceived my own already
hanging on my arm (where I had no doubt unwittingly
placed it), and that the one presented me was but its exact
counterpart in every, in even the minutest possible particular.   The singular being who had so disastrously exposed
me had been muffled, I remembered, in a cloak, and none
had been worn at all by any of the members of our party
with the exception of myself.   Retaining some presence of
mind, I took the one offered me by Preston, placed it
unnoticed over my own, left the apartment with a resolute
scowl of defiance, and next morning, ere dawn of day, commenced a hurried journey from Oxford to the Continent in
a perfect agony of horror and of shame.

I fled in vain.   My evil destiny pursued me as if in
exultation, and proved indeed that the exercise of its
mysterious dominion had as yet only begun.   Scarcely
had I set foot in Paris ere I had fresh evidence of the
detestable interest taken by this Wilson in my concerns.

Years flew while I experienced no relief. Villain !—at
Rome, with how untimely, yet with how spectral an
officiousness, stepped he in between me and my ambition !
At Vienna, too—at Berlin—and at Moscow ! Where, in
truth, had I *not* bitter cause to curse him within my heart ?
From his inscrutable tyranny did I at length flee, panic-
stricken, as from a pestilence ; and to the very ends of
the earth *I fled in vain.*

And again and again, in secret communion with my own
spirit, would I demand the questions, " Who is he ?—
whence came he ?—and what are his objects ? " But no
answer was there found. And now I scrutinised, with a
minute scrutiny, the forms, and the methods, and the
leading traits of his impertinent supervision. But even
here there was very little upon which to base a conjecture.
It was noticeable, indeed, that in no one of the multiplied
instances in which he had of late crossed my path had he
so crossed it except to frustrate those schemes, or to disturb
those actions, which, if fully carried out, might have
resulted in bitter mischief. Poor justification this, in
truth, for an authority so imperiously assumed ! Poor
indemnity for natural rights of self-agency so pertinaciously,
so insultingly denied !

I had also been forced to notice that my tormentor for a
very long period of time (while scrupulously and with
miraculous dexterity maintaining his whim of an identity
of apparel with myself) had so contrived it, in the execution
of his varied interference with my will, that I saw not at
any moment the features of his face. Be Wilson what he
might, *this* at least was but the veriest of affectation or of
folly. Could he for an instant have supposed that in my
admonisher at Eton—in the destroyer of my honour at
Oxford—in him who thwarted my ambition at Rome,
my revenge at Paris, my passionate love at Naples, or
what he falsely termed my avarice in Egypt,—that in this,
my arch-enemy and evil genius, I could fail to recognise
the William Wilson of my school-boy days,—the namesake,
the companion, the rival,—the hated and dreaded rival at
Dr. Bransby's ? Impossible !—But let me hasten to the
last eventful scene of the drama.

Thus far had I succumbed supinely to this imperious
domination. The sentiment of deep awe with which I
habitually regarded the elevated character, the majestic

wisdom, the apparent omnipresence and omnipotence of
Wilson, added to a feeling of even terror, with which
certain other traits in his nature and assumptions inspired
me, had operated hitherto to impress me with an idea of
my own utter weakness and helplessness, and to suggest
an implicit, although bitterly reluctant submission to his
arbitrary will. But of late days I had given myself up
entirely to wine, and its maddening influence upon my
hereditary temper rendered me more and more impatient
of control. I began to murmur,—to hesitate,—to resist.
And was it only fancy which induced me to believe that,
with the increase of my own firmness, that of my tormentor
underwent a proportional diminution ? Be this as it may,
I now began to feel the inspiration of a burning hope, and
at length nurtured in my secret thoughts a stern and
desperate resolution that I would submit no longer to be
enslaved.

It was at Rome, during the Carnival of 18—, that I
attended a masquerade in the palazzo of the Neapolitan
Duke Di Broglio. I had indulged more freely than usual
in the excesses of the wine-table, and now the suffocating
atmosphere of the crowded rooms irritated me beyond
endurance. The difficulty, too, of forcing my way through
the mazes of the company contributed not a little to the
ruffling of my temper ; for I was anxiously seeking (let me
not say with what unworthy motive) the young, the gay,
the beautiful wife of the aged and doting Di Broglio.
With a too unscrupulous confidence she had previously
communicated to me the secret of the costume in which
she would be habited, and now, having caught a glimpse
of her person, I was hurrying to make my way into her
presence. At this moment I felt a light hand placed upon
my shoulder, and that ever-remembered, low, damnable
whisper within my ear.

In an absolute frenzy of wrath I turned at once upon him
who had thus interrupted me, and seized him violently by
the collar. He was attired, as I had expected, in a costume
altogether similar to my own ; wearing a Spanish cloak
of blue velvet, begirt about the waist with a crimson belt
sustaining a rapier. A mask of black silk entirely covered
his face.

" Scoundrel ! " I said, in a voice husky with rage, while
every syllable I uttered seemed as new fuel to my fury ;

" scoundrel ! impostor ! accursed villain ! you shall not—
you *shall not* dog me unto death ! Follow me, or I will
stab you where you stand ! "—and I broke my way from
the ball-room into a small ante-chamber adjoining, dragging
him unresistingly with me as I went.

Upon entering, I thrust him furiously from me. He
staggered against the wall, while I closed the door with an
oath, and commanded him to draw. He hesitated but for
an instant ; then, with a slight sigh, drew in silence, and
put himself upon his defence.

The contest was brief indeed. I was frantic with every
species of wild excitement, and felt within my single arm
the energy and power of a multitude. In a few seconds I
forced him by sheer strength against the wainscoting, and
thus, getting him at mercy, plunged my sword, with brute
ferocity, repeatedly through and through his bosom.

At that instant some person tried the latch of the door.
I hastened to prevent an intrusion, and then immediately
returned to my dying antagonist. But what human
language can adequately portray *that* astonishment, *that*
horror which possessed me at the spectacle then presented
to view ? The brief moment in which I averted my eyes
had been sufficient to produce apparently a material
change in the arrangements at the upper or farther end of
the room. A large mirror—so at first it seemed to me in
my confusion—now stood where none had been perceptible
before ; and, as I stepped up to it in extremity of terror,
mine own image, but with features all pale and dabbled in
blood, advanced to meet me with a feeble and tottering gait.

Thus it appeared, I say, but was not. It was my
antagonist—it was Wilson who then stood before me in
the agonies of his dissolution. His mask and cloak lay
where he had thrown them upon the floor. Not a thread
in all his raiment—not a line in all the marked and singular
lineaments of his face which was not, even in the most
absolute identity, *mine own !*

It was Wilson ; but he spoke no longer in a whisper, and
I could have fancied that I myself was speaking while he
said :

" *You have conquered and I yield. Yet, henceforward art
thou also dead—dead to the World, to Heaven, and to Hope !
In me didst thou exist—and, in my death, see by this image,
which is thine own, how utterly thou hast murdered thyself.*"

THE FACTS IN THE CASE OF M. VALDEMAR

OF course I shall not pretend to consider it any matter for wonder that the extraordinary case of M. Valdemar has excited discussion. It would have been a miracle had it not—especially under the circumstances. Through the desire of all parties concerned to keep the affair from the public, at least for the present, or until we had further opportunities for investigation—through our endeavours to effect this—a garbled or exaggerated account made its way into society, and became the source of many unpleasant misrepresentations ; and, very naturally, of a great deal of disbelief.

It is now rendered necessary that I give the *facts*—as far as I comprehend them myself. They are, succinctly, these :—

My attention, for the last three years, had been repeatedly drawn to the subject of mesmerism ; and, about nine months ago, it occurred to me, quite suddenly, that in the series of experiments made hitherto, there had been a very remarkable and most unaccountable omission—no person had as yet been mesmerised *in articulo mortis*. It remained to be seen, first, whether, in such condition, there existed in the patient any susceptibility to the magnetic influence ; secondly, whether, if any existed, it was impaired or increased by the condition ; thirdly, to what extent, or for how long a period, the encroachments of Death might be arrested by the process. There were other points to be ascertained, but these most excited my curiosity—the last in especial, from the immensely important character of its consequences.

In looking around me for some subject by whose means I might test these particulars, I was brought to think of my friend, M. Ernest Valdemar, the well-known compiler of the *Bibliotheca Forensica*, and author (under the *nom de plume* of Issachar Marx) of the Polish versions of *Wallenstein* and *Gargantua*. M. Valdemar, who has resided principally at Harlem, N. Y., since the year 1839, is (or was) particularly noticeable for the extreme spareness of his person—his lower limbs much resembling those of John Randolph ; and, also, for the whiteness of his whiskers, in violent contrast to the blackness of his hair—the latter, in consequence, being very generally mistaken for a wig. His temperament was markedly nervous, and rendered him a good subject for mesmeric experiment. On two or three occasions I had put him to sleep with little difficulty, but was disappointed in other results which his peculiar constitution had naturally led me to anticipate. His will was at no period positively, or thoroughly, under my control ; and in regard to *clairvoyance*, I could accomplish with him nothing to be relied upon. I always attributed my failure at these points to the disordered state of his health. For some months previous to my becoming acquainted with him, his physicians had declared him in a confirmed phthisis. It was his custom, indeed, to speak calmly of his approaching dissolution, as of a matter neither to be avoided nor regretted.

When the ideas to which I have alluded first occurred to me, it was of course very natural that I should think of M. Valdemar. I knew the steady philosophy of the man too well to apprehend any scruples from *him* ; and he had no relatives in America who would be likely to interfere. I spoke to him frankly upon the subject ; and, to my surprise, his interest seemed vividly excited. I say to my surprise ; for, although he had always yielded his person freely to my experiments, he had never before given me any tokens of sympathy with what I did. His disease was of that character which would admit of exact calculation in respect to the epoch of its termination in death ; and it was finally arranged between us that he would send for me about twenty-four hours before the period announced by his physicians as that of his decease.

It is now rather more than seven months since I received, from M. Valdemar himself, the subjoined note :—

" MY DEAR P——, You may as well come *now*. D—— and F—— are agreed that I cannot hold out beyond to-morrow midnight ; and I think they have hit the time very nearly.   VALDEMAR."

I received this note within half-an-hour after it was written, and in fifteen minutes more I was in the dying man's chamber. I had not seen him for ten days, and was appalled by the fearful alteration which the brief interval had wrought in him. His face wore a leaden hue ; the eyes were utterly lustreless ; and the emaciation was so extreme, that the skin had been broken through by the cheek-bones. His expectoration was excessive. The pulse was barely perceptible. He retained, nevertheless, in a very remarkable manner, both his mental power and a certain degree of physical strength. He spoke with distinctness—took some palliative medicines without aid— and, when I entered the room, was occupied in pencilling memoranda in a pocket-book. He was propped up in the bed by pillows. Doctors D—— and F—— were in attendance. After pressing Valdemar's hand, I took these gentlemen aside, and obtained from them a minute account of the patient's condition. The left lung had been for eighteen months in a semi-osseous or cartilaginous state, and was, of course, entirely useless for all purposes of vitality. The right, in its upper portion, was also partially, if not thoroughly, ossified, while the lower region was merely a mass of purulent tubercles, running one into another. Several extensive perforations existed ; and, at one point, permanent adhesion to the ribs had taken place. These appearances in the right lobe were of comparatively recent date. The ossification had proceeded with very unusual rapidity ; no sign of it had been discovered a month before, and the adhesion had only been observed during the three previous days. Independently of the phthisis, the patient was suspected of aneurism of the aorta ; but on this point the osseous symptoms rendered an exact diagnosis impossible. It was the opinion of both physicians that M. Valdemar would die about midnight on the morrow (Sunday). It was then seven o'clock on Saturday evening.

On quitting the invalid's bedside to hold conversation with myself, Doctors D—— and F—— had bidden him a final farewell. It had not been their intention to return ; but, at my request, they agreed to look in upon the patient about ten the next night.

When they had gone, I spoke freely with M. Valdemar on the subject of his approaching dissolution, as well as, more particularly, of the experiment proposed. He still professed himself quite willing and even anxious to have it made, and urged me to commence it at once. A male and a female nurse were in attendance; but I did not feel myself altogether at liberty to engage in a task of this character with no more reliable witnesses than these people, in case of sudden accident, might prove. I therefore postponed operations until about eight the next night, when the arrival of a medical student, with whom I had some acquaintance (Mr. Theodore L——l), relieved me from further embarrassment. It had been my design, originally, to wait for the physicians; but I was induced to proceed, first, by the urgent entreaties of M. Valdemar, and secondly, by my conviction that I had not a moment to lose, as he was evidently sinking fast.

Mr. L——l was so kind as to accede to my desire that he would take notes of all that occurred; and it is from his memoranda that what I now have to relate is, for the most part, either condensed or copied *verbatim*.

It wanted about five minutes of eight when, taking the patient's hand, I begged him to state, as distinctly as he could, to Mr. L——l, whether he (M. Valdemar) was entirely willing that I should make the experiment of mesmerising him in his then condition.

He replied feebly, yet quite audibly, " Yes, I wish to be mesmerised "—adding immediately afterwards, " I fear you have deferred it too long."

While he spoke thus, I commenced the passes which I had already found most effectual in subduing him. He was evidently influenced with the first lateral stroke of my hand across his forehead; but although I exerted all my powers, no further perceptible effect was induced until some minutes after ten o'clock, when Doctors D—— and F—— called, according to appointment. I explained to them, in a few words, what I designed, and as they opposed no objection, saying that the patient was already in the death agony, I proceeded without hesitation—exchanging, however, the lateral passes for downward ones, and directing my gaze entirely into the right eye of the sufferer.

By this time his pulse was imperceptible and his breathing was stertorous, and at intervals of half a minute.

This condition was nearly unaltered for a quarter of an hour. At the expiration of this period, however, a natural, although a very deep sigh, escaped the bosom of the dying man, and the stertorous breathing ceased—that is to say, its stertorousness was no longer apparent ; the intervals were undiminished. The patient's extremities were of an icy coldness.

At five minutes before eleven I perceived unequivocal signs of the mesmeric influence. The glassy roll of the eye was changed for that expression of uneasy *inward* examination which is never seen except in cases of sleep-waking, and which it is quite impossible to mistake. With a few rapid lateral passes I made the lids quiver, as in incipient sleep, and with a few more I closed them altogether. I was not satisfied, however, with this, but continued the manipulations vigorously, and with the fullest exertion of the will, until I had completely stiffened the limbs of the slumberer, after placing them in a seemingly easy position. The legs were at full length ; the arms were nearly so, and reposed on the bed at a moderate distance from the loins. The head was very slightly elevated.

When I had accomplished this, it was fully midnight, and I requested the gentlemen present to examine M. Valdemar's condition. After a few experiments, they admitted him to be in an unusually perfect state of mesmeric trance. The curiosity of both the physicians was greatly excited. Dr. D—— resolved at once to remain with the patient all night, while Dr. F—— took leave with a promise to return at daybreak. Mr. L——l and the nurses remained.

We left M. Valdemar entirely undisturbed until about three o'clock in the morning, when I approached him, and found him in precisely the same condition as when Dr. F—— went away—that is to say, he lay in the same position. The pulse was imperceptible ; the breathing was gentle (scarcely noticeable, unless through the application of a mirror to the lips) ; the eyes were closed naturally ; and the limbs were as rigid and as cold as marble. Still, the general appearance was certainly not that of death.

As I approached M. Valdemar I made a kind of half effort to influence his right arm into pursuit of my own, as I passed the latter gently to and fro above his person. In such experiments with this patient I had never perfectly succeeded before, and assuredly I had little thought of succeeding now ; but to my astonishment, his arm very readily, although feebly, followed every direction I assigned it with mine. I determined to hazard a few words of conversation.

" M. Valdemar," I said, " are you asleep ? " He made no answer, but I perceived a tremor about the lips, and was thus induced to repeat the question, again and again. At its third repetition, his whole frame was agitated by a very slight shivering ; the eyelids unclosed themselves so far as to display a white line of a ball ; the lips moved sluggishly, and from between them, in a barely audible whisper, issued the words—

" Yes ; asleep now. Do not wake me !—let me die so ! "

I here felt the limbs and found them as rigid as ever. The right arm, as before, obeyed the direction of my hand. I questioned the sleep-waker again—

" Do you still feel pain in the breast, M. Valdemar ? "

The answer now was immediate, but even less audible than before—

" No pain—I am dying."

I did not think it advisable to disturb him further just then, and nothing more was said or done until the arrival of Dr. F——, who came a little before sunrise, and expressed unbounded astonishment at finding the patient still alive. After feeling the pulse and applying a mirror to the lips, he requested me to speak to the sleep-waker again. I did so, saying—

" M. Valdemar, do you still sleep ? "

As before, some minutes elapsed ere a reply was made ; and during the interval the dying man seemed to be collecting his energies to speak. At my fourth repetition of the question, he said very faintly, almost inaudibly—

" Yes ; still asleep—dying."

It was now the opinion, or rather the wish, of the physicians, that M. Valdemar should be suffered to remain undisturbed in his present apparently tranquil condition, until death should supervene—and this, it was generally agreed, must now take place within a few minutes. I concluded, however, to speak to him once more, and merely repeated my previous question.

While I spoke, there came a marked change over the countenance of the sleep-waker. The eyes rolled themselves slowly open, the pupils disappearing upwardly ; the skin generally assumed a cadaverous hue, resembling not so much parchment as white paper ; and the circular hectic spots which, hitherto, had been strongly defined in the centre of each cheek, *went out* at once. I use this expression, because the suddenness of their departure put me in mind of nothing so much as the extinguishment of a candle by a puff of the breath. The upper lip, at the same time, writhed itself away from the teeth, which it had previously covered completely ; while the lower jaw fell with an audible jerk, leaving the mouth widely extended, and disclosing in full view the swollen and blackened tongue. I presume that no member of the party then present had been unaccustomed to death-bed horrors ; but so hideous beyond conception was the appearance of M. Valdemar at this moment, that there was a general shrinking back from the region of the bed.

I now feel that I have reached a point of this narrative at which every reader will be startled into positive disbelief. It is my business, however, simply to proceed.

There was no longer the faintest sign of vitality in M. Valdemar ; and concluding him to be dead, we were consigning him to the charge of the nurses, when a strong vibratory motion was observable in the tongue. This continued for perhaps a minute. At the expiration of this period, there issued from the distended and motionless jaws a voice—such as it would be madness in me to attempt describing. There are, indeed, two or three epithets which might be considered as applicable to it in part ; I might say, for example, that the sound was harsh, and broken, and hollow ; but the hideous whole is indescribable, for the simple reason that no similar sounds have ever jarred upon the ear of humanity. There were two particulars, nevertheless, which I thought then, and still think, might fairly be stated as characteristic of the intonation—as well adapted to convey some idea of its unearthly peculiarity. In the first place, the voice seemed to reach our ears—at least mine—from a vast distance, or from some deep cavern within the earth. In the second place, it impressed me (I fear, indeed, that it will be impossible to make myself comprehended) as gelatinous or glutinous matters impress the sense of touch.

I have spoken both of " sound " and of " voice." I mean to say that the sound was one of distinct—of even wonderfully, thrillingly distinct—syllabification. M. Valdemar *spoke*—obviously in reply to the question I had propounded to him a few minutes before. I had asked him, it will be remembered, if he still slept. He now said—

" Yes—no—I *have been* sleeping—and now—now—*I am dead.*"

No person present even affected to deny, or attempted to repress, the unutterable, shuddering horror which these few words, thus uttered, were so well calculated to convey.   Mr. L——l (the student) swooned.   The nurses immediately left the chamber, and could not be induced to return.   My own impressions I would not pretend to render intelligible to the reader.   For nearly an hour, we busied ourselves, silently—without the utterance of a word—in endeavours to revive Mr. L——l.   When he came to himself, we addressed ourselves again to an investigation of M. Valdemar's condition.

It remained in all respects as I have last described it, with the exception that the mirror no longer afforded evidence of respiration.   An attempt to draw blood from the arm failed.   I should mention, too, that this limb was no further subject to my will.   I endeavoured in vain to make it follow the direction of my hand.   The only real indication, indeed, of the mesmeric influence was now found in the vibratory movement of the tongue, whenever I addressed M. Valdemar a question.   He seemed to be making an effort to reply, but had no longer sufficient volition   To queries put to him by any other person than myself he seemed utterly insensible—although I endeavoured to place each member of the company in mesmeric *rapport* with him.   I believe that I have now related all that is necessary to an understanding of the sleep-waker's state at this epoch.   Other nurses were procured ; and at ten o'clock I left the house in company with the two physicians and Mr. L——l.

In the afternoon we all called again to see the patient. His condition remained precisely the same.   We had now some discussion as to the propriety and feasibility of awakening him ;   but we had little difficulty in agreeing that no good purpose would be served by so doing.   It was evident that, so far, death (or what is usually termed death) had been arrested by the mesmeric process.   It seemed clear to us all that to awaken M. Valdemar would be merely to insure his instant, or at least his speedy dissolution.

From this period until the close of last week—*an interval of nearly seven months*—we continued to make daily calls at M. Valdemar's house, accompanied, now and then, by medical and other friends. All this time the sleep-waker remained *exactly* as I have last described him. The nurses' attentions were continual.

It was on Friday last that we finally resolved to make the experiment of awakening, or attempting to awaken him ; and it is the (perhaps) unfortunate result of this latter experiment which has given rise to so much discussion in private circles—to so much of what I cannot help thinking unwarranted popular feeling.

For the purpose of relieving M. Valdemar from the mesmeric trance, I made use of the customary passes. These for a time were unsuccessful. The first indication of revival was afforded by a partial descent of the iris. It was observed, as especially remarkable, that this lowering of the pupil was accompanied by the profuse outflowing of a yellowish ichor (from beneath the lids) of a pungent and highly offensive odour.

It was now suggested that I should attempt to influence the patient's arm as heretofore. I made the attempt and failed. Dr. F—— then intimated a desire to have me put a question. I did so, as follows—

" M. Valdemar, can you explain to us what are your feelings or wishes now ? "

There was an instant return of the hectic circles on the cheeks ; the tongue quivered, or rather rolled violently in the mouth (although the jaws and lips remained rigid as before) ; and at length the same hideous voice which I have already described, broke forth—

" For God's sake !—quick !—quick—put me to sleep— or quick !—waken me !—quick !—*I say to you that I am dead !* "

I was thoroughly unnerved, and for an instant remained undecided what to do. At first I made an endeavour to re-compose the patient ; but, failing in this through total abeyance of the will, I retraced my steps, and as earnestly struggled to awaken him. In this attempt I soon saw that I should be successful—or at least I soon fancied that my success would be complete—and I am sure that all in the room were prepared to see the patient awaken.

For what really occurred, however, it is quite impossible that any human being could have been prepared.

As I rapidly made the mesmeric passes, amid ejaculations of " Dead ! dead ! " absolutely *bursting* from the tongue and not from the lips of the sufferer, his whole frame at once —within the space of a single minute, or even less, shrunk —crumbled—absolutely *rotted* away beneath my hands. Upon the bed, before that whole company, there lay a nearly liquid mass of loathsome—of detestable putridity.

THE ISLAND OF THE FAY

Nullus enim locus sine genio est.—SERVIUS.

" *La musique*," says Marmontel, in those *Contes Moraux* * which, in all our translations, we have insisted upon calling *Moral Tales* as if in mockery of their spirit—" *la musique est le seul des talents qui jouissent de lui-même ; tous les autres veulent des témoins.*" He here confounds the pleasure derivable from sweet sounds with the capacity for creating them. No more than any other *talent*, is that for music susceptible of complete enjoyment, where there is no second party to appreciate its exercise. And it is only in common with other talents that it produces *effects* which may be fully enjoyed in solitude. The idea which the *raconteur* has either failed to entertain clearly, or has sacrificed in its expression to his national love of *point*, is, doubtless, the very tenable one that the higher order of music is the most thoroughly estimated when we are exclusively alone. The proposition, in this form, will be admitted at once by those who love the lyre for its own sake, and for its spiritual uses. But there is one pleasure still within the reach of fallen mortality—and perhaps only one—which owes even more than does music to the accessory sentiment of seclusion. I mean the happiness experienced in the contemplation of natural scenery. In truth, the man who would behold aright the glory of God upon earth must in solitude behold that glory. To me, at least, the presence—not of human

* *Moraux* is here derived from *mœurs* and its meaning is *fashionable,* or, more strictly, " of manners."

life only, but of life in any other form than that of the
green things which grow upon the soil and are voiceless—
is a stain upon the landscape—is at war with the genius of
the scene. I love, indeed, to regard the dark valleys, and
the grey rocks, and the waters that silently smile, and the
forests that sigh in uneasy slumbers, and the proud watchful
mountains that look down upon all—I love to regard these
as themselves but the colossal members of one vast animate
and sentient whole—a whole whose form (that of the sphere)
is the most perfect and most inclusive of all ; whose path
is among associate planets ; whose meek handmaiden is
the moon ; whose mediate sovereign is the sun ; whose
life is eternity ; whose thought is that of a God ; whose
enjoyment is knowledge ; whose destinies are lost in
immensity ; whose cognisance of ourselves is akin with
our own cognisance of the *animalculæ* which infest the
brain—a being which we, in consequence, regard as purely
inanimate and material, much in the same manner as these
animalculæ must thus regard us.

Our telescopes and our mathematical investigations
assure us on every hand—notwithstanding the cant of the
more ignorant of the priesthood—that space, and therefore
that bulk, is an important consideration in the eyes of
the Almighty. The cycles in which the stars move are those
best adapted for the evolution, without collision, of the
greatest possible number of bodies. The forms of those
bodies are accurately such as, within a given surface, to
include the greatest possible amount of matter ;—while
the surfaces themselves are so disposed as to accommodate
a denser population than could be accommodated on the
same surfaces otherwise arranged. Nor is it any argument
against bulk being an object with God, that space itself is
infinite ; for there may be an affinity of matter to fill it.
And since we see clearly that the endowment of matter with
vitality is a principle—indeed as far as our judgments
extend, the *leading* principle in the operations of Deity—
it is scarcely logical to imagine it confined to the regions of
the minute, where we daily trace it, and not extending to
those of the august. As we find cycle within cycle without
end—yet all revolving around one far-distant centre which
is the Godhead, may we not analogically suppose, in the
same manner, life within life, the less within the greater,
and all within the Spirit Divine ? In short, we are madly

erring, through self-esteem, in believing man, in either his temporal or future destinies, to be of more moment in the universe than that vast " clod of the valley " which he tills and contemns, and to which he denies a soul for no more profound reason than that he does not behold it in operation.*

These fancies, and such as these, have always given to my meditations among the mountains, and the forests, by the rivers and the ocean, a tinge of what the everyday world would not fail to term the fantastic. My wanderings amid such scenes have been many, and far-searching, and often solitary ; and the interest with which I have strayed through many a dim deep valley, or gazed into the reflected Heaven of many a bright lake, has been an interest greatly deepened by the thought that I have strayed and gazed *alone*. What flippant Frenchman † was it who said, in allusion to the well-known work of Zimmerman, that, " *la solitude est une belle chose ; mais il faut quelqu'un pour vous dire que la solitude est une belle chose.*" The epigram cannot be gainsaid ; but the necessity is a thing that does not exist.

It was during one of my lonely journeyings, amid a far-distant region of mountain locked within mountain, and sad rivers and melancholy tarns writhing or sleeping within all—that I chanced upon a certain rivulet and island. I came upon them suddenly in the leafy June, and threw myself upon the turf, beneath the branches of an unknown odorous shrub, that I might doze as I contemplated the scene. I felt that thus only should I look upon it—such was the character of phantasm which it wore.

On all sides—save to the west, where the sun was about sinking—arose the verdant walls of the forest. The little river which turned sharply in its course, and was thus immediately lost to sight, seemed to have no exit from its prison, but to be absorbed by the deep green foliage of the trees to the east—while in the opposite quarter (so it appeared to me as I lay at length and glanced upward) there poured down noiselessly and continuously into the valley, a rich golden and crimson waterfall from the sunset fountains of the sky.

About midway in the short vista which my dreamy

* Speaking of the tides, Pomponius Mela, in his treatise *De Situ Orbis*, says, " Either the world is a great animal, or," etc.
  † Balzac—in substance—I do not remember the words.

vision took in, one small circular island, profusely verdured, reposed upon the bosom of the stream.

> So blended bank and shadow there,
> That each seemed pendulous in air—

so mirror-like was the glassy water, that it was scarcely possible to say at what point upon the slope of the emerald turf its crystal dominion began.

My position enabled me to include in a single view both the eastern and western extremities of the islet ; and I observed a singularly-marked difference in their aspects. The latter was all one radiant harem of garden beauties. It glowed and blushed beneath the eye of the slant sunlight, and fairly laughed with flowers. The grass was short, springy, sweet-scented, and Asphodel-interspersed. The trees were lithe, mirthful, erect—bright, slender, and graceful—of eastern figure and foliage, with bark smooth, glossy, and parti-coloured. There seemed a deep sense of life and joy about all ; and although no airs blew from out the Heavens, yet everything had motion through the gentle sweepings to and fro of innumerable butterflies, that might have been mistaken for tulips with wings.*

The other or eastern end of the isle was whelmed in the blackest shade. A sombre, yet beautiful and peaceful gloom, here pervaded all things. The trees were dark in colour and mournful in form and attitude—wreathing themselves into sad, solemn, and spectral shapes, that conveyed ideas of mortal sorrow and untimely death. The grass wore the deep tint of the cypress, and the heads of its blades hung droopingly, and, hither and thither among it, were many small unsightly hillocks, low, and narrow, and not very long, that had the aspect of graves, but were not ; although over and all about them the rue and rosemary clambered. The shade of the trees fell heavily upon the water, and seemed to bury itself therein, impregnating the depths of the element with darkness. I fancied that each shadow, as the sun descended lower and lower, separated itself sullenly from the trunk that gave it birth, and thus became absorbed by the stream ; while other shadows issued momently from the trees, taking the place of their predecessors thus entombed.

* Florem putares nare per liquidum æthera.—P. Commire.

This idea, having once seized upon my fancy, greatly excited it, and I lost myself forthwith in reverie. " If ever island were enchanted,"—said I to myself—" this is it. This is the haunt of the few gentle Fays who remain from the wreck of the race. Are these green tombs theirs ?— or do they yield up their sweet lives as mankind yield up their own ? In dying, do they not rather waste away mournfully ; rendering unto God little by little their existence, as these trees render up shadow after shadow, exhausting their substance unto dissolution ? What the wasting tree is to the water that imbibes its shade, growing thus blacker by what it preys upon, may not the life of the Fay be to the death which engulfs it ? "

As I thus mused, with half-shut eyes, while the sun sank rapidly to rest, and eddying currents careered round and round the island, bearing upon their bosom large, dazzling, white flakes of the bark of the sycamore—flakes which, in their multiform positions upon the water, a quick imagination might have converted into anything it pleased —while I thus mused, it appeared to me that the form of one of those very Fays about whom I had been pondering, made its way slowly into the darkness from out the light at the western end of the island. She stood erect, in a singularly fragile canoe, and urged it with the mere phantom of an oar. While within the influence of the lingering sunbeams, her attitude seemed indicative of joy—but sorrow deformed it as she passed within the shade. Slowly she glided along, and at length rounded the islet and re-entered the region of light. " The revolution which has just been made by the Fay," continued I musingly—" is the cycle of the brief year of her life. She has floated through her winter and through her summer. She is a year nearer unto Death : for I did not fail to see that as she came into the shade, her shadow fell from her, and was swallowed up in the dark water, making its blackness more black."

And again the boat appeared, and the Fay ; but about the attitude of the latter there was more of care and uncertainty, and less of ecstatic joy. She floated again from out of the light and into the gloom (which deepened momently), and again her shadow fell from her into the ebony water and became absorbed into its blackness. And again and again she made the circuit of the island (while

D

the sun rushed down to his slumbers), and at each issuing
into the light, there was more sorrow about her person,
while it grew feebler, and far fainter, and more indistinct ;
and at each passage into the gloom, there fell from her
a darker shade, which became whelmed in a shadow more
black. But at length, when the sun had utterly departed,
the Fay, now the mere ghost of her former self, went
disconsolately with her boat into the region of the ebony
flood,—and that she issued thence I cannot say,—for
darkness fell over all things, and I beheld her magical figure
no more.

THE SPHINX

DURING the dread reign of the Cholera in New York, I had
accepted the invitation of a relative to spend a fortnight
with him in the retirement of his *cottage orné* on the banks
of the Hudson. He had here around us all the ordinary
means of summer amusement ; and what with rambling
in the woods, sketching, boating, fishing, bathing, music,
and books, we should have passed the time pleasantly
enough, but for the fearful intelligence which reached us
every morning from the populous city. Not a day elapsed
which did not bring us news of the decease of some acquaintance. Then, as the fatality increased, we learned to expect daily the loss of some friend. At length we trembled
at the approach of every messenger. The very air from
the South seemed to us redolent with death. That palsy-
ing thought, indeed, took entire possession of my soul. I
could neither speak, think, nor dream of anything else.
My host was of a less excitable temperament, and, although
greatly depressed in spirits, exerted himself to sustain my
own. His richly philosophical intellect was not at any
time affected by unrealities. To the substances of terror
he was sufficiently alive, but of its shadows he had no
apprehension.

His endeavours to arouse me from the condition of
abnormal gloom into which I had fallen, were frustrated
in great measure, by certain volumes which I had found

in his library. These were of a character to force into
germination whatever seeds of hereditary superstition lay
latent in my bosom. I had been reading these books
without his knowledge, and thus he was often at a loss to
account for the forcible impressions which had been made
upon my fancy.

A favourite topic with me was the popular belief in omens
—a belief which, at this one epoch of my life, I was almost
seriously disposed to defend. On this subject we had
long and animated discussions—he maintaining the utter
groundlessness of faith in such matters—I contending that
a popular sentiment arising with absolute spontaneity—that
is to say, without apparent traces of suggestion—had in
itself the unmistakable elements of truth, and was entitled
to much respect.

The fact is, that soon after my arrival at the cottage,
there had occurred to myself an incident so entirely inexplicable, and which had in it so much of the portentous
character, that I might well have been excused for regarding
it as an omen. It appalled, and at the same time so
confounded and bewildered me, that many days elapsed
before I could make up my mind to communicate the
circumstance to my friend.

Near the close of an exceedingly warm day, I was
sitting, book in hand, at an open window, commanding,
through a long vista of the river banks, a view of a distant
hill, the face of which nearest my position, had been
denuded, by what is termed a land-slide, of the principal
portion of its trees. My thoughts had been long wandering from the volume before me to the gloom and desolation
of the neighbouring city. Uplifting my eyes from the
page, they fell upon the naked face of the hill, and upon an
object—upon some living monster of hideous conformation,
which very rapidly made its way from the summit to the
bottom, disappearing finally in the dense forest below.
As this creature first came in sight, I doubted my own
sanity—or at least the evidence of my own eyes ; and
many minutes passed before I succeeded in convincing
myself that I was neither mad nor in a dream. Yet when
I describe the monster (which I distinctly saw, and calmly
surveyed through the whole period of its progress), my
readers, I fear, will feel more difficulty in being convinced
of these points than even I did myself.

Estimating the size of the creature by comparison with the diameter of the large trees near which it passed—the few giants of the forest which had escaped the fury of the land-slide—I concluded it to be far larger than any ship of the line in existence. I say ship of the line, because the shape of the monster suggested the idea—the hull of one of our seventy-fours might convey a very tolerable conception of the general outline. The mouth of the animal was situated at the extremity of a proboscis some sixty or seventy feet in length, and about as thick as the body of an ordinary elephant. Near the root of this trunk was an immense quantity of black shaggy hair—more than could have been supplied by the coats of a score of buffaloes ; and projecting from this hair downwardly and laterally, sprang two gleaming tusks not unlike those of the wild boar, but of infinitely greater dimension. Extending forward, parallel with the proboscis, and on each side of it, was a gigantic staff, thirty or forty feet in length, formed seemingly of pure crystal, and in shape a perfect prism :— it reflected in the most gorgeous manner the rays of the declining sun. The trunk was fashioned like a wedge with the apex to the earth. From it there were outspread two pairs of wings—each wing nearly one hundred yards in length—one pair being placed above the other, and all thickly covered with metal scales ; each scale apparently some ten or twelve feet in diameter. I observed that the upper and lower tiers of wings were connected by a strong chain. But the chief peculiarity of this horrible thing, was the representation of a *Death's Head*, which covered nearly the whole surface of its breast, and which was as accurately traced in glaring white, upon the dark ground of the body, as if it had been there carefully designed by an artist. While I regarded this terrific animal, and more especially the appearance on its breast, with a feeling of horror and awe—with a sentiment of forthcoming evil, which I found it impossible to quell by any effort of the reason, I perceived the huge jaws at the extremity of the proboscis suddenly expand themselves, and from them there proceeded a sound so loud and so expressive of woe, that it struck upon my nerves like a knell, and as the monster disappeared at the foot of the hill, I fell at once, fainting, to the floor.

Upon recovering, my first impulse of course was to inform

my friend of what I had seen and heard—and I can scarcely explain what feeling of repugnance it was, which, in the end, operated to prevent me.

At length, one evening, some three or four days after the occurrence, we were sitting together in the room in which I had seen the apparition—I occupying the same seat at the same window, and he lounging on a sofa near at hand. The association of the place and time impelled me to give him an account of the phenomenon. He heard me to the end—at first laughed heartily—and then lapsed into an excessively grave demeanour, as if my insanity was a thing beyond suspicion. At this instant I again had a distinct view of the monster—to which, with a shout of absolute terror, I now directed his attention. He looked eagerly—but maintained that he saw nothing —although I designated minutely the course of the creature, as it made its way down the naked face of the hill.

I was now immeasurably alarmed, for I considered the vision either as an omen of my death, or, worse, as the forerunner of an attack of mania. I threw myself passionately back in my chair, and for some moments buried my face in my hands. When I uncovered my eyes, the apparition was no longer visible.

My host, however, had in some degree resumed the calmness of his demeanour, and questioned me very rigorously in respect to the conformation of the visionary creature. When I had fully satisfied him on this head, he sighed deeply, as if relieved of some intolerable burden, and went on to talk, with what I thought a cruel calmness, of various points of speculative philosophy, which had heretofore formed subject of discussion between us. I remember his insisting very especially (among other things) upon the idea that the principal source of error in all human investigations, lay in the liability of the understanding to underrate or to overvalue the importance of an object, through mere misadmeasurement of its propinquity. " To estimate properly, for example," he said, " the influence to be exercised on mankind at large by the thorough diffusion of Democracy, the distance of the epoch at which such diffusion may possibly be accomplished, should not fail to form an item in the estimate. Yet can you tell me one writer on the subject of government, who has ever thought this particular branch of the subject worthy of discussion at all ? "

He here paused for a moment, stepped to a book-case, and brought forth one of the ordinary synopses of Natural History. Requesting me then to exchange seats with him, that he might better distinguish the fine print of the volume, he took my arm-chair at the window, and, opening the book, resumed his discourse very much in the same tone as before.

" But for your exceeding minuteness," he said, " in describing the monster, I might never have had it in my power to demonstrate to you what it was. In the first place, let me read to you a school-boy account of the genus *Sphinx*, of the family *Crepuscularia*, of the order *Lepidoptera*, of the class of *Insecta*—or insects. The account runs thus :

" Four membraneous wings covered with little coloured scales of a metallic appearance ; mouth forming a rolled proboscis, produced by an elongation of the jaws, upon the sides of which are found the rudiments of mandibles and downy palpi ; the inferior wings retained to the superior by a stiff hair ; antennæ in the form of an elongated club, prismatic ; abdomen pointed. The Death's-headed Sphinx has occasioned much terror among the vulgar, at times, by the melancholy kind of cry which it utters, and the insignia of death which it wears upon its corselet."

He here closed the book and leaned forward in the chair, placing himself accurately in the position which I had occupied at the moment of beholding " the monster."

" Ah, here it is ! " he presently exclaimed—" it is reascending the face of the hill, and a very remarkable-looking creature, I admit it to be. Still, it is by no means so large or so distant as you imagined it ; for the fact is that, as it wriggles its way up this thread, which some spider has wrought along the window-sash, I find it to be about the sixteenth of an inch in its extreme length, and also about the sixteenth of an inch distant from the pupil of my eye."

MS. FOUND IN A BOTTLE

" Qui n'a plus qu'un moment à vivre
N'a plus rien à dissimuler."
—QUINAULT, *Atys*.

OF my country and of my family I have little to say.
Ill usage and length of years have driven me from the
one, and estranged me from the other. Hereditary wealth
afforded me an education of no common order, and a
contemplative turn of mind enabled me to methodise the
stores which early study diligently garnered up. Beyond
all things, the works of the German moralists gave me a
great delight ; not from my ill-advised admiration of their
eloquent madness, but from the ease with which my habits
of rigid thought enabled me to detect their falsities. I have
often been reproached with the aridity of my genius ; a
deficiency of imagination has been imputed to me as a
crime ; and the Pyrrhonism of my opinions has at all
times rendered me notorious. Indeed, a strong relish for
physical philosophy has, I fear, tinctured my mind with a
very common error of this age—I mean the habit of
referring occurrences, even the least susceptible of such
reference, to the principles of that science. Upon the
whole, no person could be less liable than myself to be led
away from the severe precincts of truth by the *ignes fatui*
of superstition. I have thought proper to premise thus
much, lest the incredible tale I have to tell should be considered rather the raving of a crude imagination, than the
positive experience of a mind to which the reveries of fancy
have been a dead letter and a nullity.

After many years spent in foreign travel, I sailed in
the year 18—, from the port of Batavia, in the rich and
populous island of Java, on a voyage to the Archipelago
of the Sunda Islands. I went as passenger—having no
other inducement than a kind of nervous restlessness which
haunted me as a fiend.

Our vessel was a beautiful ship of about four hundred
tons, copper-fastened, and built at Bombay of Malabar
teak. She was freighted with cotton-wool and oil, from
the Lachadive Islands. We had also on board coir, jaggeree,
ghee, cocoa-nuts, and a few cases of opium. The

stowage was clumsily done, and the vessel consequently crank.

We got under way with a mere breath of wind, and for many days stood along the eastern coast of Java, without any other incident to beguile the monotony of our course than the occasional meeting with some of the small grabs of the Archipelago to which we were bound.

One evening, leaning over the taffrail, I observed a very singular isolated cloud, to the N.W. It was remarkable, as well for its colour, as from its being the first we had seen since our departure from Batavia. I watched it attentively until sunset, when it spread all at once to the eastward and westward, girting in the horizon with a narrow strip of vapour, and looking like a long line of low beach. My notice was soon afterwards attracted by the dusky-red appearance of the moon, and the peculiar character of the sea. The latter was undergoing a rapid change, and the water seemed more than usually transparent. Although I could distinctly see the bottom, yet, heaving the lead, I found the ship in fifteen fathoms. The air now became intolerably hot, and was loaded with spiral exhalations similar to those arising from heated iron. As night came on, every breath of wind died away, and a more entire calm it is impossible to conceive. The flame of a candle burned upon the poop without the least perceptible motion, and a long hair, held between the finger and thumb, hung without the possibility of detecting a vibration. However, as the captain said he could perceive no indication of danger, and as we were drifting in bodily to shore, he ordered the sails to be furled, and the anchor let go. No watch was set, and the crew, consisting principally of Malays, stretched themselves deliberately upon deck. I went below—not without a full presentiment of evil. Indeed, every appearance warranted me in apprehending a simoom. I told the captain my fears ; but he paid no attention to what I said, and left me without deigning to give a reply. My uneasiness, however, prevented me from sleeping, and about midnight I went upon deck. As I placed my foot upon the upper step of the companion-ladder, I was startled by a loud, humming noise, like that occasioned by the rapid revolution of a mill-wheel, and before I could ascertain its meaning, I found the ship quivering to its centre. In the next instant, a wilderness

of foam hurled us upon our beam-ends, and, rushing over
us fore and aft, swept the entire decks from stem to stern.

The extreme fury of the blast proved, in a great measure,
the salvation of the ship. Although completely water-
logged, yet, as her masts had gone by the board, she
rose, after a minute, heavily from the sea, and, staggering
awhile beneath the immense pressure of the tempest,
finally righted.

By what miracle I escaped destruction, it is impossible
to say. Stunned by the shock of the water, I found
myself, upon recovery, jammed in between the stern-post
and rudder. With great difficulty I gained my feet, and
looking dizzily around, was at first struck with the idea of
our being among breakers ; so terrific, beyond the wildest
imagination, was the whirlpool of mountainous and foaming
ocean within which we were engulfed. After a while, I
heard the voice of an old Swede, who had shipped with us
at the moment of leaving port. I hallooed to him with all
my strength, and presently he came reeling aft. We soon
discovered that we were the sole survivors of the accident.
All on deck, with the exeeption of ourselves, had been
swept overboard ; the captain and mates must have
perished as they slept, for the cabins were deluged with
water. Without assistance, we could expect to do little
for the security of the ship, and our exertions were at first
paralysed by the momentary expectation of going down.
Our cable had, of course, parted like pack-thread, at the
first breath of the hurricane, or we should have been
instantaneously overwhelmed. We scudded with frightful
velocity before the sea, and the water made clear breaches
over us. The framework of our stern was shattered
excessively, and, in almost every respect, we had received
considerable injury ; but to our extreme joy we found the
pumps unchoked, and that we had made no great shifting
of our ballast. The main fury of the blast had already
blown over, and we apprehended little danger from the
violence of the wind ; but we looked forward to its total
cessation with dismay, well believing, that in our shattered
condition, we should inevitably perish in the tremendous
swell which would ensue. But this very just apprehension
seemed by no means likely to be soon verified. For five
entire days and nights—during which our only subsistence
was a small quantity of jaggeree, procured with great

difficulty from the forecastle—the hulk flew at a rat
defying computation, before rapidly succeeding flaws o
wind, which without equalling the first violence of th
simoom, were still more terrific than any tempest I ha
before encountered.   Our course for the first four days wa:
with trifling variations, S.E. and by S. ; and we must hav
run down the coast of New Holland.   On the fifth day th
cold became extreme, although the wind had hauled roun
a point more to the northward.   The sun arose with
sickly yellow lustre, and clambered a very few degree
above the horizon—emitting no decisive light.   Ther
were no clouds apparent, yet the wind was upon th
increase, and blew with a fitful and unsteady fury.   Abou
noon, as nearly as we could guess, our attention was agai
arrested by the appearance of the sun.   It gave out n
light, properly so called, but a dull and sullen glow withou
reflection, as if all its rays were polarised.   Just befor
sinking within the turgid sea, its central fires suddenly wen
out, as if hurriedly extinguished by some unaccountabl
power.   It was a dim, silver-like rim, alone, as it rushe
down the unfathomable ocean.

We waited in vain for the arrival of the sixth day—
that day to me has not arrived—to the Swede, neve
did arrive.   Thenceforward we were enshrouded in pitch
darkness, so that we could not have seen an object a
twenty paces from the ship.   Eternal night continued t
envelop us, all unrelieved by the phosphoric sea-brillianc
to which we had been accustomed in the tropics.   W
observed, too, that, although the tempest continued to rag
with unabated violence, there was no longer to be dis
covered the usual appearance of surf, or foam, which ha
hitherto attended us.   All around were horror, and thic
gloom, and a black sweltering desert of ebony.   Super
stitious terror crept by degrees into the spirit of the ol
Swede, and my own soul was wrapped up in silent wonder
We neglected all care of the ship, as worse than useless
and securing ourselves, as well as possible, to the stum
of the mizzen-mast, looked out bitterly into the worl
of ocean.   We had no means of calculating time, no
could we form any guess of our situation.   We were
however, well aware of having made farther to the south
ward than any previous navigators, and felt great amaze
ment at not meeting with the usual impediments of ice

In the meantime every moment threatened to be our last—
every mountainous billow hurried to overwhelm us. The
swell surpassed anything I had imagined possible, and that
we were not instantly buried is a miracle. My companion
spoke of the lightness of our cargo, and reminded me of the
excellent qualities of our ship ; but I could not help feeling
the utter hopelessness of hope itself, and prepared myself
gloomily for that death which I thought nothing could
defer beyond an hour, as with every knot of way the ship
made, the swelling of the black stupendous seas became
more dismally appalling. At times we gasped for breath
at an elevation beyond the albatross—at times became
dizzy with the velocity of our descent into some watery
hell, where the air grew stagnant, and no sound disturbed
the slumbers of the kraken.

We were at the bottom of one of these abysses, when a
quick scream from my companion broke fearfully upon the
night. " See ! see ! " cried he, shrieking in my ears,
" Almighty God ! see ! see ! " As he spoke, I became
aware of a dull, sullen glare of red light which streamed
down the sides of the vast chasm where we lay, and threw
a fitful brilliancy upon our deck. Casting my eyes upwards, I beheld a spectacle which froze the current of my
blood. At a terrific height directly above us, and upon the
very verge of the precipitous descent, hovered a gigantic
ship, of perhaps four thousand tons. Although upreared
upon the summit of a wave more than a hundred times her
own altitude, her apparent size still exceeded that of any
ship of the line or East Indiaman in existence. Her huge
hull was of a deep dingy black, unrelieved by any of the
customary carvings of a ship. A single row of brass cannon
protruded from her open ports, and dashed from their
polished surfaces the fires of innumerable battle-lanterns
which swung to and fro about her rigging. But what
mainly inspired us with horror and astonishment, was that
she bore up under a press of sail in the very teeth of that
supernatural sea, and of that ungovernable hurricane.
When we first discovered her, her bows were alone to be
seen, as she rose slowly from the dim and horrible gulf
beyond her. For a moment of intense terror she paused
upon the giddy pinnacle, as if in contemplation of her own
sublimity, then trembled and tottered, and—came down.

At this instant, I know not what sudden self-possession

came over my spirit. Staggering as far aft as I could, I awaited fearlessly the ruin that was to overwhelm. Our own vessel was at length ceasing from her struggles, and sinking with her head to the sea. The shock of the descending mass struck her, consequently, in that portion of her frame which was nearly under water, and the inevitable result was to hurl me, with irresistible violence, upon the rigging of the stranger.

As I fell, the ship hove in stays, and went about ; and to the confusion ensuing I attributed my escape from the notice of the crew. With little difficulty I made my way, unperceived, to the main hatchway, which was partially open, and soon found an opportunity of secreting myself in the hold. Why I did so I can hardly tell. An indefinite sense of awe, which at first sight of the navigators of the ship had taken hold of my mind, was perhaps the principle of my concealment. I was unwilling to trust myself with a race of people who had offered, to the cursory glance I had taken, so many points of vague novelty, doubt, and apprehension. I therefore thought proper to contrive a hiding-place in the hold. This I did by removing a small portion of the shifting-boards, in such a manner as to afford me a convenient retreat between the huge timbers of the ship.

I had scarcely completed my work, when a footstep in the hold forced me to make use of it. A man passed by my place of concealment with a feeble and unsteady gait. I could not see his face, but had an opportunity of observing his general appearance. There was about it an evidence of great age and infirmity. His knees tottered beneath a load of years, and his entire frame quivered under the burthen. He muttered to himself, in a low broken tone, some words of a language which I could not understand, and groped in a corner among a pile of singular-looking instruments, and decayed charts of navigation. His manner was a wild mixture of the peevishness of second childhood and the solemn dignity of a god. He at length went on deck, and I saw him no more.

.   .   .   .

A feeling, for which I have no name, has taken possession of my soul—a sensation which will admit of no analysis, to which the lessons of bygone time are inadequate, and

for which I fear futurity itself will offer me no key. To a
mind constituted like my own, the latter consideration is
an evil. I shall never—I know that I shall never—be
satisfied with regard to the nature of my conceptions.
Yet it is not wonderful that these conceptions are indefinite,
since they have their origin in sources so utterly novel.
A new sense—a new entity is added to my soul.

    .   .   .   .

It is long since I first trod the deck of this terrible ship,
and the rays of my destiny are, I think, gathering to a
focus. Incomprehensible men! Wrapped up in meditations of a kind which I cannot divine, they pass me by
unnoticed. Concealment is utter folly on my part, for the
people *will not* see. It was but just now that I passed
directly before the eyes of the mate ; it was no long while
ago that I ventured into the captain's own private cabin,
and took thence the materials with which I write, and have
written. I shall from time to time continue this journal.
It is true that I may not find an opportunity of trans-
mitting it to the world, but I will not fail to make the
endeavour. At the last moment I will enclose the MS. in
a bottle, and cast it within the sea.

    .   .   .   .

An incident has occurred which has given me new room
for meditation. Are such things the operation of un-
governed chance ? I had ventured upon deck and thrown
myself down, without attracting any notice, among a pile
of ratlin-stuff and old sails, in the bottom of the yawl.
While musing upon the singularity of my fate, I unwittingly daubed with a tar-brush the edges of a neatly-
folded studding-sail which lay near me on a barrel. The
studding-sail is now bent upon the ship, and the thoughtless
touches of the brush are spread out into the word
DISCOVERY.

I have made many observations lately upon the structure
of the vessel. Although well armed, she is not, I think, a
ship of war. Her rigging, build, and general equipment,
all negative a supposition of this kind. What she *is not*,
I can easily perceive ; what she *is*, I fear it is impossible
to say. I know not how it is, but in scrutinising her
strange model and singular cast of spars, her huge size and

overgrown suits of canvas, her severely simple bow and antiquated stern, there will occasionally flash across my mind a sensation of familiar things, and there is always mixed up with such indistinct shadows of recollection, an unaccountable memory of old foreign chronicles and ages long ago.

. . . .

I have been looking at the timbers of the ship. She is built of a material to which I am a stranger. There is a peculiar character about the wood which strikes me as rendering it unfit for the purpose to which it has been applied. I mean its extreme *porousness*, considered independently of the worm-eaten condition which is a consequence of navigation in these seas, and apart from the rottenness attendant upon age. It will appear, perhaps, an observation somewhat over-curious, but this wood would have every characteristic of Spanish oak, if Spanish oak were distended by any unnatural means.

In reading the above sentence, a curious apothegm of an old weather-beaten Dutch navigator comes full upon my recollection. " It is as sure," he was wont to say, when any doubt was entertained of his veracity, " as sure as there is a sea where the ship itself will grow in bulk like the living body of the seaman."

. . . .

About an hour ago I made bold to trust myself among a group of the crew. They paid me no manner of attention, and, although I stood in the very midst of them all, seemed utterly unconscious of my presence. Like the one I had at first seen in the hold, they all bore about them the marks of a hoary old age. Their knees trembled with infirmity ; their shoulders were bent double with decrepitude ; their shrivelled skins rattled in the wind ; their voices were low, tremulous, and broken ; their eyes glistened with the rheum of years ; and their grey hairs streamed terribly in the tempest. Around them, on every part of the deck, lay scattered mathematical instruments of the most quaint and obsolete construction.

. . . .

I mentioned, some time ago, the bending of a studding-sail. From that period, the ship, being thrown dead off the wind, has continued her terrific course due south, with every rag of canvas packed upon her, from her truck to her lower studding-sail booms, and rolling every moment her top-gallant yard-arms into the most appalling hell of water which it can enter into the mind of man to imagine. I have just left the deck, where I find it impossible to maintain a footing, although the crew seem to experience little inconvenience. It appears to me a miracle of miracles that our enormous bulk is not swallowed up at once and for ever. We are surely doomed to hover continually upon the brink of eternity, without taking a final plunge into the abyss. From billows a thousand times more stupendous than any I have ever seen, we glide away with the facility of the arrowy sea-gull ; and the colossal waters rear their heads above us like demons of the deep, but like demons confined to simple threats, and forbidden to destroy. I am led to attribute these frequent escapes to the only natural cause which can account for such effect. I must suppose the ship to be within the influence of some strong current, or impetuous under-tow.

I have seen the captain face to face, and in his own cabin, but, as I expected, he paid me no attention. Although in his appearance there is, to a casual observer, nothing which might bespeak him more or less than man, still a feeling of irrepressible reverence and awe mingled with the sensation of wonder with which I regarded him. In stature, he is nearly my own height ; that is, about five feet eight inches. He is of a well-knit and compact frame of body, neither robust nor remarkable otherwise. But it is the singularity of the expression which reigns upon the face—it is the intense, the wonderful, the thrilling evidence of old age so utter, so extreme, which excites within my spirit a sense—a sentiment ineffable. His forehead, although little wrinkled, seems to bear upon it the stamp of a myriad of years. His grey hairs are records of the past, and his greyer eyes are sibyls of the future. The cabin floor was thickly strewn with strange, iron-clasped folios, and mouldering instruments of science, and obsolete long-forgotten charts. His head was bowed down upon his hands, and he pored, with a fiery, unquiet eye, over a paper which I took to be a commission, and which, at all events, bore the signature of a monarch. He muttered to himself—as did the first seaman whom I saw in the hold—some low peevish syllables of a foreign tongue ; and although the speaker was close at my elbow, his voice seemed to reach my ears from the distance of a mile.

•   •   •   •   •   •   •

The ship and all in it are imbued with the spirit of Eld. The crew glide to and fro like the ghosts of buried centuries ; their eyes have an eager and uneasy meaning ; and when their fingers fall athwart my path in the wild glare of the battle-lanterns, I feel as I have never felt before, although I have been all my life a dealer in antiquities, and have imbibed the shadows of fallen columns at Balbec, and Tadmor, and Persepolis, until my very soul has become a ruin.

•   •   •   •   •   •   •

When I look around me, I feel ashamed of my former apprehensions. If I trembled at the blast which has hitherto attended us, shall I not stand aghast at a warring of wind and ocean, to convey any idea of which, the words tornado and simoom are trivial and ineffective ?   All in the immediate vicinity of the ship is the blackness of eternal night, and a chaos of foamless water ; but, about a league on either side of us, may be seen, indistinctly, and at intervals, stupendous ramparts of ice, towering away into the desolate sky, and looking like the walls of the universe.

•   •   •   •   •   •   •

As I imagined, the ship proves to be in a current— if that appellation can properly be given to a tide which, howling and shrieking by the white ice, thunders on to the southward with a velocity like the headlong dashing of a cataract.

•   •   •   •   •   •   •

To conceive the horror of my sensations is, I presume, utterly impossible ; yet a curiosity to penetrate the mysteries of these awful regions predominates even over my despair, and will reconcile me to the most hideous aspect of death.   It is evident that we are hurrying onwards to some exciting knowledge—some never-to-be-imparted secret, whose attainment is destruction. Perhaps this current leads us to the southern pole itself. It must be confessed that a supposition apparently so wild has every probability in its favour.

.   .   .   .

The crew pace the deck with unquiet and tremulous step ; but there is upon their countenance an expression more of the eagerness of hope than of the apathy of despair. In the meantime the wind is still in our poop, and, as we carry a crowd of canvas, the ship is at times lifted bodily from out the sea ! Oh, horror upon horror !—the ice opens suddenly to the right, and to the left, and we are whirling dizzily, in immense concentric circles, round and round the borders of a gigantic amphitheatre, the summit of whose walls is lost in the darkness and the distance. But little time will be left me to ponder upon my destiny ! The circles rapidly grow small—we are plunging madly within the grasp of the whirlpool—and amid a roaring, and bellowing, and thundering of ocean and tempest, the ship is quivering—O God ! and——going down !

Note.—The " MS. Found in a Bottle " was originally published in 1831 ; and it was not until many years afterwards that I became acquainted with the maps of Mercator, in which the ocean is represented as rushing, by four mouths, into the (northern) Polar Gulf, to be absorbed into the bowels of the earth ; the Pole itself being represented by a black rock, towering to a prodigious height.

ELEONORA

" Sub conservatione formæ specificæ salva anima."

–RAYMOND LULLY.

I AM come of a race noted for vigour of fancy and ardour of passion. Men have called me mad, but the question is not yet settled whether madness is or is not the loftiest intelligence, whether much that is glorious, whether all that is profound, does not spring from disease of thought, from *moods* of mind exalted at the expense of the general intellect. They who dream by day are cognisant of many things which escape those who dream only by night. In their grey visions they obtain glimpses of eternity, and thrill, in waking, to find that they have been upon the verge of the great secret. In snatches they learn something of the wisdom which is of good, and more of the mere knowledge which is of evil. They penetrate, however rudderless or compassless, into the vast ocean of the " light ineffable," and again, like the adventures of the Nubian geographer, " *agressi sunt mare tenebrarum, quid in eo esset exploraturi.*"

We will say, then, that I am mad. I grant, at least, that there are two distinct conditions of my mental existence, the condition of a lucid reason not to be disputed, and belonging to the memory of events forming the first epoch of my life, and a condition of shadow and doubt, appertaining to the present, and to the recollection of what constitutes the second great era of my being. Therefore, what I shall tell of the earlier period, believe ; and to what I may relate of the later time, give only such credit as may seem due ; or doubt it altogether ; or, if doubt it ye cannot, then play unto its riddle the Œdipus.

She whom I loved in youth, and of whom I now pen calmly and distinctly these remembrances, was the sole daughter of the only sister of my mother long departed. Eleonora was the name of my cousin. We had always dwelt together, beneath a tropical sun, in the Valley of the Many-Coloured Grass. No unguided footstep ever came upon that vale, for it lay far away up among a range of giant hills that hung beetling around about it, shutting out the sunlight from its sweetest recesses. No path was trodden in its vicinity ; and to reach our happy home there was need of putting back with force the foliage of many thousands of forest trees, and of crushing to death the glories of many millions of fragrant flowers. Thus it was that we lived all alone, knowing nothing of the world without the valley—I, and my cousin, and her mother.

From the dim regions beyond the mountains at the upper end of our encircled domain, there crept out a narrow and deep river, brighter than all save the eyes of Eleonora ; and winding stealthily about in mazy courses, it passed away at length through a shadowy gorge, among hills still dimmer than those whence it had issued. We called it the " River of Silence," for there seemed to be a hushing influence in its flow. No murmur arose from its bed, and so gently it wandered along that the pearly pebbles upon which we loved to gaze, far down within its bosom, stirred not at all, but lay in a motionless content, each in its own old station, shining on gloriously for ever.

The margin of the river, and of the many dazzling rivulets that glided through devious ways into its channel, as well as the spaces that extended from the margins away down into the depths of the streams until they reached the bed of pebbles at the bottom, these spots, not less than the whole surface of the valley, from the river to the mountains that girdled it in, were carpeted all by a soft green grass, thick, short, perfectly even, and vanilla-perfumed, but so besprinkled throughout with the yellow buttercup, the white daisy, the purple violet, and the ruby-red asphodel, that its exceeding beauty spoke to our hearts in loud tones of the love and of the glory of God.

And here and there, in groves about this grass, like wildernesses of dreams, sprang up fantastic trees, whose tall slender stems stood not upright, but slanted gracefully towards the light that peered at noon-day into the centre of the valley. Their bark was speckled with the vivid alternate splendour of ebony and silver, and was smoother than all save the cheeks of Eleonora ; so that but for the brilliant green of the huge leaves that spread from their summits in long tremulous lines, dallying with the zephyrs, one might have fancied them giant serpents of Syria doing homage to their sovereign the sun.

Hand in hand about this valley, for fifteen years, roamed I with Eleonora before love entered within our hearts. It was one evening at the close of the third lustrum of her life, and of the fourth of my own, that we sat locked in each other's embrace, beneath the serpent-like trees, and looked down within the waters of the River of Silence at our images therein. We spoke no words during the rest of that sweet day, and our words even upon the morrow were tremulous and few. We had drawn the god Eros from that wave, and now we felt that he had enkindled within us the fiery souls of our forefathers. The passions which had for centuries distinguished our race came thronging with the fancies for which they had been equally noted, and together breathed a delirious bliss over the Valley of the Many-Coloured Grass. A change fell upon all things. Strange, brilliant flowers, star-shaped, burst out upon the trees where no flowers had been known before. The tints of the green carpet deepened, and when, one by one, the white daisies shrank away, there sprang up in place of them, ten by ten of the ruby-red asphodel. And life arose in our paths, for the tall flamingo, hitherto unseen, with all gay glowing birds, flaunted his scarlet plumage before us. The golden and silver fish haunted the river, out of the bosom of which issued, little by little, a murmur that swelled at length into a lulling melody more divine than that of the harp of Æolus, sweeter than all save the voice of Eleonora. And now, too, a voluminous cloud, which we had long watched in the regions of Hesper, floated out thence, all gorgeous in crimson and gold, and settling in peace above us, sank day by day lower and lower until its edges rested upon the tops of the mountains, turning all their dimness into magnificence, and shutting us up as if for ever within a magic prison-house of grandeur and of glory.

The loveliness of Eleonora was that of the Seraphim ; but she was a maiden artless and innocent as the brief life she had led among the flowers. No guile disguised the fervour of love which animated her heart, and she examined with me its inmost recesses as we walked together in the Valley of the Many-Coloured Grass, and discoursed of the mighty changes which had lately taken place therein.

At length, having spoken one day, in tears, of the last sad change which must befall humanity, she thenceforward dwelt only upon this one sorrowful theme, interweaving it into all our converse, as, in the songs of the bard of

Schiraz, the same images are found occurring again and again in every impressive variation of phrase.

She had seen that the finger of Death was upon her bosom—that, like the ephemeron, she had been made perfect in loveliness only to die ; but the terrors of the grave to her lay solely in a consideration which she revealed to me one evening at twilight by the banks of the River of Silence. She grieved to think that, having entombed her in the Valley of the Many-Coloured Grass, I would quit for ever its happy recesses, transferring the love which now was so passionately her own to some maiden of the outer and everyday world. And then and there I threw myself hurriedly at the feet of Eleonora, and offered up a vow to herself and to Heaven, that I would never bind myself in marriage to any daughter of Earth—that I would in no manner prove recreant to her dear memory, or to the memory of the devout affection with which she had blessed me. And I called the Mighty Ruler of the Universe to witness the pious solemnity of my vow. And the curse which I invoked of *Him* and of her, a saint in Elusion, should I prove traitorous to that promise, involved a penalty the exceeding great horror of which will not permit me to make record of it here. And the bright eyes of Eleonora grew brighter at my words ; and she sighed as if a deadly burthen had been taken from her breast ; and she trembled and very bitterly wept ; but she made acceptance of the vow (for what was she but a child ?), and it made easy to her the bed of her death. And she said to me, not many days afterwards, tranquilly dying, that, because of what I had done for the comfort of her spirit, she would watch over me in that spirit when departed, and, if so it were permitted her, return to me visibly in the watches of the night ; but, if this thing were indeed beyond the power of the souls in Paradise, that she would at least give me frequent indications of her presence ; sighing upon me in the evening winds, or filling the air which I breathed with perfume from the censers of the angels. And, with these words upon her lips, she yielded up her innocent life, putting an end to the first epoch of my own.

Thus far I have faithfully said. But as I pass the barrier in Time's path, formed by the death of my beloved, and proceed with the second era of my existence, I feel that a shadow gathers over my brain, and I mistrust the perfect sanity of the record. But let me on.—Years dragged themselves along heavily, and still I dwelled within the Valley of the Many-Coloured Grass ; but a second change had come upon all things. The star-shaped flowers shrank into the stems of the trees, and appeared no more. The tints of the green carpet faded ; and, one by one, the ruby-red asphodels withered away ; and there sprang up, in place of them, ten by ten, dark, eye-like violets, that writhed uneasily and were ever encumbered with dew. And Life departed from our paths ; for the tall flamingo flaunted no longer his scarlet plumage before us, but flew sadly from the vale into the hills, with all the gay glowing birds that had arrived in his company. And the golden and silver fish swam down through the gorge at the lower end of our domain, and bedecked the sweet river never again. And the lulling melody that had been softer than the wind-harp of Æolus, and more divine than all save the voice of Eleonora, it died little by little away, in murmurs growing lower and lower, until the stream returned, at length, utterly into the solemnity of its original silence ; and then, lastly, the voluminous cloud uprose, and, abandoning the tops of the mountains to the dimness of old, fell back into the regions of Hesper, and took away all its manifold golden and gorgeous glories from the Valley of the Many-Coloured Grass.

Yet the promises of Eleonora were not forgotten ; for I heard the sounds of the swinging of the censers of the angels ; and streams of a holy perfume floated ever and ever about the valley ; and at lone hours, when my heart beat heavily, the winds that bathed my brow came unto me laden with soft sighs ; and indistinct murmurs filled often the night air ; and once—oh, but once only ! I was awakened from a slumber, like the slumber of death, by the pressing of spiritual lips upon my own.

But the void within my heart refused, even thus, to be filled. I longed for the love which had before filled it to overflowing. At length the valley *pained* me through its memories of Eleonora, and I left it for ever for the vanities and the turbulent triumphs of the world.

*   *   *   *   *   *

I found myself within a strange city, where all things

might have served to blot from recollection the sweet dreams I had dreamed so long in the Valley of the Many-Coloured Grass. The pomps and pageantries of a stately court, and the mad clangour of arms, and the radiant loveliness of woman, bewildered and intoxicated my brain. But as yet my soul had proved true to its vows, and the indications of the presence of Eleonora were still given me in the silent hours of the night. Suddenly, these manifestations ceased ; and the world grew dark before mine eyes ; and I stood aghast at the burning thoughts which possessed—at the terrible temptations which beset me ; for there came from some far, far distant and unknown land, into the gay court of the king I served, a maiden to whose beauty my whole recreant heart yielded at once—at whose footstool I bowed down without a struggle in the most ardent, in the most abject worship of love. What indeed was my passion for the young girl of the valley in comparison with the fervour and the delirium, and the spirit-lifting ecstasy of adoration with which I poured out my whole soul in tears at the feet of the ethereal Ermengarde ? —Oh, bright was the seraph Ermengarde ! and in that knowledge I had room for none other.—Oh, divine was the angel Ermengarde ! and as I looked down into the depths of her memorial eyes, I thought only of them—and *of her*.

I wedded ;—nor dreaded the curse I had invoked ; and its bitterness was not visited upon me. And once—but once again in the silence of the night, there came through my lattice the soft sighs which had forsaken me ; and they modelled themselves into familiar and sweet voice, saying—

"Sleep in peace !—for the Spirit of Love reigneth and ruleth, and, in taking to thy passionate heart her who is Ermengarde, thou art absolved, for reasons which shall be made known to thee in Heaven, of thy vows unto Eleonora."

A DESCENT INTO THE MAELSTRÖM

" The ways of God in Nature, as in Providence, are not as *our* ways ; nor are the models that we frame any way commensurate to the vastness, profundity, and unsearchableness of His works, *which have a depth in them greater than the well of Democritus.*"— JOSEPH GLANVILLE.

WE had now reached the summit of the loftiest crag. For some minutes the old man seemed too much exhausted to speak.

" Not long ago," said he at length, " and I could have guided you on this route as well as the youngest of my sons ; but, about three years past, there happened to me an event such as never happened before to mortal man —or at least such as no man ever survived to tell of— and the six hours of deadly terror which I then endured have broken me up body and soul. You suppose me a *very* old man—but I am not. It took less than a single day to change these hairs from a jetty black to white, to weaken my limbs, and to unstring my nerves, so that I tremble at the least exertion, and am frightened at a shadow. Do you know I can scarcely look over this little cliff without getting giddy ? "

The " little cliff," upon whose edge he had so care- lessly thrown himself down to rest, that the weightier portion of his body hung over it, while he was only kept from falling by the tenure of his elbow on its extreme and slippery edge—this " little cliff " arose, a sheer unobstructed precipice of black shining rock, some fifteen or sixteen hundred feet from the world of crags beneath us. Nothing would have tempted me to within half-a-dozen yards of its brink. In truth, so deeply was I excited by the perilous position of my companion, that I fell at full length upon the ground, clung to the shrubs around me, and dared not even glance upward at the sky—while I struggled in vain to divest myself of the idea that the very foundations of the mountain were in danger from the fury of the winds. It was long before I could reason myself into sufficient courage to sit up and look out into the distance.

" You must get over these fancies," said the guide, ' for I have brought you here that you might have the

best possible view of the scene of that event I mentioned—
and to tell you the whole story with the spot just under
your eye."

"We are now," he continued, in that particularising
manner which distinguished him—" we are now close
upon the Norwegian coast—in the sixty-eighth degree
of latitude—in the great province of Nordland—and
in the dreary district of Lofoden. The mountain upon
whose top we sit is Helseggen, the Cloudy. Now raise
yourself up a little higher—hold on to the grass if you feel
giddy—so—and look out, beyond the belt of vapour
beneath us, into the sea."

I looked dizzily, and beheld a wide expanse of ocean,
whose waters wore so inky a hue as to bring at once to
my mind the Nubian geographer's account of the *Mare
Tenebrarum*. A panorama more deplorably desolate no
human imagination can conceive. To the right and left,
as far as the eye could reach, there lay out-stretched,
like ramparts of the world, lines of horribly black and
beetling cliff, whose character of gloom was but the more
forcibly illustrated by the surf which reared high up
against it its white and ghastly crest, howling and shrieking
for ever. Just opposite the promontory upon whose apex
we were placed, and at a distance of some five or six miles
out at sea, there was visible a small, bleak-looking island ;
or, more properly, its position was discernible through
the wilderness of surge in which it was enveloped. About
two miles nearer the land, arose another of smaller size,
hideously craggy and barren, and encompassed at various
intervals by a cluster of dark rocks.

The appearance of the ocean, in the space between the
more distant island and the shore, had something very
unusual about it. Although, at the time, so strong a gale
was blowing landward that a brig in the remote offing
lay to under a double-reefed trysail, and constantly plunged
her whole hull out of sight, still there was here nothing
like a regular swell, but only a short, quick, angry cross
dashing of water in every direction—as well in the teeth
of the wind as otherwise. Of foam there was little except
in the immediate vicinity of the rocks.

"The island in the distance," resumed the old man,
" is called by the Norwegians Vurrgh. The one midway
is Moskoe. That a mile to the northward is Ambaaren.

Yonder are Islesen, Hotholm, Keildhelm, Suarven, and Buckholm. Farther off—between Moskoe and Vurrgh—are Otterholm, Flimen, Sandflesen, and Stockholm. These are the true names of the places—but why it has been thought necessary to name them at all, is more than either you or I can understand. Do you hear anything ? Do you see any change in the water ? "

We had now been about ten minutes upon the top of Helseggen, to which we had ascended from the interior of Lofoden, so that we had caught no glimpse of the sea until it had burst upon us from the summit. As the old man spoke, I became aware of a loud and gradually increasing sound, like the moaning of a vast herd of buffaloes upon an American prairie ; and at the same moment I perceived what seamen term the *chopping* character of the ocean beneath us, was rapidly changing into a current which set to the eastward. Even while I gazed, this current acquired a monstrous velocity. Each moment added to its speed—to its headlong impetuosity. In five minutes the whole sea, as far as Vurrgh, was lashed into ungovernable fury ; but it was between Moskoe and the coast that the main uproar held its sway. Here the vast bed of the waters, seamed and scarred into a thousand conflicting channels, burst suddenly into frenzied convulsion—heaving, boiling, hissing—gyrating in gigantic and innumerable vortices, and all whirling and plunging on to the eastward with a rapidity which water never elsewhere assumes, except in precipitous descents.

In a few minutes more, there came over the scene another radical alteration. The general surface grew somewhat more smooth, and the whirlpools, one by one, disappeared, while prodigious streaks of foam became apparent where none had been seen before. These streaks, at length, spreading out to a great distance, and entering into combination, took unto themselves the gyratory motion of the subsided vortices, and seemed to form the germ of another more vast. Suddenly—very suddenly—this assumed a distinct and definite existence, in a circle of more than a mile in diameter. The edge of the whirl was represented by a broad belt of gleaming spray ; but no particle of this slipped into the mouth of the terrific funnel, whose interior, as far as the eye could fathom it, was a smooth, shining, and jet-black wall of water, inclined to the horizon at an angle of some forty-five degrees, speeding dizzily round and round with a swaying and sweltering motion, and sending forth to the winds an appalling voice, half-shriek, half-roar, such as not even the mighty cataract of Niagara ever lifts up in its agony to Heaven.

The mountain trembled to its very base, and the rock rocked. I threw myself upon my face, and clung to the scant herbage in an excess of nervous agitation.

" This," said I at length, to the old man—" this *can* be nothing else than the great whirlpool of the Maelström."

" So it is sometimes termed," said he. " We Norwegians call it the Moskoe-ström, from the island of Moskoe in the midway."

The ordinary accounts of this vortex had by no means prepared me for what I saw. That of Jonas Ramus, which is perhaps the most circumstantial of any, cannot impart the faintest conception either of the magnificence, or of the horror of the scene—or of the wild bewildering sense of *the novel* which confounds the beholder. I am not sure from what point of view the writer in question surveyed it, nor at what time ; but it could neither have been from the summit of Helseggen, nor during a storm. There are some passages of his description, nevertheless, which may be quoted for their details, although their effect is exceedingly feeble in conveying an impression of the spectacle.

" Between Lofoden and Moskoe," he says, " the depth of the water is between thirty-six and forty fathoms ; but on the other side, toward Ver (Vurrgh), this depth decreases so as not to afford a convenient passage for a vessel, without the risk of splitting on the rocks, which happens even in the calmest weather. When it is flood, the stream runs up the country between Lofoden and Moskoe with a boisterous rapidity ; but the roar of its impetuous ebb to the sea is scarce equalled by the loudest and most dreadful cataracts, the noise being heard several leagues off ; and the vortices or pits are of such an extent and depth, that if a ship comes within its attraction, it is inevitably absorbed and carried down to the bottom, and there beat to pieces against the rocks ; and when the water relaxes, the fragments thereof are thrown up again. But these intervals of tranquillity are only at the turn of the ebb and flood, and in calm weather, and last but a quarter of an hour, its violence gradually returning. When the stream is most boisterous, and its fury heightened by a storm, it is dangerous to come within a Norway mile of it. Boats, yachts, and ships have been carried away by not guarding against it before they were within its reach. It likewise happens frequently, that whales come too near the stream, and are overpowered by its violence ; and then it is impossible to describe their howlings and bellowings in their fruitless struggles to disengage themselves. A bear once, attempting to swim from Lofoden to Moskoe, was caught by the stream and borne down, while he roared terribly, so as to be heard on shore. Large stocks of firs and pine trees, after being absorbed by the current, rise again broken and torn to such a degree as if bristles grew upon them. This plainly shows the bottom to consist of craggy rocks, among which they are whirled to and fro. This stream is regulated by the flux and reflux of the sea— it being constantly high and low water every six hours. In the year 1645, early in the morning of Sexagesima Sunday, it raged with such noise and impetuosity that the very stones of the houses on the coast fell to the ground.''

In regard to the depth of the water, I could not see how this could have been ascertained at all in the immediate vicinity of the vortex. The " forty fathoms " must have reference only to portions of the channel close upon the shore either of Moskoe or Lofoden. The depth in the centre of the Moskoe-ström must be immeasurably greater ; and no better proof of this fact is necessary than can be obtained from even the sidelong glance into the abyss of the whirl which may be had from the highest crag of Helseggen. Looking down from this pinnacle upon the howling Phlegethon below, I could not help smiling at the simplicity with which the honest Jonas Ramus records, as a matter difficult of belief, the anecdotes of the whales and the bears ; for it appeared to me, in fact, a self-evident thing, that the largest ships of the line in existence, coming within the influence of that deadly attraction, could resist it as little as a feather the hurricane, and must disappear bodily and at once.

The attempts to account for the phenomenon—some of which, I remember, seemed to me sufficiently plausible in perusal—now wore a very different and unsatisfactory aspect. The idea generally received is that this, as well as three smaller vortices among the Faroe Islands, " have no other cause than the collision of waves rising and falling, at flux and reflux, against a ridge of rocks and shelves, which confines the water so that it precipitates itself like a cataract ; and thus the higher the flood rises, the deeper must the fall be, and the natural result of all is a whirlpool or vortex, the prodigious suction of which is sufficiently known by lesser experiments."—These are the words of the *Encyclopædia Britannica.* Kircher and others imagine that in the centre of the channel of the Maelström is an abyss penetrating the globe, and issuing in some very remote part—the Gulf of Bothnia being somewhat decidedly named in one instance. This opinion, idle in itself, was the one to which, as I gazed, my imagination most readily assented ; and, mentioning it to the guide, I was rather surprised to hear him say that, although it was the view almost universally entertained of the subject by the Norwegians, it nevertheless was not his own. As to the former notion, he confessed his inability to comprehend it ; and here I agreed with him—for, however conclusive on paper, it becomes altogether unintelligible, and even absurd, amid the thunder of the abyss.

" You have had a good look at the whirl now," said the old man, " and if you will creep round this crag, so as to get in its lee, and deaden the roar of the water, I will tell you a story that will convince you I ought to know something of the Moskoe-ström."

I placed myself as desired, and he proceeded.

" Myself and my two brothers once owned a schooner-rigged smack of about seventy tons burden, with which we were in the habit of fishing among the islands beyond Moskoe, nearly to Vurrgh. In all violent eddies at sea there is good fishing, at proper opportunities, if one has only the courage to attempt it ; but among the whole of the Lofoden coastmen, we three were the only ones who made a regular business of going out to the islands, as I tell you. The usual grounds are a great way lower down to the southward. There fish can be got at all hours, without much risk, and therefore these places are preferred. The choice spots over here among the rocks, however, not only yield the finest variety, but in far greater abundance ; so that we often got in a single day, what the more timid of the craft could not scrape together in a week. In fact, we made it a matter of desperate speculation—the risk of life standing instead of labour, and courage answering for capital.

" We kept the smack in a cove about five miles higher up the coast than this ; and it was our practice, in fine weather, to take advantage of the fifteen minutes' slack to push across the main channel of the Moskoe-ström, far above the pool, and then drop down upon anchorage somewhere near Otterholm, or Sandflesen, where the eddies are not so violent as elsewhere. Here we used to remain until nearly time for slack-water again, when we weighed and made for home. We never set out upon this expedition without a steady side wind for going and coming—one that we felt sure would not fail us before our return—and we seldom made a miscalculation upon this point. Twice, during six years, we were forced to stay all night at anchor on account of a dead calm, which is a rare thing indeed just about here ; and once we had to remain on the grounds nearly a week, starving to death, owing to a gale which blew up shortly after our arrival, and made the channel too boisterous to be thought of. Upon this occasion we should have been driven out to sea in spite of everything (for the whirlpools threw us round and round so violently, that, at length, we fouled our anchor and dragged it), if it had not been that we drifted into one of the innumerable cross currents—here to-day and gone to-morrow—which drove us under the lee of Flimen, where, by good luck, we brought up.

" I could not tell you the twentieth part of the difficulties we encountered ' on the ground '—it is a bad spot to be in, even in good weather—but we made shift always to run the gauntlet of the Moskoe-ström itself without accident ; although at times my heart has been in my mouth when we happened to be a minute or so behind or before the slack. The wind sometimes was not as strong as we thought it at starting, and then we made rather less way than we could wish, while the current rendered the smack unmanageable. My eldest brother had a son eighteen years old, and I had two stout boys of my own. These would have been of great assistance at such times, in using the sweeps, as well as afterwards in fishing—but, somehow, although we ran the risk ourselves, we had not the heart to let the young ones get into danger—for, after all said and done, it *was* a horrible danger, and that is the truth.

" It is now within a few days of three years since what I
am going to tell you occurred. It was on the 10th of July
18—, a day which the people of this part of the world will
never forget—for it was one in which blew the most terrible
hurricane that ever came out of the heavens. And yet all
the morning, and indeed until late in the afternoon, there
was a gentle and steady breeze from the south-west, while
the sun shone brightly, so that the oldest seaman among
us could not have foreseen what was to follow.

" The three of us—my two brothers and myself—had
crossed over to the islands about two o'clock P.M., and soon
nearly loaded the smack with fine fish, which, we all remarked, were more plenty that day than we had ever
known them. It was just seven, *by my watch,* when we
weighed and started for home, so as to make the worst of
the Ström at slack-water, which we knew would be at eight.

" We set out with a fresh wind on our starboard quarter,
and for some time spanked along at a great rate, never
dreaming of danger, for indeed we saw not the slightest
reason to apprehend it. All at once we were taken aback
by a breeze from over Helseggen. This was most unusual
—something that had never happened to us before—and
I began to feel a little uneasy, without exactly knowing
why. We put the boat on the wind, but could make no
headway at all for the eddies, and I was upon the point of
proposing to return to the anchorage, when, looking astern,
we saw the whole horizon covered with a singular copper-
coloured cloud that rose with the most amazing velocity.

" In the meantime the breeze that had headed us off
fell away, and we were dead becalmed, drifting about
in every direction. This state of things, however, did not
last long enough to give us time to think about it. In
less than a minute the storm was upon us—in less than
two the sky was entirely overcast—and what with this
and the driving spray, it became suddenly so dark that we
could not see each other in the smack.

" Such a hurricane as then blew it is folly to attempt
describing. The oldest seamen in Norway never experienced anything like it. We had let our sails go by the run
before it cleverly took us ; but, at the first puff, both our
masts went by the board as if they had been sawed off—
the mainmast taking with it my youngest brother, who
had lashed himself to it for safety.

"Our boat was the lightest feather of a thing that ever sat upon water. It had a complete flush deck, with only a small hatch near the bow, and this hatch it had always been our custom to batten down when about to cross the Ström, by way of precaution against the chopping seas. But for this circumstance we should have foundered at once—for we lay entirely buried for some moments. How my elder brother escaped destruction I cannot say, for I never had an opportunity of ascertaining. For my part, as soon as I had let the foresail run, I threw myself flat on deck, with my feet against the narrow gunwale of the bow, and with my hands grasping a ring-bolt near the foot of the foremast. It was mere instinct that prompted me to do this—which was undoubtedly the very best thing I could have done—for I was too much flurried to think.

"For some moments we were completely deluged, as I say, and all this time I held my breath, and clung to the bolt. When I could stand it no longer, I raised myself upon my knees, still keeping hold with my hands, and thus got my head clear. Presently our little boat gave herself a shake, just as a dog does in coming out of the water, and thus rid herself, in some measure, of the seas. I was now trying to get the better of the stupor that had come over me, and to collect my senses, so as to see what was to be done, when I felt somebody grasp my arm. It was my elder brother, and my heart leaped for joy, for I had made sure that he was overboard ; but the next moment all this joy was turned into horror, for he put his mouth close to my ear, and screamed out the word ' *Moskoe-ström !* '

"No one ever will know what my feelings were at that moment. I shook from head to foot as if I had the most violent fit of the ague. I knew what he meant by that one word well enough—I knew what he wished to make me understand. With the wind that now drove us on, we were bound for the whirl of the Ström, and nothing could save us !

"You perceive that in crossing the Ström *channel*, we always went a long way up above the whirl, even in the calmest weather, and then had to wait and watch carefully for the slack—but now we were driving right upon the pool itself, and in such a hurricane as this ! ' To be sure,' I thought, ' we shall get there just about the slack—there is some little hope in that '—but in the next moment I cursed

myself for being so great a fool as to dream of hope at all.
I knew very well that we were doomed, had we been ten
times a ninety-gun ship.

" By this time the first fury of the tempest had spent
itself, or perhaps we did not feel it so much, as we scudded
before it, but at all events the seas, which at first had been
kept down by the wind, and lay flat and frothing, now got
up into absolute mountains. A singular change, too, had
come over the heavens. Around in every direction it was
still as black as pitch, but nearly overhead there burst out,
all at once, a circular rift of clear sky—as clear as I ever
saw—and of a deep bright blue—and through it there
blazed forth the full moon with a lustre that I never before
knew her to wear. She lit up everything about us with
the greatest distinctness—but, O God, what a scene it was
to light up !

" I now made one or two attempts to speak to my
brother—but in some manner which I could not understand, the din had so increased that I could not make him
hear a single word, although I screamed at the top of my
voice in his ear. Presently he shook his head, looking as
pale as death, and held up one of his fingers, as if to say
' *listen !* '

" At first I could not make out what he meant—but
soon a hideous thought flashed upon me. I dragged my
watch from its fob. It was not going. I glanced at its
face by the moonlight, and then burst into tears as I flung
it far away into the ocean. *It had run down at seven
o'clock ! We were behind the time of the slack, and the whirl
of the Ström was in full fury !*

" When a boat is well built, properly trimmed, and not
deep laden, the waves in a strong gale, when she is going
large, seem always to slip from beneath her—which appears
very strange to a landsman—and this is what is called
riding, in sea phrase.

" Well, so far we had ridden the swells very cleverly ;
but presently a gigantic sea happened to take us right
under the counter, and bore us with it as it rose—up—up
—as if into the sky. I would not have believed that any
wave could rise so high. And then down we came with a
sweep, a slide, and a plunge, that made me feel sick and
dizzy, as if I was falling from some lofty mountain-top
in a dream. But while we were up I had thrown a quick

glance around—and that one glance was all-sufficient. I saw our exact position in an instant. The Moskoe-ström whirlpool was about a quarter of a mile dead ahead—but no more like the everyday Moskoe-ström, than the whirl as you now see it, is like a mill-race. If I had not known where we were, and what we had to expect, I should not have recognised the place at all. As it was, I involuntarily closed my eyes in horror. The lids clenched themselves together as if in a spasm.

" It could not have been more than two minutes afterwards until we suddenly felt the waves subside, and were enveloped in foam. The boat made a sharp half turn to larboard, and then shot off in its new direction like a thunderbolt. At the same moment the roaring noise of the water was completely drowned in a kind of shrill shriek—such a sound as you might imagine given out by the water-pipes of many thousand steam-vessels, letting off their steam all together. We were now in the belt of surf that always surrounds the whirl ; and I thought, of course, that another moment would plunge us into the abyss—down which we could only see indistinctly on account of the amazing velocity with which we were borne along. The boat did not seem to sink into the water at all, but to skim like an air-bubble upon the surface of the surge. Her starboard side was next the whirl, and on the larboard arose the world of ocean we had left. It stood like a huge writhing wall between us and the horizon.

" It may appear strange, but now, when we were in the very jaws of the gulf, I felt more composed than when we were only approaching it. Having made up my mind to hope no more, I got rid of a great deal of that terror which unmanned me at first. I supposed it was despair that strung my nerves.

" It may look like boasting—but what I tell you is truth—I began to reflect how magnificent a thing it was to die in such a manner, and how foolish it was in me to think of so paltry a consideration as my own individual life, in view of so wonderful a manifestation of God's power. I do believe that I blushed with shame when this idea crossed my mind. After a little while I became possessed with the keenest curiosity about the whirl itself. I positively felt a *wish* to explore its depths, even at the sacrifice I was going to make ; and my principal grief was that I

should never be able to tell my old companions on shore
about the mysteries I should see. These, no doubt, were
singular fancies to occupy a man's mind in such extremity
—and I have often thought since, that the revolutions of
the boat around the pool might have rendered me a little
light-headed.

" There was another circumstance which tended to
restore my self-possession ; and this was the cessation of
the wind, which could not reach us in our present situation
—for, as you saw yourself, the belt of surf is considerably
lower than the general bed of the ocean, and this latter
now towered above us, a high, black, mountainous ridge.
If you have never been at sea in a heavy gale, you can
form no idea of the confusion of mind occasioned by the
wind and spray together. They blind, deafen, and strangle
you, and take away all power of action or reflection. But
we were now, in a great measure, rid of these annoyances
—just as death-condemned felons in prison are allowed
petty indulgences, forbidden them while their doom is yet
uncertain.

" How often we made the circuit of the belt it is impossible to say. We careered round and round for perhaps
an hour, flying rather than floating, getting gradually
more and more into the middle of the surge, and then
nearer and nearer to its horrible inner edge. All this time
I had never let go of the ring-bolt. My brother was at
the stern, holding on to a small empty water-cask, which
had been securely lashed under the coop of the counter,
and was the only thing on deck that had not been swept
overboard when the gale first took us. As we approached
the brink of the pit he let go his hold upon this, and made
for the ring, from which, in the agony of his terror, he
endeavoured to force my hands, as it was not large enough
to afford us both a secure grasp. I never felt deeper grief
than when I saw him attempt this act—although I knew
he was a madman when he did it—a raving maniac through
sheer fright. I did not care, however, to contest the point
with him. I knew it could make no difference whether
either of us held on at all ; so I let him have the bolt, and
went astern to the cask. This there was no great difficulty
in doing ; for the smack flew round steadily enough, and
upon an even keel—only swaying to and fro, with the
immense sweeps and swelters of the whirl. Scarcely had

I secured myself in my new position, when we gave a wild
lurch to starboard, and rushed headlong into the abyss.
I muttered a hurried prayer to God, and thought all was
over.

" As I felt the sickening sweep of the descent, I had
instinctively tightened my hold upon the barrel, and
closed my eyes. For some seconds I dared not open them
—while I expected instant destruction, and wondered
that I was not already in my death-struggles with the
water. But moment after moment elapsed. I still lived.
The sense of falling had ceased ; and the motion of the
vessel seemed much as it had been before, while in the
belt of foam, with the exception that she now lay more
along. I took courage and looked once again upon the
scene.

" Never shall I forget the sensations of awe, horror,
and admiration with which I gazed about me. The boat
appeared to be hanging, as if by magic, midway down,
upon the interior surface of a funnel, vast in circumference,
prodigious in depth, and whose perfectly smooth sides
might have been mistaken for ebony, but for the bewildering
rapidity with which they spun around, and for the gleaming
and ghastly radiance they shot forth, as the rays of the full
moon, from that circular rift amid the clouds which I have
already described, streamed in a flood of golden glory along
the black walls, and far away down into the inmost recesses
of the abyss.

" At first I was too much confused to observe anything
accurately. The general burst of terrific grandeur was all
that I beheld. When I recovered myself a little, however,
my gaze fell instinctively downward. In this direction I
was able to obtain an unobstructed view, from the manner
in which the smack hung on the inclined surface of the pool.
She was quite upon an even keel—that is to say, her deck
lay in a plane parallel with that of the water—but this
latter sloped at an angle of more than forty-five degrees,
so that we seemed to be lying upon our beam-ends. I
could not help observing, nevertheless, that I had scarcely
more difficulty in maintaining my hold and footing in this
situation, than if we had been upon a dead level ; and
this, I suppose, was owing to the speed at which we
revolved.

" The rays of the moon seemed to search the very

bottom of the profound gulf; but still I could make out
nothing distinctly, on account of a thick mist in which
everything there was enveloped, and over which there
hung a magnificent rainbow, like that narrow and tottering
bridge which Mussulmans say is the only pathway between
Time and Eternity. This mist, or spray, was no doubt
occasioned by the clashing of the great walls of the funnel,
as they all met together at the bottom—but the yell that
went up to the heavens from out of that mist, I dare not
attempt to describe.

"Our first slide into the abyss itself, from the belt of
foam above, had carried us to a great distance down the
slope; but our farther descent was by no means proportionate. Round and round we swept—not with any
uniform movement—but in dizzying swings and jerks,
that sent us sometimes only a few hundred yards—sometimes nearly the complete circuit of the whirl. Our
progress downward, at each revolution, was slow, but very
perceptible.

"Looking about me upon the wide waste of liquid
ebony on which we were thus borne, I perceived that our
boat was not the only object in the embrace of the whirl.
Both above and below us were visible fragments of vessels,
large masses of building timber and trunks of trees, with
many smaller articles, such as pieces of house furniture,
broken boxes, barrels and staves. I have already described
the unnatural curiosity which had taken the place of my
original terrors. It appeared to grow upon me as I drew
nearer and nearer to my dreadful doom. I now began to
watch, with a strange interest, the numerous things that
floated in our company. I *must* have been delirious—for
I even sought *amusement* in speculating upon the relative
velocities of their several descents toward the foam below.
' This fir tree,' I found myself at one time saying, ' will
certainly be the next thing that takes the awful plunge
and disappears,' and then I was disappointed to find that
the wreck of a Dutch merchant ship overtook it and went
down before. At length, after making several guesses of
this nature, and being deceived in all—this fact—the fact
of my invariable miscalculation, set me upon a train of
reflection that made my limbs again tremble, and my
heart beat heavily once more.

"It was not a new terror that thus affected me, but

the dawn of a more exciting *hope*. This hope arose partly
from memory and partly from present observation. I
called to mind the great variety of buoyant matter that
strewed the coast of Lofoden, having been absorbed and
then thrown forth by the Moskoe-ström. By far the
greater number of the articles were shattered in the most
extraordinary way—so chafed and roughened as to have
the appearance of being stuck full of splinters—but then I
distinctly recollected that there were *some* of them which
were not disfigured at all. Now I could not account for
this difference except by supposing that the roughened
fragments were the only ones which had been *completely
absorbed*—that the others had entered the whirl at so late
a period of the tide, or, from some reason, had descended
so slowly after entering, that they did not reach the bottom
before the turn of the flood came, or of the ebb as the case
might be. I conceived it possible, in either instance, that
they might thus be whirled up again to the level of the
ocean, without undergoing the fate of those which had
been drawn in more early or absorbed more rapidly. I
made, also, three important observations. The first was,
that as a general rule, the larger the bodies were, the more
rapid their descent—the second, that, between two masses
of equal extent, the one spherical, and the other *of any
other shape*, the superiority in speed of descent was with
the sphere—the third, that, between two masses of equal
size, the one cylindrical, and the other of any other shape,
the cylinder was absorbed the more slowly. Since my
escape, I have had several conversations on this subject
with an old schoolmaster of the district ; and it was from
him that I learned the use of the words ' cylinder ' and
' sphere.' He explained to me—although I have forgotten
the explanation—how what I observed was, in fact, the
natural consequence of the forms of the floating fragments
—and showed me how it happened that a cylinder, swimming in a vortex, offered more resistance to its suction, and
was drawn in with greater difficulty than an equally bulky
body of any form whatever.*

"There was one startling circumstance which went
a great way in enforcing these observations, and rendering
me anxious to turn them to account, and this was that,

---

* See ARCHIMEDES, *De Incidentibus in Fluido*, lib. 2.

at every revolution, we passed something like a barrel, or else the yard or the mast of a vessel, while many of these things, which had been on our level when I first opened my eyes upon the wonders of the whirlpool, were now high up above us, and seemed to have moved but little from their original station.

" I no longer hesitated what to do. I resolved to lash myself securely to the water cask upon which I now held, to cut it loose from the counter, and to throw myself with it into the water. I attracted my brother's attention by signs, pointed to the floating barrels that came near us, and did everything in my power to make him understand what I was about to do. I thought at length that he comprehended my design—but whether this was the case or not, he shook his head despairingly, and refused to move from his station by the ring-bolt. It was impossible to reach him ; the emergency admitted of no delay ; and so, with a bitter struggle, I resigned him to his fate, fastened myself to the cask by means of the lashings which secured it to the counter, and precipitated myself with it into the sea, without another moment's hesitation.

" The result was precisely what I had hoped it might be. As it is myself who now tells you this tale—as you see that I *did* escape—and as you are already in possession of the mode in which this escape was effected, and must therefore anticipate all that I have further to say—I will bring my story quickly to conclusion. It might have been an hour, or thereabout, after my quitting the smack, when, having descended to a vast distance beneath me, it made three or four wild gyrations in rapid succession, and, bearing my loved brother with it, plunged headlong, at once and for ever, into the chaos of foam below. The barrel to which I was attached sunk very little farther than half the distance between the bottom of the gulf and the spot at which I leaped overboard, before a great change took place in the character of the whirlpool. The slope of the sides of the vast funnel became momentarily less and less steep, the gyrations of the whirl grew gradually less and less violent. By degrees, the froth and the rainbow disappeared, and the bottom of the gulf seemed slowly to uprise. The sky was clear, the winds had gone down, and the full moon was setting radiantly in the west, when I found myself on the surface of the ocean, in full view of the shores of Lofoden, and above the spot where the pool of the Moskoe-ström *had been*. It was the hour of the slack —but the sea still heaved in mountainous waves from the effects of the hurricane. I was borne violently into the channel of the Ström, and in a few minutes, was hurried down the coast into the ' grounds ' of the fishermen. A boat picked me up—exhausted from fatigue—and (now that the danger was removed)—speechless from the memory of its horror. Those who drew me on board were my old mates and daily companions—but they knew me no more than they would have known a traveller from the spirit-land. My hair, which had been raven-black the day before, was as white as you see it now. They say, too, that the whole expression of my countenance had changed. I told them my story—they did not believe it. I now tell it to *you*—and I can scarcely expect you to put more faith in it than did the merry fishermen of Lofoden."

THE CONVERSATION OF EIROS AND CHARMION

Πῦρ σοι προσοίσω.

" I will bring thee the fire."

—EURIPIDES, *Andromache.*

EIROS.   Why do you call me Eiros ?

CHARMION.   So henceforward will you always be called. You must forget, too, *my* earthly name, and speak to me as Charmion.

EIROS.   This is indeed no dream !

CHARMION.   Dreams are with us no more ; but of these mysteries anon. I rejoice to see you looking life-like and rational. The film of the shadow has already passed from off your eyes. Be of heart, and fear nothing. Your allotted days of stupor have expired ; and, to-morrow, I will myself induct you into the full joys and wonders of your novel existence.

EIROS.   True, I feel no stupor, none at all. The wild sickness and the terrible darkness have left me, and I hear no longer that mad, rushing, horrible sound, "like the voice of many waters." Yet my senses are bewildered, Charmion, with the keenness of their perception of *the new*.

CHARMION. A few days will remove all this;—but I fully understand you, and feel for you. It is now ten earthly years since I underwent what you undergo, yet the remembrance of it hangs by me still. You have now suffered all of pain, however, which you will suffer in Aidenn.

EIROS. In Aidenn?

CHARMION. In Aidenn.

EIROS. Oh, God!—pity me, Charmion!—I am overburdened with the majesty of all things—of the unknown now known—of the speculative Future merged in the august and certain Present.

CHARMION. Grapple not now with such thoughts. To-morrow we will speak of this. Your mind wavers, and its agitation will find relief in the exercise of simple memories. Look not around, nor forward—but back. I am burning with anxiety to hear the details of that stupendous event which threw you among us. Tell me of it. Let us converse of familiar things, in the old familiar language of the world which has so fearfully perished.

EIROS. Most fearfully, fearfully!—this is indeed no dream.

CHARMION. Dreams are no more. Was I much mourned, my Eiros?

EIROS. Mourned, Charmion?—oh, deeply. To that last hour of all, there hung a cloud of intense gloom and devout sorrow over your household.

CHARMION. And that last hour—speak of it. Remember that, beyond the naked fact of the catastrophe itself, I know nothing. When, coming out from among mankind, I passed into Night through the Grave—at that period, if I remember aright, the calamity which overwhelmed you was utterly unanticipated. But, indeed, I knew little of the speculative philosophy of the day.

EIROS. The individual calamity was, as you say, entirely unanticipated; but analogous misfortunes had been long a subject of discussion with astronomers. I need scarce tell you, my friend, that even when you left us, men had agreed to understand those passages in the most holy writings which speak of the final destruction of all things by fire, as having reference to the orb of the earth alone. But in regard to the immediate agency of the ruin, speculation had been at fault from that epoch in astronomical knowledge in which the comets were divested of the terrors of flame. The very moderate density of these bodies had been well established. They had been observed to pass among the satellites of Jupiter, without bringing about any sensible alteration either in the masses or in the orbits of these secondary planets. We had long regarded the wanderers as vapoury creations of inconceivable tenuity, and as altogether incapable of doing injury to our substantial globe, even in the event of contact. But contact was not in any degree dreaded ; for the elements of all the comets were accurately known. That among *them* we should look for the agency of the threatened fiery destruction had been for many years considered an inadmissible idea. But wonders and wild fancies had been, of late days, strangely rife among mankind ; and although it was only with a few of the ignorant that actual apprehension prevailed, upon the announcement by astronomers of a *new* comet, yet this announcement was generally received with I know not what of agitation and mistrust.

The elements of the strange orb were immediately calculated, and it was at once conceded by all observers, that its path, at perihelion, would bring it into very close proximity with the earth. There were two or three astronomers, of secondary note, who resolutely maintained that a contact was inevitable. I cannot very well express to you the effect of this intelligence upon the people. For a few short days they would not believe an assertion which their intellect, so long employed among worldly considerations, could not in any manner grasp. But the truth of a vitally important fact soon makes its way into the understanding of even the most stolid. Finally, all men saw that astronomical knowledge lied not, and they awaited the comet. Its approach was not, at first, seemingly rapid ; nor was its appearance of very unusual character. It was of a dull red, and had little perceptible train. For seven or eight days we saw no material increase in its apparent diameter, and but a partial alteration in its colour. Meanwhile the ordinary affairs of men were discarded, and all interests absorbed in a growing discussion, instituted by the philosophic, in respect to the cometary nature.

Even the grossly ignorant aroused their sluggish capacities to such considerations. The learned *now* gave their intellect—their soul—to no such points as the allaying of fear, or to the sustenance of loved theory. They sought —they panted for right views. They groaned for perfected knowledge. *Truth* arose in the purity of her strength and exceeding majesty, and the wise bowed down and adored.

That material injury to our globe or to its inhabitants would result from the apprehended contact, was an opinion which hourly lost ground among the wise ; and the wise were now freely permitted to rule the reason and the fancy of the crowd. It was demonstrated, that the density of the comet's *nucleus* was far less than that of our rarest gas ; and the harmless passage of a similar visitor among the satellites of Jupiter was a point strongly insisted upon, and which served greatly to allay terror. Theologists, with an earnestness fear-enkindled, dwelt upon the biblical prophecies, and expounded them to the people with a directness and simplicity of which no previous instance had been known. That the final destruction of the earth must be brought about by the agency of fire, was urged with a spirit that enforced everywhere conviction and that the comets were of no fiery nature (as all men now knew) was a truth which relieved all, in a great measure, from the apprehension of the great calamity foretold. It is noticeable that the popular prejudices and vulgar errors in regard to pestilences and wars—errors which were wont to prevail upon every appearance of a comet—were now altogether unknown. As if by some sudden convulsive exertion, reason had at once hurled superstition from her throne. The feeblest intellect had derived vigour from excessive interest.

What minor evils might arise from the contact were points of elaborate question. The learned spoke of slight geological disturbances, of probable alterations in climate, and consequently in vegetation ; of possible magnetic and electric influences. Many held that no visible or perceptible effect would in any manner be produced. While such discussions were going on, their subject gradually approached, growing larger in apparent diameter, and of a more brilliant lustre. Mankind grew paler as it came. All human operations were suspended.

There was an epoch in the course of the general sentiment

when the comet had attained, at length, a size surpassing
that of any previously recorded visitation. The people
now, dismissing any lingering hope that the astronomers
were wrong, experienced all the certainty of evil. The
chimerical aspect of their terror was gone. The hearts of
the stoutest of our race beat violently within their bosoms.
A very few days sufficed, however, to merge even such
feelings in sentiments more unendurable. We could no
longer apply to the strange orb any *accustomed* thoughts.
Its *historical* attributes had disappeared. It oppressed
us with a hideous *novelty* of emotion. We saw it not as
an astronomical phenomenon in the heavens, but as an
incubus upon our hearts, and a shadow upon our brains.
It had taken, with inconceivable rapidity, the character
of a gigantic mantle of rare flame, extending from horizon
to horizon.

Yet a day, and men breathed with greater freedom.
It was clear that we were already within the influence of the
comet ; yet we lived. We even felt an unusual elasticity
of frame and vivacity of mind. The exceeding tenuity of
the object of our dread was apparent ; for all heavenly
objects were plainly visible through it. Meantime, our
vegetation had perceptibly altered ; and we gained faith,
from this predicted circumstance, in the foresight of the
wise. A wild luxuriance of foliage, utterly unknown
before, burst out upon every vegetable thing.

Yet another day—and the evil was not altogether upon
us. It was now evident that its nucleus would first reach
us. A wild change had come over all men ; and the first
sense of *pain* was the wild signal for general lamentation
and horror. This first sense of pain lay in a rigorous constriction of the breast and lungs, and an insufferable dryness
of the skin. It could not be denied that our atmosphere
was radically affected ; the conformation of this atmosphere and the possible modifications to which it might be
subjected, were now the topics of discussion. The result
of investigation sent an electric thrill of the intensest
horror through the universal heart of man.

It had been long known that the air which encircled us was
a compound of oxygen and nitrogen gases, in the proportion
of twenty-one measures of oxygen, and seventy-nine of
nitrogen, in every one hundred of the atmosphere. Oxygen,
which was the principle of combustion, and the vehicle

of heat, was absolutely necessary to the support of animal life, and was the most powerful and energetic agent in nature. Nitrogen, on the contrary, was incapable of supporting either animal life or flame. An unnatural excess of oxygen would result, it had been ascertained, in just such an elevation of the animal spirits as we had latterly experienced. It was the pursuit, the extension of the idea, which had engendered awe. What would be the result of *a total extraction of the nitrogen*? A combustion irresistible, all-devouring, omni-prevalent, immediate;— the entire fulfilment, in all their minute and terrible details, of the fiery and horror-inspiring denunciations of the prophecies of the Holy Book.

Why need I paint, Charmion, the now disenchained frenzy of mankind? That tenuity in the comet which had previously inspired us with hope, was now the source of the bitterness of despair. In its impalpable gaseous character we clearly perceived the consummation of Fate. Meantime a day again passed, bearing away with it the last shadow of Hope. We gasped in the rapid modification of the air. The red blood bounded tumultuously through its strict channels. A furious delirium possessed all men; and, with arms rigidly outstretched toward the threatening heavens, they trembled and shrieked aloud. But the nucleus of the destroyer was now upon us: even here in Aidenn, I shudder while I speak. Let me be brief—brief as the ruin that overwhelmed. For a moment there was a wild lurid light alone, visiting and penetrating all things. Then—let us bow down, Charmion, before the excessive majesty of the great God!—then, there came a shouting and pervading sound, as if from the mouth itself of HIM; while the whole incumbent mass of ether in which we existed, burst at once into a species of intense flame, for whose surpassing brilliancy and all-fervid heat even the angels in the high Heaven of pure knowledge have no name. Thus ended all.

THE MURDERS IN THE RUE MORGUE

" What song the Syrens sang, or what name Achilles assumed
when he hid himself among women, although puzzling questions,
are not beyond *all* conjecture."—SIR THOMAS BROWNE.

THE mental features discoursed of as the analytical,
are, in themselves, but little susceptible of analysis. We
appreciate them only in their effects. We know of them,
among other things, that they are always to their possessor,
when inordinately possessed, a source of the liveliest
enjoyment. As the strong man exults in his physical
ability, delighting in such exercises as call his muscles into
action, so glories the analyst in that moral activity which
disentangles. He derives pleasure from even the most
trivial occupations bringing his talent into play. He is fond
of enigmas, of conundrums, of hieroglyphics ; exhibiting
in his solutions of each a degree of acumen which appears
to the ordinary apprehension preternatural. His results,
brought about by the very soul and essence of method,
have, in truth, the whole air of intuition.

The faculty of re-solution is possibly much invigorated
by mathematical study, and especially by that highest
branch of it which, unjustly, and merely on account of its
retrograde operations, has been called, as if *par excellence*,
analysis. Yet to calculate is not in itself to analyse. A
chess-player, for example, does the one, without effort at
the other. It follows that the game of chess, in its effects
upon mental character, is greatly misunderstood. I am
not now writing a treatise, but simply prefacing a somewhat peculiar narrative by observations very much at random ; I will, therefore, take occasion to assert that the
higher powers of the reflective intellect are more decidedly
and more usefully tasked by the unostentatious game of
draughts than by all the elaborate frivolity of chess. In
this latter, where the pieces have different and bizarre
motions, with various and variable values, what is only
complex, is mistaken (a not unusual error) for what is
profound. The *attention* is here called powerfully into play.
If it flag for an instant, an oversight is committed, resulting
in injury or defeat. The possible moves being not only

manifold, but involute, the chances of such oversights are multiplied ; and in nine cases out of ten, it is the more concentrative rather than the more acute player who conquers. In draughts, on the contrary, where the moves are *unique* and have but little variation, the probabilities of inadvertence are diminished, and the mere attention being left comparatively unemployed, what advantages are obtained by either party are obtained by superior acumen. To be less abstract—Let us suppose a game of draughts where the pieces are reduced to four kings, and where, of course, no oversight is to be expected. It is obvious that here the victory can be decided (the players being at all equal) only by some *recherché* movement, the result of some strong exertion of the intellect. Deprived of ordinary resources, the analyst throws himself into the spirit of his opponent, identifies himself therewith, and not unfrequently sees thus, at a glance, the sole methods (sometimes indeed absurdly simple ones) by which he may seduce into error or hurry into miscalculation.

Whist has long been noted for its influence upon what is termed the calculating power ; and men of the highest order of intellect have been known to take an apparently unaccountable delight in it, while eschewing chess as frivolous. Beyond doubt there is nothing of a similar nature so greatly tasking the faculty of analysis. The best chess-player in Christendom *may* be little more than the best player of chess ; but proficiency in whist implies capacity for success in all these more important undertakings where mind struggles with mind. When I say proficiency, I mean that perfection in the game which includes a comprehension of *all* the sources whence legitimate advantage may be derived. These are not only manifold, but multiform, and lie frequently among recesses of thought altogether inaccessible to the ordinary understanding. To observe attentively is to remember distinctly ; and, so far, the concentrative chess-player will do very well at whist ; while the rules of Hoyle (themselves based upon the mere mechanism of the game) are sufficiently and generally comprehensible. Thus to have a retentive memory, and to proceed by " the book," are points commonly regarded as the sum total of good playing. But it is in matters beyond the limits of mere rule that the skill of the analyst is evinced. He makes, in silence, a host of observations and inferences. So, perhaps, do his companions ; and the difference in the extent of the information obtained, lies not so much in the validity of the inference as in the quality of the observation. The necessary knowledge is that of *what* to observe. Our player confines himself not at all ; nor, because the game is the object, does he reject deductions from things external to the game. He examines the countenance of his partner, comparing it carefully with that of each of his opponents. He considers the mode of assorting the cards in each hand ; often counting trump by trump, and honour by honour, through the glances bestowed by their holders upon each. He notes every variation of face as the play progresses, gathering a fund of thought from the differences in the expression of certainty, of surprise, of triumph, or chagrin. From the manner of gathering up a trick he judges whether the person taking it can make another in the suit. He recognises what is played through feint, by the air with which it is thrown upon the table. A casual or inadvertent word ; the accidental dropping or turning of a card, with the accompanying anxiety or carelessness in regard to its concealment ; the counting of the tricks, with the order of their arrangement ; embarrassment, hesitation, eagerness or trepidation—all afford, to his apparently intuitive perception, indications of the true state of affairs. The first two or three rounds having been played, he is in full possession of the contents of each hand, and thenceforward puts down his cards with as absolute a precision of purpose as if the rest of the party had turned outward the faces of their own.

The analytical power should not be confounded with simple ingenuity ; for while the analyst is necessarily ingenious, the ingenious man is often remarkably incapable of analysis. The constructive or combining power, by which ingenuity is usually manifested, and to which the phrenologists (I believe erroneously) have assigned a separate organ, supposing it a primitive faculty, has been so frequently seen in those whose intellect bordered otherwise upon idiotcy, as to have attracted general observation among writers on morals. Between ingenuity and the analytic ability there exists a difference far greater, indeed, than that between the fancy and the imagination, but of a character very strictly analogous. It will be found, in fact, that the ingenious are always fanciful, and the *truly* imaginative never otherwise than analytic.

The narrative which follows will appear to the reader somewhat in the light of a commentary upon the propositions just advanced.

Residing in Paris during the spring and part of the summer of 18—, I there became acquainted with a Monsieur C. Auguste Dupin. This young gentleman was of an excellent—indeed of an illustrious family, but, by a variety of untoward events, had been reduced to such poverty that the energy of his character succumbed beneath it, and he ceased to bestir himself in the world, or to care for the retrieval of his fortunes. By courtesy of his creditors there still remained in his possession a small remnant of his patrimony ; and, upon the income arising from this, he managed, by means of a rigorous economy, to procure the necessaries of life, without troubling himself about its superfluities. Books, indeed, were his sole luxuries, and in Paris these are easily obtained.

Our first meeting was at an obscure library in the Rue Montmartre, where the accident of our both being in search of the same very rare and very remarkable volume, brought us into closer communion. We saw each other again and again. I was deeply interested in the little family history which he detailed to me with all that candour which a Frenchman indulges whenever mere self is the theme. I was astonished, too, at the vast extent of his reading ; and, above all, I felt my soul enkindled within me by the wild fervour, and the vivid freshness of his imagination. Seeking in Paris the objects I then sought, I felt that the society of such a man would be to me a treasure beyond price ; and this feeling I frankly confided to him. It was at length arranged that we should live together during my stay in the city ; and as my worldly circumstances were somewhat less embarrassed than his own, I was permitted to be at the expense of renting, and furnishing in a style which suited the rather fantastic gloom of our common temper, a time-eaten and grotesque mansion, long deserted through superstitions into which we did not inquire, and tottering to its fall in a retired and desolate portion of the Faubourg St. Germain.

Had the routine of our life at this place been known to the world, we should have been regarded as madmen

—although, perhaps, as madmen of a harmless nature. Our seclusion was perfect. We admitted no visitors. Indeed the locality of our retirement had been carefully kept a secret from my own former associates; and it had been many years since Dupin had ceased to know or be known in Paris. We existed within ourselves alone.

It was a freak of fancy in my friend (for what else shall I call it ?) to be enamoured of the night for her own sake ; and into this *bizarrerie,* as into all his others, I quietly fell, giving myself up to his wild whims with a perfect abandon. The sable divinity would not herself dwell with us always ; but we could counterfeit her presence. At the first dawn of the morning we closed all the massy shutters of our old building ; lighted a couple of tapers which, strongly perfumed, threw out only the ghastliest and feeblest of rays. By the aid of these we then busied our souls in dreams—reading, writing, or conversing, until warned by the clock of the advent of the true Darkness. Then we sallied forth into the streets, arm in arm, continuing the topics of the day, or roaming far and wide until a late hour, seeking, amid the wild lights and shadows of the populous city, that infinity of mental excitement which quiet observation can afford.

At such times I could not help remarking and admiring (although from his rich ideality I had been prepared to expect it) a peculiar analytic ability in Dupin. He seemed, too, to take an eager delight in its exercise—if not exactly in its display—and did not hesitate to confess the pleasure thus derived. He boasted to me, with a low chuckling laugh, that most men, in respect to himself, wore windows in their bosoms, and was wont to follow up such assertions by direct and very startling proofs of his intimate knowledge of my own. His manner at these moments was frigid and abstract ; his eyes were vacant in expression ; while his voice, usually a rich tenor, rose into a treble which would have sounded petulantly, but for the deliberateness and entire distinctness of the enunciation. Observing him in these moods, I often dwelt meditatively upon the old philosophy of the Bi-Part Soul, and amused myself with the fancy of a double Dupin—the creative and the resolvent.

Let it not be supposed, from what I have just said,

hat I am detailing any mystery, or penning any romance.
Vhat I have described in the Frenchman, was merely
he result of an excited, or perhaps of a diseased intelligence.
But of the character of his remarks at the periods in
question an example will best convey the idea.

We were strolling one night down a long dirty street,
n the vicinity of the Palais Royal. Being both, appar-
ntly, occupied with thought, neither of us had spoken
a syllable for fifteen minutes at least. All at once Dupin
broke forth with these words—

" He is a very little fellow, that's true, and would do
better for the *Théâtre des Variétés.*"

" There can be no doubt about that," I replied unwittingly, and not at first observing (so much had I
been absorbed in reflection) the extraordinary manner in
which the speaker had chimed in with my meditations.
In an instant afterwards I recollected myself, and my
astonishment was profound.

" Dupin," said I, gravely, " this is beyond my comprehension. I do not hesitate to say that I am amazed,
and can scarcely credit my senses. How was it possible
you should know I was thinking of —— ? " Here I
paused, to ascertain beyond a doubt whether he really
knew of whom I thought.

" Of Chantilly," said he ; " why do you pause ? You
were remarking to yourself that his diminutive figure
unfitted him for tragedy."

This was precisely what had formed the subject of
my reflections. Chantilly was a quondam cobbler of the
Rue St. Denis, who, becoming stage-mad, had attempted
the *rôle* of Xerxes, in Crébillon's tragedy so called, and
been notoriously pasquinaded for his pains.

" Tell me, for Heaven's sake," I exclaimed, " the method
—if method there is—by which you have been enabled
to fathom my soul in this matter." In fact I was even
more startled than I would have been willing to express.

" It was the fruiterer," replied my friend, " who brought
you to the conclusion that the mender of soles was not
of sufficient height for Xerxes *et id genus omne.*"

" The fruiterer !—you astonish me—I know no fruiterer
whomsoever."

" The man who ran up against you as we entered the
street—it may have been fifteen minutes ago."

I now remembered that, in fact, a fruiterer, carrying
upon his head a large basket of apples, had nearly thrown
me down, by accident, as we passed from the Rue C——
into the thoroughfare where we stood ; but what this
had to do with Chantilly I could not possibly understand

There was not a particle of *charlatanerie* about Dupin
" I will explain," he said, " and that you may compre
hend all clearly, we will first retrace the course of you
meditations, from the moment in which I spoke to you
until that of the *rencontre* with the fruiterer in question
The larger links of the chain run thus—Chantilly, Orion
Dr. Nichols, Epicurus, Stereotomy, the street stones, the
fruiterer."

There are few persons who have not, at some period
of their lives, amused themselves in retracing the step
by which particular conclusions of their own minds have
been attained. The occupation is often full of interest
and he who attempts it for the first time is astonished
by the apparently illimitable distance and incoherence
between the starting-point and the goal. What, then
must have been my amazement when I heard the French
man speak what he had just spoken, and when I could
not help acknowledging that he had spoken the truth
He continued—

" We had been talking of horses, if I remember aright
just before leaving the Rue C——. This was the last
subject we discussed. As we crossed into the street, a
fruiterer, with a large basket upon his head, brushing
quickly past us, thrust you upon a pile of paving-stones
collected at a spot where the causeway is undergoing
repair. You stepped upon one of the loose fragments
slipped, slightly strained your ankle, appeared vexed or
sulky, muttered a few words, turned to look at the pile
and then proceeded in silence. I was not particularly
attentive to what you did ; but observation has become
with me, of late, a species of necessity.

" You kept your eyes upon the ground—glancing
with a petulant expression, at the holes and ruts in the
pavement (so that I saw you were still thinking of the
stones), till we reached the little alley called Lamartine
which has been paved, by way of experiment, with the
overlapping and riveted blocks. Here your countenance
brightened up, and, perceiving your lips move, I could not

doubt that you murmured the word ' stereotomy,' a term
very affectedly applied to this species of pavement. I
knew that you could not say to yourself ' stereotomy '
without being brought to think of atomies, and thus of
the theories of Epicurus ; and since, when we discussed
this subject not very long ago, I mentioned to you how
singularly, yet with how little notice, the vague guesses
of that noble Greek had met with confirmation in the
late nebular cosmogony, I felt that you could not avoid
casting your eyes upward to the great nebula in Orion,
and I certainly expected that you would do so. You
did look up ; and I was now assured that I had correctly
followed your steps. But in that bitter tirade upon
Chantilly, which appeared in yesterday's *Musée*, the
satirist, making some disgraceful allusions to the cobbler's
change of name upon assuming the buskin, quoted a
Latin line about which we have often conversed. I mean
the line

' Perdidit antiquum litera prima sonum.'

I had told you that this was in reference to Orion, formerly
written Urion ; and, from certain pungencies connected
with this explanation, I was aware that you could not
have forgotten it. It was clear, therefore, that you
would not fail to combine the two ideas of Orion and
Chantilly. That you did combine them I saw by the
character of the smile which passed over your lips. You
thought of the poor cobbler's immolation. So far, you
had been stooping in your gait ; but now I saw you draw
yourself up to your full height. I was then sure that you
reflected upon the diminutive figure of Chantilly. At
this point I interrupted your meditations to remark that
as, in fact, he *was* a very little fellow, that Chantilly,
he would do better at the *Théâtre des Variétés*."

Not long after this, we were looking over an evening
edition of the *Gazette des Tribunaux* when the following
paragraphs arrested our attention :—

" EXTRAORDINARY MURDERS.—This morning, about
three o'clock, the inhabitants of the Quartier St. Roch
were aroused from sleep by a succession of terrific shrieks,
issuing, apparently, from the fourth story of a house
in the Rue Morgue, known to be in the sole occupancy
of one Madame L'Espanaye, and her daughter, Mademoiselle

Camille L'Espanaye. After some delay, occasioned by a
fruitless attempt to procure admission in the usual manner,
the gateway was broken in with a crowbar, and eight or
ten of the neighbours entered, accompanied by two
gendarmes. By this time the cries had ceased; but, as
the party rushed up the first flight of stairs, two or more
rough voices, in angry contention, were distinguished,
and seemed to proceed from the upper part of the house.
As the second landing was reached, these sounds, also,
had ceased, and everything remained perfectly quiet.
The party spread themselves, and hurried from room
to room. Upon arriving at a large back chamber in
the fourth story (the door of which, being found locked,
with the key inside, was forced open), a spectacle presented
itself which struck every one present not less with horror
than with astonishment.

  "The apartment was in the wildest disorder—the
furniture broken and thrown about in all directions.
There was only one bedstead ; and from this the bed had
been removed, and thrown into the middle of the floor.
On a chair lay a razor, besmeared with blood. On the
hearth were two or three long and thick tresses of grey
human hair, also dabbled in blood, and seeming to have
been pulled out by the roots. Upon the floor were found
four napoleons, an ear-ring of topaz, three large silver
spoons, three smaller of *métal d'Alger*, and two bags,
containing nearly four thousand francs in gold. The
drawers of a bureau, which stood in one corner, were open,
and had been, apparently, rifled, although many articles
still remained in them. A small iron safe was discovered
under the *bed* (not under the bedstead). It was open, with
a key still in the door. It had no contents beyond a few
old letters, and other papers of little consequence.

  "Of Madame L'Espanaye no traces were here seen ;
but an unusual quantity of soot being observed in the
fireplace, a search was made in the chimney, and (horrible
to relate !) the corpse of the daughter, head downward,
was dragged therefrom ; it having been thus forced up
the narrow aperture for a considerable distance. The
body was quite warm. Upon examining it, many excoriations were perceived, no doubt occasioned by the violence
with which it had been thrust up and disengaged. Upon
the face were many severe scratches, and, upon the throat,

dark bruises, and deep indentations of finger nails, as if the deceased had been throttled to death.

"After a thorough investigation of every portion of the house, without further discovery, the party made its way into a small paved yard in the rear of the building, where lay the corpse of the old lady, with her throat so entirely cut that, upon an attempt to raise her, the head fell off. The body, as well as the head, was fearfully mutilated—the former so much so as scarcely to retain any semblance of humanity.

"To this horrible mystery there is not as yet, we believe, the slightest clue."

The next day's paper had these additional particulars :—

"THE TRAGEDY IN THE RUE MORGUE.—Many individuals have been examined in relation to this most extraordinary and frightful affair " [the word ' *affaire* ' has not yet in France that levity of import which it conveys with us], " but nothing whatever has transpired to throw light upon it. We give below all the material testimony elicited.

"*Pauline Dubourg*, laundress, deposes that she has known both the deceased for three years, having washed for them during that period. The old lady and her daughter seemed on good terms—very affectionate towards each other. They were excellent pay. Could not speak in regard to their mode or means of living. Believed that Madame L. told fortunes for a living. Was reputed to have money put by. Never met any persons in the house when she called for the clothes or took them home. Was sure that they had no servant in employ. There appeared to be no furniture in any part of the building, except in the fourth story.

"*Pierre Moreau*, tobacconist, deposes that he has been in the habit of selling small quantities of tobacco and snuff to Madame L'Espanaye for nearly four years. Was born in the neighbourhood, and has always resided there. The deceased and her daughter had occupied the house in which the corpses were found for more than six years. It was formerly occupied by a jeweller, who under-let the upper rooms to various persons. The house was the property of Madame L. She became dissatisfied with the abuse of the premises by her tenant, and moved into them herself, refusing to let any portion. The old lady was childish.

Witness had seen the daughter some five or six times during the six years. The two lived an exceedingly retired life —were reputed to have money. Had heard it said among the neighbours that Madame L. told fortunes—did not believe it. Had never seen any person enter the door except the old lady and her daughter, a porter once or twice, and a physician some eight or ten times.

" Many other persons, neighbours, gave evidence to the same effect. No one was spoken of as frequenting the house. It was not known whether there were any living connections of Madame L. and her daughter. The shutters of the front windows were seldom opened. Those in the rear were always closed, with the exception of the large back room, fourth story. The house was a good house— not very old.

" *Isidore Mustè*, *gendarme*, deposes that he was called to the house about three o'clock in the morning, and found some twenty or thirty persons at the gateway, endeavouring to gain admittance. Forced it open, at length, with a bayonet—not with a crowbar. Had but little difficulty in getting it open, on account of its being a double or folding gate, and bolted neither at bottom nor top. The shrieks were continued until the gate was forced—and then suddenly ceased. They seemed to be screams of some person (or persons) in great agony—were loud and drawn out, not short and quick. Witness led the way upstairs. Upon reaching the first landing, heard two voices in loud and angry contention—the one a gruff voice, the other much shriller—a very strange voice. Could distinguish some words of the former, which was that of a Frenchman. Was positive that it was not a woman's voice. Could distinguish the words ' *sacré* ' and ' *diable*.' The shrill voice was that of a foreigner. Could not be sure whether it was the voice of a man or of a woman. Could not make out what was said, but believed the language to be Spanish. The state of the room and of the bodies was described by this witness as we described them yesterday.

" *Henri Duval*, a neighbour, and by trade a silversmith, deposes that he was one of the party who first entered the house. Corroborates the testimony of Mustè in general. As soon as they forced an entrance, they reclosed the door, to keep out the crowd, which collected very fast, notwithstanding the lateness of the hour. The shrill voice, this witness thinks, was that of an Italian. Was certain it was not French. Could not be sure that it was a man's voice. It might have been a woman's. Was not acquainted with the Italian language. Could not distinguish the words, but was convinced by the intonation that the speaker was an Italian. Knew Madame L. and her daughter. Had conversed with both frequently. Was sure that the shrill voice was not that of either of the deceased.

" —— *Odenheimer, restaurateur.* This witness volunteered his testimony. Not speaking French, was examined through an interpreter. Is a native of Amsterdam. Was passing the house at the time of the shrieks. They lasted for several minutes—probably ten. They were long and loud—very awful and distressing. Was one of those who entered the building. Corroborated the previous evidence in every respect but one. Was sure that the shrill voice was that of a man—of a Frenchman. Could not distinguish the words uttered. They were loud and quick—unequal—spoken apparently in fear as well as in anger. The voice was harsh—not so much shrill as harsh. Could not call it a shrill voice. The gruff voice said repeatedly ' *sacré*,' ' *diable*,' and once ' *mon Dieu*.'

" *Jules Mignaud,* banker, of the firm of Mignaud et Fils, Rue Deloraine. Is the elder Mignaud. Madame L'Espanaye had some property. Had opened an account with his banking house in the spring of the year —— (eight years previously). Made frequent deposits in small sums. Had checked for nothing until the third day before her death, when she took out in person the sum of 4000 francs. This sum was paid in gold, and a clerk sent home with the money.

" *Adolphe Le Bon,* clerk to Mignaud et Fils, deposes that on the day in question, about noon, he accompanied Madame L'Espanaye to her residence with the 4000 francs put up in two bags. Upon the door being opened, Mademoiselle L. appeared and took from his hands one of the bags, while the old lady relieved him of the other. He then bowed and departed. Did not see any person in the street at the time. It is a by-street—very lonely.

" *William Bird,* tailor, deposes that he was one of the party who entered the house. Is an Englishman. Has lived in Paris two years. Was one of the first to ascend the stairs. Heard the voices in contention. The gruff voice was that of a Frenchman. Could make out several words, but cannot now remember all. Heard distinctly ' sacré ' and ' mon Dieu.' There was a sound at the moment as if of several persons struggling—a scraping and scuffling sound. The shrill voice was very loud—louder than the gruff one. Is sure that it was not the voice of an Englishman. Appeared to be that of a German. Might have been a woman's voice. Does not understand German.

" Four of the above-named witnesses, being recalled, deposed that the door of the chamber in which was found the body of Mademoiselle L. was locked on the inside when the party reached it. Everything was perfectly silent—no groans or noises of any kind. Upon forcing the door no person was seen. The windows, both of the back and front room, were down and firmly fastened from within. A door between the two rooms was closed, but not locked. The door leading from the front room into the passage was locked, with the key on the inside. A small room in the front of the house, on the fourth story, at the head of the passage, was open, the door being ajar. This room was crowded with old beds, boxes, and so forth. These were carefully removed and searched. There was not an inch of any portion of the house which was not carefully searched. Sweeps were sent up and down the chimneys. The house was a four-story one, with garrets (mansardes). A trap-door on the roof was nailed down very securely— did not appear to have been opened for years. The time elapsing between the hearing of the voices in contention and the breaking open of the room door, was variously stated by the witnesses. Some made it as short as three minutes—some as long as five. The door was opened with difficulty.

" Alfonzo Garcio, undertaker, deposes that he resides in the Rue Morgue. Is a native of Spain. Was one of the party who entered the house. Did not proceed upstairs. Is nervous, and was apprehensive of the consequences of agitation. Heard the voices in contention. The gruff voice was that of a Frenchman. Could not distinguish what was said. The shrill voice was that of an Englishman —is sure of this. Does not understand the English language, but judges by the intonation.

" Alberto Montani, confectioner, deposes that he was

among the first to ascend the stairs. Heard the voices in
question. The gruff voice was that of a Frenchman.
Distinguished several words. The speaker appeared to
be expostulating. Could not make out the words of the
shrill voice. Spoke quick and unevenly. Thinks it the
voice of a Russian. Corroborates the general testimony.
Is an Italian. Never conversed with a native of Russia.

   " Several witnesses, recalled, here testified that the
chimneys of all the rooms on the fourth story were too
narrow to admit the passage of a human being. By
' sweeps ' were meant cylindrical sweeping-brushes, such
as are employed by those who clean chimneys. These
brushes were passed up and down every flue in the house.
There is no back passage by which any one could have
descended while the party proceeded upstairs. The body
of Mademoiselle L'Espanaye was so firmly wedged in the
chimney that it could not be got down until four or five
of the party united their strength.

   " *Paul Dumas*, physician, deposes that he was called
to view the bodies about daybreak. They were both
then lying on the sacking of the bedstead in the chamber
where Mademoiselle L. was found. The corpse of the
young lady was much bruised and excoriated. The fact
that it had been thrust up the chimney would sufficiently
account for these appearances. The throat was greatly
chafed. There were several deep scratches just below
the chin, together with a series of livid spots which were
evidently the impression of fingers. The face was fearfully
discoloured, and the eyeballs protruded. The tongue had
been partially bitten through. A large bruise was discovered upon the pit of the stomach, produced, apparently,
by the pressure of a knee. In the opinion of M. Dumas,
Mademoiselle L'Espanaye had been throttled to death by
some person or persons unknown. The corpse of the
mother was horribly mutilated. All the bones of the
right leg and arm were more or less shattered. The left
tibia much splintered, as well as all the ribs of the left side.
Whole body dreadfully bruised and discoloured. It was
not possible to say how the injuries had been inflicted. A
heavy club of wood, or a broad bar of iron—a chair—any
large, heavy, and obtuse weapon would have produced
such results, if wielded by the hands of a very powerful
man. No woman could have inflicted the blows with any

weapon. The head of the deceased, when seen by witness
was entirely separated from the body, and was also greatly
shattered. The throat had evidently been cut with some
very sharp instrument—probably with a razor.

" *Alexandre Etienne*, surgeon, was called with M. Dumas
to view the bodies. Corroborated the testimony, and the
opinions of M. Dumas.

" Nothing further of importance was elicited, although
several other persons were examined. A murder so
mysterious, and so perplexing in all its particulars, was
never before committed in Paris—if indeed a murder has
been committed at all. The police are entirely at fault
—an unusual occurrence in affairs of this nature. There
is not, however, the shadow of a clue apparent."

The evening edition of the paper stated that the greatest
excitement still continued in the Quartier St. Roch—that
the premises in question had been carefully re-searched
and fresh examinations of witnesses instituted, but all
to no purpose. A postscript, however, mentioned that
Adolphe Le Bon had been arrested and imprisoned—
although nothing appeared to criminate him, beyond the
facts already detailed.

Dupin seemed singularly interested in the progress of
this affair—at least so I judged from his manner, for he
made no comments. It was only after the announcement
that Le Bon had been imprisoned, that he asked me my
opinion respecting the murders.

I could merely agree with all Paris in considering them
an insoluble mystery. I saw no means by which it would
be possible to trace the murderer.

" We must not judge of the means," said Dupin, " by
this shell of an examination. The Parisian police, so
much extolled for acumen, are cunning, but no more.
There is no method in their proceedings, beyond the
method of the moment. They make a vast parade of
measures ; but, not unfrequently, these are so ill adapted
to the objects proposed, as to put us in mind of Monsieur
Jourdain's calling for his *robe-de-chambre—pour mieux
entendre la musique*. The results attained by them are
not unfrequently surprising, but, for the most part, are
brought about by simple diligence and activity. When
these qualities are unavailing, their schemes fail. Vidocq,
for example, was a good guesser, and a persevering man,

But, without educated thought, he erred continually by the very intensity of his investigations. He impaired his vision by holding the object too close. He might see, perhaps, one or two points with unusual clearness, but in so doing, he, necessarily, lost sight of the matter as a whole. Thus there is such a thing as being too profound. Truth is not always in a well. In fact, as regards the more important knowledge, I do believe that she is invariably superficial. The depth lies in the valleys where we seek her, and not upon the mountain-top where she is found. The modes and sources of this kind of error are well typified in the contemplation of the heavenly bodies. To look at a star by glances—to view it in a sidelong way, by turning toward it the exterior portions of the retina (more susceptible of feeble impressions of light than the interior), is to behold the star distinctly—is to have the best appreciation of its lustre—a lustre which grows dim just in proportion as we turn our vision *fully* upon it. A greater number of rays actually fall upon the eye in the latter case, but, in the former, there is the more refined capacity for comprehension. By undue profundity we perplex and enfeeble thought ; and it is possible to make even Venus herself vanish from the firmament by a scrutiny too sustained, too concentrated, or too direct.

" As for these murders, let us enter into some examinations for ourselves, before we make up an opinion respecting them. An inquiry will afford us amusement " [I thought this an odd term, so applied, but said nothing], " and, besides, Le Bon once rendered me a service for which I am not ungrateful. We will go and see the premises with our own eyes. I know G——, the Prefect of Police, and shall have no difficulty in obtaining the necessary permission."

The permission was obtained, and we proceeded at once to the Rue Morgue. This is one of those miserable thoroughfares which intervene between the Rue Richelieu and the Rue St. Roch. It was late in the afternoon when we reached it ; as this quarter is at a great distance from that in which we resided. The house was readily found ; for there were still many persons gazing up at the closed shutters, with an objectless curiosity, from the opposite side of the way. It was an ordinary Parisian house, with a gateway, on one side of which was a glazed watch-box,

with a sliding panel in the window, indicating a *loge d*
concierge. Before going in we walked up the street, turned
down an alley, and then, again turning, passed in the rear
of the building—Dupin, meanwhile, examining the whole
neighbourhood, as well as the house, with a minuteness of
attention for which I could see no possible object.

Retracing our steps, we came again to the front of the
dwelling, rang, and having shown our credentials, were
admitted by the agents in charge. We went upstairs—
into the chamber where the body of Mademoiselle L'Espanaye had been found, and where both the deceased still lay.
The disorders of the room had, as usual, been suffered to
exist. I saw nothing beyond what had been stated in
the *Gazette des Tribunaux*. Dupin scrutinised everything—
not excepting the bodies of the victims. We then went into
the other rooms, and into the yard ; a gendarme accompanying us throughout. The examination occupied us
until dark, when we took our departure. On our way
home my companion stepped in for a moment at the
office of one of the daily papers.

I have said that the whims of my friend were manifold,
and that *Je les ménagais*—for this phrase there is no
English equivalent. It was his humour, now, to decline
all conversation on the subject of the murders, until about
noon the next day. He then asked me, suddenly, if I had
observed anything *peculiar* at the scene of the atrocity.

There was something in his manner of emphasising
the word " peculiar," which caused me to shudder, without
knowing why.

" No, nothing *peculiar*," I said ; " nothing more, at
least, than we both saw stated in the paper."

" The *Gazette*," he replied, " has not entered, I fear,
into the unusual horror of the thing. But dismiss the
idle opinions of this print. It appears to me that this
mystery is considered insoluble, for the very reason which
should cause it to be regarded as easy of solution—I mean
for the *outré* character of its features. The police are confounded by the seeming absence of motive—not for the
murder itself—but for the atrocity of the murder. They
are puzzled, too, by the seeming impossibility of reconciling
the voices heard in contention, with the facts that no one
was discovered upstairs but the assassinated Mademoiselle
L'Espanaye, and that there were no means of egress with-

out the notice of the party ascending. The wild disorder of the room ; the corpse thrust, with the head downward, up the chimney ; the frightful mutilation of the body of the old lady ; these considerations, with those just mentioned, and others which I need not mention, have sufficed to para-lyse the powers, by putting completely at fault the boasted acumen of the government agents. They have fallen into the gross but common error of confounding the unusual with the abstruse. But it is by these deviations from the plane of the ordinary, that reason feels its way, if at all, in its search for the true. In investigations such as we are now pursuing, it should not be so much asked ' what has occurred ? ' as ' what has occurred that has never occurred before ? ' In fact, the facility with which I shall arrive, or have arrived, at the solution of this mystery, is in the direct ratio of its apparent insolubility in the eyes of the police."

I stared at the speaker in mute astonishment.

" I am now awaiting," continued he, looking toward the door of our apartment—" I am now awaiting a person who, although perhaps not the perpetrator of these butcheries, must have been in some measure implicated in their perpetration. Of the worst portion of the crimes committed, it is probable that he is innocent. I hope that I am right in this supposition ; for upon it I build my expectation of reading the entire riddle. I look for the man here—in this room—every moment. It is true that he may not arrive ; but the probability is that he will. Should he come, it will be necessary to detain him. Here are pistols ; and we both know how to use them when occasion demands their use."

I took the pistols, scarcely knowing what I did, or believing what I heard, while Dupin went on, very much as if in a soliloquy. I have already spoken of his abstract manner at such times. His discourse was addressed to myself ; but his voice, although by no means loud, had that intonation which is commonly employed in speaking to some one at a great distance. His eyes, vacant in expression, regarded only the wall.

" That the voices heard in contention," he said, " by the party upon the stairs, were not the voices of the women themselves, was fully proved by the evidence. This relieves us of all doubt upon the question whether the old lady could have first destroyed the daughter, and afterward have committed suicide. I speak of this point chiefly for the sake of method ; for the strength of Madame L'Espanaye would have been utterly unequal to the task of thrusting her daughter's corpse up the chimney as it was found ; and the nature of the wounds upon her own person entirely precludes the idea of self-destruction. Murder, then, has been committed by some third party ; and the voices of this third party were those heard in contention. Let me now advert—not to the whole testimony respecting these voices—but to what was *peculiar* in that testimony. Did you observe anything peculiar about it ? "

I remarked that, while all the witnesses agreed in supposing the gruff voice to be that of a Frenchman, there was much disagreement in regard to the shrill, or, as one individual termed it, the harsh voice.

" That was the evidence itself," said Dupin, " but it was not the peculiarity of the evidence. You have observed nothing distinctive. Yet there *was* something to be observed. The witnesses, as you remark, agreed about the gruff voice ; they were here unanimous. But in regard to the shrill voice, the peculiarity is—not that they disagreed—but that, while an Italian, an Englishman, a Spaniard, a Hollander, and a Frenchman attempted to describe it, each one spoke of it as that *of a foreigner.* Each is sure that it was not the voice of one of his own countrymen. Each likens it—not to the voice of an individual of any nation with whose language he is conversant—but the converse. The Frenchman supposes it the voice of a Spaniard, and ' might have distinguished some words *had he been acquainted with the Spanish.*' The Dutchman maintains it to have been that of a Frenchman ; but we find it stated that, ' *not understanding French, this witness was examined through an interpreter.*' The Englishman thinks it the voice of a German, and ' *does not understand German.*' The Spaniard ' is sure ' that it was that of an Englishman, but ' judges by the intonation ' altogether, ' *as he has no knowledge of the English.*' The Italian believes it the voice of a Russian, but ' *has never conversed with a native of Russia.*' A second Frenchman differs, moreover, with the first, and is positive that the voice was that of an Italian ; but, *not being cognisant of that*

tongue, is, like the Spaniard, ' convinced by the intonation.'
Now, how strangely unusual must that voice have really
been, about which such testimony as this *could* have been
elicited !—in whose *tones*, even, denizens of the five great
divisions of Europe could recognise nothing familiar !
You will say that it might have been the voice of an Asiatic
—of an African. Neither Asiatics nor Africans abound in
Paris ; but, without denying the inference, I will now
merely call your attention to three points. The voice is
termed by one witness ' harsh rather than shrill.' It is
represented by two others to have been ' quick and *unequal*.'
No words—no sound resembling words—were by any witness mentioned as distinguishable.

" I know not," continued Dupin, " what impression I
may have made, so far, upon your own understanding ;
but I do not hesitate to say that legitimate deductions
even from this portion of the testimony—the portion
respecting the gruff and shrill voices—are in themselves
sufficient to engender a suspicion which should give direction to all further progress in the investigation of the
mystery. I said ' legitimate deductions ' ; but my meaning is not thus fully expressed. I designed to imply that
the deductions are the *sole* proper ones, and that the
suspicion arises *inevitably* from them as the single result.
What the suspicion is, however, I will not say just yet.
I merely wish you to bear in mind that, with myself, it
was sufficiently forcible to give a definite form—a certain
tendency—to my inquiries in the chamber.

" Let us now transport ourselves, in fancy, to this
chamber. What shall we first seek here ? The means
of egress employed by the murderers. It is not too much
to say that neither of us believe in preternatural events.
Madame and Mademoiselle L'Espanaye were not destroyed
by spirits. The doers of the deed were material, and
escaped materially. Then how ? Fortunately, there is
but one mode of reasoning upon the point, and that mode
must lead us to a definite decision. Let us examine, each
by each, the possible means of egress. It is clear that the
assassins were in the room where Mademoiselle L'Espanaye
was found, or at least in the room adjoining, when the party
ascended the stairs. It is, then, only from these two
apartments that we have to seek issues. The police have
laid bare the floors, the ceilings, and the masonry of the

F

walls, in every direction. No *secret* issues could have escaped their vigilance. But, not trusting to *their* eyes, I examined with my own. There were, then, *no* secret issues. Both doors leading from the rooms into the passage were securely locked, with the keys inside. Let us turn to the chimneys. These, although of ordinary width for some eight or ten feet above the hearths, will not admit, throughout their extent, the body of a large cat. The impossibility of egress, by means already stated, being thus absolute, we are reduced to the windows. Through those of the front room no one could have escaped without notice from the crowd in the street. The murderers *must* have passed, then, through those of the back room. Now, brought to this conclusion in so unequivocal a manner as we are, it is not our part, as reasoners, to reject it on account of apparent impossibilities. It is only left for us to prove that these apparent ' impossibilities ' are, in reality, not such.

" There are two windows in the chamber. One of them is unobstructed by furniture, and is wholly visible. The lower portion of the other is hidden from view by the head of the unwieldy bedstead which is thrust close up against it. The former was found securely fastened from within. It resisted the utmost force of those who endeavoured to raise it. A large gimlet hole had been pierced in its frame to the left, and a very stout nail was found fitted therein, nearly to the head. Upon examining the other window, a similar nail was seen similarly fitted in it ; and a vigorous attempt to raise this sash, failed also. The police were now entirely satisfied that egress had not been in these directions. And, *therefore*, it was thought a matter of supererogation to withdraw the nails and open the windows.

" My own examination was somewhat more particular, and was so for the reason I have just given—because here it was, I knew, that all apparent impossibilities *must* be proved to be not such in reality.

" I proceeded to think thus—*à posteriori*. The murderers *did* escape from one of these windows. This being so, they could not have re-fastened the sashes from the inside, as they were found fastened—the consideration which put a stop, through its obviousness, to the scrutiny of the police in this quarter. Yet the sashes *were* fastened.

They *must*, then, have the power of fastening themselves. There was no escape from this conclusion. I stepped to the unobstructed casement, withdrew the nail with some difficulty, and attempted to raise the sash. It resisted all my efforts, as I had anticipated. A concealed spring must, I now knew, exist ; and this corroboration of my idea convinced me that my premises, at least, were correct, however mysterious still appeared the circumstances attending the nails. A careful search soon brought to light the hidden spring. I pressed it, and, satisfied with the discovery, forbore to upraise the sash.

" I now replaced the nail and regarded it attentively. A person passing out through this window might have reclosed it, and the spring would have caught—but the nail could not have been replaced. The conclusion was plain, and again narrowed in the field of my investigations. The assassins *must* have escaped through the other window. Supposing, then, the springs upon each sash to be the same, as was probable, there *must* be found a difference between the nails, or at least between the modes of their fixture. Getting upon the sacking of the bedstead, I looked over the head-board minutely at the second casement. Passing my hand down behind the board, I readily discovered and pressed the spring, which was, as I had supposed, identical in character with its neighbour. I now looked at the nail. It was as stout as the other, and apparently fitted in the same manner—driven in nearly up to the head.

" You will say that I was puzzled ; but, if you think so, you must have misunderstood the nature of the inductions. To use a sporting phrase, I had not been once ' at fault.' The scent had never for an instant been lost. There was no flaw in any link of the chain. I had traced the secret to its ultimate result—and that result was *the nail*. It had, I say, in every respect, the appearance of its fellow in the other window ; but this fact was an absolute nullity (conclusive as it might seem to be) when compared with the consideration that here, at this point, terminated the clue. ' There *must* be something wrong,' I said, ' about the nail.' I touched it ; and the head, with about a quarter of an inch of the shank, came off in my fingers. The rest of the shank was in the gimlet hole, where it had been broken off. The fracture was an old one (for its edges were incrusted with rust), and had apparently been accomplished by the blow of a hammer, which had partially embedded, in the top of the bottom sash, the head portion of the nail. I now carefully replaced this head portion in the indentation whence I had taken it, and the resemblance to a perfect nail was complete— the fissure was invisible. Pressing the spring, I gently raised the sash for a few inches ; the head went up with it, remaining firm in its bed. I closed the window, and the semblance of the whole nail was again perfect.

" The riddle, so far, was now unriddled. The assassin had escaped through the window which looked upon the bed. Dropping of its own accord upon his exit (or perhaps purposely closed), it had become fastened by the spring : and it was the retention of this spring which had been mistaken by the police for that of the nail—further inquiry being thus considered unnecessary.

" The next question is that of the mode of descent. Upon this point I had been satisfied in my walk with you around the building. About five feet and a half from the casement in question there runs a lightning-rod. From this rod it would have been impossible for any one to reach the window itself, to say nothing of entering it. I observed, however, that the shutters of the fourth story were of the peculiar kind called by Parisian carpenters *ferrades*—a kind rarely employed at the present day, but frequently seen upon very old mansions at Lyons and Bordeaux. They are in the form of an ordinary door (a single, not a folding door), except that the lower half is latticed or worked in open trellis—thus affording an excellent hold for the hands. In the present instance these shutters are fully three feet and a half broad. When we saw them from the rear of the house, they were both about half open—that is to say, they stood off at right angles from the wall. It is probable that the police, as well as myself, examined the back of the tenement ; but, if so, in looking at these *ferrades* in the line of their breadth (as they must have done), they did not perceive this great breadth itself, or, at all events, failed to take it into due consideration. In fact, having once satisfied themselves that no egress could have been made in this quarter, they would naturally bestow here a very cursory examination. It was clear to me, however, that the shutter belonging to the window at the head of the bed, would, if swung fully back to the wall, reach to within two feet of the lightning-rod. It was also evident that, by exertion of a very unusual degree of activity and courage, an entrance into the window, from the rod, might have been thus effected. By reaching to the distance of two feet and a half (we now suppose the shutter open to its whole extent) a robber might have taken a firm grasp upon the trellis-work. Letting go, then, his hold upon the rod, placing his feet securely against the wall, and springing boldly from it, he might have swung the shutter so as to close it, and, if we imagine the window open at the time, might even have swung himself into the room.

" I wish you to bear especially in mind that I have spoken of a *very* unusual degree of activity as requisite to success in so hazardous and so difficult a feat. It is my design to show you, first, that the thing might possibly have been accomplished ; but, secondly and *chiefly*, I wish to impress upon your understanding the *very extraordinary*—the almost preternatural character of that agility which could have accomplished it.

" You will say, no doubt, using the language of the law, that ' to make out my case,' I should rather undervalue, than insist upon a full estimation of the activity required in this matter. This may be the practice in law, but it is not the usage of reason. My ultimate object is only the truth. My immediate purpose is to lead you to place in juxtaposition, that *very unusual* activity of which I have just spoken, with that *very peculiar* shrill (or harsh) and *unequal* voice, about whose nationality no two persons could be found to agree, and in whose utterance no syllabification could be detected."

At these words a vague and half-formed conception of the meaning of Dupin flitted over my mind. I seemed to be on the verge of comprehension, without power to comprehend—as men, at times, find themselves upon the brink of remembrance, without being able in the end, to remember. My friend went on with his discourse.

" You will see," he said, " that I have shifted the question from the mode of egress to that of ingress. It was my design to convey the idea that both were effected in the same manner, at the same point. Let us now revert to the interior of the room. Let us survey the appearances here. The drawers of the bureau, it is said, had been rifled, although many articles of apparel still remained within them. The conclusion here is absurd. It is a mere guess—a very silly one—and no more. How are we to know that the articles found in the drawers were not all these drawers had originally contained ? Madame L'Espanaye and her daughter lived an exceedingly retired life—saw no company—seldom went out—had little use for numerous changes of habiliment. Those found were at least of as good quality as any likely to be possessed by these ladies. If a thief had taken any, why did he not take the best—why did he not take all ? In a word, why did he abandon four thousand francs in gold to encumber himself with a bundle of linen ? The gold *was* abandoned. Nearly the whole sum mentioned by Monsieur Mignaud, the banker, was discovered, in bags, upon the floor. I wish you, therefore, to discard from your thoughts the blundering idea of *motive*, engendered in the brains of the police by that portion of the evidence which speaks of money delivered at the door of the house. Coincidences ten times as remarkable as this (the delivery of the money, and murder committed within three days upon the party receiving it), happen to all of us every hour of our lives, without attracting even momentary notice. Coincidences, in general, are great stumbling-blocks in the way of that class of thinkers who have been educated to know nothing of the theory of probabilities—that theory to which the most glorious objects of human research are indebted for the most glorious of illustration. In the present instance, had the gold been gone, the fact of its delivery three days before would have formed something more than a coincidence. It would have been corroborative of this idea of motive. But, under the real circumstances of the case, if we are to suppose gold the motive of this outrage, we must also imagine the perpetrator so vacillating an idiot as to have abandoned his gold and his motive together.

" Keeping now steadily in mind the points to which I have drawn your attention—that peculiar voice, that unusual agility, and that startling absence of motive in a murder so singularly atrocious as this—let us glance at the butchery itself. Here is a woman strangled to death by manual strength, and thrust up a chimney, head downward. Ordinary assassins employ no such modes of murder as this. Least of all, do they thus dispose of the murdered. In the manner of thrusting the corpse up the chimney, you will admit that there was something *excessively outré*—something altogether irreconcilable with our common notions of human action, even when we suppose the actors the most depraved of men. Think, too, how great must have been that strength which could have thrust the body *up* such an aperture so forcibly that the united vigour of several persons was found barely sufficient to drag it *down* !

" Turn, now, to other indications of the employment of a vigour most marvellous. On the hearth were thick tresses—very thick tresses—of grey human hair. These had been torn out by the roots. You are aware of the great force necessary in tearing thus from the head even twenty or thirty hairs together. You saw the locks in question as well as myself. Their roots (a hideous sight !) were clotted with fragments of the flesh of the scalp— sure token of the prodigious power which had been exerted in uprooting perhaps half a million of hairs at a time. The throat of the old lady was not merely cut, but the head absolutely severed from the body : the instrument was a mere razor. I wish you also to look at the *brutal* ferocity of these deeds. Of the bruises upon the body of Madame L'Espanaye I do not speak. Monsieur Dumas, and his worthy coadjutor Monsieur Etienne, have pronounced that they were inflicted by some obtuse instrument ; and so far these gentlemen are very correct. The obtuse instrument was clearly the stone pavement in the yard, upon which the victim had fallen from the window which looked in upon the bed. This idea, however simple it may now seem, escaped the police for the same reason that the breadth of the shutters escaped them—because, by the affair of the nails, their perceptions had been hermetically sealed against the possibility of the windows having ever been opened at all.

" If now, in addition to all these things, you have properly reflected upon the odd disorder of the chamber, we have gone so far as to combine the ideas of an agility astounding, a strength superhuman, a ferocity brutal, a butchery without motive, a *grotesquerie* in horror absolutely alien from humanity, and a voice foreign in tone to the ears of men of many nations, and devoid of all distinct or intelligible syllabification. What result, then, has ensued ? What impression have I made upon your fancy ? "

I felt a creeping of the flesh as Dupin asked me the question. " A madman," I said, " has done this deed—some raving maniac escaped from a neighbouring *Maison de Santé.*"

" In some respects," he replied, " your idea is not irrelevant. But the voices of madmen, even in their wildest paroxysms, are never found to tally with that peculiar voice heard upon the stairs. Madmen are of some nation, and their language, however incoherent in its words, has always the coherence of syllabification. Besides, the hair of a madman is not such as I now hold in my hand. I disentangled this little tuft from the rigidly clutched fingers of Madame L'Espanaye. Tell me what you can make of it."

" Dupin," I said, completely unnerved ; " this hair is most unusual—this is no *human* hair."

" I have not asserted that it is," said he ; " but, before we decide this point, I wish you to glance at the little sketch I have here traced upon this paper. It is a *facsimile* drawing of what has been described in one portion of the testimony as ' dark bruises, and deep indentations of finger nails,' upon the throat of Mademoiselle L'Espanaye, and in another (by Messrs. Dumas and Etienne), as a ' series of livid spots, evidently the impression of fingers.'

" You will perceive," continued my friend, spreading out the paper upon the table before us, " that this drawing gives the idea of a firm and fixed hold. There is no *slipping* apparent. Each finger has retained—possibly until the death of the victim—the fearful grasp by which it originally embedded itself. Attempt, now, to place all your fingers, at the same time, in the respective impressions as you see them."

I made the attempt in vain.

" We are possibly not giving this matter a fair trial," he said. " The paper is spread out upon a plane surface ; but the human throat is cylindrical. Here is a billet of wood. the circumference of which is about that of the throat. Wrap the drawing round it, and try the experiment again."

" I did so ; but the difficulty was even more obvious than before. " This," I said, " is the mark of no human hand."

" Read now," replied Dupin, " this passage from Cuvier."

It was a minute anatomical and generally descriptive account of the large fulvous Ourang-Outang of the East Indian Islands. The gigantic stature, the prodigious strength and activity, the wild ferocity, and the imitative propensities of these mammalia are sufficiently well known to all. I understood the full horrors of the murder at once.

" The description of the digits," said I, as I made an end of reading, " is in exact accordance with this drawing. I see that no animal but an Ourang-Outang, of the species here mentioned, could have impressed the indentations as you have traced them. This tuft of tawny hair, too, is identical in character with that of the beast of Cuvier. But I cannot possibly comprehend the particulars of this frightful mystery. Besides, there were *two* voices heard in contention, and one of them was unquestionably the voice of a Frenchman."

" True ; and you will remember an expression attributed almost unanimously, by the evidence, to this voice —the expression ' *Mon Dieu !* ' This, under the circumstances, has been justly characterised by one of the witnesses (Montani, the confectioner) as an expression of remonstrance or expostulation. Upon these two words, therefore, I have mainly built my hopes of a full solution of the riddle. A Frenchman was cognisant of the murder. It is possible—indeed it is far more than probable—that he was innocent of all participation in the bloody transactions which took place. The Ourang-Outang may have escaped from him. He may have traced it to the chamber ; but, under the agitating circumstances which ensued, he could never have re-captured it. It is still at large. I will not pursue these guesses—for I have no right to call them more—since the shades of reflection upon which they are based are scarcely of sufficient depth to be appreciable to my own intellect, and since I could not pretend to make them intelligible to the understanding of another.

F*

We will call them guesses, then, and speak of them as such. If the Frenchman in question is indeed, as I suppose, innocent of this atrocity, this advertisement, which I left last night, upon our return home, at the office of *Le Monde* (a paper devoted to the shipping interest, and much sought by sailors), will bring him to our residence."

He handed me a paper, and I read thus :—

" CAUGHT—*In the Bois de Boulogne, early in the morning of the* ——*inst.* [the morning of the murder], *a very large, tawny Ourang-Outang of the Bornese species. The owner (who is ascertained to be a sailor, belonging to a Maltese vessel), may have the animal again, upon identifying it satisfactorily, and paying a few charges arising from its capture and keeping. Call at No.* ——, *Rue* ——, *Faubourg St. Germain—au troisième.*"

" How was it possible," I asked, " that you should know the man to be a sailor, and belonging to a Maltese vessel ? "

" I do *not* know it," said Dupin. " I am not *sure* of it. Here, however, is a small piece of ribbon, which from its form, and from its greasy appearance, has evidently been used in tying the hair in one of those long *queues* of which sailors are so fond. Moreover, this knot is one which few besides sailors can tie, and is peculiar to the Maltese. I picked the ribbon up at the foot of the lightning-rod. It could not have belonged to either of the deceased. Now if, after all, I am wrong in my induction from this ribbon, that the Frenchman was a sailor belonging to a Maltese vessel, still I can have done no harm in saying what I did in the advertisement. If I am in error, he will merely suppose that I have been misled by some circumstance into which he will not take the trouble to inquire. But if I am right, a great point is gained. Cognisant although innocent of the murder, the Frenchman will naturally hesitate about replying to the advertisement—about demanding the Ourang-Outang. He will reason thus : ' I am innocent ; I am poor ; my Ourang-Outang is of great value—to one in my circumstances a fortune of itself—why should I lose it through idle apprehensions of danger ? Here it is within my grasp. It was found in the Bois de Boulogne—at a vast distance

from the scene of that butchery. How can it ever be
suspected that a brute beast should have done the deed ?
The police are at fault—they have failed to procure the
slightest clue. Should they even trace the animal, it
would be impossible to prove me cognisant of the murder,
or to implicate me in guilt on account of that cognisance.
Above all, *I am known*. The advertiser designates me
as the possessor of the beast. I am not sure to what
limit his knowledge may extend. Should I avoid claiming
a property of so great value, which it is known that I
possess, I will render the animal at least liable to suspicion.
It is not my policy to attract attention either to myself
or to the beast. I will answer the advertisement, get
the Ourang-Outang, and keep it close until this matter
has blown over.' "

At this moment we heard a step upon the stairs.

" Be ready," said Dupin, " with your pistols, but neither
use them nor show them until at a signal from myself."

The front door of the house had been left open, and the
visitor had entered, without ringing, and advanced several
steps upon the staircase. Now, however, he seemed to
hesitate. Presently we heard him descending. Dupin was
moving quickly to the door, when we again heard him coming
up. He did not turn back a second time, but stepped
up with decision, and rapped at the door of our chamber.

" Come in," said Dupin, in a cheerful and hearty tone.

A man entered. He was a sailor, evidently—a tall,
stout, and muscular-looking person, with a certain dare-
devil expression of countenance, not altogether unprepos-
sessing. His face, greatly sunburnt, was more than half
hidden by whisker and mustachio. He had with him a
huge oaken cudgel, but appeared to be otherwise unarmed.
He bowed awkwardly, and bade us " good evening," in
French accents, which, although somewhat Neufchatelish,
were still sufficiently indicative of a Parisian origin.

" Sit down, my friend," said Dupin. " I suppose you
have called about the Ourang-Outang. Upon my word,
I almost envy you the possession of him ; a remarkably
fine, and no doubt a very valuable animal. How old do
you suppose him to be ? "

The sailor drew a long breath, with the air of a man
relieved of some intolerable burden, and then replied, in
an assured tone—

" I have no way of telling—but he can't be more than four or five years old. Have you got him here ? "

" Oh no ; we had no conveniences for keeping him here. He is at a livery stable in the Rue Dubourg, just by. You can get him in the morning. Of course you are prepared to identify the property ? "

" To be sure I am, sir."

" I shall be sorry to part with him," said Dupin.

" I don't mean that you should be at all this trouble for nothing, sir," said the man. " Couldn't expect it. Am very willing to pay a reward for the finding of the animal—that is to say, anything in reason."

" Well," replied my friend, " that is all very fair, to be sure. Let me think !—what should I have ? Oh ! I will tell you. My reward shall be this. You shall give me all the information in your power about these murders in the Rue Morgue."

Dupin said the last words in a very low tone, and very quietly. Just as quietly, too, he walked toward the door, locked it, and put the key in his pocket. He then drew a pistol from his bosom, and placed it, without the least flurry, upon the table.

The sailor's face flushed up as if he were struggling with suffocation. He started to his feet and grasped his cudgel ; but the next moment he fell back into his seat, trembling violently, and with the countenance of death itself. He spoke not a word. I pitied him from the bottom of my heart.

" My friend," said Dupin, in a kind tone, " you are alarming yourself unnecessarily—you are indeed. We mean you no harm whatever. I pledge you the honour of a gentleman, and of a Frenchman, that we intend you no injury. I perfectly well know that you are innocent of the atrocities in the Rue Morgue. It will not do, how-ever, to deny that you are in some measure implicated in them. From what I have already said, you must know that I have had means of information about this matter —means of which you could never have dreamed. Now the thing stands thus. You have done nothing which you could have avoided—nothing, certainly, which renders you culpable. You were not even guilty of robbery, when you might have robbed with impunity. You have nothing to conceal. You have no reason for concealment. On the other hand, you are bound by every principle of honour to confess all you know. An innocent man is now imprisoned, charged with that crime of which you can point out the perpetrator."

The sailor had recovered his presence of mind, in a great measure, while Dupin uttered these words ; but his original boldness of bearing was all gone.

" So help me God," said he, after a brief pause, " I *will* tell you all I know about this affair ; but I do not expect you to believe one half I say—I would be a fool indeed if I did. Still, I *am* innocent, and I will make a clean breast if I die for it."

What he stated was, in substance, this. He had lately made a voyage to 'the Indian Archipelago. A party, of which he formed one, landed at Borneo, and passed into the interior on an excursion of pleasure. Himself and a companion had captured the Ourang-Outang. This companion dying, the animal fell into his own exclusive possession. After great trouble, occasioned by the intractable ferocity of his captive during the home voyage, he at length succeeded in lodging it safely at his own residence in Paris, where, not to attract toward himself the unpleasant curiosity of his neighbours, he kept it carefully secluded, until such time as it should recover from a wound in the foot, received from a splinter on board ship. His ultimate design was to sell it.

Returning home from some sailors' frolic on the night, or rather in the morning of the murder, he found the beast occupying his own bedroom, into which it had broken from a closet adjoining, where it had been, as was thought, securely confined. Razor in hand, and fully lathered, it was sitting before a looking-glass, attempting the operation of shaving, in which it had no doubt previously watched its master through the key-hole of the closet. Terrified at the sight of so dangerous a weapon in the possession of an animal so ferocious, and so well able to use it, the man, for some moments, was at a loss what to do. He had been accustomed, however, to quiet the creature, even in its fiercest moods, by the use of a whip, and to this he now resorted. Upon sight of it, the Ourang-Outang sprang at once through the door of the chamber, down the stairs, and thence, through a window, unfortunately open, into the street.

The Frenchman followed in despair; the ape, razor still in hand, occasionally stopping to look back and gesticulate at its pursuer, until the latter had nearly come up with it. It then again made off. In this manner the chase continued for a long time. The streets were profoundly quiet, as it was nearly three o'clock in the morning. In passing down an alley in the rear of the Rue Morgue, the fugitive's attention was arrested by a light gleaming from the open window of Madame L'Espanaye's chamber, in the fourth story of her house. Rushing to the building, it perceived the lightning-rod, clambered up with inconceivable agility, grasped the shutter, which was thrown fully back against the wall, and, by its means, swung itself directly upon the head-board of the bed. The whole feat did not occupy a minute. The shutter was kicked open again by the Ourang-Outang as it entered the room.

The sailor, in the meantime, was both rejoiced and perplexed. He had strong hopes of now recapturing the brute, as it could scarcely escape from the trap into which it had ventured, except by the rod, where it might be intercepted as it came down. On the other hand, there was much cause for anxiety as to what it might do in the house. This latter reflection urged the man still to follow the fugitive. A lightning-rod is ascended without difficulty, especially by a sailor; but, when he had arrived as high as the window, which lay far to his left, his career was stopped; the most that he could accomplish was to reach over so as to obtain a glimpse of the interior of the room. At this glimpse he nearly fell from his hold through excess of horror. Now it was that those hideous shrieks arose upon the night, which had startled from slumber the inmates of the Rue Morgue. Madame L'Espanaye and her daughter, habited in their night clothes, had apparently been occupied in arranging some papers in the iron chest already mentioned, which had been wheeled into the middle of the room. It was open, and its contents lay beside it on the floor. The victims must have been sitting with their backs toward the window; and, from the time elapsing between the ingress of the beast and the screams, it seems probable that it was not immediately perceived. The flapping-to of the shutter would naturally have been attributed to the wind.

As the sailor looked in, the gigantic animal had seized

Madame L'Espanaye by the hair (which was loose, as she had been combing it), and was flourishing the razor about her face, in imitation of the motions of a barber. The daughter lay prostrate and motionless ; she had swooned. The screams and struggles of the old lady (during which the hair was torn from her head) had the effect of changing the probably pacific purposes of the Ourang-Outang into those of wrath. With one determined sweep of its muscular arm it nearly severed her head from her body. The sight of blood inflamed its anger into frenzy. Gnashing its teeth, and flashing fire from its eyes, it flew upon the body of the girl, and embedded its fearful talons in her throat, retaining its grasp until she expired. Its wandering and wild glances fell at this moment upon the head of the bed, over which the face of its master, rigid with horror, was just discernible. The fury of the beast, who no doubt bore still in mind the dreaded whip, was instantly converted into fear. Conscious of having deserved punishment, it seemed desirous of concealing its bloody deeds, and skipped about the chamber in an agony of nervous agitation ; throwing down and breaking the furniture as it moved, and dragging the bed from the bedstead. In conclusion, it seized first the corpse of the daughter, and thrust it up the chimney, as it was found ; then that of the old lady, which it immediately hurled through the window headlong.

As the ape approached the casement with its mutilated burden, the sailor shrank aghast to the rod, and rather gliding than clambering down it, hurried at once home —dreading the consequences of the butchery, and gladly abandoning, in his terror, all solicitude about the fate of the Ourang-Outang. The words heard by the party upon the staircase were the Frenchman's exclamations of horror and affright, commingled with the fiendish jabberings of the brute.

I have scarcely anything to add. The Ourang-Outang must have escaped from the chamber, by the rod, just before the breaking of the door. It must have closed the window as it passed through it. It was subsequently caught by the owner himself, who obtained for it a very large sum at the *Jardin des Plantes*. Le Bon was instantly released upon our narration of the circumstances (with some comments from Dupin) at the *bureau* of the Prefect of Police. This functionary, however well disposed to my friend, could not altogether conceal his chagrin at the turn which affairs had taken, and was fain to indulge in a sarcasm or two, about the propriety of every person minding his own business.

" Let him talk," said Dupin, who had not thought it necessary to reply. " Let him discourse ; it will ease his conscience. I am satisfied with having defeated him in his own castle. Nevertheless, that he failed in the solution of this mystery is by no means that matter for wonder which he supposes it ; for, in truth, our friend the Prefect is somewhat too cunning to be profound. In his wisdom is no *stamen*. It is all head and no body, like the pictures of the goddess Laverna—or, at best, all head and shoulders, like a codfish. But he is a good creature after all. I like him especially for one master-stroke of cant, by which he has attained his reputation for ingenuity. I mean the way he has ' *de nier ce qui est, et d'expliquer ce qui n'est pas.*' " *

THE MYSTERY OF MARIE ROGÊT †

A SEQUEL TO " THE MURDERS IN THE RUE MORGUE "

" Es giebt eine Reihe idealischer Begebenheiten, die der Wirklichkeit parallel lauft. Selten fallen sie zusammen. Menschen und zufalle modificiren gewohulich die idealische Begebenheit, so dass sie unvollkommen erscheint, und ihre Folgen gleichfalls unvollkommen sind. So bei der Reformation ; statt des Protestantismus kam das Lutherthum hervor."

(" There are ideal series of events which run parallel with the real ones. They rarely coincide. Men and circumstances generally modify the ideal train of events, so that it seems imperfect, and its consequences are equally imperfect. Thus with the Reformation ; instead of Protestantism came Lutheranism."—NOVALIS, *Moral Ansichten.*)

THERE are few persons, even amongst the calmest thinkers, who have not occasionally been startled into a vague yet thrilling half-credence in the supernatural, by *coincidences* of so seemingly marvellous a character that, as *mere* coincidences, the intellect has been unable to receive them. Such

* Rousseau, *Nouvelle Héloïse.*

† Upon the original publication of " Marie Rogêt," the footnotes now appended were considered unnecessary ; but the lapse of

sentiments—for the half credences of which I speak have never the full force of *thought*—such sentiments are seldom thoroughly stifled unless by reference to the doctrine of chance, or, as it is technically termed, the Calculus of Probabilities. Now this Calculus is, in its essence, purely mathematical ; and thus we have the anomaly of the most rigidly exact in science applied to the shadow and spirituality of the most intangible in speculation.

The extraordinary details which I am now called upon to make public, will be found to form, as regards sequence of time, the primary branch of a series of scarcely intelligible *coincidences*, whose secondary or concluding branch will be recognised by all readers in the late murder of MARY CECILIA ROGERS, at New York.

When, in an article entitled " The Murders in the Rue Morgue," I endeavoured, about a year ago, to depict some very remarkable features in the mental character of my friend, the Chevalier C. Auguste Dupin, it did not occur to me that I should ever resume the subject. This depicting of character constituted my design ; and this design was thoroughly fulfilled in the wild train of circumstances brought to instance Dupin's idiosyncrasy. I might have adduced other examples, but I should have proven no more. Late events, however, in their

several years since the tragedy upon which the tale is based, renders it expedient to give them, and also to say a few words in explanation of the general design. A young girl, Mary Cecilia Rogers, was murdered in the vicinity of New York ; and although her death occasioned an intense and long-enduring excitement, the mystery attending it had remained unsolved at the period when the present paper was written and published (November 1842). Herein, under pretence of relating the fate of a Parisian *grisette*, the author has followed, in minute detail, the essential, while merely paralleling the unessential facts of the real murder of Mary Rogers. Thus all argument founded upon the fiction is applicable to the truth : and the investigation of the truth was the object.

The " Mystery of Marie Rogêt " was composed at a distance from the scene of the atrocity, and with no other means of investigation than the newspapers afforded. Thus much escaped the writer of which he could have availed himself had he been upon the spot, and visited the localities. It may not be improper to record, nevertheless, that the confessions of *two* persons (one of them the Madame Deluc of the narrative), made at different periods, long subsequent to the publication, confirmed, in full, not only the general conclusion, but absolutely *all* the chief hypothetical details by which that conclusion was attained.

surprising development, have startled me into some further
details, which will carry with them the air of extorted
confession.   Hearing what I have lately heard, it would be
indeed strange should I remain silent in regard to what I
both heard and saw so long ago.

Upon the winding up of the tragedy involved in the
deaths of Madame L'Espanaye and her daughter, the
Chevalier dismissed the affair at once from his attention,
and relapsed into his old habits of moody reverie.   Prone,
at all times, to abstraction, I readily fell in with his humour ;
and continuing to occupy our chambers in the Faubourg
Saint Germain, we gave the Future to the winds, and
slumbered tranquilly in the Present, weaving the dull
world around us into dreams.

But these dreams were not altogether uninterrupted.
It may readily be supposed that the part played by my
friend, in the drama at the Rue Morgue, had not failed of
its impression upon the fancies of the Parisian police.
With its emissaries, the name of Dupin had grown into a
household word.   The simple character of those inductions
by which he had disentangled the mystery never having
been explained even to the Prefect, or to any other individual than myself, of course it is not surprising that the
affair was regarded as little less than miraculous, or that
the Chevalier's analytical abilities acquired for him the
credit of intuition.   His frankness would have led him to
disabuse every inquirer of such prejudice ; but his indolent
humour forbade all further agitation of a topic whose
interest to himself had long ceased.   It thus happened
that he found himself the cynosure of the pol ial eyes ;
and the cases were not few in which attempt was made to
engage his services at the Prefecture.   One of the most
remarkable instances was that of the murder of a young
girl named Marie Rogêt.

This event occurred about two years after the atrocity
in the Rue Morgue.   Marie, whose Christian and family
name will at once arrest attention from their resemblance
to those of the unfortunate " cigar-girl," was the only
daughter of the widow Estelle Rogêt.   The father had
died during the child's infancy, and from the period of
his death, until within eighteen months before the
assassination which forms the subject of our narrative,
the mother and daughter had dwelt together in the Rue

Pavée Saint Andrée ; * Madame there keeping a *pension*,
assisted by Marie. Affairs went on thus until the latter
had attained her twenty-second year, when her great
beauty attracted the notice of a perfumer, who occupied
one of the shops in the basement of the Palais Royal,
and whose custom lay chiefly among the desperate adventurers infesting that neighbourhood. Monsieur Le
Blanc † was not unaware of the advantages to be derived
from the attendance of the fair Marie in his perfumery ;
and his liberal proposals were accepted eagerly by the girl,
although with somewhat more of hesitation by Madame.

The anticipations of the shopkeeper were realised, and
his rooms soon became notorious through the charms of
the sprightly *grisette*. She had been in his employ about
a year, when her admirers were thrown into confusion
by her sudden disappearance from the shop. Monsieur
Le Blanc was unable to account for her absence, and
Madame Rogêt was distracted with anxiety and terror.
The public papers immediately took up the theme, and
the police were upon the point of making serious investigations, when, one fine morning, after the lapse of a week,
Marie, in good health, but with a somewhat saddened
air, made her re-appearance at her usual counter in the
perfumery. All inquiry, except that of a private character,
was of course immediately hushed. Monsieur Le Blanc
professed total ignorance, as before. Marie, with Madame,
replied to all questions, that the last week had been spent
at the house of a relation in the country. Thus the affair
died away, and was generally forgotten ; for the girl,
ostensibly to relieve herself from the impertinence of
curiosity, soon bade a final adieu to the perfumer, and
sought the shelter of her mother's residence in the Rue
Pavée Saint Andrée.

It was about five months after this return home, that
her friends were alarmed by her sudden disappearance
for the second time. Three days elapsed, and nothing
was heard of her. On the fourth her corpse was found
floating in the Seine, ‡ near the shore which is opposite
the Quartier of the Rue Saint Andrée, and at a point not
very far distant from the secluded neighbourhood of the
Barrière du Roule. §

* Nassau Street.   † Anderson.   ‡ The Hudson.
§ Weehawken.

The atrocity of this murder (for it was at once evident that murder had been committed), the youth and beauty of the victim, and, above all, her previous notoriety, conspired to produce intense excitement in the minds of the sensitive Parisians. I can call to mind no similar occurrence producing so general and so intense an effect. For several weeks, in the discussion of this one absorbing theme, even the momentous political topics of the day were forgotten. The Prefect made unusual exertions; and the powers of the whole Parisian police were, of course, tasked to the utmost extent.

Upon the first discovery of the corpse, it was not supposed that the murderer would be able to elude, for more than a very brief period, the inquisition which was immediately set on foot. It was not until the expiration of a week that it was deemed necessary to offer a reward; and even then this reward was limited to a thousand francs. In the meantime the investigation proceeded with vigour, if not always with judgment, and numerous individuals were examined to no purpose; while, owing to the continual absence of all clue to the mystery, the popular excitement greatly increased. At the end of the tenth day it was thought advisable to double the sum originally proposed; and, at length, the second week having elapsed without leading to any discoveries, and the prejudice which always exists in Paris against the police having given vent to itself in several serious *émeutes*, the Prefect took it upon himself to offer the sum of twenty thousand francs " for the conviction of the assassin," or, if more than one should prove to have been implicated, " for the conviction of any one of the assassins." In the proclamation setting forth this reward, a full pardon was promised to any accomplice who should come forward in evidence against his fellow; and to the whole was appended, wherever it appeared, the private placard of a committee of citizens, offering ten thousand francs, in addition to the amount proposed by the Prefecture. The entire reward thus stood at no less than thirty thousand francs, which will be regarded as an extraordinary sum when we consider the humble condition of the girl, and the great frequency, in large cities, of such atrocities as the one described.

No one doubted now that the mystery of this murder

would be immediately brought to light. But although, in one or two instances, arrests were made which promised elucidation, yet nothing was elicited which could implicate the parties suspected ; and they were discharged forthwith. Strange as it may appear, the third week from the discovery of the body had passed, and passed without any light being thrown upon the subject, before even a rumour of the events which had so agitated the public mind reached the ears of Dupin and myself. Engaged in researches which had absorbed our whole attention, it had been nearly a month since either of us had gone abroad, or received a visitor, or more than glanced at the leading political articles in one of the daily papers. The first intelligence of the murder was brought us by G——, in person. He called upon us early in the afternoon of the 13th of July 18—, and remained with us until late in the night. He had been piqued by the failure of all his endeavours to ferret the assassins. His reputation —so he said, with a peculiarly Parisian air—was at stake. Even his honour was concerned. The eyes of the public were upon him ; and there was really no sacrifice which he would not be willing to make for the development of the mystery. He concluded a somewhat droll speech with a compliment upon what he was pleased to term the *tact* of Dupin, and made him a direct, and certainly a liberal proposition, the precise nature of which I do not feel at liberty to disclose, but which has no bearing upon the proper subject of my narrative.

The compliment my friend rebutted as best he could, but the proposition he accepted at once, although its advantages were altogether provisional. This point being settled, the Prefect broke forth at once into explanations of his own views, interspersing them with long comments upon the evidence; of which latter we were not yet in possession. He discoursed much, and beyond doubt learnedly ; while I hazarded an occasional suggestion as the night wore drowsily away. Dupin, sitting steadily in his accustomed arm-chair, was the embodiment of respectful attention. He wore spectacles during the whole interview ; and an occasional glance beneath their green glasses sufficed to convince me that he slept not the less soundly, because silently, throughout the seven or eight leaden-footed hours which immediately preceded the departure of the Prefect.

In the morning I procured, at the Prefecture, a full report of all the evidence elicited, and, at the various newspaper offices, a copy of every paper in which, from first to last, had been published any decisive information in regard to this sad affair. Freed from all that was positively disproved, this mass of information stood thus :—

Marie Rogêt left the residence of her mother, in the Rue Pavée Saint Andrée, about nine o'clock in the morning of Sunday, June the 22nd, 18—. In going out she gave notice to a Monsieur Jacques St. Eustache,* and to him only, of her intention to spend the day with an aunt who resided in the Rue des Drômes. The Rue des Drômes is a short and narrow but populous thoroughfare, not far from the banks of the river, and at a distance of some two miles in the most direct course possible from the *pension* of Madame Rogêt. St. Eustache was the accepted suitor of Marie, and lodged, as well as took his meals, at the *pension*. He was to have gone for his betrothed at dusk, and to have escorted her home. In the afternoon, however, it came on to rain heavily ; and, supposing that she would remain all night at her aunt's (as she had done under similar circumstances before), he did not think it necessary to keep his promise. As night drew on, Madame Rogêt (who was an infirm old lady, seventy years of age) was heard to express a fear " that she should never see Marie again " ; but this observation attracted little attention at the time.

On Monday, it was ascertained that the girl had not been to the Rue des Drômes ; and when the day elapsed without tidings of her, a tardy search was instituted at several points in the city and its environs. It was not, however, until the fourth day from the period of her disappearance that anything satisfactory was ascertained respecting her. On this day (Wednesday, the 25th of June), a Monsieur Beauvais,† who, with a friend, had been making inquiries for Marie near the Barrière du Roule, on the shore of the Seine which is opposite the Rue Pavée Saint Andrée, was informed that a corpse had just been towed ashore by some fishermen, who had found it floating in

* Payne.   † Crommelin.

the river. Upon seeing the body, Beauvais, after some hesitation, identified it as that of the perfumery girl. His friend recognised it more promptly.

The face was suffused with dark blood, some of which issued from the mouth. No foam was seen, as in the case of the merely drowned. There was no discoloration in the cellular tissue. About the throat were bruises and impressions of fingers. The arms were bent over on the chest, and were rigid. The right hand was clenched ; the left partially open. On the left wrist were two circular excoriations, apparently the effect of ropes, or of a rope in more than one volution. A part of the right wrist, also, was much chafed, as well as the back throughout its extent, but more especially at the shoulder-blades. In bringing the body to the shore the fishermen had attached to it a rope, but none of the excoriations had been effected by this. The flesh of the neck was much swollen. There were no cuts apparent, or bruises which appeared the effect of blows. A piece of lace was found tied so tightly around the neck as to be hidden from sight ; it was completely buried in the flesh, and was fastened by a knot which lay just under the left ear. This alone would have sufficed to produce death. The medical testimony spoke confidently of the virtuous character of the deceased. She had been subjected, it said, to brutal violence. The corpse was in such condition when found that there could have been no difficulty in its recognition by friends.

The dress was much torn and otherwise disordered. In the outer garment, a slip, about a foot wide, had been torn upward from the bottom hem to the waist, but not torn off. It was wound three times around the waist, and secured by a sort of hitch in the back. The dress immediately beneath the frock was of fine muslin ; and from this a slip eighteen inches wide had been torn entirely out—torn very evenly and with great care. It was found around her neck, fitting loosely, and secured with a hard knot. Over this muslin slip and the slip of lace, the strings of a bonnet were attached, the bonnet being appended. The knot by which the strings of the bonnet were fastened, was not a lady's, but a slip or sailor's knot.

After the recognition of the corpse, it was not, as usual, taken to the Morgue (this formality being superfluous), but hastily interred not far from the spot at which it was brought ashore. Through the exertions of Beauvais the matter was industriously hushed up, as far as possible ; and several days had elapsed before any public emotion resulted. A weekly paper,* however, at length took up the theme ; the corpse was disinterred, and a re-examination instituted ; but nothing was elicited beyond what has been already noted. The clothes, however, were now submitted to the mother and friends of the deceased, and fully identified as those worn by the girl upon leaving home.

Meantime, the excitement increased hourly. Several individuals were arrested and discharged. St. Eustache fell especially under suspicion ; and he failed, at first, to give an intelligible account of his whereabouts during the Sunday on which Marie left home. Subsequently, however, he submitted to Monsieur G——, affidavits, accounting satisfactorily for every hour of the day in question. As time passed and no discovery ensued, a thousand contradictory rumours were circulated, and journalists busied themselves in *suggestions*. Among these, the one which attracted the most notice, was the idea that Marie Rogêt still lived—that the corpse found in the Seine was that of some other unfortunate. It will be proper that I submit to the reader some passages which embody the suggestion alluded to. These passages are *literal* translations from *L'Etoile,*† a paper conducted, in general, with much ability :—

" Mademoiselle Rogêt left her mother's house on Sunday morning, June the 22nd, 18—, with the ostensible purpose of going to see her aunt, or some other connection, in the Rue des Drômes. From that hour nobody is proved to have seen her. There is no trace or tidings of her at all. . . . There has no person, whatever, come forward, so far, who saw her at all, on that day, after she left her mother's door. . . . Now, though we have no evidence that Marie Rogêt was in the land of the living after nine o'clock on Sunday, June the 22nd, we have proof that, up to that hour, she was alive. On Wednesday noon, at twelve, a female body was discovered afloat on the

* The *N. Y. Mercury.*
† The *N. Y. Brother Jonathan,* edited by H. Hastings Weld, Esq.

shore of the Barrière du Roule. This was, even if we presume that Marie Rogêt was thrown into the river within three hours after she left her mother's house, only three days from the time she left her home—three days to an hour. But it is folly to suppose that the murder, if murder was committed on her body, could have been consummated soon enough to have enabled her murderers to throw the body into the river before midnight. Those who are guilty of such horrid crimes, choose darkness rather than light. . . . Thus we see that if the body found in the river *was* that of Marie Rogêt, it could only have been in the water two and a half days, or three at the outside. All experience has shown that drowned bodies, or bodies thrown into the water immediately after death by violence, require from six to ten days for sufficient decomposition to take place to bring them to the top of the water. Even where a cannon is fired over a corpse, and it rises before at least five or six days' immersion, it sinks again, if let alone. Now, we ask, what was there in this case to cause a departure from the ordinary course of nature ? . . . If the body had been kept in its mangled state on shore until Tuesday night, some trace would be found on shore of the murderers. It is a doubtful point, also, whether the body would be so soon afloat, even were it thrown in after having been dead two days. And, furthermore, it is exceedingly improbable that any villains who had committed such a murder as is here supposed, would have thrown the body in without weight to sink it, when such a precaution could have so easily been taken."

The editor here proceeds to argue that the body must have been in the water " not three days merely, but, at least, five times three days," because it was so far decomposed that Beauvais had great difficulty in recognising it. This latter point, however, was fully disproved. I continue the translation :—

" What, then, are the facts on which M. Beauvais says that he has no doubt the body was that of Marie Rogêt ? He ripped up the gown sleeve, and says he found marks which satisfied him of the identity. The public generally supposed those marks to have consisted

of some description of scars. He rubbed the arm and
found *hair* upon it—something as indefinite, we think,
as can readily be imagined—as little conclusive as finding
an arm in the sleeve. M. Beauvais did not return that
night, but sent word to Madame Rogêt, at seven o'clock
on Wednesday evening, that an investigation was still
in progress respecting her daughter. If we allow that
Madame Rogêt, from her age and grief, could not go over
(which is allowing a great deal), there certainly must
have been some one who would have thought it worth
while to go over and attend the investigation, if they
thought the body was that of Marie. Nobody went over.
There was nothing said or heard about the matter in the
Rue Pavée Saint Andrée, that reached even the occupants
of the same building. M. St. Eustache, the lover and
intended husband of Marie, who boarded in her mother's
house, deposes that he did not hear of the discovery of
the body of his intended until the next morning, when
M. Beauvais came into his chamber and told him of it.
For an item of news like this, it strikes us it was very
coolly received."

In this way the journal endeavoured to create the
impression of an apathy on the part of the relatives of
Marie, inconsistent with the supposition that these relatives
believed the corpse to be hers. Its insinuations amount
to this—that Marie, with the connivance of her friends,
had absented herself from the city for reasons involving
a charge against her chastity ; and that these friends,
upon the discovery of a corpse in the Seine, somewhat
resembling that of the girl, had availed themselves of
the opportunity to impress the public with the belief of
her death. But *L'Etoile* was again over-hasty. It was
distinctly proved that no apathy, such as was imagined,
existed ; that the old lady was exceedingly feeble, and so
agitated as to be unable to attend to any duty ; that
St. Eustache, so far from receiving the news coolly, was
distracted with grief, and bore himself so frantically, that
M. Beauvais prevailed upon a friend and relative to take
charge of him, and prevent his attending the examination
at the disinterment. Moreover, although it was stated
by *L'Etoile* that the corpse was reinterred at the public
expense—that an advantageous offer of private sepulture

was absolutely declined by the family—and that no member of the family attended the ceremonial—although, I say, all this was asserted by *L'Etoile* in furtherance of the impression it designed to convey—yet *all* this was satisfactorily disproved. In a subsequent number of the paper, an attempt was made to throw suspicion upon Beauvais himself. The editor says :—

"Now, then, a change comes over the matter. We are told that, on one occasion, while a Madame B—— was at Madame Rogêt's house, M. Beauvais, who was going out, told her that a gendarme was expected there, and that she, Madame B., must not say anything to the gendarme until he returned, but let the matter be for him. . . . In the present posture of affairs, M. Beauvais appears to have the whole matter locked up in his head. A single step cannot be taken without M. Beauvais ; for, go which way you will, you run against him. . . . For some reason, he determined that nobody shall have anything to do with the proceedings but himself, and he has elbowed the male relatives out of the way, according to their representations, in a very singular manner. He seems to have been very much averse to permitting the relatives to see the body."

By the following fact, some colour was given to the suspicion thus thrown upon Beauvais. A visitor at his office, a few days prior to the girl's disappearance, and during the absence of its occupant, had observed *a rose* in the keyhole of the door, and the name "*Marie*" inscribed upon a slate which hung near at hand.

The general impression, so far as we were enabled to glean it from the newspapers, seemed to be, that Marie had been the victim of *a gang* of desperadoes—that by these she had been borne across the river, maltreated and murdered. *Le Commerciel*,* however, a print of extensive influence, was earnest in combating this popular idea. I quote a passage or two from its columns :—

"We are persuaded that pursuit has hitherto been on a false scent, so far as it has been directed to the Barrière du Roule. It is impossible that a person so well known

* *N. Y. Journal of Commerce.*

to thousands as this young woman was, should have passed three blocks without some one having seen her ; and any one who saw her would have remembered it, for she interested all who knew her. It was when the streets were full of people, when she went out. . . . It is impossible that she could have gone to the Barrière du Roule, or to the Rue des Drômes, without being recognised by a dozen persons ; yet no one has come forward who saw her outside of her mother's door, and there is no evidence, except the testimony concerning her expressed intentions, that she did go out at all. Her gown was torn, bound round her, and tied ; and by that the body was carried as a bundle. If the murder had been committed at the Barrière du Roule, there would have been no necessity for any such arrangement. The fact that the body was found floating near the Barrière, is no proof as to where it was thrown into the water. . . . A piece of one of the unfortunate girl's petticoats, two feet long and one foot wide, was torn out and tied under her chin around the back of her head, probably to prevent screams. This was done by fellows who had no pocket-handkerchiefs."

A day or two before the Prefect called upon us, however, some important information reached the police, which seemed to overthrow, at least, the chief portion of *Le Commerciel's* argument. Two small boys, sons of a Madame Deluc, while roaming among the woods near the Barrière du Roule, chanced to penetrate a close thicket, within which were three or four large stones, forming a kind of seat, with a back and footstool. On the upper stone lay a white petticoat ; on the second a silk scarf. A parasol, gloves, and a pocket-handkerchief were also here found. The handkerchief bore the name " Marie Rogêt." Fragments of dress were discovered on the brambles around. The earth was trampled, the bushes were broken, and there was every evidence of a struggle. Between the thicket and the river, the fences were found taken down, and the ground bore evidence of some heavy burden having been dragged along it.

A weekly paper, *Le Soleil*,* had the following comments upon this discovery—comments which merely echoed the sentiments of the whole Parisian press :—

* *Philadelphia Saturday Evening Post.*

" The things had all evidently been there at least three or four weeks ; they were all mildewed down hard with the action of the rain, and stuck together from mildew. The grass had grown around and over some of them. The silk on the parasol was strong, but the threads of it were run together within. The upper part, where it had been doubled and folded, was all mildewed and rotten, and tore on its being opened. . . . The pieces of her frock torn out by the bushes were about three inches wide and six inches long. One part was the hem of the frock, and it had been mended ; the other piece was part of the skirt, not the hem. They looked like strips torn off, and were on the thorn bush, about a foot from the ground. . . . There can be no doubt, therefore, that the spot of this appalling outrage has been discovered."

Consequent upon this discovery, new evidence appeared. Madame Deluc testified that she keeps a roadside inn not far from the bank of the river, opposite the Barrière du Roule. The neighbourhood is secluded—particularly so. It is the usual Sunday resort of blackguards from the city, who cross the river in boats. About three o'clock, in the afternoon of the Sunday in question, a young girl arrived at the inn, accompanied by a young man of dark complexion. The two remained here for some time. On their departure, they took the road to some thick woods in the vicinity. Madame Deluc's attention was called to the dress worn by the girl on account of its resemblance to one worn by a deceased relative. A scarf was particularly noticed. Soon after the departure of the couple, a gang of miscreants made their appearance, behaved boisterously, ate and drank without making payment, followed in the route of the young man and girl, returned to the inn about dusk, and recrossed the river as if in great haste.

It was soon after dark, upon this same evening, that Madame Deluc, as well as her eldest son, heard the screams of a female in the vicinity of the inn. The screams were violent but brief. Madame D. recognised not only the scarf which was found in the thicket, but the dress which was discovered upon the corpse. An omnibus-driver, Valence,* now also testified that he saw Marie Rogêt

* Adam.

cross a ferry on the Seine, on the Sunday in question, in company with a young man of dark complexion. He, Valence, knew Marie, and could not be mistaken in her identity. The articles found in the thicket were fully identified by the relatives of Marie.

The items of evidence and information thus collected by myself, from the newspapers, at the suggestion of Dupin, embraced only one more point—but this was a point of seemingly vast consequence. It appears that, immediately after the discovery of the clothes as above described, the lifeless, or nearly lifeless body of St. Eustache, Marie's betrothed, was found in the vicinity of what all now supposed the scene of the outrage. A phial labelled "laudanum," and emptied, was found near him. His breath gave evidence of the poison. He died without speaking. Upon his person was found a letter, briefly stating his love for Marie, with his design of self-destruction.

" I need scarcely tell you," said Dupin, as he finished the perusal of my notes, " that this is a far more intricate case than that of the Rue Morgue ; from which it differs in one important respect. This is an *ordinary*, although an atrocious instance of crime. There is nothing peculiarly *outré* about it. You will observe that, for this reason, the mystery has been considered easy, when, for this reason, it should have been considered difficult of solution. Thus, at first, it was thought unnecessary to offer a reward. The myrmidons of G—— were able at once to comprehend how and why such an atrocity *might have been* committed. They could picture to their imaginations a mode —many modes—and a motive—many motives ; and because it was not impossible that either of these numerous modes and motives *could* have been the actual one, they have taken it for granted that one of them *must*. But the ease with which these variable fancies were entertained, and the very plausibility which each assumed, should have been understood as indicative rather of the difficulties than of the facilities which must attend elucidation. I have before observed that it is by prominences above the plane of the ordinary, that reason feels her way, if at all, in her search for the true, and that the proper question in cases such as this, is not so much ' what has occurred ? ' as ' what has occurred that has never occurred before ? '

In the investigations at the house of Madame L'Espanaye,* the agents of G—— were discouraged and confounded by that very *unusualness* which, to a properly regulated intellect, would have afforded the surest omen of success ; while this same intellect might have been plunged in despair at the ordinary character of all that met the eye in the case of the perfumery girl, and yet told of nothing but easy triumph to the functionaries of the Prefecture.

" In the case of Madame L'Espanaye and her daughter, there was, even at the beginning of our investigation, no doubt that murder had been committed. The idea of suicide was excluded at once. Here, too, we are freed, at the commencement, from all supposition of self-murder. The body found at the Barrière du Roule, was found under such circumstances as to leave us no room for embarrassment upon this important point. But it has been suggested that the corpse discovered is not that of the Marie Rogêt for the conviction of whose assassin, or assassins, the reward is offered, and respecting whom, solely, our agreement has been arranged with the Prefect. We both know this gentleman well. It will not do to trust him too far. If, dating our inquiries from the body found, and thence tracing a murderer, we yet discover this body to be that of some other individual than Marie ; or if, starting from the living Marie, we find her, yet find her unassassinated—in either case we lose our labour ; since it is Monsieur G—— with whom we have to deal. For our own purpose, therefore, if not for the purpose of justice, it is indispensable that our first step should be the determination of the identity of the corpse with the Marie Rogêt who is missing.

" With the public the arguments of *L'Etoile* have had weight ; and that the journal itself is convinced of their importance would appear from the manner in which it commences one of its essays upon the subject : ' Several of the morning papers of the day,' it says, ' speak of the *conclusive* article in Monday's *Etoile*.' To me, this article appears conclusive of little beyond the zeal of its inditer. We should bear in mind that, in general, it is the object of our newspapers rather to create a sensation—to make a point—than to further the cause of truth. The latter end is only pursued when it seems coincident with the

* See " The Murders in the Rue Morgue."

former. The print which merely falls in with ordinary opinion (however well-founded this opinion may be) earns for itself no credit with the mob. The mass of the people regard as profound only him who suggests *pungent contradictions* of the general idea. In ratiocination, not less than in literature, it is the *epigram* which is the most immediately and the most universally appreciated. In both, it is of the lowest order of merit.

" What I mean to say is, that it is the mingled epigram and melodrame of the idea that Marie Rogêt still lives, rather than any true plausibility in this idea, which have suggested it to *L'Etoile*, and secured it a favourable reception with the public. Let us examine the heads of this journal's argument ; endeavouring to avoid the incoherence with which it is originally set forth.

" The first aim of the writer is to show, from the brevity of the interval between Marie's disappearance and the finding of the floating corpse, that this corpse cannot be that of Marie. The reduction of this interval to its smallest possible dimension, becomes thus, at once, an object with the reasoner. In the rash pursuit of this object, he rushes into mere assumption at the outset. ' It is folly to suppose,' he says, ' that the murder, if murder was committed on her body, could have been consummated soon enough to have enabled her murderers to throw the body into the river before midnight.' We demand at once, and very naturally, *why ?* Why is it folly to suppose that the murder was committed *within five minutes* after the girl's quitting her mother's house ? Why is it folly to suppose that the murder was committed at any given period of the day ? There have been assassinations at all hours. But, had the murder taken place at any moment between nine o'clock in the morning of Sunday, and a quarter before midnight, there would still have been time enough ' to throw the body into the river before midnight.' This assumption, then, amounts precisely to this—that the murder was not committed on Sunday at all—and, if we allow *L'Etoile* to assume this, we may permit it any liberties whatever. The paragraph beginning ' It is folly to suppose that the murder,' etc., however it appears as printed in *L'Etoile*, may be imagined to have existed actually *thus* in the brain of its inditer : ' It is folly to suppose that the murder, if murder was committed

on the body, could have been committed soon enough
to have enabled her murderers to throw the body into
the river before midnight ; it is folly, we say, to suppose
all this, and to suppose at the same time (as we are resolved
to suppose), that the body was *not* thrown in until *after*
midnight '—a sentence sufficiently inconsequential in
itself, but not so utterly preposterous as the one printed.

" Were it my purpose," continued Dupin, " merely to
make out a case against this passage of *L'Etoile's* argument,
I might safely leave it where it is.   It is not, however,
with *L'Etoile* that we have to do, but with the truth.   The
sentence in question has but one meaning, as it stands ;
and this meaning I have fairly stated : but it is material
that we go behind the mere words for an idea which these
words have obviously intended, and failed to convey.   It
was the design of the journalist to say that, at whatever
period of the day or night of Sunday this murder was
committed, it was improbable that the assassins would have
ventured to bear the corpse to the river before midnight.
And herein lies, really, the assumption of which I complain.
It is assumed that the murder was committed at such a
position, and under such circumstances that *the bearing it*
to the river became necessary.   Now, the assassination
might have taken place upon the river's brink, or on the
river itself ; and, thus, the throwing the corpse in the
water might have been resorted to, at any period of the day
or night, as the most obvious and most immediate mode of
disposal.   You will understand that I suggest nothing here
as probable, or as coincident with my own opinion.   My
design, so far, has no reference to the facts of the case.   I
wish merely to caution you against the whole tone of
L'Etoile's suggestion, by calling your attention to its *ex
parte* character at the outset.

" Having prescribed thus a limit to suit its own preconceived notions ; having assumed that, if this were the
body of Marie, it could have been in the water but a very
brief time ; the journal goes on to say :—

" ' All experience has shown that drowned bodies, or
bodies thrown into the water immediately after death by
violence, require from six to ten days for sufficient decomposition to take place to bring them to the top of the water.
Even when a cannon is fired over a corpse, and it rises

before at least five or six days' immersion, it sinks again if let alone.'

" These assertions have been tacitly received by every paper in Paris, with the exception of *Le Moniteur*.* This latter print endeavours to combat that portion of the paragraph which has reference to ' drowned bodies ' only, by citing some five or six instances in which the bodies of individuals known to be drowned were found floating after the lapse of less time than is insisted upon by *L'Etoile*. But there is something excessively unphilosophical in the attempt on the part of *Le Moniteur*, to rebut the general assertion of *L'Etoile*, by a citation of particular instances militating against that assertion. Had it been possible to adduce fifty instead of five examples of bodies found floating at the end of two or three days, these fifty examples could still have been properly regarded only as exceptions to *L'Etoile's* rule, until such time as the rule itself should be confuted. Admitting the rule (and this *Le Moniteur* does not deny, insisting merely upon its exceptions), the argument of *L'Etoile* is suffered to remain in full force ; for this argument does not pretend to involve more than a question of the *probability* of the body having risen to the surface in less than three days ; and this probability will be in favour of *L'Etoile's* position until the instances so childishly adduced shall be sufficient in number to establish an antagonistical rule.

" You will see at once that all argument upon this head should be urged, if at all, against the rule itself, and for this end we must examine the *rationale* of the rule. Now the human body, in general, is neither much lighter nor much heavier than the water of the Seine ; that is to say, the specific gravity of the human body, in its natural condition, is about equal to the bulk of fresh water which it displaces. The bodies of fat and fleshy persons, with small bones, and of women generally, are lighter than those of the lean and large-boned, and of men ; and the specific gravity of the water of a river is somewhat influenced by the presence of the tide from sea. But, leaving this tide out of the question, it may be said that *very* few human bodies will sink at all, even in fresh water, *of their own accord.* Almost any one, falling into a river, will be enabled to float, if he

* The New York *Commercial Advertiser*.

suffer the specific gravity of the water fairly to be adduced
in comparison with his own—that is to say, if he suffer
his whole person to be immersed with as little exception
as possible. The proper position for one who cannot swim,
is the upright position of the walker on land, with the head
thrown fully back, and immersed ; the mouth and nostrils
alone remaining above the surface. Thus circumstanced,
we shall find that we float without difficulty and without
exertion. It is evident, however, that the gravities of the
body, and of the bulk of water displaced, are very nicely
balanced, and that a trifle will cause either to preponderate.
An arm, for instance, uplifted from the water, and thus
deprived of its support, is an additional weight sufficient
to immerse the whole head, while the accidental aid of the
smallest piece of timber will enable us to elevate the head
so as to look about. Now, in the struggles of one unused
to swimming, the arms are invariably thrown upwards,
while an attempt is made to keep the head in its usual
perpendicular position. The result is the immersion of
the mouth and nostrils, and the inception, during efforts
to breathe while beneath the surface, of water into the lungs.
Much is also received into the stomach, and the whole
body becomes heavier by the difference between the weight
of the air originally distending these cavities, and that of
the fluid which now fills them. This difference is sufficient
to cause the body to sink, as a general rule ; but it is
insufficient in the cases of individuals with small bones
and an abnormal quantity of flaccid or fatty matter.
Such individuals float even after drowning.

" The corpse, being supposed at the bottom of the river,
will there remain until, by some means, its specific gravity
again becomes less than that of the bulk of water which
it displaces. This effect is brought about by decomposition,
or otherwise. The result of decomposition is the generation
of gas, distending the cellular tissues and all the cavities,
and giving the *puffed* appearance which is so horrible.
When this distension has so far progressed that the bulk
of the corpse is materially increased without a corresponding
increase of *mass* or weight, its specific gravity becomes
less than that of the water displaced, and it forthwith
makes its appearance at the surface. But decomposition
is modified by innumerable circumstances—is hastened
or retarded by innumerable agencies ; for example, by

the heat or cold of the season, by the mineral impregnation or purity of the water, by its depth or shallowness, by its currency or stagnation, by the temperament of the body, by its infection or freedom from disease before death. Thus it is evident that we can assign no period, with anything like accuracy, at which the corpse shall rise through decomposition. Under certain conditions this result would be brought about within an hour ; under others, it might not take place at all. There are chemical infusions by which the animal frame can be preserved *for ever* from corruption ; the bi-chloride of mercury is one. But, apart from decomposition, there may be, and very usually is, generation of gas within the stomach, from the acetous fermentation of vegetable matter (or within other cavities from other causes) sufficient to induce a distension which will bring the body to the surface. The effect produced by the firing of a cannon is that of simple vibration. This may either loosen the corpse from the soft mud or ooze in which it is embedded, thus permitting it to rise when other agencies have already prepared it for so doing ; or it may overcome the tenacity of some putrescent portions of the cellular tissue, allowing the cavities to distend under the influence of the gas.

" Having thus before us the whole philosophy of this subject, we can easily test by it the assertions of *L'Etoile*. ' All experience shows,' says this paper, ' that drowned bodies, or bodies thrown into the water immediately after death by violence, require from six to ten days for sufficient decomposition to take place to bring them to the top of the water. Even when a cannon is fired over a corpse, and it rises before at least five or six days' immersion, it sinks again if let alone.'

" The whole of this paragraph must now appear a tissue of inconsequence and incoherence. All experience does *not* show that ' drowned bodies ' *require* from six to ten days for sufficient decomposition to take place to bring them to the surface. Both science and experience show that the period of their rising is, and necessarily must be, indeterminate. If, moreover, a body has risen to the surface through firing of cannon, it will *not* ' sink again if let alone,' until decomposition has so far progressed as to permit the escape of the generated gas. But I wish to call your attention to the distinction which is made between

' drowned bodies,' and ' bodies thrown into the water immediately after death by violence.' Although the writer admits the distinction, he yet includes them all in the same category. I have shown how it is that the body of a drowning man becomes specifically heavier than its bulk of water, and that he would not sink at all, except for the struggles by which he elevates his arms above the surface, and his gasps for breath while beneath the surface —gasps which supply by water the place of the original air in the lungs. But these struggles and these gasps would not occur in the body ' thrown into the water immediately after death by violence.' Thus, in the latter instance, *the body, as a general rule, would not sink at all*—a fact of which *L'Etoile* is evidently ignorant. When decomposition had proceeded to a very great extent—when the flesh had in a great measure left the bones—then, indeed, but not *till* then, should we lose sight of the corpse.

"And now what are we to make of the argument, that the body found could not be that of Marie Rogêt, because three days only having elapsed, the body was found floating ? If drowned, being a woman, she might never have sunk ; or having sunk, might have reappeared in twenty-four hours, or less. But no one supposes her to have been drowned ; and, dying before being thrown into the river, she might have been found floating at any period afterwards whatever.

" ' But,' says *L'Etoile*, ' if the body had been kept in its mangled state on shore until Tuesday night, some trace would be found on shore of the murderers.' Here it is at first difficult to perceive the intention of the reasoner. He means to anticipate what he imagines would be an objection to his theory—viz., that the body was kept on shore two days, suffering rapid decomposition—*more* rapid than if immersed in water. He supposes that, had this been the case, it *might* have appeared at the surface on the Wednesday, and thinks that *only* under such circumstances it could so have appeared. He is accordingly in haste to show that it *was not* kept on shore ; for, if so, ' some trace would be found on shore of the murderers.' I presume you smile at the *sequitur*. You cannot be made to see how the mere *duration* of the corpse on the shore could operate to *multiply traces* of the assassins. Nor can I.

" ' And furthermore, it is exceedingly improbable,'

continues our journal, 'that any villains who had committed such a murder as is here supposed, would have thrown the body in without weight to sink it, when such a precaution could have so easily been taken.' Observe, here, the laughable confusion of thought! No one —not even *L'Etoile*—disputes the murder committed *on the body found*. The marks of violence are too obvious. It is our reasoner's object merely to show that this body is not Marie's. He wishes to prove that *Marie* is not assassinated—not that the corpse was not. Yet his observation proves only the latter point. Here is a corpse without weight attached. Murderers, casting it in, would not have failed to attach a weight. Therefore it was not thrown in by murderers. This is all which is proved, if anything is. The question of identity is not even approached, and *L'Etoile* has been at great pains merely to gainsay now what it has admitted only a moment before. 'We are perfectly convinced,' it says, 'that the body found was that of the murdered female.'

" Nor is this the sole instance, even in this division of his subject, where our reasoner unwittingly reasons against himself. His evident object, I have already said, is to reduce, as much as possible, the interval between Marie's disappearance and the finding of the corpse. Yet we find him *urging* the point that no person saw the girl from the moment of her leaving her mother's house. 'We have no evidence,' he says, 'that Marie Rogêt was in the land of the living after nine o'clock on Sunday, June the 22nd.' As his argument is obviously an *ex parte* one, he should, at least, have left this matter out of sight ; for had any one been known to see Marie, say on Monday, or on Tuesday, the interval in question would have been much reduced, and, by his own ratiocination, the probability much diminished of the corpse being that of the *grisette*. It is, nevertheless, amusing to observe that *L'Etoile* insists upon its point in the full belief of its furthering its general argument.

" Reperuse now that portion of this argument which has reference to the identification of the corpse by Beauvais. In regard to the *hair* upon the arm, *L'Etoile* has been obviously disingenuous. M. Beauvais, not being an idiot, could never have urged, in identification of the corpse, simply *hair upon its arm*. No arm is *without* hair.

The *generality* of the expression of *L'Etoile* is a mere perversion of the witness's phraseology. He must have spoken of some *peculiarity* in this hair. It must have been a peculiarity of colour, of quantity, of length, or of situation.

"'Her foot,' says the journal, 'was small—so are thousands of feet. Her garter is no proof whatever—nor is her shoe—for shoes and garters are sold in packages. The same may be said of the flowers in her hat. One thing upon which M. Beauvais strongly insists is, that the clasp on the garter found had been set back to take it in. This amounts to nothing ; for most women find it proper to take a pair of garters home and fit them to the size of the limbs they are to encircle, rather than to try them in the store where they purchase.' Here it is difficult to suppose the reasoner in earnest. Had M. Beauvais, in his search for the body of Marie, discovered a corpse corresponding in general size and appearance to the missing girl, he would have been warranted (without reference to the question of habiliment at all) in forming an opinion that his search had been successful. If, in addition to the point of general size and contour, he had found upon the arm a peculiar hairy appearance which he had observed upon the living Marie, his opinion might have been justly strengthened ; and the increase of positiveness might well have been in the ratio of the peculiarity, or unusualness, of the hairy mark. If, the feet of Marie being small, those of the corpse were also small, the increase of probability that the body was that of Marie would not be an increase in a ratio merely arithmetical, but in one highly geometrical, or accumulative. Add to all this, shoes such as she had been known to wear upon the day of her disappearance, and, although these shoes may be ' sold in packages,' you so far augment the probability as to verge upon the certain. What, of itself, would be no evidence of identity, becomes, through its corroborative position, proof most sure. Give us, then, flowers in the hat corresponding to those worn by the missing girl, and we seek for nothing further. If only *one* flower, we seek for nothing further—what then if two or three, or more ? Each successive one is multiple evidence—proof not *added* to proof, but *multiplied* by hundreds or thousands. Let us now discover, upon the deceased, garters such as the living used, and it is almost folly to proceed. But these garters are found to be tightened, by the setting back of a clasp, in just such a manner as her own had been tightened by Marie shortly previous to her leaving home. It is now madness or hypocrisy to doubt. What *L'Etoile* says in respect to this abbreviation of the garters being an usual occurrence, shows nothing beyond its own pertinacity in error. The elastic nature of the clasp-garter is self-demonstration of the *unusual ness* of the abbreviation. What is made to adjust itself, must of necessity require foreign adjustment but rarely. It must have been by an accident, in its strictest sense, that these garters of Marie needed the tightening described. They alone would have amply established her identity. But it is not that the corpse was found to have the garters of the missing girl, or found to have her shoes, or her bonnet, or the flowers of her bonnet, or her feet, or a peculiar mark upon the arm, or her general size and appearance—it is that the corpse had each and *all collectively*. Could it be proved that the editor of *L'Etoile really* entertained a doubt, under the circumstances, there would be no need, in his case, of a commission *de lunatico inquirendo*. He has thought it sagacious to echo the small-talk of the lawyers, who, for the most part, content themselves with echoing the rectangular precepts of the courts. I would here observe that very much of what is rejected as evidence by a court, is the best of evidence to the intellect. For the court, guiding itself by the general principles of evidence —the recognised and *booked* principles—is averse from swerving at particular instances. And this steadfast adherence to principle, with rigorous disregard of the conflicting exception, is a sure mode of attaining the *maximum* of attainable truth, in any long sequence of time. The practice, *en masse*, is therefore philosophical ; but it is not the less certain that it engenders vast individual error.*

" In respect to the insinuations levelled at Beauvais,

* " A theory based on the qualities of an object, will prevent its being unfolded according to its objects ; and he who arranges topics in reference to their causes, will cease to value them according to their results. Thus the jurisprudence of every nation will show that, when law becomes a science and a system, it ceases to be justice. The errors into which a blind devotion to *principles* of classification has led the common law, will be seen by observing how often the legislature has been obliged to come forward to restore the equity its scheme had lost."—LANDOR.

you will be willing to dismiss them in a breath. You have already fathomed the true character of this good gentleman. He is a *busybody*, with much of romance and little of wit. Any one so constituted will readily so conduct himself, upon occasion of *real* excitement, as to render himself liable to suspicion on the part of the over-acute, or the ill-disposed. M. Beauvais (as it appears from your notes) had some personal interviews with the editor of *L'Etoile*, and offended him by venturing an opinion that the corpse, notwithstanding the theory of the editor, was, in sober fact, that of Marie. 'He persists,' says the paper, 'in asserting the corpse to be that of Marie, but cannot give a circumstance, in addition to those which we have commented upon, to make other believe.' Now, without readverting to the fact that stronger evidence 'to make others believe,' could *never* have been adduced, it may be remarked that a man may very well be understood to believe, in a case of this kind, without the ability to advance a single reason for the belief of a second party. Nothing is more vague than impressions of individual identity. Each man recognises his neighbour, yet there are few instances in which any one is prepared *to give a reason* for his recognition. The editor of *L'Etoile* had no right to be offended at M. Beauvais' unreasoning belief.

" The suspicious circumstances which invest him will be found to tally much better with my hypothesis of *romantic busybodyism*, than with the reasoner's suggestion of guilt. Once adopting the more charitable interpretation, we shall find no difficulty in comprehending the rose in the keyhole; the ' Marie ' upon the slate ; the ' elbowing the male relatives out of the way ' ; the ' aversion to permitting them to see the body ' ; the caution given to Madame B——, that she must hold no conversation with the gendarme until his return (Beauvais') ; and, lastly, his apparent determination ' that nobody should have anything to do with the proceedings except himself.' It seems to me unquestionable that Beauvais was a suitor of Marie's ; that she coquetted with him ; and that he was ambitious of being thought to enjoy her fullest intimacy and confidence. I shall say nothing more upon this point ; and, as the evidence fully rebuts the assertion of *L'Etoile*, touching the matter of *apathy* on the part of the mother and other relatives—an apathy inconsistent with the

G*

supposition of their believing the corpse to be that of the perfumery girl—we shall now proceed as if the question of *identity* were settled to our perfect satisfaction."

"And what," I here demanded, "do you think of the opinions of *Le Commerciel* ? "

"That, in spirit, they are far more worthy of attention than any which have been promulgated upon the subject. The deductions from the premises are philosophical and acute ; but the premises, in two instances at least, are founded in imperfect observation. *Le Commerciel* wishes to intimate that Marie was seized by some gang of low ruffians not far from her mother's door. ' It is impossible,' it urges, ' that a person so well known to thousands as this young woman was, should have passed three blocks without some one having seen her.' This is the idea of a man long resident in Paris—a public man—and one whose walks to and fro in the city have been mostly limited to the vicinity of the public offices. He is aware that *he* seldom passes so far as a dozen blocks from his own *bureau*, without being recognised and accosted. And, knowing the extent of his personal acquaintance with others, and of others with him, he compares his notoriety with that of the perfumery girl, finds no great difference between them, and reaches at once the conclusion that she, in her walks, would be equally liable to recognition with himself in his. This could only be the case were her walks of the same unvarying, methodical character, and within the same *species* of limited region as are his own. He passes to and fro, at regular intervals, within a confined periphery, abounding in individuals who are led to observation of his person through interest in the kindred nature of his occupation with their own. But the walks of Marie may, in general, be supposed discursive. In this particular instance, it will be understood as most probable, that she proceeded upon a route of more than average diversity from her accustomed ones. The parallel which we imagine to have existed in the mind of *Le Commerciel* would only be sustained in the event of the two individuals traversing the whole city. In this case, granting the personal acquaintances to be equal, the chances would be also equal that an equal number of personal rencounters would be made. For my own part, I should hold it not only as possible, but as very far more than probable, that Marie might have

proceeded, at any given period, by any one of the many
routes between her own residence and that of her aunt,
without meeting a single individual whom she knew, or by
whom she was known. In viewing this question in its
full and proper light, we must hold steadily in mind the
great disproportion between the personal acquaintances
of even the most noted individual in Paris, and the entire
population of Paris itself.

" But whatever force there may still appear to be in
the suggestion of *Le Commerciel*, will be much diminished
when we take into consideration *the hour* at which the girl
went abroad. ' It was when the streets were full of people,'
says *Le Commerciel*, ' that she went out.' But not so.
It was at nine o'clock in the morning. Now at nine o'clock
of every morning in the week, *with the exception of Sunday*,
the streets of the city are, it is true, thronged with people.
At nine on Sunday, the populace are chiefly within doors
preparing for church. No observing person can have failed
to notice the peculiarly deserted air of the town, from about
eight until ten on the morning of every Sabbath. Between ten and eleven the streets are thronged, but not at
so early a period as that designated.

" There is another point at which there seems a deficiency of *observation* on the part of *Le Commerciel*. ' A
piece,' it says, ' of one of the unfortunate girl's petticoats,
two feet long, and one foot wide, was torn out and tied
under her chin, and around the back of her head, probably
to prevent screams. This was done by fellows who had
no pocket-handkerchiefs.' Whether this idea is, or is not
well founded, we will endeavour to see hereafter ; but by
' fellows who have no pocket-handkerchiefs,' the editor
intends the lowest class of ruffians. These, however, are
the very description of people who will always be found to
have handkerchiefs even when destitute of shirts. You
must have had occasion to observe how absolutely indispensable, of late years, to the thorough blackguard, has
become the pocket-handkerchief."

" And what are we to think," I asked, " of the article
in *Le Soleil* ? "

" That it is a vast pity its inditer was not born a parrot
—in which case he would have been the most illustrious
parrot of his race. He has merely repeated the individual
items of the already published opinion ; collecting them,

with a laudable industry, from this paper and from that. 'The things had all *evidently* been there,' he says, 'at least three or four weeks, and there can be *no doubt* that the spot of this appalling outrage has been discovered.' The facts here re-stated by *Le Soleil*, are very far indeed from removing my own doubts upon this subject, and we will examine them more particularly hereafter in connection with another division of the theme.

"At present we must occupy ourselves with other investigations. You cannot fail to have remarked the extreme laxity of the examination of the corpse. To be sure the question of identity was readily determined, or should have been ; but there were other points to be ascertained. Had the body been in any respect *despoiled*? Had the deceased any articles of jewellery about her person upon leaving home ? if so, had she any when found ? These are important questions utterly untouched by the evidence ; and there are others of equal moment, which have met with no attention. We must endeavour to satisfy ourselves by personal inquiry. The case of St. Eustache must be re-examined. I have no suspicion of this person ; but let us proceed methodically. We will ascertain beyond a doubt the validity of the affidavits in regard to his whereabouts on the Sunday. Affidavits of this character are readily made matter of mystification. Should there be nothing wrong here, however, we will dismiss St. Eustache from our investigations. His suicide, however corroborative of suspicion, were there found to be deceit in the affidavits, is, without such deceit, in no respect an unaccountable circumstance, or one which need cause us to deflect from the line of ordinary analysis.

"In that which I now propose, we will discard the interior points of this tragedy, and concentrate our attention upon its outskirts. Not the least usual error, in investigations such as this, is the limiting of inquiry to the immediate, with total disregard of the collateral or circumstantial events. It is the malpractice of the courts to confine evidence and discussion to the bounds of apparent relevancy. Yet experience has shown, and a true philosophy will always show, that a vast, perhaps the larger portion of truth, arises from the seemingly irrelevant. It is through the spirit of this principle, if not precisely through its letter, that modern science resolved to *calculate upon the unforeseen.* But perhaps you do not comprehend me. The history of human knowledge has so uninterruptedly shown that to collateral, or incidental, or accidental events we are indebted for the most numerous and most valuable discoveries, that it has at length become necessary, in any prospective view of improvement, **to** make not only large, but the largest allowances for **inven**tions that shall arise by chance, and quite out of the range of ordinary expectation. It is no longer philosophical to base, upon what has been, a vision of what is to be. *Accident* is admitted as a portion of the substructure. We make chance a matter of absolute calculation. We subject the unlooked-for and unimagined, to the mathematical formulæ of the schools.

" I repeat that it is no more than fact, that the *larger* portion of all truth has sprung from the collateral ; and it is but in accordance with the spirit of the principle involved in this fact, that I would divert inquiry, in the present case, from the trodden and hitherto unfruitful ground of the event itself, to the cotemporary circumstances which surround it. While you ascertain the validity of the affidavits, I will examine the newspapers more generally than you have as yet done. So far, we have only reconnoitred the field of investigation ; but it will be strange indeed if a comprehensive survey, such as I propose, of the public prints, will not afford us some minute points which shall establish a *direction* for inquiry."

In pursuance of Dupin's suggestions, I made scrupulous examination of the affair of the affidavits. The result was a firm conviction of their validity, and of the consequent innocence of St. Eustache. In the meantime my friend occupied himself, with what seemed to me a minuteness altogether objectless, in a scrutiny of the various newspaper files. At the end of a week he placed before me the following extracts :—

" About three years and a half ago, a disturbance very similar to the present was caused by the disappearance of this same Marie Rogêt, from the *parfumerie* of Monsieur Le Blanc in the Palais Royal. At the end of a week, however, she reappeared at her customary *comptoir*, as well as ever, with the exception of a slight paleness not altogether usual. It was given out by Monsieur Le Blanc and her mother, that she had merely been on a visit to some friend in the country ; and the affair was speedily hushed up. We presume that the present absence is a freak of the same nature, and that, at the expiration of a week, or perhaps of a month, we shall have her among us again."—*Evening Paper*, Monday, June 23.*

" An evening journal of yesterday, refers to a former mysterious disappearance of Mademoiselle Rogêt. It is well known that, during the week of her absence from Le Blanc's *parfumerie*, she was in the company of a young naval officer, much noted for his debaucheries. A quarrel, it is supposed, providentially led to her return home. We have the name of the Lothario in question, who is, at present, stationed in Paris, but, for obvious reasons, forbear to make it public."—*Le Mercurie*, Tuesday Morning, June 24.†

" An outrage of the most atrocious character was perpetrated near this city the day before yesterday. A gentleman, with his wife and daughter, engaged about dusk the services of six young men, who were idly rowing a boat to and fro near the banks of the Seine, to convey him across the river. Upon reaching the opposite shore, the three passengers stepped out, and had proceeded so far as to be beyond the view of the boat, when the daughter discovered that she had left in it her parasol. She returned for it, was seized by the gang, carried out into the stream, gagged, brutally treated, and finally taken to the shore at a point not far from that at which she had originally entered the boat with her parents. The villains have escaped for the time, but the police are upon their trail, and some of them will soon be taken."—*Morning Paper*, June 25. ‡

" We have received one or two communications, the object of which is to fasten the crime of the late atrocity upon Mennais ; § but as this gentleman has been fully exonerated by a legal inquiry, and as the arguments of our several correspondents appear to be more zealous than profound, we do not think it advisable to make them public."—*Morning Paper*, June 28. ||

---

* *N. Y. Express.*   † *N. Y. Herald.*   ‡ *N. Y. Courier and Inquirer.*
§ Mennais was one of the parties originally suspected and arrested, but discharged through total lack of evidence.
|| *N. Y. Courier and Inquirer.*

" We have received several forcibly written communications, apparently from various sources, and which go far
to render it a matter of certainty that the unfortunate
Marie Rogêt has become a victim of one of the numerous
bands of blackguards which infest the vicinity of the city
upon Sunday. Our own opinion is decidedly in favour
of this supposition. We shall endeavour to make room
for some of these arguments hereafter."—*Evening Paper*,
June 30.*

" On Monday, one of the bargemen connected with the
revenue service, saw an empty boat floating down the
Seine. Sails were lying in the bottom of the boat. The
bargemen towed it under the barge office. The next morning it was taken from thence, without the knowledge of
any of the officers. The rudder is now at the barge office."
—*Le Diligence*, Thursday, June 26. †

Upon reading these various extracts, they not only
seemed to be irrelevant, but I could perceive no mode
in which any one of them could be brought to bear upon
the matter in hand. I waited for some explanation from
Dupin.

" It is not my present design," he said, " to *dwell* upon
the first and second of these extracts. I have copied them
chiefly to show you the extreme remissness of the police,
who, as far as I can understand from the Prefect, have not
troubled themselves, in any respect, with an examination
of the naval officer alluded to. Yet it is mere folly to say
that between the first and second disappearance of Marie,
there is no *supposable* connection. Let us admit the first
elopement to have resulted in a quarrel between the lovers,
and the return home of the betrayed. We are now prepared to view a second *elopement* (if we *know* that an elopement has again taken place) as indicating a renewal of the
betrayer's advances, rather than as the result of new proposals by a second individual—we are prepared to regard
it as a ' making up ' of the old amour, rather than as the
commencement of a new one. The chances are ten to
one, that he who had once eloped with Marie, would again
propose an elopement, rather than that she to whom
proposals of elopement had been made by one individual,
should have them made to her by another. And here let me

* *N. Y. Evening Post.*   † *N. Y. Standard.*

call your attention to the fact, that the time elapsing
between the first ascertained, and the second supposed
elopement, is a few months more than the general period
of the cruises of our men-of-war. Had the lover been
interrupted in his first villainy by the necessity of departure
to sea, and had he seized the first moment of his return
to renew the base designs not yet altogether accomplished
—or not yet altogether accomplished *by him* ? Of all
these things we know nothing.

" You will say, however, that, in the second instance,
there was *no* elopement as imagined. Certainly not—but
are we prepared to say that there was not the frustrated
design ? Beyond St. Eustache, and perhaps Beauvais,
we find no recognised, no open, no honourable suitors of
Marie. Of none other is there anything said. Who, then,
is the secret lover, of whom the relatives (*at least most of
them*) know nothing, but whom Marie meets upon the
morning of Sunday, and who is so deeply in her confidence,
that she hesitates not to remain with him until the shades
of the evening descend, amid the solitary groves of the
Barrière du Roule ? Who is that secret lover, I ask, of
whom, at least, *most* of the relatives know nothing ? And
what means the singular prophecy of Madame Rogêt on
the morning of Marie's departure—' I fear that I shall
never see Marie again ' ?

" But if we cannot imagine Madame Rogêt privy to
the design of elopement, may we not at least suppose this
design entertained by the girl ? Upon quitting home,
she gave it to be understood that she was about to visit her
aunt in the Rue des Drômes, and St. Eustache was requested to call for her at dark. Now, at first glance, this
fact strongly militates against my suggestion ; but let us
reflect. That she *did* meet some companion, and proceed
with him across the river, reaching the Barrière du Roule
at so late an hour as three o'clock in the afternoon, is
known. But in consenting so to accompany this individual
(*for whatever purpose—to her mother known or unknown*),
she must have thought of her expressed intention when
leaving home, and of the surprise and suspicion aroused
in the bosom of her affianced suitor, St. Eustache, when,
calling for her at the hour appointed, in the Rue des
Drômes, he should find that she had not been there, and
when, moreover, upon returning to the *pension* with this

alarming intelligence, he should become aware of her continued absence from home. She must have thought of these things, I say. She must have foreseen the chagrin of St. Eustache, the suspicion of all. She could not have thought of returning to brave this suspicion ; but the suspicion becomes a point of trivial importance to her, if we suppose her *not* intending to return.

" We may imagine her thinking thus—' I am to meet a certain person for the purpose of elopement, or for certain other purposes known only to myself. It is necessary that there be no chance of interruption—there must be sufficient time given us to elude pursuit—I will give it to be understood that I shall visit and spend the day with my aunt at the Rue des Drômes—I will tell St. Eustache not to call for me until dark—in this way, my absence from home for the longest possible period, without causing suspicion or anxiety, will be accounted for, and I shall gain more time than in any other manner. If I bid St. Eustache call for me at dark, he will be sure not to call before ; but, if I wholly neglect to bid him call, my time for escape will be diminished, since it will be expected that I return the earlier, and my absence will the sooner excite anxiety. Now, if it were my design to return *at all*—if I had in contemplation merely a stroll with the individual in question— it would not be my policy to bid St. Eustache call ; for, calling he will be *sure* to ascertain that I have played him false—a fact of which I might keep him for ever in ignorance, by leaving home without notifying him of my intention, by returning before dark, and by then stating that I had been to visit my aunt in the Rue des Drômes. But, as it is my design *never* to return—or not for some weeks— or not until certain concealments are effected—the gaining of time is the only point about which I need give myself any concern.'

" You have observed, in your notes, that the most general opinion in relation to this sad affair is, and was from the first, that the girl had been the victim of *a gang* of blackguards. Now, the popular opinion, under certain conditions, is not to be disregarded. When arising of itself—when manifesting itself in a strictly spontaneous manner—we should look upon it as analogous with that *intuition* which is the idiosyncrasy of the individual man of genius. In ninety-nine cases from the hundred I would

abide by its decision. But it is important that we find
no palpable traces of *suggestion*. The opinion must be
rigorously *the public's own* ; and the distinction is often
exceedingly difficult to perceive and to maintain.   In the
present instance, it appears to me that this ' public opinion,'
in respect to *a gang*, has been superinduced by the collateral
event which is detailed in the third of my extracts.   All
Paris is excited by the discovered corpse of Marie, a girl
young, beautiful, and notorious.   This corpse is found,
bearing marks of violence, and floating in the river.   But
it is now made known that, at the very period, or about
the very period, in which it is supposed that the girl was
assassinated, an outrage similar in nature to that endured
by the deceased, although less in extent, was perpetrated,
by a gang of young ruffians, upon the person of a second
young female.   Is it wonderful that the one known atrocity
should influence the popular judgment in regard to the
other unknown ?   This judgment awaited direction, and
the known outrage seemed so opportunely to afford it.
Marie, too, was found in the river ; and upon this very
river was this known outrage committed.   The connection
of the two events had about it so much of the palpable, that
the true wonder would have been a *failure* of the populace
to appreciate and to seize it.   But, in fact, the one atrocity,
known to be so committed, is, if anything, evidence that
the other, committed at a time nearly coincident, was *not*
so committed.   It would have been a miracle indeed, if,
while a gang of ruffians were perpetrating, at a given
locality, a most unheard-of wrong, there should have been
another similar gang, in a similar locality, in the same city,
under the same circumstances, with the same means and
appliances, engaged in a wrong of precisely the same aspect,
at precisely the same period of time !   Yet in what, if
not in this marvellous train of coincidence, does the accidentally *suggested* opinion of the populace call upon us to
believe ?

    " Before proceeding farther, let us consider the supposed
scene of the assassination, in the thicket at the Barrière du
Roule.   This thicket, although dense, was in the close
vicinity of a public road.   Within were three or four large
stones, forming a kind of seat, with a back and footstool.
On the upper stone was discovered a white petticoat ; on
the second, a silk scarf.   A parasol, gloves, and a pocket-

handkerchief, were also here found. The handkerchief bore the name, ' Marie Roget.' Fragments of dress were seen on the branches around. The earth was trampled, the bushes were broken, and there was every evidence of a violent struggle.

" Notwithstanding the acclamation with which the discovery of this thicket was received by the press, and the unanimity with which it was supposed to indicate the precise scene of the outrage, it must be admitted that there was some very good reason for doubt. That it *was* the scene, I may or I may not believe—but there was excellent reason for doubt. Had the *true* scene been, as *Le Commerciel* suggested, in the neighbourhood of the Rue Pavée Saint Andrée, the perpetrators of the crime, supposing them still resident in Paris, would naturally have been stricken with terror at the public attention thus acutely directed into the proper channel ; and, in certain classes of minds, there would have arisen, at once, a sense of the necessity of some exertion to redivert this attention. And thus, the thicket of the Barrière du Roule having been already suspected, the idea of placing the articles where they were found, might have been naturally entertained. There is no real evidence, although *Le Soleil* so supposes, that the articles discovered had been more than a very few days in the thicket ; while there is much circumstantial proof that they could not have remained there, without attracting attention, during the twenty days elapsing between the fatal Sunday and the afternoon upon which they were found by the boys. ' They were all *mildewed* down hard,' says *Le Soleil*, adopting the opinions of its predecessors, ' with the action of the rain, and stuck together from *mildew*. The grass had grown around and over some of them. The silk of the parasol was strong, but the threads of it were run together within. The upper part, where it had been doubled and folded, was all *mildewed* and rotten, and tore on being opened.' In respect to the grass having ' grown around and over some of them,' it is obvious that the fact could only have been ascertained from the words, and thus from the recollections, of two small boys ; for these boys removed the articles and took them home before they had been seen by a third party. But grass will grow, especially in warm and damp weather (such as was that of the period of the murder), as much as

two or three inches in a single day. A parasol lying upon
a newly turfed ground, might, in a single week, be entirely
concealed from sight by the upspringing grass. And
touching that *mildew* upon which the editor of *Le Soleil* so
pertinaciously insists that he employs the word no less than
three times in the brief paragraph just quoted, is he really
unaware of the nature of this *mildew* ? Is he to be told
that it is one of the many classes of fungus, of which the
most ordinary feature is its upspringing and decadence
within twenty-four hours ?

" Thus we see, at a glance, that what has been most
triumphantly adduced in support of the idea that the
articles had been ' for at least three or four weeks ' in the
thicket, is most absurdly null as regards any evidence of
that fact. On the other hand, it is exceedingly difficult
to believe that these articles could have remained in the
thicket specified, for a longer period than a single week—
for a longer period than from one Sunday to the next.
Those who know anything of the vicinity of Paris, know the
extreme difficulty of finding *seclusion* unless at a great
distance from its suburbs. Such a thing as an unexplored,
or even an unfrequently visited recess, amid its woods or
groves, is not for a moment to be imagined. Let any one
who, being at heart a lover of nature, is yet chained by
duty to the dust and heat of this great metropolis—let any
such one attempt, even during the week-days, to slake
his thirst for solitude amid the scenes of natural loveliness
which immediately surround us. At every second step,
he will find the growing charm dispelled by the voice and
personal intrusion of some ruffian or party of carousing
blackguards. He will seek privacy amid the densest foliage,
all in vain. Here are the very nooks where the unwashed
most abound—here are the temples most desecrate. With
sickness of the heart the wanderer will flee back to
the polluted Paris as to a less odious because less incongruous sink of pollution. But if the vicinity of the city
is so beset during the working days of the week, how
much more so on the Sabbath ! It is now especially that,
released from the claims of labour, or deprived of the
customary opportunities of crime, the town blackguard
seeks the precincts of the town, not through love of the
rural, which in his heart he despises, but by way of escape
from the restraints and conventionalities of society. He

desires less the fresh air and the green trees, than the utter
licence of the country. Here, at the roadside inn, or
beneath the foliage of the woods, he indulges, unchecked
by any eye except those of his boon companions, in all
the mad excess of a counterfeit hilarity—the joint off-
spring of liberty and of rum. I say nothing more than what
must be obvious to every dispassionate observer, when I
repeat that the circumstance of the articles in question
having remained undiscovered, for a longer period than
from one Sunday to another, in *any* thicket in the immediate
neighbourhood of Paris, is to be looked upon as little less
than miraculous.

" But there are not wanting other grounds for the
suspicion that the articles were placed in the thicket with
the view of diverting attention from the real scene of
the outrage. And, first, let me direct your notice to the
date of the discovery of the articles. Collate this with the
date of the fifth extract made by myself from the newspapers. You will find that the discovery followed, almost
immediately, the urgent communications sent to the
evening paper. These communications, although various,
and apparently from various sources, tended all to the same
point—viz., the directing of attention to *a gang* as the perpetrators of the outrage, and to the neighbourhood of the
Barrière du Roule as its scene. Now here, of course, the
suspicion is not that, in consequence of these communications, or of the public attention by them directed, the articles
were found by the boys ; but the suspicion might and may
well have been, that the articles were not *before* found by
the boys, for the reason that the articles had not before been
in the thicket ; having been deposited there only at so late
a period as at the date, or shortly prior to the date of the
communications, by the guilty authors of these communications themselves.

" This thicket was a singular—an exceedingly singular
one. It was unusually dense. Within its naturally
walled enclosure were three extraordinary stones, *forming
a seat with a back and footstool*. And this thicket, so full
of a natural art, was in the immediate vicinity, *within a
few rods*, of the dwelling of Madame Deluc, whose boys
were in the habit of closely examining the shrubberies
about them in search of the bark of the sassafras. Would
it be a rash wager—a wager of one thousand to one—

that *a day* never passed over the heads of these boys without finding at least one of them ensconced in the umbrageous hall, and enthroned upon its natural throne ? Those who would hesitate at such a wager, have either never been boys themselves, or have forgotten the boyish nature. I repeat—it is exceedingly hard to comprehend how the articles could have remained in this thicket, undiscovered, for a longer period than one or two days ; and that thus there is good ground for suspicion, in spite of the dogmatic ignorance of *Le Soleil*, that they were, at a comparatively late date, deposited where found.

" But there are still other and stronger reasons for believing them so deposited, than any which I have as yet urged. And now, let me beg your notice to the highly artificial arrangement of the articles. On the *upper* stone lay a white petticoat ; on the *second* a silk scarf ; scattered around, were a parasol, gloves, and a pocket-handkerchief bearing the name, ' Marie Rogêt.' Here is just such an arrangement as would *naturally* be made by a not over acute person wishing to dispose the articles *naturally*. But it is by no means a *really* natural arrange-ment. I should rather have looked to see the things *all* lying on the ground and trampled under foot. In the narrow limits of that bower, it would have been scarcely possible that the petticoat and scarf should have retained a position upon the stones, when subjected to the brushing to and fro of many struggling persons. ' There was evidence,' it is said, ' of a struggle ; and the earth was trampled, the bushes were broken '—but the petticoat and scarf are found deposited as if upon shelves. ' The pieces of the frock torn out by the bushes were about three inches wide and six inches long. One part was the hem of the frock, and it had been mended. They *looked like strips torn off.*' Here, inadvertently, *Le Soleil* has employed an exceedingly suspicious phrase. The pieces, as described, do indeed ' look like strips torn off ' ; but purposely and by hand. It is one of the rarest of accidents that a piece is ' torn off,' from any garment such as is now in question, by the agency *of a thorn*. From the very nature of such fabrics, a thorn or nail becoming entangled in them, tears them rectangularly—divides them into two longitudinal rents, at right angles with each other, and meeting at an apex where the thorn

enters—but it is scarcely possible to conceive the piece
' torn off.' I never so knew it, nor did you. To tear a piece
off from such fabric, two distinct forces, in different
directions, will be, in almost every case, required. If
there be two edges to the fabric—if, for example, it be
a pocket-handkerchief, and it is desired to tear from it
a slip, then, and then only will the one force serve the
purpose. But in the present case the question is of a
dress, presenting but one edge. To tear a piece from
the interior, where no edge is presented, could only be
effected by a miracle through the agency of thorns, and
no *one* thorn could accomplish it. But, even where an
edge is presented, two thorns will be necessary, operating,
the one in two distinct directions, and the other in one.
And this in the supposition that the edge is unhemmed.
If hemmed, the matter is nearly out of the question. We
thus see the numerous and great obstacles in the way of
pieces being ' torn off ' through the simple agency of
' thorns '; yet we are required to believe not only that
one piece but that many have been so torn. ' And one
part,' too, ' *was the hem of the frock* ' ! Another piece
was ' *part of the skirt, not the hem* '—that is to say, was
torn completely out through the agency of thorns, from
the unedged interior of the dress ! These, I say, are
things which one may well be pardoned for disbelieving ;
yet, taken collectedly, they form, perhaps, less of reasonable
ground for suspicion, than the one startling circumstance
of the articles having been left in this thicket at all, by
any *murderers* who had enough precaution to think of
removing the corpse. You will not have apprehended
me rightly, however, if you suppose it my design to *deny*
this thicket as the scene of the outrage. There might have
been a wrong *here*, or, more possibly, an accident at
Madame Deluc's. But, in fact, this is a part of minor
importance. We are not engaged in an attempt to discover
the scene, but to produce the perpetrators of the murder.
What I have adduced, notwithstanding the minuteness
with which I have adduced it, has been with the view, first,
to show the folly of the positive and headlong assertions of
Le Soleil, but secondly and chiefly, to bring you, by the
most natural route, to a further contemplation of the
doubt whether this assassination has, or has not, been the
work of *a gang*.

"We will resume this question by mere allusion to the revolting details of the surgeon examined at the inquest. It is only necessary to say that his published *inferences*, in regard to the number of the ruffians, have been properly ridiculed as unjust and totally baseless, by all the reputable anatomists of Paris. Not that the matter *might not* have been as inferred, but that there was no ground for the inference—was there not much for another ?

"Let us reflect now upon 'the traces of a struggle'; and let me ask what these traces have been supposed to demonstrate. A gang. But do they not rather demonstrate the absence of a gang? What *struggle* could have taken place—what struggle so violent and so enduring as to have left its 'traces' in all directions —between a weak and defenceless girl and the *gang* of ruffians imagined ? The silent grasp of a few rough arms and all would have been over, the victim must have been absolutely passive at their will. You will here bear in mind that the arguments urged against the thicket as the scene, are applicable, in chief part, only against it as the scene of an outrage committed by *more than a single individual*. If we imagine but one violator, we can conceive, and thus only conceive, the struggle of so violent and so obstinate a nature as to have left the 'traces' apparent.

"And again. I have already mentioned the suspicion to be excited by the fact that the articles in question were suffered to remain *at all* in the thicket where discovered. It seems almost impossible that these evidences of guilt should have been accidentally left where found. There was sufficient presence of mind (it is supposed) to remove the corpse; and yet a more positive evidence than the corpse itself (whose features might have been quickly obliterated by decay), is allowed to lie conspicuously in the scene of the outrage—I allude to the handkerchief with the *name* of the deceased. If this was accident, it was not the accident *of a gang*. We can imagine it only the accident of an individual. Let us see. An individual has committed the murder. He is alone with the ghost of the departed. He is appalled by what lies motionless before him. The fury of his passion is over, and there is abundant room in his heart for the natural awe of the deed. His is none of that confidence which the presence

of numbers inevitably inspires. He is *alone* with the dead. He trembles and is bewildered. Yet there is a necessity for disposing of the corpse. He bears it to the river, but leaves behind him the other evidences of guilt ; for it is difficult, if not impossible to carry all the burden at once, and it will be easy to return for what is left. But in his toilsome journey to the water his fears redouble within him. The sounds of life encompass his path. A dozen times he hears or fancies the step of an observer. Even the very lights from the city bewilder him. Yet, in time, and by long and frequent pauses of deep agony, he reaches the river's brink, and disposes of his ghastly charge—perhaps through the medium of a boat. But *now* what treasure does the world hold— what threat of vengeance could it hold out—which would have power to urge the return of that lonely murderer over that toilsome and perilous path, to the thicket and its blood-chilling recollections ? He returns *not*, let the consequences be what they may. He *could* not return if he would. His sole thought is immediate escape. He turns his back *for ever* upon those dreadful shrubberies, and flees. as from the wrath to come.

" But how with a gang ? Their number would have inspired them with confidence ; if, indeed, confidence is ever wanting in the breast of the arrant blackguard ; and of arrant blackguards alone are the supposed *gangs* ever constituted. Their number, I say, would have prevented the bewildering and unreasoning terror which I have imagined to paralyse the single man. Could we suppose an oversight in one, or two, or three, this oversight would have been remedied by a fourth. They would have left nothing behind them ; for their number would have enabled them to carry *all* at once. There would have been no need of *return*.

" Consider now the circumstance that, in the outer garment of the corpse when found, ' a slip, about a foot wide, had been torn upward from the bottom hem to the waist, wound three times round the waist, and secured by a sort of hitch in the back.' This was done with the obvious design of affording *a handle* by which to carry the body. But would any *number* of men have dreamed of resorting to such an expedient ? To three or four, the limbs of the corpse would have afforded not only a

sufficient, but the best possible hold. The device is that
of a single individual ; and this brings us to the fact
that ' between the thicket and the river, the rails of the
fences were found taken down, and the ground bore evident
traces of some heavy burden having been dragged along it ' !
But would a *number* of men have put themselves to the
superfluous trouble of taking down a fence, for the purpose
of dragging through it a corpse which they might have
lifted over any fence in an instant ? Would a *number* of
men have so *dragged* a corpse at all as to have left evident
traces of the dragging ?

"And here we must refer to an observation of *Le
Commerciel* ; an observation upon which I have already,
in some measure, commented. ' A piece,' says this
journal, ' of one of the unfortunate girl's petticoats was
torn out and tied under her chin, and around the back
of her head, probably to prevent screams. This was
done by fellows who had no pocket-handkerchiefs.'

" I have before suggested that a genuine blackguard
is never *without* a pocket-handkerchief. But it is not
to this fact that I now especially advert. That it was
not through want of a handkerchief for the purpose
imagined by *Le Commerciel*, that this bandage was employed, is rendered apparent by the handkerchief left in
the thicket ; and that the object was not ' to prevent
screams' appears, also, from the bandage having been
employed in preference to what would so much better have
answered the purpose. But the language of the evidence
speaks of the strip in question as ' found around the
neck, fitting loosely, and secured with a hard knot.' These
words are sufficiently vague, but differ materially from
those of *Le Commerciel*. The slip was eighteen inches
wide, and therefore, although of muslin, would form a
strong band when folded or rumpled longitudinally. And
thus rumpled it was discovered. My inference is this.
The solitary murderer, having borne the corpse, for some
distance (whether from the thicket or elsewhere), by
means of the bandage *hitched* around its middle, found
the weight, in this mode of procedure, too much for his
strength. He resolved to drag the burthen—the evidence
goes to show that it was dragged. With this object in
view, it became necessary to attach something like a
rope to one of the extremities. It could be best attached

about the neck, where the head would prevent it slipping off. And now the murderer bethought him, unquestionably, of the bandage about the loins. He would have used this, but for its volution about the corpse, the *hitch* which embarrassed it, and the reflection that it had not been ' torn off ' from the garment. It was easier to tear a new slip from the petticoat. He tore it, made it fast about the neck, and so *dragged* his victim to the brink of the river. That this ' bandage,' only attainable with trouble and delay, and but imperfectly answering its purpose—that this bandage was employed *at all*, demonstrates that the necessity for its employment sprang from circumstances arising at a period when the handkerchief was no longer attainable—that is to say, arising, as we have imagined, after quitting the thicket (if the thicket it was), and on the road between the thicket and the river.

" But the evidence, you will say, of Madame Deluc (!) points especially to the presence of *a gang*, in the vicinity of the thicket, at or about the epoch of the murder. This I grant. I doubt if there were not a *dozen* gangs, such as described by Madame Deluc, in and about the vicinity of the Barrière du Roule at *or about* the period of this tragedy. But the gang which has drawn upon itself the pointed animadversion, although the somewhat tardy and very suspicious evidence of Madame Deluc, is the *only* gang which is represented by that honest and scrupulous old lady as having eaten her cakes and swallowed her brandy, without putting themselves to the trouble of making her payment. *Et hinc illæ iræ ?*

" But what *is* the precise evidence of Madame Deluc ? ' A gang of miscreants made their appearance, behaved boisterously, ate and drank without making payment, followed in the route of the young man and girl, returned to the inn *about dusk*, and recrossed the river as if in great haste.'

" Now this ' great haste ' very possibly seemed *greater* haste in the eyes of Madame Deluc, since she dwelt lingeringly and lamentingly upon her violated cakes and ale —cakes and ale for which she might still have entertained a faint hope of compensation. Why, otherwise, since it was *about dusk*, should she make a point of the *haste* ? It is no cause for wonder, surely, that even a gang of blackguards should make *haste* to get home, when a wide river is to be crossed in small boats, when storm impends, and when night *approaches*.

" I say *approaches* ; for the night had *not yet arrived*. It was only *about dusk* that the indecent haste of these ' miscreants ' offended the sober eyes of Madame Deluc. But we are told that it was upon this very evening that Madame Deluc, as well as her eldest son, ' heard the screams of a female in the vicinity of the inn.' And in what words does Madame Deluc designate the period of the evening at which these screams were heard ? It was ' *soon after dark*,' she says. But ' soon *after* dark,' is at least *dark* ; and ' *about dusk* ' is as certainly daylight. Thus it is abundantly clear that the gang quitted the Barrière du Roule *prior* to the screams overheard (?) by Madame Deluc. And although, in all the many reports of the evidence, the relative expressions in question are distinctly and invariably employed just as I have employed them in this conversation with yourself, no notice whatever of the gross discrepancy has, as yet, been taken by any of the public journals, or by any of the myrmidons of police.

" I shall add but one to the arguments against *a gang* ; but this *one* has, to my own understanding at least, a weight altogether irresistible. Under the circumstances of large reward offered, and full pardon to any king's evidence, it is not to be imagined, for a moment, that some member of *a gang* of low ruffians, or of any body of men, would not long ago have betrayed his accomplices. Each one of a gang so placed is not so much greedy of reward, or anxious for escape, as *fearful of betrayal*. He betrays eagerly and early that *he may not himself be betrayed*. That the secret has not been divulged, is the very best of proof that it is, in fact, a secret. The horrors of this dark deed are known only to *one*, or two, living human beings, and to God.

" Let us sum up now the meagre yet certain fruits of our long analysis. We have attained the idea either of a fatal accident under the roof of Madame Deluc, or of a murder perpetrated, in the thicket at the Barrière du Roule, by a lover, or at least by an intimate and secret associate of the deceased. This associate is of swarthy complexion. This complexion, the ' hitch ' in the bandage, and the sailor's knot ' with which the bonnet-ribbon is tied, point

to a seaman. His companionship with the deceased, a gay,
but not an abject young girl, designates him as above the
grade of the common sailor. Here the well-written and
urgent communications to the journals are much in the way
of corroboration. The circumstance of the first elopement,
as mentioned by *Le Mercurie*, tends to blend the idea of
this seaman with that of the ' naval officer ' who is first
known to have led the unfortunate into crime.

   " And here, most fitly, comes the consideration of the
continued absence of him of the dark complexion. Let
me pause to observe that the complexion of this man is
dark and swarthy ; it was no common swarthiness which
constituted the *sole* point of remembrance, both as regards
Valence and Madame Deluc. But why is this man absent ?
Was he murdered by the gang ?   If so, why are there only
traces of the assassinated *girl* ? The scene of the two out-
rages will naturally be supposed identical. And where is
his corpse ? The assassins would most probably have
disposed of both in the same way. But it may be said
that this man lives, and is deterred from making himself
known, through dread of being charged with the murder.
This consideration might be supposed to operate upon him
now—at this late period—since it has been given in evidence
that he was seen with Marie—but it would have had no force
at the period of the deed. The first impulse of an innocent
man would have been to announce the outrage, and to
aid in identifying the ruffians. This, *policy* would have
suggested. He had been seen with the girl. He had
crossed the river with her in an open ferry-boat. The
denouncing of the assassins would have appeared, even to
an idiot, the surest and sole means of relieving himself
from suspicion. We cannot suppose him, on the night
of the fatal Sunday, both innocent himself and incognisant
of an outrage committed. Yet only under such circumstances is it possible to imagine that he would have failed,
if alive, in the denouncement of the assassins.

   " And what means are ours of attaining the truth ?
We shall find these means multiplying and gathering
distinctness as we proceed. Let us sift to the bottom this
affair of the first elopement. Let us know the full history
of ' the officer,' with his present circumstances, and his
whereabouts at the precise period of the murder. Let us
carefully compare with each other the various communica-

tions sent to the evening paper, in which the object was to inculpate *a gang*. This done, let us compare these communications, both as regards style and MS., with those sent to the morning paper, at a previous period, and insisting so vehemently upon the guilt of Mennais. And, all this done, let us again compare these various communications with the known MSS. of the officer. Let us endeavour to ascertain, by repeated questionings of Madame Deluc and her boys, as well as of the omnibus-driver, Valence, something more of the personal appearance and bearing of the ' man of dark complexion.' Queries, skilfully directed, will not fail to elicit, from some of these parties, information on this particular point (or upon others)—information which the parties themselves may not even be aware of possessing. And let us now trace *the boat* picked up by the bargeman on the morning of Monday, the 23rd of June, and which was removed from the barge-office, without the cognisance of the officer in attendance, and *without the rudder*, at some period prior to the discovery of the corpse. With a proper caution and perseverance we shall infallibly trace this boat ; for not only can the bargeman who picked it up identify it, but the *rudder is at hand*. The rudder *of a sail-boat* would not have been abandoned, without inquiry, by one altogether at ease in heart. And here let me pause to insinuate a question. There was no *advertisement* of the picking up of this boat. It was silently taken to the barge-office, and as silently removed. But its owner or employer—how *happened* he, at so early a period as Tuesday morning, to be informed, without the agency of advertisement, of the locality of the boat taken up on Monday, unless we imagine some connection with the *navy*—some personal permanent connection leading to cognisance of its minute interests—its petty local news ?

" In speaking of the lonely assassin dragging his burden to the shore, I have already suggested the probability of his availing himself *of a boat*. Now we are to understand that Marie Rogêt *was* precipitated from a boat. This would naturally have been the case. The corpse could not have been trusted to the shallow waters of the shore. The peculiar marks on the back and shoulders of the victim tell of the bottom ribs of a boat. That the body was found without weight is also corroborative of the idea. If thrown from the shore a weight would have been attached. We can only account for its absence by supposing the murderer to have neglected the precaution of supplying himself with it before pushing off. In the act of consigning the corpse to the water, he would unquestionably have noticed his oversight; but then no remedy would have been at hand. Any risk would have been preferred to a return to that accursed shore. Having rid himself of his ghastly charge, the murderer would have hastened to the city. There, at some obscure wharf, he would have leaped on land. But the boat—would he have secured it ? He would have been in too great haste for such things as securing a boat. Moreover, in fastening it to the wharf, he would have felt as if securing evidence against himself. His natural thought would have been to cast from him, as far as possible, all that had held connection with his crime. He would not only have fled from the wharf, but he would not have permitted *the boat* to remain. Assuredly he would have cast it adrift. Let us pursue our fancies. In the morning, the wretch is stricken with unutterable horror at finding that the boat has been picked up and detained at a locality which he is in the daily habit of frequenting—at a locality, perhaps, which his duty compels him to frequent. The next night, *without daring to ask for the rudder*, he removes it. Now *where* is that rudderless boat ? Let it be one of our first purposes to discover. With the first glimpse we obtain of it, the dawn of our success shall begin. This boat shall guide us, with a rapidity which will surprise even ourselves, to him who employed it in the midnight of the fatal Sabbath. Corroboration will rise upon corroboration, and the murderer will be traced."

[For reasons which we shall not specify, but which to many readers will appear obvious, we have taken the liberty of here omitting, from the MSS. placed in our hands, such portion as details the *following up* of the apparently slight clue obtained by Dupin. We feel it advisable only to state, in brief, that the result desired was brought to pass ; and that the Prefect fulfilled punctually, although with reluctance, the terms of his compact with the Chevalier. Mr. Poe's article concludes with the following words.—*Eds.**]

* Of the magazine in which the article was originally published.

It will be understood that I speak of coincidence *and no more*. What I have said above upon this topic must suffice. In my own heart there dwells no faith in præternature. That Nature and its God are two, no man who thinks will deny. That the latter, creating the former, can, at will, control or modify it, is all unquestionable. I say " at will " ; for the question is of will, and not, as the insanity of logic has assumed, of power. It is not that the Deity *cannot* modify His laws, but that we insult Him in imagining a possible necessity for modification. In their origin these laws were fashioned to embrace *all* contingencies which *could* lie in the Future. With God all is *Now*.

I repeat, then, that I speak of these things only as of coincidences. And further : in what I relate it will be seen that between the fate of the unhappy Marie Cecilia Rogers, so far as that fate is known, and the fate of one Marie Rogêt up to a certain epoch in her history, there has existed a parallel in the contemplation of whose wonderful exactitude the reason becomes embarrassed. I say all this will be seen. But let it not for a moment be supposed that, in proceeding with the sad narrative of Marie from the epoch just mentioned, and in tracing to its *dénouement* the mystery which enshrouded her, it is my covert design to hint at an extension of the parallel, or even to suggest that the measures adopted in Paris for the discovery of the assassin of a *grisette*, or measures founded in any similar ratiocination, would produce any similar result.

For, in respect to the latter branch of the supposition, it should be considered that the most trifling variation in the facts of the two cases might give rise to the most important miscalculations, by diverting thoroughly the two courses of events ; very much as, in arithmetic, an error which, in its own individuality, may be inappreciable, produces, at length, by dint of multiplication at all points of the process, a result enormously at variance with truth. And, in regard to the former branch, we must not fail to hold in view that the very Calculus of Probabilities to which I have referred, forbids all idea of the extension of the parallel—forbids it with a positiveness strong and decided just in proportion as this parallel has already been long-drawn and exact. This is one of those anomalous propositions which, seemingly appealing to thought altogether apart from the mathematical, is yet one which only the mathematician can fully entertain.   Nothing, for example, is more difficult than to convince the merely general reader that the fact of sixes having been thrown twice in succession by a player at dice, is sufficient cause for betting the largest odds that sixes will not be thrown in the third attempt. A suggestion to this effect is usually rejected by the intellect at once.   It does not appear that the two throws which have been completed, and which lie now absolutely in the Past, can have influence upon the throw which exists only in the Future.   The chance for throwing sixes seems to be precisely as it was at any ordinary time—that is to say, subject only to the influence of the various other throws which may be made by the dice.   And this is a reflection which appears so exceedingly obvious that attempts to controvert it are received more frequently with a derisive smile than with anything like respectful attention.   The error here involved—a gross error redolent of mischief— I cannot pretend to expose within the limits assigned me at present ; and with the philosophical it needs no exposure. It may be sufficient here to say that it forms one of an infinite series of mistakes which arise in the path of Reason through her propensity for seeking truth *in detail.*

THE PURLOINED LETTER

" Nil sapientiæ odiosius acumine nimio."—Seneca.

At Paris, just after dark one gusty evening in the autumn of 18—, I was enjoying the twofold luxury of meditation and a meerschaum, in company with my friend, C. Auguste Dupin, in his little back library or book-closet, *au troisième,* No. 33 Rue Dunôt, Faubourg St. Germain.   For one hour at least we had maintained a profound silence ; while each, to any casual observer, might have seemed intently and exclusively occupied with the curling eddies of smoke that oppressed the atmosphere of the chamber.   For myself, however, I was mentally discussing certain topics which had formed matter for conversation between us at an earlier period of the evening ; I mean the affair of the Rue Morgue, and the mystery attending the murder of Marie Rogêt. I looked upon it, therefore, as something of a coincidence, when the door of our apartment was thrown open and admitted our old acquaintance, Monsieur G——, the Prefect of the Parisian police.

We gave him a hearty welcome ; for there was nearly half as much of the entertaining as of the contemptible about the man, and we had not seen him for several years. We had been sitting in the dark, and Dupin now arose for the purpose of lighting a lamp, but sat down again, without doing so, upon G.'s saying that he had called to consult us, or rather to ask the opinion of my friend, about some official business which had occasioned a great deal of trouble.

" If it is any point requiring reflection," observed Dupin, as he forbore to enkindle the wick, " we shall examine it to better purpose in the dark."

" That is another of your odd notions," said the Prefect, who had a fashion of calling everything " odd " that was beyond his comprehension, and thus lived amid an absolute legion of " oddities."

" Very true," said Dupin, as he supplied his visitor with a pipe, and rolled towards him a comfortable chair.

" And what is the difficulty now ? " I asked.   " Nothing more in the assassination way, I hope ? "

" Oh, no ; nothing of that nature.   The fact is, the business is *very* simple indeed, and I make no doubt that we can manage it sufficiently well ourselves ; but then I thought Dupin would like to hear the details of it, because it is so excessively *odd*."

" Simple and odd," said Dupin.

" Why, yes ; and not exactly that, either.   The fact is, we have all been a good deal puzzled because the affair *is* so simple, and yet baffles us altogether."

" Perhaps it is the very simplicity of the thing which puts you at fault," said my friend.

" What nonsense you *do* talk ! " replied the Prefect, laughing heartily.

" Perhaps the mystery is a little *too* plain," said Dupin.

" Oh, good heavens ! who ever heard of such an idea ? "

" A little *too* self-evident."

"Ha! ha! ha!—ha! ha! ha!—ho! ho! ho!" roared our visitor, profoundly amused; "O Dupin, you will be the death of me yet!"

"And what, after all, *is* the matter on hand?" I asked.

"Why, I will tell you," replied the Prefect, as he gave a long, steady, and contemplative puff, and settled himself in his chair. "I will tell you in a few words; but, before I begin, let me caution you that this is an affair demanding the greatest secrecy, and that I should most probably lose the position I now hold, were it known that I confided it to any one."

"Proceed," said I.

"Or not," said Dupin.

"Well, then; I have received personal information, from a very high quarter, that a certain document of the last importance has been purloined from the royal apartments. The individual who purloined it is known; this beyond a doubt; he was seen to take it. It is known, also, that it still remains in his possession."

"How is this known?" asked Dupin.

"It is clearly inferred," replied the Prefect, "from the nature of the document, and from the non-appearance of certain results which would at once arise from its passing *out* of the robber's possession—that is to say, from his employing it as he must design in the end to employ it."

"Be a little more explicit," I said.

"Well, I may venture so far as to say that the paper gives its holder a certain power in a certain quarter where such power is immensely valuable." The Prefect was fond of the cant of diplomacy.

"Still I do not quite understand," said Dupin.

"No? Well; the disclosure of the document to a third person, who shall be nameless, would bring in question the honour of a personage of most exalted station; and this fact gives the holder of the document an ascendency over the illustrious personage whose honour and peace are so jeopardised."

"But this ascendency," I interposed, "would depend upon the robber's knowledge of the loser's knowledge of the robber. Who would dare——"

"The thief," said G., "is the Minister D——, who dares all things, those unbecoming as well as those becoming a man. The method of the theft was not less ingenious than bold. The document in question—a letter, to be frank—had been received by the personage robbed while alone in the royal *boudoir*. During its perusal she was suddenly interrupted by the entrance of the other exalted personage from whom especially it was her wish to conceal it. After a hurried and vain endeavour to thrust it in a drawer, she was forced to place it, open as it was, upon a table. The address, however, was uppermost, and, the contents thus unexposed, the letter escaped notice. At this juncture enters the Minister D——. His lynx eye immediately perceives the paper, recognises the handwriting of the address, observes the confusion of the personage addressed, and fathoms her secret. After some business transactions, hurried through in his ordinary manner, he produces a letter somewhat similar to the one in question, opens it, pretends to read it, and then places it in close juxtaposition to the other. Again he converses, for some fifteen minutes, upon the public affairs. At length, in taking leave, he takes also from the table the letter to which he had no claim. Its rightful owner saw, but, of course, dared not call attention to the act, in the presence of the third personage who stood at her elbow. The Minister decamped, leaving his own letter —one of no importance—upon the table."

" Here, then," said Dupin to me, " you have precisely what you demand to make the ascendency complete— the robber's knowledge of the loser's knowledge of the robber."

" Yes," replied the Prefect ; " and the power thus attained has, for some months past, been wielded, for political purposes, to a very dangerous extent. The personage robbed is more thoroughly convinced, every day, of the necessity of reclaiming her letter. But this, of course, cannot be done openly. In fine, driven to despair, she has committed the matter to me."

" Than whom," said Dupin, amid a perfect whirlwind of smoke, " no more sagacious agent could, I suppose, be desired, or even imagined."

" You flatter me," replied the Prefect ; " but it is possible that some such opinion may have been entertained."

" It is clear," said I, " as you observe, that the letter is still in the possession of the Minister ; since it is this possession, and not any employment of the letter, which bestows the power. With the employment the power departs."

"True," said G. ; "and upon this conviction I proceeded. My first care was to make thorough search of the Minister's hotel ; and here my chief embarrassment lay in the necessity of searching without his knowledge. Beyond all things, I have been warned of the danger which would result from giving him reason to suspect our design."

"But," said I, "you are quite *au fait* in these investigations. The Parisian police have done this thing often before."

"Oh yes ; and for this reason I did not despair. The habits of the Minister gave me, too, a great advantage. He is frequently absent from home all night. His servants are by no means numerous. They sleep at a distance from their master's apartment, and, being chiefly Neapolitans, are readily made drunk. I have keys, as you know, with which I can open any chamber or cabinet in Paris. For three months a night has not passed, during the greater part of which I have not been engaged, personally, in ransacking the D—— Hotel. My honour is interested, and, to mention a great secret, the reward is enormous. So I did not abandon the search until I had become fully satisfied that the thief is a more astute man than myself. I fancy that I have investigated every nook and corner of the premises in which it is possible that the paper can be concealed."

"But is it not possible," I suggested, "that although the letter may be in possession of the Minister, as it unquestionably is, he may have concealed it elsewhere than upon his own premises ? "

"This is barely possible," said Dupin. "The present peculiar condition of affairs at court, and especially of those intrigues in which D—— is known to be involved, would render the instant availability of the document— its susceptibility of being produced at a moment's notice —a point of nearly equal importance with its possession."

"Its susceptibility of being produced ? " said I.

"That is to say, of being *destroyed*," said Dupin.

"True," I observed ; "the paper is clearly then upon the premises. As for its being upon the person of the Minister, we may consider that as out of the question."

"Entirely," said the Prefect. "He has been twice waylaid, as if by footpads, and his person rigorously searched under my own inspection."

"You might have spared yourself this trouble," said Dupin. "D——, I presume, is not altogether a fool, and, if not, must have anticipated these waylayings, as a matter of course."

"Not *altogether* a fool," said G. ; "but then he's a poet, which I take to be only one remove from a fool."

"True," said Dupin, after a long and thoughtful whiff from his meerschaum, "although I have been guilty of certain doggerel myself."

"Suppose you detail," said I, "the particulars of your search."

"Why, the fact is we took our time, and we searched *everywhere*. I have had long experience in these affairs. I took the entire building, room by room ; devoting the nights of a whole week to each. We examined, first, the furniture of each apartment. We opened every possible drawer ; and I presume you know that, to a properly trained police agent, such a thing as a *secret* drawer is impossible. Any man is a dolt who permits a 'secret' drawer to escape him in a search of this kind. The thing is *so* plain. There is a certain amount of bulk—of space —to be accounted for in every cabinet. Then we have accurate rules. The fiftieth part of a line could not escape us. After the cabinets we took the chairs. The cushions we probed with the fine long needles you have seen me employ. From the tables we removed the tops."

"Why so ? "

"Sometimes the top of a table, or other similarly arranged piece of furniture, is removed by the person wishing to conceal an article ; then the leg is excavated, the article deposited within the cavity, and the top replaced. The tops and bottoms of bedposts are employed in the same way."

"But could not the cavity be detected by sounding ? " I asked.

"By no means, if, when the article is deposited, a sufficient wadding of cotton be placed around it. Besides, in our case, we were obliged to proceed without noise."

"But you could not have removed—you could not have taken to pieces *all* articles of furniture in which it would have been possible to make a deposit in the manner you mention. A letter may be compressed into a thin spiral roll, not differing much in shape or bulk from a large knitting-needle, and in this form it might be inserted into the rung of a chair, for example. You did not take to pieces all the chairs ? "

" Certainly not ; but we did better—we examined the rungs of every chair in the hotel, and, indeed, the jointings of every description of furniture, by the aid of a most powerful microscope. Had there been any traces of recent disturbance we should not have failed to detect it instantly. A single grain of gimlet-dust, for example, would have been as obvious as an apple. Any disorder in the glueing—any unusual gaping in the joints—would have sufficed to ensure detection."

" I presume you looked to the mirrors, between the boards and the plates, and you probed the beds and the bedclothes, as well as the curtains and carpets."

" That of course ; and when we had absolutely completed every particle of the furniture in this way, then we examined the house itself. We divided its entire surface into compartments, which we numbered, so that none might be missed ; then we scrutinised each individual square inch throughout the premises, including the two houses immediately adjoining, with the microscope, as before."

" The two houses adjoining ! " I exclaimed ; " you must have had a great deal of trouble."

" We had ; but the reward offered is prodigious."

" You include the *grounds* about the houses ? "

" All the grounds are paved with brick. They gave us comparatively little trouble. We examined the moss between the bricks, and found it undisturbed."

" You looked among D——'s papers, of course, and into the books of the library ? "

" Certainly ; we opened every package and parcel ; we not only opened every book, but we turned over every leaf in each volume, not contenting ourselves with a mere shake, according to the fashion of some of our police officers. We also measured the thickness of every book-*cover*, with the most accurate admeasurement, and applied to each the most jealous scrutiny of the microscope. Had any of the bindings been recently meddled with, it would have been utterly impossible that the fact should have escaped observation. Some five or six volumes, just from the hands of the binder, we carefully probed longitudinally, with the needles."

" You explored the floors beneath the carpets ? "

" Beyond doubt. We removed every carpet, and examined the boards with the microscope."

" And the paper on the walls ? "

" Yes."

" You looked into the cellars ? "

" We did."

" Then," I said, " you have been making a miscalculation, and the letter is *not* upon the premises, as you suppose."

" I fear you are right there," said the Prefect. " And now, Dupin, what would you advise me to do ? "

" To make a thorough research of the premises."

" That is absolutely needless," replied G——. " I am not more sure that I breathe than I am that the letter is not at the hotel."

" I have no better advice to give you," said Dupin. " You have, of course, an accurate description of the letter ? "

" Oh yes ! " And here the Prefect, producing a memorandum-book, proceeded to read aloud a minute account of the internal, and especially of the external appearance of the missing document. Soon after finishing the perusal of this description, he took his departure more entirely depressed in spirits than I had ever known the good gentleman before.

In about a month afterwards he paid us another visit, and found us occupied very nearly as before. He took a pipe and a chair and entered into some ordinary conversation. At length I said—

" Well, but G——, what of the purloined letter ? I presume you have at last made up your mind that there is no such thing as overreaching the Minister ? "

" Confound him, say I—yes ; I made the re-examination, however, as Dupin suggested—but it was all labour lost, as I knew it would be."

" How much was the reward offered, did you say ? " asked Dupin.

" Why, a very great deal—a *very* liberal reward—I don't like to say how much, precisely ; but I *will* say, that I wouldn't mind giving my individual cheque for fifty thousand francs to any one who could obtain me that letter. The fact is, it is becoming of more and more importance every day ; and the reward has been lately doubled. If it were trebled, however, I could do no more than I have done."

" Why, yes," said Dupin, drawlingly, between the whiffs of his meerschaum, " I really—think, G——, you have not exerted yourself—to the utmost—in this matter. You might—do a little more, I think, eh ? "

" How ?—in what way ? "

" Why—puff, puff,—you might—puff, puff—employ counsel in the matter, eh ?—puff, puff, puff. Do you remember the story they tell of Abernethy ? "

" No ; hang Abernethy ! "

" To be sure ! hang him and welcome. But once upon a time, a certain rich miser conceived the design of sponging upon this Abernethy for a medical opinion. Getting up, for this purpose, an ordinary conversation in a private company, he insinuated his case to the physician, as that of an imaginary individual.

" ' We will suppose,' said the miser, ' that his symptoms are such and such ; now, doctor, what would *you* have directed him to take ? '

" ' Take ! ' said Abernethy, ' why, take *advice*, to be sure.' "

" But," said the Prefect, a little discomposed, " I am *perfectly* willing to take advice, and to pay for it. I would *really* give fifty thousand francs to any one who would aid me in the matter."

" In that case," replied Dupin, opening a drawer, and producing a cheque-book, " you may as well fill me up a cheque for the amount mentioned. When you have signed it, I will hand you the letter."

I was astounded. The Prefect appeared absolutely thunderstricken. For some minutes he remained speechless and motionless, looking incredulously at my friend with open mouth, and eyes that seemed starting from their sockets ; then, apparently recovering himself in some measure, he seized a pen, and after several pauses and vacant stares, finally filled up and signed a cheque for fifty thousand francs, and handed it across the table to Dupin. The latter examined it carefully and deposited

H*

it in his pocket-book ; then, unlocking an *escritoire*, took thence a letter and gave it to the Prefect. This functionary grasped it in a perfect agony of joy, opened it, with a trembling hand, cast a rapid glance at its contents, and then, scrambling and struggling to the door, rushed at length unceremoniously from the room and from the house, without having uttered a syllable since Dupin had requested him to fill up the cheque.

When he had gone, my friend entered into some explanations.

" The Parisian police," he said, " are exceedingly able in their way. They are persevering, ingenious, cunning, and thoroughly versed in the knowledge which their duties seem chiefly to demand. Thus, when G—— detailed to us his mode of searching the premises at the Hôtel D——, I felt entire confidence in his having made a satisfactory investigation—so far as his labours extended."

" So far as his labours extended ? " said I.

" Yes," said Dupin. " The measures adopted were not only the best of their kind, but carried out to absolute perfection. Had the letter been deposited within the range of their search, these fellows would, beyond a question, have found it."

I merely laughed—but he seemed quite serious in all that he said.

" The measures, then," he continued, " were good in their kind, and well executed ; their defect lay in their being inapplicable to the case, and to the man. A certain set of highly ingenious resources are, with the Prefect, a sort of Procrustean bed, to which he forcibly adapts his designs. But he perpetually errs by being too deep or too shallow for the matter in hand ; and many a school-boy is a better reasoner than he. I knew one about eight years of age, whose success at guessing in the game of ' even and odd ' attracted universal admiration. This game is simple, and is played with marbles. One player holds in his hand a number of these toys, and demands of another whether that number is even or odd. If the guess is right, the guesser wins one ; if wrong, he loses one. The boy to whom I allude won all the marbles of the school. Of course he had some principle of guessing ; and this lay in mere observation and admeasurement of the astuteness of his opponents. For example, an arrant simpleton is his opponent, and, holding up his closed hand, asks, ' Are they even or odd ? ' Our school-boy replies ' Odd,' and loses ; but upon the second trial he wins, for he then says to himself, ' The simpleton had them even upon the first trial, and his amount of cunning is just sufficient to make him have them odd upon the second ; I will therefore guess odd '—he guesses odd, and wins. Now, with a simpleton a degree above the first, he would have reasoned thus : ' This fellow finds that in the first instance I guessed odd, and, in the second, he will propose to himself, upon the first impulse, a simple variation from even to odd, as did the first simpleton ; but then a second thought will suggest that this is too simple a variation, and finally he will decide upon putting it even as before. I will therefore guess even '—he guesses even, and wins. Now this mode of reasoning in the school-boy, whom his fellows termed ' lucky '—what, in its last analysis, is it ? "

" It is merely," I said, " an identification of the reasoner's intellect with that of his opponent."

" It is," said Dupin ; " and upon inquiring of the boy by what means he effected the *thorough* identification in which his success consisted, I received answer as follows : ' When I wish to find out how wise, or how stupid, or how good, or how wicked is any one, or what are his thoughts at the moment, I fashion the expression of my face, as accurately as possible, in accordance with the expression of his, and then wait to see what thoughts or sentiments arise in my mind or heart, as if to match or correspond with the expression.' This response of the schoolboy lies at the bottom of all the spurious profundity which has been attributed to Rochefoucauld, to La Bougive, to Machiavelli, and to Campanella."

" And the identification," I said, " of the reasoner's intellect with that of his opponent, depends, if I understand you aright, upon the accuracy with which the opponent's intellect is admeasured."

" For its practical value it depends upon this," replied Dupin ; " and the Prefect and his cohort fail so frequently, first, by default of his identification, and, secondly, by ill-admeasurement, or rather through non-admeasurement, of the intellect with which they are engaged. They consider only their *own* ideas of ingenuity ; and, in searching for anything hidden, advert only to the modes in which *they*

would have hidden it. They are right in this much—that
their own ingenuity is a faithful representative of that of
the mass ; but when the cunning of the individual felon is
diverse in character from their own, the felon foils them, of
course. This always happens when it is above their own,
and very usually when it is below. They have no variation
of principle in their investigations ; at best, when urged
by some unusual emergency—by some extraordinary reward—they extend or exaggerate their old modes of
practice, without touching their principles. What, for
example, in this case of D——, has been done to vary the
principle of action ? What is all this boring, and probing,
and sounding, and scrutinising with the microscope, and
dividing the surface of the building into registered square
inches—what is it all but an exaggeration *of the application*
of the one principle or set of principles of search, which
are based upon the one set of notions regarding human
ingenuity, to which the Prefect, in the long routine of
his duty, has been accustomed ? Do you not see he has
taken it for granted that *all* men proceed to conceal a
letter—not exactly in a gimlet-hole bored in a chair-leg—
but, at least, in *some* out-of-the-way hole or corner suggested by the same tenor of thought which would urge a
man to secrete a letter in a gimlet-hole bored in a chair-
leg ? And do you not see also, that such *recherchés* nooks
for concealment are adapted only for ordinary occasions,
and would be adopted only by ordinary intellects ; for,
in all cases of concealment, a disposal of the article concealed—a disposal of it in this *recherché* manner—is, in the
very first instance, presumable and presumed ; and thus
its discovery depends, not at all upon the acumen, but
altogether upon the mere care, patience, and determination
of the seekers ; and where the case is of importance—or,
what amounts to the same thing in the policial eyes, when
the reward is of magnitude—the qualities in question
have *never* been known to fail. You will now understand
what I meant in suggesting that, had the purloined letter
been hidden anywhere within the limits of the Prefect's
examination—in other words, had the principle of its
concealment been comprehended within the principles of
the Prefect—its discovery would have been a matter altogether beyond question. This functionary, however, has
been thoroughly mystified ; and the remote source of his

defeat lies in the supposition that the Minister is a fool, because he has acquired renown as a poet. All fools are poets—this the Prefect *feels* ; and he is merely guilty of a *non distributio medii* in thence inferring that all poets are fools."

" But is this really the poet ? " I asked. " There are two brothers, I know ; and both have attained reputation in letters. The Minister, I believe, has written learnedly on the Differential Calculus. He is a mathematician, and no poet."

" You are mistaken ; I know him well ; he is both. As poet *and* mathematician, he would reason well ; as mere mathematician, he could not have reasoned at all, and thus would have been at the mercy of the Prefect."

" You surprise me," I said, " by these opinions, which have been contradicted by the voice of the world. You do not mean to set at naught the well-digested idea of centuries. The mathematical reason has long been re- garded as *the* reason *par excellence*."

" ' *Il y a à parier*,' " replied Dupin, quoting from Cham- fort, " ' *que toute idée publique, toute convention reçue, est une sottise, car elle a convenue au plus grand nombre*.' The mathematicians, I grant you, have done their best to promulgate the popular error to which you allude, and which is none the less an error for its promulgation as truth. With an art worthy a better cause, for example, they have insinuated the term ' analysis ' into application to algebra. The French are the originators of this particu- lar deception ; but if a term is of any importance—if words derive any value from applicability—then ' analysis ' con- veys ' algebra ' about as much as, in Latin, ' *ambitus* ' implies ' ambition,' ' *religio* ' ' religion,' or ' *homines honesti* ' a set of *honourable* men."

" You have a quarrel on hand, i see," said I, " with some of the algebraists of Paris ; but proceed."

" I dispute the availability, and thus the value, of that reason which is cultivated in any especial form other than the abstractly logical. I dispute, in particular, the reason educed by mathematical study. The mathematics are the science of form and quantity ; mathematical reasoning is merely logic applied to observation upon form and quantity. The great error lies in supposing that even the truths of what is called *pure* algebra, are abstract or general truths.

And this error is so egregious that I am confounded at the
universality with which it has been received. Mathematical
axioms are *not* axioms of general truth. What is true of
relation—of form and quantity—is often grossly false in
regard to morals, for example. In this latter science it
is very usually *un*true that the aggregated parts are equal
to the whole. In chemistry also the axiom fails. In the
consideration of motive it fails ; for two motives, each of
a given value, have not, necessarily, a value when united,
equal to the sum of their values apart. There are numerous
other mathematical truths which are only truths within
the limits of *relation*. But the mathematician argues,
from his *finite truths*, through habit, as if they were of
an absolutely general applicability—as the world indeed
imagines them to be. Bryant, in his very learned ' Mytho-
logy,' mentions an analogous source of error, when he says
that ' although the Pagan fables are not believed, yet we
forget ourselves continually, and make inferences from
them as existing realities.' With the algebraists, however,
who are Pagans themselves, the ' Pagan fables ' *are* believed, and the inferences are made, not so much through
lapse of memory, as through an unaccountable addling of
the brains. In short, I never yet encountered the mere
mathematician who could be trusted out of equal roots,
or one who did not clandestinely hold it as a point of his
faith that $x^2 + px$ was absolutely and unconditionally equal
to q. Say to one of these gentlemen, by way of experiment,
if you please, that you believe occasions may occur where
$x^2 + px$ is *not* altogether equal to q, and, having made him
understand what you mean, get out of his reach as speedily
as convenient, for, beyond doubt, he will endeavour to
knock you down.

" I mean to say," continued Dupin, while I merely
laughed at his last observations, " that if the Minister
had been no more than a mathematician, the Prefect
would have been under no necessity of giving me this
cheque. I knew him, however, as both mathematician
and poet, and my measures were adapted to his capacity,
with reference to the circumstances by which he was
surrounded. I knew him as a courtier, too, and as a bold
intriguant. Such a man, I considered, could not fail to be
aware of the ordinary policial modes of action. He could
not have failed to anticipate—and events have proved that

he did not fail to anticipate—the waylayings to which he was subjected. He must have foreseen, I reflected, the secret investigations of his premises. His frequent absences from home at night, which were hailed by the Prefect as certain aids to his success, I regarded only as ruses, to afford opportunity for thorough search to the police, and thus the sooner to impress them with the conviction to which G——, in fact, did finally arrive—the conviction that the letter was not upon the premises. I felt, also, that the whole train of thought, which I was at some pains in detailing to you just now, concerning the invariable principle of policial action in searches for articles concealed—I felt that this whole train of thought would necessarily pass through the mind of the Minister. It would imperatively lead him to despise all the ordinary *nooks* of concealment. *He* could not, I reflected, be so weak as not to see that the most intricate and remote recess of his hotel would be as open as his commonest closets to the eyes, to the probes, to the gimlets, and to the microscopes of the Prefect. I saw, in fine, that he would be driven, as a matter of course, to *simplicity*, if not deliberately induced to it as a matter of choice. You will remember, perhaps, how desperately the Prefect laughed when I suggested, upon our first interview, that it was just possible this mystery troubled him so much on account of its being so *very* self-evident."

" Yes," said I, " I remember his merriment well. I really thought he would have fallen into convulsions."

" The material world," continued Dupin, " abounds with very strict analogies to the immaterial ; and thus some colour of truth has been given to the rhetorical dogma, that metaphor, or simile, may be made to strengthen an argument, as well as to embellish a description. The principle of the *vis inertiæ*, for example, seems to be identical in physics and metaphysics. It is not more true in the former, that a large body is with more difficulty set in motion than a smaller one, and that its subsequent momentum is commensurate with this difficulty, than it is, in the latter, that intellects of the vaster capacity, while more forcible, more constant, and more eventful in their movements than those of inferior grade, are yet the less readily moved, and more embarrassed and full of hesitation in the first few steps of their progress. Again, have you ever noticed which of the street signs over the shop-doors are the most attractive of attention ? "

" I have never given the matter a thought," I said.

" There is a game of puzzles," he resumed, " which is played upon a map. One party playing requires another to find a given word—the name of town, river, state or empire—any word, in short, upon the motley and perplexed surface of the chart. A novice in the game generally seeks to embarrass his opponents by giving them the most minutely lettered names ; but the adept selects such words as stretch, in large characters, from one end of the chart to the other. These, like the over-largely lettered signs and placards of the street, escape observation by dint of being excessively obvious ; and here the physical oversight is precisely analogous with the moral inapprehension by which the intellect suffers to pass unnoticed those considerations which are too obtrusively and too palpably self-evident. But this is a point, it appears, somewhat above or beneath the understanding of the Prefect. He never once thought it probable, or possible, that the Minister had deposited the letter immediately beneath the nose of the whole world, by way of best preventing any portion of that world from perceiving it.

" But the more I reflected upon the daring, dashing, and discriminating ingenuity of D——; upon the fact that the document must always have been at hand, if he intended to use it to good purpose ; and upon the decisive evidence, obtained by the Prefect, that it was not hidden within the limits of that dignitary's ordinary search—the more satisfied I became that, to conceal this letter, the Minister had resorted to the comprehensive and sagacious expedient of not attempting to conceal it at all.

" Full of these ideas, I prepared myself with a pair of green spectacles, and called one fine morning, quite by accident, at the Ministerial hotel. I found D—— at home, yawning, lounging, and dawdling, as usual, and pretending to be in the last extremity of ennui. He is, perhaps, the most really energetic human being now alive—but that is only when nobody sees him.

" To be even with him, I complained of my weak eyes, and lamented the necessity of the spectacles, under cover of which I cautiously and thoroughly surveyed the whole apartment, while seemingly intent only upon the conversation of my host.

" I paid especial attention to a large writing-table near which he sat, and upon which lay confusedly some miscellaneous letters and other papers, with one or two musical instruments and a few books. Here, however, after a long and very deliberate scrutiny, I saw nothing to excite particular suspicion.

" At length my eyes, in going the circuit of the room, fell upon a trumpery filigree card-rack of pasteboard, that hung dangling by a dirty blue ribbon, from a little brass knob just beneath the middle of the mantelpiece. In this rack, which had three or four compartments, were five or six visiting cards and a solitary letter. This last was much soiled and crumpled. It was torn nearly in two, across the middle—as if a design, in the first instance, to tear it entirely up as worthless, had been altered, or stayed, in the second. It had a large black seal, bearing the D—— cipher *very* conspicuously, and was addressed, in a diminutive female hand, to D——, the Minister, himself. It was thrust carelessly, and even, as it seemed, contemptuously, into one of the uppermost divisions of the rack.

" No sooner had I glanced at this letter, than I concluded it to be that of which I was in search. To be sure, it was, to all appearance, radically different from the one of which the Prefect had read us so minute a description. Here the seal was large and black, with the D—— cipher ; there it was small and red, with the ducal arms of the S—— family. Here, the address, to the Minister, was diminutive and feminine ; there the superscription, to a certain royal personage, was markedly bold and decided ; the size alone formed a point of correspondence. But then the *radicalness* of these differences, which was excessive ; the dirt ; the soiled and torn condition of the paper, so inconsistent with the *true* methodical habits of D——, and so suggestive of a design to delude the beholder into an idea of the worthlessness of the document ; these things, together with the hyperobtrusive situation of this document, full in the view of every visitor, and thus exactly in accordance with the conclusions to which I had previously arrived ; these things, I say, were strongly corroborative of suspicion, in one who came with the intention to suspect.

" I protracted my visit as long as possible, and, while

I maintained a most animated discussion with the Minister, upon a topic which I knew well had never failed to interest and excite him, I kept my attention really riveted upon the letter. In this examination, I committed to memory its external appearance and arrangement in the rack; and also fell, at length, upon a discovery, which set at rest whatever trivial doubt I might have entertained. In scrutinising the edges of the paper, I observed them to be more *chafed* than seemed necessary. They presented the *broken* appearance which is manifested when a stiff paper, having been once folded and pressed with a folder, is refolded in a reversed direction, in the same creases or edges which had formed the original fold. This discovery was sufficient. It was clear to me that the letter had been turned, as a glove, inside out, redirected and resealed. I bade the Minister good-morning, and took my departure at once, leaving a gold snuff-box upon the table.

" The next morning I called for the snuff-box, when we resumed, quite eagerly, the conversation of the preceding day. While thus engaged, however, a loud report, as if of a pistol, was heard immediately beneath the windows of the hotel, and was succeeded by a series of fearful screams, and the shoutings of a terrified mob. D—— rushed to a casement, threw it open, and looked out. In the meantime, I stepped to the card-rack, took the letter, put it in my pocket, and replaced it by a fac-simile (so far as regards externals) which I had carefully prepared at my lodgings—imitating the D—— cipher, very readily, by means of a seal formed of bread.

" The disturbance in the street had been occasioned by the frantic behaviour of a man with a musket. He had fired it among a crowd of women and children. It proved, however, to have been without ball, and the fellow was suffered to go his way as a lunatic or a drunkard. When he had gone, D—— came from the window, whither I had followed him immediately upon securing the object in view. Soon afterwards I bade him farewell. The pretended lunatic was a man in my own pay."

" But what purpose had you," I asked, " in replacing the letter by a fac-simile ? Would it not have been better, at the first visit, to have seized it openly, and departed ? "

" D——," replied Dupin, " is a desperate man, and a

man of nerve. His hotel, too, is not without attendants devoted to his interests. Had I made the wild attempt you suggest, I might never have left the Ministerial presence alive. The good people of Paris might have heard of me no more. But I had an object apart from these considerations. You know my political prepossessions. In this matter, I act as a partisan of the lady concerned. For eighteen months the Minister has had her in his power. She has now him in hers—since, being unaware that the letter is not in his possession, he will proceed with his exactions as if it was. Thus will he inevitably commit himself, at once, to his political destruction. His downfall, too, will not be more precipitate than awkward. It is all very well to talk about the *facilis descensus Averni*; but in all kinds of climbing, as Catalani said of singing, it is far more easy to get up than to come down. In the present instance I have no sympathy—at least no pity—for him who descends. He is that *monstrum horrendum*, an unprincipled man of genius. I confess, however, that I should like very well to know the precise character of his thoughts, when, being defied by her whom the Prefect terms ' a certain personage,' he is reduced to opening the letter which I left for him in the card-rack."

" How ? did you put anything particular in it ? "

" Why—it did not seem altogether right to leave the interior blank—that would have been insulting. D——, at Vienna once, did me an evil turn, which I told him, quite good-humouredly, that I should remember. So, as I knew he would feel some curiosity in regard to the identity of the person who had outwitted him, I thought it a pity not to give him a clue. He is well acquainted with my MS., and I just copied into the middle of the blank sheet the words :—

" ' ——Un dessein si funeste,
S'il n'est digne d'Atrée, est digne de Thyeste.'

They are to be found in Crébillon's *Atrée*."

THE THOUSAND-AND-SECOND TALE
OF SCHEHERAZADE

Truth is stranger than fiction.—*Old Saying*.

HAVING had occasion, lately, in the course of some oriental investigations, to consult the *Tellmenow Isitsoörnot*,* a work which (like the Zohar of Simeon Jochaides) is scarcely known at all, even in Europe, and which has never been quoted to my knowledge, by any American—if we except, perhaps, the author of the *Curiosities of American Literature* ;—having had occasion, I say, to turn over some pages of the first-mentioned very remarkable work, I was not a little astonished to discover that the literary world has hitherto been strangely in error respecting the fate of the vizier's daughter, Scheherazade, as that fate is depicted in the *Arabian Nights*, and that the *dénouement* there given. if not altogether inaccurate, as far as it goes, is at least to blame in not having gone very much farther.

For full information on this interesting topic, I must refer the inquisitive reader to the *Isitsoörnot* itself : but, in the meantime, I shall be pardoned for giving a summary of what I there discovered.

It will be remembered that, in the usual version of the tales, a certain monarch, having good cause to be jealous of his queen, not only puts her to death, but makes a vow by his beard and the prophet, to espouse each night the most beautiful maiden in his dominions, and the next morning to deliver her up to the executioner.

Having fulfilled this vow for many years to the letter, and with a religious punctuality and method that conferred great credit upon him as a man of devout feelings and excellent sense, he was interrupted one afternoon (no doubt at his prayers) by a visit from his grand vizier, to whose daughter, it appears, there had occurred an idea.

Her name was Scheherazade, and her idea was, that she would either redeem the land from the depopulating tax upon its beauty, or perish, after the approved fashion of all heroines, in the attempt.

* Tell me now, Is it so or not ?

Accordingly, and although we do not find it to be leap-year (which makes the sacrifice more meritorious), she deputes her father, the grand vizier, to make an offer to the king of her hand. This hand the king eagerly accepts —(he had intended to take it at all events, and had put off the matter from day to day, only through fear of the vizier) —but, in accepting it now, he gives all parties very distinctly to understand that, grand vizier or no grand vizier, he has not the slightest design of giving up one iota of his vow or of his privileges. When, therefore, the fair Scheherazade insisted upon marrying the king, and did actually marry him despite her father's excellent advice not to do anything of the kind—when she would and did marry him, I say, will I nill I, it was with her beautiful black eyes as thoroughly open as the nature of the case would allow.

It seems, however, that this politic damsel (who had been reading Machiavelli, beyond doubt) had a very ingenious little plot in her mind. On the night of the wedding she contrived, upon I forget what specious pretence, to have her sister occupy a couch sufficiently near that of the royal pair to admit of easy conversation from bed to bed ; and, a little before cock-crowing, she took care to awaken the good monarch, her husband (who bore her none the worse will because he intended to wring her neck on the morrow) ; —she managed to awaken him, I say (although, on account of a capital conscience and an easy digestion, he slept well), by the profound interest of a story (about a rat and a black cat, I think) which she was narrating (all in an undertone, of course,) to her sister. When the day broke, it so happened that this history was not altogether finished, and that Scheherazade, in the nature of things, could not finish it just then, since it was high time for her to get up and be bowstrung—a thing very little more pleasant than hanging, only a trifle more genteel.

The king's curiosity, however, prevailing, I am sorry to say, even over his sound religious principles, induced him for this once to postpone the fulfilment of his vow until next morning, for the purpose and with the hope of hearing that night how it fared in the end with the black cat (a black cat I think it was) and the rat.

The night having arrived, however, the Lady Scheherazade not only put the finishing stroke to the black cat and the rat (the rat was blue), but before she well knew what she was about, found herself deep in the intricacies of a narration, having reference (if I am not altogether mistaken) to a pink horse (with green wings) that went, in a violent manner, by clock-work, and was wound up with an indigo key. With this history the king was even more profoundly interested than with the other, and as the day broke before its conclusion (notwithstanding all the queen's endeavours to get through with it in time for the bow-stringing), there was again no resource but to postpone that ceremony as before, for twenty-four hours. The next night there happened a similar accident with a similar result ; and then the next—and then again the next ; so that, in the end, the good monarch, having been unavoidably deprived of all opportunity to keep his vow during a period of no less than one-thousand and one nights, either forgets it altogether by the expiration of this time or gets himself absolved of it in the regular way, or (what is more probable) breaks it outright as well as the head of his father confessor. At all events, Scheherazade, who, being lineally descended from Eve, fell heir, perhaps, to the whole seven baskets of talk which the latter lady, we all know, picked up from under the trees in the garden of Eden—Scheherazade, I say, finally triumphed, and the tariff upon beauty was repealed.

Now, this conclusion (which is that of the story as we have it upon record) is, no doubt, excessively proper and pleasant—but, alas ! like a great many pleasant things, is more pleasant than true ; and I am indebted altogether to the *Isitsoörnot* for the means of correcting the error. " *Le mieux*," says a French proverb, " *est l'ennemi du bien*," and, in mentioning that Scheherazade had inherited the seven baskets of talk, I should have added that she put them out at compound interest until they amounted to seventy-seven.

" My dear sister," said she, on the thousand-and-second night [I quote the language of the *Isitsoörnot*, at this point, *verbatim*], " my dear sister," said she, " now that all this little difficulty about the bowstring has blown over, and that this odious tax is so happily repealed, I feel that I have been guilty of great indiscretion in withholding from you and the king (who, I am sorry to say, snores—a thing no gentleman would do) the full conclusion of the history of Sinbad the sailor. This person went through numerous other and more interesting adventures than those which I related ; but the truth is, I felt sleepy on the particular night of their narration, and so was seduced into cutting them short—a grievous piece of misconduct, for which I only trust that Allah will forgive me. But even yet it is not too late to remedy my great neglect, and as soon as I have given the king a pinch or two in order to wake him up so far that he may stop making that horrible noise, I will forthwith entertain you (and him if he pleases) with the sequel of this very remarkable story."

Hereupon the sister of Scheherazade, as I have it from the *Isitsoörnot*, expressed no very particular intensity of gratification ; but the king having been sufficiently pinched, at length ceased snoring, and finally said " hum ! " and then " hoo ! " when the queen understanding these words (which are no doubt Arabic) to signify that he was all attention, and would do his best not to snore any more,— the queen, I say, having arranged these matters to her satisfaction, re-entered thus, at once, into the history of Sinbad the sailor.

" ' At length in my old age,' [these are the words of Sinbad himself, as retailed by Scheherazade]—' at length, in my old age, and after enjoying many years of tranquillity at home, I became once more possessed with a desire of visiting foreign countries ; and one day, without acquainting any of my family with my design, I packed up some bundles of such merchandise as was most precious and least bulky, and, engaging a porter to carry them, went with him down to the seashore, to await the arrival of any chance vessel that might convey me out of the kingdom into some region which I had not as yet explored.

" ' Having deposited the packages upon the sands, we sat down beneath some trees and looked out into the ocean in the hope of perceiving a ship, but during several hours we saw none whatever. At length I fancied that I could hear a singular buzzing or humming sound, and the porter, after listening awhile, declared that he also could distinguish it. Presently it grew louder, and then still louder, so that we could have no doubt that the object which caused it was approaching us. At length, on the edge of the horizon, we discovered a black speck, which rapidly increased in size until we made it out to be a vast monster, swimming with a great part of its body above the surface

of the sea. It came towards us with inconceivable swiftness, throwing up huge waves of foam around its breast,
and illuminating all that part of the sea through which it
passed, with a long line of fire that extended far off into
the distance.

"'As the thing drew near we saw it very distinctly.
Its length was equal to that of three of the loftiest trees
that grow, and it was as wide as the great hall of audience
in your palace, O most sublime and munificent of the Caliphs.
Its body, which was unlike that of ordinary fishes, was as
solid as a rock, and of a jetty blackness throughout all
that portion of it which floated above the water, with the
exception of a narrow blood-red streak that completely
begirdled it. The belly, which floated beneath the surface,
and of which we could get only a glimpse now and then
as the monster rose and fell with the billows, was entirely
covered with metallic scales, of a colour like that of the
moon in misty weather. The back was flat and nearly
white, and from it there extended upwards six spines,
about half the length of the whole body.

"'This horrible creature had no mouth that we could
perceive; but, as if to make up for this deficiency, it was
provided with at least four score of eyes, that protruded
from their sockets like those of the green dragon-fly, and
were arranged all around the body in two rows, one above
the other, and parallel to the blood-red streak, which seemed
to answer the purpose of an eyebrow. Two or three of
these dreadful eyes were much larger than the others, and
had the appearance of solid gold.

"'Although this beast approached us, as I have before
said, with the greatest rapidity, it must have been moved
altogether by necromancy—for it had neither fins like a fish,
nor web-feet like a duck, nor wings like the sea-shell which
is blown along in the manner of a vessel; nor yet did it
writhe itself forward as do the eels. Its head and its tail
were shaped precisely alike, only, not far from the latter,
were two small holes that served for nostrils, and through
which the monster puffed out its thick breath with
prodigious violence, and with a shrieking disagreeable
noise.

"'Our terror at beholding this hideous thing was very
great; but it was even surpassed by our astonishment
when, upon getting a nearer look, we perceived upon the

creature's back a vast number of animals about the size
and shape of men, and altogether much resembling them,
except that they wore no garments (as men do), being
supplied (by nature no doubt) with an ugly, uncomfortable
covering, a good deal like cloth, but fitting so tight to the
skin as to render the poor wretches laughably awkward
and put them apparently to severe pain. On the very tips
of their heads were certain square-looking boxes, which,
at first sight, I thought might have been intended to answer
as turbans, but I soon discovered that they were excessively
heavy and solid, and I therefore concluded they were
contrivances designed, by their great weight, to keep the
heads of the animals steady and safe upon their shoulders.
Around the necks of the creatures were fastened black
collars (badges of servitude, no doubt), such as we keep on
our dogs, only much wider and infinitely stiffer, so that it
was quite impossible for these poor victims to move their
heads in any direction without moving the body at the
same time ; and thus they were doomed to perpetual
contemplation of their noses—a view puggish and snubby
in a wonderful, if not positively in an awful degree.

" ' When the monster had nearly reached the shore
where we stood, it suddenly pushed out one of its eyes to
a great extent, and emitted from it a terrible flash of fire,
accompanied by a dense cloud of smoke and a noise that I
can compare to nothing but thunder. As the smoke
cleared away, we saw one of the odd man-animals standing
near the head of the large beast with a trumpet in his hand,
through which (putting it to his mouth) he presently
addressed us in loud, harsh and disagreeable accents, that,
perhaps, we should have mistaken for language had they
not come altogether through the nose.

" ' Being thus evidently spoken to, I was at a loss how
to reply, as I could in no manner understand what was
said ; and in this difficulty I turned to the porter, who
was near swooning through affright, and demanded of him
his opinion as to what species of monster it was, what it
wanted, and what kind of creatures those were that so
swarmed upon its back. To this the porter replied, as
well as he could for trepidation, that he had once before
heard of this sea-beast ; that it was a cruel demon, with
bowels of sulphur and blood of fire, created by evil genii
as the means of inflicting misery upon mankind ; that the

things upon its back were vermin, such as sometimes infest cats and dogs, only a little larger and more savage ; and that these vermin had their uses, however evil—for, through the torture they caused the beast by their nibblings and stingings, it was goaded into that degree of wrath which was requisite to make it roar and commit ill, and so fulfil the vengeful and malicious designs of the wicked genii.

" ' This account determined me to take to my heels, and, without once even looking behind me, I ran at full speed up into the hills, while the porter ran equally fast, although nearly in an opposite direction, so that, by these means, he finally made his escape with my bundles, of which I have no doubt he took excellent care—although this is a point I cannot determine, as I do not remember that I ever beheld him again.

" ' For myself, I was so hotly pursued by a swarm of the men-vermin (who had come to the shore in boats) that I was very soon overtaken, bound hand and foot, and conveyed to the beast, which immediately swam out again into the middle of the sea.

" ' I now bitterly repented my folly in quitting a comfortable home to peril my life in such adventures as this ; but regret being useless, I made the best of my condition and exerted myself to secure the good-will of the man-animal that owned the trumpet, and who appeared to exercise authority over his fellows. I succeeded so well in this endeavour that, in a few days, the creature bestowed upon me various tokens of its favour, and, in the end, even went to the trouble of teaching me the rudiments of what it was vain enough to denominate its language ; so that, at length, I was enabled to converse with it readily, and came to make it comprehend the ardent desire I had of seeing the world.

" ' " Washish squashish squeak, Sinbad, hey-diddle, diddle, grunt unt grumble, hiss, fiss, whiss," said he to me, one day after dinner—but I beg a thousand pardons, I had forgotten that your majesty is not conversant with the dialect of the Cockneighs (so the man-animals were called ; I presume because their language formed the connecting link between that of the horse and that of the rooster). With your permission, I will translate. " Washish, squashish," and so forth :—that is to say, " I am happy to find, my dear Sinbad, that you are really a very excellent fellow ; we are

now about doing a thing which is called circumnavigating
the globe ; and since you are so desirous of seeing the world,
I will strain a point and give you a free passage upon the
back of the beast." ' "

When the Lady Scheherazade had proceeded thus far,
relates the *Isitsoörnot*, the king turned over from his left
side to his right, and said—

" It is, in fact, *very* surprising, my dear queen, that you
omitted, hitherto, these latter adventures of Sinbad. Do
you know I think them exceedingly entertaining and
strange ? "

The king having thus expressed himself, we are told, the
fair Scheherazade resumed her history in the following
words :—

" Sinbad went on in this manner, with his narrative to the
Caliph—' I thanked the man-animal for its kindness, and
soon found myself very much at home on the beast, which
swam at a prodigious rate through the ocean ; although
the surface of the latter is, in that part of the world, by no
means flat, but round like a pomegranate, so that he went—
so to say—either up hill or down hill all the time.' "

" That, I think, was very singular," interrupted the king.

" Nevertheless, it is quite true," replied Scheherazade.

" I have my doubts," rejoined the king ; " but, pray, be
so good as to go on with the story."

" I will," said the queen. " ' The beast,' continued
Sinbad to the Caliph, ' swam, as I have related, up hill and
down hill, until, at length, we arrived at an island, many
hundreds of miles in circumference, but which, nevertheless,
had been built in the middle of the sea by a colony of little
things like caterpillars.' " *

" Hum ! " said the king.

" ' Leaving this island,' said Sinbad—(for Scheherazade, it
must be understood, took no notice of her husband's ill-
mannered ejaculation)—' leaving this island, we came to
another where the forests were of solid stone, and so hard
that they shivered to pieces the finest-tempered axes with
which we endeavoured to cut them down.' " †

---

* The corallites.

† " One of the most remarkable natural curiosities in Texas is
a petrified forest, near the head of Pasigno river. It consists of
several hundred trees, in an erect position, all turned to stone.
Some trees, now growing, are partly petrified. This is a startling

"Hum!" said the king, again; but Scheherazade, paying him no attention, continued in the language of Sinbad.

" ' Passing beyond this last island, we reached a country where there was a cave that ran to the distance of thirty or forty miles within the bowels of the earth, and that contained a greater number of far more spacious and more magnificent palaces than are to be found in all Damascus and Bagdad. From the roofs of these palaces there hung myriads of gems, like diamonds, but larger than men ; and in among the streets of towers and pyramids and temples, there flowed immense rivers as black as ebony and swarming with fish that had no eyes.' " *

fact for natural philosophers, and must cause them to modify the existing theory of petrifaction."—KENNEDY. [*Texas*, I. p. 120.]

This account, at first discredited, has since been corroborated by the discovery of a completely petrified forest, near the head waters of the Chayenne, or Chienne river, which has its source in the Black Hills of the Rocky chain.

There is scarcely, perhaps, a spectacle on the surface of the globe more remarkable, either in a geological or picturesque point of view, than that presented by the petrified forest, near Cairo. The traveller, having passed the tombs of the caliphs, just beyond the gates of the city, proceeds to the southward, nearly at right angles to the road across the desert to Suez, and after having travelled some ten miles up a low barren valley, covered with sand, gravel, and sea shells, fresh as if the tide had retired but yesterday, crosses a low range of sandhills, which has for some distance run parallel to his path. The scene now presented to him is beyond conception singular and desolate. A mass of fragments of trees, all converted into stone, and when struck by his horse's hoof ringing like cast iron, is seen to extend itself for miles and miles around him, in the form of a decayed and prostrate forest. The wood is of a dark brown hue, but retains its form in perfection, the pieces being from one to fifteen feet in length, and from half a foot to three feet in thickness, strewed so closely together, as far as the eye can reach, that an Egyptian donkey can scarcely thread its way through amongst them, and so natural that, were it in Scotland or Ireland, it might pass without remark for some enormous drained bog, on which the exhumed trees lay rotting in the sun. The roots and rudiments of the branches are, in many cases, nearly perfect, and in some the worm-holes eaten under the bark are readily recognisable. The most delicate of the sap vessels, and all the finer portions of the centre of the wood, are perfectly entire, and bear to be examined with the strongest magnifiers. The whole are so thoroughly silicified as to scratch glass and be capable of receiving the highest polish.—*Asiatic Magazine*. [Vol. III. p. 359 : Third Series.]

* The Mammoth Cave of Kentucky.

" Hum ! " said the king.

" ' We then swam into a region of the sea where we found a lofty mountain, down whose sides there streamed torrents of melted metal, some of which were twelve miles wide and sixty miles long ; * while from an abyss on the summit, issued so vast a quantity of ashes that the sun was entirely blotted out from the heavens, and it became darker than the darkest midnight ; so that, when we were even at the distance of a hundred and fifty miles from the mountain, it was impossible to see the whitest object, however close we held it to our eyes.' " †

" Hum ! " said the king.

" ' After quitting this coast, the beast continued his voyage until we met with a land in which the nature of things seemed reversed—for we here saw a great lake, at the bottom of which, more than a hundred feet beneath the surface of the water, there flourished in full leaf a forest of tall and luxuriant trees.' " ‡

" Hoo ! " said the king.

" ' Some hundred miles farther on brought us to a climate where the atmosphere was so dense as to sustain iron or steel, just as our own does feathers.' " §

" Fiddle de dee," said the king.

" ' Proceeding still in the same direction, we presently arrived at the most magnificent region in the whole world.

* In Iceland, 1783.

† " During the eruption of Hecla, in 1766, clouds of this kind produced such a degree of darkness that, at Glaumba, which is more than fifty leagues from the mountain, people could only find their way by groping. During the eruption of Vesuvius, in 1794, at Caserta, four leagues distant, people could only walk by the light of torches. On the first of May, 1812, a cloud of volcanic ashes and sand, coming from a volcano in the island of St. Vincent, covered the whole of Barbadoes, spreading over it so intense a darkness that, at mid-day, in the open air, one could not perceive the trees or other objects near him, or even a white handkerchief placed at the distance of six inches from the eye."—MURRAY, p. 215, *Phil. edit.* [I. *Encyclopædia of Geography.*]

‡ " In the year 1790, in the Caraccas, during an earthquake, a portion of the granite soil sank and left a lake eight hundred yards in diameter, and from eighty to a hundred feet deep. It was a part of the Forest of Aripao which sank, and the trees remained green for several months under the water."—MURRAY, p. 221. *[Encyc. of Geog.]*

§ The hardest steel ever manufactured may, under the action of a blow-pipe, be reduced to an impalpable powder, which will float readily in the atmospheric air.

Through it there meandered a glorious river for several thousands of miles. This river was of unspeakable depth, and of a transparency richer than that of amber. It was from three to six miles in width ; and its banks, which arose on either side to twelve hundred feet in perpendicular height, were crowned with ever-blossoming trees and perpetual sweet-scented flowers that made the whole territory one gorgeous garden ; but the name of this luxuriant land was the kingdom of Horror, and to enter it was inevitable death.' " *

" Humph ! " said the king.

" ' We left this kingdom in great haste, and, after some days, came to another, where we were astonished to perceive myriads of monstrous animals with horns resembling scythes upon their heads. These hideous beasts dig for themselves vast caverns in the soil, of a funnel shape, and line the sides of them with rocks, so disposed one upon the other that they fall instantly, when trodden upon by other animals, thus precipitating them into the monsters' dens, where their blood is immediately sucked, and their carcasses afterwards hurled contemptuously out to an immense distance from the caverns of death.' " †

" Pooh ! " said the king.

" ' Continuing our progress, we perceived a district abounding with vegetables that grew not upon any soil but in the air. ‡ There were others that sprang from the substance of other vegetables ; § others that derived their sustenance from the bodies of living animals ; ‖ and then,

* The region of the Niger. See SIMMOND's *Colonial Magazine.*

† The *Myrmeleon*—lion-ant. The term " monster " is equally applicable to small abnormal things and to great, while such epithets as " vast " are merely comparative. The cavern of the myrmeleon is *vast* in comparison with the hole of the common red ant. A grain of silex is, also, a " rock."

‡ The *Epidendron, Flos Aeris,* of the family of the *Orchideæ,* grows with merely the surface of its roots attached to a tree or other object, from which it derives no nutriment—subsisting altogether upon air.

§ The *Parasites,* such as the wonderful *Rafflesia Arnoldi.*

‖ Schouw advocates a class of plants that grow upon living animals—the *Plantæ Epizoæ.* Of this class are the *Fuci* and *Algæ.*

Mr. J. B. Williams, of Salem, Mass., presented the " National Institute " with an insect from New Zealand, with the following description :—" ' *The Hotte,*' a decided caterpillar, or worm, is found growing at the foot of the *Rata* tree, with a plant growing again, there were others that glowed all over with intense fire ; * others that moved from place to place at pleasure, † and what is still more wonderful, we discovered flowers that lived and breathed and moved their limbs at will, and had, moreover, the detestable passion of mankind for enslaving other creatures, and confining them in horrid and solitary prisons until the fulfilment of appointed tasks.' " ‡

" Pshaw ! " said the king.

" ' Quitting this land, we soon arrived at another in which the bees and the birds are mathematicians of such genius and erudition, that they give daily instructions in the science of geometry to the wise men of the empire.   The king of the place having offered a reward for the solution of two very difficult problems, they were solved upon the spot—the one by the bees, and the other by the birds ; but

out of its head. This most peculiar and most extraordinary insect travels up both the *Rata* and *Puriri* trees, and entering into the top, eats its way, perforating the trunk of the tree until it reaches the root ; it then comes out of the root, and dies, or remains dormant, and the plant propagates out of its head ; the body remains perfect and entire, of a harder substance than when alive. From this insect the natives make a colouring for tattooing."

* In mines and natural caves we find a species of cryptogamous *fungus* that emits an intense phosphorescence.

† The *orchis, scabius* and *vallisneria.*

‡ " The corolla of this flower (*Aristolochia Clematitis*), which is tubular, but terminating upwards in a ligulate limb, is inflated into a globular figure at the base. The tubular part is internally beset with stiff hairs, pointing downwards. The globular part contains the pistil, which consists merely of a germen and stigma, together with the surrounding stamens. But the stamens, being shorter than even the germen, cannot discharge the pollen so as to throw it upon the stigma, as the flower stands always upright till after impregnation. And hence, without some additional and peculiar aid, the pollen must necessarily fall down to the bottom of the flower.

Now, the aid that Nature has furnished in this case, is that of the *Tipula Pennicornis*, a small insect, which entering the tube of the corolla in quest of honey, descends to the bottom, and rummages about till it becomes quite covered with pollen ; but, not being able to force its way out again, owing to the downward position of the hairs, which converge to a point like the wires of a mouse-trap, and being somewhat impatient of its confinement, it brushes backwards and forwards, trying every corner, till, after repeatedly traversing the stigma, it covers it with pollen sufficient for its impregnation, in consequence of which the flower soon begins to droop and the hairs to shrink to the side of the tube, effecting an easy passage for the escape of the insect."—REV. P. KEITH, *System of Physiological Botany.*

the king keeping their solutions a secret, it was only after
the most profound researches and labour, and the writing
of an infinity of big books, during a long series of years,
that the men-mathematicians at length arrived at the
identical solutions which had been given upon the spot by
the bees and by the birds.' " *

"Oh my!" said the king.

" 'We had scarcely lost sight of this empire when we
found ourselves close upon another, from whose shores
there flew over our heads a flock of fowls a mile in breadth
and two hundred and forty miles long ; so that, although
they flew a mile during every minute, it required no
less than four hours for the whole flock to pass over
us—in which there were several millions of millions of
fowls.' " †

"Oh fy!" said the king.

" 'No sooner had we got rid of these birds, which
occasioned us great annoyance, than we were terrified by the
appearance of a fowl of another kind, and infinitely larger
than even the rocs which I met in my former voyages ;
for it was bigger than the biggest of the domes upon your
seraglio, oh, most Munificent of Caliphs. This terrible

---

* The bees—ever since bees were—have been constructing their
cells with just such sides, in just such number, and at just such
inclination, as it has been demonstrated (in a problem involving
the profoundest mathematical principles) are the very sides, in the
very number, and at the very angles which will afford the creatures
the most room that is compatible with the greatest stability of
structure.

During the latter part of the last century, the question arose
among mathematicians—"to determine the best form that can
be given to the sails of a windmill, according to their varying
distances from the revolving vanes, and likewise from the centres
of revolution." This is an excessively complex problem ; for it
is, in other words, to find the best possible position at an infinity
of varied distances, and at an infinity of points on the arm. There
were a thousand futile attempts to answer the query on the part
of the most illustrious mathematicians ; and when, at length, an
undeniable solution was discovered, men found that the wings of
a bird had given it with absolute precision, ever since the first bird
had traversed the air.

† He observed a flock of pigeons betwixt Frankfort and the
Indiana territory, one mile at least in breadth ; it took up four
hours in passing ; which, at the rate of one mile per minute, gives
a length of 240 miles ; and, supposing three pigeons to each square
yard, gives 2,230,272,000 pigeons.—*Travels in Canada and the
United States,* by LIEUT. F. HALL.

fowl had no head that we could perceive, but was fashioned entirely of belly, which was of a prodigious fatness and roundness, of a soft-looking substance, smooth, shining, and striped with various colours.   In its talons, the monster was bearing away to his eyrie in the heavens, a house from which it had knocked off the roof, and in the interior of which we distinctly saw human beings, who, beyond doubt, were in a state of frightful despair at the horrible fate which awaited them.   We shouted with all our might, in the hope of frightening the bird into letting go of its prey ; but it merely gave a snort or puff, as if of rage, and then let fall upon our heads a heavy sack which proved to be filled with sand.' "

" Stuff ! " said the king.

" ' It was just after this adventure that we encountered a continent of immense extent and of prodigious solidity, but which, nevertheless, was supported entirely upon the back of a sky-blue cow that had no fewer than four hundred horns.' " *

" *That*, now, I believe," said the king, " because I have read something of the kind before, in a book."

" ' We passed immediately beneath this continent (swimming in between the legs of the cow), and, after some hours, found ourselves in a wonderful country indeed, which, I was informed by the man-animal, was his own native land, inhabited by things of his own species.   This elevated the man-animal very much in my esteem ; and in fact, I now began to feel ashamed of the contemptuous familiarity with which I had treated him ; for I found that the man-animals in general were a nation of the most powerful magicians, who lived with worms in their brains,† which, no doubt, served to stimulate them by their painful writhings and wrigglings to the most miraculous efforts of imagination.' "

" Nonsense ! " said the king.

" ' Among the magicians, were domesticated several animals of very singular kinds ; for example, there was a huge horse whose bones were iron and whose blood was

* " The earth is upheld by a cow of a blue colour, having horns four hundred in number."—SALE's *Koran*.

† " The *Entozoa*, or intestinal worms, have repeatedly been observed in the muscles, and in the cerebral substance of men."— See WYATT's *Physiology*, p. 143.

I

boiling water. In place of corn, he had black stones for his usual food ; and yet, in spite of so hard a diet, he was so strong and swift that he would drag a load more weighty than the grandest temple in this city, at a rate surpassing that of the flight of most birds.' " *

" Twattle ! " said the king.

" ' I saw, also, among these people a hen without feathers, but bigger than a camel ; instead of flesh and bone she had iron and brick ; her blood, like that of the horse (to whom in fact she was nearly related), was boiling water ; and like him she ate nothing but wood or black stones. This hen brought forth very frequently, a hundred chickens in the day ; and, after birth, they took up their residence for several weeks within the stomach of their mother.' " †

" Fal lal ! " said the king.

" ' One of this nation of mighty conjurors created a man out of brass and wood, and leather, and endowed him with such ingenuity that he would have beaten at chess, all the race of mankind with the exception of the great Caliph, Haroun Alraschid. ‡   Another of these magi constructed (of like material) a creature that put to shame even the genius of him who made it ; for so great were its reasoning powers that, in a second, it performed calculations of so vast an extent that they would have required the united labour of fifty thousand fleshly men for a year. §   But a still more wonderful conjuror fashioned for himself a mighty thing that was neither man nor beast, but which had brains of lead intermixed with a black matter like pitch, and fingers that it employed with such incredible speed and dexterity that it would have had no trouble in writing out twenty thousand copies of the Koran in an hour ; and this with so exquisite a precision, that in all the copies there should not be found one to vary from another by the breadth of the finest hair. This thing was of prodigious strength, so that it erected or overthrew the mightiest empires at a breath ; but its power was exercised equally for evil and for good.' "

---

* On the Great Western Railway, between London and Exeter, a speed of 71 miles per hour has been attained. A train weighing 90 tons was whirled from Paddington to Didcot (53 miles) in 51 minutes.

† The *Eccaleobion*.

‡ Maelzel's Automaton Chess-player.

§ Babbage's Calculating Machine.

" Ridiculous ! " said the king.

" ' Among this nation of necromancers tnere was also one who had in his veins the blood of the salamanders ; for he made no scruple of sitting down to smoke his chibouque in a red-hot oven until his dinner was thoroughly roasted upon its floor.* Another had the faculty of converting the common metals into gold, without even looking at them during the process.† Another had such delicacy of touch that he made a wire so fine as to be invisible. ‡ Another had such quickness of perception that he counted all the separate motions of an elastic body, while it was springing backwards and forwards at the rate of nine hundred millions of times in a second.' " §

" Absurd ! " said the king.

" ' Another of these magicians, by means of a fluid that nobody ever yet saw, could make the corpses of his friends brandish their arms, kick out their legs, fight, or even get up and dance at his will. ‖ Another had cultivated his voice to so great an extent that he could have made himself heard from one end of the earth to the other. ¶ Another had so long an arm that he could sit down in Damascus and indite a letter at Bagdad—or indeed at any distance whatsoever.** Another commanded the lightning to come down to him out of the heavens, and it came at his call, and served him for a plaything when it came. Another took two loud sounds and out of them made a silence. Another constructed a deep darkness out of two brilliant lights. †† Another made ice in a red-hot

* Chabert, and since him, a hundred others.

† The Electrotype [Electroplate ?].

‡ Wollaston made of platinum for the field of views in a telescope a wire one eighteen-thousandth part of an inch in thickness. It could be seen only by means of the microscope.

§ Newton demonstrated that the retina beneath the influence of the violet ray of the spectrum, vibrated 900,000,000 of times in a second.

‖ The Voltaic pile.

¶ The Electro Telegraph transmits intelligence instantaneously —at least so far as regards any distance upon the earth.

** The Electro Telegraph Printing Apparatus.

†† Common experiments in Natural Philosophy. If two red rays rom two luminous points be admitted into a dark chamber so as to fall on a white surface, and differ in their length by 0·0000258 of an inch, their intensity is doubled. So also if the difference in length be any whole-number multiple of that fraction. A multiple by 2¼, 3¼, etc., gives an intensity equal to one ray only ; but a

furnace.* Another directed the sun to paint his portrait, and the sun did.† Another took this luminary with the moon and the planets, and having first weighed them with scrupulous accuracy, probed into their depths and found out the solidity of the substance of which they are made. But the whole nation is, indeed, of so surprising a necromantic ability, that not even their infants, nor their commonest cats and dogs, have any difficulty in seeing objects that do not exist at all, or that for twenty thousand years before the birth of the nation itself, had been blotted out from the face of creation.' " ‡

"Preposterous!" said the king.

"'The wives and daughters of these incomparably great and wise magi,'" continued Scheherazade, without being in any manner disturbed by these frequent and most

multiple by $2\frac{1}{2}$, $3\frac{1}{2}$, etc., gives the result of total darkness. In violet rays similar effects arise when the difference in length is 0·000157 of an inch; and with all other rays the results are the same—the difference varying with a uniform increase from the violet to the red.

Analogous experiments in respect to sound produce analogous results.

* Place a platina crucible over a spirit lamp, and keep it a red heat; pour in some sulphuric acid, which, though the most volatile of bodies at a common temperature, will be found to become completely fixed in a hot crucible, and not a drop evaporates—being surrounded by an atmosphere of its own, it does not, in fact, touch the sides. A few drops of water are now introduced, when the acid immediately coming in contact with the heated sides of the crucible, flies off in sulphurous acid vapour, and so rapid is its progress, that the caloric of the water passes off with it, which falls a lump of ice to the bottom; by taking advantage of the moment before it is allowed to re-melt, it may be turned out a lump of ice from a red-hot vessel.

† The Daguerreotype.

‡ Although light travels 200,000 miles in a second, the distance of what we suppose to be the nearest fixed star (Sirius) is so inconceivably great, that its rays would require at least three years to reach the earth. For stars beyond this 20—or even 1000 years —would be a moderate estimate. Thus, if they had been annihilated 20 or 1000 years ago, we might still see them to-day, by the light which started from their surfaces, 20 or 1000 years in the past time. That many which we see daily are really extinct, is not impossible—not even improbable. [Broadway Journal Note.]

The elder Herschel maintains that the light of the faintest nebulæ seen through his great telescope, must have taken 3,000,000 years in reaching the earth. Some, made visible by Lord Ross's instrument must, then, have required at least 20,000,000. [Griswold Note.]

ungentlemanly interruptions on the part of her husband—
" ' the wives and daughters of these eminent conjurors are
everything that is accomplished and refined ; and would
be everything that is interesting and beautiful, but for an
unhappy fatality that besets them, and from which not
even the miraculous power of their husbands and fathers
has, hitherto, been adequate to save. Some fatalities
come in certain shapes, and some in others—but this of
which I speak, has come in the shape of a crotchet.' "

" A what ? " said the king.

" ' A crotchet,' " said Scheherazade. " ' One of the evil
genii who are perpetually upon the watch to inflict ill, has
put it into the heads of these accomplished ladies that the
thing which we describe as personal beauty, consists altogether in the protuberance of the region which lies not
very far below the small of the back.—Perfection of loveliness, they say, is in the direct ratio of the extent of this
hump. Having been long possessed of this idea, and
bolsters being cheap in that country, the days have long
gone by since it was possible to distinguish a woman from
a dromedary——' "

" Stop ! " said the king,—" I can't stand that, and I
won't. You have already given me a dreadful headache
with your lies. The day, too, I perceive, is beginning to
break. How long have we been married ?—my conscience
is getting to be troublesome again. And then that dromedary touch—do you take me for a fool ? Upon the whole
you might as well get up and be throttled."

These words, as I learn from the *Isitsoörnot*, both grieved
and astonished Scheherazade ; but, as she knew the king
to be a man of scrupulous integrity, and quite unlikely to
forfeit his word, she submitted to her fate with a good
grace. She derived, however, great consolation (during
the tightening of the bowstring), from the reflection that
much of the history remained still untold, and that the
petulance of her brute of a husband had reaped for him a
most righteous reward, in depriving him of many inconceivable adventures.

THE FALL OF THE HOUSE OF USHER

" Son cœur est un luth suspendu ;
Sitôt qu'on le touche il résonne."
—De Béranger.

DURING the whole of a dull, dark, and soundless day in the autumn of the year, when the clouds hung oppressively low in the heavens, I had been passing alone, on horseback, through a singularly dreary tract of country ; and at length found myself, as the shades of evening drew on, within view of the melancholy House of Usher. I know not how it was—but, with the first glimpse of the building, a sense of insufferable gloom pervaded my spirit. I say insufferable ; for the feeling was unrelieved by any of that half-pleasurable, because poetic, sentiment, with which the mind usually receives even the sternest natural images of the desolate or terrible. I looked upon the scene before me—upon the mere house, and the simple landscape features of the domain—upon the bleak walls—upon the vacant eye-like windows—upon a few rank sedges—and upon a few white trunks of decayed trees—with an utter depression of soul which I can compare to no earthly sensation more properly than to the after-dream of the reveller upon opium—the bitter lapse into everyday life—the hideous dropping off of the veil. There was an iciness, a sinking, a sickening of the heart—an unredeemed dreariness of thought which no goading of the imagination could torture into aught of the sublime. What was it— I paused to think—what was it that so unnerved me in the contemplation of the House of Usher ? It was a mystery all insoluble ; nor could I grapple with the shadowy fancies that crowded upon me as I pondered. I was forced to fall back upon the unsatisfactory conclusion, that while, beyond doubt, there *are* combinations of very simple natural objects which have the power of thus affecting us, still the analysis of this power lies among considerations beyond our depth. It was possible, I reflected, that a mere different arrangement of the particulars of the scene, of the details of the picture, would be sufficient to modify, or perhaps to annihilate its capacity for sorrowful impression ; and, acting upon this idea, I reined my horse to the precipitous brink of a black and lurid tarn that lay in unruffled lustre by the dwelling, and gazed down—but with a shudder even more thrilling than before—upon the remodelled and inverted images of the grey sedge, and the ghastly tree-stems, and the vacant and eye-like windows.

Nevertheless, in this mansion of gloom I now proposed to myself a sojourn of some weeks. Its proprietor, Roderick Usher, had been one of my boon companions in boyhood ; but many years had elapsed since our last meeting. A letter, however, had lately reached me in a distant part of the country—a letter from him—which, in its wildly importunate nature, had admitted of no other than the personal reply. The MS. gave evidence of nervous agitation. The writer spoke of acute bodily illness—of a mental disorder which oppressed him—and of an earnest desire to see me, as his best, and indeed his only personal friend, with a view of attempting, by the cheerfulness of my society, some alleviation of his malady. It was the manner in which all this, and much more, was said—it was the apparent *heart* that went with his request —which allowed me no room for hesitation ; and I accordingly obeyed forthwith what I still considered a very singular summons.

Although, as boys, we had been even intimate associates, yet I really knew little of my friend. His reserve had been always excessive and habitual. I was aware, however, that his very ancient family had been noted, time out of mind, for a peculiar sensibility of temperament, displaying itself, through long ages, in many works of exalted art, and manifested, of late, in repeated deeds of munificent yet unobtrusive charity, as well as in a passionate devotion to the intricacies, perhaps even more than to the orthodox and easily recognisable beauties of musical science. I had learned, too, the very remarkable fact, that the stem of the Usher race, all time-honoured as it was, had put forth, at no period, any enduring branch ; in other words, that the entire family lay in the direct line of descent, and had always, with very trifling and very temporary variation, so lain. It was this deficiency, I considered, while running over in thought the perfect keeping of the character of the premises with the accredited character of the people, and while speculating upon the possible influence which the one, in the long lapse of centuries, might have exercised upon the other—it was this deficiency, perhaps, of collateral issue, and the consequent undeviating transmission, from sire to son, of the patrimony with the name, which had, at length, so identified the two as to merge the original title of the estate in the quaint and equivocal appellation of the " House of Usher "—an appellation which seemed to include, in the minds of the peasantry who used it, both the family and the family mansion.

I have said that the sole effect of my somewhat childish experiment—that of looking down within the tarn—had been to deepen the first singular impression. There can be no doubt that the consciousness of the rapid increase of my superstition—for why should I not so term it ?— served mainly to accelerate the increase itself. Such, I have long known, is the paradoxical law of all sentiments having terror as a basis. And it might have been for this reason only, that, when I again uplifted my eyes to the house itself, from its image in the pool, there grew in my mind a strange fancy—a fancy so ridiculous, indeed, that I but mention it to show the vivid force of the sensations which oppressed me. I had so worked upon my imagination as really to believe that about the whole mansion and domain there hung an atmosphere peculiar to themselves and their immediate vicinity—an atmosphere which had no affinity with the air of heaven, but which had reeked up from the decayed trees, and the grey wall, and the silent tarn—a pestilent and mystic vapour, dull, sluggish, faintly discernible, and leaden-hued.

Shaking off from my spirit what *must* have been a dream, I scanned more narrowly the real aspect of the building. Its principal feature seemed to be that of an excessive antiquity. The discoloration of ages had been great. Minute fungi overspread the whole exterior, hanging in a fine tangled webwork from the eaves. Yet all this was apart from any extraordinary dilapidation. No portion of the masonry had fallen ; and there appeared to be a wild inconsistency between its still perfect adaptation of parts, and the crumbling condition of the individual stones. In this there was much that reminded me of the specious totality of old woodwork which has rotted for long years in some neglected vault, with no disturbance from the breath of the external air. Beyond this indication of extensive decay, however, the fabric gave little token of instability. Perhaps the eye of a scrutinising observer might have discovered a barely perceptible fissure, which, extending from the roof of the building in front, made its way down the wall in a zigzag direction, until it became lost in the sullen waters of the tarn.

Noticing these things, I rode over a short causeway to the house. A servant in waiting took my horse, and I entered the Gothic archway of the hall. A valet, of stealthy step, thence conducted me, in silence, through many dark and intricate passages in my progress to the studio of his master. Much that I encountered on the way contributed, I know not how, to heighten the vague sentiments of which I have already spoken. While the objects around me—while the carvings of the ceilings, the sombre tapestries of the walls, the ebon blackness of the floors, and the phantasmagoric armorial trophies which rattled as I strode, were but matters to which, or to such as which, I had been accustomed from my infancy—while I hesitated not to acknowledge how familiar was all this—I still wondered to find how unfamiliar were the fancies which ordinary images were stirring up. On one of the staircases I met the physician of the family. His countenance, I thought, wore a mingled expression of low cunning and perplexity. He accosted me with trepidation and passed on. The valet now threw open a door and ushered me into the presence of his master.

The room in which I found myself was very large and lofty. The windows were long, narrow, and pointed, and at so vast a distance from the black oaken floor as to be altogether inaccessible from within. Feeble gleams of encrimsoned light made their way through the trellised panes, and served to render sufficiently distinct the more prominent objects around; the eye, however, struggled in vain to reach the remoter angles of the chamber, or the recesses of the vaulted and fretted ceiling. Dark draperies hung upon the walls. The general furniture was profuse, comfortless, antique, and tattered. Many books and musical instruments lay scattered about, but failed to give any vitality to the scene. I felt that I breathed an atmosphere of sorrow. An air of stern, deep, and irredeemable gloom hung over and pervaded all.

Upon my entrance, Usher arose from a sofa on which he had been lying at full length, and greeted me with a vivacious warmth, which had much in it, I at first thought, of an overdone cordiality—of the constrained effort of the *ennuyé* man of the world. A glance, however, at his countenance, convinced me of his perfect sincerity. We sat down ; and for some moments, while he spoke not, I gazed upon him with a feeling half of pity, half of awe. Surely, man had never before so terribly altered, in so brief a period, as had Roderick Usher ! It was with difficulty that I could bring myself to admit the identity of the wan being before me with the companion of my early boyhood. Yet the character of his face had been at all times remarkable. A cadaverousness of complexion ; an eye large, liquid, and luminous beyond comparison ; lips somewhat thin and very pallid, but of a surpassingly beautiful curve ; a nose of a delicate Hebrew model, but with a breadth of nostril unusual in similar formations ; a finely moulded chin, speaking, in its want of prominence, of a want of moral energy ; hair of a more than weblike softness and tenuity ; these features, with an inordinate expansion above the regions of the temple, made up altogether a countenance not easily to be forgotten. And now in the mere exaggeration of the prevailing character of these features, and of the expression they were wont to convey, lay so much of change that I doubted to whom I spoke. The now ghastly pallor of the skin, and the now miraculous lustre of the eye, above all things startled and even awed me. The silken hair, too, had been suffered to grow all unheeded, and as, in its wild gossamer texture, it floated rather than fell about the face, I could not, even with effort, connect its Arabesque expression with any idea of simple humanity.

In the manner of my friend I was at once struck with an incoherence—an inconsistency ; and I soon found this to arise from a series of feeble and futile struggles to overcome an habitual trepidancy—an excessive nervous agitation. For something of this nature I had indeed been prepared, no less by his letter, than by reminiscences of certain boyish traits, and by conclusions deduced from his peculiar physical conformation and temperament. His action was alternately vivacious and sullen. His voice varied rapidly from a tremulous indecision (when the animal spirits seemed utterly in abeyance) to that species of energetic concision—that abrupt, weighty, unhurried, and hollow-sounding enunciation—that leaden, self-balanced, and perfectly modulated guttural utterance, which may be observed in the lost drunkard, or the irreclaimable eater of opium, during the periods of his most intense excitement.

It was thus that he spoke of the object of my visit, of his earnest desire to see me, and of the solace he expected me to afford him. He entered, at some length, into what he conceived to be the nature of his malady. It was, he said, a constitutional and a family evil, and one for which he despaired to find a remedy—a mere nervous affection, he immediately added, which would undoubtedly soon pass off. It displayed itself in a host of unnatural sensations. Some of these, as he detailed them, interested and bewildered me ; although, perhaps, the terms, and the general manner of the narration had their weight. He suffered much from a morbid acuteness of the senses ; the most insipid food was alone endurable ; he could wear only garments of certain texture ; the odours of all flowers were oppressive ; his eyes were tortured by even a faint light ; and there were but peculiar sounds, and these from stringed instruments, which did not inspire him with horror.

To an anomalous species of terror I found him a bounden slave. " I shall perish," said he, " I *must* perish in this deplorable folly. Thus, thus, and not otherwise, shall I be lost. I dread the events of the future, not in themselves, but in their results. I shudder at the thought of any, even the most trivial, incident, which may operate upon this intolerable agitation of soul. I have, indeed, no abhorrence of danger, except in its absolute effect—in terror. In this unnerved—in this pitiable condition—I feel that the period will sooner or later arrive when I must abandon life and reason together, in some struggle with the grim phantasm, FEAR."

I learned, moreover, at intervals, and through broken and equivocal hints, another singular feature of his mental condition. He was enchained by certain superstitious impressions in regard to the dwelling which he tenanted, and whence, for many years, he had never ventured forth—

in regard to an influence whose supposititious force was conveyed in terms too shadowy here to be restated—an influence which some peculiarities in the mere form and substance of his family mansion, had, by dint of long sufferance, he said, obtained over his spirit—an effect which the *physique* of the grey walls and turrets, and of the dim tarn into which they all looked down, had at length brought about upon the *morale* of his existence.

He admitted, however, although with hesitation, that much of the peculiar gloom which thus afflicted him could be traced to a more natural and far more palpable origin— to the severe and long-continued illness—indeed to the evidently approaching dissolution—of a tenderly beloved sister—his sole companion for long years—his last and only relative on earth. " Her decease," he said, with a bitterness which I can never forget, " would leave him (him the hopeless and the frail) the last of the ancient race of the Ushers." While he spoke, the Lady Madeline (for so was she called) passed slowly through a remote portion of the apartment, and, without having noticed my presence, disappeared. I regarded her with an utter astonishment not unmingled with dread—and yet I found it impossible to account for such feelings. A sensation of stupor oppressed me, as my eyes followed her retreating steps. When a door at length closed upon her, my glance sought instinctively and eagerly the countenance of the brother—but he had buried his face in his hands, and I could only perceive that a far more than ordinary wanness had overspread the emaciated fingers, through which trickled many passionate tears.

The disease of the Lady Madeline had long baffled the skill of her physicians. A settled apathy, a gradual wasting away of the person, and frequent although transient affections of a partially cataleptical character, were the unusual diagnosis. Hitherto she had steadily borne up against the pressure of her malady, and had not betaken herself finally to bed ; but, on the closing in of the evening of my arrival at the house, she succumbed (as her brother told me at night with inexpressible agitation) to the prostrating power of the destroyer ; and I learned that the glimpse I had obtained of her person would thus probably be the last I should obtain—that the lady, at least while living, would be seen by me no more.

For several days ensuing, her name was unmentioned by either Usher or myself ; and during this period I was busied in earnest endeavours to alleviate the melancholy of my friend. We painted and read together ; or I listened, as if in a dream, to the wild improvisations of his speaking guitar. And thus, as a closer and still closer intimacy admitted me more unreservedly into the recesses of his spirit, the more bitterly did I perceive the futility of all attempt at cheering a mind from which darkness, as if an inherent positive quality, poured forth upon all objects of the moral and physical universe, in one unceasing radiation of gloom.

I shall ever bear about me a memory of the many solemn hours I thus spent alone with the master of the House of Usher. Yet I should fail in any attempt to convey an idea of the exact character of the studies, or of the occupations, in which he involved me, or led me the way. An excited and highly distempered ideality threw a sulphureous lustre over all. His long improvised dirges will ring for ever in my ears. Among other things, I hold painfully in mind a certain singular perversion and amplification of the wild air of the last waltz of Von Weber. From the paintings over which his elaborate fancy brooded, and which grew, touch by touch, into vaguenesses at which I shuddered the more thrillingly, because I shuddered knowing not why—from these paintings (vivid as their images now are before me) I would in vain endeavour to educe more than a small portion which should lie within the compass of merely written words. By the utter simplicity, by the nakedness of his designs, he arrested and overawed attention. If ever mortal painted an idea, that mortal was Roderick Usher. For me at least—in the circumstances then surrounding me—there arose out of the pure abstractions which the hypochondriac contrived to throw upon his canvas, an intensity of intolerable awe, no shadow of which felt I ever yet in the contemplation of the certainly glowing yet too concrete reveries of Fuseli.

One of the phantasmagoric conceptions of my friend, partaking not so rigidly of the spirit of abstraction, may be shadowed forth, although feebly, in words. A small picture presented the interior of an immensely long and rectangular vault or tunnel, with low walls, smooth, white, and without interruption or device. Certain accessory points of the design served well to convey the idea that this excavation lay at an exceeding depth below the surface of the earth. No outlet was observed in any portion of its vast extent, and no torch, or other artificial source of light, was discernible ; yet a flood of intense rays rolled throughout, and bathed the whole in a ghastly and inappropriate splendour.

I have just spoken of that morbid condition of the auditory nerve which rendered all music intolerable to the sufferer, with the exception of certain effects of stringed instruments. It was, perhaps, the narrow limits to which he thus confined himself upon the guitar, which gave birth, in great measure, to the fantastic character of his performances. But the fervid facility of his impromptus could not be so accounted for. They must have been, and were, in the notes, as well as in the words, of his wild fantasias (for he not unfrequently accompanied himself with rhymed verbal improvisations), the result of that intense mental collectedness and concentration to which I have previously alluded as observable only in particular moments of the highest artificial excitement. The words of one of these rhapsodies I have easily remembered. I was, perhaps, the more forcibly impressed with it, as he gave it, because, in the under or mystic current of its meaning, I fancied that I perceived, and for the first time, a full consciousness on the part of Usher, of the tottering of his lofty reason upon her throne. The verses, which were entitled " The Haunted Palace," ran very nearly, if not accurately, thus :—

I

In the greenest of our valleys,
By good angels tenanted,
Once a fair and stately palace—
Radiant palace—reared its head.
In the monarch Thought's dominion—
It stood there !
Never seraph spread a pinion
Over fabric half so fair.

II

Banners yellow, glorious, golden,
On its roof did float and flow
(This—all this—was in the olden
Time long ago) ;

And every gentle air that dallied,
    In that sweet day,
Along the ramparts plumed and pallid,
    A winged odour went away.

III

Wanderers in that happy valley
    Through two luminous windows saw
Spirits moving musically
    To a lute's well-tunèd law,
Round about a throne, where sitting
    (Porphyrogene !)
In state his glory well befitting,
    The ruler of the realm was seen.

IV

And all with pearl and ruby glowing
    Was the fair palace door,
Through which came flowing, flowing, flowing
    And sparkling evermore,
A troop of Echoes, whose sweet duty
    Was but to sing,
In voices of surpassing beauty,
    The wit and wisdom of their king.

V

But evil things, in robes of sorrow,
    Assailed the monarch's high estate.
(Ah, let us mourn, for never morrow
    Shall dawn upon him, desolate !)
And, round about his home, the glory
    That blushed and bloomed
Is but a dim-remembered story
    Of the old time entombed.

VI

And travellers now within that valley,
    Through the red-litten windows, see
Vast forms that move fantastically
    To a discordant melody ;
While, like a rapid ghastly river,
    Through the pale door,
A hideous throng rush out for ever,
    And laugh—but smile no more.

I well remember that suggestions arising from this ballad
led us into a train of thought wherein there became manifest
an opinion of Usher's, which I mention not so much on
account of its novelty (for other men have thought thus),
as on account of the pertinacity with which he maintained

it. This opinion, in its general form, was that of the
sentience of all vegetable things. But, in his disordered
fancy, the idea had assumed a more daring character, and
trespassed, under certain conditions, upon the kingdom of
inorganisation. I lack words .to express the full extent,
or the earnest *abandon* of his persuasion. The belief,
however, was connected (as I have previously hinted)
with the grey stones of the home of his forefathers. The
conditions of the sentience had been here, he imagined,
fulfilled in the method of collocation of these stones—in the
order of their arrangement, as well as in that of the many
fungi which overspread them, and of the decayed trees
which stood around—above all, in the long undisturbed
endurance of this arrangement, and in its reduplication
in the still waters of the tarn. Its evidence—the evidence
of the sentience—was to be seen, he said (and I here
started as he spoke), in the gradual yet certain condensation of an atmosphere of their own about the waters and
the walls. The result was discoverable, he added, in that
silent, yet importunate and terrible influence which for
centuries had moulded the destinies of his family, and
which made *him* what I now saw him—what he was. Such
opinions need no comment, and I will make none.

Our books—the books which, for years, had formed
no small portion of the mental existence of the invalid
—were, as might be supposed, in strict keeping with this
character of phantasm. We pored together over such
works as the *Ververt et Chartreuse* of Gresset ; the *Bel-
phegor* of Machiavelli ; the *Heaven and Hell* of Sweden-
borg ; the *Subterranean Voyage of Nicholas Klimn,* by
Holberg ; the *Chiromancy* of Robert Flud, of Jean D'Inda-
giné, and of De la Chambre ; the *Journey into the Blue
Distance* of Tieck ; and the *City of the Sun* of Campanella.
One favourite volume was a small octavo edition of the
Directorium Inquisitorium, by the Dominican Eymeric de
Gironne ; and there were passages in Pomponius Mela,
about the old African Satyrs and Œgipans, over which
Usher would sit dreaming for hours. His chief delight,
however, was found in the perusal of an exceedingly
rare and curious book in quarto Gothic—the manual of
a forgotten church—the *Vigiliæ Mortuorum secundum
Chorum Ecclesiæ Maguntinæ.*

I could not help thinking of the wild ritual of this work,

and of its probable influence upon the hypochondriac,
when, one evening, having informed me abruptly that the
Lady Madeline was no more, he stated his intention of
preserving her corpse for a fortnight (previously to its final
interment), in one of the numerous vaults within the main
walls of the building. The worldly reason, however,
assigned for this singular proceeding, was one which I did
not feel at liberty to dispute. The brother had been led
to his resolution (so he told me) by consideration of the
unusual character of the malady of the deceased, of certain
obtrusive and eager inquiries on the part of her medical
men, and of the remote and exposed situation of the
burial-ground of the family. I will not deny that when
I called to mind the sinister countenance of the person
whom I met upon the staircase, on the day of my arrival
at the house, I had no desire to oppose what I regarded
as at best but a harmless, and by no means an unnatural,
precaution.

At the request of Usher, I personally aided him in the
arrangements for the temporary entombment. The body
having been encoffined, we two alone bore it to its rest.
The vault in which we placed it (and which had been so
long unopened that our torches, half smothered in its
oppressive atmosphere, gave us little opportunity for
investigation) was small, damp, and entirely without
means of admission for light ; lying, at great depth, immediately beneath that portion of the building in which was
my own sleeping apartment. It had been used, apparently,
in remote feudal times, for the worst purposes of a donjon-
keep, and, in latter days, as a place of deposit for powder,
or some other highly combustible substance, as a portion
of its floor, and the whole interior of a long archway through
which we reached it, were carefully sheathed with copper.
The door, of massive iron, had been, also, similarly protected. Its immense weight caused an unusually sharp
grating sound, as it moved upon its hinges.

Having deposited our mournful burden upon tressels
within this region of horror, we partially turned aside
the yet unscrewed lid of the coffin, and looked upon the
face of the tenant. A striking similitude between the
brother and sister now first arrested my attention ; and
Usher, divining, perhaps, my thoughts, murmured out some
few words from which I learned that the deceased and

himself had been twins, and that sympathies of a scarcely
intelligible nature had always existed between them.   Our
glances, however, rested not long upon the dead—for we
could not regard her unawed.   The disease which had thus
entombed the lady in the maturity of youth, had left, as
usual in all maladies of a strictly cataleptical character,
the mockery of a faint blush upon the bosom and the face,
and that suspiciously lingering smile upon the lip which is so
terrible in death.   We replaced and screwed down the
lid, and, having secured the door of iron, made our way,
with toil, into the scarcely less gloomy apartments of the
upper portion of the house.

And now, some days of bitter grief having elapsed,
an observable change came over the features of the mental
disorder of my friend.   His ordinary manner had vanished.
His ordinary occupations were neglected or forgotten.
He roamed from chamber to chamber with hurried, unequal,
and objectless step.   The pallor of his countenance had
assumed, if possible, a more ghastly hue—but the luminous-
ness of his eye had utterly gone out.   The more occasional
huskiness of his tone was heard no more ; and a tremulous
quaver, as if of extreme terror, habitually characterised
his utterance.   There were times, indeed, when I thought
his unceasingly agitated mind was labouring with some
oppressive secret, to divulge which he struggled for the
necessary courage.   At times, again, I was obliged to
resolve all into the mere inexplicable vagaries of madness,
for I beheld him gazing upon vacancy for long hours, in
an attitude of the profoundest attention, as if listening
to some imaginary sound.   It was no wonder that his condition terrified—that it infected me.   I felt creeping upon
me, by slow yet certain degrees, the wild influences of his
own fantastic yet impressive superstitions.

It was, especially, upon retiring to bed late in the night
of the seventh or eighth day after the placing of the Lady
Madeline within the donjon, that I experienced the full
power of such feelings.   Sleep came not near my couch—
while the hours waned and waned away.   I struggled to
reason off the nervousness which had dominion over me.
I endeavoured to believe that much, if not all of what I felt,
was due to the bewildering influence of the gloomy furniture
of the room—of the dark and tattered draperies, which,
tortured into motion by the breath of a rising tempest,

THE FALL OF THE HOUSE OF USHER   255

swayed fitfully to and fro upon the walls, and rustled uneasily about the decorations of the bed. But my efforts were fruitless. An irrepressible tremor gradually pervaded my frame ; and, at length, there sat upon my very heart an incubus of utterly causeless alarm. Shaking this off with a gasp and a struggle, I uplifted myself upon the pillows, and, peering earnestly within the intense darkness of the chamber, hearkened—I know not why, except that an instinctive spirit prompted me—to certain low and indefinite sounds which came, through the pauses of the storm, at long intervals, I knew not whence. Overpowered by an intense sentiment of horror, unaccountable yet unendurable, I threw on my clothes with haste (for I felt that I should sleep no more during the night), and endeavoured to arouse myself from the pitiable condition into which I had fallen, by pacing rapidly to and fro through the apartment.

I had taken but few turns in this manner, when a light step on an adjoining staircase arrested my attention. I presently recognised it as that of Usher. In an instant afterward he rapped with a gentle touch, at my door, and entered, bearing a lamp. His countenance was, as usual, cadaverously wan—but, moreover, there was a species of mad hilarity in his eyes—an evidently restrained hysteria in his whole demeanour. His air appalled me—but anything was preferable to the solitude which I had so long endured, and I even welcomed his presence as a relief.

" And you have not seen it ? " he said abruptly, after having stared about him for some moments in silence —" you have not then seen it ?—but, stay ! you shall." Thus speaking, and having carefully shaded his lamp, he hurried to one of the casements, and threw it freely open to the storm.

The impetuous fury of the entering gust nearly lifted us from our feet. It was, indeed, a tempestuous yet sternly beautiful night, and one wildly singular in its terror and its beauty. A whirlwind had apparently collected its force in our vicinity ; for there were frequent and violent alterations in the direction of the wind ; and the exceeding density of the clouds (which hung so low as to press upon the turrets of the house) did not prevent our perceiving the life-like velocity with which they flew careering from all points against each other, without passing away into the distance. I say that even their exceeding density did not prevent our perceiving this— yet we had no glimpse of the moon or stars—nor was there any flashing forth of the lightning. But the under surfaces of the huge masses of agitated vapour, as well as all terrestrial objects immediately around us, were glowing in the unnatural light of a faintly luminous and distinctly visible gaseous exhalation which hung about and enshrouded the mansion.

" You must not—you shall not behold this ! " said I, shudderingly, to Usher, as I led him, with a gentle violence from the window to a seat. " These appearances, which bewilder you, are merely electrical phenomena not uncommon—or it may be that they have their ghastly origin in the rank miasma of the tarn. Let us close this casement—the air is chilling and dangerous to your frame. Here is one of your favourite romances. I will read, and you shall listen—and so we will pass away this terrible night together."

The antique volume which I had taken up was the *Mad Trist* of Sir Launcelot Canning ; but I had called it a favourite of Usher's more in sad jest than in earnest ; for, in truth, there is little in its uncouth and unimaginative prolixity which could have had interest for the lofty and spiritual ideality of my friend. It was, however, the only book immediately at hand ; and I indulged a vague hope that the excitement which now agitated the hypochondriac, might find relief (for the history of mental disorder is full of similar anomalies) even in the extremeness of the folly which I should read. Could I have judged, indeed, by the wild overstrained air of vivacity with which he hearkened, or apparently hearkened, to the words of the tale, I might well have congratulated myself upon the success of my design.

I had arrived at that well-known portion of the story where Ethelred, the hero of the Trist, having sought in vain for peaceable admission into the dwelling of the hermit, proceeds to make good an entrance by force. Here, it will be remembered, the words of the narrative run thus :—

" And Ethelred, who was by nature of a doughty heart, and who was now mighty withal, on account of the powerfulness of the wine which he had drunken, waited no longer to hold parley with the hermit, who, in sooth, was of an obstinate and maliceful turn, but, feeling the rain upon his shoulders, and fearing the rising of the tempest, uplifted his mace outright, and, with blows, made quickly room in the plankings of the door for his gauntleted hand; and now pulling therewith sturdily, he so cracked, and ripped, and tore all asunder, that the noise of the dry and hollow-sounding wood alarummed and reverberated throughout the forest."

At the termination of this sentence I started, and for a moment paused; for it appeared to me (although I at once concluded that my excited fancy had deceived me) —it appeared to me that, from some very remote portion of the mansion, there came, indistinctly, to my ears, what might have been, in its exact similarity of character, the echo (but a stifled and dull one certainly) of the very cracking and ripping sound which Sir Launcelot had so particularly described. It was, beyond doubt, the coincidence alone which had arrested my attention; for, amid the rattling of the sashes of the casements, and the ordinary commingled noises of the still increasing storm, the sound, in itself, had nothing, surely, which should have interested or disturbed me. I continued the story :—

"But the good champion Ethelred, now entering within the door, was sore enraged and amazed to perceive no signal of the maliceful hermit; but, in the stead thereof, a dragon of a scaly and prodigious demeanour, and of a fiery tongue, which sate in guard before a palace of gold, with a floor of silver; and upon the wall there hung a shield of shining brass with this legend enwritten :—

'Who entereth herein, a conqueror hath bin;
Who slayeth the dragon, the shield he shall win.'

And Ethelred uplifted his mace, and struck upon the head of the dragon, which fell before him, and gave up his pesty breath, with a shriek so horrid and harsh, and withal so piercing, that Ethelred had fain to close his ears with his hands against the dreadful noise of it, the like whereof was never before heard."

Here again I paused abruptly, and now with a feeling of wild amazement—for there could be no doubt whatever that, in this instance, I did actually hear (although from

what direction it proceeded I found it impossible to say)
a low and apparently distant, but harsh, protracted, and
most unusual screaming or grating sound—the exact
counterpart of what my fancy had already conjured up
for the dragon's unnatural shriek as described by the
romancer.

Oppressed as I certainly was, upon the occurrence of this
second and most extraordinary coincidence, by a thousand
conflicting sensations, in which wonder and extreme terror
were predominant, I still retained sufficient presence of
mind to avoid exciting, by any observation, the sensitive
nervousness of my companion. I was by no means
certain that he had noticed the sound in question ; although, assuredly, a strange alteration had, during the
last few minutes, taken place in his demeanour. From
a position fronting my own, he had gradually brought
round his chair, so as to sit with his face to the door of
the chamber ; and thus I could but partially perceive
his features, although I saw that his lips trembled as if
he were murmuring inaudibly. His head had dropped
upon his breast—yet I knew that he was not asleep, from
the wide and rigid opening of the eye as I caught a glance
of it in profile. The motion of his body, too, was at
variance with this idea—for he rocked from side to side with
a gentle yet constant and uniform sway. Having rapidly
taken notice of all this, I resumed the narrative of Sir
Launcelot, which thus proceeded :—

" And now, the champion, having escaped from the
terrible fury of the dragon, bethinking himself of the
brazen shield, and of the breaking up of the enchantment
which was upon it, removed the carcass from out of the
way before him, and approached valorously over the
silver pavement of the castle to where the shield was upon
the wall ; which in sooth tarried not for his full coming,
but fell down at his feet upon the silver floor, with a mighty
great and terrible ringing sound."

No sooner had these syllables passed my lips, than—
as if a shield of brass had indeed, at the moment, fallen
heavily upon a floor of silver—I became aware of a distinct,
hollow, metallic, and clangorous, yet apparently muffled
reverberation. Completely unnerved, I leaped to my feet ;
but the measured rocking movement of Usher was undisturbed. I rushed to the chair in which he sat. His

eyes were bent fixedly before him, and throughout his whole countenance there reigned a stony rigidity. But, as I placed my hand upon his shoulder, there came a strong shudder over his whole person ; a sickly smile quivered on his lips ; and I saw that he spoke in a low, hurried, and gibbering murmur, as if unconscious of my presence. Bending closely over him, I at length drank in the hideous import of his words.

" Not hear it ?—yes, I hear it, and *have* heard it. Long —long—long—many minutes, many hours, many days, have I heard it—yet I dared not—oh, pity me, miserable wretch that I am !—I dared not—I *dared* not speak ! *We have put her living in the tomb !* Said I not that my senses were acute ? I *now* tell you that I heard her first feeble movements in the hollow coffin. I heard them— many, many days ago—yet I dared not—*I dared not speak !* And now—to-night—Ethelred—ha ! ha !—the breaking of the hermit's door, and the death-cry of the dragon, and the clangour of the shield !—say, rather, the rending of her coffin, and the grating of the iron hinges of her prison, and her struggles within the coppered archway of the vault ! Oh, whither shall I fly ? Will she not be here anon ? Is she not hurrying to upbraid me for my haste ? Have I not heard her footstep on the stair ? Do I not distinguish that heavy and horrible beating of her heart ? Madman ! "—here he sprang furiously to his feet, and shrieked out his syllables, as if in the effort he were giving up his soul—" *Madman ! I tell you that she now stands without the door !* "

As if in the superhuman energy of his utterance there had been found the potency of a spell—the huge antique panels to which the speaker pointed threw slowly back, upon the instant, their ponderous and ebony jaws. It was the work of the rushing gust—but then without those doors there *did* stand the lofty and enshrouded figure of the Lady Madeline of Usher. There was blood upon her white robes, and the evidence of some bitter struggle upon every portion of her emaciated frame. For a moment she remained trembling and reeling to and fro upon the threshold—then, with a low moaning cry, fell heavily inward upon the person of her brother, and in her violent and now final death-agonies, bore him to the floor a corpse, and a victim to the terrors he had anticipated.

From that chamber, and from that mansion, I fled aghast. The storm was still abroad in all its wrath as I found myself crossing the old causeway. Suddenly there shot along the path a wild light, and I turned to see whence a gleam so unusual could have issued ; for the vast house and its shadows were alone behind me. The radiance was that of the full, setting, and blood-red moon, which now shone vividly through that once barely-discernible fissure, of which I have before spoken as extending from the roof of the building, in a zigzag direction, to the base. While I gazed, this fissure rapidly widened —there came a fierce breath of the whirlwind—the entire orb of the satellite burst at once upon my sight—my brain reeled as I saw the mighty walls rushing asunder —there was a long tumultuous shouting sound like a voice of a thousand waters—and the deep and dank tarn at my feet closed sullenly and silently over the fragments of the " House of Usher."

THE UNPARALLELED ADVENTURE OF ONE HANS PFAALL

With a heart of furious fancies,
Whereof I am commander,
With a burning spear, *and a horse of air*,
To the wilderness I wander.
—*Tom o' Bedlam's Song.*

By late accounts from Rotterdam, that city seems to be in a high state of philosophical excitement. Indeed, phenomena have there occurred of a nature so completely unexpected, so entirely novel, so utterly at variance with preconceived opinions, as to leave no doubt on my mind that long ere this all Europe is in an uproar, all physics in a ferment, all reason and astronomy together by the ears.

It appears that on the ——— day of ——— (I am not positive about the date), a vast crowd of people, for purposes not specifically mentioned, were assembled in the

great square of the Exchange, in the well-conditioned
city of Rotterdam. The day was warm—unusually so
for the season—there was hardly a breath of air stirring ;
and the multitude were in no bad humour at being now
and then besprinkled with friendly showers of momentary
duration, that fell from large white masses of cloud profusely distributed about the blue vault of the firmament.
Nevertheless, about noon, a slight but remarkable agitation
became apparent in the assembly ; the clattering of ten
thousand tongues succeeded ; and, in an instant afterwards, ten thousand faces were upturned towards the
heavens, ten thousand pipes descended simultaneously
from the corners of ten thousand mouths, and a shout
which could be compared to nothing but the roaring of
Niagara, resounded long, loudly and furiously, through
all the city and through all the environs of Rotterdam.

The origin of this hubbub soon became sufficiently
evident. From behind the huge bulk of those sharply
defined masses of cloud already mentioned, was seen
slowly to emerge into an open area of blue space, a queer,
heterogeneous, but apparently solid substance, so oddly
shaped, so whimsically put together, as not to be in any
manner comprehended, and never to be sufficiently admired,
by the host of sturdy burghers, who stood open-mouthed
below. What could it be ? In the name of all the devils
in Rotterdam, what could it possibly portend ? No one
knew, no one could imagine ; no one—not even the
burgomaster Mynheer Superbus Von Underduk—had the
slightest clue by which to unravel the mystery ; so, as
nothing more reasonable could be done, every one, to a
man, replaced his pipe carefully in the corner of his mouth,
and maintaining an eye steadily upon the phenomenon,
puffed, paused, waddled about, and grunted significantly
—then waddled back, grunted, paused, and finally—
puffed again.

In the meantime, however, lower and still lower towards
the goodly city, came the object of so much curiosity, and
the cause of so much smoke. In a very few minutes it
arrived near enough to be accurately discerned. It
appeared to be—yes ! it *was* undoubtedly a species of
balloon ; but surely no *such* balloon had ever been seen in
Rotterdam before. For who, let me ask, ever heard of a
balloon manufactured entirely of dirty newspapers ? No

man in Holland certainly ; yet here, under the very noses
of the people, or rather at some distance *above* their noses,
was the identical thing in question, and composed—I
have it on the best authority—of the precise material
which no one had ever before known to be used for a similar
purpose. It was an egregious insult to the good sense of
the burghers of Rotterdam. As to the shape of the
phenomenon, it was even still more reprehensible ; being
little or nothing better than a huge fool's-cap turned upside
down. And this similitude was regarded as by no means
lessened, when upon nearer inspection, the crowd saw a
large tassel depending from its apex, and, around the upper
rim or base of the cone, a circle of little instruments,
resembling sheep-bells, which kept up a continual tinkling to
the tune of Betty Martin. But, still worse, suspended by blue
ribbons to the end of this fantastic machine, there hung by
way of car, an enormous drab beaver hat, with a brim
superlatively broad, and a hemispherical crown with a
black band and a silver buckle. It is, however, somewhat
remarkable that many citizens of Rotterdam swore to
having seen the same hat repeatedly before ; and indeed
the whole assembly seemed to regard it with eyes of
familiarity ; while the vrow Grettel Pfaall upon sight of
it uttered an exclamation of joyful surprise, and declared
it to be the identical hat of her good man himself. Now
this was a circumstance the more to be observed, as Pfaall
with three companions had actually disappeared from
Rotterdam about five years before, in a very sudden and
unaccountable manner, and up to the date of this narrative
all attempts at obtaining intelligence concerning them had
failed. To be sure, some bones, which were thought to be
human, mixed up with a quantity of odd-looking rubbish,
had been lately discovered in a retired situation to the east
of the city ; and some people went so far as to imagine
that in this spot a foul murder had been committed, and
that the sufferers were in all probability Hans Pfaall and
his associates. But to return.

The balloon (for such no doubt it was) had now descended
to within a hundred feet of the earth, allowing the crowd
below a sufficiently distinct view of the person of its occupant. This was in truth a very singular body. He could
not have been more than two feet in height ; but this
altitude, little as it was, would have been sufficient to

destroy his equilibrium, and tilt him over the edge of his tiny car, but for the intervention of a circular rim reaching as high as the breast, and rigged on to the cords of the balloon. The body of the little man was more than proportionally broad, giving to his entire figure a rotundity highly absurd. His feet, of course, could not be seen at all. His hands were enormously large. His hair was grey, and collected into a *queue* behind. His nose was prodigiously long, crooked and inflammatory ; his eyes full, brilliant, and acute ; his chin and cheeks, although wrinkled with age, were broad, puffy, and double ; but of ears of any kind there was not a semblance to be discovered upon any portion of his head. This odd little gentleman was dressed in a loose surtout of sky-blue satin, with tight breeches to match, fastened with silver buckles at the knees. His vest was of some bright yellow material ; a white taffety cap was set jauntily on one side of his head ; and, to complete his equipment, a blood-red silk handkerchief enveloped his throat, and fell down in a dainty manner upon his bosom, in a fantastic bow-knot of super-eminent dimensions.

Having descended, as I said before, to about one hundred feet from the surface of the earth, the little old gentleman was suddenly seized with a fit of trepidation, and appeared disinclined to make any nearer approach to *terra firma*. Throwing out, therefore, a quantity of sand from a canvas bag, which he lifted with great difficulty, he became stationary in an instant. He then proceeded, in a hurried and agitated manner, to extract from a side pocket in his surtout a large morocco pocket-book. This he poised suspiciously in his hand ; then eyed it with an air of extreme surprise, and was evidently astonished at its weight. He at length opened it, and, drawing therefrom a huge letter sealed with red sealing-wax and tied carefully with red tape, let it fall precisely at the feet of the burgomaster Superbus Von Underduk. His Excellency stooped to pick it up. But the aeronaut, still greatly discomposed, and having apparently no further business to detain him in Rotterdam, began at this moment to make busy preparations for departure ; and it being necessary to discharge a portion of ballast to enable him to re-ascend, the half-dozen bags which he threw out, one after another, without taking the trouble to empty their contents, tumbled, every one of

them, most unfortunately, upon the back of the burgomaster, and rolled him over and over no less than half-a-
dozen times, in the face of every individual in Rotterdam.
It is not to be supposed, however, that the great Underduk
suffered this impertinence on the part of the little old man
to pass off with impunity. It is said, on the contrary, that
during each of his half-dozen circumvolutions, he emitted
no less than half-a-dozen distinct and furious whiffs from
his pipe, to which he held fast the whole time with all his
might, and to which he intends holding fast—God willing
—until the day of his decease.

In the meantime the balloon arose like a lark, and, soaring
far away above the city, at length drifted quietly behind a
cloud similar to that from which it had so oddly emerged,
and was thus lost for ever to the wondering eyes of the good
citizens of Rotterdam. All attention was now directed to
the letter, the descent of which, and the consequences
attending thereupon, had proved so fatally subversive of
both person and personal dignity to his Excellency Von
Underduk. That functionary, however, had not failed,
during his circumgyratory movements, to bestow a thought
upon the important object of securing the epistle, which was
seen, upon inspection, to have fallen into the most proper
hands, being actually addressed to himself and Professor
Rubadub, in their official capacities of President and Vice-
President of the Rotterdam College of Astronomy. It was
accordingly opened by those dignitaries upon the spot, and
found to contain the following extraordinary, and, indeed,
very serious communication :—

*To their Excellencies Von Underduk and Rubadub, President
and Vice-President of the States' College of Astronomers, in
the City of Rotterdam.*

Your Excellencies may perhaps be able to remember an
humble artisan, by name Hans Pfaall, and by occupation a
mender of bellows, who, with three others, disappeared from
Rotterdam, about five years ago, in a manner which must
have been considered unaccountable. If, however, it so
please your Excellencies, I, the writer of this communication, am the identical Hans Pfaall himself. It is well known
to most of my fellow-citizens that for the period of forty
years I continued to occupy the little square brick building
at the head of the alley called Sauerkraut, in which I

resided at the time of my disappearance. My ancestors have also resided therein time out of mind—they, as well as myself, steadily following the respectable and indeed lucrative profession of mending of bellows ; for, to speak the truth, until, of late years, that the heads of all the people have been set agog with politics, no better business than my own could an honest citizen of Rotterdam either desire or deserve. Credit was good, employment was never wanting, and there was no lack of either money or good will. But, as I was saying, we soon began to feel the effects of liberty, and long speeches, and radicalism, and all that sort of thing. People who were formerly the very best customers in the world had now not a moment of time to think of us at all. They had as much as they could do to read about the revolutions, and keep up with the march of intellect and the spirit of the age. If a fire wanted fanning, it could readily be fanned with a newspaper ; and as the Government grew weaker, I have no doubt that leather and iron acquired durability in proportion ; for in a very short time there was not a pair of bellows in all Rotterdam that ever stood in need of a stitch or required the assistance of a hammer. This was a state of things not to be endured. I soon grew as poor as a rat, and, having a wife and children to provide for, my burdens at length became intolerable, and I spent hour after hour in reflecting upon the most convenient method of putting an end to my life. Duns, in the meantime, left me little leisure for contemplation. My house was literally besieged from morning till night. There were three fellows in particular, who worried me beyond endurance, keeping watch continually about my door, and threatening me with the law. Upon these three I vowed the bitterest revenge, if ever I should be so happy as to get them within my clutches ; and I believe nothing in the world but the pleasure of this anticipation prevented me from putting my plan of suicide into immediate execution, by blowing my brains out with a blunderbuss. I thought it best, however, to dissemble my wrath, and treat them with promises and fair words, until, by some good turn of fate, an opportunity of vengeance should be afforded me.

One day, having given them the slip, and feeling more than usually dejected, I continued for a long time to wander about the most obscure streets without object, until at length I chanced to stumble against the corner of a bookseller's stall. Seeing a chair close at hand for the use of customers, I threw myself doggedly into it, and, hardly knowing why, opened the pages of the first volume which came within my reach. It proved to be a small pamphlet treatise on Speculative Astronomy, written either by Professor Encke of Berlin, or by a Frenchman of somewhat similar name. I had some little tincture of information on matters of this nature, and soon became more and more absorbed in the contents of the book—reading it actually through twice before I awoke to a recollection of what was passing around me. By this time it began to grow dark, and I directed my steps towards home. But the treatise (in conjunction with a discovery in pneumatics, lately communicated to me as an important secret by a cousin from Nantz) had made an indelible impression on my mind ; and as I sauntered along the dusky streets, I revolved carefully over in memory the wild and sometimes unintelligible reasonings of the writer. There are some particular passages which affected my imagination in an extraordinary manner. The longer I meditated upon these, the more intense grew the interest which had been excited within me. The limited nature of my education in general, and more especially my ignorance on subjects connected with natural philosophy, so far from rendering me diffident of my own ability to comprehend what I had read, or inducing me to mistrust the many vague notions which had arisen in consequence, merely served as a farther stimulus to imagination ; and I was vain enough, or perhaps reasonable enough, to doubt whether those crude ideas which, arising in ill-regulated minds, have all the appearance, may not often in effect possess all the force, the reality, and other inherent properties of instinct or intuition.

It was late when I reached home, and I went immediately to bed. My mind, however, was too much occupied to sleep, and I lay the whole night buried in meditation. Arising early in the morning, I repaired eagerly to the bookseller's stall, and laid out what little ready money I possessed in the purchase of some volumes of Mechanics and Practical Astronomy. Having arrived at home safely with these, I devoted every spare moment to their perusal, and soon made such proficiency in studies of this nature as

I thought sufficient for the execution of a certain design with which either the devil or my better genius had inspired me. In the intervals of this period I made every endeavour to conciliate the three creditors who had given me so much annoyance. In this I finally succeeded, partly by selling enough of my household furniture to satisfy a moiety of their claim, and partly by a promise of paying the balance upon completion of a little project which I told them I had in view, and for assistance in which I solicited their services. By these means (for they were ignorant men) I found little difficulty in gaining them over to my purpose.

Matters being thus arranged, I contrived, by the aid of my wife, and with the greatest secrecy and caution, to dispose of what property I had remaining, and to borrow in small sums, under various pretences, and without giving any attention, I am ashamed to say, to my future means of repayment, no inconsiderable quantity of ready money. With the means thus accruing I proceeded to procure, at intervals, cambric muslin, very fine, in pieces of twelve yards each ; twine ; a lot of varnish of caoutchouc ; a large and deep basket of wicker-work, made to order ; and several other articles necessary in the construction and equipment of a balloon of extraordinary dimensions. This I directed my wife to make up as soon as possible, and gave her all requisite information as to the particular method of proceeding. In the meantime I worked up the twine into network of sufficient dimensions, rigged it with a hoop and the necessary cords, and made purchase of numerous instruments and materials for experiment in the upper regions of the upper atmosphere. I then took opportunities of conveying by night, to a retired situation east of Rotterdam, five iron-bound casks, to contain about fifty gallons each, and one of a larger size ; six tin tubes, three inches in diameter, properly shaped, and ten feet in length ; a quantity of a *particular metallic substance, or semi-metal,* which I shall not name, and a dozen demijohns of *a very common acid.* The gas to be formed from these latter materials is a gas never yet generated by any other person than myself, or at least never applied to any similar purpose. I can only venture to say here, that it is *a constituent of azote,* so long considered irreducible, and that its density is about 37·4 times *less than that of hydrogen.* It is taste-

less, but not odourless ; burns, when pure, with a greenish
flame, and instantaneously fatal to animal life.   Its full
secret I would make no difficulty in disclosing, but that it
of right belongs, as I have before hinted, to a citizen of
Nantz, in France, by whom it was conditionally communicated to myself.   The same individual submitted to me,
without being at all aware of my intentions, a method of
constructing balloons from the membrane of a certain
animal, through which substance any escape of gas was
nearly an impossibility.   I found it, however, altogether
too expensive, and was not sure, upon the whole, whether
cambric muslin, with a coating of gum-caoutchouc, was not
equally as good.   I mention this circumstance, because I
think it probable that hereafter the individual in question
may attempt a balloon ascension with the novel gas and
material I have spoken of, and I do not wish to deprive
him of the honour of a very singular invention.

On the spot which I intended each of the smaller casks
to occupy respectively during the inflation of the balloon,
I privately dug a small hole ; the holes forming in this
manner a circle twenty-five feet in diameter.   In the centre
of this circle, being the station designed for the large cask,
I also dug a hole of greater depth.   In each of the five
smaller holes I deposited a canister containing fifty pounds,
and in the larger one a keg holding one hundred and fifty
pounds, of cannon-powder.   These—the keg and the
canisters—I connected in a proper manner with covered
trains ; and having let into one of the canisters the end of
about four feet of slow-match, I covered up the hole, and
placed the cask over it, leaving the other end of the match
protruding about an inch, and barely visible beyond the
cask.   I then filled up the remaining holes, and placed the
barrels over them in their destined situation.

Besides the articles above enumerated, I conveyed to the
dépôt, and there secreted, one of M. Grimm's improvements
upon the apparatus for condensation of the atmospheric air.
I found this machine, however, to require considerable
alteration before it could be adapted to the purposes to
which I intended making it applicable.   But, with severe
labour and unremitting perseverance, I at length met with
entire success in all my preparations.   My balloon was soon
completed.   It would contain more than forty thousand
cubic feet of gas ; would take me up easily, I calculated,

with all my implements, and, if I managed rightly, with one hundred and seventy-five pounds of ballast into the bargain. It had received three coats of varnish, and I found the cambric muslin to answer all the purposes of silk itself, being quite as strong and a good deal less expensive.

Everything being now ready, I exacted from my wife an oath of secrecy in relation to all my actions from the day of my first visit to the bookseller's stall ; and promising, on my part, to return as soon as circumstances would permit, I gave her what little money I had left, and bade her farewell. Indeed, I had no fear on her account. She was what people call a notable woman, and could manage matters in the world without my assistance. I believe, to tell the truth, she always looked upon me as an idle body—a mere make-weight, good for nothing but building castles in the air, and was rather glad to get rid of me. It was a dark night when I bade her good-bye, and taking with me, as *aides-de-camp*, the three creditors who had given me so much trouble, we carried the balloon, with the car and accoutrements, by a roundabout way, to the station where the other articles were deposited. We there found them all unmolested, and I proceeded immediately to business.

It was the first of April. The night, as I said before, was dark ; there was not a star to be seen ; and a drizzling rain, falling at intervals, rendered us very uncomfortable But my chief anxiety was concerning the balloon, which, in spite of the varnish with which it was defended, began to grow rather heavy with the moisture ; the powder also was liable to damage. I therefore kept my three duns working with great diligence, pounding down ice around the central cask, and stirring the acid in the others. They did not cease, however, importuning me with questions as to what I intended to do with all this apparatus, and expressed much dissatisfaction at the terrible labour I made them undergo. They could not perceive (so they said) what good was likely to result from their getting wet to the skin, merely to take a part in such horrible incantations. I began to get uneasy, and worked away with all my might ; for I verily believe the idiots supposed that I had entered into a compact with the devil, and that, in short, what I was now doing was nothing better than it should be. I was, therefore, in great fear of their leaving me altogether. I contrived, however, to pacify them by promises of payment of all scores in full, as soon as I could bring the present business to a termination. To these speeches they gave, of course, their own interpretation ; fancying, no doubt, that at all events I should come into possession of vast quantities of ready money ; and provided I paid them all I owed, and a trifle more, in consideration of their services, I dare say they cared very little what became of either my soul or my carcass.

In about four hours and a half I found the balloon sufficiently inflated. I attached the car, therefore, and put all my implements in it—a telescope ; a barometer, with some important modifications ; a thermometer ; an electrometer ; a compass ; a magnetic needle ; a seconds watch ; a bell ; a speaking-trumpet, etc., etc., etc., also a globe of glass, exhausted of air, and carefully closed with a stopper, not forgetting the condensing-apparatus, some unslacked lime, a stick of sealing-wax, a copious supply of water, and a large quantity of provisions, such as pemmican, in which much nutriment is contained in comparatively little bulk. I also secured in the car a pair of pigeons and a cat.

It was now nearly daybreak, and I thought it high time to take my departure. Dropping a lighted cigar on the ground, as if by accident, I took the opportunity, in stooping to pick it up, of igniting privately the piece of slow match, the end of which, as I said before, protruded a little beyond the lower rim of one of the smaller casks. This manœuvre was totally unperceived on the part of the three duns ; and, jumping into the car, I immediately cut the single cord which held me to the earth, and was pleased to find that I shot upwards with inconceivable rapidity, carrying with all ease one hundred and seventy-five pounds of leaden ballast, and able to have carried up as many more. As I left the earth, the barometer stood at thirty inches, and the centigrade thermometer at 19°.

Scarcely, however, had I attained the height of fifty yards, when, roaring and rumbling up after me in the most tumultuous and terrible manner, came so dense a hurricane of fire, and gravel, and burning wood, and blazing metal, and mangled limbs, that my very heart sunk within me, and I fell down in the bottom of the car, trembling with terror. Indeed, I now perceived that I had entirely overdone the business, and that the main consequences of the shock were yet to be experienced. Accordingly in less than a second, I felt all the blood in my body rushing to my temples, and, immediately thereupon, a concussion, which I shall never forget, burst abruptly through the night, and seemed to rip the very firmament asunder. When I afterwards had time for reflection, I did not fail to attribute the extreme violence of the explosion as regarded myself, to its proper cause—my situation directly above it, and in the line of its greatest power. But at the time, I thought only of preserving my life. The balloon at first collapsed, then furiously expanded, then whirled round and round with sickening velocity, and finally, reeling and staggering like a drunken man, hurled me over the rim of the car, and left me dangling, at a terrific height, with my head downward, and my face outward, by a piece of slender cord about three feet in length, which hung accidentally through a crevice near the bottom of the wicker-work, and in which, as I fell, my left foot became most providentially entangled. It is impossible—utterly impossible—to form any adequate idea of the horror of my situation. I gasped convulsively for breath—a shudder resembling a fit of the ague agitated every nerve and muscle in my frame—I felt my eyes starting from their sockets—a horrible nausea overwhelmed me—and at length I lost all consciousness in a swoon.

How long I remained in this state it is impossible to say. It must, however, have been no inconsiderable time, for when I partially recovered the sense of existence, I found the day breaking, the balloon at a prodigious height over a wilderness of ocean, and not a trace of land to be discovered far and wide within the limits of the vast horizon. My sensations, however, upon thus recovering, were by no means so replete with agony as might have been anticipated. Indeed, there was much of madness in the calm survey which I began to take of my situation. I drew up to my eyes each of my hands, one after the other, and wondered what occurrence could have given rise to the swelling of the veins, and the horrible blackness of the finger-nails. I afterwards carefully examined my head, shaking it repeatedly, and feeling it with minute attention, until I succeeded in satisfying myself that it was not, as I had more than half suspected, larger than my balloon. Then, in a knowing manner, I felt in both my breeches pockets,

and, missing therefrom a set of tablets and a toothpick
case, endeavoured to account for their disappearance, and,
not being able to do so, felt inexpressibly chagrined. It
now occurred to me that I suffered great uneasiness in the
joint of my left ankle, and a dim consciousness of my
situation began to glimmer through my mind. But,
strange to say, I was neither astonished nor horror-stricken.
If I felt any emotion at all, it was a kind of chuckling
satisfaction at the cleverness I was about to display in
extricating myself from this dilemma ; and never for a
moment did I look upon my ultimate safety as a question
susceptible of doubt. For a few minutes I remained
wrapped in the profoundest meditation. I have a distinct
recollection of frequently compressing my lips, putting my
forefinger to the side of my nose, and making use of other
gesticulations and grimaces common to men who, at ease
in their arm-chairs, meditate upon matters of intricacy or
importance. Having, as I thought, sufficiently collected
my ideas, I now, with great caution and deliberation, put
my hands behind my back, and unfastened the large iron
buckle which belonged to the waistband of my pantaloons.
This buckle had three teeth, which, being somewhat rusty,
turned with great difficulty on their axis. I brought
them, however, after some trouble, at right angles to the
body of the buckle, and was glad to find them remain
firm in that position. Holding within my teeth the
instrument thus obtained, I now proceeded to untie the
knot of my cravat. I had to rest several times before I
could accomplish this manœuvre ; but it was at length
accomplished. To one end of the cravat I then made fast
the buckle, and the other end I tied, for greater security,
tightly around my wrist. Drawing now my body upwards,
with a prodigious exertion of muscular force I succeeded,
at the very first trial, in throwing the buckle over the car,
and entangling it, as I had anticipated, in the circular rim
of the wicker-work.

My body was now inclined towards the side of the car,
at an angle of about forty-five degrees ; but it must not be
understood that I was therefore only forty-five degrees
below the perpendicular. So far from it, I still lay nearly
level with the plane of the horizon ; for the change of
situation which I had acquired had forced the bottom of
the car considerably outward from my position, which was

accordingly one of the most imminent peril. It should be remembered, however, that when I fell, in the first instance, from the car, if I had fallen with my face turned toward the balloon, instead of turned outwardly from it, as it actually was—or if, in the second place, the cord by which I was suspended had chanced to hang over the upper edge, instead of through a crevice near the bottom of the car—I say it may readily be conceived that, in either of these supposed cases, I should have been unable to accomplish even as much as I had now accomplished, and the disclosures now made would have been utterly lost to posterity. I had therefore every reason to be grateful ; although, in point of fact, I was still too stupid to be anything at all, and hung for perhaps a quarter of an hour in that extraordinary manner, without making the slightest farther exertion, and in a singularly tranquil state of idiotic enjoyment. But this feeling did not fail to die rapidly away, and thereunto succeeded horror, and dismay, and a sense of utter helplessness and ruin. In fact, the blood so long accumulating in the vessels of my head and throat, and which had hitherto buoyed up my spirits with delirium, had now begun to retire within their proper channels, and the distinctness which was thus added to my perception of the danger merely served to deprive me of the self-possession and the courage to encounter it. But this weakness was, luckily for me, of no very long duration. In good time came to my rescue the spirit of despair, and, with frantic cries and struggles, I jerked my way bodily upwards, till, at length, clutching with a vice-like grip the long-desired rim, I writhed my person over it, and fell headlong and shuddering within the car.

It was not until some time afterward that I recovered myself sufficiently to attend to the ordinary cares of the balloon. I then, however, examined it with attention, and found it, to my great relief, uninjured. My implements were all safe, and, fortunately, I had lost neither ballast nor provisions. Indeed, I had so well secured them in their places, that such an accident was entirely out of the question. Looking at my watch, I found it six o'clock. I was still rapidly ascending, and the barometer gave a present altitude of three and three-quarter miles. Immediately beneath me in the ocean lay a small black object, slightly oblong in shape, seemingly about the size of a

domino, and in every respect bearing a great resemblance
to one of those toys. Bringing my telescope to bear upon
it, I plainly discerned it to be a British ninety-four gun
ship, close-hauled, and pitching heavily in the sea with
her head to the W.S.W. Besides this ship, I saw nothing
but the ocean and the sky, and the sun, which had long
risen.

It is now high time that I should explain to your Excellencies the object of my voyage. Your Excellencies will
bear in mind that distressed circumstances in Rotterdam
had at length driven me to the resolution of committing
suicide. It was not, however, that to life itself I had any
positive disgust, but that I was harassed beyond endurance
by the adventitious miseries attending my situation. In
this state of mind, wishing to live, yet wearied with life, the
treatise at the stall of the bookseller, backed by the oppor-
tune discovery of my cousin of Nantz, opened a resource to
my imagination. I then finally made up my mind. I
determined to depart, yet live—to leave the world, yet
continue to exist—in short, to drop enigmas, I resolved, let
what would ensue, to force a passage, if I could, *to the moon.*
Now, lest I should be supposed more of a madman than I
actually am, I will detail, as well as I am able, the considerations which led me to believe that an achievement of
this nature, although without doubt difficult and full of
danger, was not absolutely, to a bold spirit, beyond the
confines of the possible.

The moon's actual distance from the earth was the first
thing to be attended to. Now, the mean or average
interval between the *centres* of the two planets is 59·9643
of the earth's equatorial *radii*, or only about 237,000 miles.
I say the mean or average interval ; but it must be borne
in mind, that the form of the moon's orbit being an ellipse
of eccentricity amounting to no less than 0·05484 of the
major semi-axis of the ellipse itself, and the earth's centre
being situated in its focus, if I could, in any manner,
contrive to meet the moon in its perigee, the above-men-
tioned distance would be materially diminished. But to
say nothing at present of this possibility, it wás very
certain that, at all events, from the 237,000 miles I would
have to deduct the *radius* of the earth, say 4000, and the
radius of the moon, say 1080, in all 5080, leaving an actual
interval to be traversed, under average circumstances, of

231,920 miles. Now this, I reflected, was no very extra-ordinary distance. Travelling on the land has been repeatedly accomplished at the rate of sixty miles per hour, and, indeed, a much greater speed may be antici-pated ; but even at this velocity, it would take me no more than 161 days to reach the surface of the moon. There were, however, many particulars inducing me to believe that my average rate of travelling might possibly very much exceed that of sixty miles per hour ; and as these considerations did not fail to make a deep impression upon my mind, I will mention them more fully hereafter.

The next point to be regarded was one of far greater importance. From indications afforded by the barometer, we find that, in ascensions from the surface of the earth, we have, at the height of 1000 feet, left below us about one-thirtieth of the entire mass of atmospheric air ; that at 10,600, we have ascended through nearly one-third ; and that at 18,000, which is not far from the elevation of Cotopaxi, we have surmounted one-half the material, or, at all events, one-half the *ponderable* body of air incumbent upon our globe. It is also calculated that at an altitude not exceeding the hundredth part of the earth's diameter— that is, not exceeding eighty miles—the rarefaction would be so excessive that animal life could in no manner be sustained, and, moreover, that the most delicate means we possess of ascertaining the presence of the atmosphere would be inadequate to assure us of its existence. But I did not fail to perceive that these latter calculations are founded altogether on our experimental knowledge of the properties of air, and the mechanical laws regulating its dilation and compression, in what may be called, com-paratively speaking, *the immediate vicinity* of the earth itself ; and, at the same time, it is taken for granted that animal life is and must be essentially *incapable of modifica-tion* at any given unattainable distance from the surface. Now, all such reasoning and from such *data*, must of course be simply analogical. The greatest height ever reached by man was that of 25,000 feet, attained in the aëronautic expedition of Messieurs Gay-Lussac and Biot. This is a moderate altitude, even when compared with the eighty miles in question ; and I could not help thinking that the subject admitted room for doubt and great latitude for speculation.

But, in point of fact, an ascension being made to any given altitude, the ponderable quantity of air surmounted in any *farther* ascension is by no means in proportion to the additional height ascended, as may be plainly seen from what has been stated before, but in a *ratio* constantly decreasing. It is therefore evident that, ascend as high as we may, we cannot, literally speaking, arrive at a limit beyond which *no* atmosphere is to be found. It *must exist*, I argued ; although it *may* exist in a state of infinite rarefaction.

On the other hand, I was aware that arguments have not been wanting to prove the existence of a real and definite limit to the atmosphere, beyond which there is absolutely no air whatsoever. But a circumstance which has been left out of view by those who contend for such a limit, seemed to me, although no positive refutation of their creed, still a point worthy very serious investigation. On comparing the intervals between the successive arrivals of Encke's comet at its perihelion, after giving credit, in the most exact manner, for all the disturbances due to the attractions of the planets, it appears that the periods are gradually diminishing ; that is to say, the major axis of the comet's ellipse is growing shorter, in a slow but perfectly regular decrease. Now, this is precisely what ought to be the case, if we suppose a resistance experienced from the comet from an extremely *rare ethereal medium* pervading the regions of its orbit. For it is evident that such a medium must, in retarding the comet's velocity, increase its centripetal, by weakening its centrifugal force. In other words, the sun's attraction would be constantly attaining greater power, and the comet would be drawn nearer at every revolution. Indeed, there is no other way of accounting for the variation in question. But again : The real diameter of the same comet's nebulosity is observed to contract rapidly as it approaches the sun, and dilate with equal rapidity in its departure towards its aphelion. Was I not justifiable in supposing, with M. Valz, that this apparent condensation of volume has its origin in the compression of the same ethereal medium I have spoken of before, and which is dense in proportion to its vicinity to the sun ? The lenticular-shaped phenomenon, also, called the zodiacal light, was a matter worthy of attention. This radiance, so apparent in the tropics, and which cannot be mistaken for any meteoric lustre, extends from the horizon obliquely upwards, and follows generally the direction of the sun's equator. It appeared to me evidently in the nature of a rare atmosphere extending from the sun outwards, beyond the orbit of Venus at least, and I believed indefinitely further.* Indeed, this medium I could not suppose confined to the path of the comet's ellipse, or to the immediate neighbourhood of the sun. It was easy, on the contrary, to imagine it pervading the entire regions of our planetary system, condensed into what we call atmosphere at the planets themselves, and perhaps at some of them modified by considerations purely geological ; that is to say, modified or varied in its proportions (or absolute nature) by matters volatilised from the respective orbs.

Having adopted this view of the subject, I had little farther hesitation. Granting that on my passage I should meet with atmosphere *essentially* the same as at the surface of the earth, I conceived that, by means of the very ingenious apparatus of M. Grimm, I should readily be enabled to condense it in sufficient quantity for the purposes of respiration. This would remove the chief obstacle in a journey to the moon. I had, indeed, spent some money and great labour in adapting the apparatus to the object intended, and confidently looked forward to its successful application, if I could manage to complete the voyage within any reasonable period. This brings me back to the *rate* at which it would be possible to travel.

It is true that balloons, in the first stage of their ascensions from the earth, are known to rise with a velocity comparatively moderate. Now, the power of elevation lies altogether in the superior gravity of the atmospheric air compared with the gas in the balloon ; and, at first sight, it does not appear probable that, as the balloon acquires altitude, and consequently arrives successively in atmospheric *strata* of densities rapidly diminishing—I say, it does not appear at all reasonable that, in this its progress upward, the original velocity should be accelerated. On the other hand, I was not aware that, in any recorded ascension, a *diminution* had been proved to be apparent in the absolute rate of ascent ; although such should have

---

* The zodiacal light is probably what the ancients called *Trabes*. *Emicant Trabes quos docos vocant.* Pliny, lib. 2, p. 26.

been the case, if on account of nothing else, on account of
the escape of gas through balloons ill constructed, and
varnished with no better material than the ordinary
varnish. It seemed, therefore, that the effect of such
escape was only sufficient to counterbalance the effect of
the acceleration attained in the diminishing of the balloon's
distance from the gravitating centre. I now considered
that, provided in my passage I found the *medium* I had
imagined, and provided it should prove to be *essentially*
what we denominate atmospheric air, it could make comparatively little difference at what extreme state of rarefaction I should discover it—that is to say, in regard to
my power of ascending ; for thé gas in the balloon would
not only be itself subject to similar rarefaction (in proportion
to the occurrence of which, I could suffer an escape of so
much as would be requisite to prevent explosion), but,
being what it was, would, at all events, continue specifically
lighter that any compound whatever of mere nitrogen and
oxygen. Thus there was a chance—in fact, there was a
strong probability—that, *at no epoch of my ascent, I should
reach a point where the united weights of my immense balloon,
the inconceivably rare gas within it, the car, and its contents,
should equal the weight of the mass of the surrounding atmosphere displaced ;* and this will be readily understood
as the sole condition upon which my upward flight would
be arrested. But, if this point were even attained, I could
dispense with ballast and other weight to the amount of
nearly 300 pounds. In the meantime, the force of gravitation would be constantly diminishing in proportion to the
squares of the distances, and so, with a velocity prodigiously
accelerating, I should at length arrive in those distant
regions where the force of the earth's attraction would be
superseded by that of the moon.

There was another difficulty, however, which occasioned
me some little disquietude. It has been observed, that, in
balloon ascensions to any considerable height, besides the
pain attending respiration, great uneasiness is experienced
about the head and body, often accompanied with bleeding at the nose, and other symptoms of an alarming
kind, and growing more and more inconvenient in proportion to the altitude attained.* This was a reflection

* Since the original publication of " Hans Pfaall," I find that Mr.
Green, of Nassau balloon notoriety, and other late aëronauts, deny

of a nature somewhat startling. Was it not probable that these symptoms would increase until terminated by death itself ? I finally thought not. Their origin was to be looked for in the progressive removal of the *customary* atmospheric pressure upon the surface of the body, and consequent distension of the superficial blood-vessels—not in any positive disorganisation of the animal system, as in the case of difficulty in breathing, where the atmospheric density is *chemically insufficient* for the due renovation of blood in a ventricle of the heart. Unless for default of this renovation, I could see no reason, therefore, why life could not be sustained even in a *vacuum* ; for the expansion and compression of chest, commonly called breathing, is action purely muscular, and the *cause*, not the *effect*, of respiration. In a word, I conceived that, as the body should become habituated to the want of atmospheric pressure, these sensations of pain would gradually diminish ; and to endure them while they continued, I relied with confidence upon the iron hardihood of my constitution.

Thus, may it please your Excellencies, I have detailed some, though by no means all, the considerations which led me to form the project of a lunar voyage. I shall now proceed to lay before you the result of an attempt so apparently audacious in conception, and, at all events, so utterly unparalleled in the annals of mankind.

Having attained the altitude before mentioned—that is to say, three miles and three quarters—I threw out from the car a quantity of feathers, and found that I still ascended with sufficient rapidity ; there was, therefore, no necessity for discharging any ballast. I was glad of this, for I wished to retain with me as much weight as I could carry, for the obvious reason that I could not be *positive* either about the gravitation or the atmospheric density of the moon. I as yet suffered no bodily inconvenience, breathing with great freedom, and feeling no pain whatever in the head. The cat was lying very demurely upon my coat, which I had taken off, and eyeing the pigeons with an air of *nonchalance.* These latter being tied by the leg, to prevent their escape, were busily employed in picking up

the assertions of Humboldt, in this respect, and speak of a *decreasing* inconvenience,—precisely in accordance with the theory here urged.

some grains of rice scattered for them in the bottom of the car.

At twenty minutes past six o'clock, the barometer showed an elevation of 26,400 feet, or five miles to a fraction. The prospect seemed unbounded. Indeed, it is very easily calculated, by means of spherical geometry, how great an extent of the earth's area I beheld. The convex surface of any segment of a sphere is, to the entire surface of the sphere itself, as the versed sine of the segment to the diameter of the sphere. Now, in my case, the versed sine—that is to say, the *thickness* of the segment beneath me—was about equal to my elevation, or the elevation of the point of sight above the surface. " As five miles, then, to eight thousand," would express the proportion of the earth's area seen by me. In other words, I beheld as much as a sixteen-hundredth part of the whole surface of the globe. The sea appeared unruffled as a mirror, although, by means of the telescope, I could perceive it to be in a state of violent agitation. The ship was no longer visible, having drifted away, apparently, to the eastward. I now began to experience, at intervals, severe pain in the head, especially about the ears—still, however, breathing with tolerable freedom. The cat and pigeons seemed to suffer no inconvenience whatever.

At twenty minutes before seven, the balloon entered a long series of dense cloud, which put me to great trouble, by damaging my condensing-apparatus, and wetting me to the skin. This was, to be sure, a singular *rencontre*, for I had not believed it possible that a cloud of this nature could be sustained at so great an elevation. I thought it best, however, to throw out two five-pound pieces of ballast, reserving still a weight of one hundred and sixty-five pounds. Upon so doing I soon rose above the difficulty, and perceived immediately that I had obtained a great increase in my rate of ascent. In a few seconds after my leaving the cloud, a flash of vivid lightning shot from one end of it to the other, and caused it to kindle up, throughout its vast extent, like a mass of ignited charcoal. This, it must be remembered, was in the broad light of day. No fancy may picture the sublimity which might have been exhibited by a similar phenomenon taking place amid the darkness of the night. Hell itself might then have found a fitting image. Even as it was, my hair stood on end, while

I gazed afar down within the yawning abysses, letting imagination descend, and stalk about in the strange vaulted halls, and ruddy gulfs, and red ghastly chasms of the hideous and unfathomable fire. I had indeed made a narrow escape. Had the balloon remained a very short time longer within the cloud—that is to say, had not the inconvenience of getting wet determined me to discharge the ballast—my destruction might, and probably would, have been the consequence. Such perils, although little considered, are perhaps the greatest which must be encountered in balloons. I had by this time, however, attained too great an elevation to be any longer uneasy on this head.

I was now rising rapidly, and by seven o'clock the barometer indicated an altitude of no less than nine miles and a half. I began to find great difficulty in drawing my breath. My head, too, was excessively painful; and, having felt for some time a moisture about my cheeks, I at length discovered it to be blood, which was oozing quite fast from the drums of my ears. My eyes, also, gave me great uneasiness. Upon passing the hand over them they seemed to have protruded from their sockets in no inconsiderable degree; and all objects in the car, and even the balloon itself, appeared distorted to my vision. These symptoms were more than I had expected, and occasioned me some alarm. At this juncture, very imprudently, and without consideration, I threw out from the car three five-pound pieces of ballast. The accelerated rate of ascent thus obtained carried me too rapidly, and without sufficient gradation, into a highly rarefied *stratum* of the atmosphere, and the result had nearly proved fatal to my expedition and to myself. I was suddenly seized with a spasm which lasted for more than five minutes, and even when this, in a measure, ceased, I could catch my breath only at long intervals, and in a gasping manner—bleeding all the while copiously at the nose and ears, and even slightly at the eyes. The pigeons, appearing distressed in the extreme, struggled to escape, while the cat mewed piteously, and, with her tongue hanging out of her mouth, staggered to and fro in the car as if under the influence of poison. I now too late discovered the great rashness of which I had been guilty in discharging the ballast, and my agitation was excessive. I anticipated nothing less than death,

and death in a few minutes. The physical suffering I
underwent contributed also to render me nearly incapable
of making any exertion for the preservation of my life.
I had, indeed, little power of reflection left, and the violence
of the pain in my head seemed to be greatly on the increase.
Thus I found that my senses would shortly give way
altogether, and I had already clutched one of the valve-
ropes with the view of attempting a descent, when the
recollection of the trick I had played the three creditors,
and the possible consequences to myself should I return,
operated to deter me for the moment. I lay down in the
bottom of the car, and endeavoured to collect my faculties.
In this I so far succeeded as to determine upon the experiment of losing blood. Having no lancet, however, I was
constrained to perform the operation in the best manner
I was able, and finally succeeded in opening a vein in my
left arm, with the blade of my penknife. The blood had
hardly commenced flowing when I experienced a sensible
relief, and by the time I had lost about half a moderate
basin-full, most of the worst symptoms had abandoned me
entirely. I nevertheless did not think it expedient to
attempt getting on my feet immediately ; but, having tied
up my arm as well as I could, I lay still for about a quarter
of an hour. At the end of this time I arose, and found
myself freer from absolute *pain* of any kind than I had been
during the last hour and a quarter of my ascension. The
difficulty of breathing, however, was diminished in a very
slight degree, and I found that it would soon be positively
necessary to make use of my condenser. In the meantime, looking towards the cat, who was again snugly stowed
away upon my coat, I discovered, to my infinite surprise,
that she had taken the opportunity of my indisposition to
bring into light a litter of three little kittens. This was
an addition to the number of passengers on my part altogether unexpected; but I was pleased at the occurrence.
It would afford me a chance of bringing to a kind of test
the truth of a surmise which more than anything else
had influenced me in attempting this ascension. I had
imagined that the *habitual* endurance of the atmospheric
pressure at the surface of the earth was the cause, or
nearly so, of the pain attending animal existence at a
distance above the surface. Should the kittens be found
to suffer uneasiness *in an equal degree with their mother,*

I must consider my theory in fault, but a failure to do so I should look upon as a strong confirmation of my idea.

By eight o'clock I had actually attained an elevation of seventeen miles above the surface of the earth. Thus it seemed to me evident that my rate of ascent was not only on the increase, but that the progression would have been apparent in a slight degree even had I not discharged the ballast which I did. The pains in my head and ears returned at intervals with violence, and I still continued to bleed occasionally at the nose ; but, upon the whole, I suffered much less than might have been expected. I breathed, however, at every moment with more and more difficulty, and each inhalation was attended with a troublesome spasmodic action of the chest. I now unpacked the condensing-apparatus, and got it ready for immediate use.

The view of the earth, at this period of my ascension, was beautiful indeed. To the westward, the northward, and the southward, as far as I could see, lay a boundless sheet of apparently unruffled ocean, which every moment gained a deeper and deeper tint of blue. At a vast distance to the eastward, although perfectly discernible, extended the islands of Great Britain, the entire Atlantic coasts of France and Spain, with a small portion of the northern part of the continent of Africa. Of individual edifices not a trace could be discovered, and the proudest cities of mankind had utterly faded away from the face of the earth.

What mainly astonished me, in the appearance of things below, was the seeming concavity of the surface of the globe. I had, thoughtlessly enough, expected to see its real *convexity* become evident as I ascended ; but a very little reflection sufficed to explain the discrepancy. A line, dropped from my position perpendicularly to the earth, would have formed the perpendicular of a right-angled triangle, of which the base would have extended from the right-angle to the horizon, and the hypothenuse from the horizon to my position. But my height was little or nothing in comparison with my prospect. In other words, the base and hypothenuse of the supposed triangle would, in my case, have been so long, when compared to the perpendicular, that the two former might have been regarded as nearly parallel. In this manner the horizon of the aëronaut appears always to be *upon a level* with the car. But as the point immediately beneath him seems, and is,

at a great distance below him, it seems, of course, also at a
great distance below the horizon.   Hence the impression
of concavity ; and this impression must remain until the
elevation shall bear so great a proportion to the prospect
that the apparent parallelism of the base and hypothenuse
disappears.

The pigeons about this time seeming to undergo much
suffering, I determined upon giving them their liberty.   I
first untied one of them, a beautiful grey-mottled pigeon,
and placed him upon the rim of the wicker-work.   He
appeared extremely uneasy, looking anxiously around him,
fluttering his wings, and making a loud cooing noise, but
could not be persuaded to trust himself from the car.   I
took him up at last, and threw him to about half-a-dozen
yards from the balloon.   He made, however, no attempt
to descend, as I had expected, but struggled with great
vehemence to get back, uttering at the same time very
shrill and piercing cries.   He at length succeeded in regaining his former station on the rim, but had hardly done so
when his head dropped upon his breast, and he fell dead
within the car.   The other one did not prove so unfortunate.
To prevent his following the example of his companion, and
accomplishing a return, I threw him downwards with all
my force, and was pleased to find him continue his descent
with great velocity, making use of his wings with ease, and
in a perfectly natural manner.   In a very short time he
was out of sight, and I have no doubt he reached home
in safety.   Puss, who seemed in a great measure recovered
from her illness, now made a hearty meal of the dead bird,
and then went to sleep with much apparent satisfaction.
Her kittens were quite lively, and so far evinced not the
slightest sign of any uneasiness.

At a quarter past eight, being able no longer to draw
breath without the most intolerable pain, I proceeded
forthwith to adjust around the car the apparatus belonging
to the condenser.   This apparatus will require some little
explanation, and your Excellencies will please to bear in
mind that my object, in the first place, was to surround
myself and car entirely with a barricade against the highly-
rarefied atmosphere in which I was existing, with the intention of introducing within this barricade, by means of
my condenser, a quantity of this same atmosphere sufficiently condensed for the purpose of respiration.   With

this object in view, I had prepared a very strong, perfectly air-tight, but flexible gum-elastic bag. In this bag, which was of sufficient dimensions, the entire car was in a manner placed. That is to say, it (the bag) was drawn over the whole bottom of the car, up its sides, and so on, along the outside of the ropes, to the upper rim, or hoop, where the net-work is attached. Having pulled the bag up in this way, and formed a complete enclosure on all sides, and at bottom, it was now necessary to fasten up its top, or mouth, by passing its material over the hoop of the net-work—in other words, between the net-work and the hoop. But if the net-work were separated from the hoop to admit this passage, what was to sustain the car in the meantime ? Now, the net-work was not permanently fastened to the hoop, but attached by a series of running loops or nooses. I therefore undid only a few of these loops at one time, leaving the car suspended by the remainder. Having thus inserted a portion of the cloth forming the upper part of the bag, I re-fastened the loops—not to the hoop, for that would have been impossible, since the cloth now intervened—but to a series of large buttons, affixed to the cloth itself, about three feet below the mouth of the bag ; the intervals between the buttons having been made to correspond to the intervals between the loops. This done, a few more of the loops were unfastened from the rim, a farther portion of the cloth introduced, and the disengaged loops then connected with their proper buttons. In this way it was possible to insert the whole upper part of the bag between the net-work and the hoop. It is evident that the hoop would now drop down within the car, while the whole weight of the car itself, with all its contents, would be held up merely by the strength of the buttons. This, at first sight, would seem an inadequate dependence ; but it was by no means so, for the buttons were not only very strong in themselves, but so close together that a very slight portion of the whole weight was supported by any one of them. Indeed, had the car and contents been three times heavier than they were, I should not have been at all uneasy. I now raised up the hoop again within the covering of gum-elastic, and propped it at nearly its former height by means of three light poles prepared for the occasion. This was done, of course, to keep the bag distended at the top, and to pre-serve the lower part of the net-work in its proper situation.

All that now remained was to fasten up the mouth of the enclosure; and this was readily accomplished by gathering the folds of the material together, and twisting them up very tightly on the inside by means of a kind of stationary *tourniquet*.

In the sides of the covering thus adjusted round the car had been inserted three circular panes of thick but clear glass, through which I could see without difficulty around me in every horizontal direction. In that portion of the cloth forming the bottom was likewise a fourth window of the same kind, and corresponding with a small aperture in the floor of the car itself. This enabled me to see perpendicularly down, but having found it impossible to place any similar contrivance overhead, on account of the peculiar manner of closing up the opening there, and the consequent wrinkles in the cloth, I could expect to see no objects situated directly in my zenith. This, of course, was a matter of little consequence ; for, had I even been able to place a window at top, the balloon itself would have prevented my making any use of it.

About a foot below one of the side windows was a circular opening three inches in diameter, and fitted with a brass rim adapted in its inner edge to the windings of a screw. In this rim was screwed the large tube of the condenser, the body of the machine being, of course, within the chamber of gum-elastic. Through this tube a quantity of the rare atmosphere circumjacent being drawn by means of a *vacuum* created in the body of the machine, was thence discharged, in a state of condensation, to mingle with the thin air already in the chamber. This operation, being repeated several times, at length filled the chamber with atmosphere proper for all the purposes of respiration. But, in so confined a space, it would in a short time necessarily become foul and unfit for use from frequent contact with the lungs. It was then ejected by a small valve at the bottom of the car, the dense air readily sinking into the thinner atmosphere below. To avoid the inconvenience of making a total *vacuum* at any moment within the car, this purification was never accomplished all at once, but in a gradual manner ; the valve being opened only for a few seconds, then closed again, until one or two strokes from the pump of the condenser had supplied the place of the atmosphere ejected. For the sake of experiment I had put

the cat and kittens in a small basket, and suspended it outside the car to a button at the bottom, close to the valve,
through which I could feed them at any moment when
necessary. I did this at some little risk, and before closing
the mouth of the chamber, by reaching under the car with
one of the poles before mentioned, to which a hook had
been attached. As soon as dense air was admitted in the
chamber, the hoop and poles became unnecessary ; the
expansion of the enclosed atmosphere powerfully distending
the gum-elastic.

By the time I had fully completed these arrangements,
and filled the chamber as explained, it wanted only ten
minutes of nine o'clock. During the whole period of my
being thus employed, I endured the most terrible distress
from difficulty of respiration ; and bitterly did I repent the
negligence, or rather foolhardiness, of which I had been
guilty, in putting off to the last moment a matter of so
much importance. But, having at length accomplished it,
I soon began to reap the benefit of my invention. Once
again I breathed with perfect freedom and ease ; and,
indeed, why should I not ? I was also agreeably surprised
to find myself in a great measure relieved from the violent
pains which had hitherto tormented me. A slight headache, accompanied with a sensation of fulness or distension
about the wrists, the ankles, and the throat, was nearly all
of which I had now to complain. Thus it seemed evident
that a greater part of the uneasiness attending the removal
of atmospheric pressure had actually worn off, as I had expected, and that much of the pain endured for the last two
hours should have been attributed altogether to the effects
of a deficient respiration.

At twenty minutes before nine o'clock—that is to say, a
short time prior to my closing up the mouth of the chamber
—the mercury attained its limit, or ran down in the barometer, which, as I mentioned before, was one of an extended
construction. It then indicated an altitude on my part
of 132,000 feet, or five-and-twenty miles ; and I consequently surveyed at that time an extent of the earth's
area amounting to no less than the three-hundred-and-
twentieth part of its entire superficies. At nine o'clock I
had again lost sight of land to the eastward, but not before
I became aware that the balloon was drifting rapidly to the
N.N.W. The ocean beneath me still retained its apparent

concavity, although my view was often interrupted by the
masses of cloud which floated to and fro.

At half-past nine I tried the experiment of throwing out
a handful of feathers through the valve. They did not float
as I had expected ; but dropped down perpendicularly,
like a bullet, *en masse*, and with the greatest velocity—being
out of sight in a very few seconds. I did not at first know
what to make of this extraordinary phenomenon ; not
being able to believe that my rate of ascent had, of a sudden,
met with so prodigious an acceleration. But it soon occurred to me that the atmosphere was now far too rare to
sustain even the feathers ; that they actually fell, as they
appeared to do, with great rapidity ; and that I had been
surprised by the united velocities of their descent and my
own elevation.

By ten o'clock I found that I had very little to occupy
my immediate attention. Affairs went on swimmingly,
and I believed the balloon to be going upwards with a speed
increasing momently, although I had no longer any means
of ascertaining the progression of the increase. I suffered
no pain or uneasiness of any kind, and enjoyed better spirits
than I had at any period since my departure from Rotterdam ; busying myself now in examining the state of my
various apparatus, and now in regenerating the atmosphere
within the chamber. This latter point I determined to
attend to àt regular intervals of forty minutes, more on
account of the preservation of my health than from so
frequent a renovation being absolutely necessary. In the
meanwhile I could not help making anticipations. Fancy
revelled in the wild and dreamy regions of the moon.
Imagination, feeling herself for once unshackled, roamed
at will among the ever-changing wonders of a shadowy
and unstable land. Now there were hoary and time-
honoured forests, and craggy precipices, and waterfalls
tumbling with a loud noise into abysses without a bottom.
Then I came suddenly into still noonday solitudes, where
no wind of heaven ever intruded, and where vast meadows
of poppies, and slender, lily-looking flowers spread themselves out a weary distance, all silent and motionless for
ever. Then again I journeyed far down away into another
country where it was all one dim and vague lake, with a
boundary-line of clouds. But fancies such as these were
not the sole possessors of my brain. Horrors of a nature

most stern and most appalling would too frequently obtrude
themselves upon my mind, and shake the innermost depths
of my soul with the bare supposition of their possibility.
Yet I would not suffer my thoughts for any length of time
to dwell upon these latter speculations, rightly judging the
real and palpable dangers of the voyage sufficient for my
undivided attention.

At five o'clock P.M., being engaged in regenerating the
atmosphere within the chamber, I took that opportunity of
observing the cat and kittens through the valve. The
cat herself appeared to suffer again very much, and I had
no hesitation in attributing her uneasiness chiefly to a
difficulty in breathing ; but my experiment with the
kittens had resulted very strangely. I had expected,
of course, to see them betray a sense of pain, although in
a less degree than their mother ; and this would have
been sufficient to confirm my opinion concerning the
habitual endurance of atmospheric pressure. But I was
not prepared to find them, upon close examination, evidently enjoying a high degree of health, breathing with
the greatest ease and perfect regularity, and evincing
not the slightest sign of any uneasiness. I could only
account for all this by extending my theory, and supposing
that the highly rarefied atmosphere around, might perhaps
not be, as I had taken for granted, chemically insufficient
for the purposes of life, and that a person born in such
a *medium* might, possibly, be unaware of any inconvenience
attending its inhalation, while, upon removal to the
denser *strata* near the earth, he might endure tortures of
a similar nature to those I had so lately experienced. It
has since been to me a matter of deep regret that an
awkward accident, at this time, occasioned me the loss of
my little family of cats, and deprived me of the insight
into this matter which a continued experiment might have
afforded. In passing my hand through the valve, with a
cup of water for the old puss, the sleeve of my shirt became
entangled in the loop which sustained the basket, and
thus, in a moment, loosened it from the bottom. Had
the whole actually vanished into air, it could not have shot
from my sight in a more abrupt and instantaneous manner.
Positively, there could not have intervened the tenth part
of a second between the disengagement of the basket and
its absolute disappearance with all that it contained. My

good wishes followed it to the earth, but, of course, I had
no hope that either cat or kittens would live to tell the
tale.

At six o'clock I perceived a great portion of the earth's
visible area to the eastward involved in thick shadow, which
continued to advance with great rapidity, until, at five
minutes before seven, the whole surface in view was
enveloped in the darkness of night. It was not, however,
until long after this time that the rays of the setting sun
ceased to illumine the balloon ; and this circumstance,
although of course fully anticipated, did not fail to give
me an infinite deal of pleasure. It was evident that, in
the morning, I should behold the rising luminary many
hours at least before the citizens of Rotterdam, in spite
of their situation so much farther to the eastward, and
thus, day after day, in proportion to the height ascended,
would I enjoy the light of the sun for a longer and a longer
period. I now determined to keep a journal of my passage,
reckoning the days from one to twenty-four hours continuously, without taking into consideration the intervals
of darkness.

At ten o'clock, feeling sleepy, I determined to lie down
for the rest of the night; but here a difficulty presented
itself which, obvious as it may appear, had escaped my
attention up to the very moment of which I am now
speaking. If I went to sleep as I proposed, how could the
atmosphere in the chamber be regenerated in the *interim* ?
To breathe it for more than an hour, at the farthest, would
be a matter of impossibility ; or, even if this term could
be extended to an hour and a quarter, the most ruinous
consequences might ensue. The consideration of this
dilemma gave me no little disquietude ; and it will hardly
be believed that, after the dangers I had undergone, I
should look upon this business in so serious a light as to
give up all hope of accomplishing my ultimate design, and
finally make up my mind to the necessity of a descent ; but
this hesitation was only momentary. I reflected that man
is the veriest slave of custom, and that many points in the
routine of his existence are deemed *essentially* important
which are only so *at all* by his having rendered them habitual.
It was very certain that I could not do without sleep ; but
I might easily bring myself to feel no inconvenience from
being awakened at intervals of an hour during the whole

period of my repose. It would require but five minutes at most to regenerate the atmosphere in the fullest manner ; and the only real difficulty was to contrive a method of arousing myself at the proper moment for so doing. But this was a question which, I am willing to confess, occasioned me no little trouble in its solution. To be sure, I had heard of a student who, to prevent his falling asleep over his books, held in one hand a ball of copper, the din of whose descent into a basin of the same metal on the floor beside his chair served effectually to startle him up, if at any moment he should be overcome with drowsiness. My own case, however, was very different indeed, and left me no room for any similar idea ; for I did not wish to keep awake, but to be aroused from slumber at regular intervals of time. I at length hit upon the following expedient, which, simple as it may seem, was hailed by me, at the moment of discovery, as an invention fully equal to that of the telescope, the steam-engine, or the art of printing itself.

It is necessary to premise that the balloon, at the elevation now attained, continued its course upwards with an even and undeviating ascent, and the car consequently followed with a steadiness so perfect that it would have been impossible to detect in it the slightest vacillation. This circumstance favoured me greatly in the project I now determined to adopt. My supply of water had been put on board in kegs containing five gallons each, and ranged very securely around the interior of the car. I unfastened one of these, and taking two ropes, tied them tightly across the rim of the wicker-work from one side to the other, placing them about a foot apart and parallel, so as to form a kind of shelf, upon which I placed the keg, and steadied it in a horizontal position. About eight inches immediately below these ropes, and four feet from the bottom of the car, I fastened another shelf, but made of thin plank, being the only similar piece of wood I had. Upon this latter shelf, and exactly beneath one of the rims of the keg, a small earthen pitcher was deposited. I now bored a hole in the end of the keg over the pitcher, and fitted in a plug of soft wood, cut in a tapering or conical shape. This plug I pushed in or pulled out, as might happen, until, after a few experiments, it arrived at that exact degree of tightness at which the water, oozing

from the hole, and falling into the pitcher below, would fill
the latter to the brim in the period of sixty minutes. This,
of course, was a matter briefly and easily ascertained,
by noticing the proportion of the pitcher filled in any given
time. Having arranged all this, the rest of the plan is
obvious. My bed was so contrived upon the floor of
the car as to bring my head, in lying down, immediately
below the mouth of the pitcher. It was evident that, at
the expiration of an hour, the pitcher, getting full, would
be forced to run over, and to run over at the mouth, which
was somewhat lower than the rim. It was also evident
that the water, thus falling from a height of more than
four feet, could not do otherwise than fall upon my face, and
that the sure consequence would be to waken me up instantaneously, even from the soundest slumber in the world.

It was fully eleven by the time I had completed these
arrangements, and I immediately betook myself to bed,
with full confidence in the efficiency of my invention. Nor
in this matter was I disappointed. Punctually every
sixty minutes was I aroused by my trusty chronometer,
when, having emptied the pitcher into the bung-hole of
the keg, and performed the duties of the condenser, I
retired again to bed. These regular interruptions to my
slumber caused me even less discomfort than I had anticipated ; and when I finally arose for the day, it was seven
o'clock, and the sun had already attained many degrees
above the line of my horizon.

April 3rd.—I found the balloon at an immense height
indeed, and the earth's convexity had now become strikingly
manifest. Below me in the ocean lay a cluster of black
specks, which undoubtedly were islands. Overhead, the
sky was of a jetty black, and the stars were brilliantly
visible ; indeed, they had been so constantly since the
first day of ascent. Far away to the northward I perceived
a thin, white, and exceedingly brilliant line, or streak, on
the edge of the horizon, and I had no hesitation in supposing
it to be the southern disc of the ices of the Polar sea. My
curiosity was greatly excited, for I had hopes of passing on
much farther to the north, and might possibly, at some
period, find myself placed directly above the Pole itself.
I now lamented that my great elevation would, in this case,
prevent my taking as accurate a survey as I could wish.
Much, however, might be ascertained.

Nothing else of an extraordinary nature occurred during the day. My apparatus all continued in good order, and the balloon still ascended without any perceptible vacillation. The cold was intense, and obliged me to wrap up closely in an overcoat. When darkness came over the earth, I betook myself to bed, although it was for many hours afterwards broad daylight all around my immediate situation. The water-clock was punctual in its duty, and I slept until next morning soundly, with the exception of the periodical interruption.

April 4th.—Arose in good health and spirits, and was astonished at the singular change which had taken place in the appearance of the sea. It had lost, in a great measure, the deep tint of blue it had hitherto worn, being now of a greyish-white, and of a lustre dazzling to the eye. The convexity of the ocean had become so evident, that the entire mass of the distant water seemed to be tumbling headlong over the abyss of the horizon, and I found myself listening on tiptoe for the echoes of the mighty cataract. The islands were no longer visible ; whether they had passed down the horizon to the south-east, or whether my increasing elevation had left them out of sight, it is impossible to say. I was inclined, however, to the latter opinion. The rim of ice to the northward was growing more and more apparent. Cold by no means so intense. Nothing of importance occurred, and I passed the day in reading, having taken care to supply myself with books.

April 5th.—Beheld the singular phenomenon of the sun rising while nearly the whole visible surface of the earth continued to be involved in darkness. In time, however, the light spread itself over all, and I again saw the line of ice to the northward. It was now very distinct, and appeared of a much darker hue than the waters of the ocean. I was evidently approaching it, and with great rapidity. Fancied I could again distinguish a strip of land to the eastward, and one also to the westward, but could not be certain. Weather moderate. Nothing of any consequence happened during the day. Went early to bed.

April 6th.—Was surprised at finding the rim of ice at a very moderate distance, and an immense field of the same material stretching away off to the horizon in the north. It was evident that if the balloon held its present

course, it would soon arrive above the Frozen Ocean, and
I had now little doubt of ultimately seeing the Pole.
During the whole of the day I continued to near the
ice. Towards night the limits of my horizon very suddenly
and materially increased, owing undoubtedly to the
earth's form being that of an oblate spheroid, and my
arriving above the flattened regions in the vicinity of the
Arctic circle. When darkness at length overtook me, I
went to bed in great anxiety, fearing to pass over the
object of so much curiosity when I should have no opportunity of observing it.

April 7th.—Arose early, and, to my great joy, at length
beheld what there could be no hesitation in supposing
the northern Pole itself. It was there, beyond a doubt,
and immediately beneath my feet ; but, alas ! I had
now ascended to so vast a distance that nothing could
with accuracy be discerned. Indeed, to judge from the
progression of the numbers indicating my various altitudes,
respectively, at different periods, between six A.M. on the
second of April, and twenty minutes before nine A.M. of the
same day (at which time the barometer ran down), it might
be fairly inferred that the balloon had now, at four o'clock
in the morning of April the seventh, reached a height of
not less, certainly, than 7,254 miles above the surface of
the sea. This elevation may appear immense ; but the
estimate upon which it is calculated gave a result in all
probability far inferior to the truth. At all events, I
undoubtedly beheld the whole of the earth's major
diameter ; the entire northern hemisphere lay beneath
me like a chart orthographically projected ; and the
great circle of the equator itself formed the boundary
line of my horizon. Your Excellencies may, however,
readily imagine that the confined regions hitherto unexplored within the limits of the Arctic circle, although
situated directly beneath me, and therefore seen without
any appearance of being foreshortened, were still, in
themselves, comparatively too diminutive, and at too
great a distance from the point of sight, to admit of any
very accurate examination. Nevertheless, what could be
seen was of a nature singular and exciting. Northwardly
from that huge rim before mentioned, and which, with
slight qualification, may be called the limit of human
discovery in these regions, one unbroken, or nearly un-

broken sheet of ice continues to extend. In the first
few degrees of this its progress, its surface is very sensibly
flattened, farther on depressed into a plane, and finally,
becoming *not a little concave*, it terminates, at the Pole
itself, in a circular centre, sharply defined, whose apparent
diameter subtended at the balloon an angle of about
sixty-five seconds, and whose dusky hue, varying in
intensity, was at all times darker than any other spot
upon the visible hemisphere, and occasionally deepened
into the most absolute blackness. Farther than this
little could be ascertained. By twelve o'clock the circular
centre had materially decreased in circumference, and by
seven P.M. I lost sight of it entirely ; the balloon passing
over the western limb of the ice, and floating away rapidly
in the direction of the equator.

April 8th.—Found a sensible diminution in the earth's
apparent diameter, besides a material alteration in its
general colour and appearance. The whole visible area
partook in different degrees of a tint of pale yellow, and
in some portions had acquired a brilliancy even painful
to the eye. My view downwards was also considerably
impeded by the dense atmosphere in the vicinity of the
surface being loaded with clouds, between whose masses
I could only now and then obtain a glimpse of the earth
itself. This difficulty of direct vision had troubled me
more or less for the last forty-eight hours ; but my present
enormous elevation brought closer together, as it were, the
floating bodies of vapour, and the inconvenience became,
of course, more and more palpable in proportion to my
ascent. Nevertheless, I could easily perceive that the
balloon now hovered above the range of great lakes in
the continent of North America, and was holding a course
due south, which would soon bring me to the tropics.
This circumstance did not fail to give me the most heart-
felt satisfaction, and I hailed it as a happy omen of ultimate
success. Indeed, the direction I had hitherto taken had
filled me with uneasiness ; for it was evident that, had I
continued it much longer, there would have been no
possibility of my arriving at the moon at all, whose orbit
is inclined to the ecliptic at only the small angle of 5
degrees, 8 minutes, 48 seconds. Strange as it may seem,
it was only at this late period that I began to understand
the great error I had committed in not taking my

departure from earth at some point *in the plane of the lunar ellipse.*

April 9th.—To-day, the earth's diameter was greatly diminished, and the colour of the surface assumed hourly a deeper tint of yellow. The balloon kept steadily on her course to the southward, and arrived at nine P.M. over the northern edge of the Mexican Gulf.

April 10th.—I was suddenly aroused from slumber, about five o'clock this morning, by a loud, crackling, and terrific sound, for which I could in no manner account. It was of very brief duration, but, while it lasted, resembled nothing in the world of which I had any previous experience. It is needless to say that I became excessively alarmed, having, in the first instance, attributed the noise to the bursting of the balloon. I examined all my apparatus, however, with great attention, and could discover nothing out of order. Spent a great part of the day in meditating upon an occurrence so extraordinary, but could find no means whatever of accounting for it. Went to bed dissatisfied, and in a state of great anxiety and agitation.

April 11th.—Found a startling diminution in the apparent diameter of the earth, and a considerable increase, now observable for the first time, in that of the moon itself, which wanted only a few days of being full. It now required long and excessive labour to condense within the chamber sufficient atmospheric air for the sustenance of life.

April 12th.—A singular alteration took place in regard to the direction of the balloon, and, although fully anticipated, afforded me the most unequivocal delight. Having reached, in its former course, about the twentieth parallel of southern latitude, it turned off suddenly, at an acute angle, to the eastward, and thus proceeded throughout the day, keeping nearly, if not altogether, *in the exact plane of the lunar ellipse.* What was worthy of remark, a very perceptible vacillation in the car was a consequence of this change of route—a vacillation which prevailed, in a more or less degree, for a period of many hours.

April 13th.—Was again very much alarmed by a repetition of the loud crackling noise which terrified me on the tenth. Thought long upon the subject, but was unable to form any satisfactory conclusion. Great decrease in

the earth's apparent diameter, which now subtended
from the balloon an angle of very little more than twenty-
five degrees. The moon could not be seen at all, being
nearly in my zenith. I still continued in the plane of
the ellipse, but made little progress to the eastward.

April 14th.—Extremely rapid decrease in the diameter
of the earth. To-day I became strongly impressed with
the idea, that the balloon was now actually running up the
line of apsides to the point of perigee—in other words,
holding the direct course which would bring it immediately
to the moon in that part of its orbit the nearest to the
earth. The moon itself was directly overhead, and consequently hidden from my view. Great and long-continued
labour necessary for the condensation of the atmosphere.

April 15th.—Not even the outlines of continents and
seas could now be traced upon the earth with distinctness.
About twelve o'clock I became aware, for the third time,
of that appalling sound which had astonished me before.
It now, however, continued for some moments, and
gathered intensity as it continued. At length, while,
stupefied and terror-stricken, I stood in expectation of
I knew not what hideous destruction, the car vibrated
with excessive violence, and a gigantic and flaming mass
of some material which I could not distinguish came with
a voice of a thousand thunders, roaring and booming by
the balloon. When my fears and astonishment had in
some degree subsided, I had little difficulty in supposing
it to be some mighty volcanic fragment ejected from that
world to which I was so rapidly approaching, and, in all
probability, one of that singular class of substances occasionally picked up on the earth, and termed meteoric
stones for want of a better appellation.

April 16th.—To-day, looking upwards as well as I could,
through each of the side windows alternately, I beheld, to
my great delight, a very small portion of the moon's disk
protruding, as it were, on all sides beyond the huge circumference of the balloon. My agitation was extreme, for I
had now little doubt of soon reaching the end of my perilous
voyage. Indeed, the labour now required by the condenser had increased to a most oppressive degree, and
allowed me scarcely any respite from exertion. Sleep was
a matter nearly out of the question. I became quite ill,
and my frame trembled with exhaustion. It was impossible

that human nature could endure this state of intense
suffering much longer. During the now brief interval of
darkness a meteoric stone again passed in my vicinity,
and the frequency of these phenomena began to occasion
me much apprehension.

April 17*th*.—This morning proved an epoch in my
voyage. It will be remembered, that, on the thirteenth,
the earth subtended an angular breadth of twenty-five
degrees. On the fourteenth this had greatly diminished ;
on the fifteenth, a still more rapid decrease was observable ;
and, on retiring for the night of the sixteenth, I had noticed
an angle of no more than about seven degrees and fifteen
minutes. What, therefore, must have been my amazement, on awakening from a brief and disturbed slumber
on the morning of this day, the seventeenth, at finding
the surface beneath me so suddenly and wonderfully
augmented in volume, as to subtend no less than thirty-
nine degrees in apparent angular diameter ! I was thunder-
struck ! No words can give any adequate idea of the
extreme, the absolute horror and astonishment, with
which I was seized, possessed, and altogether overwhelmed
My knees tottered beneath me—my teeth chattered—my
hair started up on end. " The balloon, then, had actually
burst ! " These were the first tumultuous ideas which
hurried through my mind : " The balloon had positively
burst !—I was falling—falling with the most impetuous
the most unparalleled velocity ! To judge from the
immense distance already so quickly passed over, it
could not be more than ten minutes at farthest before
I should meet the surface of the earth, and be hurled into
annihilation ! " But at length reflection came to my
relief. I paused ; I considered ; and I began to doubt
The matter was impossible, I could not in any reason
have so rapidly come down. Besides, although I was
evidently approaching the surface below me, it was with
a speed by no means commensurate with the velocity
had at first conceived. This consideration served to
calm the perturbation of my mind, and I finally succeeded
in regarding the phenomenon in its proper point of view
In fact, amazement must have fairly deprived me of my
senses, when I could not see the vast difference in appearance between the surface below me and the surface of
my mother earth. The latter was indeed over my head

and completely hidden by the balloon, while the moon—
the moon itself in all its glory—lay beneath me, and at my
feet.

The stupor and surprise produced in my mind by this
extraordinary change in the posture of affairs, was, perhaps,
after all, that part of the adventure least susceptible of
explanation. For the *bouleversement* in itself was not only
natural and inevitable, but had been long actually anticipated, as a circumstance to be expected whenever I should
arrive at the exact point of my voyage where the attraction
of the planet should be superseded by the attraction of
the satellite—or, more precisely, where the gravitation of
the balloon towards the earth should be less powerful than
its gravitation towards the moon. To be sure, I rose from
a sound slumber, with all my senses in confusion, to the
contemplation of a very startling phenomenon, and one
which, although expected, was not expected at the moment.
The revolution itself must, of course, have taken place in
an easy and gradual manner, and it is by no means clear
that had I even been awake at the time of the occurrence,
I should have been made aware of it by any *internal*
evidence of an inversion—that is to say, by any inconvenience or disarrangement, either about my person or about
my apparatus.

It is almost needless to say, that, upon coming to a due
sense of my situation, and emerging from the terror which
had absorbed every faculty of my soul, my attention was,
in the first place, wholly directed to the contemplation of
the general physical appearance of the moon. It lay
beneath me like a chart—and although I judged it to be
still at no inconsiderable distance, the indentures of its
surface were defined to my vision with a most striking and
altogether unaccountable distinctness. The entire absence of
ocean or sea, and indeed of any lake or river, or body of water
whatsoever, struck me, at the first glance, as the most extraordinary feature in its geological condition. Yet, strange
to say, I beheld vast level regions of a character decidedly
alluvial, although by far the greater portion of the hemisphere in sight was covered with innumerable volcanic
mountains, conical in shape, and having more the appearance of artificial than of natural protuberances. The
highest among them does not exceed three and three-
quarter miles in perpendicular elevation ; but a map of the

volcanic districts of the Campi Phlegræi would afford to your Excellencies a better idea of their general surface than any unworthy description I might think proper to attempt. The greater part of them were in a state of evident irruption, and gave me fearfully to understand their fury and their power, by the repeated thunders of the miscalled meteoric stones, which now rushed upwards by the balloon with a frequency more and more appalling.

April 18*th.*—To-day I found an enormous increase in the moon's apparent bulk—and the evidently accelerated velocity of my descent began to fill me with alarm. It will be remembered that, in the earliest stage of my speculations upon the possibility of a passage to the moon, the existence in its vicinity of an atmosphere dense in proportion to the bulk of the planet had entered largely into my calculations ; this, too, in spite of many theories to the contrary, and, it may be added, in spite of a general disbelief in the existence of any lunar atmosphere at all. But, in addition to what I have already urged in regard to Enckes' comet, and the zodiacal light, I had been strengthened in my opinion by certain observations of Mr. Schroeter, of Lilienthal. He observed the moon, when two days and a half old, in the evening soon after sunset, before the dark part was visible, and continued to watch it until it became visible. The two cusps appeared tapering in a very sharp faint prolongation, each exhibiting its farthest extremity faintly illuminated by the solar rays, before any part of the dark hemisphere was visible. Soon afterwards, the whole dark limb became illuminated. This prolongation of the cusps beyond the semicircle, I thought must have arisen from the refraction of the sun's rays by the moon's atmosphere. I computed, also, the height of the atmosphere (which could refract light enough in its dark hemisphere to produce a twilight more luminous than the light reflected from the earth when the moon is about 32° from the new) to be 1,356 Paris feet ; in this view, I supposed the greatest height capable of refracting the solar ray, to be 5,376 feet. My ideas upon this topic had also received confirmation by a passage in the eighty-second volume of the *Philosophical Transactions*, in which it is stated that, at an occultation of Jupiter's satellites, the third disappeared after having been about one or two seconds of time

indistinct, and the fourth became indiscernible near the limb.*

Upon the resistance, or, more properly, upon the support of an atmosphere, existing in the state of density imagined, I had, of course, entirely depended for the safety of my ultimate descent. Should I, then, after all, prove to have been mistaken, I had in consequence nothing better to expect, as a *finale* to my adventure, than being dashed into atoms against the rugged surface of the satellite. And, indeed, I had now every reason to be terrified. My distance from the moon was comparatively trifling, while the labour required by the condenser was diminished not at all, and I could discover no indication whatever of a decreasing rarity in the air.

April 19th.—This morning, to my great joy, about nine o'clock—the surface of the moon being frightfully near, and my apprehensions excited to the utmost—the pump of my condenser gave evident tokens of an alteration in the atmosphere. By ten I had reason to believe its density considerably increased. By eleven very little labour was necessary at the apparatus; and at twelve o'clock, with some hesitation, I ventured to unscrew the *tourniquet,* when, finding no inconvenience from having done so, I finally threw open the gum-elastic chamber, and unrigged it from around the car. As might have been expected, spasms and violent headache were the immediate consequences of an experiment so precipitate and full of danger. But these and other difficulties attending respiration, as they were by no means so great as to put me in peril of my life,

---

* Hevelius writes that he has several times found in skies perfectly clear, when even stars of the sixth and seventh magnitude were conspicuous, that, at the same altitude of the moon, at the same elongation from the earth, and with one and the same excellent telescope, the moon and its maculæ did not appear equally lucid at all times. From the circumstances of the observation, it is evident that the cause of this phenomenon is not either in our air, in the tube, in the moon, or in the eye of the spectator, but must be looked for in something (an atmosphere ?) existing about the moon.

Cassini frequently observed Saturn, Jupiter, and the fixed stars, when approaching the moon to occultation, to have their circular figure changed into an oval one ; and, in other occultations, he found no alteration of figure at all. Hence it might be supposed, that at some times, and not at others, there is a dense matter encompassing the moon, wherein the rays of the stars are refracted.

K

I determined to endure as I best could in consideration of my leaving them behind me momently in my approach to the denser *strata* near the moon. This approach, however, was still impetuous in the extreme ; and it soon became alarmingly certain that although I had probably not been deceived in the expectation of an atmosphere dense in proportion to the mass of the satellite, still I had been wrong in supposing this density, even at the surface, at all adequate to the support of the great weight contained in the car of my balloon. Yet this *should* have been the case, and in an equal degree as at the surface of the earth, the actual gravity of bodies at either planet supposed in the ratio of the atmospheric condensation. That it *was not* the case, however, my precipitous downfall gave testimony enough ; *why* it was not so, can only be explained by a reference to those possible geological disturbances to which I have formerly alluded. At all events, I was now close upon the planet, and coming down with the most terrible impetuosity. I lost not a moment, accordingly, in throwing overboard first my ballast, then my water-kegs, then my condensing-apparatus and gum-elastic chamber, and finally every article within the car. But it was all to no purpose. I still fell with horrible rapidity, and was now not more than half a mile from the surface. As a last resource, therefore, having got rid of my coat, hat, and boots, I cut loose from the balloon *the car itself*, which was of no inconsiderable weight, and thus, clinging with both hands to the net-work, I had barely time to observe that the whole country, as far as the eye could reach, was thickly interspersed with diminutive habitations, ere I tumbled headlong into the very heart of a fantastical-looking city, and into the middle of a vast crowd of ugly little people, who none of them uttered a single syllable, or gave themselves the least trouble to render me assistance, but stood, like a parcel of idiots, grinning in a ludicrous manner, and eyeing me and my balloon askant, with their arms set akimbo. I turned from them in contempt, and, gazing upwards at the earth so lately left, and left perhaps for ever, beheld it like a huge, dull, copper shield, above two degrees in diameter, fixed immovably in the heavens overhead, and tipped on one of its edges with a crescent border of the most brilliant gold. No traces of land or water could be discovered, and the whole was clouded with variable spots, and belted with tropical and equatorial zones.

Thus, may it please your Excellencies, after a series of great anxieties, unheard-of dangers, and unparalleled escapes, I had, at length, on the nineteenth day of my departure from Rotterdam, arrived in safety at the conclusion of a voyage undoubtedly the most extraordinary, and the most momentous, ever accomplished, undertaken or conceived by any denizen of earth. But my adventures yet remain to be related. And, indeed, your Excellencies may well imagine that, after a residence of five years upon a planet not only deeply interesting in its own peculiar character, but rendered doubly so by its intimate connection, in capacity of satellite, with the world inhabited by man, I may have intelligence for the private ear of the States' College of Astronomers of far more importance than the details, however wonderful, of the mere *voyage* which so happily concluded. This is, in fact, the case. I have much, very much which it would give me the greatest pleasure to communicate. I have much to say of the climate of the planet ; of its wonderful alternations of heat and cold ; of unmitigated and burning sunshine for one fortnight, and more than polar frigidity for the next ; of a constant transfer of moisture, by distillation like that *in vacuo*, from the point beneath the sun to the point the farthest from it ; of a variable zone of running water ; of the people themselves ; of their manners, customs, and political institutions ; of their peculiar physical constructions ; of their ugliness ; of their want of ears, those useless appendages in an atmosphere so peculiarly modified ; of their consequent ignorance of the use and properties of speech ; of their substitute for speech in a singular method of inter-communication ; of the incomprehensible connection between each particular individual in the moon with some particular individual on the earth—a connection analogous with, and depending upon, that of the orbs of the planet and the satellite, and by means of which the lives and destinies of the inhabitants of the one are interwoven with the lives and destinies of the inhabitants of the other ; and, above all, if it so please your Excellencies, above all, of those dark and hideous mysteries which lie in the outer regions of the moon—regions which, owing to the almost miraculous accordance of the satellite's

rotation on its own axis with its sidereal revolution about
the earth, have never yet been turned, and, by God's mercy,
never shall be turned, to the scrutiny of the telescopes
of man. All this, and more—much more—would I most
willingly detail. But, to be brief, I must have my reward.
I am pining for a return to my family and to my home ;
and as the price of any farther communications on my part,
in consideration of the light which I have it in my power
to throw upon many very important branches of physical
and metaphysical science, I must solicit, through the
influence of your honourable body, a pardon for the crime
of which I have been guilty in the death of the creditors
upon my departure from Rotterdam. This, then, is the
object of the present paper. Its bearer, an inhabitant of
the moon, whom I have prevailed upon, and properly
instructed, to be my messenger to the earth, will await
your Excellencies' pleasure, and return to me with the
pardon in question, if it can in any manner be obtained.

I have the honour to be, etc., your Excellencies' very
humble servant,

HANS PFAALL.

Upon finishing the perusal of this very extraordinary
document, Professor Rubadub, it is said, dropped his pipe
upon the ground in the extremity of his surprise, and
Mynheer Superbus Von Underduk, having taken off his
spectacles, wiped them, and deposited them in his pocket,
so far forgot both himself and his dignity as to turn round
three times upon his heel in the quintessence of astonishment and admiration. There was no doubt about the matter
—the pardon should be obtained. So at least swore, with a
round oath, Professor Rubadub, and so finally thought the
illustrious Von Underduk, as he took the arm of his brother
in science, and, without saying a word, began to make the
best of his way home to deliberate upon the measures to be
adopted. Having reached the door, however, of the burgomaster's dwelling, the professor ventured to suggest that
as the messenger had thought proper to disappear (no doubt
frightened to death by the savage appearance of the
burghers of Rotterdam), the pardon would be of little use,
as no one but a man of the moon would undertake a voyage
to so vast a distance. To the truth of this observation the
burgomaster assented, and the matter was therefore at an

end. Not so, however, rumours and speculations. The
letter, having been published, gave rise to a variety of gossip
and opinion. Some of the over-wise even made themselves
ridiculous by decrying the whole business as nothing better
than a hoax. But hoax, with these sort of people, is, I
believe, a general term for all matters above their comprehension. For my part, I cannot conceive upon what data
they have founded such an accusation. Let us see what
they say :—

Imprimis. That certain wags in Rotterdam have certain especial antipathies to certain burgomasters and
astronomers.

Secondly. That an odd little dwarf and bottle conjurer,
both of whose ears, for some misdemeanour, have been cut
off close to his head, has been missing for several days from
the neighbouring city of Bruges.

Thirdly. That the newspapers which were stuck all over
the little balloon were newspapers of Holland, and therefore could not have been made in the moon. They were
dirty papers—very dirty ; and Gluck, the printer, would
take his Bible oath to their having been printed in Rotterdam.

Fourthly. That Hans Pfaall himself, the drunken
villain, and the three very idle gentlemen styled his creditors, were all seen, no longer than two or three days ago, in
a tippling-house in the suburbs, having just returned, with
money in their pockets, from a trip beyond the sea.

Lastly. That it is an opinion very generally received,
or which ought to be generally received, that the College
of Astronomers in the city of Rotterdam, as well as all
other colleges in all other parts of the world—not to mention colleges and astronomers in general—are, to say the
least of the matter, not a whit better, nor greater, nor
wiser than they ought to be.

THE PIT AND THE PENDULUM

" Impia tortorum longas hic turba furores
Sanguinis innocui, non satiata, aluit.
Sospite nunc patria, fracto nunc funeris antro,
Mors ubi dira fuit vita salusque patent."

[*Quatrain composed for the gates of a market to be erected upon the
site of the Jacobin Club House at Paris.*]

I WAS sick—sick unto death with that long agony ; and
when they at length unbound me, and I was permitted
to sit, I felt that my senses were leaving me.   The sentence
—the dread sentence of death—was the last of distinct
accentuation which reached my ears.   After that, the
sound of the inquisitorial voices seemed merged in one
dreamy indeterminate hum.   It conveyed to my soul the
idea of *revolution*—perhaps from its association in fancy
with the burr of a mill-wheel.   This only for a brief period ;
for presently I heard no more.   Yet, for a while, I saw ;
but with how terrible an exaggeration ! I saw the lips of
the black-robed judges.   They appeared to me white—
whiter than the sheet upon which I trace these words—
and thin even to grotesqueness ; thin with the intensity of
their expression of firmness—of immovable resolution—of
stern contempt of human torture.   I saw that the decrees
of what to me was Fate, were still issuing from those lips.
I saw them writhe with a deadly locution.   I saw them
fashion the syllables of my name ; and I shuddered because
no sound succeeded.   I saw, too, for a few moments of
delirious horror, the soft and nearly imperceptible waving
of the sable draperies which enwrapped the walls of the
apartment.   And then my vision fell upon the seven tall
candles upon the table.   At first they wore the aspect of
charity, and seemed white slender angels who would save
me ; but then, all at once, there came a most deadly
nausea over my spirit, and I felt every fibre in my frame
thrill as if I had touched the wire of a galvanic battery,
while the angel forms became meaningless spectres, with
heads of flame, and I saw that from them there would be
no help.   And then there stole into my fancy, like a rich
musical note, the thought of what sweet rest there must

be in the grave. The thought came gently and stealthily, and it seemed long before it attained full appreciation ; but just as my spirit came at length properly to feel and entertain it, the figures of the judges vanished, as if magically, from before me ; the tall candles sank into nothingness ; their flames went out utterly ; the blackness of darkness supervened ; all sensations appeared swallowed up in a mad rushing descent as of the soul into Hades. Then silence, and stillness, and night were the universe.

I had swooned ; but still will not say that all of consciousness was lost. What of it there remained I will not attempt to define, or even to describe ; yet all was not lost. In the deepest slumber—no ! In delirium— no ! In a swoon—no ! In death—no ! even in the grave all *is not* lost. Else there is no immortality for man. Arousing from the most profound of slumbers, we break the gossamer web of *some* dream. Yet in a second afterward (so frail may that web have been) we remember not that we have dreamed. In the return to life from the swoon there are two stages : first, that of the sense of mental or spiritual ; secondly, that of the sense of physical existence. It seems probable that if, upon reaching the second stage, we could recall the impressions of the first, we should find these impressions eloquent in memories of the gulf beyond. And that gulf is—what ? How at least shall we distinguish its shadows from those of the tomb ? But if the impressions of what I have termed the first stage are not, at will, recalled, yet, after long interval, do they not come unbidden, while we marvel whence they come ? He who has never swooned, is not he who finds strange palaces and wildly familiar faces in coals that glow ; is not he who beholds floating in mid-air the sad visions that the many may not view ; is not he who ponders over the perfume of some novel flower ; is not he whose brain grows bewildered with the meaning of some musical cadence which has never before arrested his attention.

Amid frequent and thoughtful endeavours to remember ; amid earnest struggles to regather some token of the state of seeming nothingness into which my soul had lapsed, there have been moments when I have dreamed of success ; there have been brief, very brief periods when I have conjured up remembrances which the lucid reason of a later epoch assures me could have had reference only to that condition of seeming unconsciousness. These shadows of memory tell, indistinctly, of tall figures that lifted and bore me in silence down—down—still down—till a hideous dizziness oppressed me at the mere idea of the interminableness of the descent. They tell also of a vague horror at my heart, on account of that heart's unnatural stillness. Then comes a sense of sudden motionlessness throughout all things; as if those who bore me (a ghastly train!) had outrun, in their descent, the limits of the limitless, and paused from the wearisomeness of their toil. After this I call to mind flatness and dampness; and then all is *madness* —the madness of a memory which busies itself among forbidden things.

Very suddenly there came back to my soul motion and sound—the tumultuous motion of the heart, and, in my ears, the sound of its beating. Then a pause, in which all is blank. Then again sound, and motion, and touch—a tingling sensation pervading my frame. Then the mere consciousness of existence, without thought—a condition which lasted long. Then, very suddenly, *thought*, and shuddering terror, and earnest endeavour to comprehend my true state. Then a strong desire to lapse into insensibility. Then a rushing revival of soul and a successful effort to move. And now a full memory of the trial, of the judges, of the sable draperies, of the sentence, of the sickness, of the swoon. Then entire forgetfulness of all that followed; of all that a later day and much earnestness of endeavour have enabled me vaguely to recall.

So far, I had not opened my eyes. I felt that I lay upon my back, unbound. I reached out my hand, and it fell heavily upon something damp and hard. There I suffered it to remain for many minutes, while I strove to imagine where and *what* I could be. I longed, yet dared not to employ my vision. I dreaded the first glance at objects around me. It was not that I feared to look upon things horrible, but that I grew aghast lest there should be *nothing* to see. At length, with a wild desperation at heart, I quickly unclosed my eyes. My worst thoughts, then, were confirmed. The blackness of eternal night encompassed me. I struggled for breath. The intensity of the darkness seemed to oppress and stifle me. The atmosphere was intolerably close. I still lay quietly, and made effort to exercise my reason. I brought to mind the inquisitorial proceedings, and attempted from that point to deduce my real condition. The sentence had passed ; and it appeared to me that a very long interval of time had since elapsed. Yet not for a moment did I suppose myself actually dead. Such a supposition, notwithstanding what we read in fiction, is altogether inconsistent with real existence—but where and in what state was I ? The condemned to death, I knew, perished usually at the *autos da fé,* and one of these had been held on the very night of the day of my trial. Had I been remanded to my dungeon, to await the next sacrifice, which would not take place for many months ? This I at once saw could not be. Victims had been in immediate demand. Moreover, my dungeon, as well as all the condemned cells at Toledo, had stone floors, and light was not altogether excluded.

A fearful idea now suddenly drove the blood in torrents upon my heart, and for a brief period I once more relapsed into insensibility. Upon recovering, I at once started to my feet, trembling convulsively in every fibre. I thrust my arms wildly above and around me in all directions. I felt nothing ; yet dreaded to move a step, lest I should be impeded by the walls of a *tomb.* Perspiration burst from every pore, and stood in cold beads upon my forehead. The agony of suspense grew at length intolerable, and I cautiously moved forward, with my arms extended, and my eyes straining from their sockets, in the hope of catching some faint ray of light. I proceeded for many paces ; but still all was blackness and vacancy. I breathed more freely. It seemed evident that mine was not, at least, the most hideous of fates.

And now, as I still continued to step cautiously onward, there came thronging upon my recollection a thousand vague rumours of the horrors of Toledo. Of the dungeons there had been strange things narrated—fables I had always deemed them—but yet strange, and too ghastly to repeat, save in a whisper. Was I left to perish of starvation in this subterranean world of darkness ; or what fate, perhaps even more fearful, awaited me ? That the result would be death, and a death of more than customary bitterness, I knew too well the character of my judges to doubt. The mode and the hour were all that occupied or distracted me.

K*

My outstretched hands at length encountered some solid obstruction. It was a wall, seemingly of stone masonry—very smooth, slimy, and cold. I followed it up, stepping with all the careful distrust with which certain antique narratives had inspired me. This process, however, afforded me no means of ascertaining the dimensions of my dungeon, as I might make its circuit, and return to the point whence I set out, without being aware of the fact, so perfectly uniform seemed the wall. I therefore sought the knife which had been in my pocket, when led into the inquisitorial chamber, but it was gone; my clothes had been exchanged for a wrapper of coarse serge. I had thought of forcing the blade in some minute crevice of the masonry, so as to identify my point of departure. The difficulty, nevertheless, was but trivial; although, in the disorder of my fancy, it seemed at first insuperable. I tore a part of the hem from the robe and placed the fragment at full length, and at right angles to the wall. In groping my way around the prison, I could not fail to encounter this rag upon completing the circuit. So, at least, I thought; but I had not counted upon the extent of the dungeon, or upon my own weakness. The ground was moist and slippery. I staggered onward for some time, when I stumbled and fell. My excessive fatigue induced me to remain prostrate; and sleep soon overtook me as I lay.

Upon awaking, and stretching forth an arm, I found beside me a loaf and a pitcher with water. I was too much exhausted to reflect upon this circumstance, but ate and drank with avidity. Shortly afterward I resumed my tour around the prison, and, with much toil, came at last upon the fragment of the serge. Up to the period when I fell, I had counted fifty-two paces, and, upon resuming my walk, I had counted forty-eight more—when I arrived at the rag. There were in all, then, a hundred paces; and, admitting two paces to the yard, I presumed the dungeon to be fifty yards in circuit. I had met, however, with many angles in the wall, and thus I could form no guess at the shape of the vault; for vault I could not help supposing it to be.

I had little object—certainly no hope—in these researches; but a vague curiosity prompted me to continue them. Quitting the wall, I resolved to cross the area of the cnclosure. At first, I proceeded with extreme caution, for the floor, although seemingly of solid material, was treacherous with slime. At length, however, I took courage, and did not hesitate to step firmly—endeavouring to cross in as direct a line as possible. I had advanced some ten or twelve paces in this manner, when the remnant of the torn hem of my robe became entangled between my legs. I stepped on it, and fell violently on my face.

In the confusion attending my fall, I did not immediately apprehend a somewhat startling circumstance, which yet, in a few seconds afterward, and while I still lay prostrate, arrested my attention. It was this : my chin rested upon the floor of the prison, but my lips, and the upper portion of my head, although seemingly at a less elevation than the chin, touched nothing. At the same time, my forehead seemed bathed in a clammy vapour, and the peculiar smell of decayed fungus arose to my nostrils. I put forward my arm, and shuddered to find that I had fallen at the very brink of a circular pit, whose extent, of course, I had no means of ascertaining at the moment. Groping about the masonry just below the margin, I succeeded in dislodging a small fragment, and let it fall into the abyss. For many seconds I hearkened to its reverberations as it dashed against the sides of the chasm in its descent. At length, there was a sullen plunge into water, succeeded by loud echoes. At the same moment, there came a sound re-sembling the quick opening, and as rapid closing of a door overhead, while a faint gleam of light flashed suddenly through the gloom, and as suddenly faded away.

I saw clearly the doom which had been prepared for me, and congratulated myself upon the timely accident by which I had escaped. Another step before my fall, and the world had seen me no more. And the death just avoided was of that very character which I had regarded as fabulous and frivolous in the tales respecting the In-quisition. To the victims of its tyranny, there was the choice of death with its direst physical agonies, or death with its most hideous moral horrors. I had been reserved for the latter. By long suffering my nerves had been unstrung, until I trembled at the sound of my own voice, and had become in every respect a fitting subject for the species of torture which awaited me.

Shaking in every limb, I groped my way back to the

wall—resolving there to perish rather than risk the terrors of the wells, of which my imagination now pictured many in various positions about the dungeon. In other conditions of mind, I might have had courage to end my misery at once, by a plunge into one of these abysses ; but now I was the veriest of cowards. Neither could I forget what I had read of these pits—that the *sudden* extinction of life formed no part of their most horrible plan.

Agitation of spirit kept me awake for many long hours ; but at length I again slumbered. Upon arousing, I found by my side, as before, a loaf and a pitcher of water. A burning thirst consumed me, and I emptied the vessel at a draught. It must have been drugged—for scarcely had I drunk, before I became irresistibly drowsy. A deep sleep fell upon me—a sleep like that of death. How long it lasted, of course, I know not ; but when, once again, I unclosed my eyes, the objects around me were visible. By a wild, sulphureous lustre, the origin of which I could not at first determine, I was enabled to see the extent and aspect of the prison.

In its size I had been greatly mistaken. The whole circuit of its walls did not exceed twenty-five yards. For some minutes this fact occasioned me a world of vain trouble ; vain indeed—for what could be of less importance, under the terrible circumstances which environed me, than the mere dimensions of my dungeon ? But my soul took a wild interest in trifles, and I busied myself in endeavours to account for the error I had committed in my measurement. The truth at length flashed upon me. In my first attempt at exploration I had counted fifty-two paces, up to the period when I fell ; I must then have been within a pace or two of the fragment of serge ; in fact, I had nearly performed the circuit of the vault. I then slept—and, upon awaking, I must have returned upon my steps—thus supposing the circuit nearly double what it actually was. My confusion of mind prevented me from observing that I began my tour with the wall to the left, and ended it with the wall to the right.

I had been deceived, too, in respect to the shape of the enclosure. In feeling my way, I had found many angles, and thus deduced an idea of great irregularity ; so potent is the effect of total darkness upon one arousing from lethargy or sleep ! The angles were simply those of a few

slight depressions, or niches, at odd intervals. The general
shape of the prison was square. What I had taken for
masonry seemed now to be iron, or some other metal, in
huge plates, whose sutures or joints occasioned the depression. The entire surface of this metallic enclosure
was rudely daubed in all the hideous and repulsive devices
to which the charnel superstition of the monks has given
rise. The figures of fiends in aspects of menace, with
skeleton forms, and other more really fearful images, overspread and disfigured the walls. I observed that the
outlines of these monstrosities were sufficiently distinct,
but that the colours seemed faded and blurred, as if from
the effects of a damp atmosphere. I now noticed the floor,
too, which was of stone. In the centre yawned the circular
pit from whose jaws I had escaped ; but it was the only
one in the dungeon.

All this I saw indistinctly and by much effort—for my
personal condition had been greatly changed during
slumber. I now lay upon my back, and at full length,
on a species of low framework of wood. To this I was
securely bound by a long strap resembling a surcingle.
It passed in many convolutions about my limbs and body,
leaving at liberty only my head and my left arm to such
extent, that I could, by dint of much exertion, supply
myself with food from an earthen dish which lay by my
side on the floor. I saw, to my horror, that the pitcher
had been removed. I say, to my horror—for I was consumed with intolerable thirst. This thirst it appeared to
be the design of my persecutors to stimulate—for the food
in the dish was meat pungently seasoned.

Looking upward, I surveyed the ceiling of my prison.
It was some thirty or forty feet overhead, and constructed
much as the side walls. In one of its panels a very singular
figure riveted my whole attention. It was the painted
figure of Time as he is commonly represented, save that, in
lieu of a scythe, he held what, at a casual glance, I supposed
to be the pictured image of a huge pendulum, such as we
see on antique clocks. There was something, however, in
the appearance of this machine which caused me to regard
it more attentively. While I gazed directly upward at it
(for its position was immediately over my own), I fancied
that I saw it in motion. In an instant afterward the fancy
was confirmed. Its sweep was brief, and, of course, slow.

I watched it for some minutes, somewhat in fear, but more in wonder. Wearied at length with observing its dull movement, I turned my eyes upon the other objects in the cell.

A slight noise attracted my notice, and looking to the floor, I saw several enormous rats traversing it. They had issued from the well, which lay just within view to my right. Even then, while I gazed, they came up in troops, hurriedly, with ravenous eyes, allured by the scent of the meat. From this it required much effort and attention to scare them away.

It might have been half-an-hour, perhaps even an hour (for I could take but imperfect note of time) before I again cast my eyes upward. What I then saw, confounded and amazed me. The sweep of the pendulum had increased in extent by nearly a yard. As a natural consequence, its velocity was also much greater. But what mainly disturbed me, was the idea that it had perceptibly *descended*. I now observed—with what horror it is needless to say—that its nether extremity was formed of a crescent of glittering steel, about a foot in length from horn to horn ; the horns upward, and the under edge evidently as keen as that of a razor. Like a razor also, it seemed massy and heavy, tapering from the edge into a solid and broad structure above. It was appended to a weighty rod of brass, and the whole *hissed* as it swung through the air.

I could no longer doubt the doom prepared for me by monkish ingenuity in torture. My cognisance of the pit had become known to the inquisitorial agents—*the pit*, whose horrors had been destined for so bold a recusant as myself—*the pit*, typical of hell, and regarded by rumour as the Ultima Thule of all their punishments. The plunge into this pit I had avoided by the merest of accidents, and I knew that surprise, or entrapment into torment, formed an important portion of all the grotesquerie of these dungeon deaths. Having failed to fall, it was no part of the demon plan to hurl me into the abyss ; and thus (there being no alternative) a different and a milder destruction awaited me. Milder ! I half smiled in my agony as I thought of such application of such a term.

What boots it to tell of the long, long hours of horror more than mortal, during which I counted the rushing oscillations of the steel ! Inch by inch—line by line—with a descent

only appreciable at intervals that seemed ages—down and
still down it came! Days passed—it might have been
that many days passed—ere it swept so closely over me as
to fan me with its acrid breath. The odour of the sharp
steel forced itself into my nostrils. I prayed—I wearied
heaven with my prayer for its more speedy descent. I
grew frantically mad, and struggled to force myself upward
against the sweep of the fearful scimitar. And then I fell
suddenly calm, and lay smiling at the glittering death, as a
child at some rare bauble.

There was another interval of utter insensibility; it
was brief; for, upon again lapsing into life, there had been
no perceptible descent in the pendulum. But it might have
been long—for I knew there were demons who took note of
my swoon, and who could have arrested the vibration at
pleasure. Upon my recovery, too, I felt very—oh, inexpressibly—sick and weak, as if through long inanition.
Even amid the agonies of that period the human nature
craved food. With painful effort I outstretched my left arm
as far as my bonds permitted, and took possession of the
small remnant which had been spared me by the rats. As I
put a portion of it within my lips, there rushed to my mind a
half-formed thought of joy—of hope. Yet what business
had *I* with hope? It was, as I say, a half-formed thought
—man has many such, which are never completed. I felt
that it was of joy—of hope; but I felt also that it had
perished in its formation. In vain I struggled to perfect—
to regain it. Long suffering had nearly annihilated all my
ordinary powers of mind. I was an imbecile—an idiot.

The vibration of the pendulum was at right angles to my
length. I saw that the crescent was designed to cross the
region of the heart. It would fray the serge of my robe—
it would return and repeat its operations—again—and
again. Notwithstanding its terrifically wide sweep (some
thirty feet or more), and the hissing vigour of its descent,
sufficient to sunder these very walls of iron, still the fraying
of my robe would be all that, for several minutes, it would
accomplish. And at this thought I paused. I dared not
go farther than this reflection. I dwelt upon it with a
pertinacity of attention—as if, in so dwelling, I could
arrest *here* the descent of the steel. I forced myself to
ponder upon the sound of the crescent as it should pass
across the garment—upon the peculiar thrilling sensation

which the friction of cloth produces on the nerves. I pondered upon all this frivolity until my teeth were on edge.

Down—steadily down it crept. I took a frenzied pleasure in contrasting its downward with its lateral velocity. To the right—to the left—far and wide—with the shriek of a damned spirit ! to my heart, with the stealthy pace of the tiger ! I alternately laughed and howled, as the one or the other idea grew predominant.

Down—certainly, relentlessly down ! It vibrated within three inches of my bosom ! I struggled violently— furiously—to free my left arm. This was free only from the elbow to the hand. I could reach the latter, from the platter beside me, to my mouth, with great effort, but no farther. Could I have broken the fastenings above the elbow, I would have seized and attempted to arrest the pendulum. I might as well have attempted to arrest an avalanche !

Down—still unceasingly—still inevitably down ! I gasped and struggled at each vibration. I shrunk convulsively at its every sweep. My eyes followed its outward or upward whirls with the eagerness of the most unmeaning despair ; they closed themselves spasmodically at the descent, although death would have been a relief, oh, how unspeakable ! Still I quivered in every nerve to think how slight a sinking of the machinery would precipitate that keen, glistening axe upon my bosom. It was *hope* that prompted the nerve to quiver—the frame to shrink. It was *hope*—the hope that triumphs on the rack— that whispers to the death-condemned even in the dungeons of the Inquisition.

I saw that some ten or twelve vibrations would bring the steel in actual contact with my robe—and with this observation there suddenly came over my spirit all the keen, collected calmness of despair. For the first time during many hours—or perhaps days—I *thought*. It now occurred to me, that the bandage, or surcingle, which enveloped me, was *unique*. I was tied by no separate cord. The first stroke of the razor-like crescent athwart any portion of the band, would so detach it that it might be unwound from my person by means of my left hand. But how fearful, in that case, the proximity of the steel ! The result of the slightest struggle, how deadly ! Was it likely, moreover, that the minions of the torturer had not foreseen and provided for this possibility ? Was it probable that the bandage crossed my bosom in the track of the pendulum ? Dreading to find my faint, and, as it seemed, my last hope frustrated, I so far elevated my head as to obtain a distinct view of my breast. The surcingle enveloped my limbs and body close in all directions—*save in the path of the destroying crescent.*

Scarcely had I dropped my head back into its original position, when there flashed upon my mind what I cannot better describe than as the unformed half of that idea of deliverance to which I have previously alluded, and of which a moiety only floated indeterminately through my brain when I raised food to my burning lips. The whole thought was now present—feeble, scarcely sane, scarcely definite— but still entire. I proceeded at once, with the nervous energy of despair, to attempt its execution.

For many hours the immediate vicinity of the low framework upon which I lay, had been literally swarming with rats. They were wild, bold, ravenous—their red eyes glaring upon me as if they waited but for motionlessness on my part to make me their prey. " To what food," I thought, " have they been accustomed in the well ? "

They had devoured, in spite of all my efforts to prevent them, all but a small remnant of the contents of the dish. I had fallen into an habitual see-saw, or wave of the hand, about the platter ; and at length the unconscious uniformity of the movement deprived it of effect. In their voracity, the vermin frequently fastened their sharp fangs in my fingers. With the particles of the oily and spicy viand which now remained, I thoroughly rubbed the bandage wherever I could reach it ; then, raising my hand from the floor, I lay breathlessly still.

At first, the ravenous animals were startled and terrified at the change—at the cessation of movement. They shrank alarmedly back ; many sought the well. But this was only for a moment. I had not counted in vain upon their voracity. Observing that I remained without motion, one or two of the boldest leaped upon the framework, and smelt at the surcingle. This seemed the signal for a general rush. Forth from the well they hurried in fresh troops. They clung to the wood—they overran it, and leaped in hundreds upon my person. The measured move-

ment of the pendulum disturbed them not at all. Avoid
ing its strokes, they busied themselves with the anointed
bandage. They pressed—they swarmed upon me in ever
accumulating heaps. They writhed upon my throat;
their cold lips sought my own; I was half stifled by their
thronging pressure; disgust, for which the world has no
name, swelled my bosom, and chilled, with a heavy clamminess, my heart. Yet one minute, and I felt that the
struggle would be over. Plainly I perceived the loosening
of the bandage. I knew that in more than one place it must
be already severed. With a more than human resolution I
lay still.

Nor had I erred in my calculations—nor had I endured
in vain. I at length felt that I was *free*. The surcingle
hung in ribands from my body. But the stroke of the
pendulum already pressed upon my bosom. It had
divided the serge of the robe. It had cut through the linen
beneath. Twice again it swung, and a sharp sense of pain
shot through every nerve. But the moment of escape had
arrived. At a wave of my hand my deliverers hurried
tumultuously away. With a steady movement—cautious,
sidelong, shrinking, and slow—I slid from the embrace of
the bandage and beyond the reach of the scimitar. For
the moment, at least, *I was free*.

Free!—and in the grasp of the Inquisition! I had
scarcely stepped from my wooden bed of horror upon
the stone floor of the prison, when the motion of the hellish
machine ceased, and I beheld it drawn up, by some invisible
force, through the ceiling. This was a lesson which I took
desperately to heart. My every motion was undoubtedly
watched. Free!—I had but escaped death in one form
of agony, to be delivered unto worse than death in some
other. With that thought I rolled my eyes nervously
around on the barriers of iron that hemmed me in. Something unusual—some change which, at first, I could not
appreciate distinctly—it was obvious, had taken place
in the apartment. For many minutes of a dreamy and
trembling abstraction, I busied myself in vain, unconnected
conjecture. During this period, I became aware, for the
first time, of the origin of the sulphureous light which illumined the cell. It proceeded from a fissure, about half an
inch in width, extending entirely around the prison at the
base of the walls, which thus appeared, and were com-

pletely separated from the floor. I endeavoured, but of course in vain, to look through the aperture.

As I arose from the attempt, the mystery of the alteration in the chamber broke at once upon my understanding. I have observed that, although the outlines of the figures upon the walls were sufficiently distinct, yet the colours seemed blurred and indefinite. These colours had now assumed, and were momentarily assuming, a startling and most intense brilliancy, that gave to the spectral and fiendish portraitures an aspect that might have thrilled even firmer nerves than my own. Demon eyes, of a wild and ghastly vivacity, glared upon me in a thousand directions, where none had been visible before, and gleamed with the lurid lustre of a fire that I could not force my imagination to regard as unreal.

Unreal! Even while I breathed there came to my nostrils the breath of the vapour of heated iron! A suffocating odour pervaded the prison! A deeper glow settled each moment in the eyes that glared at my agonies! A richer tint of crimson diffused itself over the pictured horrors of blood. I panted! I gasped for breath! There could be no doubt of the design of my tormentors—oh! most unrelenting! oh! most demoniac of men! I shrank from the glowing metal to the centre of the cell. Amid the thought of the fiery destruction that impended, the idea of the coolness of the well came over my soul like balm. I rushed to its deadly brink. I threw my straining vision below. The glare from the enkindled roof illumined its inmost recesses. Yet, for a wild moment, did my spirit refuse to comprehend the meaning of what I saw. At length it forced—it wrestled its way into my soul—it burned itself in upon my shuddering reason. Oh! for a voice to speak!—oh! horror!— oh! any horror but this! With a shriek, I rushed from the margin, and buried my face in my hands—weeping bitterly.

The heat rapidly increased, and once again I looked up, shuddering as with a fit of the ague. There had been a second change in the cell—and now the change was obviously in the *form*. As before, it was in vain that I at first endeavoured to appreciate or understand what was taking place. But not long was I left in doubt. The inquisitorial vengeance had been hurried by my twofold

escape, and there was to be no more dallying with the King
of Terrors. The room had been square. I saw that two
of its iron angles were now acute—two, consequently,
obtuse. The fearful difference quickly increased with a low
rumbling or moaning sound. In an instant the apartment
had shifted its form into that of a lozenge. But the alteration stopped not here—I neither hoped nor desired it to
stop. I could have clasped the red walls to my bosom as
a garment of eternal peace. " Death," I said, " any death
but that of the pit ! " Fool ! might I not have known
that *into the pit* it was the object of the burning iron to
urge me ? Could I resist its glow ? or if even that, could
I withstand its pressure ? And now, flatter and flatter
grew the lozenge, with a rapidity that left me no time for
contemplation. Its centre, and of course, its greatest
width, came just over the yawning gulf. I shrank back—
but the closing walls pressed me resistlessly onward. At
length for my seared and writhing body there was no
longer an inch of foothold on the firm floor of the prison.
I struggled no more, but the agony of my soul found vent in
one loud, long, and final scream of despair. I felt that I
tottered upon the brink—I averted my eyes——

There was a discordant hum of human voices ! There
was a loud blast as of many trumpets ! There was a harsh
grating as of a thousand thunders ! The fiery walls rushed
back ! An outstretched arm caught my own as I fell,
fainting, into the abyss. It was that of General Lasalle.
The French army had entered Toledo. The Inquisition was
in the hands of its enemies.

THE DOMAIN OF ARNHEIM

" The garden like a lady fair was cut,
    That lay as if she slumbered in delight,
And to the open skies her eyes did shut.
    The azure fields of Heaven were 'sembled right
    In a large round, set with the flowers of light.
The flowers-de-luce, and the round sparks of dew,
That hung upon their azure leaves, did shew
Like twinkling stars, that sparkle in the evening blue."
                                                —GILES FLETCHER.

FROM his cradle to his grave a gale of prosperity bore my friend Ellison along. Nor do I use the word prosperity in its mere worldly sense. I mean it as synonymous with happiness. The person of whom I speak seemed born for the purpose of foreshadowing the doctrines of Turgot, Price, Priestley, and Condorcet—of exemplifying by individual instance what has been deemed the chimera of the perfectionists. In the brief existence of Ellison I fancy that I have seen refuted the dogma, that in man's very nature lies some hidden principle, the antagonist of bliss. An anxious examination of his career has given me to understand that in general, from the violation of a few simple laws of humanity, arises the wretchedness of mankind—that as a species we have in our possession the as yet unwrought elements of content—and that, even now, in the present darkness and madness of all thought on the great question of the social condition, it is not impossible that man, the individual, under certain unusual and highly fortuitous conditions, may be happy.

With opinions such as these my young friend, too, was fully imbued ; and thus it is worthy of observation that the uninterrupted enjoyment which distinguished his life was, in great measure, the result of preconcert. It is indeed evident, that with less of the instinctive philosophy, which now and then stands so well in the stead of experience, Mr. Ellison would have found himself precipitated by the very extraordinary success of his life into the common vortex of unhappiness which yawns for those of pre-eminent endowments. But it is by no means my object to pen an essay on happiness. The ideas of my friend may be summed up in a few words. He admitted but four elementary principles, or, more strictly, conditions of bliss. That which he considered chief was (strange to say !) the simple and purely physical one of free exercise in the open air. " The health," he said, " attainable by other means is scarcely worth the name." He instanced the ecstasies of the fox-hunter, and pointed to the tillers of the earth, the only people who, as a class, can be fairly considered happier than others. His second condition was the love of woman. His third, and most difficult of realisation, was the contempt of ambition. His fourth was an object of unceasing pursuit ; and he held that, other things being equal, the extent of attainable happiness was in proportion to the spirituality of this object.

Ellison was remarkable in the continuous profusion of good gifts lavished upon him by fortune. In personal grace and beauty he exceeded all men. His intellect was of that order to which the acquisition of knowledge is less a labour than an intuition and a necessity. His family was one of the most illustrious of the empire. His bride was the loveliest and most devoted of women. His possessions had been always ample ; but, on the attainment of his majority, it was discovered that one of those extraordinary freaks of fate had been played in his behalf which startle the whole social world amid which they occur, and seldom fail radically to alter the moral constitution of those who are their objects.

It appears that, about a hundred years before Mr. Ellison's coming of age, there had died, in a remote province, one Mr. Seabright Ellison. This gentleman had amassed a princely fortune, and, having no immediate connections, conceived the whim of suffering his wealth to accumulate for a century after his decease. Minutely and sagaciously directing the various modes of investment, he bequeathed the aggregate amount to the nearest of blood bearing the name Ellison, who should be alive at the end of the hundred years. Many attempts had been made to set aside this singular bequest ; their *ex post facto* character rendered them abortive ; but the attention of a jealous government was aroused, and a legislative act finally obtained, forbidding all similar accumulations. This act, however, did not prevent young Ellison from entering into possession, on his twenty-first birthday, as the heir of his ancestor

Seabright, of a fortune of *four hundred and fifty millions of dollars.**

When it had become known that such was the enormous wealth inherited, there were, of course, many speculations as to the mode of its disposal. The magnitude and the immediate availability of the sum bewildered all who thought on the topic. The possessor of any *appreciable* amount of money might have been imagined to perform any one of a thousand things. With riches merely surpassing those of any citizen, it would have been easy to suppose him engaging to supreme excess in the fashionable extravagances of his time—or busying himself with political intrigue—or aiming at ministerial power—or purchasing increase of nobility—or collecting large museums of *virtu*—or playing the munificent patron of letters, of science, of art—or endowing and bestowing his name upon extensive institutions of charity. But for the inconceivable wealth in the actual possession of the heir, these objects and all ordinary objects were felt to afford too limited a field. Recourse was had to figures, and these but sufficed to confound. It was seen that, even at three per cent., the annual income of the inheritance amounted to no less than thirteen millions and five hundred thousand dollars ; which was one million and one hundred and twenty-five thousand per month ; or thirty-six thousand nine hundred and eighty-six per day; or one thousand five hundred and forty-one per hour ; or six and twenty dollars for every minute that flew. Thus the usual track of supposition was thoroughly broken up. Men knew not what to imagine. There were some who even conceived that Mr. Ellison would divest himself of at least one-half of his fortune, as of utterly superfluous opulence—enriching whole troops of his relatives by division of his superabund-

—————————

, * An incident, similar in outline to the one here imagined, occurred not very long ago in England. The name of the fortunate heir was Thelluson. I first saw an account of this matter in the *Tour* of Prince Puckler Muskau, who makes the sum inherited *ninety millions of pounds,* and justly observes that " in the contemplation of so vast a sum, and of the services to which it might be applied, there is something even of the sublime." To suit the views of this article I have followed the Prince's statement, although a grossly exaggerated one. The germ, and in fact the commencement of the present paper was published many years ago—previous to the issue of the first number of Sue's admirable *Juif Errant,* which may possibly have been suggested to him by Muskau's account.

ance. To the nearest of these he did, in fact, abandon the very unusual wealth which was his own before the inheritance.

I was not surprised, however, to perceive that he had long made up his mind on a point which had occasioned so much discussion to his friends. Nor was I greatly astonished at the nature of his decision. In regard to individual charities he had satisfied his conscience. In the possibility of any improvement, properly so called, being effected by man himself in the general condition of man, he had (I am sorry to confess) little faith. Upon the whole, whether happily or unhappily, he was thrown back, in very great measure, upon self.

In the widest and noblest sense he was a poet. He comprehended, moreover, the true character, the august aims, the supreme majesty and dignity of the poetic sentiment. The fullest, if not the sole proper satisfaction of this sentiment he instinctively felt to lie in the creation of novel forms of beauty. Some peculiarities, either in his early education or in the nature of his intellect, had tinged with what is termed materialism all his ethical speculations ; and it was this bias, perhaps, which led him to believe that the most advantageous at least, if not the sole legitimate field for the poetic exercise, lies in the creation of novel moods of purely *physical* loveliness. Thus it happened he became neither musician nor poet—if we use this latter term in its everyday acceptation. Or it might have been that he neglected to become either, merely in pursuance of his idea that in contempt of ambition is to be found one of the essential principles of happiness on earth. Is it not, indeed, possible that, while a high order of genius is necessarily ambitious, the highest is above that which is termed ambition ? And may it not thus happen that many far greater than Milton have contentedly remained " mute and inglorious " ? I believe that the world has never seen—and that, unless through some series of accidents goading the noblest order of mind into distasteful exertion, the world will never see—that full extent of triumphant execution, in the richer domains of art, of which the human nature is absolutely capable.

Ellison became neither musician nor poet ; although no man lived more profoundly enamoured of music and poetry. Under other circumstances than those which

invested him, it is not impossible that he would have become
a painter. Sculpture, although in its nature rigorously
poetical, was too limited in its extent and consequences,
to have occupied, at any time, much of his attention. And
I have now mentioned all the provinces in which the
common understanding of the poetic sentiment has declared
it capable of expatiating. But Ellison maintained that
the richest, the truest, and most natural, if not altogether
the most extensive province, had been unaccountably
neglected. No definition had spoken of the landscape-
gardener as of the poet ; yet it seemed to my friend that
the creation of the landscape-garden offered to the proper
Muse the most magnificent of opportunities. Here, indeed,
was the fairest field for the display of imagination in the
endless combining of forms of novel beauty ; the elements
to enter into combination being, by a vast superiority, the
most glorious which the earth could afford. In the multiform and multicolour of the flower and the tree, he recognised the most direct and energetic efforts of Nature at
physical loveliness. And in the direction or concentration
of this effort—or, more properly, in its adaptation to the
eyes which were to behold it on earth—he perceived that he
should be employing the best means—labouring to the
greatest advantage—in the fulfilment, not only of his own
destiny as poet, but of the august purposes for which the
Deity had implanted the poetic sentiment in man.

  " Its adaptation to the eyes which were to behold it on
earth." In his explanation of this phraseology, Mr.
Ellison did much towards solving what has always seemed
to me an enigma—I mean the fact (which none but the
ignorant dispute) that no such combination of scenery
exists in nature as the painter of genius may produce.
No such paradises are to be found in reality as have glowed
on the canvas of Claude. In the most enchanting of natural
landscapes there will always be found a defect or an excess
—many excesses and defects. While the component parts
may defy, individually, the highest skill of the artist, the
arrangement of these parts will always be susceptible of
improvement. In short, no position can be attained on
the wide surface of the *natural* earth, from which an
artistical eye, looking steadily, will not find matter of offence
in what is termed the " composition " of the landscape.
And yet how unintelligible is this ! In all other matters

we are justly instructed to regard nature as supreme.
With her details we shrink from competition. Who shall
presume to imitate the colours of the tulip, or to improve
the proportions of the lily of the valley ? The criticism
which says, of sculpture or portraiture, that here nature
is to be exalted or idealised rather than imitated, is in error.
No pictorial or sculptural combinations of points of human
loveliness do more than approach the living and breathing
beauty. In landscape alone is the principle of the critic
true ; and having felt its truth here, it is but the headlong
spirit of generalisation which has led him to pronounce it
true throughout all the domains of art. Having, I say,
felt its truth here ; for the feeling is no affectation or
chimera. The mathematics afford no more absolute
demonstrations than the sentiment of his art yields the
artist. He not only believes, but positively knows, that
such and such apparently arbitrary arrangements of matter
constitute, and alone constitute, the true beauty. His
reasons, however, have not yet been matured into expression. It remains for a more profound analysis than the
world has yet seen, fully to investigate and express them.
Nevertheless he is confirmed in his instinctive opinions
by the voice of all his brethren. Let a " composition "
be defective ; let an emendation be wrought in its mere
arrangement of form ; let this emendation be submitted
to every artist in the world ; by each will its necessity be
admitted. And even far more than this : in remedy of
the defective composition each insulated member of the
fraternity would have suggested the identical emendation.

I repeat that in landscape arrangements alone is the
physical nature susceptible of exaltation, and that therefore
her susceptibility of improvement at this one point was a
mystery I had been unable to solve. My own thoughts
on the subject had rested in the idea that the primitive
intention of nature would have so arranged the earth's
surface as to have fulfilled at all points man's sense of
perfection in the beautiful, the sublime, or the picturesque ;
but that this primitive intention had been frustrated by
the known geological disturbances—disturbances of form
and colour-grouping, in the correction or allaying of which
lies the soul of art. The force of this idea was much
weakened, however, by the necessity which it involved of
considering the disturbances abnormal and unadapted to

any purpose. It was Ellison who suggested that they were prognostic of *death*. He thus explained :—Admit the earthly immortality of man to have been the first intention. We have then the primitive arrangement of the earth's surface adapted to his blissful estate, as not existent but designed. The disturbances were the preparations for his subsequently conceived deathful condition.

" Now," said my friend, " what we regard as exaltation of the landscape may be really such, as respects only the moral or human *point of view*. Each alternation of the natural scenery may possibly effect a blemish in the picture, if we can suppose this picture viewed at large—in mass— from some point distant from the earth's surface, although not beyond the limits of its atmosphere. It is easily understood that what might improve a closely-scrutinised detail, may at the time injure a general or more distantly observed effect. There *may* be a class of beings, human once, but now invisible to humanity, to whom, from afar, our disorder may seem order—our unpicturesqueness picturesque ; in a word, the earth-angels, for whose scrutiny more especially than our own, and for whose death-refined appreciation of the beautiful, may have been set in array by God the wide landscape-gardens of the hemispheres."

In the course of discussion, my friend quoted some passages from a writer on landscape-gardening, who has been supposed to have well treated his theme :—

" There are properly but two styles of landscape-garden-ing—the natural and the artificial. One seeks to recall the original beauty of the country, by adapting its means to the surrounding scenery ; cultivating trees in harmony with the hills or plain of the neighbouring land ; detecting and bringing into practice those nice relations of size, proportion, and colour which, hid from the common ob-server, are revealed everywhere to the experienced student of nature. The result of the natural style of gardening is seen rather in the absence of all defects and incongruities —in the prevalence of a healthy harmony and order—than in the creation of any special wonders or miracles. The artificial style has as many varieties as there are different tastes to gratify. It has a certain general relation to the various styles of building. There are the stately avenues and retirements of Versailles ; Italian terraces ; and a various mixed old-English style, which bears some relation

to the Domestic Gothic or English Elizabethan architecture.   Whatever may be said against the abuses of the
artificial landscape-gardening, a mixture of pure art in a
garden scene adds to it a great beauty.   This is partly
pleasing to the eye, by the show of order and design, and
partly moral.   A terrace with an old moss-covered balustrade calls up at once to the eye the fair forms that have
passed there in other days.   The slightest exhibition of
art is an evidence of care and human interest."

"From what I have already observed," said Ellison,
" you will understand that I reject the idea, here expressed,
of recalling the original beauty of the country.   The
original beauty is never so great as that which may be
introduced.   Of course, everything depends on the selec-
tion of a spot with capabilities.   What is said about
detecting and bringing into practice nice relations of
size, proportion, and colour is one of those mere vaguenesses of speech which serve to veil inaccuracy of thought.
The phrase quoted may mean anything, or nothing, and
guides in no degree.   That the true result of the natural
style of gardening is seen rather in the absence of all
defects and incongruities than in the creation of any
special wonders or miracles, is a proposition better suited
to the grovelling apprehension of the herd than to the
fervid dreams of the man of genius.   The negative merit
suggested appertains to that hobbling criticism which,
in letters, would elevate Addison into apotheosis.   In
truth, while that virtue which consists in the mere avoid-
ance of vice appeals directly to the understanding, and
can thus be circumscribed in *rule*, the loftier virtue, which
flames in creation, can be apprehended in its results alone.
Rule applies but to the merits of denial—to the excellences
which refrain.   Beyond these, the critical art can but
suggest.   We may be instructed to build a ' Cato,' but we
are in vain told *how* to conceive a Parthenon or an
' Inferno.'   The thing done, however—the wonder accomplished—and the capacity for apprehension becomes
universal.   The sophists of the negative school who,
through inability to create, have scoffed at creation, are
now found the loudest in applause.   What, in its chrysalis
condition of principle, affronted their demure reason,
never fails, in its maturity of accomplishment, to extort
admiration from their instinct of beauty.

" The author's observations on the artificial style," continued Ellison, " are less objectionable. A mixture of pure art in a garden scene adds to it a great beauty. This is just ; as also is the reference to the sense of human interest. The principle expressed is incontrovertible—but there *may* be something beyond it. There may be an object in keeping with the principle—an object unattainable by the means ordinarily possessed by individuals, yet which, if attained, would lend a charm to the landscape-garden, far surpassing that which a sense of merely human interest could bestow. A poet, having very unusual pecuniary resources, might, while retaining the necessary idea of art, or culture, or, as our author expresses it, of interest, so imbue his designs at once with extent and novelty of beauty as to convey the sentiment of spiritual interference. It will be seen that, in bringing about such result, he secures all the advantages of interest or *design*, while relieving his work of the harshness or technicality of the worldly *art*. In the most rugged of wildernesses —in the most savage of the scenes of pure nature—there is apparent the *art* of a creator ; yet this art is apparent to reflection only ; in no respect has it the obvious force of a feeling. Now, let us suppose this sense of the Almighty design to be *one step depressed*—to be brought into something like harmony or consistency with the sense of human art —to form an intermedium between the two ;—let us imagine, for example, a landscape whose combined vastness and definitiveness—whose united beauty, magnificence, and *strangeness*, shall convey the idea of care, or culture, or superintendence, on the part of beings superior, yet akin to humanity—then the sentiment of *interest* is preserved, while the art intervolved is made to assume the air of an intermediate or secondary nature—a nature which is not God, nor an emanation from God, but which still is nature in the sense of the handiwork of the angels that hover between man and God."

It was in devoting his enormous wealth to the embodiment of a vision such as this—in the free exercise in the open air ensured by the personal superintendence of his plans—in the unceasing object which these plans afforded, in the high spirituality of the object, in the contempt of ambition which it enabled him truly to feel, in the perennial springs with which it gratified, without possibility of satiating, that one master-passion of his soul, the thirst for beauty ; above all, it was in the sympathy of a woman, not unwomanly, whose loveliness and love enveloped his existence in the purple atmosphere of Paradise, that Ellison thought to find, *and found*, exemption from the ordinary cares of humanity, with a far greater amount of positive happiness than ever glowed in the rapt day-dreams of De Staël.

I despair of conveying to the reader any distinct conception of the marvels which my friend did actually accomplish. I wish to describe, but am disheartened by the difficulty of description, and hesitate between detail and generality. Perhaps the better course will be to unite the two in their extremes.

Mr. Ellison's first step regarded, of course, the choice of a locality ; and scarcely had he commenced thinking on this point, when the luxuriant nature of the Pacific Islands arrested his attention. In fact he had made up his mind for a voyage to the South Seas, when a night's reflection induced him to abandon the idea. " Were I misanthropic," he said, " such a *locale* would suit me. The thoroughness of its insulation and seclusion, and the difficulty of ingress and egress, would in such case be the charm of charms ; but as yet I am not Timon. I wish the composure but not the depression of solitude. There must remain with me a certain control over the extent and duration of my repose. There will be frequent hours in which I shall need, too, the sympathy of the poetic in what I have done. Let me seek then a spot not far from a populous city—whose vicinity also will best enable me to execute my plans."

In search of a suitable place so situated Ellison travelled for several years, and I was permitted to accompany him. A thousand spots with which I was enraptured he rejected without hesitation for reasons which satisfied me in the end that he was right. We came at length to an elevated table-land of wonderful fertility and beauty, affording a panoramic prospect very little less in extent than that of Ætna, and, in Ellison's opinion as well as my own, surpassing the far-famed view from that mountain in all the true elements of the picturesque.

" I am aware," said the traveller, as he drew a sigh of deep delight after gazing on this scene, entranced, for nearly an hour, " I know that here, in my circumstances, nine-tenths of the most fastidious of men would rest content. This panorama is indeed glorious, and I should rejoice in it but for the excess of its glory. The taste of all the architects I have ever known leads them, for the sake of ' prospect,' to put up buildings on hill-tops. The error is obvious. Grandeur in any of its moods, but especially in that of extent, startles, excites—and then fatigues, depresses. For the occasional scene nothing can be better—for the constant view nothing worse. And, in the constant view, the most objectionable phase of grandeur is that of extent ; the worst phase of extent that of distance. It is at war with the sentiment and with the sense of *seclusion*—the sentiment and sense which we seek to humour in ' retiring to the country.' In looking from the summit of a mountain we cannot help feeling *abroad* in the world. The heart-sick avoid distant prospects as a pestilence."

It was not until towards the close of the fourth year of our search that we found a locality with which Ellison professed himself satisfied. It is of course needless to say *where* was the locality. The late death of my friend, in causing his domain to be thrown open to certain classes of visitors, has given to *Arnheim* a species of secret and subdued if not solemn celebrity, similar in kind, although infinitely superior in degree, to that which so long distinguished Fonthill.

The usual approach to Arnheim was by the river. The visitor left the city in the early morning. During the forenoon he passed between shores of a tranquil and domestic beauty, on which grazed innumerable sheep, their white fleeces spotting the vivid green of rolling meadows. By degrees the idea of cultivation subsided into that of merely pastoral care. This slowly became merged in a sense of retirement—this again in a consciousness of solitude. As the evening approached the channel grew more narrow ; the banks more and more precipitous , and these latter were clothed in richer, more profuse, and more sombre foliage. The water increased in transparency. The stream took a thousand turns, so that at no moment could its gleaming surface be seen for a greater distance than a furlong. At every instant the vessel seemed imprisoned within an enchanted circle, having insuperable and impenetrable walls of foliage, a roof of ultra-marine satin, and *no* floor—the keel balancing itself with admirable nicety on that of a phantom bark which, by some accident having been turned upside down, floated in constant company with the substantial one for the purpose of sustaining it. The channel now became a *gorge*— although the term is somewhat inapplicable, and I employ it merely because the language has no word which better represents the most striking—not the most distinctive— feature of the scene. The character of gorge was maintained only in the height and parallelism of the shores ; it was lost altogether in their other traits. The walls of the ravine (through which the clear water still tranquilly flowed) arose to an elevation of a hundred and occasionally of a hundred and fifty feet, and inclined so much towards each other as in a great measure to shut out the light of day ; while the long plume-like moss which depended densely from the intertwining shrubberies overhead gave the whole chasm an air of funereal gloom. The windings became more frequent and intricate, and seemed often as if returning in upon themselves, so that the voyager had long lost all idea of direction. He was, moreover, enwrapt in an exquisite sense of the strange. The thought of nature still remained, but her character seemed to have undergone modification ; there was a weird symmetry, a thrilling uniformity, a wizard propriety, in these her works. Not a dead branch—not a withered leaf—not a stray pebble—not a patch of the brown earth was anywhere visible. The crystal water welled up against the clean granite or the unblemished moss with a sharpness of outline that delighted while it bewildered the eye.

Having threaded the mazes of this channel for some hours, the gloom deepening every moment, a sharp and unexpected turn of the vessel brought it suddenly, as if dropped from heaven, into a circular basin of very considerable extent when compared with the width of the gorge. It was about two hundred yards in diameter, and girt in at all points but one, that immediately fronting the vessel as it entered, by hills equal in general height to the walls of the chasm, although of a thoroughly different character. Their sides sloped from the water's edge at an angle of some forty-five degrees, and they were clothed from base to summit—not a perceptible point escaping—

drapery of the most gorgeous flower blossoms ; scarcely
reen leaf being visible among the sea of odorous and
tuating colour. This basin was of great depth, but
transparent was the water that the bottom, which
ned to consist of a thick mass of small round alabaster
bles, was distinctly visible by glimpses, that is to say,
enever the eye could permit itself *not* to see far down
the inverted heaven the duplicate blooming of the
s. On these latter there were no trees, nor even shrubs
any size. The impressions wrought on the observer
e those of richness, warmth, colour, quietude, uni-
nity, softness, delicacy, daintiness, voluptuousness,
a miraculous extremeness of culture that suggested
ams of a new race of fairies, laborious, tasteful,
gnificent, and fastidious ; but as the eye traced upward
myriad-tinted slope, from its sharp junction with the
er to its myriad termination amid the folds of over-
ging cloud, it became indeed difficult not to fancy
anoramic cataract of rubies, sapphires, opals, and
en onyxes, rolling silently out of the sky.

he visitor, shooting suddenly into this bay from out
gloom of the ravine, is delighted, but astounded by
full orb of the declining sun, which he had supposed
e already far below the horizon, but which now con-
ts him and forms the sole termination of an otherwise
tless vista seen through another chasm-like rift in the

ut here the voyager quits the vessel which has borne
so far, and descends into a light canoe of ivory, stained
arabesque devices in vivid scarlet, both within and
out. The poop and beak of this boat arise high
ve the water with sharp points, so that the general
is that of an irregular crescent. It lies on the surface
e bay with the proud grace of a swan. On its ermined
reposes a single feathery paddle of satin-wood ; but
arsman or attendant is to be seen. The guest is
en to be of good cheer—that the fates will take care
im. The larger vessel disappears, and he is left alone
he canoe, which lies apparently motionless in the
lle of the lake. While he considers what course to
ue, however, he becomes aware of a gentle movement
he fairy bark. It slowly swings itself around until
row points towards the sun. It advances with a

L

gentle but gradually accelerated velocity, while the sli,
ripples it creates seem to break about the ivory si
in divinest melody—seem to offer the only possible
planation of the soothing yet melancholy music for wh
unseen origin the bewildered voyager looks around I
in vain.

The canoe steadily proceeds, and the rocky gate of
vista is approached, so that its depths can be more distinc
seen. To the right arise a chain of lofty hills rudely a
luxuriantly wooded. It is observed, however, that
trait of exquisite *cleanness* where the bank dips into
water still prevails. There is not one token of the us
river *débris*. To the left the character of the scene
softer and more obviously artificial. Here the bank slo
upward from the stream in a very gentle ascent, formin
broad sward of grass, of a texture resembling nothing
much as velvet, and of a brilliancy of green which wo
bear comparison with the tint of the purest emera
This *plateau* varies in width from ten to three hund
yards ; reaching from the river bank to a wall, fifty 1
high, which extends in an infinity of curves, but follow
the general direction of the river until lost in the dista
to the westward. This wall is of one continuous ro
and has been formed by cutting perpendicularly the o
rugged precipice of the stream's southern bank ; but
trace of the labour has been suffered to remain. '
chiselled stone has the hue of ages, and is profusely o'
hung and overspread with the ivy, the coral honeysuc
the eglantine, and the clematis. The uniformity of
top and bottom lines of the wall is fully relieved by
casional trees of gigantic height, growing singly or in sr
groups, both along the *plateau* and in the domain beb
the wall, but in close proximity to it ; so that frequ
limbs (of the black walnut especially) reach over and
their pendent extremities into the water. Farther b
within the domain the vision is impeded by an impenetra
screen of foliage.

These things are observed during the canoe's grac
approach to what I have called the gate of the vista.
drawing nearer to this, however, its chasm-like appeara
vanishes ; a new outlet from the bay is discovered to
left, in which direction the wall is also seen to sweep,
following the general course of the stream. Down

w opening the eye cannot penetrate very far ; for the
ream, accompanied by the wall, still bends to the left
til both are swallowed up by the leaves.

The boat, nevertheless, glides magically into the winding
annel ; and here the shore opposite the wall is found
resemble that opposite the wall in the straight vista.
fty hills, rising occasionally into mountains, and covered
th vegetation in wild luxuriance, still shut in the scene.
Floating gently onward, but with a velocity slightly
gmented, the voyager, after many short turns, finds his
ogress apparently barred by a gigantic gate or rather
or of burnished gold, elaborately carved and fretted,
d reflecting the direct rays of the now fast sinking sun
th an effulgence that seems to wreathe the whole sur-
inding forest in flames. This gate is inserted in the
ty wall ; which here appears to cross the river at right
gles. In a few moments, however, it is seen that the
in body of the water still sweeps in a gentle and ex-
sive curve to the left, the wall following it as before,
ile a stream of considerable volume, diverging from the
incipal one, makes its way with a slight ripple, under
e door, and is thus hidden from sight. The canoe falls
o the lesser channel and approaches the gate. Its
nderous wings are slowly and musically expanded. The
at glides between them, and commences a rapid descent
o a vast amphitheatre entirely begirt with purple
untains, whose bases are laved by a gleaming river
oughout the full extent of their circuit. Meantime the
ole Paradise of Arnheim bursts upon the view. There
a gush of entrancing melody ; there is an oppressive
se of strange sweet odour ;—there is a dream-like
ermingling to the eye of tall slender Eastern trees, bosky
ubberies, flocks of golden and crimson birds, lily-fringed
es, meadows of violets, tulips, poppies, hyacinths, and
eroses, long intertangled lines of silver streamlets, and,
springing confusedly from amid all, a mass of semi-
thic, semi-Saracenic architecture, sustaining itself as if
miracle in mid-air, glittering in the red sunlight with
undred oriels, minarets, and pinnacles ; and seeming
phantom handiwork conjointly of the Sylphs, of the
ries, of the Genii, and of the Gnomes.

LANDOR'S COTTAGE

A PENDANT TO " THE DOMAIN OF ARNHEIM "

DURING a pedestrian tour last summer through one or tw
of the river counties of New York, I found myself, as t
day declined, somewhat embarrassed about the road I w
pursuing. The land undulated very remarkably ; and r
path for the last hour had wound about and about so co
fusedly in its effort to keep in the valleys, that I no long
knew in what direction lay the sweet village of B—
where I had determined to stop for the night. The s
had scarcely *shone*, strictly speaking, during the da
which nevertheless had been unpleasantly warm.
smoky mist, resembling that of the Indian summer, e
veloped all things, and, of course, added to my uncertaint
Not that I cared much about the matter. If I did not I
upon the village before sunset, or even before dark, it w
more than possible that a little Dutch farm-house,
something of that kind, would soon make its appearan
although, in fact, the neighbourhood (perhaps on accou
of being more picturesque than fertile) was very spars
inhabited. At all events, with my knapsack for a pillo
and my hound as a sentry, a bivouac in the open air v
just the thing which would have amused me. I saunter
on, therefore, quite at ease, Ponto taking charge of r
gun, until at length, just as I had begun to consider whet
the numerous little glades that led hither and thither w
intended to be paths at all, I was conducted by one of t
most promising of them into an unquestionable carria
track. There could be no mistaking it. The traces
light wheels were evident ; and although the tall shrubber
and overgrown undergrowth met overhead, there was
obstruction whatever below, even to the passage of
Virginian mountain waggon, the most aspiring vehicle
take it, of its kind. The road, however, except in bei
open through the wood, if wood be not too weighty a na
for such an assemblage of light trees, and except in t
particulars of evident wheel-tracks, bore no resembla
to any road I had before seen. The tracks of which
speak were but faintly perceptible, having been impress

upon the firm, yet pleasantly moist surface of what looked more like green Genoese velvet than anything else. It was grass, clearly, but grass such as we seldom see out of England, so short, so thick, so even, and so vivid in colour. Not a single impediment lay in the wheel-rut, not even a chip or a dead twig. The stones that once obstructed the way had been carefully *placed*, not thrown, along the sides of the lane, so as to define its boundaries at bottom with a kind of half-precise, half-negligent, and wholly picturesque definition. Clumps of wild flowers grew everywhere luxuriantly in the interspaces.

What to make of all this, of course, I knew not. Here was *art* undoubtedly; *that* did not surprise me; all roads, in the ordinary sense, are works of art; nor can I say there was much to wonder at in the mere *excess* of art manifested; all that seemed to have been done, might have been done *here*, with such natural " capabilities " as they have it in the books on Landscape Gardening), with very little labour and expense. No, it was not the amount but the *character* of the art which caused me to take a seat on one of the blossomy stones, and gaze up and down this fairy-like avenue for half-an-hour or more in bewildered admiration. One thing became more and more evident the longer I gazed : an artist, and one with a most scrupulous eye for form, had superintended all these arrangements. The greatest care had been taken to pre-serve a due medium between the neat and graceful on the one hand, and the *pittoresco*, in the true sense of the Italian term, on the other. There were few straight, and no long uninterrupted lines. The same effect of cur-vature or of colour appeared twice usually but not oftener, at any one point of view. Everywhere was variety in uniformity. It was a piece of " composition," in which the most fastidiously critical taste could scarcely have suggested an emendation.

I had turned to the right as I entered this road, and now, arising, I continued in the same direction. The path was so serpentine that at no moment could I trace its course for more than two or three paces in advance. Its character did not undergo any material change.

Presently the murmur of water fell gently upon my ear, and in a few moments afterwards, as I turned with the road somewhat more abruptly than hitherto, I became

aware that a building of some kind lay at the foot of a
gentle declivity just before me. I could see nothing
distinctly on account of the mist which occupied all the
little valley below. A gentle breeze, however, now arose,
as the sun was about descending; and while I remained
standing on the brow of the slope, the fog gradually became
dissipated into wreaths, and so floated over the scene.

As it came fully into view, thus *gradually* as I describe it,
piece by piece, here a tree, there a glimpse of water, and
here again the summit of a chimney, I could scarcely help
fancying that the whole was one of the ingenious illusions
sometimes exhibited under the name of " vanishing
pictures."

By the time, however, that the fog had thoroughly
disappeared, the sun had made its way down behind the
gentle hills, and thence, as if with a slight *chassez* to the
south, had come again fully into sight, glaring with a
purplish lustre through a chasm that entered the valley
from the west. Suddenly, therefore, and as if by the hand
of magic, this whole valley and everything in it became
brilliantly visible.

The first *coup d'œil*, as the sun slid into the position
described, impressed me very much as I have been impressed when a boy by the concluding scene of some well
arranged theatrical spectacle or melodrama. Not even
the monstrosity of colour was wanting, for the sunlight
came out through the chasm, tinted all orange and purple;
while the vivid green of the grass in the valley was reflected
more or less upon all objects, from the curtain of vapour
that still hung overhead, as if loth to take its total departure
from a scene so enchantingly beautiful.

The little vale into which I thus peered down from under
the fog canopy could not have been more than four hundred
yards long; while in breadth it varied from fifty to one
hundred and fifty, or perhaps two hundred. It was most
narrow at its northern extremity, opening out as it tended
southwardly, but with no very precise regularity. The
widest portion was within eighty yards of the southern
extreme. The slopes which encompassed the vale could not
fairly be called hills, unless at their northern face. Here
a precipitous ledge of granite arose to a height of some
ninety feet; and, as I have mentioned, the valley at this
point was not more than fifty feet wide; but as the visitor

roceeded southwardly from this cliff, he found on his
ght hand and on his left declivities at once less high, less
recipitous, and less rocky. All, in a word, sloped and
oftened to the south; and yet the whole vale was en-
irdled by eminences, more or less high, except at two
oints. One of these I have already spoken of. It lay
onsiderably to the north of west, and was where the
etting sun made its way, as I have before described, into
ae amphitheatre, through a cleanly-cut natural cleft in
ae granite embankment; this fissure might have been ten
ards wide at its widest point, so far as the eye could trace
. It seemed to lead up, up, like a natural causeway,
ato the recesses of unexplored mountains and forests.
he other opening was directly at the southern end of the
ale. Here, generally, the slopes were nothing more than
entle inclinations, extending from east to west about one
undred and fifty yards. In the middle of this extent was
depression, level with the ordinary floor of the valley.
s regards vegetation, as well as in respect to everything
se, the scene *softened and sloped* to the south. To the
orth, on the craggy precipice, a few paces from the verge,
sprang the magnificent trunks of numerous hickories,
ack walnuts, and chestnuts, interspersed with occasional
ak; and the strong lateral branches thrown out by the
alnuts especially, spread far over the edge of the cliff.
roceeding southwardly, the explorer saw at first the
me class of trees, but less and less lofty and Salvatorish
character; then he saw the gentler elm, succeeded
y the sassafras and locust—these again by the softer
aden, redbud, catalpa, and maple—these yet again by
ill more graceful and more modest varieties. The whole
ce of the southern declivity was covered with wild
rubbery alone, an occasional silver willow or white
plar excepted. In the bottom of the valley itself (for
must be borne in mind that the vegetation hitherto
entioned grew only on the cliffs or hill-sides) were to be
en three insulated trees. One was an elm of fine size
d exquisite form; it stood guard over the southern gate
the vale. Another was a hickory, much larger than the
n, and altogether a much finer tree, although both were
ceedingly beautiful; it seemed to have taken charge of
e north-western entrance, springing from a group of rocks
the very jaws of the ravine, and throwing its graceful

body, at an angle of nearly forty-five degrees, far out int
the sunshine of the amphitheatre. About thirty yard
east of this tree stood, however, the pride of the valley
and beyond all question the most magnificent tree I hav
ever seen, unless perhaps among the cypresses of the Itchia
tuckanee. It was a triple-stemmed tulip-tree—the *Liric
dendron tulipiferum*—one of the natural order of magnolia
Its three trunks separated from the parent at about thre
feet from the soil, and, diverging very slightly and gradually
were not more than four feet apart at the point where th
largest stem shot out into foliage : this was at an elevatio
of about eighty feet. The whole height of the princip
division was one hundred and twenty feet. Nothing ca
surpass in beauty the form or the glossy vivid green of th
leaves of the tulip-tree. In the present instance they wei
fully eight inches wide ; but their glory was altogethe
eclipsed by the gorgeous splendour of the profuse blossom
Conceive, closely congregated, a million of the largest an
most resplendent tulips ! Only thus can the reader ge
any idea of the picture I would convey. And then tl
stately grace of the clean, delicately-granulated column
stems, the largest four feet in diameter at twenty fro
the ground. The innumerable blossoms, mingling wit
those of other trees scarcely less beautiful, althoug
infinitely less majestic, filled the valley with more tha
Arabian perfumes.

The general floor of the amphitheatre was *grass* of tl
same character as that I had found in the road ; if an
thing, more deliciously soft, thick, velvety, and miraculous
green. It was hard to conceive how all this beauty ha
been attained.

I have spoken of the two openings into the vale. Fro
the one to the north-west issued a rivulet, which can
gently murmuring and slightly foaming down the ravin
until it dashed against the group of rocks out of whi
sprang the insulated hickory. Here, after encircling tl
tree, it passed on a little to the north of east, leaving t
tulip tree some twenty feet to the south, and making
decided alteration in its course until it came near t
midway between the eastern and western boundaries
the valley. At this point, after a series of sweeps,
turned off at right angles and pursued a generally southe
direction, meandering as it went, until it became lost in

mall lake of irregular figure (although roughly oval) that
ay gleaming near the lower extremity of the vale. This
akelet was, perhaps, a hundred yards in diameter at its
widest part. No crystal could be clearer than its waters.
Its bottom, which could be distinctly seen, consisted altogether of pebbles brilliantly white. Its banks, of the
emerald grass already described, *rounded*, rather than
sloped, off into the clear heaven below ; and *so* clear was
his heaven, so perfectly at times did it reflect all objects
above it, that where the true bank ended and where the
mimic one commenced, it was a point of no little difficulty
o determine. The trout and some other varieties of fish,
with which this pond seemed to be almost inconveniently
crowded, had all the appearance of veritable flying-fish.
It was almost impossible to believe that they were not
absolutely suspended in the air. A light birch canoe,
hat lay placidly on the water, was reflected in its minutest
ibres with a fidelity unsurpassed by the most exquisitely
polished mirror. A small island, fairly laughing with
flowers in full bloom, and affording little more space than
ust enough for a picturesque little building, seemingly a
fowl-house—arose from the lake not far from its northern
shore—to which it was connected by means of an inconceivably light-looking and yet very primitive bridge. It
was formed of a single broad and thick plank of the tulip
wood. This was forty feet long, and spanned the interval
between shore and shore with a slight but very perceptible
arch, preventing all oscillation. From the southern ex-
reme of the lake issued a continuation of the rivulet, which,
after meandering for perhaps thirty yards, finally passed
through the " depression " (already described) in the middle
of the southern declivity, and tumbling down a sheer
precipice of a hundred feet, made its devious and unnoticed
way to the Hudson.

The lake was deep—at some points thirty feet—but the
rivulet seldom exceeded three, while its greatest width was
about eight. Its bottom and banks were as those of the
pond—if a defect could have been attributed to them, in
point of picturesqueness, it was that of excessive *neatness*.

The expanse of the green turf was relieved, here and
here, by an occasional showy shrub, such as the hydrangea,
or the common snow-ball, or the aromatic syringa ; or
more frequently by a clump of geraniums blossoming

gorgeously in great varieties. These latter grew in pot
which were carefully buried in the soil, so as to give th
plants the appearance of being indigenous. Besides al
this the lawn's velvet was exquisitely spotted with sheep
a considerable flock of which roamed about the vale, i
company with three tamed deer, and a vast number o
brilliantly-plumed ducks. A very large mastiff seeme
to be in vigilant attendance upon these animals, each an
all.

Along the eastern and western cliffs—where, towards th
upper portion of the amphitheatre, the boundaries wer
more or less precipitous—grew ivy in great profusion—
so that only here and there could even a glimpse of th
naked rock be obtained. The northern precipice, in lik
manner, was almost entirely clothed by grape-vines o
rare luxuriance, some springing from the soil at the base o
the cliff, and others from ledges on its face.

The slight elevation which formed the lower boundar
of this little domain was crowned by a neat stone wal
of sufficient height to prevent the escape of the deer
Nothing of the fence kind was observable elsewhere ; fo
nowhere else was an artificial enclosure needed : any stra
sheep, for example, which should attempt to make its wa
out of the vale by means of the ravine, would find its pro
gress arrested, after a few yards' advance, by the precipitou
ledge of rock over which tumbled the cascade that ha
arrested my attention as I first drew near the domain. I
short, the only ingress or egress was through a gate occupy
ing a rocky pass in the road, a few paces below the point a
which I stopped to reconnoitre the scene.

I have described the brook as meandering very irregularl
through the whole of its course. Its two *general* directions
as I have said, were first from west to east, and then fror
north to south. At the *turn*, the stream, sweeping back
wards, made an almost circular *loop*, so as to form a penin
sula which was *very* nearly an island, and which include
about the sixteenth of an acre. On this peninsula stoo
a dwelling-house—and when I say that this house, like th
infernal terrace seen by Vathek, " *était d'une architectur
inconnue dans les annales de la terre,*" I mean merely tha
its *tout ensemble* struck me with the keenest sense of com
bined novelty and propriety—in a word, of *poetry*—(fo
than in the words just employed, I could scarcely giv

of poetry in the abstract, a more rigorous definition)—
and I do *not* mean that the merely *outré* was perceptible in
any respect.

In fact, nothing could well be more simple—more utterly
unpretending than this cottage. Its marvellous *effect*
lay altogether in its artistic arrangement *as a picture*. I
could have fancied, while I looked at it, that some eminent
landscape-painter had built it with his brush.

The point of view from which I first saw the valley was
not *altogether*, although it was nearly, the best point from
which to survey the house. I will, therefore, describe
it as I afterwards saw it—from a position on the stone wall
at the southern extreme of the amphitheatre.

The main building was about twenty-four feet long and
sixteen broad—certainly not more. Its total height, from
the ground to the apex of the roof, could not have exceeded
eighteen feet. To the west end of this structure was
attached one about a third smaller in all its proportions—
the line of its front standing back about two yards from
that of the larger house ; and the line of its roof, of course,
being considerably depressed below that of the roof adjoining. At right angles to these buildings, and from the rear
of the main one—not exactly in the middle—extended a
third compartment, very small—being, in general, one-
third less than the western wing. The roofs of the two
larger were very steep—sweeping down from the ridge-
beam with a long concave curve, and extending at least
four feet beyond the walls in front, so as to form the roofs
of two piazzas. These latter roofs, of course, needed no
support ; but as they had the *air* of needing it, slight and
perfectly plain pillars were inserted at the corners alone.
The roof of the northern wing was merely an extension of a
portion of the main roof. Between the chief building and
western wing arose a very tall and rather slender square
chimney of hard Dutch bricks, alternately black and red—
a slight cornice of projecting bricks at the top. Over the
gables, the roofs also projected very much—in the main
building about four feet to the east and two to the west.
The principal door was not exactly in the main division,
being a little to the east—while the two windows were to the
west. These latter did not extend to the floor, but were
much longer and narrower than usual—they had single
shutters like doors—the panes were of lozenge form, but

quite large. The door itself had its upper half of glass, also in lozenge panes—a movable shutter secured it at night. The door to the west wing was in its gable, and quite simple ; a single window looked out to the south. There was no external door to the north wing, and it also had only one window to the east.

The blank wall of the eastern gable was relieved by stairs (with a balustrade) running diagonally across it—the ascent being from the south. Under cover of the widely-projecting eave these steps gave access to a door leading into the garret, or rather loft—for it was lighted only by a single window to the north, and seemed to have been intended as a store-room.

The piazzas of the main building and western wing had no floors, as is usual ; but at the doors and at each window, large, flat, irregular slabs of granite lay imbedded in the delicious turf, affording comfortable footing in all weather. Excellent paths of the same material—not *nicely* adapted, but with the velvety sod filling frequent intervals between the stones, led hither and thither from the house, to a crystal spring about five paces off, to the road, or to one or two outhouses that lay to the north, beyond the brook, and were thoroughly concealed by a few locusts and catalpas.

Not more than six steps from the main door of the cottage stood the dead trunk of a fantastic pear-tree, so clothed from head to foot in the gorgeous bignonia blossoms that one required no little scrutiny to determine what manner of sweet thing it could be. From various arms of this tree hung cages of different kinds. In one, a large wicker cylinder with a ring at top, revelled a mocking-bird ; in another, an oriole ; in a third, the impudent bobalink— while three or four more delicate prisons were loudly vocal with canaries.

The pillars of the piazza were enwreathed in jasmine and sweet honeysuckle, while from the angle formed by the main structure and its west wing in front sprang a grape-vine of unexampled luxuriance. Scorning all restraint, it had clambered first to the lower roof, then to the higher, and along the ridge of this latter it continued to writhe on, throwing out tendrils to the right and left, until at length it fairly attained the east gable, and fell trailing over the stairs.

The whole house, with its wings, was constructed of the

-fashioned Dutch shingles, broad, and with unrounded
rners. It is a peculiarity of this material to give houses
ilt of it the appearance of being wider at bottom than at
), after the manner of Egyptian architecture; and in
e present instance this exceedingly picturesque effect was
led by numerous pots of gorgeous flowers that almost
compassed the base of the buildings.

The shingles were painted a dull grey, and the happiness
th which this neutral tint melted into the vivid green of
e tulip tree leaves that partially overshadowed the cottage
n readily be conceived by an artist.

From the position near the stone wall, as described, the
ildings were seen at great advantage, for the south-
tern angle was thrown forward, so that the eye took
at once the whole of the two fronts, with the picturesque
tern gable, and at the same time obtained just a sufficient
mpse of the northern wing, with parts of a pretty roof
the spring-house, and nearly half of a light bridge that
inned the brook in the near vicinity of the main buildings.

I did not remain very long on the brow of the hill,
hough long enough to make a thorough survey of the
ne at my feet. It was clear that I had wandered from
e road to the village, and I had thus good travellers'
:use to open the gate before me and inquire my way at
events; so, without more ado, I proceeded.

The road, after passing the gate, seemed to lie upon a
:ural ledge, sloping gradually down along the face of the
·th-eastern cliffs. It led me on to the foot of the northern
cipice, and thence over the bridge, round by the eastern
·le to the front door. In this progress, I took notice that
sight of the out-houses could be obtained.

As I turned the corner of the gable the mastiff bounded
vards me in stern silence, but with the eye and the whole
of a tiger. I held him out my hand, however, in token
amity, and I never yet knew the dog who was proof
·inst such an appeal to his courtesy. He not only shut
mouth and wagged his tail, but absolutely offered me
paw, afterwards extending his civilities to Ponto.

As no bell was discernible, I rapped with my stick against.
door which stood half open. Instantly a figure ad-
·ced to the threshold—that of a young woman about
·nty-eight years of age—slender, or rather slight, and
·ewhat above the medium height. As she approached

with a certain *modest decision* of step altogether indescr
able, I said to myself, " Surely here I have found the p
fection of natural in contra-distinction from artific
grace." The second impression which she made on n
but by far the more vivid of the two, was that of *enthusias*
So intense an expression of *romance*, perhaps I should c
it, or of unworldliness, as that which gleamed from b
deep-set eyes, had never so sunk into my heart of hea
before. I know not how it is, but this peculiar expressi
of the eye, wreathing itself occasionally into the lips, is t
most powerful, if not absolutely the *sole* spell, which riv
my interest in woman. " *Romance*," provided my read
fully comprehend what I would here imply by the word
" romance " and " womanliness " seem to me convertil
terms, and, after all, what man truly *loves* in woman
simply her *womanhood*. The eyes of Annie (I heard so
one from the interior call her " Annie, darling ! ") w
" spiritual grey," her hair a light chestnut ; this is al
had time to observe of her.

At her most courteous of invitations I entered, passi
first into a tolerably wide vestibule. Having come mai
to *observe*, I took notice that to my right, as I stepped
was a window such as those in front of the house, to the le
a door leading into the principal room, while, oppos
me, an *open* door enabled me to see a small apartme
just the size of the vestibule, arranged as a study, a
having a large *bow* window looking to the north.

Passing into the parlour I found myself with *Mr. Lan*
for this I afterwards found was his name. He was ci
even cordial, in his manner, but just then I was m
intent on observing the arrangements of the dwelli
which had so much interested me than the personal appe
ance of the tenant.

The north wing I now saw was a bedchamber, its d
opened into the parlour. West of this door was a sin
window looking towards the brook. At the west end
the parlour were a fireplace and a door leading into t
west wing, probably a kitchen.

Nothing could be more rigorously simple than the fur
ture of the parlour. On the floor was an ingrain carpet
excellent texture, a white ground spotted with small circu
green figures. At the windows were curtains of sno
white jaconet muslin ; they were tolerably full, and hu

sively, perhaps rather formally, in sharp parallel plaits
ne floor—*just* to the floor. The walls were papered with
rench paper of great delicacy, a silver ground with a
t green cord running zigzag throughout. Its expanse
relieved merely by three of Julien's exquisite litho-
hs *à trois crayons*, fastened to the wall without frames.
of these drawings was a scene of Oriental luxury, or
er voluptuousness ; another was a " carnival piece,"
ted beyond compare ; the third was a Greek female
d : a face so divinely beautiful, and yet of an expression
rovokingly indeterminate, never before arrested my
ntion.

ne more substantial furniture consisted of a round table,
w chairs (including a large rocking-chair), and a sofa,
ather " settee " ; its material was plain maple painted
camy white, slightly interstriped with green ; the seat
ine. The chairs and table were " to match," but the
s of all had evidently been designed by the same brain
h planned " the grounds "—it is impossible to conceive
hing more graceful.

a the table were a few books, a large, square, crystal
le of some novel perfume, a plain ground-glass *astral*
solar) lamp with an Italian shade, and a large vase of
endently-blooming flowers. Flowers, indeed, of gor-
s colours and delicate odour formed the sole mere
ation of the apartment. The fireplace was nearly
ation with a vase of brilliant geranium. On a triangular
in each angle of the room stood also a similar vase,
d only as to its lovely contents. One or two smaller
uets adorned the mantel, and late violets clustered
t the open windows.

is not the purpose of this work to do more than give, in
il, a picture of Landor's residence—*as I found it.*

THE PREMATURE BURIAL

There are certain themes of which the interest is
absorbing, but which are too entirely horrible for
purposes of legitimate fiction. These the mere roman
must eschew, if he do not wish to offend, or to dis
They are with propriety handled only when the sev
and majesty of truth sanctify and sustain them.
thrill, for example, with the most intense of " pleasu
pain," over the accounts of the Passage of the Bere
of the Earthquake at Lisbon, of the Plague at Lor
of the Massacre of St. Bartholomew, or of the stifli
the hundred and twenty-three prisoners in the Black
at Calcutta. But, in these accounts, it is the fact—
the reality—it is the history which excites. As invent
we should regard them with simple abhorrence.

I have mentioned some few of the more promi
and august calamities on record ; but in these it is
extent, not less than the character of the calamity, w
so vividly impresses the fancy. I need not remind
reader that, from the long and weird catalogue of hu
miseries, I might have selected many individual insta
more replete with essential suffering than any of t
vast generalities of disaster. The true wretched
indeed—the ultimate woe—is particular, not diffuse.
the ghastly extremes of agony are endured by man
unit, and never by man the mass—for this let us t
a merciful God !

To be buried while alive is, beyond question, the
terrific of these extremes which has ever fallen to th
of mere mortality. That it has frequently, very freque
so fallen, will scarcely be denied by those who think.
boundaries which divide Life from Death are at
shadowy and vague. Who shall say where the one
and where the other begins ? We know that there
diseases in which occur total cessations of all the appa
functions of vitality, and yet in which these cessation
merely suspensions, properly so called. They are
temporary pauses in the incomprehensible mechanism
certain period elapses, and some unseen myste

principle again sets in motion the magic pinions and the wizard wheels. The silver cord was not for ever loosed, nor the golden bowl irreparably broken. But where, meantime, was the soul ?

Apart, however, from the inevitable conclusion, *à priori*, that such causes must produce such effects—that the well-known occurrence of such cases of suspended animation must naturally give rise, now and then, to premature interments—apart from this consideration, we have the direct testimony of medical and ordinary experience, to prove that a vast number of such interments have actually taken place. I might refer at once, if necessary, to a hundred well-authenticated instances. One of very remarkable character, and of which the circumstances may be fresh in the memory of some of my readers, occurred, not very long ago, in the neighbouring city of Baltimore, where it occasioned a painful, intense, and widely extended excitement. The wife of one of the most respectable citizens—a lawyer of eminence and a member of Congress —was seized with a sudden and unaccountable illness, which completely baffled the skill of her physicians. After much suffering, she died, or was supposed to die. No one suspected, indeed, or had reason to suspect, that she was not actually dead. She presented all the ordinary appearances of death. The face assumed the usual pinched and sunken outline. The lips were of the usual marble pallor. The eyes were lustreless. There was no warmth. Pulsation had ceased. For three days the body was preserved unburied, during which it had acquired a stony rigidity. The funeral, in short, was hastened, on account of the rapid advance of what was supposed to be decomposition.

The lady was deposited in her family vault, which, for three subsequent years, was undisturbed. At the expiration of this term, it was opened for the reception of a sarcophagus—but, alas ! how fearful a shock awaited the husband, who, personally, threw open the door. As its portals swung outwardly back, some white-apparelled object fell rattling within his arms. It was the skeleton of his wife in her yet unmouldered shroud.

A careful investigation rendered it evident that she had revived within two days after her entombment—that her struggles within the coffin had caused it to fall from a ledge, or shelf, to the floor, where it was so broken as to permit her escape. A lamp which had been accidentally left, full of oil, within the tomb, was found empty ; it might have been exhausted, however, by evaporation. On the uppermost of the steps which led down into the dread chamber, was a large fragment of the coffin, with which it seemed that she had endeavoured to arrest attention, by striking the iron door. While thus occupied, she probably swooned, or possibly died, through sheer terror ; and, in falling, her shroud became entangled in some ironwork which projected interiorly. Thus she remained, and thus she rotted, erect.

In the year 1810, a case of living inhumation happened in France, attended with circumstances which go far to warrant the assertion that truth is, indeed, stranger than fiction. The heroine of the story was a Mademoiselle Victorine Lafourcade, a young girl of illustrious family, of wealth, and of great personal beauty. Among her numerous suitors was Julien Bossuet, a poor *litterateur*, or journalist, of Paris. His talents and general amiability had recommended him to the notice of the heiress, by whom he seems to have been truly beloved ; but her pride of birth decided her, finally, to reject him, and to wed a Monsieur Renelle, a banker, and a diplomatist of some eminence. After marriage, however, this gentleman neglected, and, perhaps, even more positively ill-treated her. Having passed with him some wretched years, she died—at least her condition so closely resembled death as to deceive every one who saw her. She was buried—not in a vault —but in an ordinary grave in the village of her nativity. Filled with despair, and still inflamed by the memory of a profound attachment, the lover journeys from the capital to the remote province in which the village lies, with the romantic purpose of disinterring the corpse, and possessing himself of its luxuriant tresses. He reaches the grave. At midnight he unearths the coffin, opens it, and is in the act of detaching the hair, when he is arrested by the unclosing of the beloved eyes. In fact, the lady had been buried alive. Vitality had not altogether departed ; and she was aroused, by the caresses of her lover, from the lethargy which had been mistaken for death. He bore her frantically to his lodgings in the village. He employed certain powerful restoratives suggested by no little medical learning. In fine, she revived. She recognised her preserver. She remained with him until, by slow degrees, she fully recovered her original health. Her woman's heart was not adamant, and this last lesson of love sufficed to soften it. She bestowed it upon Bossuet. She returned no more to her husband, but concealing from him her resurrection, fled with her lover to America. Twenty years afterwards, the two returned to France, in the persuasion that time had so greatly altered the lady's appearance, that her friends would be unable to recognise her. They were mistaken, however ; for, at the first meeting, Monsieur Renelle did actually recognise and make claim to his wife. This claim she resisted ; and a judicial tribunal sustained her in her resistance ; deciding that the peculiar circumstances, with the long lapse of years, had extinguished, not only equitably, but legally, the authority of the husband.

The *Chirurgical Journal* of Leipsic—a periodical of high authority and merit, which some American bookseller would do well to translate and republish—records, in a late number, a very distressing event of the character in question.

An officer of artillery, a man of gigantic stature and of robust health, being thrown from an unmanageable horse, received a very severe contusion upon the head, which rendered him insensible at once ; the skull was slightly fractured ; but no immediate danger was apprehended. Trepanning was accomplished successfully. He was bled, and many other of the ordinary means of relief were adopted. Gradually, however, he fell into a more and more hopeless state of stupor ; and, finally, it was thought that he died.

The weather was warm ; and he was buried, with indecent haste, in one of the public cemeteries. His funeral took place on Thursday. On the Sunday following, the grounds of the cemetery were, as usual, much thronged with visitors ; and about noon, an intense excitement was created by the declaration of a peasant, that, while sitting upon the grave of the officer, he had distinctly felt a commotion of the earth, as if occasioned by some one struggling beneath. At first, little attention was paid to the man's asseveration ; but his evident terror, and the dogged obstinacy with which he persisted in his story, had at length their natural effect upon the crowd. Spades were hurriedly procured, and the grave, which was shamefully shallow, was, in a few minutes, so far thrown open that the head of its occupant appeared. He was then, seemingly, dead ; but he sat nearly erect within his coffin, the lid of which, in his furious struggles, he had partially uplifted.

He was forthwith conveyed to the nearest hospital, and there pronounced to be still living, although in an asphytic condition. After some hours he revived, recognised individuals of his acquaintance, and, in broken sentences, spoke of his agonies in the grave.

From what he related, it was clear that he must have been conscious of life for more than an hour, while inhumed, before lapsing into insensibility. The grave was carelessly and loosely filled with an exceedingly porous soil ; and thus some air was necessarily admitted. He heard the footsteps of the crowd overhead, and endeavoured to make himself heard in turn. It was the tumult within the grounds of the cemetery, he said, which appeared to awaken him from a deep sleep—but no sooner was he awake than he became fully aware of the awful horrors of his position.

This patient, it is recorded, was doing well, and seemed to be in a fair way of ultimate recovery, but fell a victim to the quackeries of medical experiment. The galvanic battery was applied, and he suddenly expired in one of those ecstatic paroxysms which, occasionally, it superinduces.

The mention of the galvanic battery, nevertheless, recalls to my memory a well-known and very extraordinary case in point, where its action proved the means of restoring to animation a young attorney of London, who had been interred for two days. This occurrred in 1831, and created, at the time, a very profound sensation wherever it was made the subject of converse.

The patient, Mr. Edward Stapleton, had died, apparently, of typhus fever, accompanied with some anomalous symptoms which had excited the curiosity of his medical attendants. Upon his seeming decease, his friends were requested to sanction a *post-mortem* examination, but declined to permit it. As often happens, when such refusals are made, the practitioners resolved to disinter the body and dissect it at leisure, in private. Arrangements were easily effected with some of the numerous corps of body-snatchers with which London abounds ; and, upon the third night after the funeral, the supposed corpse was unearthed from a grave eight feet deep, and deposited in the operating chamber of one of the private hospitals.

An incision of some extent had been actually made in the abdomen, when the fresh and undecayed appearance of the subject suggested an application of the battery. One experiment succeeded another, and the customary effects supervened, with nothing to characterise them in any respect, except, upon one or two occasions, a more than ordinary degree of life-likeness in the convulsive action.

It grew late. The day was about to dawn ; and it was thought expedient, at length, to proceed at once to the dissection. A student, however, was especially desirous of testing a theory of his own, and insisted upon applying the battery to one of the pectoral muscles. A rough gash was made, and a wire hastily brought in contact ; when the patient, with a hurried, but quite unconvulsive movement, arose from the table, stepped into the middle of the floor, gazed about him uneasily for a few seconds, and then —spoke. What he said was unintelligible ; but words were uttered ; the syllabification was distinct. Having spoken, he fell heavily to the floor.

For some moments all were paralysed with awe—but the urgency of the case soon restored them their presence of mind. It was seen that Mr. Stapleton was alive, although in a swoon. Upon exhibition of ether he revived and was rapidly restored to health, and to the society of his friends —from whom, however, all knowledge of his resuscitation was withheld, until a relapse was no longer to be apprehended. Their wonder—their rapturous astonishment— may be conceived.

The most thrilling peculiarity of this incident, nevertheless, is involved in what Mr. S. himself asserts. He declares that at no period was he altogether insensible—that, dully and confusedly, he was aware of everything which happened to him, from the moment in which he was pronounced *dead* by his physicians, to that in which he fell swooning to the floor of the hospital. " I am alive," were the uncomprehended words which, upon recognising the locality of the dissecting-room, he had endeavoured, in his extremity, to utter.

It were an easy matter to multiply such histories as these—but I forbear—for, indeed, we have no need of such to establish the fact that premature interments occur. When we reflect how very rarely, from the nature of the case, we have it in our power to detect them, we must admit that they may *frequently* occur without our cognisance. Scarcely, in truth, is a graveyard ever encroached upon, for any purpose, to any great extent, that skeletons are not found in postures which suggest the most fearful of suspicions.

Fearful indeed the suspicion—but more fearful the doom ! It may be asserted, without hesitation, that *no* event is so terribly well adapted to inspire the supremeness of bodily and of mental distress, as is burial before death. The unendurable oppression of the lungs—the stifling fumes of the damp earth—the clinging to the death garments—the rigid embrace of the narrow house—the blackness of the absolute Night—the silence like a sea that overwhelms—the unseen but palpable presence of the Conqueror Worm—these things, with thoughts of the air and grass above, with memory of dear friends who would fly to save us if but informed of our fate, and with consciousness that of this fate they can *never* be informed—that our hopeless portion is that of the really dead—these considerations, I say, carry into the heart, which still palpitates, a degree of appalling and intolerable horror from which the most daring imagination must recoil. We know of nothing so agonising upon Earth—we can dream of nothing half so hideous in the realms of the nethermost Hell. And thus all narratives upon this topic have an interest profound ; an interest, nevertheless, which, through the sacred awe of the topic itself, very properly and very peculiarly depends upon our conviction of the *truth* of the matter narrated. What I have now to tell, is of my own actual knowledge—of my own positive and personal experience.

For several years I had been subject to attacks of the singular disorder which physicians have agreed to term catalepsy, in default of a more definite title. Although both the immediate and the predisposing causes, and even the actual diagnosis of this disease, are still mysteries, its obvious and apparent character is sufficiently well understood. Its variations seem to be chiefly of degree.

Sometimes the patient lies, for a day only, or even for a shorter period, in a species of exaggerated lethargy. He is senseless and externally motionless ; but the pulsation of the heart is still faintly perceptible ; some traces of warmth remain ; a slight colour lingers within the centre of the cheek ; and, upon application of a mirror to the lips, we can detect a torpid, unequal, and vacillating action of the lungs. Then, again, the duration of the trance is for weeks—even for months ; while the closest scrutiny, and the most rigorous medical tests, fail to establish any material distinction between the state of the sufferer and what we conceive of absolute death. Very usually, he is saved from premature interment solely by the knowledge of his friends that he has been previously subject to catalepsy, by the consequent suspicion excited, and, above all, by the non-appearance of decay. The advances of the malady are, luckily, gradual. The first manifestations, although marked, are unequivocal. The fits grow successively more and more distinctive, and endure each for a longer term than the preceding. In this lies the principal security from inhumation. The unfortunate whose *first* attack should be of the extreme character which is occasionally seen, would almost inevitably be consigned alive to the tomb.

My own case differed in no important particular from those mentioned in medical books. Sometimes, without any apparent cause, I sank, little by little, into a condition of semi-syncope, or half-swoon ; and, in this condition, without pain, without ability to stir, or strictly speaking, to think, but with a dull lethargic consciousness of life and of the presence of those who surrounded my bed, I remained, until the crisis of the disease restored me, suddenly, to perfect sensation. At other times I was quickly and impetuously smitten. I grew sick, and numb, and chilly, and dizzy, and so fell prostrate at once. Then, for weeks, all was void, and black, and silent, and Nothing became the universe. Total annihilation could be no more. From these latter attacks I awoke, however, with a gradation slow in proportion to the suddenness of the seizure. Just as the day dawns to the friendless and houseless beggar who roams the streets throughout the long desolate winter night—just so tardily—just so wearily—just so cheerily came back the light of the Soul to me.

Apart from the tendency to trance, however, my general health appeared to be good ; nor could I perceive that it was at all affected by the one prevalent malady—unless, indeed, an idiosyncrasy in an ordinary *sleep* may be looked upon as superinduced. Upon awaking from slumber, I could never gain, at once, thorough possession of my senses, and always remained, for many minutes, in much bewilderment and perplexity—the mental faculties in general, but the memory in especial, being in a condition of absolute abeyance.

In all that I endured there was no physical suffering, but of moral distress an infinitude. My fancy grew charnel. I talked " of worms, of tombs and epitaphs." I was lost in reveries of death, and the idea of premature burial held continual possession of my brain. The ghastly danger to which I was subjected haunted me day and night. In the former, the torture of meditation was excessive—in the latter, supreme. When the grim darkness overspread the earth, then, with very horror of thought, I shook—shook as the quivering plumes upon the hearse. When nature could endure wakefulness no longer, it was with a struggle that I consented to sleep—for I shuddered to reflect that, upon awaking, I might find myself the tenant of a grave. And when, finally, I sank into slumber, it was only to rush at once into a world of phantasms, above which, with vast, sable, over-shadowing wings, hovered, predominant, the one sepulchral Idea.

From the innumerable images of gloom which thus oppressed me in dreams, I select for record but a solitary vision. Methought I was immersed in a cataleptic trance of more than usual duration and profundity. Suddenly there came an icy hand upon my forehead, and an impatient, gibbering voice whispered the word " Arise ! " within my ear.

I sat erect. The darkness was total. I could not see the figure of him who had aroused me. I could call to mind neither the period at which I had fallen into the trance, nor the locality in which I then lay. While I remained motionless, and busied in endeavours to collect my thoughts, the cold hand grasped me fiercely by the wrist, shaking it petulantly, while the gibbering voice said again—

"Arise ! did I not bid thee arise ? "

"And who," I demanded, " art thou ? "

" I have no name in the regions which I inhabit," replied the voice mournfully ; " I was mortal, but am fiend.   I was merciless, but am pitiful.   Thou dost feel that I shudder.   My teeth chatter as I speak, yet it is not with the chilliness of the night—of the night without end.   But this hideousness is insufferable.   How canst *thou* tranquilly sleep ?   I cannot rest for the cry of these great agonies.   These sights are more than I can bear.   Get thee up !   Come with me into the outer Night, and let me unfold to thee the graves.   Is not this a spectacle of woe ?   Behold ! "

I looked ; and the unseen figure, which still grasped me by the wrist, had caused to be thrown open the graves of all mankind ; and from each issued the faint phosphoric radiance of decay, so that I could see into the innermost recesses, and there view the shrouded bodies in their sad and solemn slumbers with the worm.   But, alas !   the real sleepers were fewer, by many millions, than those who slumbered not at all ; and there was a feeble struggling ; and there was a general sad unrest ; and from out the depths of the countless pits there came a melancholy rustling from the garments of the buried.   And, of those who seemed tranquilly to repose, I saw that a vast number had changed, in a greater or less degree, the rigid and uneasy position in which they had originally been entombed.   And the voice again said to me, as I gazed—

" Is it not—oh, is it *not* a pitiful sight ? "   But, before I could find words to reply, the figure had ceased to grasp my wrist, the phosphoric lights expired, and the graves were closed with a sudden violence, while from out them arose a tumult of despairing cries, saying again, " Is it not—O God ! is it *not* a very pitiful sight ? "

Phantasies such as these, presenting themselves at night, extended their terrific influence far into my waking hours.   My nerves became thoroughly unstrung, and I fell a prey to perpetual horror.   I hesitated to ride, or to walk, or to indulge in any exercise that would carry me from home.   In fact, I no longer dared trust myself out of the immediate presence of those who were aware of my proneness to catalepsy, lest, falling into one of my usual fits, I should be buried before my real condition could be ascertained. I doubted the care, the fidelity of my dearest friends. I dreaded that, in some trance of more than customary duration, they might be prevailed upon to regard me as irrecoverable. I even went so far as to fear that, as I occasioned much trouble, they might be glad to consider any very protracted attack as sufficient excuse for getting rid of me altogether. It was in vain they endeavoured to reassure me by the most solemn promises. I exacted the most sacred oaths, that under no circumstances they would bury me until decomposition had so materially advanced as to render further preservation impossible. And, even then, my mortal terrors would listen to no reason—would accept no consolation. I entered into a series of elaborate precautions. Among other things, I had the family vault so remodelled as to admit of being readily opened from within. The slightest pressure upon a long lever that extended far into the tomb would cause the iron portals to fly back. There were arrangements also for the free admission of air and light, and convenient receptacles for food and water, within immediate reach of the coffin intended for my reception. This coffin was warmly and softly padded, and was provided with a lid, fashioned upon the principle of the vault-door, with the addition of springs so contrived that the feeblest movement of the body would be sufficient to set it at liberty. Besides all this, there was suspended from the roof of the tomb a large bell, the rope of which, it was designed, should extend through a hole in the coffin, and so be fastened to one of the hands of the corpse. But, alas! what avails the vigilance against the Destiny of man? Not even these well-contrived securities sufficed to save from the uttermost agonies of living inhumation a wretch to these agonies foredoomed!

There arrived an epoch—as often before there had arrived—in which I found myself emerging from total unconsciousness into the first feeble and indefinite sense of existence. Slowly—with a tortoise gradation—approached the faint grey dawn of the psychal day. A torpid uneasiness. An apathetic endurance of dull pain. No care—no hope—no effort. Then, after long interval,

a ringing in the ears ; then, after a lapse still longer, a
prickling or tingling sensation in the extremities ; then
a seemingly eternal period of pleasurable quiescence,
during which the awakening feelings are struggling into
thought ; then a brief re-sinking into nonentity ; then
a sudden recovery. At length the slight quivering of
an eyelid, and immediately thereupon an electric shock
of a terror, deadly and indefinite, which sends the blood
in torrents from the temples to the heart. And now the
first positive effort to think. And now the first endeavour
to remember. And now a partial and evanescent success.
And now the memory has so far regained its dominion,
that, in some measure, I am cognisant of my state.
I feel that I am not awaking from ordinary sleep. I
recollect that I have been subject to catalepsy. And
now, at last, as if by the rush of an ocean, my shuddering
spirit is overwhelmed by the one grim Danger—by the
one spectral and ever-prevalent Idea.

For some minutes after this fancy possessed me, I
remained without motion. And why ? I could not
summon courage to move. I dared not make the effort
which was to satisfy me of my fate—and yet there was
something at my heart which whispered me *it was sure*.
Despair—such as no other species of wretchedness ever
calls into being—despair alone urged me, after long irresolu-
tion, to uplift the heavy lids of my eyes. I uplifted them.
It was dark—all dark. I knew that the fit was over.
I knew that the crisis of my disorder had long passed.
I knew that I had now fully recovered the use of my
visual faculties—and yet it was dark—all dark—the
intense and utter raylessness of the Night that endureth
for evermore.

I endeavoured to shriek ; and my lips and my parched
tongue moved convulsively together in the attempt—
but no voice issued from the cavernous lungs, which,
oppressed as if by the weight of some incumbent mountain,
gasped and palpitated, with the heart, at every elaborate
and struggling inspiration.

The movement of the jaws, in this effort to cry aloud,
showed me that they were bound up, as is usual with
the dead. I felt, too, that I lay upon some hard substance ;
and by something similar my sides were, also, closely
compressed. So far, I had not ventured to stir any of

my limbs—but now I violently threw up my arms, which had been lying at length, with the wrists crossed. They struck a solid wooden substance, which extended above my person at an elevation of not more than six inches from my face. I could no longer doubt that I reposed within a coffin at last.

And now, amid all my infinite miseries, came sweetly the cherub Hope—for I thought of my precautions. I writhed, and made spasmodic exertions to force open the lid; it would not move. I felt my wrists for the bell-rope; it was not to be found. And now the Comforter fled for ever, and a still sterner Despair reigned triumphant; for I could not help perceiving the absence of the paddings which I had so carefully prepared—and then, too, there came suddenly to my nostrils the strong peculiar odour of moist earth. The conclusion was irresistible. I was *not* within the vault. I had fallen into a trance while absent from home—while among strangers—when, or how, I could not remember—and it was they who had buried me as a dog—nailed up in some common coffin—and thrust, deep, deep, and for ever, into some ordinary and nameless *grave*.

As this awful conviction forced itself, thus, into the innermost chambers of my soul, I once again struggled to cry aloud. And in this second endeavour I succeeded. A long, wild, and continuous shriek, or yell, of agony, resounded through the realms of the subterrene Night.

" Hillo ! hillo, there ! " said a gruff voice, in reply.

" What the devil's the matter now ? " said a second.

" Get out o' that ! " said a third.

" What do you mean by yowling in that ere kind of style, like a cattymount ? " said a fourth ; and hereupon I was seized and shaken without ceremony, for several minutes, by a junto of very rough-looking individuals. They did not arouse me from my slumber—for I was wide awake when I screamed—but they restored me to full possession of my memory.

This adventure occurred near Richmond, in Virginia. Accompanied by a friend, I had proceeded, upon a gunning expedition, some miles down the banks of James River. Night approached, and we were overtaken by a storm. The cabin of a small sloop lying at anchor in the stream, and laden with garden mould, afforded us the only available shelter. We made the best of it, and passed the night on board. I slept in one of the only two berths in the vessel—and the berths of a sloop of sixty or seventy tons need scarcely be described. That which I occupied had no bedding of any kind. Its extreme width was eighteen inches. The distance of its bottom from the deck overhead, was precisely the same. I found it a matter of exceeding difficulty to squeeze myself in. Nevertheless, I slept soundly ; and the whole of my vision—for it was no dream, and no nightmare—arose naturally from the circumstances of my position—from my ordinary bias of thought—and from the difficulty, to which I have alluded, of collecting my senses, and especially of regaining my memory, for a long time after awaking from slumber. The men who shook me were the crew of the sloop, and some labourers engaged to unload it. From the load itself came the earthy smell. The bandage about the jaws was a silk handkerchief in which I bound up my head, in default of my customary nightcap.

The tortures endured, however, were indubitably quite equal, for the time, to those of actual sepulture. They were fearfully—they were inconceivably hideous ; but out of evil proceeded good ; for their very excess wrought in my spirit an inevitable revulsion. My soul acquired tone—acquired temper. I went abroad. I took vigorous exercise. I breathed the free air of heaven. I thought upon other subjects than death. I discarded my medical books. *Buchan* I burned. I read no *Night Thoughts*— no fustian about churchyards—no bugaboo tales—*such as this*. In short I became a new man, and lived a man's life. From that memorable night I dismissed for ever my charnel apprehensions, and with them vanished the cataleptic disorder, of which, perhaps, they had been less the consequence than the cause.

There are moments when, even to the sober eye of Reason, the world of our sad Humanity may assume the semblance of a Hell—but the imagination of man is no Carathis, to explore with impunity its every cavern. Alas ! the grim legion of sepulchral terrors cannot be regarded as altogether fanciful—but, like the Demons in whose company Afrasiab made his voyage down the Oxus, they must sleep, or they will devour us—they must be suffered to slumber, or we perish.

THE ASSIGNATION

" Stay for me there ! I will not fail
To meet thee in that hollow vale."

Exequy on the death of his wife, by HENRY KING, *Bishop of Chichester.*

ILL-FATED and mysterious man !—bewildered in the brilliancy of thine own imagination, and fallen in the flames of thine own youth ! Again in fancy I behold thee ! Once more thy form hath risen before me !—not—O not as thou art—in the cold valley and shadow—but as thou *shouldst be* —squandering away a life of magnificent meditation in that city of dim visions, thine own Venice—which is a starbeloved Elysium of the sea, and the wide windows of whose Palladian palaces look down with a deep and bitter meaning upon the secrets of her silent waters. Yes ! I repeat it— as thou *shouldst be.* There are surely other worlds than this—other thoughts than the thoughts of the multitude— other speculations than the speculations of the sophist. Who then shall call thy conduct into question ? who blame thee for thy visionary hours, or denounce those occupations as a wasting away of life, which were but the overflowings of thine everlasting energies ?

It was at Venice, beneath the covered archway there called the *Ponte di Sospiri*, that I met for the third or fourth time the person of whom I speak. It is with a confused recollection that I bring to mind the circumstances of that meeting. Yet I remember—ah ! how should I forget ? —the deep midnight, the Bridge of Sighs, the beauty of woman, and the Genius of Romance, that stalked up and down the narrow canal.

It was a night of unusual gloom. The great clock of the Piazza had sounded the fifth hour of the Italian evening. The square of the Campanile lay silent and deserted, and the lights in the old Ducal Palace were dying fast away. I was returning home from the Piazzetta by way of the Grand Canal. But as my gondola arrived opposite the mouth of the canal San Marco, a female voice from its recesses broke suddenly upon the night in one wild, hysterical, and long-continued shriek. Startled at the sound, I sprang upon my feet ; while the gondolier, letting slip

his single oar, lost it in the pitchy darkness beyond a
chance of recovery, and we were consequently left to the
guidance of the current which here sets from the greater
into the smaller channel. Like some huge and sable-
feathered condor, we were slowly drifting down towards
the Bridge of Sighs, when a thousand flambeaux flashing
from the windows, and down the staircases of the Ducal
Palace, turned all at once that deep gloom into a livid and
preternatural day.

A child, slipping from the arms of its own mother, had
fallen from an upper window of the lofty structure into the
deep and dim canal. The quiet waters had closed placidly
over their victim ; and although my own gondola was the
only one in sight, many a stout swimmer, already in the
stream, was seeking in vain upon the surface the treasure
which was to be found, alas ! only within the abyss. Upon
the broad black marble flagstones at the entrance of the
palace, and a few steps above the water, stood a figure
which none who then saw can have ever since forgotten.
It was the Marchesa Aphrodite—the adoration of all Venice
—the gayest of the gay—the most lovely where all were
beautiful—but still the young wife of the old and intriguing
Mentoni, and the mother of that fair child, her first and
only one, who now, deep beneath the murky water, was
thinking in bitterness of heart upon her sweet caresses,
and exhausting its little life in struggles to call upon her
name.

She stood alone. Her small, bare, and silvery feet
gleamed in the black marble beneath her. Her hair, not
as yet more than half loosened for the night from its ball-
room array, clustered amid a shower of diamonds round
and round her classical head, in curls like those of the young
hyacinth. A snowy-white and gauze-like drapery seemed
to be nearly the sole covering to her delicate form ; but the
mid-summer and midnight air was hot, sullen, and still,
and no motion in the statue-like form itself stirred even the
folds of that raiment of very vapour which hung around
it as the heavy marble hangs around the Niobe. Yet—
strange to say !—her large lustrous eyes were not turned
downwards upon that grave wherein her brightest hope
lay buried—but riveted in a widely different direction !
The prison of the Old Republic is, I think, the stateliest
building in all Venice ; but how could that lady gaze so

fixedly upon it, when beneath her lay stifling her own child ? Yon dark gloomy niche, too, yawns right opposite her chamber window—what then *could* there be in its shadows, in its architecture, in its ivy-wreathed and solemn cornices—that the Marchesa di Mentoni had not wondered at a thousand times before ? Nonsense !—Who does not remember, that at such a time as this, the eye, like a shattered mirror, multiplies the images of its sorrow, and sees in innumerable far-off places, the woe which is close at hand ?

Many steps above the Marchesa, and within the arch of the water-gate, stood, in full dress, the Satyr-like figure of Mentoni himself. He was occasionally occupied in thrumming a guitar, and seemed *ennuyé* to the very death, as at intervals he gave directions for the recovery of his child. Stupefied and aghast I had myself no power to move from the upright position I had assumed upon first hearing the shriek, and must have presented to the eyes of the agitated group a spectral and ominous appearance, as with pale countenance and rigid limbs I floated down among them in that funereal gondola.

All efforts proved in vain. Many of the most energetic in the search were relaxing their exertions, and yielding to a gloomy sorrow. There seemed but little hope for the child (how much less then for the mother !) ; but now, from the interior of that dark niche which has been already mentioned as forming a part of the Old Republican prison, and as fronting the lattice of the Marchesa, a figure muffled in a cloak stepped out within reach of the light, and pausing a moment upon the verge of the giddy descent, plunged headlong into the canal. As in an instant afterwards he stood with the still living and breathing child within his grasp upon the marble flagstones by the side of the Marchesa, his cloak heavy with the drenching water became unfastened, and, falling in folds about his feet, discovered to the wonder-stricken spectators the graceful person of a very young man, with the sound of whose name the greater part of Europe was then ringing.

No word spoke the deliverer. But the Marchesa ! She will now receive her child—she will press it to her heart —she will cling to its little form, and smother it with her caresses. Alas ! *another's* arms have taken it from the stranger—*another's* arms have taken it away, and borne t afar off, unnoticed, into the palace ! And the Marchesa ! Her lip—her beautiful lip trembles : tears are gathering in her eyes—those eyes which, like Pliny's acanthus, are ' soft and almost liquid." Yes ! tears are gathering in those eyes—and see ! the entire woman thrills thoughout he soul, and the statue has started into life ! The pallor of the marble countenance, the swelling of the marble bosom, the very purity of the marble feet, we behold suddenly flushed over with a tide of ungovernable crimson ; and a slight shudder quivers about her delicate frame, as a gentle air at Napoli about the rich silver lilies in the grass.

Why *should* that lady blush ? To this demand there is no answer—except that having left, in the eager haste and error of a mother's heart, the privacy of her own *boudoir*, she has neglected to enthral her tiny feet in their slippers, and utterly forgotten to throw over her Venetian shoulders that drapery which is their due. What other possible reason could there have been for her so blushing ?—for the glance of those wild appealing eyes ?—for the unusual tumult of that throbbing bosom ?—for the convulsive pressure of that trembling hand ?—that hand which fell, as Mentoni turned into the palace, accidentally, upon the hand of the stranger. What reason could there have been for the low—the singularly low tone of those unmeaning words which the lady uttered hurriedly in bidding him adieu ? " Thou hast conquered," she said, " or the murmurs of the water deceived me ; thou hast conquered— one hour after sunrise—we shall meet—so let it be ! "

· · · · · · ·

The tumult had subsided, the lights had died away within the palace, and the stranger whom I now recognised stood alone upon the flags. He shook with inconceivable agitation, and his eye glanced around in search of a gondola. I could not do less than offer him the service of my own ; and he accepted the civility. Having obtained an oar at the water-gate, we proceeded together to his residence, while he rapidly recovered his self-possession, and spoke of our former slight acquaintance in terms of great apparent cordiality.

There are some subjects upon which I take pleasure in being minute. The person of the stranger—let me call him by this title, who to all the world was still a stranger

M

—the person of the stranger is one of these subjects. In height he might have been below rather than above the medium size : although there were moments of intense passion when his frame actually *expanded* and belied the assertion. The light, almost slender, symmetry of his figure promised more of that ready activity which he evinced at the Bridge of Sighs, than of that Herculean strength which he has been known to wield without an effort upon occasions of more dangerous emergency. With the mouth and chin of a deity—singular, wild, full, liquid eyes, whose shadows varied from pure hazel to intense and brilliant jet—and a profusion of curling black hair, from which a forehead of unusual breadth gleamed forth at intervals all light and ivory—his were features than which I have seen none more classically regular, except, perhaps, the marble ones of the Emperor Commodus. Yet his countenance was, nevertheless, one of those which all men have seen at some period of their lives, and have never afterwards seen again. It had no peculiar—it had no settled predominant expression to be fastened upon the memory ; a countenance seen and instantly forgotten—but forgotten with a vague and never-ceasing desire of recalling it to mind. Not that the spirit of each rapid passion failed, at any time, to throw its own distinct image upon the mirror of that face—but that the mirror, mirror-like, retained no vestige of the passion when the passion had departed.

Upon leaving him on the night of our adventure, he solicited me, in what I thought an urgent manner, to call upon him *very* early the next morning. Shortly after sunrise I found myself accordingly at his Palazzo, one of those huge structures of gloomy, yet fantastic pomp, which tower above the waters of the Grand Canal in the vicinity of the Rialto. I was shown up a broad winding staircase of mosaics into an apartment whose unparalleled splendour burst through the opening door with an actual glare, making me blind and dizzy with luxuriousness.

I knew my acquaintance to be wealthy. Report had spoken of his possessions in terms which I had even ventured to call terms of ridiculous exaggeration. But as I gazed about me, I could not bring myself to believe that the wealth of any subject in Europe could have supplied the princely magnificence which burned and blazed around.

Although, as I say, the sun had arisen, yet the room

was still brilliantly lighted up. I judge from this circumstance, as well as from an air of exhaustion in the countenance of my friend, that he had not retired to bed during the whole of the preceding night. In the architecture and embellishments of the chamber, the evident design had been to dazzle and astound. Little attention had been paid to the *decora* of what is technically called *keeping*, or to the proprieties of nationality. The eye wandered from object to object, and rested upon none—neither the *grotesques* of the Greek painters, nor the sculptures of the best Italian days, nor the huge carvings of untutored Egypt. Rich draperies in every part of the room trembled to the vibration of low, melancholy music, whose origin was not to be discovered. The senses were oppressed by mingled and conflicting perfumes, reeking up from strange convolute censers, together with multitudinous flaring and flickering tongues of emerald and violet fire. The rays of the newly-risen sun poured in upon the whole, through windows, formed each of a single pane of crimson-tinted glass. Glancing to and fro, in a thousand reflections, from curtains which rolled from their cornices like cataracts of molten silver, the beams of natural glory mingled at length fitfully with the artificial light, and lay weltering in subdued masses upon a carpet of rich, liquid-looking cloth of Chili gold.

"Ha! ha! ha!—ha! ha! ha!"—laughed the proprietor, motioning me to a seat as I entered the room, and throwing himself back at full-length upon an ottoman. "I see," said he, perceiving that I could not immediately reconcile myself to the *bienséance* of so singular a welcome —"I see you are astonished at my apartment—at my statues—my pictures—my originality of conception in architecture and upholstery! absolutely drunk, eh, with my magnificence? But pardon me, my dear sir (here his tone of voice dropped to the very spirit of cordiality), pardon me for my uncharitable laughter. You appeared so *utterly* astonished. Besides, some things are so completely ludicrous that a man *must* laugh or die. To die laughing must be the most glorious of all glorious deaths! Sir Thomas More—a very fine man was Sir Thomas More— Sir Thomas More died laughing, you remember. Also in the *Absurdities* of Ravisius Textor there is a long list of characters who came to the same magnificent end. Do

you know, however," continued he, musingly, "that at
Sparta (which is now Palæochori), at Sparta, I say, to the
west of the citadel, among a chaos of scarcely visible ruins,
is a kind of *socle* upon which are still legible the letters
ΛΑΞΜ. They are undoubtedly part of ΓΕΛΑΞΜΑ.
Now, at Sparta were a thousand temples and shrines to a
thousand different divinities. How exceedingly strange
that the altar of Laughter should have survived all the
others ! But in the present instance," he resumed, with a
singular alteration of voice and manner, " I have no right
to be merry at your expense. You might well have been
amazed. Europe cannot produce anything so fine as this
my little regal cabinet. My other apartments are by no
means of the same order—mere *ultras* of fashionable
insipidity. This is better than fashion—is it not ? Yet
this has but to be seen to become the rage—that is with
those who could afford it at the cost of their entire patrimony. I have guarded, however, against any such
profanation. With one exception you are the only human
being, besides myself and my *valet,* who has been admitted
within the mysteries of these imperial precincts since they
have been bedizened as you see ! "

I bowed in acknowledgment—for the overpowering
sense of splendour, and perfume, and music, together
with the unexpected eccentricity of his address and
manner, prevented me from expressing in words my
appreciation of what I might have construed into a
compliment.

" Here," he resumed, arising and leaning on my arm as
he sauntered around the apartment, " here are paintings
from the Greeks to Cimabue, and from Cimabue to the
present hour. Many are chosen, as you see, with little
deference to the opinions of Virtû. They are all, however,
fitting tapestry for a chamber such as this. Here, too, are
some *chefs d'œuvre* of the unknown great ; and here un-
finished designs by men celebrated in their day, whose
very names the perspicacity of the academies has left to
silence and to me. What think you," said he, turning
abruptly as he spoke—" what think you of this Madonna
della Pieta ? "

. " It is Guido's own," I said, with all the enthusiasm of
my nature, for I had been poring intently over its surpassing loveliness. " It is Guido's own !—how *could* you

have obtained it ? she is undoubtedly in painting what the Venus is in sculpture."

" Ha ! " said he, thoughtfully, " the Venus—the beautiful Venus ?—the Venus of the Medici ?—she of the diminutive head and the gilded hair ? Part of the left arm (here his voice dropped so as to be heard with difficulty) and all the right are restorations ; and in the coquetry of that right arm lies, I think, the quintessence of all affectation. Give *me* the Canova ! The Apollo, too, is a copy—there can be no doubt of it—blind fool that I am who cannot behold the boasted inspiration of the Apollo ! I cannot help—pity me !—I cannot help preferring the Antinous. Was it not Socrates who said that the statuary found his statue in the block of marble ? Then Michael Angelo was by no means original in his couplet—

> ' Non ha l'ottimo artista alcun concetto
> Che un marmo solo in se non circonscriva.' "

It has been or should be remarked that in the manner of the true gentleman we are always aware of a difference from the bearing of the vulgar, without being at once precisely able to determine in what such difference consists. Allowing the remark to have applied in its full force to the outward demeanour of my acquaintance, I felt it on that eventful morning still more fully applicable to his moral temperament and character. Nor can I better define that peculiarity of spirit which seemed to place him so essentially apart from all other human beings, than by calling it a *habit* of intense and continual thought pervading even his most trivial actions—intruding upon his moments of dalliance, and interweaving itself with his very flashes of merriment—like adders which writhe from out the eyes of the grinning masks in the cornices around the temples of Persepolis.

I could not help, however, repeatedly observing through the mingled tone of levity and solemnity with which he rapidly descanted upon matters of little importance, a certain air of trepidation—a degree of nervous *unction* in action and in speech—an unquiet excitability of manner which appeared to me at all times unaccountable, and upon some occasions even filled me with alarm. Frequently, too, pausing in the middle of a sentence whose commencement he had apparently forgotten, he seemed tc be listening in the deepest attention as if either in momentary expectation of a visitor, or to sounds which must have had existence in his imagination alone.

It was during one of these reveries or pauses of apparent abstraction, that, in turning over a page of the poet and scholar Politian's beautiful tragedy, *The Orfeo* (the first native Italian tragedy), which lay near me upon an ottoman, I discovered a passage underlined in pencil. It was a passage towards the end of the third act—a passage of the most heart-stirring excitement—a passage which, although tainted with impurity, no man shall read without a thrill of novel emotion—no woman without a sigh. The whole page was blotted with fresh tears ; and upon the opposite interleaf were the following English lines, written in a hand so very different from the peculiar characters of my acquaintance, that I had some difficulty in recognising it as his own :—

Thou wast that all to me, love,
    For which my soul did pine—
A green isle in the sea, love,
    A fountain and a shrine,
All wreathed with fairy fruits and flowers ;
    And all the flowers were mine.

Ah, dream too bright to last !
    Ah, starry Hope, that didst arise
But to be overcast !
    A voice from out the future cries,
" Onward ! "—but o'er the past
    (Dim gulf !) my spirit hovering lies,
Mute—motionless—aghast !

For alas ! alas ! with me
    The light of life is o'er.
" No more—no more—no more,"
    (Such language holds the solemn sea
To the sands upon the shore),
    Shall bloom the thunder-blasted tree,
Or the stricken eagle soar !

Now all my hours are trances ;
    And all my nightly dreams
Are where thy dark eye glances,
    And where thy footstep gleams—
In what ethereal dances—
    By what Italian streams !

Alas ! for that accursed time
They bore thee o'er the billow,
From Love to titled age and crime,
And an unholy pillow !—
From me, and from our misty clime,
Where weeps the silver willow !

That these lines were written in English—a language
with which I had not believed their author acquainted—
afforded me little matter for surprise.   I was too well aware
of the extent of his acquirements, and of the singular
pleasure he took in concealing them from observation, to be
astonished at any similar discovery ; but the place of
date, I must confess, occasioned me no little amazement.
It had been originally written in *London*, and afterwards
carefully overscored—not, however, so effectually as to
conceal the word from a scrutinising eye.   I say this
occasioned me no little amazement ; for I well remember
that, in a former conversation with my friend, I particularly
inquired if he had at any time met in London the Marchesa
di Mentoni (who for some years previous to her marriage
had resided in that city), when his answer, if I mistake
not, gave me to understand that he had never visited the
metropolis of Great Britain.   I might as well here mention
that I have more than once heard (without, of course,
giving credit to a report involving so many improbabilities)
that the person of whom I speak, was not only by birth,
but in education, an *Englishman*.

"There is one painting," said he, without being aware
of my notice of the tragedy—" there is still one painting
which you have not seen."   And throwing aside a drapery,
he discovered a full-length portrait of the Marchesa
Aphrodite.

Human art could have done no more in the delineation
of her superhuman beauty.   The same ethereal figure
which stood before me the preceding night upon the steps
of the Ducal Palace, stood before me once again.   But in
the expression of the countenance, which was beaming
all over with smiles, there still lurked (incomprehensible
anomaly !) that fitful stain of melancholy which will ever
be found inseparable from the perfection of the beautiful.
Her right arm lay folded over her bosom.   With her left
she pointed downward to a curiouslv-fashioned vase.   One

small, fairy foot, alone visible, barely touched the earth ;
and, scarcely discernible in the brilliant atmosphere which
seemed to encircle and enshrine her loveliness, floated a
pair of the most delicately-imagined wings. My glance
fell from the painting to the figure of my friend, and the
vigorous words of Chapman's *Bussy D'Ambois* quivered
instinctively upon my lips :—

> " He is up
> There like a Roman statue !   He will stand
> 'Till Death hath made him marble ! "

" Come," he said at length, turning towards a table of
richly enamelled and massive silver, upon which were a
few goblets fantastically stained, together with two large
Etruscan vases, fashioned in the same extraordinary model
as that in the foreground of the portrait, and filled with
what I supposed to be Johannisberger. " Come," he said
abruptly, " let us drink ! It is early—but let us drink.
It is *indeed* early," he continued, musingly, as a cherub
with a heavy golden hammer made the apartment ring
with the first hour after sunrise : " it is *indeed* early—but
what matters it ? let us drink !   Let us pour out an offering
to yon solemn sun which these gaudy lamps and censers
are so eager to subdue ! "   And, having made me pledge
him in a bumper, he swallowed in rapid succession several
goblets of the wine.

" To dream," he continued, resuming the tone of his
desultory conversation, as he held up to the rich light of
a censer one of the magnificent vases—" to dream has
been the business of my life. I have therefore framed for
myself, as you see, a bower of dreams. In the heart of
Venice could I have erected a better ? You behold around
you, it is true, a medley of architectural embellishments.
The chastity of Ionia is offended by antediluvian devices,
and the sphinxes of Egypt are outstretched upon carpets
of gold. Yet the effect is incongruous to the timid alone.
Proprieties of place, and especially of time, are the bug-
bears which terrify mankind from the contemplation of
the magnificent. Once I was myself a decorist ; but that
sublimation of folly has palled upon my soul. All this is
now the fitter for my purpose. Like these arabesque
censers, my spirit is writhing in fire, and the delirium of this
scene is fashioning me for the wilder visions of that land of

real dreams whither I am now rapidly departing." He here paused abruptly, bent his head to his bosom, and seemed to listen to a sound which I could not hear. At length, erecting his frame, he looked upwards, and ejaculated the lines of the Bishop of Chichester :—

> " Stay for me there !   I will not fail
> To meet thee in that hollow vale."

In the next instant, confessing the power of the wine, he threw himself at full length upon an ottoman.

A quick step was now heard upon the staircase, and a loud knock at the door rapidly succeeded. I was hastening to anticipate a second disturbance, when a page of Mentoni's household burst into the room, and faltered out, in a voice choking with emotion, the incoherent words : " My mistress !—my mistress !—Poisoned—poisoned ! Oh, beautiful—oh, beautiful Aphrodite ! "

Bewildered, I flew to the ottoman, and endeavoured to arouse the sleeper to a sense of the startling intelligence. But his limbs were rigid—his lips were livid—his lately beaming eyes were riveted in *death*. I staggered back towards the table—my hand fell upon a cracked and blackened goblet—and a consciousness of the entire and terrible truth flashed suddenly over my soul.

SHADOW

A Parable

" Yea ! though I walk through the valley of the *Shadow*."
                                    —*Psalm of David.*

Ye who read are still among the living ; but I who write shall have long since gone my way into the region of shadows. For indeed strange things shall happen, and secret things be known, and many centuries shall pass away, ere these memorials be seen of men. And, when seen, there will be some to disbelieve and some to doubt, and yet a few who will find much to ponder upon in the characters here graven with a stylus of iron.

The year had been a year of terror, and of feelings more intense than terror for which there is no name upon the earth. For many prodigies and signs had taken place, and far and wide, over sea and land, the black wings of the Pestilence were spread abroad. To those, nevertheless, cunning in the stars, it was not unknown that the heavens wore an aspect of ill ; and to me, the Greek Oinos, among others, it was evident that now had arrived the alternation of that seven hundred and ninety-fourth year when, at the entrance of Aries, the planet Jupiter is conjoined with the red ring of the terrible Saturnus. The peculiar spirit of the skies, if I mistake not greatly, made itself manifest, not only in the physical orb of the earth, but in the souls, imaginations, and meditations of mankind.

Over some flasks of the red Chian wine, within the walls of a noble hall, in a dim city called Ptolemais, we sat, at night, a company of seven. And to our chamber there was no entrance save by a lofty door of brass : and the door was fashioned by the artisan Corinnos, and, being of rare workmanship, was fastened from within. Black draperies, likewise, in the gloomy room, shut out from our view the moon, the lurid stars, and the peopleless streets— but the boding and the memory of Evil, they would not be so excluded. There were things around us and about of which I can render no distinct account—things material and spiritual—heaviness in the atmosphere—a sense of suffocation—anxiety—and, above all, that terrible state of existence which the nervous experience when the senses are keenly living and awake, and meanwhile the powers of thought lie dormant. A dead weight hung upon us. It hung upon our limbs—upon the household furniture— upon the goblets from which we drank ; and all things were depressed, and borne down thereby—all things save only the flames of the seven iron lamps which illumined our revel. Uprearing themselves in tall slender lines of light, they thus remained burning all pallid and motionless ; and in the mirror which their lustre formed upon the round table of ebony at which we sat, each of us there assembled beheld the pallor of his own countenance, and the unquiet glare in the downcast eyes of his companions. Yet we laughed and were merry in our proper way—which was hysterical ; and sang the songs of Anacreon—which are madness ; and drank deeply—although the purple wine reminded us of blood. For there was yet another tenant of our chamber in the person of young Zoilus. Dead, and at full length he lay, enshrouded ;—the genius and the demon of the scene. Alas ! he bore no portion in our mirth, save that his countenance, distorted with the plague, and his eyes in which Death had but half extinguished the fire of the pestilence, seemed to take such interest in our merriment as the dead may haply take in the merriment of those who are to die. But although I, Oinos, felt that the eyes of the departed were upon me, still I forced myself not to perceive the bitterness of their expression, and gazing down steadily into the depths of the ebony mirror, sang with a loud and sonorous voice the songs of the son of Teios. But gradually my songs they ceased, and their echoes, rolling afar off among the sable draperies of the chamber, became weak and undistinguishable, and so faded away. And lo ! from among those sable draperies where the sounds of the song departed there came forth a dark and undefined shadow—a shadow such as the moon, when low in heaven, might fashion from the figure of a man : but it was the shadow neither of man, nor of God, nor of any familiar thing. And quivering awhile among the draperies of the room, it at length rested in full view upon the surface of the door of brass. But the shadow was vague, and formless, and indefinite, and was the shadow neither of man nor God—neither God of Greece, nor God of Chaldæa, nor any Egyptian God. And the shadow rested upon the brazen doorway, and under the arch of the entablature of the door, and moved not, nor spoke any word, but there became stationary and remained. And the door whereupon the shadow rested was, if I remember aright, over against the feet of the young Zoilus enshrouded. But we, the seven there assembled, having seen the shadow as it came out from among the draperies, dared not steadily behold it, but cast down our eyes, and gazed continually into the depths of the mirror of ebony. And at length I, Oinos, speaking some low words, demanded of the shadow its dwelling and its appellation. And the shadow answered, " I am SHADOW, and my dwelling is near to the Catacombs of Ptolemais, and hard by those dim plains of Elusion which border upon the foul Charonian canal." And then did we, the seven, start from our seats in horror, and stand trembling, and shuddering, and aghast ; for the tones in the voice of the shadow were not the tones of any one being, but of a multitude of beings, and, varying in their cadences from syllable to syllable, fell duskily upon our ears in the well-remembered and familiar accents of many thousand departed friends.

THE BLACK CAT

For the most wild, yet most homely narrative which I am about to pen, I neither expect nor solicit belief. Mad indeed would I be to expect it, in a case where my very senses reject their own evidence. Yet, mad am I not— and very surely do I not dream. But to-morrow I die, and to-day I would unburden my soul. My immediate purpose is to place before the world, plainly, succinctly, and without comment, a series of mere household events. In their consequences, these events have terrified—have tortured— have destroyed me. Yet I will not attempt to expound them. To me, they have presented little but horror—to many they will seem less terrible than *baroques*. Hereafter, perhaps, some intellect may be found which will reduce my phantasm to the commonplace—some intellect more calm, more logical, and far less excitable than my own, which will perceive, in the circumstances I detail with awe, nothing more than an ordinary succession of very natural causes and effects.

From my infancy I was noted for the docility and humanity of my disposition. My tenderness of heart was even so conspicuous as to make me the jest of my companions. I was especially fond of animals, and was indulged by my parents with a great variety of pets. With these I spent most of my time, and never was so happy as when feeding and caressing them. This peculiarity of character grew with my growth, and, in my manhood, I derived from it one of my principal sources of pleasure. To those who have cherished an affection for a faithful and sagacious dog, I need hardly be at the trouble of explaining the nature or the intensity of the gratification thus derivable. There is something in the unselfish and self-sacrificing love of a brute, which goes directly to the heart of him who has had frequent occasion to test the paltry friendship and gossamer fidelity of mere *Man*.

I married early, and was happy to find in my wife a disposition not uncongenial with my own. Observing my partiality for domestic pets, she lost no opportunity of procuring those of the most agreeable kind. We had birds, gold-fish, a fine dog, rabbits, a small monkey, and *a cat*.

This latter was a remarkably large and beautiful animal, entirely black, and sagacious to an astonishing degree. In speaking of his intelligence, my wife, who at heart was not a little tinctured with superstition, made frequent allusion to the ancient popular notion, which regarded all black cats as witches in disguise. Not that she was ever *serious* upon this point—and I mention the matter at all for no better reason than that it happens, just now, to be remembered.

Pluto—this was the cat's name—was my favourite pet and playmate. I alone fed him, and he attended me wherever I went about the house. It was even with difficulty that I could prevent him from following me through the streets.

Our friendship lasted, in this manner, for several years, during which my general temperament and character— through the instrumentality of the fiend Intemperance— had (I blush to confess it) experienced a radical alteration for the worse. I grew, day by day, more moody, more irritable, more regardless of the feelings of others. I suffered myself to use intemperate language to my wife. At length, I even offered her personal violence. My pets, of course, were made to feel the change in my disposition. I not only neglected, but ill-used them. For Pluto, however, I still retained sufficient regard to restrain me from maltreating him, as I made no scruple of maltreating the rabbits, the monkey, or even the dog, when by accident, or through affection, they came in my way. But my disease grew upon me—for what disease is like alcohol ?—and at length even Pluto, who was now becoming old, and conse- quently somewhat peevish—even Pluto began to experience the effects of my ill temper.

One night, returning home, much intoxicated, from one of my haunts about town, I fancied that the cat avoided my presence. I seized him ; when, in his fright at my violence, he inflicted a slight wound upon my hand with his teeth. The fury of a demon instantly possessed me. I knew myself no longer. My original soul seemed, at once, to take its flight from my body ; and a more than fiendish malevolence, gin-nurtured, thrilled every fibre of my frame. I took from my waistcoat pocket a pen-knife, opened it, grasped the poor beast by the throat, and deliberately cut one of its eyes from the socket ! I blush, I burn, I shudder, while I pen the damnable atrocity.

When reason returned with the morning—when I had slept off the fumes of the night's debauch—I experienced a sentiment half of horror, half of remorse, for the crime of which I had been guilty ; but it was, at best, a feeble and equivocal feeling, and the soul remained untouched. I again plunged into excess, and soon drowned in wine all memory of the deed.

In the meantime the cat slowly recovered. The socket of the lost eye presented, it is true, a frightful appearance, but he no longer appeared to suffer any pain. He went about the house as usual, but, as might be expected, fled in extreme terror at my approach. I had so much of my old heart left, as to be at first grieved by this evident dislike on the part of a creature which had once so loved me. But this feeling soon gave place to irritation. And then came, as if to my final and irrevocable overthrow, the spirit of PERVERSENESS. Of this spirit philosophy takes no account. Yet I am not more sure that my soul lives, than I am that perverseness is one of the primitive impulses of the human heart—one of the indivisible primary faculties, or sentiments, which give direction to the character of man. Who has not, a hundred times, found himself committing a vile or a silly action, for no other reason than because he knows he should *not* ? Have we not a perpetual inclination, in the teeth of our best judgment, to violate that which is *Law*, merely because we understand it to be such ? This spirit of perverseness, I say, came to my final overthrow. It was this unfathomable longing of the soul *to vex itself*—to offer violence to its own nature—to do wrong for the wrong's sake only—that urged me to continue and finally to consummate the injury I had inflicted upon the unoffending brute. One morning, in cool blood, I slipped a noose about its neck and hung it to the limb of a tree—hung it with the tears streaming from my eyes, and with the bitterest remorse at my heart—hung it *because* I knew that it had loved me, and *because* I felt it had given me no reason of offence—hung it *because* I knew that in so doing I was committing a sin—a deadly sin that would so jeopardise my immortal soul as to place it—if such a thing were possible—even beyond the reach of the infinite mercy of the Most Merciful and Most Terrible God.

On the night of the day on which this cruel deed was done, I was aroused from sleep by the cry of " Fire ! " The curtains of my bed were in flames. The whole house was blazing. It was with great difficulty that my wife, a servant, and myself, made our escape from the conflagration. The destruction was complete. My entire worldly wealth was swallowed up, and I resigned myself thenceforward to despair.

I am above the weakness of seeking to establish a sequence of cause and effect between the disaster and the atrocity. But I am detailing a chain of facts, and wish not to leave even a possible link imperfect. On the day succeeding the fire, I visited the ruins. The walls, with one exception, had fallen in. This exception was found in a compartment wall, not very thick, which stood about the middle of the house, and against which had rested the head of my bed. The plastering had here, in great measure, resisted the action of the fire—a fact which I attributed to its having been recently spread. About this wall a dense crowd were collected, and many persons seemed to be examining a particular portion of it with very minute and eager attention. The words " strange ! " " singular ! " and other similar expressions, excited my curiosity. I approached and saw, as if graven in bas-relief upon the white surface, the figure of a gigantic *cat.* The impression was given with an accuracy truly marvellous. There was a rope about the animal's neck.

When I first beheld this apparition—for I could scarcely regard it as less—my wonder and my terror were extreme. But at length reflection came to my aid. The cat, I remembered, had been hung in a garden adjacent to the house. Upon the alarm of fire, this garden had been immediately filled by the crowd—by some one of whom the animal must have been cut from the tree and thrown, through an open window, into my chamber. This had probably been done with the view of arousing me from

sleep. The falling of other walls had compressed the
victim of my cruelty into the substance of the freshly-
spread plaster ; the lime of which, with the flames and
the *ammonia* from the carcass, had then accomplished the
portraiture as I saw it.

Although I thus readily accounted to my reason, if not
altogether to my conscience, for the startling fact just
detailed, it did not the less fail to make a deep impression
upon my fancy. For months I could not rid myself of the
phantasm of the cat ; and, during this period, there came
back into my spirit a half-sentiment that seemed, but was
not, remorse. I went so far as to regret the loss of the
animal, and to look about me, among the vile haunts which
I now habitually frequented, for another pet of the same
species, and of somewhat similar appearance, with which
to supply its place.

One night as I sat, half stupefied, in a den of more than
infamy, my attention was suddenly drawn to some black
object, reposing upon the head of one of the immense
hogsheads of gin, or of rum, which constituted the chief
furniture of the apartment. I had been looking steadily
at the top of this hogshead for some minutes, and what
now caused me surprise was the fact that I had not sooner
perceived the object thereupon. I approached it, and
touched it with my hand. It was a black cat—a very
large one—fully as large as Pluto, and closely resembling
him in every respect but one. Pluto had not a white hair
upon any portion of his body ; but this cat had a large,
although indefinite, splotch of white, covering nearly the
whole region of the breast.

Upon my touching him, he immediately arose, purred
loudly, rubbed against my hand, and appeared delighted
with my notice. This, then, was the very creature of
which I was in search. I at once offered to purchase it of
the landlord ; but this person made no claim to it—knew
nothing of it—had never seen it before.

I continued my caresses, and when I prepared to go home,
the animal evinced a disposition to accompany me. I permitted it to do so ; occasionally stooping and patting it as
I proceeded. When it reached the house it domesticated
itself at once, and became immediately a great favourite
with my wife.

For my own part, I soon found a dislike to it arising

within me. This was just the reverse of what I had
anticipated ; but—I know not how or why it was—its
evident fondness for myself rather disgusted and annoyed
me. By slow degrees, these feelings of disgust and annoyance rose into the bitterness of hatred. I avoided the
creature ; a certain sense of shame, and the remembrance
of my former deed of cruelty, preventing me from physically
abusing it. I did not, for some weeks, strike, or otherwise
violently ill-use it ; but gradually—very gradually—I came
to look upon it with unutterable loathing, and to flee
silently from its odious presence, as from the breath of a
pestilence.

What added, no doubt, to my hatred of the beast, was
the discovery, on the morning after I brought it home, that,
like Pluto, it also had been deprived of one of its eyes. This
circumstance, however, only endeared it to my wife, who,
as I have already said, possessed, in a high degree, that
humanity of feeling which had once been my distinguish-
ing trait, and the source of many of my simplest and purest
pleasures.

With my aversion to this cat, however, its partiality for
myself seemed to increase. It followed my footsteps with
a pertinacity which it would be difficult to make the
reader comprehend. Whenever I sat, it would crouch
beneath my chair, or spring upon my knees, covering
me with its loathsome caresses. If I arose to walk, it would
get between my feet, and thus nearly throw me down, or,
fastening its long and sharp claws in my dress, clamber,
in this manner, to my breast. At such times, although
I longed to destroy it with a blow, I was yet withheld
from so doing, partly by a memory of my former crime,
but chiefly—let me confess it at once—by absolute *dread*
of the beast.

This dread was not exactly a dread of physical evil—
and yet I should be at a loss how otherwise to define
it. I am almost ashamed to own—yes, even in this
felon's cell, I am almost ashamed to own—that the terror
and horror with which the animal inspired me, had been
heightened by one of the merest chimeras it would be
possible to conceive. My wife had called my attention,
more than once, to the character of the mark of white
hair, of which I have spoken, and which constituted the
sole visible difference between the strange beast and

the one I had destroyed. The reader will remember
that this mark, although large, had been originally very
indefinite; but, by slow degrees—degrees nearly imperceptible, and which for a long time my reason struggled
to reject as fanciful—it had, at length, assumed a rigorous
distinctness of outline. It was now the representation
of an object that I shudder to name—and for this, above
all, I loathed, and dreaded, and would have rid myself
of the monster *had I dared*—it was now, I say, the image
of a hideous—of a ghastly thing—of the GALLOWS !—oh,
mournful and terrible engine of horror and of crime—of
agony and of death !

And now was I indeed wretched beyond the wretchedness
of mere humanity. And *a brute beast*—whose fellow I
had contemptuously destroyed—*a brute beast* to work out
for *me*—for me, a man, fashioned in the image of the High
God—so much of insufferable woe ! Alas ! neither by
day nor by night knew I the blessing of rest any more !
During the former the creature left me no moment alone ;
and, in the latter, I started, hourly, from dreams of unutterable fear, to find the hot breath of *the thing* upon
my face, and its vast weight—an incarnate nightmare
that I had no power to shake off—incumbent eternally
upon my *heart* !

Beneath the pressure of torments such as these, the
feeble remnant of the good within me succumbed. Evil
thoughts became my sole intimates—the darkest and most
evil of thoughts. The moodiness of my usual temper
increased to hatred of all things and of all mankind ;
while, from the sudden, frequent, and ungovernable
outbursts of a fury to which I now blindly abandoned
myself, my uncomplaining wife, alas ! was the most
usual and the most patient of sufferers.

One day she accompanied me, upon some household
errand, into the cellar of the old building which our poverty
compelled us to inhabit. The cat followed me down
the steep stairs, and, nearly throwing me headlong,
exasperated me to madness. Uplifting an axe, and forgetting, in my wrath, the childish dread which had hitherto
stayed my hand, I aimed a blow at the animal which, of
course, would have proved instantly fatal had it descended
as I wished. But this blow was arrested by the hand of
my wife. Goaded, by the interference, into a rage more

than demoniacal, I withdrew my arm from her grasp, and buried the axe in her brain. She fell dead upon the spot, without a groan.

This hideous murder accomplished, I set myself forth-with, and with entire deliberation, to the task of concealing the body. I knew that I could not remove it from the house, either by day or by night, without the risk of being observed by the neighbours. Many projects entered my mind. At one period I thought of cutting the corpse into minute fragments, and destroying them by fire. At another, I resolved to dig a grave for it in the floor of the cellar. Again, I deliberated about casting it into the well in the yard—about packing it in a box, as if merchandise, with the usual arrangements, and so getting a porter to take it from the house. Finally I hit upon what I considered a far better expedient than either of these. I determined to wall it up in the cellar—as the monks of the Middle Ages are recorded to have walled up their victims.

For a purpose such as this the cellar was well adapted. Its walls were loosely constructed, and had lately been plastered throughout with a rough plaster, which the dampness of the atmosphere had prevented from hardening. Moreover, in one of the walls was a projection, caused by a false chimney, or fireplace, that had been filled up, and made to resemble the rest of the cellar. I made no doubt that I could readily displace the bricks at this point, insert the corpse, and wall the whole up as before, so that no eye could detect anything suspicious.

And in this calculation I was not deceived. By means of a crowbar I easily dislodged the bricks, and, having carefully deposited the body against the inner wall, I propped it in that position, while, with little trouble, I relaid the whole structure as it originally stood. Having procured mortar, sand, and hair, with every possible precau-tion, I prepared a plaster which could not be distinguished from the old, and with this I very carefully went over the new brickwork. When I had finished, I felt satisfied that all was right. The wall did not present the slightest appearance of having been disturbed. The rubbish on the floor was picked up with the minutest care. I looked around triumphantly, and said to myself, " Here at least then, my labour has not been in vain."

My next step was to look for the beast which had been the cause of so much wretchedness ; for I had, at length, firmly resolved to put it to death. Had I been able to meet with it, at the moment, there could have been no doubt of its fate ; but it appeared that the crafty animal had been alarmed at the violence of my previous anger, and forbore to present itself in my present mood. It is impossible to describe, or to imagine, the deep, the blissful sense of relief which the absence of the detested creature occasioned in my bosom. It did not make its appearance during the night—and thus for one night at least, since its introduction into the house, I soundly and tranquilly slept ; aye, *slept* even with the burden of murder upon my soul !

The second and the third day passed, and still my tormentor came not. Once again I breathed as a free man. The monster, in terror, had fled the premises for ever ! I should behold it no more ! My happiness was supreme ! The guilt of my dark deed disturbed me but little. Some few inquiries had been made, but these had been readily answered. Even a search had been instituted—but of course nothing was to be discovered. I looked upon my future felicity as secured.

Upon the fourth day of the assassination, a party of the police came, very unexpectedly, into the house, and proceeded again to make rigorous investigation of the premises. Secure, however, in the inscrutability of my place of concealment, I felt no embarrassment whatever. The officers bade me accompany them in their search. They left no nook or corner unexplored. At length, for the third or fourth time, they descended into the cellar. I quivered not in a muscle. My heart beat calmly as that of one who slumbers in innocence. I walked the cellar from end to end. I folded my arms upon my bosom, and roamed easily to and fro. The police were thoroughly satisfied, and prepared to depart. The glee at my heart was too strong to be restrained. I burned to say if but one word, by way of triumph, and to render doubly sure their assurance of my guiltlessness.

" Gentlemen," I said at last, as the party ascended the steps, " I delight to have allayed your suspicions. I wish you all health, and a little more courtesy. By-the-bye, gentlemen, this—this is a very well-constructed house."

(In the rabid desire to say something easily, I scarcely knew what I uttered at all.) " I may say an *excellently* well-constructed house. These walls—are you going, gentlemen ?—these walls are solidly put together ; " and here, through the mere frenzy of bravado, I rapped heavily, with a cane which I held in my hand, upon that very portion of the brickwork behind which stood the corpse of the wife of my bosom.

But may God shield and deliver me from the fangs of the Arch-Fiend ! No sooner had the reverberation of my blows sunk into silence, than I was answered by a voice from within the tomb !—by a cry, at first muffled and broken, like the sobbing of a child, and then quickly swelling into one long, loud, and continuous scream, utterly anomalous and inhuman—a howl—a wailing shriek, half of horror and half of triumph, such as might have arisen only out of hell, conjointly from the throats of the damned in their agony and of the demons that exult in the damnation.

Of my own thoughts it is folly to speak. Swooning, I staggered to the opposite wall. For one instant the party upon the stairs remained motionless, through extremity of terror and of awe. In the next, a dozen stout arms were toiling at the wall. It fell bodily. The corpse, already greatly decayed and clotted with gore, stood erect before the eyes of the spectators. Upon its head, with red extended mouth and solitary eye of fire, sat the hideous beast whose craft had seduced me into murder, and whose informing voice had consigned me to the hangman. I had walled the monster up within the tomb !

THE MASQUE OF THE RED DEATH

THE "Red Death" had long devastated the country.
No pestilence had ever been so fatal, or so hideous. Blood
was its Avatar and its seal—the redness and the horror of
blood. There were sharp pains, and sudden dizziness,
and then profuse bleeding at the pores, with dissolution.
The scarlet stains upon the body and especially upon the
face of the victim, were the pest ban which shut him
out from the aid and from the sympathy of his fellow-men.
And the whole seizure, progress, and termination of the
disease, were the incidents of half-an-hour.

But the Prince Prospero was happy and dauntless and
sagacious. When his dominions were half depopulated,
he summoned to his presence a thousand hale and light-
hearted friends from among the knights and dames of
his court, and with these retired to the deep seclusion of
one of his castellated abbeys. This was an extensive
and magnificent structure, the creation of the prince's
own eccentric yet august taste. A strong and lofty wall
girdled it in. This wall had gates of iron. The courtiers,
having entered, brought furnaces and massy hammers
and welded the bolts. They resolved to leave neither
of ingress or egress to the sudden impulses of despair or
of frenzy from within. The abbey was amply provisioned.
With such precautions the courtiers might bid defiance
to contagion. The external world could take care of
itself. In the meantime it was folly to grieve, or to think.
The prince had provided all the appliances of pleasure.
There were buffoons, there were improvisatori, there were
ballet-dancers, there were musicians, there was beauty,
there was wine. All these and security were within.
Without was the "Red Death."

It was toward the close of the fifth or sixth month of
his seclusion, and while the pestilence raged most furiously
abroad, that the Prince Prospero entertained his thousand
friends at a masked ball of the most unusual magnificence.

It was a voluptuous scene, that masquerade. But first
let me tell of the rooms in which it was held. There were
seven—an imperial suite. In many palaces, however,

such suites form a long and straight vista, while the folding
doors slide back nearly to the walls on either hand, so that
the view of the whole extent is scarcely impeded. Here
the case was very different, as might have been expected
from the duke's love of the bizarre. The apartments were
so irregularly disposed that the vision embraced but
little more than one at a time. There was a sharp turn at
every twenty or thirty yards, and at each turn a novel
effect. To the right and left, in the middle of each wall,
a tall and narrow Gothic window looked out upon a closed
corridor which pursued the windings of the suite. These
windows were of stained glass, whose colour varied in
accordance with the prevailing hue of the decorations
of the chamber into which it opened. That at the eastern
extremity was hung, for example, in blue—and vividly blue
were its windows. The second chamber was purple in
its ornaments and tapestries, and here the panes were
purple. The third was green throughout, and so were
the casements. The fourth was furnished and lighted
with orange—the fifth with white—the sixth with violet.
The seventh apartment was closely shrouded in black
velvet tapestries that hung all over the ceiling and down
the walls, falling in heavy folds upon a carpet of the
same material and hue. But in this chamber only the
colour of the windows failed to correspond with the decorations. The panes here were scarlet—a deep blood colour.
Now in no one of the seven apartments was there any
lamp or candelabrum, amid the profusion of golden ornaments that lay scattered to and fro, or depended from
the roof. There was no light of any kind emanating
from lamp or candle within the suite of chambers. But
in the corridors that followed the suite, there stood, opposite
to each window, a heavy tripod, bearing a brazier of fire,
that projected its rays through the tinted glass, and so
glaringly illumined the room. And thus were produced
a multitude of gaudy and fantastic appearances. But
in the western or black chamber the effect of the firelight
that streamed upon the dark hangings through the blood-
tinted panes, was ghastly in the extreme, and produced
so wild a look upon the countenances of those who entered,
that there were few of the company bold enough to set
foot within its precincts at all.

It was in this apartment, also, that there stood against

the western wall a gigantic clock of ebony. Its pendulum swung to and fro with a dull, heavy, monotonous clang; and when the minute-hand made the circuit of the face, and the hour was to be stricken, there came from the brazen lungs of the clock a sound which was clear and loud and deep and exceedingly musical; but of so peculiar a note and emphasis that, at each lapse of an hour, the musicians of the orchestra were constrained to pause, momentarily, in their performance, to hearken to the sound; and thus the waltzers perforce ceased their evolutions; and there was a brief disconcert of the whole gay company; and, while the chimes of the clock yet rang, it was observed that the giddiest grew pale, and the more aged and sedate passed their hands over their brows as if in confused reverie or meditation. But when the echoes had fully ceased, a light laughter at once pervaded the assembly; the musicians looked at each other and smiled as if at their own nervousness and folly, and made whispering vows, each to the other, that the next chiming of the clock should produce in them no similar emotion; and then, after the lapse of sixty minutes (which embrace three thousand and six hundred seconds of the Time that flies), there came yet another chiming of the clock, and then were the same disconcert and tremulousness and meditation as before.

But, in spite of these things, it was a gay and magnificent revel. The tastes of the duke were peculiar. He had a fine eye for colours and effects. He disregarded the *decora* of mere fashion. His plans were bold and fiery, and his conceptions glowed with barbaric lustre. There are some who would have thought him mad. His followers felt that he was not. It was necessary to hear and see and touch him to be *sure* that he was not.

He had directed, in great part, the movable embellishments of the seven chambers, upon occasion of this great *fête*; and it was his own guiding taste which had given character to the masqueraders. Be sure they were grotesque. There were much glare and glitter and piquancy and phantasm—much of what has been since seen in *Hernani*. There were arabesque figures with unsuited limbs and appointments. There were delirious fancies as the madman fashions. There were much of the beautiful, much of the wanton, much of the bizarre, something of the terrible, and not a little of that which might have excited disgust. To and fro in the seven chambers there stalked, in fact, a multitude of dreams. And these—the dreams—writhed in and about, taking hue from the rooms, and causing the wild music of the orchestra to seem as the echo of their steps. And, anon, there strikes the ebony clock which stands in the hall of the velvet. And then, for a moment, all is still, and all is silent save the voice of the clock. The dreams are stiff-frozen as they stand. But the echoes of the chime die away—they have endured but an instant—and a light, half-subdued laughter floats after them as they depart. And now again the music swells, and the dreams live, and writhe to and fro more merrily than ever, taking hue from the many tinted windows through which stream the rays from the tripods. But to the chamber which lies most westwardly of the seven, there are now none of the maskers who venture ; for the night is waning away ; and there flows a ruddier light through the blood-coloured panes ; and the blackness of the sable drapery appals ; and to him whose foot falls upon the sable carpet, there comes from the near clock of ebony a muffled peal more solemnly emphatic than any which reaches *their* ears who indulge in the more remote gaieties of the other apartments.

But these other apartments were densely crowded, and in them beat feverishly the heart of life. And the revel went whirlingly on, until at length there commenced the sounding of midnight upon the clock. And then the music ceased, as I have told ; and the evolutions of the waltzers were quieted ; and there was an uneasy cessation of all things as before. But now there were twelve strokes to be sounded by the bell of the clock ; and thus it happened, perhaps, that more of thought crept, with more of time, into the meditations of the thoughtful among those who revelled. And thus, too, it happened, perhaps, that before the last echoes of the last chime had utterly sunk into silence, there were many individuals in the crowd who had found leisure to become aware of the presence of a masked figure which had arrested the attention of no single individual before. And the rumour of this new presence having spread itself whisperingly around, there arose at length from the whole company a buzz, or murmur, expressive of disapprobation and surprise—then, finally, of terror, of horror, and of disgust.

In an assembly of phantasms, such as I have painted, it may well be supposed that no ordinary appearance could have excited such sensation. In truth the masquerade licence of the night was nearly unlimited ; but the figure in question had out-Heroded Herod, and gone beyond the bounds of even the prince's indefinite decorum. There are chords in the hearts of the most reckless which cannot be touched without emotion. Even with the utterly lost, to whom life and death are equally jests, there are matters of which no jests can be made. The whole company, indeed, seemed now deeply to feel that in the costume and bearing of the stranger neither wit nor propriety existed. The figure was tall and gaunt, and shrouded from head to foot in the habiliments of the grave. The mask which concealed the visage was made so nearly to resemble the countenance of a stiffened corpse that the closest scrutiny must have had difficulty in detecting the cheat. And yet all this might have been endured, if not approved, by the mad revellers around. But the mummer had gone so far as to assume the type of the Red Death. His vesture was dabbled in *blood*—and his broad brow, with all the features of the face, was besprinkled with the scarlet horror.

When the eyes of Prince Prospero fell upon this spectral image (which with a slow and solemn movement, as if more fully to sustain its *rôle*, stalked to and fro among the waltzers), he was seen to be convulsed, in the first moment, with a strong shudder either of terror or distaste ; but, in the next, his brow reddened with rage.

" Who dares ? " he demanded hoarsely of the courtiers who stood near him—" who dares insult us with this blasphemous mockery ? Seize him and unmask him—that we may know whom we have to hang at sunrise from the battlements ! "

It was in the eastern or blue chamber in which stood the Prince Prospero as he uttered these words. They rang throughout the seven rooms loudly and clearly—for the prince was a bold and robust man, and the music had become hushed at the waving of his hand.

It was in the blue room where stood the prince with a group of pale courtiers by his side. At first, as he spoke, there was a slight rushing movement of this group in the direction of the intruder, who, at the moment, was also near at hand, and now, with deliberate and stately step, made closer approach to the speaker. But from a certain nameless awe with which the mad assumptions of the mummer had inspired the whole party, there were found none who put forth hand to seize him ; so that, unimpeded, he passed within a yard of the prince's person ; and, while the vast assembly, as if with one impulse, shrank from the centres of the rooms to the walls, he made his way uninterruptedly, but with the same solemn and measured step which had distinguished him from the first, through the blue chamber to the purple—through the purple to the green—through the green to the orange— through this again to the white—and even thence to the violet, ere a decided movement had been made to arrest him. It was then, however, that the Prince Prospero, maddened with rage and the shame of his own momentary cowardice, rushed hurriedly through the six chambers, while none followed him on account of a deadly terror that had seized upon all. He bore aloft a drawn dagger, and had approached, in rapid impetuosity, to within three or four feet of the retreating figure, when the latter, having attained the extremity of the velvet apartment, turned suddenly and confronted his pursuer. There was a sharp cry—and the dagger dropped gleaming upon the sable carpet, upon which, instantly afterwards, fell prostrate in death the Prince Prospero. Then, summoning the wild courage of despair, a throng of the revellers at once threw themselves into the black apartment, and, seizing the mummer, whose tall figure stood erect and motionless within the shadow of the ebony clock, gasped in unutter- able horror at finding the grave cerements and corpse-like mask which they handled with so violent a rudeness, untenanted by any tangible form.

And now was acknowledged the presence of the Red Death. He had come like a thief in the night. And one by one dropped the revellers in the blood-bedewed halls of their revel, and died each in the despairing posture of his fall. And the life of the ebony clock went out with that of the last of the gay. And the flames of the tripods expired. And Darkness and Decay and the Red Death held illimitable dominion over all.

THE SPECTACLES

MANY years ago, it was the fashion to ridicule the idea of " love at first sight " ; but those who think, not less than those who feel deeply, have always advocated its existence. Modern discoveries, indeed, in what may be termed ethical magnetism or magneto-æsthetics, render it probable that the most natural, and, consequently, the truest and most intense of the human affections are those which arise in the heart as if by electric sympathy—in a word, that the brightest and most enduring of the psychal fetters are those which are riveted by a glance. The confession I am about to make will add another to the already almost innumerable instances of the truth of the position.

My story requires that I should be somewhat minute. I am still a very young man—not yet twenty-two years of age. My name, at present, is a very usual and rather plebeian one—Simpson. I say " at present " ; for it is only lately that I have been so called—having legislatively adopted this surname within the last year, in order to receive a large inheritance left me by a distant male relative, Adolphus Simpson, Esq. The bequest was conditioned upon my taking the name of the testator—the family, not the Christian name ; my Christian name is Napoleon Bonaparte—or, more properly, these are my first and middle appellations.

I assumed the name, Simpson, with some reluctance, as in my true patronym, Froissart, I felt a very pardonable pride—believing that I could trace a descent from the immortal author of the *Chronicles*. While on the subject of names, by-the-bye, I may mention a singular coincidence of sound attending the names of some of my immediate predecessors. My father was a Monsieur Froissart, of Paris. His wife—my mother, whom he married at fifteen —was a Mademoiselle Croissart, eldest daughter of Croissart the banker ; whose wife, again, being only sixteen when married, was the eldest daughter of one Victor Voissart. Monsieur Voissart, very singularly, had married a lady of similar name—a Mademoiselle Moissart. She, too, was

quite a child when married ; and her mother, also, Madame
Moissart, was only fourteen when led to the altar. These
early marriages are usual in France. Here, however, are
Moissart, Voissart, Croissart, and Froissart, all in the
direct line of descent. My own name, though, as I say,
became Simpson, by act of Legislature, and with so much
repugnance on my part, that, at one period, I actually
hesitated about accepting the legacy with the useless and
annoying *proviso* attached.

As to personal endowments, I am by no means deficient.
On the contrary, I believe that I am well made, and
possess what nine-tenths of the world would call a handsome face. In height I am five feet eleven. My hair is
black and curling. My nose is sufficiently good. My
eyes are large and grey ; and although, in fact, they are
weak to a very inconvenient degree, still no defect in this
regard would be suspected from their appearance. The
weakness itself, however, has always much annoyed me,
and I have resorted to every remedy—short of wearing
glasses. Being youthful and good-looking, I naturally
dislike these, and have absolutely refused to employ them.
I know nothing, indeed, which so disfigures the countenance of a young person, or so impresses every feature
with an air of demureness, if not altogether of sancti-
moniousness and of age. An eye-glass, on the other hand,
has a savour of downright foppery and affectation. I
have hitherto managed as well as I could without either.
But something too much of these merely personal details,
which, after all, are of little importance. I will content
myself with saying, in addition, that my temperament is
sanguine, rash, ardent, enthusiastic—and that all my life
I have been a devoted admirer of the women.

One night last winter I entered a box at the P——
Theatre, in company with a friend, Mr. Talbot. It was
an opera night, and the bills presented a very rare attraction, so that the house was excessively crowded. We
were in time, however, to obtain the front seats which had
been reserved for us, and into which, with some little
difficulty, we elbowed our way.

For two hours my companion, who was a musical
fanatico, gave his undivided attention to the stage ; and, in
the meantime, I amused myself by observing the audience,
which consisted, in chief part, of the very *élite* of the city.

Having satisfied myself upon this point, I was about
turning my eyes to the *prima donna*, when they were
arrested and riveted by a figure in one of the private boxes
which had escaped my observation.

If I live a thousand years I can never forget the intense
emotion with which I regarded this figure. It was that of
a female, the most exquisite I had ever beheld. The face
was so far turned toward the stage that, for some minutes
I could not obtain a view of it,—but the form was *divine*
no other word can sufficiently express its magnificent
proportion—and even the term " divine " seems ridicul-
ously feeble as I write it.

The magic of a lovely form in woman—the necromancy
of female gracefulness—was always a power which I had
found it impossible to resist ; but here was grace personi-
fied, incarnate, the *beau idéal* of my wildest and most
enthusiastic visions. The figure, almost all of which the
construction of the box permitted to be seen, was somewhat above the medium height, and nearly approached,
without positively reaching, the majestic. Its perfect
fulness and *tournure* were delicious. The head, of which
only the back was visible, rivalled in outline that of the
Greek Psyche, and was rather displayed than concealed
by an elegant cap of *gaze aérienne*, which put me in mind
of the *ventum textilem* of Apuleius. The right arm hung
over the balustrade of the box, and thrilled every nerve
of my frame with its exquisite symmetry. Its upper
portion was draperied by one of the loose open sleeves
now in fashion. This extended but little below the elbow.
Beneath it was worn an under one of some frail material,
close-fitting, and terminated by a cuff of rich lace, which
fell gracefully over the top of the hand, revealing only the
delicate fingers, upon one of which sparkled a diamond
ring, which I at once saw was of extraordinary value.
The admirable roundness of the wrist was well set off by
a bracelet which encircled it, and which also was ornamented and clasped by a magnificent *aigrette* of jewels,—
telling, in words that could not be mistaken, at once of the
wealth and fastidious taste of the wearer.

I gazed at this queenly apparition for at least half-an-
hour, as if I had been suddenly converted to stone ; and,
during this period, I felt the full force and truth of all
that has been said or sung concerning " love at first sight."

My feelings were totally different from any which I had hitherto experienced, in the presence of even the most celebrated specimens of female loveliness. An unaccountable, and what I am compelled to consider a *magnetic*, sympathy of soul for soul, seemed to rivet, not only my vision, but my whole powers of thought and feeling, upon the admirable object before me. I saw—I felt—I knew that I was deeply, madly, irrevocably in love—and this even before seeing the face of the person beloved. So intense, indeed, was the passion that consumed me, that I really believed it would have received little if any abatement had the features, yet unseen, proved of merely ordinary character ; so anomalous is the nature of the only true love—of the love at first sight—and so little really dependent is it upon the external conditions which only seem to create and control it.

While I was thus wrapped in admiration of this lovely vision, a sudden disturbance among the audience caused her to turn her head partially toward me, so that I beheld the entire profile of the face. Its beauty even exceeded my anticipations—and yet there was something about it which disappointed me without my being able to tell exactly what it was. I said " disappointed," but this is not altogether the word. My sentiments were at once quieted and exalted. They partook less of transport and more of calm enthusiasm—of enthusiastic repose. This state of feeling arose, perhaps, from the Madonna-like and matronly air of the face ; and yet I at once understood that it could not have arisen entirely from this. There was something else—some mystery which I could not develop—some expression about the countenance which slightly disturbed me while it greatly heightened my interest. In fact, I was just in that condition of mind which prepares a young and susceptible man for any act of extravagance. Had the lady been alone, I should un-doubtedly have entered her box and accosted her at all hazards ; but, fortunately, she was attended by two companions—a gentleman, and a strikingly beautiful woman, to all appearance a few years younger than herself.

I revolved in my mind a thousand schemes by which I might obtain, hereafter, an introduction to the elder lady, or, for the present, at all events, a more distinct view of her beauty. I would have removed my position to one nearer her own, but the crowded state of the theatre rendered this impossible ; and the stern decrees of Fashion had, of late, imperatively prohibited the use of the opera-glass, in a case such as this, even had I been so fortunate as to have one with me—but I had not—and was thus in despair.

At length I bethought me of applying to my companion.

" Talbot," I said, " *you* have an opera-glass. Let me have it."

" An opera-glass !—no !—what do you suppose *I* would be doing with an opera-glass ? " Here he turned impatiently toward the stage.

" But, Talbot," I continued, pulling him by the shoulder, " listen to me, will you ? Do you see the stage-box ?—there !—no, the next.—Did you ever behold as lovely a woman ? "

" She is very beautiful, no doubt," he said.

" I wonder who she can be ? "

" Why, in the name of all that is angelic, don't you *know* who she is ? ' Not to know her argues yourself unknown.' She is the celebrated Madame Lalande—the beauty of the day *par excellence*, and the talk of the whole town. Immensely wealthy too—a widow—and a great match—has just arrived from Paris."

" Do you know her ? "

" Yes—I have the honour."

" Will you introduce me ? "

" Assuredly—with the greatest pleasure ; when shall it be ? "

" To-morrow, at one, I will call upon you at B——'s."

" Very good ; and now *do* hold your tongue, *if* you can."

In this latter respect I was forced to take Talbot's advice ; for he remained obstinately deaf to every further question or suggestion, and occupied himself exclusively for the rest of the evening with what was transacting upon the stage.

In the meantime I kept my eyes riveted on Madame Lalande, and at length had the good fortune to obtain a full front view of her face. It was exquisitely lovely : this, of course, my heart had told me before, even had not Talbot fully satisfied me upon the point—but still the unintelligible something disturbed me. I finally concluded that my senses were impressed by a certain air of gravity, sadness, or, still more properly, of weariness, which took something from the youth and freshness of the countenance, only to endow it with a seraphic tenderness and majesty, and thus, of course, to my enthusiastic and romantic temperament, with an interest tenfold.

While I thus feasted my eyes, I perceived, at last, to my great trepidation, by an almost imperceptible start on the part of the lady, that she had become suddenly aware of the intensity of my gaze. Still, I was absolutely fascinated, and could not withdraw it, even for an instant. She turned aside her face, and again I saw only the chiselled contour of the back portion of the head. After some minutes, as if urged by curiosity to see if I was still looking, she gradually brought her face again around and again encountered my burning gaze. Her large dark eyes fell instantly, and a deep blush mantled her cheek. But what was my astonishment at perceiving that she not only did not a second time avert her head, but that she actually took from her girdle a double eye-glass—elevated it—adjusted it—and then regarded me through it, intently and deliberately, for the space of several minutes.

Had a thunderbolt fallen at my feet I could not have been more thoroughly astounded—astounded *only*—not offended or disgusted in the slightest degree; although an action so bold in any other woman would have been likely to offend or disgust. But the whole thing was done with so much quietude—so much *nonchalance*—so much repose—with so evident an air of the highest breeding, in short—that nothing of mere effrontery was perceptible, and my sole sentiments were those of admiration and surprise.

I observed that, upon her first elevation of the glass, she had seemed satisfied with a momentary inspection of my person, and was withdrawing the instrument, when, as if struck by a second thought, she resumed it, and so continued to regard me with fixed attention for the space of several minutes—for five minutes, at the very least, I am sure.

This action, so remarkable in an American theatre, attracted very general observation, and gave rise to an indefinite movement, or *buzz*, among the audience, which, for a moment, filled me with confusion, but produced no visible effect upon the countenance of Madame Lalande.

Having satisfied her curiosity—if such it was—she dropped the glass, and quietly gave her attention again to

N

the stage; her profile now being turned toward myself, as before. I continued to watch her unremittingly, although I was fully conscious of my rudeness in so doing. Presently I saw the head slowly and slightly change its position; and soon I became convinced that the lady, while pretending to look at the stage was, in fact, attentively regarding myself. It is needless to say what effect this conduct, on the part of so fascinating a woman, had upon my excitable mind.

Having thus scrutinised me for perhaps a quarter of an hour, the fair object of my passion addressed the gentleman who attended her, and, while she spoke, I saw distinctly, by the glances of both, that the conversation had reference to myself.

Upon its conclusion, Madame Lalande again turned toward the stage, and, for a few minutes, seemed absorbed in the performances. At the expiration of this period, however, I was thrown into an extremity of agitation by seeing her unfold, for the second time, the eye-glass which hung at her side, fully confront me as before, and, disregarding the renewed buzz of the audience, survey me, from head to foot, with the same miraculous composure which had previously so delighted and confounded my soul.

This extraordinary behaviour, by throwing me into a perfect fever of excitement—into an absolute delirium of love—served rather to embolden than to disconcert me. In the mad intensity of my devotion, I forgot everything but the presence and the majestic loveliness of the vision which confronted my gaze. Watching my opportunity, when I thought the audience were fully engaged with the opera, I at length caught the eyes of Madame Lalande, and, upon the instant, made a slight but unmistakable bow.

She blushed very deeply—then averted her eyes—then slowly and cautiously looked around, apparently to see if my rash action had been noticed—then leaned over toward the gentleman who sat by her side.

I now felt a burning sense of the impropriety I had committed, and expected nothing less than instant exposure; while a vision of pistols upon the morrow floated rapidly and uncomfortably through my brain. I was greatly and immediately relieved, however, when I saw the lady merely hand the gentleman a play-bill, without speaking; but the reader may form some feeble conception of my astonishment—of my *profound* amazement—my delirious bewilderment of heart and soul—when, instantly afterward, having again glanced furtively around, she allowed her bright eyes to set fully and steadily upon my own, and then, with a faint smile, disclosing a bright line of her pearly teeth, made two distinct, pointed, and unequivocal affirmative inclinations of the head.

It is useless, of course, to dwell upon my joy—upon my transport—upon my illimitable ecstasy of heart. If ever man was mad with excess of happiness, it was myself at that moment. I loved. This was my *first* love—so I felt it to be. It was love supreme—indescribable. It was "love at first sight"; and at first sight, too, it had been appreciated and *returned*.

Yes, returned. How and why should I doubt it for an instant. What other construction could I possibly put upon such conduct, on the part of a lady so beautiful—so wealthy—evidently so accomplished—of so high breeding —of so lofty a position in society—in every regard so entirely respectable as I felt assured was Madame Lalande ? Yes, she loved me—she returned the enthusiasm of my love, with an enthusiasm as blind—as uncompromising— as uncalculating—as abandoned—and as utterly unbounded as my own! These delicious fancies and reflections, however, were now interrupted by the falling of the dropcurtain. The audience arose; and the usual tumult immediately supervened. Quitting Talbot abruptly, I made every effort to force my way into closer proximity with Madame Lalande. Having failed in this, on account of the crowd, I at length gave up the chase, and bent my steps homeward ; consoling myself for my disappointment in not having been able to touch even the hem of her robe, by the reflection that I should be introduced by Talbot, in due form, upon the morrow.

This morrow at last came ; that is to say, a day finally dawned upon a long and weary night of impatience ; and then the hours until " one " were snail-paced, dreary, and innumerable. But even Stamboul, it is said, shall have an end, and there came an end to this long delay. The clock struck. As the last echo ceased, I stepped into B——'s and inquired for Talbot.

" Out ! " said the footman—Talbot's own.

" Out ! " I replied, staggering back half-a-dozen paces—

"let me tell you, my fine fellow, that this thing is thoroughly impossible and impracticable ; Mr. Talbot is *not* out. What do you mean ? "

"Nothing, sir ; only Mr. Talbot is not in. That's all. He rode over to S——, immediately after breakfast, and left word that he would not be in town again for a week."

I stood petrified with horror and rage. I endeavoured to reply, but my tongue refused its office. At length I turned on my heel, livid with wrath, and inwardly consigning the whole tribe of the Talbots to the innermost regions of Erebus. It was evident that my considerate friend, *il fanatico*, had quite forgotten his appointment with myself—had forgotten it as soon as it was made. At no time was he a very scrupulous man of his word. There was no help for it ; so smothering my vexation as well as I could, I strolled moodily up the street, propounding futile inquiries about Madame Lalande to every male acquaintance I met. By report she was known, I found, to all—to many by sight—but she had been in town only a few weeks, and there were very few, therefore, who claimed her personal acquaintance. These few, being still comparatively strangers, could not, or would not, take the liberty of introducing me through the formality of a morning call. While I stood thus, in despair, conversing with a trio of friends upon the all-absorbing subject of my heart, it so happened that the subject itself passed by.

"As I live, there she is ! " cried one.

"Surprisingly beautiful ! " exclaimed a second.

"An angel upon earth ! " ejaculated a third.

I looked ; and in an open carriage which approached us, passing slowly down the street, sat the enchanting vision of the opera, accompanied by the younger lady who had occupied a portion of her box.

"Her companion also wears remarkably well," said the one of my trio who had spoken first.

"Astonishingly," said the second ; " still quite a brilliant air ; but art will do wonders. Upon my word, she looks better than she did at Paris five years ago. A beautiful woman still ;—don't you think so, Froissart ?—Simpson, I mean."

"*Still !* " said I, " and why shouldn't she be ? But compared with her friend she is as a rushlight to the evening star—a glow-worm to Antares."

" Ha! ha! ha!—why, Simpson, you have an astonishing tact at making discoveries—original ones, I mean."
And here we separated, while one of the trio began humming
a gay *vaudeville*, of which I caught only the lines—

> Ninon, Ninon, Ninon à bas—
> À bas Ninon De L'Enclos !

During this little scene, however, one thing had served
greatly to console me, although it fed the passion by which
I was consumed. As the carriage of Madame Lalande
rolled by our group, I had observed that she recognised me ;
and more than this, she had blessed me, by the most
seraphic of all imaginable smiles, with no equivocal mark
of the recognition.

As for an introduction, I was obliged to abandon all hope
of it, until such time as Talbot should think proper to
return from the country. In the meantime I perseveringly
frequented every reputable place of public amusement ;
and, at length, at the theatre, where I first saw her, I had
the supreme bliss of meeting her, and of exchanging glances
with her once again. This did not occur, however, until
the lapse of a fortnight. Every day, in the *interim*, I had
inquired for Talbot at his hotel, and every day had been
thrown into a spasm of wrath by the everlasting " Not
come home yet " of his footman.

Upon the evening in question, therefore, I was in a condition little short of madness. Madame Lalande, I had been
told, was a Parisian—had lately arrived from Paris—
might she not suddenly return ?—return before Talbot
came back—and might she not be thus lost to me for ever ?
The thought was too terrible to bear. Since my future
happiness was at issue, I resolved to act with a manly
decision. In a word, upon the breaking up of the play, I
traced the lady to her residence, noted the address, and
the next morning sent her a full and elaborate letter, in
which I poured out my whole heart.

I spoke boldly, freely—in a word, I spoke with passion.
I concealed nothing—not even of my weakness. I alluded
to the romantic circumstances of our first meeting—even
to the glances which had passed between us. I went so
far as to say that I felt assured of her love ; while I offered
this assurance, and my own intensity of devotion, as two
excuses for my otherwise unpardonable conduct. As a

third, I spoke of my fear that she might quit the city before I could have the opportunity of a formal introduction. I concluded the most wildly enthusiastic epistle ever penned, with a frank declaration of my worldly circumstances—of my affluence—and with an offer of my heart and of my hand.

In an agony of expectation I awaited the reply. After what seemed the lapse of a century it came.

Yes, *actually came*. Romantic as all this may appear, I really received a letter from Madame Lalande—the beautiful, the wealthy, the idolised Madame Lalande. Her eyes—her magnificent eyes, had not belied her noble heart. Like a true Frenchwoman, as she was, she had obeyed the frank dictates of her reason—the generous impulses of her nature—despising the conventional pruderies of the world. She had *not* scorned my proposals. She had *not* sheltered herself in silence. She had *not* returned my letter unopened. She had even sent me, in reply, one penned by her own exquisite fingers. It ran thus :

" Monsieur Simpson vill pardonne me for not compose de butefulle tong of his contrée so vell as might. It is only de late dat I am arrive, and not yet ave de opportunité for to—l'étudier.

" Vid dis apologie for the maniere, I vill not say dat, hélas !— Monsieur Simpson ave guess but de too true. Need I say de more ? Hélas ! am I not ready speak de too moshe ?

" EUGÉNIE LALANDE."

This noble-spirited note I kissed a million times, and committed no doubt, on its account, a thousand other extravagances that have now escaped my memory. Still Talbot *would* not return. Alas ! could he have formed the even vaguest idea of the suffering his absence had occasioned his friend, would not his sympathising nature have flown immediately to my relief ? Still, however, he came *not*. I wrote. He replied. He was detained by urgent business—but would shortly return. He begged me not to be impatient—to moderate my transports—to read soothing books—to drink nothing stronger than Hock—and to bring the consolations of philosophy in my aid. The fool ! if he could not come himself, why, in the name of everything rational, could he not have enclosed me a letter of presentation ? I wrote him again, entreating him to forward one forthwith. My letter was returned by *that* footman, with the following endorsement in pencil. The scoundrel had joined his master in the country :

" Left S—— yesterday, for parts unknown—did not say where —or when be back—so thought best to return letter, knowing your handwriting, and as how you is always, more or less, in a hurry.
" Yours sincerely, STUBBS."

After this, it is needless to say that I devoted to the infernal deities both master and valet :—but there was little use in anger, and no consolation at all in complaint.

But I had yet a resource left, in my constitutional audacity. Hitherto it had served me well, and I now resolved to make it avail me to the end. Besides, after the correspondence which had passed between us, what act of mere informality *could* I commit, within bounds, that ought to be regarded as indecorous by Madame Lalande ? Since the affair of the letter, I had been in the habit of watching her house, and thus discovered that, about twilight, it was her custom to promenade, attended only by a negro in livery, in a public square overlooked by her windows. Here, amid the luxuriant and shadowy groves, in the grey gloom of a sweet midsummer evening, I observed my opportunity and accosted her.

The better to deceive the servant in attendance, I did this with the assured air of an old and familiar acquaintance. With a presence of mind truly Parisian, she took the cue at once, and, to greet me, held out the most bewitchingly little of hands. The valet at once fell into the rear, and now, with hearts full to overflowing, we discoursed long and unreservedly of our love.

As Madame Lalande spoke English even less fluently than she wrote it, our conversation was necessarily in French. In this sweet tongue, so adapted to passion, I gave loose to the impetuous enthusiasm of my nature, and, with all the eloquence I could command, besought her to consent to an immediate marriage.

At this impatience she smiled. She urged the old story of decorum—that bug-bear which deters so many from bliss until the opportunity for bliss has for ever gone by. I had most imprudently made it known among my friends, she observed, that I desired her acquaintance—thus that I did not possess it—thus, again, there was no possibility of concealing the date of our first knowledge of each other. And then she adverted, with a blush, to the extreme recency of this date. To wed immediately would be improper—would be indecorous—would be *outré*. All this she said with a charming air of *naïveté* which enraptured while it grieved and convinced me. She went even so far as to accuse me, laughingly, of rashness—of imprudence. She bade me remember that I really even knew not who she was—what were her prospects, her connections, her standing in society. She begged me, but with a sigh, to reconsider my proposal, and termed my love an infatuation—a will o' the wisp—a fancy or fantasy of the moment, a baseless and unstable creation rather of the imagination than of the heart. These things she uttered as the shadows of the sweet twilight gathered darkly and more darkly around us—and then, with a gentle pressure of her fairy-like hand, overthrew in a single sweet instant, all the argumentative fabric she had reared.

I replied as best I could—as only a true lover can. I spoke at length, and perseveringly of my devotion, of my passion—of her exceeding beauty, and of my own enthusiastic admiration. In conclusion, I dwelt, with a convincing energy, upon the perils that encompass the course of love—that course of true love that never did run smooth —and thus deduced the manifest danger of rendering that course unnecessarily long.

This latter argument seemed finally to soften the rigour of her determination. She relented ; but there was yet an obstacle, she said, which she felt assured I had not properly considered. This was a delicate point—for a woman to urge, especially so ; in mentioning it, she saw that she must make a sacrifice of her feelings ; still, for *me*, every sacrifice should be made. She alluded to the topic of *age*. Was I aware—was I fully aware of this discrepancy between us ? That the age of the husband should surpass by a few years—even by fifteen or twenty— the age of the wife, was regarded by the world as admissible, and indeed, as even proper : but she had always entertained the belief that the years of the wife should *never* exceed in number those of the husband. A discrepancy of this unnatural kind gave rise, too frequently, alas ! to a life of unhappiness. Now she was aware that my own age did not exceed two and twenty ; and I, on the contrary, perhaps was *not* aware that the years of my Eugénie extended very considerably beyond that number.

About all this there was a nobility of soul—a dignity of candour—which delighted—which enchanted me—which eternally riveted my chains. I could scarcely restrain the excessive transport which possessed me.

"My sweetest Eugénie," I cried, "what is all this about which you are discoursing? Your years surpass in some measure my own. But what then? The customs of the world are so many conventional follies. To those who love as ourselves, in what respect differs a year from an hour? I am twenty-two, you say; granted: indeed, you may as well call me, at once, twenty-three. Now you yourself, my dearest Eugénie, can have numbered no more than—can have numbered no more than—no more than—than—than—than——"

Here I paused for an instant, in the expectation that Madame Lalande would interrupt me by supplying her true age. But a Frenchwoman is seldom direct, and has always, by way of answering to an embarrassing query, some little practical reply of her own. In the present instance, Eugénie, who for a few moments past had seemed to be searching for something in her bosom, at length let fall upon the grass a miniature, which I immediately picked up and presented to her.

"Keep it!" she said, with one of her most ravishing smiles. "Keep it for my sake—for the sake of her whom it too flatteringly represents. Besides, upon the back of the trinket you may discover, perhaps, the very information you seem to desire. It is now, to be sure, growing rather dark—but you can examine it at your leisure in the morning. In the meantime, you shall be my escort home to-night. My friends are about holding a little musical *levée*. I can promise you, too, some good singing. We French are not nearly so punctilious as you Americans, and I shall have no difficulty in smuggling you in, in the character of an old acquaintance."

With this, she took my arm, and I attended her home. The mansion was quite a fine one, and, I believe, furnished in good taste. Of this latter point, however, I am scarcely qualified to judge; for it was just dark as we arrived; and in American mansions of the better sort lights seldom, during the heat of summer, make their appearance at this, the most pleasant period of the day. In about an hour after my arrival, to be sure, a single shaded solar lamp was lit in the principal drawing-room; and this apartment, I could thus see, was arranged with unusual good taste and even splendour; but two other rooms of the suite, and in which the company chiefly assembled, remained, during the whole evening, in a very agreeable shadow. This is a well-conceived custom, giving the party at least a choice of light or shade, and one which our friends over the water could not do better than immediately adopt.

The evening thus spent was unquestionably the most delicious of my life. Madame Lalande had not overrated the musical abilities of her friends; and the singing I here heard I had never heard excelled in any private circle out of Vienna. The instrumental performers were many and of superior talents. The vocalists were chiefly ladies, and no individual sang less than well. At length, upon a peremptory call for " Madame Lalande," she arose at once, without affectation or demur, from the *chaise longue* upon which she had sat by my side, and, accompanied by one or two gentlemen and her female friend of the opera, repaired to the piano in the main drawing-room. I would have escorted her myself, but felt that, under the circumstances of my introduction to the house, I had better remain unobserved where I was. I was thus deprived of the pleasure of seeing, although not of hearing, her sing.

The impression she produced upon the company seemed electrical—but the effect upon myself was something even more. I know not how adequately to describe it. It arose in part, no doubt, from the sentiment of love with which I was imbued; but chiefly from my conviction of the extreme sensibility of the singer. It is beyond the reach of art to endow either air or recitative with more impassioned *expression* than was hers. Her utterance of the romance in Otello—the tone with which she gave the words " *Sul mio sasso*," in the Capuletti—is ringing in my memory yet. Her lower tones were absolutely miraculous. Her voice embraced three complete octaves, extending from the contralto D to the D upper soprano, and, though sufficiently powerful to have filled the San Carlos, executed, with the minutest precision, every difficulty of vocal composition—ascending and descending scales, cadences, or *fiorituri*. In the finale of the Sonnambula, she brought about a most remarkable effect at the words :

Ah ! non guinge uman pensiero
Al contento ond 'io son piena.

Here, in imitation of Malibran, she modified the original phrase of Bellini, so as to let her voice descend to the tenor G, when, by a rapid transition, she struck the G above the treble stave, springing over an interval of two octaves.

Upon rising from the piano after these miracles of vocal execution, she resumed her seat by my side ; when I expressed to her, in terms of the deepest enthusiasm, my delight at her performance. Of my surprise I said nothing, and yet was I most unfeignedly surprised ; for a certain feebleness, or rather a certain tremulous indecision of voice in ordinary conversation, had prepared me to anticipate that, in singing, she would not acquit herself with any remarkable ability.

Our conversation was now long, earnest, uninterrupted, and totally unreserved. She made me relate many of the earlier passages of my life, and listened with breathless attention to every word of the narrative. I concealed nothing—felt that I had a right to conceal nothing—from her confiding affection. Encouraged by her candour upon the delicate point of her age, I entered, with perfect frankness, not only into a detail of my many minor vices, but made full confession of those moral and even of those physical infirmities, the disclosure of which, in demanding so much higher a degree of courage, is so much surer an evidence of love. I touched upon my college indiscretions —upon my extravagances—upon my carousals—upon my debts—upon my flirtations. I even went so far as to speak of a slightly hectic cough with which, at one time, I had been troubled—of a chronic rheumatism—of a twinge of hereditary gout—and, in conclusion, of the disagreeable and inconvenient, but hitherto carefully concealed, weakness of my eyes.

" Upon this latter point," said Madame Lalande, laughingly, " you have been surely injudicious in coming to confession ; for, without the confession, I take it for granted that no one would have accused you of the crime. By-the-bye," she continued, " have you any recollection——" and here I fancied that a blush, even through the gloom of the apartment, became distinctly visible upon her cheek—" have you any recollection, *mon cher ami*, of this little ocular assistant which now depends from my neck ? "

As she spoke, she twirled in her fingers the identical double eye-glass, which had so overwhelmed me with confusion at the opera.

" Full well—alas ! do I remember it," I exclaimed, pressing passionately the delicate hand which offered the glasses for my inspection. They formed a complex and magnificent toy, richly chased and filigreed, and gleaming with jewels which, even in the deficient light, I could not help perceiving were of high value.

" *Eh bien !* mon ami," she resumed with a certain *empressement* of manner that rather surprised me—" *Eh bien !* mon ami, you have earnestly besought of me a favour which you have been pleased to denominate priceless. You have demanded of me my hand upon the morrow. Should I yield to your entreaties—and, I may add, to the pleadings of my own bosom—would I not be entitled to demand of you a very—a very little boon in return ? "

" Name it ! " I exclaimed with an energy that had nearly drawn upon us the observation of the company, and restrained by their presence alone from throwing myself impetuously at her feet. " Name it, my beloved, my Eugénie, my own !—name it !—but, alas ! it is already yielded ere named."

" You shall conquer, then, *mon ami*," said she, " for the sake of the Eugénie whom you love, this little weakness which you have at last confessed—this weakness more moral than physical—and which, let me assure you, is so unbecoming the nobility of your real nature—so inconsistent with the candour of your usual character—and which, if permitted further control, will assuredly involve you, sooner or later, in some very disagreeable scrape. You shall conquer, for my sake, this affectation which leads you, as you yourself acknowledge, to the tacit or implied denial of your infirmity of vision. For, this infirmity you virtually deny, in refusing to employ the customary means for its relief. You will understand me to say, then, that I wish you to wear spectacles :—ah, hush !—you have already consented to wear them, *for my sake*. You shall accept the little toy which I now hold in my hand, and which, though admirable as an aid to vision, is really of no very immense value as a gem. You perceive that, by a trifling modification thus—or thus—it can be adapted to the eyes in the form of spectacles, or worn in the waistcoat pocket as an eye-glass. It is in the former mode, however, and habitually, that you have already consented to wear it *for my sake.*"

This request—must I confess it?—confused me in no little degree. But the condition with which it was coupled rendered hesitation, of course, a matter altogether out of the question.

" It is done ! " I cried, with all the enthusiasm that I could muster at the moment. " It is done—it is most cheerfully agreed. I sacrifice every feeling for your sake. To-night I wear this dear eye-glass, *as* an eye-glass, and upon my heart ; but with the earliest dawn of that morning which gives me the pleasure of calling you wife, I will place it upon my—upon my nose,—and there wear it ever afterward, in the less romantic, and less fashionable, but certainly in the more serviceable, form, which you desire."

Our conversation now turned upon the details of our arrangements for the morrow. Talbot, I learned from my betrothed, had just arrived in town. I was to see him at once, and procure a carriage. The *soirée* would scarcely break up before two ; and by this hour the vehicle was to be at the door ; when, in the confusion occasioned by the departure of the company, Madame L. could easily enter it unobserved. We were then to call at the house of a clergyman who would be in waiting ; there be married, drop Talbot, and proceed on a short tour to the East ; leaving the fashionable world at home to make whatever comments upon the matter it thought best.

Having planned all this, I immediately took leave, and went in search of Talbot, but, on the way, I could not refrain from stepping into a hotel, for the purpose of inspecting the miniature ; and this I did by the powerful aid of the glasses. The countenance was a surpassingly beautiful one ! Those large luminous eyes !—that proud Grecian nose !—those dark luxuriant curls !—" Ah ! " said I, exultingly to myself, " this is indeed the speaking image of my beloved ! " I turned the reverse, and discovered the words—" Eugénie Lalande—aged twenty-seven years and seven months."

I found Talbot at home, and proceeded at once to

acquaint him with my good fortune. He professed
excessive astonishment, of course, but congratulated me
most cordially, and proffered every assistance in his
power. In a word, we carried out our arrangement to
the letter ; and at two in the morning, just ten minutes
after the ceremony, I found myself in a close carriage with
Madame Lalande—with Mrs. Simpson, I should say—and
driving at a great rate out of town, in a direction north-
east by north, half-north.

It had been determined for us by Talbot, that, as we
were to be up all night, we should make our first stop at
C——, a village about twenty miles from the city, and
there get an early breakfast and some repose, before proceeding upon our route. At four, precisely, therefore, the
carriage drew up at the door of the principal inn. I
handed my adored wife out, and ordered breakfast forthwith. In the meantime we were shown into a small
parlour, and sat down.

It was now nearly if not altogether daylight ; and, as I
gazed, enraptured, at the angel by my side, the singular
idea came, all at once, into my head, that this was really
the very first moment since my acquaintance with the
celebrated loveliness of Madame Lalande, that I had enjoyed a near inspection of that loveliness by daylight at all.

" And now, *mon ami*," said she, taking my hand, and so
interrupting this train of reflection, " and now, *mon cher
ami*, since we are indissolubly one—since I have yielded
to your passionate entreaties, and performed my portion
of our agreement—I presume you have not forgotten that
you also have a little favour to bestow—a little promise
which it is your intention to keep. Ah ! let me see !
Let me remember ! Yes ; full easily do I call to mind the
precise words of the dear promise you made to Eugénie
last night. Listen ! You spoke thus : ' It is done !—it
is most cheerfully agreed ! I sacrifice every feeling for
your sake. To-night I wear this dear eye-glass *as* an eye-
glass, and upon my heart ; but with the earliest dawn of
that morning which gives me the privilege of calling you
wife, I will place it upon my—upon my nose,—and there
wear it ever afterward, in the less romantic, and less
fashionable, but certainly in the more serviceable, form
which you desire.' These were the exact words, my
beloved husband, were they not ? "

" They were," I said ; " you have an excellent memory ; and assuredly, my beautiful Eugénie, there is no disposition on my part to evade the performance of the trivial promise they imply. See ! Behold ? They are becoming—rather —are they not ? " And here, having arranged the glasses in the ordinary form of spectacles, I applied them gingerly in their proper position ; while Madame Simpson, adjusting her cap, and folding her arms, sat bolt upright in her chair, in a somewhat stiff and prim, and indeed, in a somewhat undignified position.

" Goodness gracious me ! " I exclaimed, almost at the very instant that the rim of the spectacles had settled upon my nose—" *My !* goodness gracious me !—why what *can* be the matter with these glasses ? " and taking them quickly off, I wiped them carefully with a silk handkerchief, and adjusted them again.

But if, in the first instance, there had occurred something which occasioned me surprise, in the second, this surprise became elevated into astonishment ; and this astonishment was profound—was extreme—indeed I may say it was horrific. What, in the name of everything hideous, did this mean ? Could I believe my eyes ?—*could* I ?— that was the question. Was that—was that—was that *rouge* ? And were those—and were those—were those *wrinkles*, upon the visage of Eugénie Lalande ? And oh ! Jupiter, and every one of the gods and goddesses, little and big !—what—what—what—*what* had become of her teeth ? I dashed the spectacles violently to the ground, and, leaping to my feet, stood erect in the middle of the floor, confronting Mrs. Simpson, with my arms set akimbo, and grinning and foaming, but, at the same time, utterly speechless with terror and with rage.

Now I have already said that Madame Eugénie Lalande— that is to say, Simpson—spoke the English language but very little better than she wrote it ; and for this reason she very properly never attempted to speak it upon ordinary occasions. But rage will carry a lady to any extreme ; and in the present case it carried Mrs. Simpson to the very extraordinary extreme of attempting to hold a conversation in a tongue that she did not altogether understand.

" Vell, monsieur," said she, after surveying me, in great apparent astonishment, for some moments—" Vell, monsieur !—and vat den ?—vat de matter now ? It is de

dance of de Saint Vitusse dut you ave ?   If not like me,
vat for vy buy de pig in de poke ? "

" You wretch ! " said I, catching my breath—" you—
you—you villainous old hag ! "

" Ag ?—ole ?—me not so *ver* ole, after all ! me not one
single day more dan de eighty-doo."

" Eighty-two ! " I ejaculated, staggering to the wall—
" eighty-two hundred thousand baboons !   The miniature
said twenty-seven years and seven months ! "

" To be sure !—dat is so !—ver true ! but den de por-
traite has been take for dese fifty-five year.   Ven I go
marry my segonde usbande, Monsieur Lalande, at dat time
I had de portrait take for my daughter by my first usbande,
Monsieur Moissart ! "

" Moissart ! " said I.

" Yes, Moissart," said she, mimicking my pronuncia-
tion, which, to speak the truth, was none of the best ;
" and vat den ?   Vat *you* know about de Moissart ? "

" Nothing, you old fright !—I know nothing about him
at all ; only I had an ancestor of that name, once upon a
time."

" Dat name ! and vat you ave for say to dat name ?
'Tis ver *goot* name ; and so is Voissart—dat is ver goot
name too.   My daughter, Mademoiselle Moissart, she marry
von Monsieur Voissart ; and de name is both *ver* respectaable
name."

" Moissart ? " I exclaimed, " and Voissart ! why, what
is it you mean ? "

" Vat I mean ?—I mean Moissart and Voissart ; and for
de matter of dat, I mean Croissart and Froissart, too, if I
only tink proper to mean it.   My daughter's daughter,
Mademoiselle Voissart, she marry von Monsieur Croissart,
and den agin, my daughter's grande-daughter, Mademoiselle Croissart, she marry von Monsieur Froissart ; and I
suppose you say dat *dat* is not von *ver* respectaable name."

" Froissart ! " said I, beginning to faint, " why surely
you don't say Moissart, and Voissart, and Croissart, and
Froissart ? "

" Yes," she replied, leaning fully back in her chair, and
stretching out her lower limbs at great length ; " yes,
Moissart, and Voissart, and Croissart, and Froissart.   But
Monsieur Froissart, he vas von *ver* big vat you call fool—
he vas von ver great big donce like yourself—for he lef

la belle France for come to dis stupide Amérique—and ven he get here he vent and ave von *ver* stupide, von *ver*, *ver* stupide sonn, so I hear, dough I not yet av ad de plaisir to meet vid him—neither me nor my companion, de Madame Stephanie Lalande. He is name de Napoleon Bonaparte Froissart, and I suppose you say dat *dat*, too, is not von *ver* respectable name."

Either the length or the nature of this speech, had the effect of working up Mrs. Simpson into a very extraordinary passion indeed : and as she made an end of it, with great labour, she jumped up from her chair like somebody bewitched, dropping upon the floor an entire universe of bustle as she jumped. Once upon her feet, she gnashed her gums, brandished her arms, rolled up her sleeves, shook her fist in my face, and concluded the performance by tearing the cap from her head, and with it an immense wig of the most valuable and beautiful black hair, the whole of which she dashed upon the ground with a yell, and there trampled and danced a fandango upon it, in an absolute ecstasy and agony of rage.

Meantime I sank aghast into the chair which she had vacated. " Moissart and Voissart ! " I repeated thoughtfully, as she cut one of her pigeon-wings, " and Croissart and Froissart ! " as she completed another—" Moissart and Voissart and Croissart and Napoleon Bonaparte Froissart !—why, you ineffable old serpent, that's *me*— that's *me*—d'ye hear ?—that's *me* "—here I screamed at the top of my voice—" that's *me-e-e* ! *I* am Napoleon Bonaparte Froissart ! and if I haven't married my great, great, grandmother, I wish I may be everlastingly confounded ! "

Madame Eugénie Lalande, *quasi* Simpson—formerly Moissart—was, in sober fact, my great, great, grandmother. In her youth she had been beautiful, and even at eighty-two, retained the majestic height, the sculptural contour of head, the fine eyes and the Grecian nose of her girlhood. By the aid of these, of pearl-powder, of rouge, of false hair, false teeth, and false *tournure*, as well as of the most skilful modistes of Paris, she contrived to hold a respectable footing among the beauties *en peu passées* of the French metropolis. In this respect, indeed, she might have been regarded as little less than the equal of the celebrated Ninon De L'Enclos.

She was immensely wealthy, and being left, for the
second time, a widow without children, she bethought
herself of my existence in America, and for the purpose
of making me her heir, paid a visit to the United States,
in company with a distant and exceedingly lovely relative
of her second husband's—a Madame Stephanie Lalande.

At the opera, my great, great, grandmother's attention
was arrested by my notice; and, upon surveying me
through her eye-glass, she was struck with a certain family
resemblance to herself. Thus interested, and knowing
that the heir she sought was actually in the city, she
made inquiries of her party respecting me. The gentleman who attended her knew my person, and told her who
I was. The information thus obtained induced her to
renew her scrutiny; and this scrutiny it was which so
emboldened me that I behaved in the absurd manner
already detailed. She returned my bow, however, under
the impression that, by some odd accident, I had discovered
her identity. When, deceived by my weakness of vision,
and the arts of the toilet, in respect to the age and charms
of the strange lady, I demanded so enthusiastically of
Talbot who she was, he concluded that I meant the younger
beauty, as a matter of course, and so informed me, with
perfect truth, that she was " the celebrated widow, Madame
Lalande."

In the street, next morning, my great, great, grandmother encountered Talbot, an old Parisian acquaintance;
and the conversation, very naturally, turned upon myself.
My deficiencies of vision were then explained; for these
were notorious, although I was entirely ignorant of their
notoriety; and my good old relative discovered, much to
her chagrin, that she had been deceived in supposing me
aware of her identity, and that I had been merely making
a fool of myself in making open love, in a theatre, to an
old woman unknown. By way of punishing me for this
imprudence, she concocted with Talbot a plot. He purposely kept out of my way to avoid giving me the introduction. My street inquiries about " the lovely widow,
Madame Lalande," were supposed to refer to the younger
lady, of course; and thus the conversation with the three
gentlemen whom I encountered shortly after leaving
Talbot's hotel will be easily explained, as also their allusion
to Ninon De L'Enclos. I had no opportunity of seeing

Madame Lalande closely during daylight, and, at her musical *soirée*, my silly weakness in refusing the aid of glasses effectually prevented me from making a discovery of her age. When " Madame Lalande " was called upon to sing, the younger lady was intended ; and it was she who arose to obey the call ; my great, great, grandmother, to further the deception, arising at the same moment and accompanying her to the piano in the main drawing-room. Had I decided upon escorting her thither, it had been her design to suggest the propriety of my remaining where I was ; but my own prudential views rendered this unnecessary. The songs which I so much admired, and which so confirmed my impression of the youth of my mistress, were executed by Madame Stephanie Lalande. The eye-glass was presented by way of adding a reproof to the hoax—a sting to the epigram of the deception. Its presentation afforded an opportunity for the lecture upon affectation with which I was so especially edified. It is almost superfluous to add that the glasses of the instrument, as worn by the old lady, had been exchanged by her for a pair better adapted to my years. They suited me, in fact, to a T.

The clergyman, who merely pretended to tie the fatal knot, was a boon companion of Talbot's, and no priest. He was an excellent " whip," however ; and having doffed his cassock to put on a greatcoat, he drove the hack which conveyed the " happy couple " out of town. Talbot took a seat at his side. The two scoundrels were thus " in at the death," and through a half open window of the back parlour of the inn, amused themselves in grinning at the *dénouement* of the drama. I believe I shall be forced to call them both out.

Nevertheless, I am *not* the husband of my great, great, grandmother ; and this is a reflection which affords me infinite relief ;—but I *am* the husband of Madame Lalande —of Madame Stephanie Lalande—with whom my good old relative, besides making me her sole heir when she dies— if ever she does—has been at the trouble of concocting me a match. In conclusion : I am done for ever with *billets doux,* and am never to be met without SPECTACLES.

THE CASK OF AMONTILLADO

THE thousand injuries of Fortunato I had borne as
best could ; but when he ventured upon insult, I vowed
revenge. You, who so well know the nature of my soul
will not suppose, however, that I gave utterance to a
threat. *At length* I would be avenged ; this was a point
definitely settled—but the very definitiveness upon which
it was resolved, precluded the idea of risk. I must not only
punish, but punish with impunity. A wrong is unredressed
when retribution overtakes its redresser. It is equally
unredressed when the avenger fails to make himself felt
as such to him who has done the wrong.

It must be understood, that neither by word nor deed
had I given Fortunato cause to doubt my good-will.
continued, as was my wont, to smile in his face, and he
did not perceive that my smile *now* was at the thought
of his immolation.

He had a weak point—this Fortunato—although in
other regards he was a man to be respected and even
feared. He prided himself on his connoisseurship in
wine. Few Italians have the true virtuoso spirit. For
the most part their enthusiasm is adapted to suit the
time and opportunity—to practise imposture upon the
British and Austrian millionaires. In painting and
gemmary Fortunato, like his countrymen, was a quack
—but in the matter of old wines he was sincere. In
this respect I did not differ from him materially : I was
skilful in the Italian vintages myself, and bought largely
whenever I could.

It was about dusk, one evening during the supreme
madness of the Carnival season, that I encountered my
friend. He accosted me with excessive warmth, for he
had been drinking much. The man wore motley. He
had on a tight-fitting parti-striped dress, and his head
was surmounted by the conical cap and bells. I was so
pleased to see him, that I thought I should never have
done wringing his hand.

I said to him, " My dear Fortunato, you are luckily
met. How remarkably well you are looking to-day ! But

I have received a pipe of what passes for Amontillado, and I have my doubts."

"How?" said he; "Amontillado? A pipe? Impossible! And in the middle of the Carnival!"

"I have my doubts," I replied; "and I was silly enough to pay the full Amontillado price without consulting you in the matter. You were not to be found, and I was fearful of losing a bargain."

"Amontillado!"

"I have my doubts."

"Amontillado!"

"And I must satisfy them."

"Amontillado!"

"As you are engaged, I am on my way to Luchesi. If any one has a critical turn, it is he. He will tell me——"

"Luchesi cannot tell Amontillado from Sherry."

"And yet some fools will have it that his taste is a match for your own."

"Come, let us go."

"Whither?"

"To your vaults."

"My friend, no; I will not impose upon your good-nature. I perceive you have an engagement. Luchesi——"

"I have no engagement; come."

"My friend, no. It is not the engagement, but the severe cold with which I perceive you are afflicted. The vaults are insufferably damp. They are encrusted with nitre."

"Let us go nevertheless. The cold is merely nothing. Amontillado! You have been imposed upon. And as for Luchesi—he cannot distinguish Sherry from Amontillado."

Thus speaking, Fortunato possessed himself of my arm. Putting on a mask of black silk, and drawing a *roquelaure* closely about my person, I suffered him to hurry me to my palazzo.

There were no attendants at home; they had absconded to make merry in honour of the time. I had told them that I should not return until the morning, and had given them explicit orders not to stir from the house. These orders were sufficient, I well knew, to ensure their immediate disappearance, one and all, as soon as my back was turned.

I took from their sconces two flambeaux, and givin
one to Fortunato, bowed him through several suites o
rooms to the archway that led into the vaults. I passe
down a long and winding staircase, requesting him t
be cautious as he followed. We came at length to th
foot of the descent, and stood together on the damp
ground of the catacombs of the Montresors.

The gait of my friend was unsteady, and the bells upor
his cap jingled as he strode.

" The pipe," said he.

" It is farther on," said I ; " but observe the whit
webwork which gleams from these cavern walls."

He turned towards me, and looked into my eyes witl
two filmy orbs that distilled the rheum of intoxication.

" Nitre ? " he asked, at length.

" Nitre," ·I replied. " How long have you had tha
cough ? "

" Ugh ! ugh ! ugh !—ugh ! ugh ! ugh !—ugh ! ugh
ugh !—ugh ! ugh ! ugh !—ugh ! ugh ! ugh ! "

My poor friend found it impossible to reply for man}
minutes.

" It is nothing," he said, at last.

" Come," I said, with decision, " we will go back ; you
health is precious. You are rich, respected, admired
beloved ; you are happy, as once I was. You are a mar
to be missed. For me it is no matter. We will go back
you will be ill, and I cannot be responsible. Besides
there is Luchesi——"

" Enough," he said, " the cough is a mere nothing ; i
will not kill me. I shall not die of a cough."

" True—true," I replied ; " and, indeed, I had n
intention of alarming you unnecessarily—but you shoul
use all proper caution. A draught of this Medoc wil
defend us from the damps."

Here I knocked off the neck of a bottle which I drev
from a long row of its fellows that lay upon the mould.

" Drink," I said, presenting him the wine.

He raised it to his lips with a leer. He paused an
nodded to me familiarly, while his bells jingled.

" I drink," he said, " to the buried that repose aroun
us."

" And I to your long life."

He again took my arm, and we proceeded.

" These vaults," he said, " are extensive."

" The Montresors," I replied, " were a great and numerous family."

" I forget your arms."

" A huge human foot d'or, in a field azure ; the foot crushes a serpent rampant whose fangs are embedded in the heel."

" And the motto ? "

" *Nemo me impune lacessit.*"

" Good ! " he said.

The wine sparkled in his eyes and the bells jingled. My own fancy grew warm with the Medoc. We had passed through walls of piled bones, with casks and puncheons intermingling, into the inmost recesses of the catacombs. I paused again, and this time I made bold to seize Fortunato by an arm above the elbow.

" The nitre ! " I said ; " see, it increases. It hangs like moss upon the vaults. We are below the river's bed. The drops of moisture trickle among the bones. Come, we will go back ere it is too late. Your cough——"

" It is nothing," he said ; " let us go on. But first, another draught of the Medoc."

I broke and reached him a flagon of De Grâve. He emptied it at a breath. His eyes flashed with a fierce light. He laughed and threw the bottle upwards with a gesticulation I did not understand.

I looked at him in surprise. He repeated the movement —a grotesque one.

" You do not comprehend ? " he said.

" Not I," I replied.

" Then you are not of the brotherhood."

" How ? "

" You are not of the masons."

" Yes, yes," I said ; " yes, yes."

" You ! Impossible ! A mason ? "

" A mason," I replied.

" A sign," he said.

" It is this," I answered, producing a trowel from beneath the folds of my *roquelaure.*

" You jest," he exclaimed, recoiling a few paces. " But let us proceed to the Amontillado."

" Be it so," I said, replacing the tool beneath the cloak, and again offering him my arm. He leaned upon it heavily.

We continued our route in search of the Amontillado. W
passed through a range of low arches, descended, passe
on, and descending again, arrived at a deep crypt, in whic
the foulness of the air caused our flambeaux rather to glo
than flame.

At the most remote end of the crypt there appeare
another less spacious. Its walls had been lined wit
human remains, piled to the vault overhead, in th
fashion of the great catacombs of Paris. Three sides o
this interior crypt were still ornamented in this manner
From the fourth the bones had been thrown down, an
lay promiscuously upon the earth, forming at one poin
a mound of some size. Within the wall thus exposed b
the displacing of the bones, we perceived a still interio
recess, in depth about four feet, in width three, in heigh
six or seven. It seemed to have been constructed for n
especial use within itself, but formed merely the interva
between two of the colossal supports of the roof of th
catacombs, and was backed by one of their circumscribin
walls of solid granite.

It was in vain that Fortunato, uplifting his dul
torch, endeavoured to pry into the depth of th
recess. Its termination the feeble light did not enabl
us to see.

"Proceed," I said; "herein is the Amontillado. A
for Luchesi——"

"He is an ignoramus," interrupted my friend, as h
stepped unsteadily forward, while I followed immediatel
at his heels. In an instant he had reached the extremit
of the niche, and finding his progress arrested by th
rock, stood stupidly bewildered. A moment more an
I had fettered him to the granite. In its surface wer
two iron staples, distant from each other about two feet
horizontally. From one of these depended a short chain
from the other a padlock. Throwing the links abou
his waist, it was but the work of a few seconds to secure it
He was too much astounded to resist. Withdrawing th
key, I stepped back from the recess.

"Pass your hand," I said, "over the wall; you canno
help feeling the nitre. Indeed it is *very* damp. Onc
more let me *implore* you to return. No? Then I mus
positively leave you. But I must first render you all th
little attentions in my power."

" The Amontillado ! " ejaculated my friend, not yet recovered from his astonishment.

" True," I replied, " the Amontillado."

As I said these words I busied myself among the pile of bones of which I have before spoken. Throwing them aside, I soon uncovered a quantity of building stone and mortar. With these materials, and with the aid of my trowel, I began vigorously to wall up the entrance of the niche.

I had scarcely laid the first tier of the masonry when I discovered that the intoxication of Fortunato had in a great measure worn off. The earliest indication I had of this was a low moaning cry from the depth of the recess. It was not the cry of a drunken man. There was then a long and obstinate silence. I laid the second tier, and the third, and the fourth ; and then I heard the furious vibrations of the chain. The noise lasted for several minutes, during which, that I might hearken to it with the more satisfaction, I ceased my labours and sat down upon the bones. When at last the clanking subsided, I resumed the trowel, and finished without interruption the fifth, the sixth, and the seventh tier. The wall was now nearly upon a level with my breast. I again paused, and holding the flambeaux over the mason-work, threw a few feeble rays upon the figure within.

A succession of loud and shrill screams, bursting suddenly from the throat of the chained form, seemed to thrust me violently back. For a brief moment I hesitated —I trembled. Unsheathing my rapier, I began to grope with it about the recess ; but the thought of an instant reassured me. I placed my hand upon the solid fabric of the catacombs, and felt satisfied. I reapproached the wall. I replied to the yells of him who clamoured. I re-echoed—I aided—I surpassed them in volume and in strength. I did this, and the clamourer grew still.

It was now midnight, and my task was drawing to a close. I had completed the eighth, the ninth, and the tenth tier. I had finished a portion of the last and the eleventh ; there remained but a single stone to be fitted and plastered in. I struggled with its weight ; I placed it partially in its destined position. But now there came from out the niche a low laugh that erected the hairs upon my head. It was succeeded by a sad voice, which I had difficulty

in recognising as that of the noble Fortunato. The voice
said—

"Ha! ha! ha!—he! he!—a very good joke indeed
—an excellent jest. We will have many a rich laugh
about it at the palazzo—he! he! he!—over our wine—
he! he! he!"

"The Amontillado!" I said.

"He! he! he!—he! he! he!—yes, the Amontillado.
But is it not getting late? Will they not be awaiting
us at the palazzo, the Lady Fortunato and the rest?
Let us be gone."

"Yes," I said, "let us be gone."

"*For the love of God, Montresor!*"

"Yes," I said, "for the love of God!"

But to these words I hearkened in vain for a reply.
I grew impatient. I called aloud—

"Fortunato!"

No answer. I called again—

"Fortunato!"

No answer still. I thrust a torch through the remaining
aperture and let it fall within. There came forth in
return only a jingling of the bells. My heart grew sick—
on account of the dampness of the catacombs. I hastened
to make an end of my labour. I forced the last stone
into its position; I plastered it up. Against the new
masonry I re-erected the old rampart of bones. For
the half of a century no mortal has disturbed them. *In
pace requiescat!*

THE OVAL PORTRAIT

THE château into which my valet had ventured to make
forcible entrance, rather than permit me, in my desperately
wounded condition, to pass a night in the open air, was
one of those piles of commingled gloom and grandeur
which have so long frowned among the Apennines, not less
in fact than in the fancy of Mrs. Radcliffe. To all appearance it had been temporarily and very lately abandoned.
We established ourselves in one of the smallest and least

mptuously furnished apartments. It lay in a remote
rret of the building. Its decorations were rich, yet
ttered and antique. Its walls were hung with tapestry
d bedecked with manifold and multiform armorial
ophies, together with an unusually great number of very
irited modern paintings in frames of rich golden
abesque. In these paintings, which depended from the
alls not only in their main surfaces, but in very many
oks which the bizarre architecture of the château
ndered necessary—in these paintings my incipient
lirium, perhaps, had caused me to take deep interest ;
that I bade Pedro to close the heavy shutters of the
om—since it was already night—to light the tongues of
tall candelabrum which stood by the head of my bed—
d to throw open far and wide the fringed curtains of
ack velvet which enveloped the bed itself. I wished all
is done that I might resign myself, if not to sleep, at
1st alternately to the contemplation of these pictures,
d the perusal of a small volume which had been found
on the pillow, and which purported to criticise and
scribe them.
Long, long I read—and devoutly, devotedly I gazed.
apidly and gloriously the hours flew by, and the deep
idnight came. The position of the candelabrum diseased me, and outreaching my hand with difficulty,
ther than disturb my slumbering valet, I placed it so
to throw its rays more fully upon the book.
But the action produced an effect altogether unantici-
ted. The rays of the numerous candles (for there were
any) now fell within a niche of the room which had
therto been thrown into deep shade by one of the bed-
sts. I thus saw in vivid light a picture all unnoticed
fore. It was the portrait of a young girl just ripening
to womanhood. I glanced at the painting hurriedly,
d then closed my eyes. Why I did this was not at first
parent even to my own perception. But while my lids
mained thus shut, I ran over in mind my reason for so
utting them. It was an impulsive movement to gain
1e for thought—to make sure that my vision had not
ceived me—to calm and subdue my fancy for a more
ber and more certain gaze. In a very few moments I
ain looked fixedly at the painting.
That I now saw aright I could not and would not doubt ;

for the first flashing of the candles upon that canvas ha
seemed to dissipate the dreamy stupor which was stealin
over my senses, and to startle me at once into waking lif

The portrait, I have already said, was that of a youn
girl. It was a mere head and shoulders, done in what
technically termed a _vignette_ manner—much in the sty
of the favourite heads of Sully. The arms, the bosor
and even the ends of the radiant hair, melted imperceptib
into the vague yet deep shadow which formed the bac
ground of the whole. The frame was oval, richly gild
and filigreed in Moresque. As a thing of art nothing cou
be more admirable than the painting itself. But it cou
have been neither the execution of the work, nor the ir
mortal beauty of the countenance, which had so sudden
and so vehemently moved me. Least of all could it ha
been that my fancy, shaken from its half slumber, ha
mistaken the head for that of a living person. I saw
once that the peculiarities of the design, of the vignettin
and of the frame, must have instantly dispelled such ide
—must have prevented even its momentary entertainmen
Thinking earnestly upon these points, I remained for a
hour, perhaps, half sitting, half reclining, with my visi
riveted upon the portrait. At length, satisfied with th
true secret of its effect, I fell back within the bed. I ha
found the spell of the picture in an absolute _life-likeness_
expression, which, at first startling, finally confounde
subdued, and appalled me. With deep and reverent awe
replaced the candelabrum in its former position. Th
cause of my deep agitation being thus shut from view,
sought eagerly the volume which discussed the paintin
and their histories. Turning to the number which desi
nated the oval portrait, I there read the vague and quai
words which follow:—

" She was a maiden of rarest beauty, and not more love
than full of glee. And evil was the hour when she sa
and loved, and wedded the painter. He, passionat
studious, austere, and having already a bride in his A
She, a maiden of rarest beauty, and not more lovely th
full of glee—all light and smiles, and frolicsome as t
young fawn ; loving and cherishing all things ; hatin
only the Art which was her rival ; dreading only the palet
and brushes and other untoward instruments which d
prived her of the countenance of her lover. It was thus

rrible thing for this lady to hear the painter speak of his
esire to portray even his young bride. But she was
imble and obedient, and sat meekly for many weeks in
ie dark high turret-chamber where the light dripped upon
ie pale canvas only from overhead. But he, the painter,
ook glory in his work, which went on from hour to hour,
id from day to day. And he was a passionate, and wild,
id moody man, who became lost in reveries ; so that he
ould not see that the light which fell so ghastlily in that
ne turret withered the health and the spirits of his bride,
ho pined visibly to all but him. Yet she smiled on and
ill on, uncomplainingly, because she saw that the painter
who had high renown) took a fervid and burning plea-
ire in his task, and wrought day and night to depict her
ho so loved him, yet who grew daily more dispirited and
eak. And in sooth some who beheld the portrait spoke
its resemblance in low words, as of a mighty marvel,
id a proof not less of the power of the painter than of his
eep love for her whom he depicted so surpassingly well.
ut at length, as the labour drew nearer to its conclusion,
ere were admitted none into the turret ; for the painter
id grown wild with the ardour of his work, and turned his
yes from the canvas rarely, even to regard the countenance
his wife. And he *would* not see that the tints which he
pread upon the canvas were drawn from the cheeks of
er who sat beside him. And when many weeks had passed,
id but little remained to do, save one brush upon the
outh and one tint upon the eye, the spirit of the lady
gain flickered up as the flame within the socket of the
mp. And then the brush was given, and then the
nt was placed ; and, for one moment, the painter stood
itranced before the work which he had wrought ; but
the next, while he yet gazed, he grew tremulous and very
illid, and aghast, and crying with a loud voice, ' This is
deed *Life* itself ! ' turned suddenly to regard his beloved :
-*She was dead !* "

THE TELL-TALE HEART

TRUE !—nervous—very, very dreadfully nervous I had bee
and am ; but why *will* you say that I am mad ? Tl
disease had sharpened my senses—not destroyed—n
dulled them. Above all was the sense of hearing acut
I heard all things in the heaven and in the earth. I hea
many things in hell. How, then, am I mad ? Hearken
and observe how healthily—how calmly I can tell you tl
whole story.

It is impossible to say how first the idea entered n
brain ; but once conceived, it haunted me day and nigh
Object there was none. Passion there was none. I lov
the old man. He had never wronged me. He had nev
given me insult. For his gold I had no desire. I think
was his eye ! yes, it was this ! One of his eyes resembl
that of a vulture—a pale blue eye, with a film over i
Whenever it fell upon me, my blood ran cold ; and so l
degrees—very gradually—I made up my mind to take tl
life of the old man, and thus rid myself of the eye for eve

Now this is the point. You fancy me mad. Madm
know nothing. But you should have seen *me.* Y
should have seen how wisely I proceeded—with wh
caution—with what foresight—with what dissimulation
went to work ! I was never kinder to the old man tha
during the whole week before I killed him. And eve
night, about midnight, I turned the latch of his door a
opened it—oh, so gently ! And then, when I had ma
an opening sufficient for my head, I put in a dark lanter
all closed, closed, so that no light shone out, and then
thrust in my head. Oh, you would have laughed to s
how cunningly I thrust it in ! I moved it slowly—ver
very slowly, so that I might not disturb the old mar
sleep. It took me an hour to place my whole head with
the opening so far that I could see him as he lay upon l
bed. Ha !—would a madman have been so wise as this
And then, when my head was well in the room, I undid tl
lantern, cautiously—oh, so cautiously—cautiously (for tl
hinges creaked) I undid it just so much that a single th
ray fell upon the vulture eye. And this I did for sev

long nights—every night just at midnight—but I found the eye always closed ; and so it was impossible to do the work ; for it was not the old man who vexed me, but his Evil Eye. And every morning, when the day broke, I went boldly into the chamber, and spoke courageously to him, calling him by name in a hearty tone, and inquiring how he had passed the night. So you see he would have been a very profound old man, indeed, to suspect that every night, just at twelve, I looked in upon him while he slept.

Upon the eighth night I was more than usually cautious in opening the door. A watch's minute hand moves more quickly than did mine. Never before that night had I *felt* the extent of my own powers—of my sagacity. I could scarcely contain my feelings of triumph. To think that there I was, opening the door, little by little, and he not even to dream of my secret deeds or thoughts. I fairly chuckled at the idea ; and perhaps he heard me—for he moved on the bed suddenly, as if startled. Now you may think that I drew back—but no. His room was as black as pitch with the thick darkness (for the shutters were close-fastened, through fear of robbers), and so I knew that he could not see the opening of the door, and I kept pushing it on steadily, steadily.

I had my head in, and was about to open the lantern, when my thumb slipped upon the tin fastening, and the old man sprang up in the bed, crying out, " Who's there ? "

I kept quite still and said nothing. For a whole hour I did not move a muscle, and in the meantime I did not hear him lie down. He was still sitting up in the bed, listening —just as I have done, night after night, hearkening to the death-watches in the wall.

Presently I heard a groan, and I knew it was the groan of mortal terror. It was not a groan of pain or of grief —oh, no !—it was the low stifled sound that arises from the bottom of the soul when overcharged with awe. I knew the sound well. Many a night, just at midnight, when all the world slept, it has welled up from my own bosom, deepening, with its dreadful echo, the terrors that distracted me. I say I knew it well. I knew what the old man felt, and pitied him, although I chuckled at heart. I knew that he had been lying awake ever since the first slight noise, when he had turned in the bed. His fears had been ever since growing upon him. He had been trying to fancy them causeless, but could not. He had been saying to himself, " It is nothing but the wind in the chimney— it is only a mouse crossing the floor," or, " It is merely a cricket which has made a single chirp." Yes, he had been trying to comfort himself with these suppositions ; but he had found all in vain. *All in vain ;* because Death, in approaching him, had stalked with his black shadow before him, and enveloped the victim. And it was the mournful influence of the unperceived shadow that caused him to feel—although he neither saw nor heard—to *feel* the presence of my head within the room.

When I had waited a long time, very patiently, without hearing him lie down, I resolved to open a little—a very, very little crevice in the lantern. So I opened it—you cannot imagine how stealthily, stealthily—until, at length, a single dim ray, like the thread of the spider, shot from out the crevice and fell upon the vulture eye.

It was open—wide, wide open—and I grew furious as I gazed upon it. I saw it with perfect distinctness—all a dull blue, with a hideous veil over it that chilled the very marrow in my bones ; but I could see nothing else of the old man's face or person, for I had directed the ray, as if by instinct, precisely upon the damned spot.

And now have I not told you that what you mistake for madness is but over-acuteness of the senses ?—now, I say, there came to my ears a low, dull, quick sound, such as a watch makes when enveloped in cotton. I knew *that* sound well, too. It was the beating of the old man's heart. It increased my fury, as the beating of a drum stimulates the soldier into courage.

But even yet I refrained and kept still. I scarcely breathed. I held the lantern motionless. I tried how steadily I could maintain the ray upon the eye. Meantime the hellish tattoo of the heart increased. It grew quicker and quicker, and louder and louder every instant. The old man's terror *must* have been extreme ! It grew louder, I say, louder every moment !—do you mark me well ? I have told you that I am nervous : so I am. And now, at the dead hour of the night, amid the dreadful silence of that old house, so strange a noise as this excited me to uncontrollable terror. Yet, for some minutes longer, I refrained and stood still. But the beating grew louder,

louder! I thought the heart must burst. And now a new anxiety seized me—the sound would be heard by a neighbour! The old man's hour had come! With a loud yell I threw open the lantern and leaped into the room. He shrieked once—once only. In an instant I dragged him to the floor, and pulled the heavy bed over him. I then smiled gaily, to find the deed so far done. But, for many minutes, the heart beat on with a muffled sound. This, however, did not vex me ; it would not be heard through the wall. At length it ceased. The old man was dead. I removed the bed and examined the corpse. Yes, he was stone, stone dead. I placed my hand upon the heart and held it there many minutes. There was no pulsation. He was stone dead. His eye would trouble me no more.

If still you think me mad, you will think so no longer when I describe the wise precautions I took for the conceal-ment of the body. The night waned, and I worked hastily, but in silence. First of all I dismembered the corpse. I cut off the head and the arms and the legs.

I then took up three planks from the flooring of the chamber and deposited all between the scantlings. I then replaced the boards so cleverly, so cunningly, that no human eye—not even *his*—could have detected anything wrong. There was nothing to wash out—no stain of any kind—no blood-spot whatever. I had been too wary for that. A tub had caught all—ha! ha!

When I had made an end of these labours, it was four o'clock—still dark as midnight. As the bell sounded the hour, there came a knocking at the street door. I went down to open it with a light heart—for what had I *now* to fear? There entered three men, who introduced them-selves, with perfect suavity, as officers of the police. A shriek had been heard by a neighbour during the night ; suspicion of foul play had been aroused ; information had been lodged at the police office, and they (the officers) had been deputed to search the premises.

I smiled—for *what* had I to fear? I bade the gentlemen welcome. The shriek, I said, was my own in a dream. The old man, I mentioned, was absent in the country. I took my visitors all over the house. I bade them search—search *well*. I led them, at length, to *his* chamber. I showed them his treasures, secure, undisturbed. In the enthusiasm of my confidence, I brought chairs into the

o

room, and desired them *here* to rest from their fatigues, while I myself, in the wild audacity of my perfect triumph, placed my own seat upon the very spot beneath which reposed the corpse of the victim.

The officers were satisfied. My *manner* had convinced them. I was singularly at ease. They sat, and while I answered cheerily, they chatted of familiar things. But, ere long, I felt myself getting pale and wished them gone. My head ached, and I fancied a ringing in my ears ; but still they sat and still chatted. The ringing became more distinct—it continued and became more distinct. I talked more freely to get rid of the feeling ; but it continued and gained definitiveness—until, at length, I found that the noise was *not* within my ears.

No doubt I now grew *very* pale ; but I talked more fluently, and with a heightened voice. Yet the sound increased—and what could I do ? It was *a low, dull, quick sound—much such a sound as a watch makes when enveloped in cotton.* I gasped for breath—and yet the officers heard it not. I talked more quickly—more vehemently ; but the noise steadily increased. I arose and argued about trifles, in a high key and with violent gesticulations ; but the noise steadily increased. Why *would* they not be gone ? I paced the floor to and fro with heavy strides, as if excited to fury by the observations of the men—but the noise steadily increased. O God ! what *could* I do ? I foamed—I raved—I swore ! I swung the chair upon which I had been sitting, and grated it upon the boards, but the noise arose over all and continually increased. It grew louder—louder—*louder* ! And still the men chatted pleasantly, and smiled. Was it possible they heard not ? Almighty God !—no, no ! They heard !— they suspected !—they *knew* !—they were making a mockery of my horror !—this I thought, and this I think. But anything was better than this agony ! Anything was more tolerable than this derision ! I could bear those hypocritical smiles no longer ! I felt that I must scream or die !—and now—again ! hark ! louder ! louder ! louder ! *louder* !——

" Villains ! " I shrieked, " dissemble no more ! I admit the deed !—tear up the planks !—here, here !—it **is the** beating of his hideous heart ! "

LIGEIA

> " And the will therein lieth, which dieth not. Who knoweth the
> mysteries of the will, with its vigour ? For God is but a great
> will pervading all things by nature of its intentness. Man doth
> not yield himself to the angels, nor unto death utterly, save only
> through the weakness of his feeble will."—JOSEPH GLANVILL.

I CANNOT, for my soul, remember how, when, or even
precisely where, I first became acquainted with the Lady
Ligeia. Long years have since elapsed, and my memory
is feeble through much suffering. Or, perhaps, I cannot
now bring these points to mind, because, in truth, the
character of my beloved, her rare learning, her singular
yet placid cast of beauty, and the thrilling and enthralling
eloquence of her low musical language, made their way
into my heart by paces so steadily and stealthily progressive, that they have been unnoticed and unknown.
Yet I believe that I met her first and most frequently in
some large, old, decaying city near the Rhine. Of her
family—I have surely heard her speak. That it is of a
remotely ancient date cannot be doubted. Ligeia ! Ligeia !
Buried in studies of a nature more than all else adapted
to deaden impressions of the outward world, it is by that
sweet word alone—by Ligeia—that I bring before mine
eyes in fancy the image of her who is no more. And now,
while I write, a recollection flashes upon me that I have
never known the paternal name of her who was my friend
and my betrothed, and who became the partner of my
studies, and finally the wife of my bosom. Was it a playful
charge on the part of my Ligeia ? or was it a test of my
strength of affection, that I should institute no inquiries
upon this point ? or was it rather a caprice of my own—
a wildly romantic offering on the shrine of the most passionate devotion ? I but indistinctly recall the fact itself—
what wonder that I have utterly forgotten the circumstances which originated or attended it ? And, indeed,
if ever that spirit which is entitled *Romance*—if ever she,
the wan and the misty-winged *Ashtophet* of idolatrous
Egypt, presided, as they tell, over marriages ill-omened,
then most surely she presided over mine.

There is one dear topic, however, on which my memory

fails me not. It is the *person* of Ligeia. In stature she was tall, somewhat slender, and, in her latter days, even emaciated. I would in vain attempt to portray the majesty, the quiet ease, of her demeanour, or the incomprehensible lightness and elasticity of her footfall. She came and departed as a shadow. I was never made aware of her entrance into my closed study, save by the dear music of her low sweet voice, as she placed her marble hand upon my shoulder. In beauty of face no maiden ever equalled her. It was the radiance of an opium-dream— an airy and spirit-lifting vision more wildly divine than the fantasies which hovered about the slumbering souls of the daughters of Delos. Yet her features were not of that regular mould which we have been falsely taught to worship in the classical labours of the heathen. " There is no exquisite beauty," says Bacon, Lord Verulam, speaking truly of all the forms and genera of beauty, " without some *strangeness* in the proportion." Yet, although I saw that the features of Ligeia were not of a classic regularity—although I perceived that her loveliness was indeed " exquisite," and felt that there was much of " strangeness " pervading it, yet I have tried in vain to detect the irregularity and to trace home my own perception of " the strange." I examined the contour of the lofty and pale forehead—it was faultless—how cold indeed that word when applied to a majesty so divine !—the skin rivalling the purest ivory, the commanding extent and repose, the gentle prominence of the regions above the temples ; and then the raven-black, the glossy, the luxuriant and naturally-curling tresses, setting forth the full force of the Homeric epithet, " hyacinthine ! " I looked at the delicate outlines of the nose—and nowhere but in the graceful medallions of the Hebrews had I beheld a similar perfection. There were the same luxurious smoothness of surface, the same scarcely perceptible tendency to the aquiline, the same harmoniously curved nostrils speaking the free spirit. I regarded the sweet mouth. Here was indeed the triumph of all things heavenly—the magnificent turn of the short upper lip—the soft, voluptuous slumber of the under—the dimples which sported, and the colour which spoke—the teeth glancing back, with a brilliancy almost startling, every ray of the holy light which fell upon them in her serene and placid, yet most

exultingly radiant of all smiles. I scrutinised the formation of the chin—and here, too, I found the gentleness of
breadth, the softness and the majesty, the fulness and the
spirituality, of the Greek—the contour which the god
Apollo revealed but in a dream, to Cleomenes, the son of
the Athenian. And then I peered into the large eyes of
Ligeia.

For eyes we have no models in the remotely antique.
It might have been, too, that in these eyes of my beloved
lay the secret to which Lord Verulam alludes. They were,
I must believe, far larger than the ordinary eyes of our
own race. They were even fuller than the fullest of the
gazelle eyes of the tribe of the valley of Nourjahad. Yet
it was only at intervals—in moments of intense excitement
—that this peculiarity became more than slightly noticeable in Ligeia. And at such moments was her beauty—
in my heated fancy thus it appeared, perhaps—the beauty
of beings either above or apart from the earth—the beauty
of the fabulous Houri of the Turk. The hue of the orbs
was the most brilliant of black, and, far over them, hung
jetty lashes of great length. The brows, slightly irregular
in outline, had the same tint. The " strangeness," however, which I found in the eyes, was of a nature distinct
from the formation, or the colour, or the brilliancy of the
features, and must, after all, be referred to the *expression*.
Ah, word of no meaning ! behind whose vast latitude of
mere sound we intrench our ignorance of so much of the
spiritual. The expression of the eyes of Ligeia—how for
long hours have I pondered upon it ! How have I, through
the whole of a midsummer night, struggled to fathom it !
What was it—that something more profound than the
well of Democritus—which lay far within the pupils of
my beloved ? what *was* it ? I was possessed with a
passion to discover. Those eyes, those large, those shining,
those divine orbs ? they became to me twin stars of Leda,
and I to them devoutest of astrologers.

There is no point, among the many incomprehensible
anomalies of the science of mind, more thrillingly exciting
than the fact—never, I believe, noticed in the schools—
that in our endeavours to recall to memory something long
forgotten, we often find ourselves *upon the very verge* of
remembrance, without being able, in the end, to remember.
And thus how frequently, in my intense scrutiny of Ligeia's

eyes, have I felt approaching the full knowledge of their expression—felt it approaching—yet not quite be mine— and so at length entirely depart! And (strange—oh, strangest mystery of all!) I found, in the commonest objects of the universe, a circle of analogies to that expression. I mean to say that, subsequently to the period when Ligeia's beauty passed into my spirit, there dwelling as in a shrine, I derived, from many existences in the material world, a sentiment such as I felt always aroused within me by her large and luminous orbs. Yet not the more could I define that sentiment, or analyse, or even steadily view it. I recognised it, let me repeat, sometimes in the survey of a rapidly growing vine—in the contemplation of a moth, a butterfly, a chrysalis, a stream of running water. I have felt it in the ocean; in the falling of a meteor. I have felt it in the glances of unusually aged people. And there are one or two stars in heaven (one especially, a star of the sixth magnitude, double and changeable, to be found near the large star in Lyra), in a telescopic scrutiny of which I have been made aware of the feeling. I have been filled with it by certain sounds from stringed instruments, and not unfrequently by passages from books. Among innumerable other instances, I well remember something in a volume of Joseph Glanvill, which (perhaps merely from its quaintness—who shall say?) never failed to inspire me with the sentiment : " And the will therein lieth, which dieth not. Who knoweth the mysteries of the will, with its vigour? For God is but a great will pervading all things by nature of its intentness. Man doth not yield him to the angels, nor unto death utterly, save only through the weakness of his feeble will."

Length of years and subsequent reflection have enabled me to trace, indeed, some remote connection between this passage in the English moralist and a portion of the character of Ligeia. An *intensity* in thought, action, or speech, was possibly, in her, a result, or at least an index, of that gigantic volition which, during our long intercourse, failed to give other and more immediate evidence of its existence. Of all the women whom I have ever known, she, the outwardly calm, the ever-placid Ligeia, was the most violently a prey to the tumultuous vultures of stern passion. And of such passion I could form no estimate, save by the miraculous expansion of those eyes which at once so delighted and appalled me—by the almost magical melody, modulation, distinctness, and placidity of her very low voice—and by the fierce energy (rendered doubly effective by contrast with her manner of utterance) of the wild words which she habitually uttered.

I have spoken of the learning of Ligeia : it was immense—such as I have never known in woman. In the classical tongues was she deeply proficient, and, as far as my own acquaintance extended in regard to the modern dialects of Europe, I have never known her at fault. Indeed upon any theme of the most admired, because simply the most abstruse of the boasted erudition of the academy, have I *ever* found Ligeia at fault ? How singularly—how thrillingly, this one point in the nature of my wife has forced itself, at this late period only, upon my attention ! I said her knowledge was such as I have never known in woman—but where breathes the man who has traversed, and successfully, *all* the wide areas of moral, physical, and mathematical science ? I saw not then what I now clearly perceive, that the acquisitions of Ligeia were gigantic, were astounding ; yet I was sufficiently aware of her infinite supremacy to resign myself, with a childlike confidence, to her guidance through the chaotic world of metaphysical investigation at which I was most busily occupied during the earlier years of our marriage. With how vast a triumph—with how vivid a delight— with how much of all that is ethereal in hope—did I *feel*, as she bent over me in studies but little sought—but less known—that delicious vista by slow degrees expanding before me, down whose long, gorgeous, and all untrodden path, I might at length pass onward to the goal of a wisdom too divinely precious not to be forbidden !

How poignant, then, must have been the grief with which, after some years, I beheld my well-grounded expectations take wings to themselves and fly away ! Without Ligeia I was but as a child groping benighted. Her presence, her readings alone, rendered vividly luminous the many mysteries of the transcendentalism in which we were immersed. Wanting the radiant lustre of her eyes, letters, lambent and golden, grew duller than Saturnian lead. And now those eyes shone less and less frequently upon the pages over which I pored. Ligeia grew ill. The wild eyes blazed with a too—too glorious effulgence ; the pale fingers became of the transparent waxen hue of the grave; and the blue veins upon the lofty forehead swelled and sank impetuously with the tides of the most gentle emotion. I saw that she must die—and I struggled desperately in spirit with the grim Azrael. And the struggles of the passionate wife were, to my astonishment, even more energetic than my own. There had been much in her stern nature to impress me with the belief that, to her, death would have come without its terrors; but not so. Words are impotent to convey any just idea of the fierceness of resistance with which she wrestled with the Shadow. I groaned in anguish at the pitiable spectacle. I would have soothed—I would have reasoned; but, in the intensity of her wild desire for life—for life—*but* for life— solace and reason were alike the uttermost of folly. Yet not until the last instance, amid the most convulsive writhings of her fierce spirit, was shaken the external placidity of her demeanour. Her voice grew more gentle— grew more low—yet I would not wish to dwell upon the wild meaning of the quietly uttered words. My brain reeled as I hearkened, entranced, to a melody more than mortal—to assumptions and aspirations which mortality had never before known.

That she loved me I should not have doubted; and I might have been easily aware that, in a bosom such as hers, love would have reigned no ordinary passion. But in death only was I fully impressed with the strength of her affection. For long hours, detaining my hand, would she pour out before me the overflowing of a heart whose more than passionate devotion amounted to idolatry. How had I deserved to be so blessed by such confessions?— how had I deserved to be so cursed with the removal of my beloved in the hour of her making them? But upon this subject I cannot bear to dilate. Let me say only, that in Ligeia's more than womanly abandonment to a love, alas! all unmerited, all unworthily bestowed, I at length recognised the principle of her longing, with so wildly earnest a desire, for the life which was now fleeing so rapidly away. It is this wild longing—it is this eager vehemence of desire for life—*but* for life—that I have no power to portray—no utterance capable of expressing.

At high noon of the day in which she departed, beckoning me, peremptorily, to her side. she bade me repeat

certain verses composed by herself not many days before.
I obeyed her. They were these :—

> Lo ! 'tis a gala night
>   Within the lonesome latter years !
> An angel throng, bewinged, bedight
>   In veils, and drowned in tears,
> Sit in a theatre, to see
>   A play of hopes and fears,
> While the orchestra breathes fitfully
>   The music of the spheres.
>
> Mimes, in the form of God on high,
>   Mutter and mumble low,
> And hither and thither fly ;
>   Mere puppets they, who come and go
> At bidding of vast formless things
>   That shift the scenery to and fro,
> Flapping from out their condor wings
>   Invisible Woe !
>
> That motley drama !—oh, be sure
>   It shall not be forgot !
> With its Phantom chased for evermore,
>   By a crowd that seize it not,
> Through a circle that ever returneth in
>   To the self-same spot ;
> And much of Madness, and more of Sin,
>   And Horror, the soul of the plot !
>
> But see, amid the mimic rout
>   A crawling shape intrude !
> A blood-red thing that writhes from out
>   The scenic solitude !
> It writhes !—it writhes !—with mortal pangs
>   The mimes become its food,
> And the seraphs sob at vermin fangs
>   In human gore imbued.
>
> Out—out are the lights—out all !
>   And over each quivering form,
> The curtain, a funeral pall,
>   Comes down with the rush of a storm—
> And the angels, all pallid and wan,
>   Uprising, unveiling, affirm
> That the play is the tragedy, " Man,"
>   And its hero, the Conqueror Worm.

" O God ! " half-shrieked Ligeia, leaping to her feet and
extending her arms aloft with a spasmodic movement, as
I made an end of these lines—" O God ! O Divine Father !
—shall these things be undeviatingly so ?—shall this con-

queror be not once conquered ?   Are we not part and parcel
in Thee ?   Who—who knoweth the mysteries of the will,
with its vigour ?   Man doth not yield him to the angels,
nor unto death utterly, save only through the weakness of
his feeble will."

And now, as if exhausted with emotion, she suffered
her white arms to fall, and returned solemnly to her bed
of death.   And as she breathed her last sighs, there came
mingled with them a low murmur from her lips.   I bent
to them my ear, and distinguished again the concluding
words of the passage in Glanvill : " *Man doth not yield him
to the angels, nor unto death utterly, save only through the
weakness of his feeble will.*"

She died ; and I, crushed into the very dust with sorrow,
could no longer endure the lonely desolation of my dwelling
in the dim and decaying city by the Rhine.   I had no
lack of what the world calls wealth.   Ligeia had brought
me far more, very far more than ordinarily falls to the lot
of mortals.   After a few months, therefore, of weary and
aimless wandering, I purchased, and put in some repair,
an abbey, which I shall not name, in one of the wildest and
least frequented portions of fair England.   The gloomy
and dreary grandeur of the building, the almost savage
aspect of the domain, the many melancholy and time-
honoured memories connected with both, had much in
unison with the feelings of utter abandonment which had
driven me into that remote and unsocial region of the
country.   Yet although the external abbey, with its
verdant decay hanging about it, suffered but little alteration, I gave way, with a child-like perversity, and per-
chance with a faint hope of alleviating my sorrows, to a
display of more than regal magnificence within.   For such
follies, even in childhood, I had imbibed a taste, and now
they came back to me as if in the dotage of grief.   Alas, I
feel how much even of incipient madness might have been
discovered in the gorgeous and fantastic draperies, in the
solemn carvings of Egypt, in the wild cornices and furniture,
in the Bedlam patterns of the carpets of tufted gold !   I
had become a bounden slave in the trammels of opium,
and my labours and my orders had taken a colouring from
my dreams.   But these absurdities I must not pause to
detail.   Let me speak only of that one chamber, ever
accursed, whither in a moment of mental alienation, I led

from the altar as my bride—as the successor of the unfor-
gotten Ligeia—the fair-haired and blue-eyed Lady Rowena
Trevanion, of Tremaine.

There is no individual portion of the architecture and
decoration of that bridal chamber which is not now visibly
before me. Where were the souls of the haughty family
of the bride, when, through thirst of gold, they permitted
to pass the threshold of an apartment *so* bedecked, a
maiden and a daughter so beloved ? I have said that
I minutely remember the details of the chamber—yet I
am sadly forgetful on topics of deep moment—and here
there was no system, no keeping, in the fantastic display,
to take hold upon the memory. The room lay in a high
turret of the castellated abbey, was pentagonal in shape,
and of capacious size. Occupying the whole southern
face of the pentagon was the sole window—an immense
sheet of unbroken glass from Venice—a single pane, and
tinted of a leaden hue, so that the rays of either the sun
or moon passing through it, fell with a ghastly lustre on
the objects within. Over the upper portion of this huge
window extended the trellis-work of an aged vine, which
clambered up the massy walls of the turret. The ceiling,
of gloomy-looking oak, was excessively lofty, vaulted, and
elaborately fretted with the wildest and most grotesque
specimens of a semi-Gothic, semi-Druidical device. From
out the most central recess of this melancholy vaulting,
depended, by a single chain of gold with long links, a huge
censer of the same metal, Saracenic in pattern, and with
many perforations so contrived that there writhed in and
out of them, as if endued with a serpent vitality, a continual succession of parti-coloured fires.

Some few ottomans and golden candelabra, of Eastern
figure, were in various stations about ; and there was the
couch, too—the bridal couch—of an Indian model, and
low, and sculptured of solid ebony, with a pall-like canopy
above. In each of the angles of the chamber stood on end
a gigantic sarcophagus of black granite, from the tombs of
the kings over against Luxor, with their aged lids full of
immemorial sculpture. But in the draping of the apartment lay, alas ! the chief fantasy of all. The lofty walls,
gigantic in height—even unproportionably so—were hung
from summit to foot, in vast folds, with a heavy and
massive-looking tapestry—tapestry of a material which

was found alike as a carpet on the floor, as a covering for
the ottomans and the ebony bed, as a canopy for the bed,
and as the gorgeous volutes of the curtains which partially
shaded the window. The material was the richest cloth
of gold. It was spotted all over, at irregular intervals, with
arabesque figures, about a foot in diameter, and wrought
upon the cloth in patterns of the most jetty black. But
these figures partook of the true character of the arabesque
only when regarded from a single point of view. By a
contrivance now common, and indeed traceable to a very
remote period of antiquity, they were made changeable
in aspect. To one entering the room, they bore the appearance of simple monstrosities ; but upon a farther advance,
this appearance gradually departed ; and, step by step, as
the visitor moved his station in the chamber, he saw himself
surrounded by an endless succession of the ghastly forms
which belong to the superstition of the Norman, or arise in
the guilty slumbers of the monk. The phantasmagoric
effect was vastly heightened by the artificial introduction
of a strong continual current of wind behind the draperies
—giving a hideous and uneasy animation to the whole.

In halls such as these—in a bridal chamber such as this—
I passed, with the Lady of Tremaine, the unhallowed hours
of the first month of our marriage—passed them with
but little disquietude. That my wife dreaded the fierce
moodiness of my temper—that she shunned me, and loved
me but little—I could not help perceiving ; but it gave
me rather pleasure than otherwise. I loathed her with a
hatred belonging more to demon than to man. My memory
flew back (oh, with what intensity of regret !) to Ligeia,
the beloved, the august, the beautiful, the entombed. I
revelled in recollections of her purity ; of her wisdom ;
of her lofty, her ethereal nature ; of her passionate, her
idolatrous love. Now, then, did my spirit fully and freely
burn with more than all the fires of her own. In the
excitement of my opium dreams (for I was habitually
fettered in the shackles of the drug) I would call aloud upon
her name, during the silence of the night, or among the
sheltered recesses of the glens by day, as if, through the wild
eagerness, the solemn passion, the consuming ardour of my
longing for the departed, I could restore her to the pathway she had abandoned—ah, *could* it be for ever ?—upon
the earth.

About the commencement of the second month of the marriage, the Lady Rowena was attacked with sudden illness, from which her recovery was slow. The fever which consumed her rendered her nights uneasy; and in her perturbed state of half-slumber, she spoke of sounds, and of motions, in and about the chamber of the turret, which I concluded had no origin save in the distemper of her fancy, or perhaps in the phantasmagoric influences of the chamber itself. She became at length convalescent —finally, well. Yet but a brief period elapsed ere a second more violent disorder again threw her upon a bed of suffering; and from this attack her frame, at all times feeble, never altogether recovered. Her illnesses were, after this epoch, of alarming character, and of more alarming recurrence, defying alike the knowledge and the great exertions of her physicians. With the increase of the chronic disease, which had thus, apparently, taken too sure hold upon her constitution to be eradicated by human means, I could not fail to observe a similar increase in the nervous irritation of her temperament, and in her excitability by trivial causes of fear. She spoke again, and now more frequently and pertinaciously, of the sounds— of the slight sounds—and of the unusual motions among the tapestries, to which she had formerly alluded.

One night, near the closing in of September, she pressed this distressing subject with more than usual emphasis upon my attention. She had just awakened from an unquiet slumber, and I had been watching, with feelings half of anxiety, half of vague terror, the workings of her emaciated countenance. I sat by the side of her ebony bed, upon one of the ottomans of India. She partly arose, and spoke, in an earnest low whisper, of sounds which she *then* heard, but which I could not hear—of motions which she *then* saw, but which I could not perceive. The wind was rushing hurriedly behind the tapestries, and I wished to show her (what, let me confess it, I could not *all* believe) that those almost inarticulate breathings, and those very gentle variations of the figures upon the wall, were but the natural effects of that customary rushing of the wind. But a deadly pallor, overspreading her face, had proved to me that my exertions to reassure her would be fruitless. She appeared to be fainting, and no attendants were within call. I remembered where was deposited a decanter of light wine which had been ordered by her physicians, and hastened across the chamber to procure it. But, as I stepped beneath the light of the censer, two circumstances of a startling nature attracted my attention. I had felt that some palpable although invisible object had passed lightly by my person ; and I saw that there lay upon the golden carpet, in the very middle of the rich lustre thrown from the censer, a shadow—a faint, indefinite shadow of angelic aspect—such as might be fancied for the shadow of a shade. But I was wild with the excitement of an immoderate dose of opium, and heeded these things but little, nor spoke of them to Rowena. Having found the wine, I recrossed the chamber, and poured out a gobletful, which I held to the lips of the fainting lady. She had now partially recovered, however, and took the vessel herself, while I sank upon an ottoman near me, with my eyes fastened upon her person. It was then that I became distinctly aware of a gentle footfall upon the carpet, and near the couch ; and in a second thereafter, as Rowena was in the act of raising the wine to her lips, I saw, or may have dreamed that I saw, fall within the goblet, as if from some invisible spring in the atmosphere of the room, three or four large drops of a brilliant and ruby-coloured fluid. If this I saw—not so Rowena. She swallowed the wine unhesitatingly, and I forbore to speak to her of a circumstance which must, after all, I considered, have been but the suggestion of a vivid imagination, rendered morbidly active by the terror of the lady, by the opium, and by the hour.

Yet I cannot conceal it from my own perception that, immediately subsequent to the fall of the ruby drops, a rapid change for the worse took place in the disorder of my wife ; so that, on the third subsequent night, the hands of her menials prepared her for the tomb, and on the fourth, I sat alone, with her shrouded body, in that fantastic chamber which had received her as my bride. Wild visions, opium-engendered, flitted, shadow-like, before me. I gazed with unquiet eye upon the sarcophagi in the angles of the room, upon the varying figures of the drapery, and upon the writhing of the parti-coloured fires in the censer overhead. My eyes then fell, as I called to mind the circumstances of a former night, to the spot beneath the glare of the censer where I had seen the faint traces of the shadow. It was there, however, no longer : and breathing with greater freedom, I turned my glances to the pallid and rigid figure upon the bed. Then rushed upon me a thousand memories of Ligeia—and then came back upon my heart, with the turbulent violence of a flood, the whole of that unutterable woe with which I had regarded *her* thus enshrouded. The night waned; and still, with a bosom full of bitter thoughts of the one only and supremely beloved, I remained gazing upon the body of Rowena.

It might have been midnight, or perhaps earlier, or later, for I had taken no note of time, when a sob, low, gentle, but very distinct, startled me from my reverie. I *felt* that it came from the bed of ebony—the bed of death. I listened in an agony of superstitious terror—but there was no repetition of the sound. I strained my vision to detect any motion in the corpse—but there was not the slightest perceptible. Yet I could not have been deceived. I *had* heard the noise, however faint, and my soul was awakened within me. I resolutely and perseveringly kept my attention riveted upon the body. Many minutes elapsed before any circumstance occurred tending to throw light upon the mystery. At length it became evident that a slight, a very feeble, and barely noticeable tinge of colour had flushed up within the cheeks, and along the sunken small veins of the eyelids. Through a species of unutterable horror and awe, for which the language of mortality has no sufficiently energetic expression, I felt my heart cease to beat, my limbs grow rigid where I sat. Yet a sense of duty finally operated to restore my self-possession. I could no longer doubt that we had been precipitate in our preparations—that Rowena still lived. It was necessary that some immediate exertion be made; yet the turret was altogether apart from the portion of the abbey tenanted by the servants—there were none within call—I had no means of summoning them to my aid without leaving the room for many minutes—and this I could not venture to do. I therefore struggled alone in my endeavours to call back the spirit still hovering. In a short period it was certain, however, that a relapse had taken place; the colour disappeared from both eyelid and cheek, leaving a wanness even more than that of marble; the lips became doubly shrivelled and pinched up in the ghastly expression of death; a repulsive clamminess and coldness overspread rapidly the surface of the body; and all the usual rigorous stiffness immediately supervened. I fell back with a shudder upon the couch from which I had been so startlingly aroused, and again gave myself up to passionate waking visions of Ligeia.

An hour thus elapsed, when (could it be possible?) I was a second time aware of some vague sound issuing from the region of the bed. I listened—in extremity of horror. The sound came again—it was a sigh. Rushing to the corpse, I saw—distinctly saw—a tremor upon the lips. In a minute afterwards they relaxed, disclosing a bright line of the pearly teeth. Amazement now struggled in my bosom with the profound awe which had hitherto reigned there alone. I felt that my vision grew dim, that my reason wandered; and it was only by a violent effort that I at length succeeded in nerving myself to the task which duty thus once more had pointed out. There was now a partial glow upon the forehead and upon the cheek and throat; a perceptible warmth pervaded the whole frame; there was even a slight pulsation at the heart. The lady *lived*; and with redoubled ardour I betook myself to the task of restoration. I chafed and bathed the temples and the hands, and used every exertion which experience, and no little medical reading, could suggest. But in vain. Suddenly, the colour fled, the pulsation ceased, the lips resumed the expression of the dead, and, in an instant afterward, the whole body took upon itself the icy chilliness, the livid hue, the intense rigidity, the sunken outline, and all the loathsome peculiarities of that which has been, for many days, a tenant of the tomb.

And again I sunk into visions of Ligeia—and again (what marvel that I shudder while I write?) *again* there reached my ears a low sob from the region of the ebony bed. But why shall I minutely detail the unspeakable horrors of that night? Why shall I pause to relate how, time after time, until near the period of the grey dawn, this hideous drama of revivification was repeated; how each terrific relapse was only into a sterner and apparently more irredeemable death; how each agony wore the aspect of a struggle with some invisible foe; and how each struggle was succeeded by I know not what of wild change in the personal appearance of the corpse? Let me hurry to a conclusion.

The greater part of the fearful night had worn away, and she who had been dead, once again stirred—and now more vigorously than hitherto, although arousing from a dissolution more appalling in its utter hopelessness than any. I had long ceased to struggle or to move, and remained sitting rigidly upon the ottoman, a helpless prey to a whirl of violent emotions, of which extreme awe was perhaps the least terrible, the least consuming. The corpse, I repeat, stirred, and now more vigorously than before. The hues of life flushed up with unwonted energy into the countenance—the limbs relaxed—and, save that the eyelids were yet pressed heavily together and that the bandages and draperies of the grave still imparted their charnel character to the figure, I might have dreamed that Rowena had indeed shaken off, utterly, the fetters of death. But if this idea was not, even then, altogether adopted, I could at least doubt no longer, when arising from the bed, tottering, with feeble steps, with closed eyes, and with the manner of one bewildered in a dream, the thing that was enshrouded advanced boldly and palpably into the middle of the apartment.

I trembled not—I stirred not—for a crowd of unutterable fancies connected with the air, the stature, the demeanour of the figure, rushing hurriedly through my brain, had paralysed—had chilled me into stone. I stirred not—but gazed upon the apparition. There was a mad disorder in my thoughts—a tumult unappeasable. Could it, indeed, be the *living* Rowena who confronted me? Could it indeed be Rowena *at all*—the fair-haired, the blue-eyed Lady Rowena Trevanion of Tremaine? Why, *why* should I doubt it? The bandage lay heavily about the mouth—but then might it not be the mouth of the breathing Lady of Tremaine? And the cheeks—there were the roses as in her noon of life—yes, these might indeed be the fair cheeks of the living Lady of Tremaine. And the chin, with its dimples, as in health, might it not be hers?—but *had she then grown taller since her malady?* What inexpressible madness seized me with that thought? One bound, and I had reached her feet! Shrinking from my touch, she let fall from her head, unloosened, the ghastly cerements which had confined it, and there streamed forth, into the rushing atmosphere of the chamber, huge masses of long and dishevelled hair; *it was blacker than the raven wings of midnight!* And now slowly opened *the eyes* of the figure which stood before me. " Here then,

at least," I shrieked aloud, " can I never—can I never
be mistaken—these are the full, and the black, and the
wild eyes—of my lost love—of the Lady—of the LADY
LIGEIA."

THE OBLONG BOX

SOME years ago, I engaged passage from Charleston,
S.C., to the city of New York, in the fine packet-ship
Independence, Captain Hardy. We were to sail on the
fifteenth of the month (June), weather permitting; and on
the fourteenth, I went on board to arrange some matters
in my state-room.

I found that we were to have a great many passengers,
including a more than usual number of ladies. On the
list were several of my acquaintances; and among other
names, I was rejoiced to see that of Mr. Cornelius Wyatt,
a young artist, for whom I entertained feelings of warm
friendship. He had been with me a fellow-student at
C—— University, where we were very much together.
He had the ordinary temperament of genius, and was
a compound of misanthropy, sensibility, and enthusiasm.
To these qualities he united the warmest and truest heart
which ever beat in a human bosom.

I observed that his name was carded upon *three* state-
rooms; and, upon again referring to the list of passengers,
I found that he had engaged passage for himself, wife,
and two sisters—his own. The state-rooms were sufficiently roomy, and each had two berths, one above the
other. These berths, to be sure, were so exceedingly
narrow as to be insufficient for more than one person;
still, I could not comprehend why there were *three* state-
rooms for these four persons. I was, just at that epoch,
in one of those moody frames of mind which make a man
abnormally inquisitive about trifles; and I confess, with
shame, that I busied myself in a variety of ill-bred and
preposterous conjectures about this matter of the super-
numerary state-room. It was no business of mine, to
be sure; but with none the less pertinacity did I occupy

myself in attempts to resolve the enigma.   At last I reached a conclusion which wrought in me great wonder why I had not arrived at it before.   "It is a servant, of course," I said; "what a fool I am not sooner to have thought of so obvious a solution!"   And then I again repaired to the list—but here I saw distinctly that *no* servant was to come with the party; although, in fact, it had been the original design to bring one—for the words "and servant" had been first written and then over-scored. "Oh, extra baggage, to be sure," I now said to myself —"something he wishes not to be put in the hold— something to be kept under his own eye—ah, I have it —a painting or so—and this is what he has been bargaining about with Nicolino, the Italian Jew."   This idea satisfied me, and I dismissed my curiosity for the nonce.

Wyatt's two sisters I knew very well, and most amiable and clever girls they were.   His wife he had newly married, and I had never yet seen her.   He had often talked about her in my presence, however, and in his usual style of enthusiasm.   He described her as of surpassing beauty, wit, and accomplishment.   I was, therefore, quite anxious to make her acquaintance.

On the day in which I visited the ship (the fourteenth), Wyatt and party were also to visit it—so the captain informed me—and I waited on board an hour longer than I had designed, in hope of being presented to the bride; but then an apology came.   "Mrs. W. was a little indisposed, and would decline coming on board until to-morrow, at the hour of sailing."

The morrow having arrived, I was going from my hotel to the wharf, when Captain Hardy met me and said that "owing to circumstances" (a stupid but convenient phrase), "he rather thought the *Independence* would not sail for a day or two, and that when all was ready, he would send up and let me know."   This I thought strange, for there was a stiff southerly breeze; but as "the circumstances" were not forthcoming, although I pumped for them with much perseverance, I had nothing to do but to return home and digest my impatience at leisure.

I did not receive the expected message from the captain for nearly a week.   It came at length, however, and I immediately went on board.   The ship was crowded with passengers, and everything was in the bustle attendant

upon making sail. Wyatt's party arrived in about ten
minutes after myself. There were the two sisters, the
bride, and the artist—the latter in one of his customary
fits of moody misanthropy. I was too well used to these,
however, to pay them any special attention. He did not
even introduce me to his wife ; this courtesy devolving,
perforce, upon his sister Marian—a very sweet and intelligent
girl, who, in a few hurried words, made us acquainted.

Mrs. Wyatt had been closely veiled ; and when she
raisea her veil, in acknowledging my bow, I confess that
I was very profoundly astonished. I should have been much
more so, however, had not long experience advised me
not to trust, with too implicit a reliance, the enthusiastic
description of my friend, the artist, when indulging in
comments upon the loveliness of woman. When beauty
was the theme, I well knew with what facility he soared
into the regions of the purely ideal.

The truth is, I could not help regarding Mrs. Wyatt
as a decidedly plain-looking woman. If not positively
ugly, she was not, I think, very far from it. She was
dressed, however, in exquisite taste—and then I had
no doubt that she had captivated my friend's heart by
the more enduring graces of the intellect and soul. She
said very few words, and passed at once into her state-
room with Mr. W.

My old inquisitiveness now returned. There was *no*
servant—*that* was a settled point. I looked, therefore,
for the extra baggage. After some delay, a cart arrived
at the wharf with an oblong pine box, which was everything
that seemed to be expected. Immediately upon its arrival
we made sail, and in a short time were safely over the bar
and standing out at sea.

The box in question was, as I say, oblong. It was
about six feet in length by two and a half in breadth ;
I observed it attentively, and like to be precise. Now
this shape was *peculiar* ; and no sooner had I seen it,
than I took credit to myself for the accuracy of my
guessing. I had reached the conclusion, it will be remembered, that the extra baggage of my friend, the artist,
would prove to be pictures, or at least a picture—for I
knew he had been for several weeks in conference with
Nicolino ; and now here was a box which, from its shape,
could possibly contain nothing in the world but a copy

of Leonardo's "Last Supper"; and a copy of this very "Last Supper," done by Rubini the younger, at Florence, I had known, for some time, to be in the possession of Nicolino. This point, therefore, I considered as sufficiently settled. I chuckled excessively when I thought of my acumen. It was the first time I had ever known Wyatt to keep from me any of his artistical secrets; but here he evidently intended to steal a march upon me, and smuggle a fine picture to New York, under my very nose; expecting me to know nothing of the matter. I resolved to quiz him well, now and hereafter.

One thing, however, annoyed me not a little. The box did *not* go into the extra state-room. It was deposited in Wyatt's own; and there, too, it remained, occupying very nearly the whole of the floor—no doubt to the exceeding discomfort of the artist and his wife; this the more especially as the tar or paint with which it was lettered in sprawling capitals emitted a strong, disagreeable, and, to *my* fancy, a peculiarly disgusting odour. On the lid were painted the words—" *Mrs. Adelaide Curtis, Albany, New York. Charge of Cornelius Wyatt, Esq. This side up. To be handled with care.*"

Now, I was aware that Mrs. Adelaide Curtis, of Albany, was the artist's wife's mother; but then I looked upon the whole address as a mystification, intended especially for myself. I made up my mind, of course, that the box and contents would never get farther north than the studio of my misanthropic friend in Chambers Street, New York.

For the first three or four days we had fine weather, although the wind was dead ahead; having chopped round to the northward, immediately upon our losing sight of the coast. The passengers were, consequently, in high spirits, and disposed to be social. I must except, however, Wyatt and his sisters, who behaved stiffly, and I could not help thinking, uncourteously to the rest of the party. *Wyatt's* conduct, I did not so much regard. He was gloomy, even beyond his usual habit—in fact he was *morose*—but in him I was prepared for eccentricity. For the sisters, however, I could make no excuse. They secluded themselves in their state-rooms during the greater part of the passage, and absolutely refused, although I repeatedly urged them, to hold communication with any person on board.

Mrs. Wyatt herself was far more agreeable. That is
to say, she was *chatty* ; and to be chatty is no slight recom
mendation at sea. She became *excessively* intimate with
most of the ladies ; and, to my profound astonishment,
evinced no equivocal disposition to coquet with the men.
She amused us all very much. I say " *amused* "—and
scarcely know how to explain myself. The truth is, I
soon found that Mrs. W. was far oftener laughed *at* than
with. The gentlemen said little about her ; but the ladies,
in a little while, pronounced her " a good-hearted thing,
rather indifferent-looking, totally uneducated, and decidedly
vulgar." The great wonder was how Wyatt had been
entrapped into such a match. Wealth was the general
solution—but this I knew to be no solution at all ; for
Wyatt had told me she neither brought him a dollar nor
had any expectations from any source whatever. " He
had married," he said, " for love, and for love only ; and
his bride was far more than worthy of his love." When
I thought of these expressions, on the part of my friend,
I confess that I felt indescribably puzzled. Could it be
possible that he was taking leave of his senses ? What
else could I think ? *He*, so refined, so intellectual, so
fastidious, with so exquisite a perception of the faulty,
and so keen an appreciation of the beautiful ! To be
sure, the lady seemed especially fond of *him*—particularly
so in his absence—when she made herself ridiculous by
frequent quotations of what had been said by her " beloved
husband, Mr. Wyatt." The word " husband " seemed
for ever—to use one of her own delicate expressions—
for ever " on the tip of her tongue." In the meantime,
it was observed by all on board, that he avoided
her in the most pointed manner, and, for the most part,
shut himself up alone in his state-room, where, in fact,
he might have been said to live altogether, leaving his
wife at full liberty to amuse herself as she thought best,
in the public society of the main cabin.

My conclusion, from what I saw and heard, was, that
the artist, by some unaccountable freak of fate, or perhaps
in some fit of enthusiastic and fanciful passion, had been
induced to unite himself with a person altogether beneath
him, and that the natural result, entire and speedy disgust,
had ensued. I pitied him from the bottom of my heart—
but could not, for that reason, quite forgive his incom-

municativeness in the matter of the " Last Supper." For his I resolved to have my revenge.

One day he came upon deck, and, taking his arm as had been my wont, I sauntered with him backwards and forwards. His gloom, however (which I considered quite natural under the circumstances), seemed entirely unabated. He said little, and that moodily, and with evident effort. I ventured a jest or two, and he made a sickening attempt at a smile. Poor fellow !—as I thought of *his* *wife*, I wondered that he could have heart to put on even the semblance of mirth. At last I ventured a home thrust. I determined to commence a series of covert insinuations, or innuendoes, about the oblong box—just to let him perceive, gradually, that I was *not* altogether the butt, or victim, of his little bit of pleasant mystification. My first observation was by way of opening a masked battery. I said something about the " peculiar shape of *that* box " ; and, as I spoke the words, I smiled knowingly, winked, and touched him gently with my forefinger in the ribs.

The manner in which Wyatt received this harmless pleasantry convinced me at once that he was mad. At first he stared at me as if he found it impossible to comprehend the witticism of my remark ; but as its point seemed slowly to make its way into his brain, his eyes in the same proportion seemed protruding from their sockets. Then he grew very red—then hideously pale— then, as if highly amused with what I had insinuated, he began a loud and boisterous laugh, which, to my astonishment, he kept up with gradually increasing vigour, for ten minutes or more. In conclusion, he fell flat and heavily upon the deck. When I ran to uplift him, to all appearance he was *dead*.

I called assistance, and, with much difficulty, we brought him to himself. Upon reviving, he spoke incoherently for some time. At length we bled him and put him to bed. The next morning he was quite recovered, so far as regarded his mere bodily health. Of his mind I say nothing, of course. I avoided him during the rest of the passage, by advice of the captain, who seemed to coincide with me altogether in my views of his insanity, but cautioned me to say nothing on this head to any person on board.

Several circumstances occurred immediately after this

fit of Wyatt's, which contributed to heighten the curiosit
with which I was already possessed. Among other thing
this : I had been nervous—drank too much strong gree
tea, and slept ill at night—in fact, for two nights I coul
not be properly said to sleep at all. Now, my state-roo
opened into the main cabin, or dining-room, as did thos
of all the single men on board. Wyatt's three rooms wer
in the after-cabin, which was separated from the main on
by a slight sliding door, never locked even at night. A
we were almost constantly on a wind, and the breeze wa
not a little stiff, the ship heeled to leeward very consider
ably ; and whenever her starboard side was to leeward
the sliding door between the cabins slid open, and s
remained, nobody taking the trouble to get up and shu
it. But my berth was in such a position, that when m
own state-room door was open, as well as the sliding doo
in question (and my own door was *always* open on accoun
of the heat), I could see into the after-cabin quite distinctly
and just at that portion of it, too, where were situated th
state-rooms of Mr. Wyatt. Well, during two nights (*no*
consecutive) while I lay awake, I clearly saw Mrs. W., abou
eleven o'clock upon each night, steal cautiously from th
state-room of Mr. W., and enter the extra room, where sh
remained until daybreak, when she was called by he
husband and went back. That they were virtually
separated was clear. They had separate apartments—
no doubt in contemplation of a more permanent divorce
and here, after all, I thought, was the mystery of the extr
state-room.

There was another circumstance, too, which interested
me much. During the two wakeful nights in question
and immediately after the disappearance of Mrs. Wyatt
into the extra state-room, I was attracted by certain
singular, cautious, subdued noises in that of her husband.
After listening to them for some time, with thoughtful
attention, I at length succeeded perfectly in translating
their import. They were sounds occasioned by the artist
in prising open the oblong box by means of a chisel and
mallet—the latter being apparently muffled or deadened
by some soft woollen or cotton substance in which its head
was enveloped.

In this manner I fancied I could distinguish the precise
moment when he fairly disengaged the lid—also, that I

:ould determine when he removed it altogether, and when he deposited it upon the lower berth in his room ; this .atter point I knew, for example, by certain slight taps which the lid made in striking against the wooden edges of the berth, as he endeavoured to lay it down very gently— there being no room for it on the floor. After this there was a dead stillness, and I heard nothing more, upon either occasion, until nearly daybreak ; unless, perhaps, I may mention a low sobbing or murmuring sound, so very much suppressed as to be nearly inaudible—if, indeed, the whole of this latter noise were not rather produced by my own imagination. I say it seemed to *resemble* sobbing or sighing—but, of course, it could not have been either. I rather think it was a ringing in my own ears. Mr. Wyatt, no doubt, according to custom, was merely giving the rein to one of his hobbies—indulging in one of his fits of artistic enthusiasm. He had opened his oblong box in order to feast his eyes on the pictorial treasure within. There was nothing in this, however, to make him *sob*. I repeat, therefore, that it must have been simply a freak of my own fancy, distempered by good Captain Hardy's green tea. Just before dawn, on each of the two nights of which I speak, I distinctly heard Mr. Wyatt replace the lid upon the oblong box, and force the nails into their old places, by means of the muffled mallet. Having done this, he issued from his state-room, fully dressed, and proceeded to call Mrs. W. from hers.

We had been at sea seven days, and were now off Cape Hatteras, when there came a tremendously heavy blow from the south-west. We were, in a measure, prepared for it, however, as the weather had been holding out threats for some time. Everything was made snug, alow and aloft ; and as the wind steadily freshened, we lay to, at length, under spanker and foretopsail, both double-reefed.

In this trim we rode safely enough for forty-eight hours —the ship proving herself an excellent sea-boat, in many respects, and shipping no water of any consequence. At the end of this period, however, the gale had freshened into a hurricane, and our after-sail split into ribbons, bringing us so much in the trough of the water that we shipped several prodigious seas, one immediately after the other. By this accident we lost three men overboard with

the caboose, and nearly the whole of the larboard bulwarks.
Scarcely had we recovered our senses before the foretopsail
went into shreds, when we got up a storm stay-sail, and
with this did pretty well for some hours, the ship heading
the sea much more steadily than before.

The gale still held on, however, and we saw no signs
of its abating. The rigging was found to be ill-fitted and
greatly strained ; and on the third day of the blow, about
five in the afternoon, our mizzen-mast, in a heavy lurch to
windward, went by the board. For an hour or more we
tried in vain to get rid of it on account of the prodigious
rolling of the ship ; and, before we had succeeded, the
carpenter came aft and announced four feet of water in
the hold. To add to our dilemma, we found the pumps
choked and nearly useless.

All was now confusion and despair—but an effort was
made to lighten the ship by throwing overboard as much
of her cargo as could be reached, and by cutting away the
two masts that remained. This we at last accomplished—
but we were still unable to do anything at the pumps ;
and, in the meantime, the leak gained on us fast.

At sundown, the gale had sensibly diminished in violence,
and, as the sea went down with it, we still entertained faint
hopes of saving ourselves in the boats. At eight P.M. the
clouds broke away to windward, and we had the advantage
of a full moon—a piece of good fortune which served
wonderfully to cheer our drooping spirits.

After incredible labour we succeeded, at length, in getting
the long-boat over the side without material accident, and
into this we crowded the whole of the crew and most of the
passengers. This party made off immediately, and, after
undergoing much suffering, finally arrived, in safety, at
Ocracoke Inlet, on the third day after the wreck.

Fourteen passengers, with the captain, remained on
board, resolving to trust their fortunes to the jolly-boat
at the stern. We lowered it without difficulty, although
it was only by a miracle that we prevented it from swamping
as it touched the water. It contained, when afloat, the
captain and his wife, Mr. Wyatt and party, a Mexican
officer, wife, four children, and myself, with a negro valet.

We had no room, of course, for anything except a few
positively necessary instruments, some provisions, and
the clothes upon our backs. No one had thought of even

THE OBLONG BOX

the astonishment of all then, when, having proceeded a
few fathoms from the ship, Mr. Wyatt stood up in the
stern-sheets. and coolly demanded of Captain Hardy that
the boat should be put back for the purpose of taking in
his oblong box !

" Sit down, Mr. Wyatt," replied the captain, somewhat
sternly, " you will capsize us if you do not sit quite still.
Our gunwale is almost in the water now."

" The box ! " vociferated Mr. Wyatt, still standing—
" the box, I say ! Captain Hardy, you cannot, you *will*
not refuse me. Its weight will be but a trifle—it is nothing
—mere nothing. By the mother who bore you—for the
love of Heaven—by your hope of salvation, I *implore* you
to put back for the box ! "

The captain, for a moment, seemed touched by the
earnest appeal of the artist ; but he regained his stern
composure, and merely said—

" Mr. Wyatt, you are mad. I cannot listen to you.
Sit down, I say, or you will swamp the boat. Stay—hold
him—seize him !—he is about to spring overboard !
There—I knew it—he is over ! "

As the captain said this, Mr. Wyatt, in fact, sprang
from the boat, and, as we were yet in the lee of the wreck,
succeeded, by almost superhuman exertion, in getting
hold of a rope which hung from the forechains. In another
moment he was on board, and rushing frantically down into
the cabin.

In the meantime, we had been swept astern of the ship,
and being quite out of her lee, were at the mercy of the
tremendous sea which was still running. We made a
determined effort to put back, but our little boat was like
a feather in the breath of the tempest. We saw at a
glance that the doom of the unfortunate artist was sealed.

As our distance from the wreck rapidly increased, the
madman (for as such only could we regard him) was seen
to emerge from the companion-way, up which, by dint of
a strength that appeared gigantic, he dragged, bodily, the
oblong box. While we gazed in the extremity of astonishment, he passed, rapidly, several turns of a three-inch rope,
first around the box and then around his body. In another
instant both body and box were in the sea—disappearing
suddenly, at once and for ever.

We lingered awhile sadly upon our oars, with our eyes riveted upon the spot. At length we pulled away. The silence remained unbroken for an hour. Finally, I hazarded a remark.

" Did you observe, captain, how suddenly they sank ? Was not that an exceedingly singular thing ? I confess that I entertained some feeble hope of his final deliverance, when I saw him lash himself to the box, and commit himself to the sea."

" They sank as a matter of course," replied the captain, " and that like a shot. They will soon rise again, however —*but not till the salt melts.*"

" The salt ! " I ejaculated.

" Hush ! " said the captain, pointing to the wife and sisters of the deceased. " We must talk of these things at some more appropriate time."

We suffered much, and made a narrow escape ; but fortune befriended *us*, as well as our mates in the long-boat. We landed, in fine, more dead than alive, after four days of intense distress, upon the beach opposite Roanoke Island. We remained here a week, were not ill-treated by the wreckers, and at length obtained a passage to New York.

About a month after the loss of the *Independence*, I happened to meet Captain Hardy in Broadway. Our conversation turned, naturally, upon the disaster, and especially upon the sad fate of poor Wyatt. I thus learned the following particulars.

The artist had engaged passage for himself, wife, two sisters, and a servant. His wife was, indeed, as she had been represented, a most lovely and most accomplished woman. On the morning of the fourteenth of June (the day in which I first visited the ship), the lady suddenly sickened and died. The young husband was frantic with grief—but circumstances imperatively forbade the deferring his voyage to New York. It was necessary to take to her mother the corpse of his adored wife, and on the other hand, the universal prejudice which would prevent his doing so openly was well known. Nine-tenths of the passengers would have abandoned the ship rather than take passage with a dead body.

In this dilemma, Captain Hardy arranged that the

corpse, being first partially embalmed, and packed, with a large quantity of salt, in a box of suitable dimensions, should be conveyed on board as merchandise. Nothing was to be said of the lady's decease ; and, as it was well understood that Mr. Wyatt had engaged passage for his wife, it became necessary that some person should personate her during the voyage. This the deceased's lady's-maid was easily prevailed on to do. The extra state-room, originally engaged for this girl, during her mistress's life, was now merely retained. In this state-room the pseudo-wife slept, of course, every night. In the day-time she performed, to the best of her ability, the part of her mistress —whose person, it had been carefully ascertained, was unknown to any of the passengers on board.

My own mistakes arose, naturally enough, through too careless, too inquisitive, and too impulsive a temperament. But of late, it is a rare thing that I sleep soundly at night. There is a countenance which haunts me, turn as I will. There is an hysterical laugh which will for ever ring within my ears.

METZENGERSTEIN

"Pestis eram vivus—moriens tua mors ero."
—Martin Luther.

Horror and fatality have been stalking abroad in all ages. Why then give a date to the story I have to tell ? Let it suffice to say, that at the period of which I speak, there existed, in the interior of Hungary, a settled although hidden belief in the doctrines of the Metempsychosis. Of the doctrines themselves—that is, of their falsity, or of their probability—I say nothing. I assert, however, that much of our incredulity (as La Bruyère says of all our unhappiness) " vient de ne pouvoir être seuls." *

* Mercier, in " L'An deux mille quatre cents quarante," seriously maintains the doctrines of the Metempsychosis, and I. D'Israeli says that " no system is so simple and so little repugnant to the understanding." Colonel Ethan Allen, the " Green Mountain Boy," is also said to have been a serious metempsychosist.

But there were some points in the Hungarian super
stition which were fast verging to absurdity. They—th
Hungarians—differed very essentially from their Easter
authorities. For example. " *The soul*," said the former—
I give the words of an acute and intelligent Parisian—" *n*
*demeure qu'une seule fois dans un corps sensible : au reste—
un cheval, un chien, un homme même, n'est que la ressem
blance peu tangible de ces animaux.*"

The families at Berlifitzing and Metzengerstein had bee
at variance for centuries. Never before were two houses
so illustrious, mutually embittered by hostility so deadly
The origin of this enmity seems to be found in the word
of an ancient prophecy—" A lofty name shall have a fearfu
fall when, as the rider over his horse, the mortality o
Metzengerstein shall triumph over the immortality o
Berlifitzing."

To be sure, the words themselves had little or no meaning
But more trivial causes have given rise—and that no lon
while ago—to consequences equally eventful. Besides, th
estates, which were contiguous, had long exercised a riva
influence in the affairs of a busy government. Moreover
near neighbours are seldom friends ; and the inhabitant
of the Castle Berlifitzing might look from their loft
buttresses into the very windows of the Palace Metzenger
stein. Least of all had the more than feudal magnificence
thus discovered, a tendency to allay the irritable feeling
of the less ancient and less wealthy Berlifitzing. Wha
wonder, then, that the words, however silly, of that pre
diction, should have succeeded in setting and keeping a
variance two families already predisposed to quarrel b
every instigation of hereditary jealousy ? The prophec
seemed to imply—if it implied anything—a final triump
on the part of the already more powerful house ; and wa
of course remembered with the more bitter animosity b
the weaker and less influential.

Wilhelm, Count Berlifitzing, although loftily descended
was, at the epoch of this narrative, an infirm and dotin
old man, remarkable for nothing but an inordinate an
inveterate personal antipathy to the family of his rival
and so passionate a love of horses, and of hunting, tha
neither bodily infirmity, great age, nor mental incapacit
prevented his daily participation in the dangers of th
chase.

Frederick, Baron Metzengerstein, was, on the other hand, not yet of age. His father, the Minister G——, died young. His mother, the Lady Mary, followed him quickly. Frederick was, at that time, in his eighteenth year. In a city, eighteen years are no long period ; but in a wilderness—in so magnificent a wilderness as that old principality, the pendulum vibrates with a deeper meaning.

From some peculiar circumstances attending the administration of his father, the young Baron, at the decease of the former, entered immediately upon his vast possessions. Such estates were seldom held before by a nobleman of Hungary. His castles were without number. The chief in point of splendour and extent was the " Palace Metzengerstein." The boundary line of his dominions was never clearly defined ; but his principal park embraced a circuit of fifty miles.

Upon the succession of a proprietor so young, with a character so well known, to a fortune so unparalleled, little speculation was afloat in regard to his probable course of conduct. And, indeed, for the space of three days, the behaviour of the heir out-Heroded Herod, and fairly surpassed the expectations of his most enthusiastic admirers. Shameful debaucheries—flagrant treacheries—unheard-of atrocities—gave his trembling vassals quickly to understand that no servile submission on their part—no punctilios of conscience on his own—were thenceforward to prove any security against the remorseless fangs of a petty Caligula. On the night of the fourth day, the stables of the Castle Berlifitzing were discovered to be on fire ; and the unanimous opinion of the neighbourhood added the crime of the incendiary to the already hideous list of the Baron's misdemeanours and enormities.

But during the tumult occasioned by this occurrence, the young nobleman himself sat apparently buried in meditation, in a vast and desolate upper apartment of the family palace of Metzengerstein. The rich although faded tapestry hangings which swung gloomily upon the walls represented the shadowy and majestic forms of a thousand illustrious ancestors. *Here*, rich-ermined priests and pontifical dignitaries, familiarly seated with the autocrat and the sovereign, put a veto on the wishes of a temporal king, or restrained with the fiat of papal supremacy the rebellious sceptre of the Arch-enemy. *There*, the dark, tall statures of the Princes Metzengerstein—their muscular war-coursers plunging over the carcasses of fallen foes—startled the steadiest nerves with their vigorous expression ; and *here*, again, the voluptuous and swan-like figures of the dames of days gone by floated away in the mazes of an unreal dance to the strains of imaginary melody.

But as the Baron listened, or affected to listen, to the gradually increasing uproar in the stables of Berlifitzing —or perhaps pondered upon some more novel, some more decided act of audacity—his eyes were turned unwittingly to the figure of an enormous, and unnaturally coloured horse, represented in the tapestry as belonging to a Saracen ancestor of the family of his rival. The horse itself, in the foreground of the design, stood motionless and statue-like—while, farther back, its discomfited rider perished by the dagger of a Metzengerstein.

On Frederick's lip arose a fiendish expression, as he became aware of the direction which his glance had, without his consciousness, assumed. Yet he did not remove it. On the contrary, he could by no means account for the overwhelming anxiety which appeared falling like a pall upon his senses. It was with difficulty that he reconciled his dreamy and incoherent feelings with the certainty of being awake. The longer he gazed the more absorbing became the spell—the more impossible did it appear that he could ever withdraw his glance from the fascination of that tapestry. But the tumult without becoming suddenly more violent, with a compulsory exertion he diverted his attention to the glare of ruddy light thrown full by the flaming stables upon the windows of the apartment.

The action, however, was but momentary ; his gaze returned mechanically to the wall. To his extreme horror and astonishment, the head of the gigantic steed had, in the meantime, altered its position. The neck of the animal before arched, as if in compassion, over the prostrate body of its lord, was now extended at full length, in the direction of the Baron. The eyes, before invisible, now wore an energetic and human expression, while they gleamed with a fiery and unusual red ; and the distended lips of the apparently enraged horse left in full view his sepulchral and disgusting teeth.

Stupefied with terror, the young nobleman tottered to

the door. As he threw it open, a flash of red light, streaming far into the chamber, flung his shadow with a clear outline against the quivering tapestry ; and he shuddered to perceive that shadow—as he staggered awhile upon the threshold—assuming the exact position, and precisely filling up the contour, of the relentless and triumphant murderer of the Saracen Berlifitzing.

To lighten the depression of his spirits, the Baron hurried into the open air. At the principal gate of the palace he encountered three equerries. With much difficulty, and at the imminent peril of their lives, they were restraining the convulsive plunges of a gigantic and fiery-coloured horse.

" Whose horse ? Where did you get him ? " demanded the youth, in a querulous and husky tone, as he became instantly aware that the mysterious steed in the tapestried chamber was the very counterpart of the furious animal before his eyes.

" He is your own property, sire," replied one of the equerries, " at least he is claimed by no other owner. We caught him flying, all smoking and foaming with rage, from the burning stables of the Castle Berlifitzing. Supposing him to have belonged to the old Count's stud of foreign horses, we led him back as an estray. But the grooms there disclaim any title to the creature ; which is strange, since he bears evident marks of having made a narrow escape from the flames."

" The letters W. V. B. are also branded very distinctly on his forehead," interrupted a second equerry ; " I supposed them, of course, to be the initials of William Von Berlifitzing—but all at the castle are positive in denying any knowledge of the horse."

" Extremely singular ! " said the young Baron, with a musing air, and apparently unconscious of the meaning of his words. " He is, as you say, a remarkable horse—a prodigious horse ! although, as you very justly observe, of a suspicious and untractable character ; let him be mine, however," he added, after a pause, " perhaps a rider like Frederick of Metzengerstein, may tame even the devil from the stables of Berlifitzing."

" You are mistaken, my lord ; the horse, as I think we mentioned, is *not* from the stables of the Count. If such had been the case, we know our duty better than to bring him into the presence of a noble of your family."

F

" True ! " observed the Baron, drily ; and at that instant a page of the bed-chamber came from the palace with a heightened colour, and a precipitate step. He whispered into his master's ear an account of the sudden disappearance of a small portion of the tapestry, in an apartment which he designated ; entering, at the same time, into particulars of a minute and circumstantial character ; but from the low tone of voice in which these latter were communicated, nothing escaped to gratify the excited curiosity of the equerries.

The young Frederick, during the conference, seemed agitated by a variety of emotions. He soon, however, recovered his composure, and an expression of determined malignancy settled upon his countenance, as he gave peremptory orders that the apartment in question should be immediately locked up, and the key placed in his own possession.

" Have you heard of the unhappy death of the old hunter, Berliitzing ? " said one of his vassals to the Baron, as, after the departure of the page, the huge steed which that nobleman had adopted as his own, plunged and curveted, with redoubled fury, down the long avenue which extended from the palace to the stables of Metzengerstein.

" No ! " said the Baron, turning abruptly toward the speaker, " dead ! say you ? "

" It is indeed true, my lord ; and, to the noble of your name, will be, I imagine, no unwelcome intelligence."

A rapid smile shot over the countenance of the listener. " How died he ? "

" In his rash exertions to rescue a favourite portion of the hunting stud, he has himself perished miserably in the flames."

" I—n—d—e—e—d— ! " ejaculated the Baron, as if slowly and deliberately impressed with the truth of some exciting idea.

" Indeed ; " repeated the vassal.

" Shocking ! " said the youth, calmly, and turned quietly into the palace.

From this date a marked alteration took place in the outward demeanour of the dissolute young Baron Frederick Von Metzengerstein. Indeed, his behaviour disappointed every expectation, and proved little in accordance with the views of many a manœuvring mamma ; while his habits and manner, still less than formerly, offered anything congenial with those of the neighbouring aristocracy. He was never to be seen beyond the limits of his own domain, and in his wide and social world, was utterly companionless —unless, indeed, that unnatural, impetuous, and fiery-coloured horse, which he henceforward continually bestrode, had any mysterious right to the title of his friend.

Numerous invitations on the part of the neighbourhood for a long time, however, periodically came in. " Will the Baron honour our festivals with his presence ? " " Will the Baron join us in a hunting of the boar ? " — " Metzengerstein does not hunt ; " " Metzengerstein will not attend," were the haughty and laconic answers.

These repeated insults were not to be endured by an imperious nobility. Such invitations became less cordial— less frequent—in time they ceased altogether. The widow of the unfortunate Count Berlifitzing was even heard to express a hope " that the Baron might be at home when he did not wish to be at home, since he disdained the company of his equals ; and ride when he did not wish to ride, since he preferred the society of a horse." This, to be sure, was a very silly explosion of hereditary pique ; and merely proved how singularly unmeaning our sayings are apt to become, when we desire to be unusually energetic.

The charitable, nevertheless, attributed the alteration in the conduct of the young nobleman to the natural sorrow of a son for the untimely loss of his parents ;—forgetting, however, his atrocious and reckless behaviour during the short period immediately succeeding that bereavement. Some there were, indeed, who suggested a too haughty idea of self-consequence and dignity. Others again (among whom may be mentioned the family physician) did not hesitate in speaking of morbid melancholy, and hereditary ill-health ; while dark hints, of a more equivocal nature, were current among the multitude.

Indeed, the Baron's perverse attachment to his lately acquired charger—an attachment which seemed to attain new strength from every fresh example of the animal's ferocious and demon-like propensities—at length became, in the eyes of all reasonable men, a hideous and unnatural fervour. In the glare of noon—at the dead hour of night —in sickness or in health—in calm or in tempest—the young Metzengerstein seemed riveted to the saddle of that colossal horse, whose intractable audacities so well accorded with his own spirit.

There were circumstances, moreover, which, coupled with late events, gave an unearthly and portentous character to the mania of the rider, and to the capabilities of the steed. The space passed over in a single leap had been accurately measured, and was found to exceed, by an astounding difference, the wildest expectations of the most imaginative. The Baron, besides, had no particular *name* for the animal, although all the rest in his collection were distinguished by characteristic appellations. His stable, too, was appointed at a distance from the rest ; and, with regard to grooming and other necessary offices, none but the owner in person had ventured to officiate, or even to enter the enclosure of that horse's particular stall. It was also to be observed, that although the three grooms, who had caught the steed as he fled from the conflagration at Berlifitzing, had succeeded in arresting his course by means of a chain-bridle and noose—yet not one of the three could with any certainty affirm that he had, during that dangerous struggle, or at any period thereafter, actually placed his hand upon the body of the beast. Instances of peculiar intelligence in the demeanour of a noble and high-spirited horse are not to be supposed capable of exciting unreasonable attention, but there were certain circumstances which intruded themselves perforce upon the most sceptical and phlegmatic ; and it is said there were times when the animal caused the gaping crowd who stood around to recoil in horror from the deep and impressive meaning of his terrible stamp—times when the young Metzengerstein turned pale and shrunk away from the rapid and searching expression of his human-looking eye.

Among all the retinue of the Baron, however, none were found to doubt the ardour of that extraordinary affection which existed on the part of the young nobleman for the fiery qualities of his horse ; at least, none but an insignificant and misshapen little page, whose deformities were in everybody's way, and whose opinions were of the least possible importance. He (if his ideas are worth mentioning at all) had the effrontery to assert that his master never vaulted into the saddle without an unaccountable and almost imperceptible shudder ; and that, upon his return from every long-continued and habitual ride, an expression of triumphant malignity distorted every muscle in his countenance.

One tempestuous night, Metzengerstein, awaking from a heavy slumber, descended like a maniac from his chamber, and, mounting in hot haste, bounded away into the mazes of the forest. An occurrence so common attracted no particular attention, but his return was looked for with intense anxiety on the part of his domestics, when, after some hours' absence, the stupendous and magnificent battlements of the Palace Metzengerstein were discovered crackling and rocking to their very foundation, under the influence of a dense and livid mass of ungovernable fire.

As the flames, when first seen, had already made so terrible a progress that all efforts to save any portion of the building were evidently futile, the astonished neighbourhood stood idly around in silent if not pathetic wonder. But a new and fearful object soon riveted the attention of the multitude, and proved how much more intense is the excitement wrought in the feelings of a crowd by the contemplation of human agony, than that brought about by the most appalling spectacles of inanimate matter.

Up the long avenue of aged oaks which led from the forest to the main entrance of the Palace Metzengerstein, a steed, bearing an unbonneted and disordered rider, was seen leaping with an impetuosity which outstripped the very Demon of the Tempest.

The career of the horseman was indisputably, on his own part, uncontrollable. The agony of his countenance, the convulsive struggle of his frame, gave evidence of super-human exertion ; but no sound, save a solitary shriek, escaped from his lacerated lips, which were bitten through and through in the intensity of terror. One instant, and the clattering of hoofs resounded sharply and shrilly above the roaring of the flames and the shrieking of the winds—another, and, clearing at a single plunge the gate-way and the moat, the steed bounded far up the tottering staircases of the palace, and, with its rider, disappeared amid the whirlwind of chaotic fire.

The fury of the tempest immediately died away, and a dead calm-sullenly succeeded. A white flame still en-

veloped the building like a shroud, and, streaming far away
into the quiet atmosphere, shot forth a glare of preternatural light ; while a cloud of smoke settled heavily over
the battlements in the distinct colossal figure of—*a
horse.*

SILENCE

A FABLE

"'Ευδουσιν δ'ορεων κορυφαι τε και φαραγγες
Πρωνες τε και χαραδραι."—ALCMAN.

"The mountain pinnacles slumber ; valleys, crags, and caves
are silent."

"LISTEN to *me,*" said the Demon, as he placed his hand
upon my head. "The region of which I speak is a dreary
region in Libya, by the borders of the River Zäire. And
there is no quiet there, nor silence.

"The waters of the river have a saffron and sickly hue ;
and they flow not onward to the sea, but palpitate for ever
and for ever beneath the red eye of the sun with a tumultuous and convulsive motion. For many miles on either
side of the river's oozy bed is a pale desert of gigantic water-
lilies. They sigh one unto the other in that solitude, and
stretch towards the heaven their long and ghastly necks,
and nod to and fro their everlasting heads. And there is
an indistinct murmur which cometh out from among them
like the rushing of subterrene water. And they sigh one
unto the other.

"But there is a boundary to their realm—the boundary
of the dark, horrible, lofty forest. There, like the waves
about the Hebrides, the low underwood is agitated continually. But there is no wind throughout the heaven.
And the tall primeval trees rock eternally hither and
thither with a crashing and mighty sound. And from
their high summits, one by one, drop everlasting dews.
And at the roots strange poisonous flowers lie writhing
in perturbed slumber. And overhead, with a rustling
and loud noise, the grey clouds rush westwardly for ever,
until they roll, a cataract, over the fiery wall of the horizon.
But there is no wind throughout the heaven. And by the
shores of the River Zäire there is neither quiet nor silence.

" It was night, and the rain fell ; and, falling, it was rain, but, having fallen, it was blood. And I stood in the morass among the tall lilies, and the rain fell upon my head—and the lilies sighed one unto the other in the solemnity of their desolation.

" And, all at once, the moon arose through the thin ghastly mist, and was crimson in colour. And mine eyes fell upon a huge grey rock which stood by the shore of the river, and was lighted by the light of the moon. And the rock was grey, and ghastly, and tall—and the rock was grey. Upon its front were characters engraven in the stone ; and I walked through the morass of water-lilies, until I came close unto the shore, that I might read the characters upon the stone. But I could not decipher them. And I was going back into the morass, when the moon shone with a fuller red, and I turned and looked again upon the rock, and upon the characters—and the characters were ' DESOLATION.'

" And I looked upwards, and there stood a man upon the summit of the rock ; and I hid myself among the water-lilies that I might discover the actions of the man. And the man was tall and stately in form, and was wrapped up from his shoulders to his feet in the toga of old Rome. And the outlines of his figure were indistinct—but his features were the features of a deity ; for the mantle of the night, and of the mist, and of the moon, and of the dew, had left uncovered the features of his face. And his brow was lofty with thought, and his eye wild with care ; and in the few furrows upon his cheek I read the fables of sorrow, and weariness, and disgust with mankind, and a longing after solitude.

" And the man sat upon the rock, and leaned his head upon his hand, and looked out upon the desolation. He looked down into the low unquiet shrubbery, and up into the tall primeval trees, and up higher at the rustling heaven, and into the crimson moon. And I lay close within shelter of the lilies, and observed the actions of the man. And the man trembled in the solitude ; but the night waned, and he sat upon the rock.

" And the man turned his attention from the heaven, and looked out upon the dreary River Zäire, and upon the yellow ghastly waters, and upon the pale legions of the water-lilies. And the man listened to the sighs of the

SILENCE.

water-lilies, and to the murmur that came up from among them. And I lay close within my covert, and observed the actions of the man. And the man trembled in the solitude ; but the night waned and he sat upon the rock.

" Then I went down into the recesses of the morass, and waded far in among the wilderness of the lilies, and called unto the hippopotami which dwelt among the fens in the recesses of the morass. And the hippopotami heard my call, and came, with the behemoth, unto the foot of the rock, and roared loudly and fearfully beneath the moon. And I lay close within my covert, and observed the actions of the man. And the man trembled in the solitude ; but the night waned, and he sat upon the rock.

" Then I cursed the elements with the curse of tumult ; and a frightful tempest gathered in the heaven, where, before, there had been no wind. And the heaven became livid with the violence of the tempest—and the rain beat upon the head of the man—and the floods of the river came down—and the river was tormented into foam—and the water-lilies shrieked within their beds—and the forest crumbled before the wind—and the thunder rolled—and the lightning fell—and the rock rocked to its foundation. And I lay close within my covert, and observed the actions of the man. And the man trembled in the solitude ; but the night waned, and he sat upon the rock.

" Then I grew angry and cursed, with the curse of *silence*, the river, and the lilies, and the wind, and the forest, and the heaven, and the thunder, and the sighs of the water-lilies. And they became accursed, and *were still*. And the moon ceased to totter up its pathway to heaven—and the thunder died away—and the lightning did not flash—and the clouds hung motionless—and the waters sunk to their level and remained—and the trees ceased to rock—and the water-lilies sighed no more—and the murmur was heard no longer from among them, nor any shadow of sound throughout the vast illimitable desert. And I looked upon the characters of the rock, and they were changed ; and the characters were ' SILENCE.'

" And mine eyes fell upon the countenance of the man, and his countenance was wan with terror. And, hurriedly, he raised his head from his hand, and stood forth upon the rock and listened. But there was no voice throughout the vast illimitable desert, and the characters upon the rock

were ' SILENCE.' And the man shuddered, and turned
his face away, and fled afar off, in haste, so that I beheld
him no more."

.   .   .   .

Now there are fine tales in the volumes of the Magi—in
the iron-bound, melancholy volumes of the Magi. Therein,
I say, are glorious histories of the heaven, and of the earth,
and of the mighty sea—and of the Genii that over-ruled
the sea, and the earth, and the lofty heaven. There was
much lore, too, in the sayings which were said by the
Sibyls ; and holy, holy things were heard of old by the
dim leaves that trembled around Dodona—but, as Allah
liveth, that fable which the Demon told me as he sat by my
side in the shadow of the tomb, I hold to be the most
wonderful of all ! And as the Demon made an end of his
story, he fell back within the cavity of the tomb and
laughed. And I could not laugh with the Demon, and he
cursed me because I could not laugh. And the lynx which
dwelleth for ever in the tomb came out therefrom, and lay
down at the feet of the Demon, and looked at him steadily
in the face.

HOP-FROG

I NEVER knew any one so keenly alive to a joke as the king
was. He seemed to live only for joking. To tell a good
story of the joke kind, and to tell it well, was the surest road
to his favour. Thus it happened that his seven ministers
were all noted for their accomplishments as jokers. They
all took after the king, too, in being large, corpulent, oily
men, as well as inimitable jokers. Whether people grow
fat by joking, or whether there is something in fat itself
which predisposes to a joke, I have never been quite able
to determine ; but certain it is that a lean joker is a *rara
avis in terris.*

About the refinements, or, as he called them, the
" ghosts " of wit, the king troubled himself very little.
He had an especial admiration for *breadth* in a jest, and
would often put up with *length*, for the sake of it. Over-

P*

niceties wearied him. He would have preferred Rabelais's *Gargantua* to the *Zadig* of Voltaire : and, upon the whole practical jokes suited his taste far better than verbal ones

At the date of my narrative, professing jesters had not altogether gone out of fashion at court. Several of the great continental " powers " still retained their "fools,' who wore motley, with caps and bells, and who were expected to be always ready with sharp witticisms, at a moment's notice, in consideration of the crumbs that fell from the royal table.

Our king, as a matter of course, retained his " fool." The fact is, he *required* something in the way of folly—if only to counterbalance the heavy wisdom of the seven wise men who were his ministers—not to mention himself.

His fool, or professional jester, was not *only* a fool, however. His value was trebled in the eyes of the king by the fact of his being also a dwarf and a cripple. Dwarfs were as common at court, in those days, as fools ; and many monarchs would have found it difficult to get through their days (days are rather longer at court than elsewhere) without both a jester to laugh *with*, and a dwarf to laugh *at*. But, as I have already observed, your jesters, in ninety-nine cases out of a hundred, are fat, round, and unwieldy— so that it was no small source of self-gratulation with our king that, in Hop-Frog (this was the fool's name) he possessed a triplicate treasure in one person.

I believe the name " Hop-Frog " was *not* that given to the dwarf by his sponsors at baptism, but it was conferred upon him, by general consent of the seven ministers, on account of his inability to walk as other men do. In fact, Hop-Frog could only get along by a sort of interjectional gait—something between a leap and a wriggle—a movement that afforded illimitable amusement, and of course consolation, to the king, for (notwithstanding the protuberance of his stomach and a constitutional swelling of the head) the king, by his whole court, was accounted a capital figure.

But although Hop-Frog, through the distortion of his legs, could move only with great pain and difficulty along a road or floor, the prodigious muscular power which nature seemed to have bestowed upon his arms, by way of compensation for deficiency in the lower limbs, enabled him to perform many feats of wonderful dexterity, where trees

or ropes were in question, or anything else to climb. At
such exercises he certainly much more resembled a squirrel,
or a small monkey, than a frog.

I am not able to say, with precision, from what country
Hop-Frog originally came. It was from some barbarous
region, however, that no person ever heard of—a vast
distance from the court of our king. Hop-Frog, and a
young girl very little less dwarfish than himself (although
of exquisite proportions, and a marvellous dancer), had
been forcibly carried off from their respective homes in
adjoining provinces, and sent as presents to the king, by
one of his ever-victorious generals.

Under these circumstances, it is not to be wondered at
that a close intimacy arose between the two little captives.
Indeed, they soon became sworn friends. Hop-Frog, who,
although he made a great deal of sport, was by no means
popular, had it not in his power to render Trippetta many
services ; but *she*, on account of her grace and exquisite
beauty (although a dwarf), was universally admired and
petted : so she possessed much influence ; and never failed
to use it, whenever she could, for the benefit of Hop-Frog.

On some grand state occasion—I forget what—the king
determined to have a masquerade ; and whenever a
masquerade, or anything of that kind, occurred at our
court, then the talents both of Hop-Frog and Trippetta
were sure to be called in play. Hop-Frog, in especial, was
so inventive in the way of getting up pageants, suggesting
novel characters and arranging costumes for masked
balls, that nothing could be done, it seems, without his
assistance.

The night appointed for the *fête* had arrived. A gorgeous hall had been fitted up, under Trippetta's eye, with
every kind of device which could possibly give *éclat* to a
masquerade. The whole court was in a fever of expectation. As for costumes and characters, it might well be
supposed that everybody had come to a decision on such
points. Many had made up their minds as to what *rôles*
they should assume, a week, or even a month, in advance ;
and, in fact, there was not a particle of indecision anywhere
—except in the case of the king and his seven ministers.
Why *they* hesitated I never could tell, unless they did it
by way of a joke. More probably, they found it difficult,
on account of being so fat, to make up their minds. At

all events, time flew ; and, as a last resource, they sent for Trippetta and Hop-Frog.

When the two little friends obeyed the summons of the king, they found him sitting at his wine with the seven members of his cabinet council ; but the monarch appeared to be in a very ill-humour. He knew that Hop-Frog was not fond of wine ; for it excited the poor cripple almost to madness ; and madness is no comfortable feeling. But the king loved his practical jokes, and took pleasure in forcing Hop-Frog to drink and (as the king called it) " to be merry."

" Come here, Hop-Frog," said he, as the jester and his friend entered the room : " swallow this bumper to the health of your absent friends " (here Hop-Frog sighed), " and then let us have the benefit of your invention. We want characters—*characters*, man—something novel—out of the way. We are wearied with this everlasting sameness. Come, drink ! the wine will brighten your wits."

Hop-Frog endeavoured, as usual, to get up a jest in reply to these advances from the king ; but the effort was too much. It happened to be the poor dwarf's birthday, and the command to drink to his " absent friends " forced the tears to his eyes. Many large, bitter drops fell into the goblet as he took it, humbly, from the hand of the tyrant.

" Ah ! ha ! ha ! ha ! " roared the latter, as the dwarf reluctantly drained the beaker. " See what a glass of good wine can do ! Why, your eyes are shining already ! "

Poor fellow ! his large eyes *gleamed* rather than shone, for the effect of wine on his excitable brain was not more powerful than instantaneous. He placed the goblet nervously on the table, and looked round upon the company with a half-insane stare. They all seemed highly amused at the success of the king's " *joke*."

" And now to business," said the prime minister, a *very* fat man.

" Yes," said the king; " come, Hop-Frog, lend us your assistance. Characters, my fine fellow ; we stand in need of characters—all of us—ha ! ha ! ha ! " and as this was seriously meant for a joke, his laugh was chorused by the seven.

Hop-Frog also laughed, although feebly and somewhat vacantly.

" Come, come," said the king, impatiently, " have you nothing to suggest ? "

" I am endeavouring to think of something *novel*," replied the dwarf, abstractedly, for he was quite bewildered by the wine.

" Endeavouring ! " cried the tyrant, fiercely ; " what do you mean by *that* ? Ah, I perceive. You are sulky, and want more wine. Here, drink this ! " and he poured out another gobletful and offered it to the cripple, who merely gazed at it, gasping for breath.

" Drink, I say ! " shouted the monster, " or by the fiends——"

The dwarf hesitated. The king grew purple with rage. The courtiers smirked. Trippetta, pale as a corpse, advanced to the monarch's seat, and, falling on her knees before him, implored him to spare her friend.

The tyrant regarded her, for some moments, in evident wonder at her audacity. He seemed quite at a loss what to do or say—how most becomingly to express his indignation. At last, without uttering a syllable, he pushed her violently from him, and threw the contents of the brimming goblet in her face.

The poor girl got up as best she could, and, not daring even to sigh, resumed her position at the foot of the table.

There was a dead silence for about half a minute, during which the falling of a leaf, or of a feather, might have been heard. It was interrupted by a low, but harsh and protracted *grating* sound which seemed to come at once from every corner of the room.

" What—what—*what* are you making that noise for ? " demanded the king, turning furiously to the dwarf.

The latter seemed to have recovered, in great measure, from his intoxication, and looked fixedly but quietly into the tyrant's face, merely ejaculated :

" I—I ? How could it have been me ? "

" The sound appeared to come from without," observed one of the courtiers. " I fancy it was the parrot at the window, whetting his bill upon his cage-wires."

" True," replied the monarch, as if much relieved by the suggestion ; " but, on the honour of a knight, I could have sworn that it was the gritting of this vagabond's teeth."

Hereupon the dwarf laughed (the king was too con-

firmed a joker to object to any one's laughing), and displayed
a set of large, powerful, and very repulsive teeth. Moreover, he avowed his perfect willingness to swallow as
much wine as desired. The monarch was pacified ; and
having drained another bumper with no very perceptible
ill effect, Hop-Frog entered at once, and with spirit, into
the plans for the masquerade.

"I cannot tell what was the association of idea," observed he, very tranquilly, and as if he had never tasted
wine in his life, "but *just after* your majesty had struck
the girl and thrown the wine in her face—*just after* your
majesty had done this, and while the parrot was making that
odd noise outside the window, there came into my mind
a capital diversion—one of my own country frolics—
often enacted among us, at our masquerades : but here
it will be new altogether. Unfortunately, however, it
requires a company of eight persons, and——"

"Here we *are* ! " cried the king, laughing at his acute
discovery of the coincidence ; "eight to a fraction—
I and my seven ministers. Come ! what is the
diversion ! "

"We call it," replied the cripple, "the Eight Chained
Ourang-Outangs, and it really is excellent sport if well
enacted."

"*We* will enact it," remarked the king, drawing himself
up, and lowering his eyelids.

"The beauty of the game," continued Hop-Frog, "lies
in the fright it occasions among the women."

"Capital ! " roared in chorus the monarch and his
ministry.

"*I* will equip you as ourang-outangs," proceeded the
dwarf ; "leave all that to me. The resemblance shall
be so striking that the company of masqueraders will
take you for real beasts—and, of course, they will be as
much terrified as astonished."

"Oh, this is exquisite ! " exclaimed the king. "Hop-
Frog ! I will make a man of you."

"The chains are for the purpose of increasing the confusion by their jangling. You are supposed to have
escaped, *en masse,* from your keepers. Your majesty
cannot conceive the *effect* produced, at a masquerade, by
eight chained ourang-outangs, imagined to be real ones
by most of the company, and rushing in with savage

cries among the crowd of delicately and gorgeously habited men and women. The *contrast* is inimitable."

" It *must* be," said the king : and the council arose hurriedly (as it was growing late), to put in execution the scheme of Hop-Frog.

His mode of equipping the party as ourang-outangs was very simple, but effective enough for his purposes. The animals in question had, at the epoch of my story, very rarely been seen in any part of the civilised world ; and as the imitations made by the dwarf were sufficiently beast-like and more than sufficiently hideous, their truth-fulness to nature was thus thought to be secured.

The king and his ministers were first encased in tight-fitting stockinette shirts and drawers. They were then saturated with tar. At this stage of the process, some one of the party suggested feathers ; but the suggestion was at once overruled by the dwarf, who soon convinced the eight, by ocular demonstration, that the hair of such a brute as the ourang-outang was much more efficiently represented by *flax*. A thick coating of the latter was accordingly plastered upon the coating of tar. A long chain was now procured. First, it was passed about the waist of the king, *and tied* ; then about another of the party, and also tied ; then about all successively, in the same manner. When this chaining arrangement was complete, and the party stood as far apart from each other as possible, they formed a circle ; and to make all things appear natural, Hop-Frog passed the residue of the chain, in two diameters, at right angles, across the circle, after the fashion adopted, at the present day, by those who capture Chimpanzees, or other large apes, in Borneo.

The grand saloon in which the masquerade was to take place, was a circular room, very lofty, and receiving the light of the sun only through a single window at top. At night (the season for which the apartment was especially designed), it was illuminated principally by a large chandelier, depending by a chain from the centre of the sky-light, and lowered, or elevated, by means of a counter-balance as usual ; but (in order not to look unsightly) this latter passed outside the cupola and over the roof.

The arrangements of the room had been left to Trippetta's superintendence ; but, in some particulars, it seems, she

had been guided by the calmer judgment of her friend
the dwarf. At his suggestion it was that, on this occasion,
the chandelier was removed. Its waxen drippings (which,
in weather so warm, it was quite impossible to prevent)
would have been seriously detrimental to the rich dresses
of the guests, who, on account of the crowded state of the
saloon, could not *all* be expected to keep from out its centre
—that is to say, from under the chandelier. Additional
sconces were set in various parts of the hall, out of the
way ; and a flambeau, emitting sweet odour, was placed
in the right hand of each of the Caryatides that stood
against the wall—some fifty or sixty altogether.

The eight ourang-outangs, taking Hop-Frog's advice,
waited patiently until midnight (when the room was
thoroughly filled with masqueraders) before making their
appearance. No sooner had the clock ceased striking,
however, than they rushed, or rather rolled in, all together
—for the impediment of their chains caused most of the
party to fall, and all to stumble as they entered.

The excitement among the masqueraders was prodigious,
and filled the heart of the king with glee. As had been
anticipated, there were not a few of the guests who supposed the ferocious-looking creatures to be beasts of
some kind in reality, if not precisely ourang-outangs.
Many of the women swooned with affright ; and had not
the king taken the precaution to exclude all weapons
from the saloon, his party might soon have expiated their
frolic in their blood. As it was, a general rush was made
for the doors ; but the king had ordered them to be locked
immediately upon his entrance ; and, at the dwarf's
suggestion, the keys had been deposited with *him.*

While the tumult was at its height, and each masquerader
attentive only to his own safety (for, in fact, there was
much *real* danger from the pressure of the excited crowd),
the chain by which the chandelier ordinarily hung, and
which had been drawn up on its removal, might have been
seen very gradually to descend, until its hooked extremity
came within three feet of the floor.

Soon after this, the king and his seven friends, having
reeled about the hall in all directions, found themselves, at
length, in its centre, and, of course, in immediate contact
with the chain. While they were thus situated, the dwarf,
who had followed closely at their heels, inciting them to

keep up the commotion, took hold of their own chain at
the intersection of the two portions which crossed the
circle diametrically and at right angles. Here, with the
rapidity of thought, he inserted the hook from which the
chandelier had been wont to depend ; and, in an instant,
by some unseen agency, the chandelier-chain was drawn
so far upward as to take the hook out of reach, and, as an
inevitable consequence, to drag the ourang-outangs together
in close connection, and face to face.

The masqueraders, by this time, had recovered, in some
measure, from their alarm ; and, beginning to regard the
whole matter as a well-contrived pleasantry, set up a loud
shout of laughter at the predicament of the apes.

" Leave them to *me* ! " now screamed Hop-Frog, his
shrill voice making itself easily heard through all the din.
" Leave them to *me*. I fancy *I* know them. If I can only
get a good look at them, *I* can soon tell who they are."

Here, scrambling over the heads of the crowd, he managed
to get to the wall ; when, seizing a flambeau from one of
the Caryatides, he returned, as he went, to the centre of
the room—leaped, with the agility of a monkey, upon the
king's head—and thence clambered a few feet up the chain
—holding down the torch to examine the group of ourang-
outangs, and still screaming, " *I* shall soon find out who
they are ! "

And now, while the whole assembly (the apes included)
were convulsed with laughter, the jester suddenly uttered
a shrill whistle ; when the chain flew violently up for about
thirty feet—dragging with it the dismayed and struggling
ourang-outangs, and leaving them suspended in mid-air
between the sky-light and the floor. Hop-Frog, clinging
to the chain as it rose, still maintained his relative position
in respect to the eight maskers, and still (as if nothing
were the matter) continued to thrust his torch down
towards them, as though endeavouring to discover who
they were.

So thoroughly astonished were the whole company
at this ascent, that a dead silence, of about a minute's
duration, ensued. It was broken by just such a low,
harsh, *grating* sound, as had before attracted the attention
of the king and his councillors, when the former threw
the wine in the face of Trippetta. But, on the present
occasion, there could be no question as to *whence* the

sound issued. It came from the fang-like teeth of the dwarf, who ground them and gnashed them as he foamed at the mouth, and glared, with an expression of maniacal rage, into the upturned countenances of the king and his seven companions.

"Ah, ha!" said at length the infuriated jester. "Ah, ha! I begin to see who these people *are*, now!" Here, pretending to scrutinise the king more closely, he held the flambeau to the flaxen coat which enveloped him, and which instantly burst into a sheet of vivid flame. In less than half a minute the whole eight ourang-outangs were blazing fiercely, amid the shrieks of the multitude who gazed at them from below, horror-stricken, and without the power to render them the slightest assistance.

At length the flames, suddenly increasing in virulence, forced the jester to climb higher up the chain, to be out of their reach; and, as he made this movement, the crowd again sank, for a brief instant, into silence. The dwarf seized his opportunity, and once more spoke:

"I now see *distinctly*," he said, "what manner of people these maskers are. They are a great king and his seven privy-councillors—a king who does not scruple to strike a defenceless girl, and his seven councillors who abet him in the outrage. As for myself, I am simply Hop-Frog, the jester—and *this is my last jest*."

Owing to the high combustibility of both the flax and the tar to which it adhered, the dwarf had scarcely made an end of his brief speech before the work of vengeance was complete. The eight corpses swung in their chains, a fetid, blackened, hideous, and indistinguishable mass. The cripple hurled his torch at them, clambered leisurely to the ceiling, and disappeared through the sky-light.

It is supposed that Trippetta, stationed on the roof of the saloon, had been the accomplice of her friend in his fiery revenge, and that, together, they effected their escape to their own country: for neither was seen again.

THE MAN OF THE CROWD

" Ce grand malheur, de ne pouvoir être seul."—LA BRUYÈRE.

IT was well said of a certain German book that *" es lässt
sich nicht lesen "*—it does not permit itself to be read.
There are some secrets which do not permit themselves
to be told. Men die nightly in their beds, wringing the
hands of ghostly confessors, and looking them piteously
in the eyes—die with despair of heart and convulsion of
throat, on account of the hideousness of mysteries which
will not *suffer themselves* to be revealed. Now and then,
alas, the conscience of man takes up a burden so heavy
in horror that it can be thrown down only into the grave.
And thus the essence of all crime is undivulged.

Not long ago, about the closing in of an evening in
autumn, I sat at the large bow window of the D—— Coffee-
House in London. For some months I had been ill in
health, but was now convalescent, and, with returning
strength, found myself in one of those happy moods which
are so precisely the converse of *ennui*—moods of the
keenest appetency, when the film from the mental vision
departs—the αχλυς ος πριν επηεν—and the intellect, electri-
fied, surpasses as greatly its every-day condition, as does the
vivid yet candid reason of Leibnitz, the mad and flimsy
rhetoric of Gorgias. Merely to breathe was enjoyment,
and I derived positive pleasure even from many of the
legitimate sources of pain. I felt a calm but inquisitive
interest in everything. With a cigar in my mouth and a
newspaper in my lap, I had been amusing myself for the
greater part of the afternoon, now in poring over advertise-
ments, now in observing the promiscuous company in the
room, and now in peering through the smoky panes into
the street.

This latter is one of the principal thoroughfares of the
city, and had been very much crowded during the whole
day. But, as the darkness came on, the throng momently
increased ; and, by the time the lamps were well lighted,
two dense and continuous tides of population were rushing
past the door. At this particular period of the evening
I had never before been in a similar situation, and the

tumultuous sea of human heads filled me, therefore, with a delicious novelty of emotion. I gave up, at length, all care of things within the hotel, and became absorbed in contemplation of the scene without.

At first my observations took an abstract and generalising turn. I looked at the passengers in masses, and thought of them in their aggregate relations. Soon, however, I descended to details, and regarded with minute interest the innumerable varieties of figure, dress, air, gait, visage, and expression of countenance.

By far the greater number of those who went by had a satisfied business-like demeanour, and seemed to be thinking only of making their way through the press. Their brows were knit, and their eyes rolled quickly ; when pushed against by fellow-wayfarers they evinced no symptom of impatience, but adjusted their clothes and hurried on. Others, still a numerous class, were restless in their movements, had flushed faces, and talked and gesticulated to themselves, as if feeling in solitude on account of the very denseness of the company around. When impeded in their progress, these people suddenly ceased muttering, but redoubled their gesticulations, and awaited, with an absent and overdone smile upon their lips, the course of the persons impeding them. If jostled, they bowed profusely to the jostlers, and appeared overwhelmed with confusion. There was nothing very distinctive about these two large classes beyond what I have noted. Their habiliments belonged to that order which is pointedly termed the decent. They were undoubtedly noblemen, merchants, attorneys, tradesmen, stock-jobbers —the Eupatrids and the commonplaces of society—men of leisure and men actively engaged in affairs of their own—conducting business upon their own responsibility. They did not greatly excite my attention.

The tribe of clerks was an obvious one ; and here I discerned two remarkable divisions. There were the junior clerks of flash houses—young gentlemen with tight coats, bright boots, well-oiled hair, and supercilious lips. Setting aside a certain dapperness of carriage, which may be termed *deskism* for want of a better word, the manner of these persons seemed to me an exact facsimile of what had been the perfection of *bon ton* about twelve or eighteen months before. They wore the cast-off graces of the gentry—and this, I believe, involves the best definition of the class.

The division of the upper clerks of staunch firms, or of the " steady old fellows," it was not possible to mistake. These were known by their coats and pantaloons of black or brown, made to sit comfortably, with white cravats and waistcoats, broad, solid-looking shoes, and thick hose or gaiters. They had all slightly bald heads, from which the right ears, long used to penholding, had an odd habit of standing off on end. I observed that they always removed or settled their hats with both hands, and wore watches, with short gold chains of a substantial and ancient pattern. Theirs was the affectation of respectability ; if indeed there be an affectation so honourable.

There were many individuals of dashing appearance, whom I easily understood as belonging to the race of swell pick-pockets, with which all great cities are infested. I watched these gentry with much inquisitiveness, and found it difficult to imagine how they should ever be mistaken for gentlemen by gentlemen themselves. Their voluminousness of wristband, with an air of excessive frankness, should betray them at once.

The gamblers, of whom I descried not a few, were still more easily recognisable. They wore every variety of dress, from that of the desperate thimblerig bully, with velvet waistcoat, fancy neckerchief, gilt chains, and filigreed buttons, to that of the scrupulously inornate clergyman, than which nothing could be less liable to suspicion. Still all were distinguished by a certain sodden swarthiness of complexion, a filmy dimness of eye, and pallor and compression of lip. There were two other traits, moreover, by which I could always detect them—a guarded lowness of tone in conversation, and a more than ordinary extension of the thumb in a direction at right angles with the fingers. Very often, in company with these sharpers, I observed an order of men somewhat different in habits, but still birds of a kindred feather. They may be defined as the gentlemen who live by their wits. They seem to prey upon the public in two battalions —that of the dandies and that of the military men. Of the first grade the leading features are long locks and smiles ; of the second frogged coats and frowns.

Descending in the scale of what is termed gentility,

I found darker and deeper themes for speculation. I saw Jew pedlars, with hawk eyes flashing from countenances whose every other feature wore only an expression of abject humility; sturdy professional street beggars scowling upon mendicants of a better stamp, whom despair alone had driven forth into the night for charity; feeble and ghastly invalids, upon whom death had placed a sure hand, and who sidled and tottered through the mob, looking every one beseechingly in the face, as if in search of some chance consolation, some lost hope; modest young girls returning from long and late labour to a cheerless home, and shrinking more tearfully than indignantly from the glances of ruffians, whose direct contact, even, could not be avoided; women of the town of all kinds and of all ages—the unequivocal beauty in the prime of her womanhood, putting one in mind of the statue in Lucian, with the surface of Parian marble, and the interior filled with filth—the loathsome and utterly lost leper in rags— the wrinkled, bejewelled and paint-begrimed beldame, making a last effort at youth—the mere child of immature form, yet, from long association, an adept in the dreadful coquetries of her trade, and burning with a rabid ambition to be ranked the equal of her elders in vice; drunkards innumerable and indescribable—some in shreds and patches, reeling, inarticulate, with bruised visage and lacklustre eyes—some in whole although filthy garments, with a slightly unsteady swagger, thick sensual lips, and heartylooking rubicund faces—others clothed in materials which had once been good, and which even now were scrupulously well brushed—men who walked with a more than naturally firm and springy step, but whose countenances were fearfully pale, whose eyes were hideously wild and red, and who clutched with quivering fingers, as they strode through the crowd, at every object which came within their reach; beside these, pie-men, porters, coal-heavers, sweeps; organ-grinders, monkey-exhibitors, and ballad-mongers, those who vended with those who sang; ragged artisans and exhausted labourers of every description, and all full of a noisy and inordinate vivacity which jarred discordantly upon the ear, and gave an aching sensation to the eye.

As the night deepened, so deepened to me the interest of the scene; for not only did the general character of the crowd materially alter (its gentler features retiring in the gradual withdrawal of the more orderly portion of the people, and its harsher ones coming out into bolder relief, as the late hour brought forth every species of infamy from its den), but the rays of the gas-lamps, feeble at first in their struggle with the dying day, had now at length gained ascendency, and threw over everything a fitful and garish lustre. All was dark yet splendid—as that ebony to which has been likened the style of Tertullian.

The wild effects of the light enchained me to an examination of individual faces ; and although the rapidity with which the world of light flitted before the window, prevented me from casting more than a glance upon each visage, still it seemed that, in my then peculiar mental state, I could frequently read, even in that brief interval of a glance, the history of long years.

With my brow to the glass, I was thus occupied in scrutinising the mob, when suddenly there came into view a countenance (that of a decrepit old man, some sixty-five or seventy years of age)—a countenance which at once arrested and absorbed my whole attention, on account of the absolute idiosyncrasy of its expression. Anything even remotely resembling that expression I had never seen before. I well remember that my first thought, upon beholding it, was that Retzch, had he viewed it, would have greatly preferred it to his own pictorial incarnations of the fiend. As I endeavoured, during the brief minute of my original survey, to form some analysis of the meaning conveyed, there arose confusedly and paradoxically within my mind, the ideas of vast mental power, of caution, of penuriousness, of avarice, of coolness, of malice, of blood-thirstiness, of triumph, of merriment, of excessive terror, of intense—of supreme despair. I felt singularly aroused, startled, fascinated. "How wild a history," I said to myself, "is written within that bosom ! " Then came a craving desire to keep the man in view—to know more of him. Hurriedly putting on an overcoat, and seizing my hat and cane, I made my way into the street, and pushed through the crowd in the direction which I had seen him take ; for he had already disappeared. With some little difficulty I at length came within sight of him, approached, and followed him closely, yet cautiously, so as not to attract his attention.

I had now a good opportunity of examining his person.

He was short in stature, very thin, and apparently very feeble. His clothes, generally, were filthy and ragged; but as he came, now and then, within the strong glare of a lamp, I perceived that his linen, although dirty, was of beautiful texture; and my vision deceived me, or, through a rent in a closely-buttoned and evidently second-hand *roquelaure* which enveloped him, I caught a glimpse both of a diamond and of a dagger. These observations heightened my curiosity, and I resolved to follow the stranger whithersoever he should go.

It was now fully nightfall, and a thick humid fog hung over the city, soon ending in a settled and heavy rain. This change of weather had an odd effect upon the crowd, the whole of which was at once put into new commotion, and overshadowed by a world of umbrellas. The waver, the jostle, and the hum increased in a tenfold degree. For my own part I did not much regard the rain—the lurking of an old fever in my system rendering the moisture somewhat too dangerously pleasant. Tying a handkerchief about my mouth, I kept on. For half-an-hour the old man held his way with difficulty along the great thoroughfare; and I here walked close at his elbow through fear of losing sight of him. Never once turning his head to look back, he did not observe me. By-and-by he passed into a cross street, which, although densely filled with people, was not quite so much thronged as the main one he had quitted. Here a change in his demeanour became evident. He walked more slowly, and with less object than before— more hesitatingly. He crossed and recrossed the way repeatedly, without apparent aim; and the press was still so thick that, at every such movement, I was obliged to follow him closely. The street was a narrow and long one, and his course lay within it for nearly an hour, during which the passengers had gradually diminished to about that number which is ordinarily seen at noon in Broadway near the park—so vast a difference is there between a London populace and that of the most frequented American city. A second turn brought us into a square, brilliantly lighted, and overflowing with life. The old manner of the stranger reappeared. His chin fell upon his breast, while his eyes rolled wildly from under his knit brows, in every direction, upon those who hemmed him in. He urged his way steadily and perseveringly. I was surprised, however, to find, upon his having made the circuit of the square, that he turned and retraced his steps. Still more was I astonished to see him repeat the same walk several times —once nearly detecting me as he came round with a sudden movement.

In this exercise he spent another hour, at the end of which we met with far less interruption from passengers than at first. The rain fell fast ; the air grew cool ; and the people were retiring to their homes. With a gesture of impatience, the wanderer passed into a by-street comparatively deserted. Down this, some quarter of a mile long, he rushed with an activity I could not have dreamed of seeing in one so aged, and which put me to much trouble in pursuit. A few minutes brought us to a large and busy bazaar, with the localities of which the stranger appeared well acquainted, and where his original demeanour again became apparent, as he forced his way to and fro, without aim, among the host of buyers and sellers.

During the hour and a half, or thereabouts, which we passed in this place, it required much caution on my part to keep him within reach without attracting his observation. Luckily I wore a pair of caoutchouc over-shoes, and could move about in perfect silence. At no moment did he see that I watched him. He entered shop after shop, priced nothing, spoke no word, and looked at all objects with a wild and vacant stare. I was now utterly amazed at his behaviour, and firmly resolved that we should not part until I had satisfied myself in some measure respecting him.

A loud-toned clock struck eleven, and the company were fast deserting the bazaar. A shopkeeper, in putting up a shutter, jostled the old man, and at the instant I saw a strong shudder come over his frame. He hurried into the street, looked anxiously around him for an instant, and then ran with incredible swiftness through many crooked and peopleless lanes, until we emerged once more upon the great thoroughfare whence we had started—the street of the D—— Hotel. It no longer wore, however, the same aspect. It was still brilliant with gas ; but the rain fell fiercely, and there were few persons to be seen. The stranger grew pale. He walked moodily some paces up the once populous avenue, then, with a heavy sigh, turned in the direction of the river, and, plunging through a great variety of devious ways, came out, at length, in view of one of the principal theatres. It was about being closed, and the audience were thronging from the doors. I saw the old man gasp as if for breath while he threw himself amid the crowd ; but I thought that the intense agony of his countenance had in some measure abated. His head again fell upon his breast ; he appeared as I had seen him at first. I observed that he now took the course in which had gone the greater number of the audience ; but, upon the whole, I was at a loss to comprehend the way-wardness of his actions.

As he proceeded, the company grew more scattered, and his old uneasiness and vacillation were resumed. For some time he followed closely a party of some ten or twelve roisterers ; but from this number one by one dropped off, until three only remained together, in a narrow and gloomy lane little frequented. The stranger paused, and, for a moment, seemed lost in thought ; then, with every mark of agitation, pursued rapidly a route which brought us to the verge of the city, amid regions very different from those we had hitherto traversed. It was the most noisome quarter of London, where everything wore the worst impress of the most deplorable poverty, and of the most desperate crime. By the dim light of an accidental lamp, tall, antique, worm-eaten, wooden tene-ments were seen tottering to their fall, in directions so many and capricious, that scarce the semblance of a passage was discernible between them. The paving-stones lay at random, displaced from their beds by the rankly-growing grass. Horrible filth festered in the dammed-up gutters. The whole atmosphere teemed with desolation. Yet, as we proceeded, the sounds of human life revived by sure degrees, and at length large bands of the most aban-doned of a London populace were seen reeling to and fro. The spirits of the old man again flickered up, as a lamp which is near its death-hour. Once more he strode onward with elastic tread. Suddenly a corner was turned, a blaze of light burst upon our sight, and we stood before one of the huge suburban temples of Intemperance—one of the palaces of the fiend, Gin.

It was now nearly daybreak ; but a number of wretched inebriates still pressed in and out of the flaunting entrance. With a half shriek of joy the old man forced a passage

ithin, resumed at once his original bearing, and stalked
ackward and forward, without apparent object, among
ıe throng.   He had not been thus long occupied, however,
efore a rush to the doors gave token that the host was
osing them for the night.   It was something even more
ıtense than despair that I then observed upon the coun-
•nance of the singular being whom I had watched so
ertinaciously.   Yet he did not hesitate in his career, but,
ith a mad energy, retraced his steps at once, to the heart
' the mighty London.   Long and swiftly he fled, while
followed him in the wildest amazement, resolute not to
)andon a scrutiny in which I now felt an interest all-
)sorbing.   The sun arose while we proceeded, and, when
e had once again reached that most thronged mart of
ıe populous town, the street of the D—— Hotel, it pre-
•nted an appearance of human bustle and activity scarcely
_ferior to what I had seen on the evening before.   And
ere, long, amid the momently increasing confusion, did I
•rsist in my pursuit of the stranger.   But, as usual, he
alked to and fro, and during the day did not pass from
ıt the turmoil of that street.   And, as the shades of the
cond evening came on, I grew wearied unto death, and,
opping fully in front of the wanderer, gazed at him
eadfastly in the face.   He noticed me not, but resumed
s solemn walk, while I, ceasing to follow, remained
)sorbed in contemplation.   " This old man," I said at
ngth, " is the type and the genius of deep crime.   He
fuses to be alone.   *He is the man of the crowd.*   It will
: in vain to follow ; for I shall learn no more of him, nor
his deeds.   The worst heart of the world is a grosser
•ok than the *Hortulus Animæ* ; and perhaps it is but
ıe of the great mercies of God that ' *es lässt sich nicht
sen.*' "

A TALE OF THE RAGGED MOUNTAIN

DURING the fall of the year 1827, while residing ne
Charlottesville, Virginia, I casually made the acquaintan
of Mr. Augustus Bedloe. This young gentleman w
remarkable in every respect, and excited in me a profoun
interest and curiosity. I found it impossible to compr
hend him either in his moral or his physical relations. (
his family I could obtain no satisfactory account. When
he came, I never ascertained. Even about his age—
although I call him a young gentleman—there was som
thing which perplexed me in no little degree. He certain
seemed young—and he made a point of speaking about h
youth—yet there were moments when I should have ha
little trouble in imagining him a hundred years of ag
But in no regard was he more peculiar than in his person
appearance. He was singularly tall and thin. He stoop
much. His limbs were exceedingly long and emaciate
His forehead was broad and low. His complexion w
absolutely bloodless. His mouth was large and flexibl
and his teeth were more wildly uneven, although soun
than I had ever before seen teeth in a human head. T
expression of his smile, however, was by no means u
pleasing, as might be supposed ; but it had no variati
whatever. It was one of profound melancholy—of
phaseless and unceasing gloom. His eyes were abnorma
large, and round like those of a cat. The pupils, too, up
any accession or diminution of light, underwent contracti
or dilation, just such as is observed in the feline tribe.
moments of excitement the orbs grew bright to a degr
almost inconceivable ; seeming to emit luminous rays, n
of a reflected but of an intrinsic lustre, as does a cand
or the sun ; yet their ordinary condition was so total
vapid, filmy, and dull, as to convey the idea of the eyes
a long-interred corpse.

These peculiarities of person appeared to cause him mu
annoyance, and he was continually alluding to them in
sort of half explanatory, half apologetic strain, whic
when I first heard it, impressed me very painfully.
soon, however, grew accustomed to it, and my uneasine
wore off. It seemed to be his design rather to insinua

han directly to assert that, physically, he had not always
een what he was—that a long series of neuralgic attacks
ad reduced him from a condition of more than usual
ersonal beauty, to that which I saw.   For many years
ast he had been attended by a physician, named Templeton
—an old gentleman, perhaps seventy years of age—whom
e had first encountered at Saratoga, and from whose
ttention, while there, he either received, or fancied that
e received, great benefit.   The result was that Bedloe,
ho was wealthy, had made an arrangement with Dr.
'empleton, by which the latter, in consideration of a
beral annual allowance, had consented to devote his time
nd medical experience exclusively to the care of the
ivalid.

Doctor Templeton had been a traveller in his younger
ays, and at Paris had become a convert, in great measure,
ɔ the doctrine of Mesmer.   It was altogether by means of
iagnetic remedies that he had succeeded in alleviating
ie acute pains of his patient ; and this success had very
aturally inspired the latter with a certain degree of confi-
ence in the opinions from which the remedies had been
duced.   The doctor, however, like all enthusiasts, had
truggled hard to make a thorough convert of his pupil,
ad finally so far gained his point as to induce the sufferer
ɔ submit to numerous experiments.   By a frequent
epetition of these, a result had arisen, which of late days
as become so common as to attract little or no attention,
ut which, at the period of which I write, had very rarely
een known in America.   I mean to say, that between
·r. Templeton and Bedloe there had grown up, little by
ttle, a very distinct and strongly-marked *rapport*, or
iagnetic relation.   I am not prepared to assert, however,
iat this *rapport* extended beyond the limits of the simple
eep-producing power ; but this power itself had attained
·eat intensity.   At the first attempt to induce the mag-
etic somnolency, the mesmerist entirely failed.   In the
fth or sixth he succeeded very partially, and after long-
ɔntinued effort.   Only at the twelfth was the triumph
ɔmplete.   After this the will of the patient succumbed
ipidly to that of the physician, so that, when I first became
cquainted with the two, sleep was brought about almost
istantaneously by the mere volition of the operator, even
hen the invalid was unaware of his presence.   It is only

now, in the year 1845, when similar miracles are witnesse
daily by thousands, that I dare venture to record th
apparent impossibility as a matter of serious fact.

The temperament of Bedloe was in the highest degre
sensitive, excitable, enthusiastic. His imagination wa
singularly vigorous and creative ; and no doubt it derive
additional force from the habitual use of morphine, whic
he swallowed in great quantity, and without which he woul
have found it impossible to exist. It was his practice t
take a very large dose of it immediately after breakfa
each morning,—or, rather, immediately after a cup
strong coffee, for he ate nothing in the forenoon,—and the
set forth alone, or attended only by a dog, upon a lor
ramble among the chain of wild and dreary hi
that lie westward and southward of Charlottesvill
and are there dignified by the title of the Ragge
Mountains.

Upon a dim, warm, misty day, toward the close
November, and during the strange *interregnum* of t
seasons which in America is termed the Indian summe
Mr. Bedloe departed as usual for the hills. The da
passed, and still he did not return.

About eight o'clock at night, having become serious
alarmed at his protracted absence, we were about setti
out in search of him, when he unexpectedly made h
appearance, in health no worse than usual, and in rath
more than ordinary spirits. The account which he gave
his expedition, and of the events which had detained hi
was a singular one indeed.

" You will remember," said he, " that it was about ni
in the morning when I left Charlottesville. I bent n
steps immediately to the mountains, and, about ten, enter
a gorge which was entirely new to me. I followed t
windings of this pass with much interest. The scene
which presented itself on all sides, although scarce
entitled to be called grand, had about it an indescriba
and to me a delicious aspect of dreary desolation. T
solitude seemed absolutely virgin. I could not h
believing that the green sods and the grey rocks upon whi
I trod had been trodden never before by the foot of a hum
being. So entirely secluded, and in fact inaccessib
except through a series of accidents, is the entrance of t
ravine, that it is by no means impossible that 1 was the fi

venturer—the very first and sole adventurer who had
er penetrated its recesses.

" The thick and peculiar mist, or smoke, which distin-
ishes the Indian summer, and which now hung heavily
er all objects, served, no doubt, to deepen the vague
pressions which these objects created. So dense was
is pleasant fog that I could at no time see more than a
zen yards of the path before me. This path was exces-
ely sinuous, and as the sun could not be seen, I soon
t all idea of the direction in which I journeyed. In the
eantime the morphine had its customary effect—that of
duing all the external world with an intensity of interest.
the quivering of a leaf—in the hue of a blade of grass—
the shape of a trefoil—in the humming of a bee—in the
aming of a dew-drop—in the breathing of the wind—
the faint odours that came from the forest—there came
whole universe of suggestion—a gay and motley train of
apsodical and immethodical thought.

" Busied in this, I walked on for several hours, during
ich the mist deepened around me to so great an extent
at at length I was reduced to an absolute groping of the
y. And now an indescribable uneasiness possessed me
a species of nervous hesitation and tremor. I feared to
ad, lest I should be precipitated into some abyss. I
nembered, too, strange stories told about these Ragged
lls, and of the uncouth and fierce races of men who
nanted their groves and caverns. A thousand vague
ncies oppressed and disconcerted me—fancies the more
tressing because vague. Very suddenly my attention
s arrested by the loud beating of a drum.

' My amazement was, of course, extreme. A drum in
se hills was a thing unknown. I could not have been
re surprised at the sound of the trump of the Archangel.
t a new and still more astounding source of interest and
plexity arose. There came a wild rattling or jingling
nd, as if of a bunch of large keys, and upon the instant
lusky-visaged and half-naked man rushed past me with
hriek. He came so close to my person that I felt his hot
ath upon my face. He bore in one hand an instru-
nt composed of an assemblage of steel rings, and
ok them vigorously as he ran. Scarcely had he dis-
peared in the mist, before, panting after him, with
n mouth and glaring eyes, there darted a huge

beast. I could not be mistaken in its character. It w
a hyena.

"The sight of this monster rather relieved than heighten
my terrors—for I now made sure that I dreamed, a
endeavoured to arouse myself to waking consciousne
I stepped boldly and briskly forward. I rubbed my ey
I called aloud. I pinched my limbs. A small spring
water presented itself to my view, and here, stooping,
bathed my hands and my head and my neck. This seem
to dissipate the equivocal sensations which had hithe
annoyed me. I arose, as I thought, a new man, and p
ceeded steadily and complacently on my unknown way.

"At length, quite overcome by exertion, and by a cert
oppressive closeness of the atmosphere, I seated mys
beneath a tree. Presently there came a feeble gleam
sunshine, and the shadow of the leaves of the tree
faintly but definitely upon the grass. At this shadow
gazed wonderingly for many minutes. Its charac
stupefied me with astonishment. I looked upward. T
tree was a palm.

"I now rose hurriedly, and in a state of fearful agitati
—for the fancy that I dreamed would serve me no long
I saw—I felt that I had perfect command of my senses
and these senses now brought to my soul a world of no
and singular sensation. The heat became all at o
intolerable. A strange odour loaded the breeze. A l
continuous murmur, like that arising from a full, but gen
flowing river, came to my ears, intermingled with
peculiar hum of multitudinous human voices.

"While I listened in an extremity of astonishm
which I need not attempt to describe, a strong and b
gust of wind bore off the incumbent fog as if by the wand
an enchanter.

"I found myself at the foot of a high mountain, a
looking down into a vast plain, through which woun
majestic river. On the margin of this river stood
Eastern-looking city, such as we read of in the *Arab
Tales*, but of a character even more singular than any th
described. From my position, which was far above
level of the town, I could perceive its every nook and cor
as if delineated on a map. The streets seemed innumera
and crossed each other irregularly in all directions, but w
rather long winding alleys than streets, and absolut

armed with inhabitants. The houses were wildly
turesque. On every hand was a wilderness of balconies,
verandas, of minarets, of shrines, and fantastically carved
els. Bazaars abounded ; and there were displayed rich
res in infinite variety and profusion—silks, muslins, the
st dazzling cutlery, the most magnificent jewels and
ns. Besides these things, were seen, on all sides, banners
d palanquins, litters with stately dames close-veiled,
phants gorgeously caparisoned, idols grotesquely hewn,
ms, banners, and gongs, spears, silver and gilded maces.
d amid the crowd, and the clamour, and the general
ricacy and confusion—amid the million of black and
low men, turbaned and robed, and of flowing beard,
re roamed a countless multitude of holy filleted bulls,
ile vast legions of the filthy but sacred ape clambered,
ittering and shrieking, about the cornices of the mosques,
clung to the minarets and oriels. From the swarming
eets to the banks of the river, there descended innumer-
e flights of steps leading to bathing places, while the
er itself seemed to force a passage with difficulty through
vast fleets of deeply burdened ships that far and wide en-
ntered its surface. Beyond the limits of the city arose,
frequent majestic groups, the palm and the cocoa, with
er gigantic and weird trees of vast age ; and here and
re might be seen a field of rice, the thatched hut of a
sant, a tank, a stray temple, a gipsy camp, or a solitary
ceful maiden taking her way, with a pitcher upon her
d, to the banks of the magnificent river.

You will say now, of course, that I dreamed ; but not
What I saw—what I heard—what I felt—what I
ught—had about it nothing of the unmistakable idio-
crasy of the dream. All was rigorously self-consistent.
first, doubting that I was really awake, I entered into a
es of tests, which soon convinced me that I really was.
w when one dreams, and, in the dream, suspects that
dreams, the suspicion *never fails to confirm itself,* and the
per is almost immediately aroused. Thus Novalis
not in saying that ' we are near waking when we dream
t we dream.' Had the vision occurred to me as I de-
be it, without my suspecting it as a dream, then a dream
night absolutely have been, but, occurring as it did,
suspected and tested as it was, I am forced to class it
ong other phenomena."

"In this I am not sure that you are wrong," obser
Dr. Templeton, "but proceed. You arose and descen
into the city."

"I arose," continued Bedloe, regarding the Doctor v
an air of profound astonishment, "I arose as you say, a
descended into the city. On my way I fell in with
immense populace, crowding through every avenue, al
the same direction, and exhibiting in every action
wildest excitement. Very suddenly, and by some inc
ceivable impulse, I became intensely imbued with perso
interest in what was going on. I seemed to feel tha
had an important part to play, without exactly und
standing what it was. Against the crowd which enviro
me, however, I experienced a deep sentiment of animos
I shrank from amid them, and, swiftly, by a circuit
path, reached and entered the city. Here all was
wildest tumult and contention. A small party of n
clad in garments half Indian, half European, and office
by gentlemen in a uniform partly British, were engaged
great odds, with the swarming rabble of the allies.
joined the weaker party, arming myself with the weap
of a fallen officer, and fighting I knew not whom with
nervous ferocity of despair. We were soon overpowe
by numbers, and driven to seek refuge in a species
kiosk. Here we barricaded ourselves, and, for the pres
were secure. From a loop-hole near the summit of
kiosk, I perceived a vast crowd, in furious agitati
surrounding and assaulting a gay palace that overhung
river. Presently, from an upper window of this pal
there descended an effeminate-looking person, by me
of a string made of the turbans of his attendants. A b
was at hand in which he escaped to the opposite bank
the river.

"And now a new object took possession of my soul.
spoke a few hurried but energetic words to my companic
and, having succeeded in gaining over a few of them to
purpose, made a frantic sally from the kiosk. We rus
amid the crowd that surrounded it. They retreated,
first, before us. They rallied, fought madly, and retrea
again. In the meantime we were borne far from
kiosk, and became bewildered and entangled among
narrow streets of tall, overhanging houses, into the rece
of which the sun had never been able to shine. The rab

pressed impetuously upon us, harassing us with their
spears, and overwhelming us with flights of arrows. These
latter were very remarkable, and resembled in some
respects the writhing creese of the Malay. They were
made to imitate the body of a creeping serpent, and were
long and black, with a poisoned barb. One of them struck
me upon the right temple. I reeled and fell. An instantaneous and dreadful sickness seized me. I struggled
—I gasped—I died."

"You will hardly persist *now*," said I, smiling, "that
the whole of your adventure was not a dream. You are
not prepared to maintain that you are dead?"

When I said these words, I of course expected some
lively sally from Bedloe in reply; but, to my astonishment,
he hesitated, trembled, became fearfully pallid, and remained silent. I looked toward Templeton. He sat erect
and rigid in his chair—his teeth chattered, and his eyes
were starting from their sockets. "Proceed!" he at
length said hoarsely to Bedloe.

"For many minutes," continued the latter, "my sole
sentiment—my sole feeling—was that of darkness and
nonentity, with the consciousness of death. At length
there seemed to pass a violent and sudden shock through
my soul, as if of electricity. With it came the sense of
elasticity and of light. This latter I felt—not saw. In an
instant I seemed to rise from the ground. But I had no
bodily, no visible, audible, or palpable presence. The
crowd had departed. The tumult had ceased. The city
was in comparative repose. Beneath me lay my corpse,
with the arrow in my temple, the whole head greatly
swollen and disfigured. But all these things I felt—not
saw. I took interest in nothing. Even the corpse seemed
a matter in which I had no concern. Volition I had none,
but appeared to be impelled into motion, and flitted
buoyantly out of the city, retracing the circuitous path
by which I had entered it. When I had attained that
point of the ravine in the mountains at which I had encountered the hyena, I again experienced a shock as of a
galvanic battery; the sense of weight, of volition, of
substance, returned. I became my original self, and bent
my steps eagerly homeward—but the past had not lost the
vividness of the real—and not now, even for an instant,
can I compel my understanding to regard it as a dream."

"Nor was it," said Templeton, with an air of deep solemnity, "yet it would be difficult to say how otherwise it should be termed. Let us suppose only, that the soul of the man of to-day is upon the verge of some stupendous psychal discoveries. Let us content ourselves with this supposition. For the rest I have some explanation to make. Here is a water-colour drawing, which I should have shown you before, but which an accountable sentiment of horror has hitherto prevented me from showing."

We looked at the picture which he presented. I saw nothing in it of an extraordinary character; but its effect upon Bedloe was prodigious. He nearly fainted as he gazed. And yet it was but a miniature portrait—a miraculously accurate one, to be sure—of his own very remarkable features. At least this was my thought as I regarded it.

"You will perceive," said Templeton, "the date of this picture—it is here, scarcely visible, in this corner—1780. In this year was the portrait taken. It is the likeness of a dead friend—a Mr. Oldeb—to whom I became much attached at Calcutta, during the administration of Warren Hastings. I was then only twenty years old. When I first saw you, Mr. Bedloe, at Saratoga, it was the miraculous similarity which existed between yourself and the painting which induced me to accost you, to seek your friendship and to bring about those arrangements which resulted in my becoming your constant companion. In accomplishing this point, I was urged partly, and perhaps principally by a regretful memory of the deceased, but also, in part by an uneasy, and not altogether horrorless curiosity respecting yourself.

"In your detail of the vision which presented itself to you amid the hills, you have described, with the minutest accuracy, the Indian city of Benares, upon the Holy River. The riots, the combat, the massacre, were the actual events of the insurrection of Cheyte Sing, which took place in 1780, when Hastings was put in imminent peril of his life. The man escaping by the string of turbans was Cheyte Sing himself. The party in the kiosk were sepoys and British officers, headed by Hastings. Of this party I was one, and did all I could to prevent the rash and fatal sally of the officer who fell, in the crowded alleys, by the poisoned arrow of a Bengalee. That officer was my dearest friend. It was Oldeb. You will perceive by these manuscripts" (here the speaker produced a note-book in which several pages appeared to have been freshly written), "that at the very period in which you fancied these things amid the hills I was engaged in detailing them upon paper here at home."

In about a week after this conversation, the following paragraphs appeared in a Charlottesville paper :

"We have the painful duty of announcing the death of Mr. AUGUSTUS BEDLO, a gentleman whose amiable manners and many virtues have long endeared him to the citizens of Charlottesville.

"Mr. B., for some years past, has been subject to neuralgia, which has often threatened to terminate fatally ; but this can be regarded only as the mediate cause of his decease. The proximate cause was one of especial singularity. In an excursion to the Ragged Mountains, a few days since, a slight cold and fever were contracted, attended with great determination of blood to the head. To relieve this, Dr. Templeton resorted to topical bleeding. Leeches were applied to the temples. In a fearfully brief period the patient died, when it appeared that, in the jar containing the leeches, had been introduced, by accident, one of the venomous vermicular sangsues which are now and then found in the neighbouring ponds. This creature fastened itself upon a small artery in the right temple. Its close resemblance to the medicinal leech caused the mistake to be overlooked until too late.

"N.B.—The poisonous sangsue of Charlottesville may always be distinguished from the medicinal leech by its blackness, and especially by its writhing or vermicular motions, which very nearly resemble those of a snake."

I was speaking with the editor of the paper in question, upon the topic of this remarkable accident, when it occurred to me to ask how it happened that the name of the deceased had been given as Bedlo.

" I presume," said I, " you have authority for this spelling, but I have always supposed the name to be written with an e at the end."

" Authority ?—no," he replied. " It is a mere typographical error. The name is Bedlo with an e, all the world over, and I never knew it to be spelt otherwise in my life."

"Then," said I mutteringly, as I turned upon my heel, "then indeed has it come to pass that one truth is stranger than any fiction—for Bedlo, without the *e*, what is it but Oldeb conversed? And this man tells me it is a typographical error."

THE IMP OF THE PERVERSE

In the consideration of the faculties and impulses—of the *prima mobilia* of the human soul, the phrenologists have failed to make room for a propensity which, although obviously existing as a radical, primitive, irreducible sentiment, has been equally overlooked by all the moralists who have preceded them. In the pure arrogance of the reason, we have all overlooked it. We have suffered its existence to escape our senses solely through want of belief—of faith;—whether it be faith in Revelation, or faith in the Kabbala. The idea of it has never occurred to us, simply because of its supererogation. We saw no *need* of impulse—for the propensity. We could not perceive its necessity. We could not understand, that is to say, we could not have understood, had the notion of this *primum mobile* ever obtruded itself;—we could not have understood in what manner it might be made to further the objects of humanity, either temporal or eternal. It cannot be denied that phrenology and, in great measure all metaphysicianism have been concocted *à priori*. The intellectual or logical man, rather than the understanding or observant man, set himself to imagine designs—to dictate purposes to God. Having thus fathomed, to his satisfaction, the intentions of Jehovah, out of these intentions he built his innumerable systems of mind. In the matter of phrenology, for example, we first determined naturally enough, that it was the design of the Deity that man should eat. We then assigned to man an organ of alimentiveness, and this organ is the scourge with which the Deity compels man, will-I nill-I, into eating. Secondly having settled it to be God's will that man should continue his species, we discovered an organ of amativeness, forthwith. And so with combativeness, with ideality, with causality, with constructiveness,—so, in short, with every organ, whether representing a propensity, a moral sentiment, or a faculty of the pure intellect. And in these arrangements of the *principia* of human action, the Spurzheimites, whether right or wrong, in part, or upon the whole, have but followed, in principle, the footsteps of their predecessors ; deducing and establishing everything from the preconceived destiny of man, and upon the ground of the objects of his Creator.

It would have been wiser, it would have been safer, to classify (if classify we must) upon the basis of what man usually or occasionally did, and was always occasionally doing, rather than upon the basis of what we took it for granted the Deity intended him to do. If we cannot comprehend God in his visible works, how then in his inconceivable thoughts, that call the works into being ? If we cannot understand him in his objective creatures, how then in his substantive moods and phases of creation ?

Induction, *à posteriori*, would have brought phrenology to admit, as an innate and primitive principle of human action, a paradoxical something, which we may call *perverseness*, for want of a more characteristic term. In the sense I intend, it is, in fact, a *mobile* without motive, a motive not *motivirt*. Through its promptings we act without comprehensible object ; or, if this shall be understood as a contradiction in terms, we may so far modify the proposition as to say, that through its promptings we act, for the reason that we should *not*. In theory, no reason can be more unreasonable ; but, in fact, there is none more strong. With certain minds, under certain conditions it becomes absolutely irresistible. I am not more certain that I breathe, than that the assurance of the wrong or error of any action is often the one unconquerable *force* which impels us, and alone impels us to its prosecution. Nor will this overwhelming tendency to do wrong for the wrong's sake, admit of analysis, or resolution into ulterior elements. It is a radical, a primitive impulse—elementary. It will be said, I am aware, that when we persist in acts because we feel we should *not* persist in them, our conduct is but a modification of that which ordinarily springs from the *combativeness* of phrenology. But a glance will show the fallacy of this idea. The phrenological combativeness has, for its essence, the necessity of self-defence. It is our safeguard against injury. Its principle regards our well-being ; and thus the desire to be well is excited simultaneously with its development. It follows, that the desire to be well must be excited simultaneously with any principle which shall be merely a modification of combativeness, but in the case of that something which I term *perverseness*, the desire to be well is not only not aroused, but a strongly antagonistical sentiment exists.

An appeal to one's own heart is, after all, the best reply to the sophistry just noticed. No one who trustingly consults and thoroughly questions his own soul, will be disposed to deny the entire radicalness of the propensity in question. It is not more incomprehensible than distinctive. There lives no man who at some period has not been tormented, for example, by an earnest desire to tantalise a listener by circumlocution. The speaker is aware that he displeases ; he has every intention to please ; he is usually curt, precise, and clear ; the most laconic and luminous language is struggling for utterance upon his tongue ; it is only with difficulty that he restrains himself from giving it flow ; he dreads and deprecates the anger of him whom he addresses ; yet, the thought strikes him, that by certain involutions and parentheses this anger may be engendered. That single thought is enough. The impulse increases to a wish, the wish to a desire, the desire to an uncontrollable longing, and the longing (to the deep regret and mortification of the speaker, and in defiance of all consequences) is indulged.

We have a task before us which must be speedily performed. We know that it will be ruinous to make delay. The most important crisis of our life calls, trumpet-tongued, for immediate energy and action. We glow, we are consumed with eagerness to commence the work, with the anticipation of whose glorious result our whole souls are on fire. It must, it shall be undertaken to-day, and yet we put it off until to-morrow ; and why ? There is no answer, except that we feel *perverse*, using the word with no comprehension of the principle. To-morrow arrives, and with it a more impatient anxiety to do our duty, but with this very increase of anxiety arrives, also, a nameless, a positively fearful, because unfathomable, craving for delay. This craving gathers strength as the moments fly. The last hour for action is at hand. We tremble with the violence of the conflict within us,—of the definite with the indefinite—of the substance with the shadow. But, if the contest has proceeded thus far, it is the shadow which prevails,—we struggle in vain. The clock strikes, and is the knell of our welfare. At the same time, it is the chanticleer-note to the ghost that has so long overawed us. It flies—it disappears—we are free. The old energy returns. We will labour *now*. Alas, it is *too late* !

We stand upon the brink of a precipice. We peer into the abyss—we grow sick and dizzy. Our first impulse is to shrink from the danger. Unaccountably we remain. By slow degrees our sickness and dizziness and horror become merged in a cloud of unnamable feeling. By gradations, still more imperceptible, this cloud assumes shape, as did the vapour from the bottle out of which arose the genius in the *Arabian Nights*. But out of this *our* cloud upon the precipice's edge, there grows into palpability, a shape, far more terrible than any genius or any demon of a tale, and yet it is but a thought, although a fearful one, and one which chills the very marrow of our bones with the fierceness of the delight of its horror. It is merely the idea of what would be our sensations during the sweeping precipitancy of a fall from such a height. And this fall—this rushing annihilation—for the very reason that it involves that one most ghastly and loathsome of all the most ghastly and loathsome images of death and suffering which have ever presented themselves to our imagination—for this very cause do we now the most vividly desire it. And because our reason violently deters us from the brink, *therefore* do we the most impetuously approach it. There is no passion in nature so demoniacally impatient as that of him who, shuddering upon the edge of a precipice, thus meditates a plunge. To indulge, for a moment, in any attempt at *thought*, is to be inevitably lost ; for reflection but urges us to forbear, and *therefore* it is, I say, that we *cannot*. If there be no friendly arm to check us, or if we fail in a sudden effort to prostrate ourselves backward from the abyss, we plunge, and are destroyed.

Examine these and similar actions as we will, we shall find them resulting solely from the spirit of the *Perverse*.

We perpetrate them merely because we feel that we should *not*. Beyond or behind this there is no intelligible principle ; and we might, indeed, deem this perverseness a direct instigation of the arch-fiend, were it not occasionally known to operate in furtherance of good.

I have said thus much, that in some measure I may answer your question—that I may explain to you why I am here—that I may assign to you something that shall have at least the faint aspect of a cause for my wearing these fetters, and for my tenanting this cell of the condemned. Had I not been thus prolix, you might either have misunderstood me altogether, or, with the rabble, have fancied me mad. As it is, you will easily perceive that I am one of the many uncounted victims of the Imp of the Perverse.

It is impossible that any deed could have been wrought with a more thorough deliberation. For weeks, for months, I pondered upon the means of the murder. I rejected a thousand schemes, because their accomplishment involved a *chance* of detection. At length, in reading some French memoirs, I found an account of a nearly fatal illness that occurred to Madame Pilau, through the agency of a candle accidentally poisoned. The idea struck my fancy at once. I knew my victim's habit of reading in bed. I knew, too, that his apartment was narrow and ill-ventilated. But I need not vex you with impertinent details. I need not describe the easy artifices by which I substituted, in his bedroom candle stand, a wax-light of my own making for the one which I there found. The next morning he was discovered dead in his bed, and the coroner's verdict was— "Death by the visitation of God."

Having inherited his estate, all went well with me for years. The idea of detection never once entered my brain. Of the remains of the fatal taper I had myself carefully disposed. I had left no shadow of a clue by which it would be possible to convict, or even suspect, me of the crime. It is inconceivable how rich a sentiment of satisfaction arose in my bosom as I reflected upon my absolute security. For a very long period of time I was accustomed to revel in this sentiment. It afforded me more real delight than all the mere worldly advantages accruing from my sin. But there arrived at length an epoch, from which the pleasurable feeling grew, by scarcely perceptible gradations, into a haunting and harassing thought. It harassed me because it haunted. I could scarcely get rid of it for an instant. It is quite a common thing to be thus annoyed with the ringing in our ears, or rather in our memories, of the burthen of some ordinary song, or some unimpressive snatches from an opera. Nor will we be the less tormented if the song in itself be good, or the opera air meritorious. In this manner, at last, I would perpetually catch myself pondering upon my security, and repeating, in a low undertone, the phrase, " I am safe."

One day, whilst sauntering along the streets, I arrested myself in the act of murmuring, half aloud, these customary syllables. In a fit of petulance I re-modelled them thus : " I am safe—I am safe—yes—if I be not fool enough to make open confession."

No sooner had I spoken these words, than I felt an icy chill creep to my heart. I had had some experience in these fits of perversity (whose nature I have been at some trouble to explain), and I remembered well that in no instance I had successfully resisted their attacks. And now my own casual self-suggestion, that I might possibly be fool enough to confess the murder of which I had been guilty, confronted me, as if the very ghost of him whom I had murdered—and beckoned me on to death.

At first, I made an effort to shake off this nightmare of the soul. I walked vigorously—faster—still faster—at length I ran. I felt a maddening desire to shriek aloud. Every succeeding wave of thought overwhelmed me with new terror, for, alas ! I well, too well, understood that to *think*, in my situation, was to be lost. I still quickened my pace. I bounded like a madman through the crowded thoroughfares. At length, the populace took the alarm and pursued me. I felt *then* the consummation of my fate. Could I have torn out my tongue, I would have done it— but a rough voice resounded in my ears—a rougher grasp seized me by the shoulder. I turned—I gasped for breath. For a moment I experienced all the pangs of suffocation ; I became blind, and deaf, and giddy ; and then some invisible fiend, I thought, struck me with his broad palm upon the back. The long-imprisoned secret burst forth from my soul.

They say that I spoke with a distinct enunciation, but with marked emphasis and passionate hurry, as if in dread of interruption before concluding the brief but pregnant sentences that consigned me to the hangman and to hell.

Having related all that was necessary for the fullest judicial conviction, I fell prostrate in a swoon.

But why shall I say more ? To-day I wear these chains, and am *here* ! To-morrow I shall be fetterless !—*but where ?*

SOME WORDS WITH A MUMMY

THE *symposium* of the preceding evening had been a little too much for my nerves. I had a wretched headache, and was desperately drowsy. Instead of going out, therefore, to spend the evening, as I had proposed, it occurred to me that I could not do a wiser thing than just eat a mouthful of supper and go immediately to bed.

A *light* supper, of course. I am exceedingly fond of Welsh rabbit. More than a pound at once, however, may not at all times be advisable. Still, there can be no material objection to two. And really between two and three, there is merely a single unit of difference. I ventured, perhaps, upon four. My wife will have it five ; but, clearly, she has confounded two very distinct affairs. The abstract number, five, I am willing to admit ; but, concretely, it has reference to bottles of brown stout, without which, in the way of condiment, Welsh rabbit is to be eschewed.

Having thus concluded a frugal meal and donned my nightcap, with the serene hope of enjoying it till noon the next day, I placed my head upon the pillow, and through the aid of a capital conscience, fell into a profound slumber forthwith.

But when were the hopes of humanity fulfilled ? I could not have completed my third snore when there came a furious ringing at the street-door bell, and then an impatient thumping at the knocker, which awakened me at once. In a minute afterward, and while I was still rubbing my eyes, my wife thrust in my face a note, from my old friend, Doctor Ponnonner. It ran thus :—

" Come to me, by all means, my dear good friend, as

soon as you receive this. Come and help us to rejoice.
At last, by long persevering diplomacy, I have gained the
assent of the Directors of the City Museum, to my examination of the Mummy—you know the one I mean. I have
permission to unswathe it, and open it, if desirable. A few
friends only will be present—you, of course. The Mummy
is now at my house, and we shall begin to unroll it at eleven
to-night.—Yours ever,   PONNONNER."

By the time I had reached the " Ponnonner," it struck
me that I was as wide awake as a man need be. I leaped
out of bed in an ecstasy, overthrowing all in my way ;
dressed myself with a rapidity truly marvellous ; and
set off, at the top of my speed, for the doctor's.

There I found a very eager company assembled. They
had been awaiting me with much impatience. The Mummy
was extended upon the dining-table ; and the moment I
entered, its examination was commenced.

It was one of a pair brought, several years previously,
by Captain Arthur Sabretash, a cousin of Ponnonner's,
from a tomb near Eleithias, in the Lybian Mountains, a
considerable distance above Thebes on the Nile. The
grottoes at this point, although less magnificent than the
Theban sepulchres, are of higher interest, on account of
affording more numerous illustrations of the private life
of the Egyptians. The chamber from which our specimen
was taken, was said to be very rich in such illustrations—
the walls being completely covered with fresco-paintings
and bas-reliefs, while statues, vases, and mosaic work of
rich patterns, indicated the vast wealth of the deceased.

The treasure had been deposited in the Museum precisely
in the same condition in which Captain Sabretash had found
it—that is to say, the coffin had not been disturbed. For
eight years it had thus stood, subject only externally to
public inspection. We had now, therefore, the complete
Mummy at our disposal ; and to those who are aware how
very rarely the unransacked antique reaches our shores, it
will be evident, at once, that we had great reason to con-
gratulate ourselves upon our good fortune.

Approaching the table, I saw on it a large box, or case,
nearly seven feet long, and perhaps three feet wide, by two
feet and a half deep. It was oblong—not coffin-shaped.
The material was at first supposed to be the wood of the

sycamore (*platanus*), but upon cutting into it, we found it to be pasteboard, or, more properly, *papier-mâché*, composed of papyrus. It was thickly ornamented with paintings, representing funeral scenes, and other mournful subjects—interspersed among which, in every variety of position, were certain series of hieroglyphical characters, intended, no doubt, for the name of the departed. By good luck, Mr Gliddon formed one of our party; and he had no difficulty in translating the letters, which were simply phonetic, and represented the word, *Allamistakeo*.

We had some difficulty in getting this case open without injury; but, having at length accomplished the task, we came to a second, coffin-shaped, and very considerably less in size than the exterior one, but resembling it precisely in every other respect. The interval between the two was filled with resin, which had, in some degree, defaced the colours of the interior box.

Upon opening this latter (which we did quite easily) we arrived at a third case, also coffin-shaped, and varying from the second one in no particular, except in that of its material, which was cedar, and still emitted the peculiar and highly aromatic odour of that wood. Between the second and the third case there was no interval—the one fitting accurately within the other.

Removing the third case, we discovered and took out the body itself. We had expected to find it, as usual, enveloped in frequent rolls or bandages of linen; but, in place of these, we found a sort of sheath, made of papyrus, and coated with a layer of plaster, thickly gilt and painted. The paintings represented subjects connected with the various supposed duties of the soul, and its presentation to different divinities, with numerous identical human figures, intended, very probably, as portraits of the persons embalmed. Extending from head to foot, was a columnar, or perpendicular inscription, in phonetic hieroglyphics, giving again his name and titles, and the names and titles of his relations.

Around the neck thus ensheathed, was a collar of cylindrical glass beads, diverse in colour, and so arranged as to form images of deities, of the scarabæus, etc., with the winged globe. Around the small of the waist was a similar collar or belt.

Stripping off the papyrus, we found the flesh in excellent

reservation, with no perceptible odour. The colour was
reddish. The skin was hard, smooth, and glossy. The
teeth and hair were in good condition. The eyes (it seemed)
had been removed, and glass ones substituted, which were
very beautiful, and wonderfully life-like, with the exception
of somewhat too determined a stare. The fingers and the
nails were brilliantly gilded.

Mr. Gliddon was of opinion, from the redness of the
epidermis, that the embalmment had been effected altogether by asphaltum ; but, on scraping the surface with a
steel instrument, and throwing into the fire some of the
powder thus obtained, the flavour of camphor and other
sweet-scented gums became apparent.

We searched the corpse very carefully for the usual
openings through which the entrails are extracted, but, to
our surprise, we could discover none. No member of the
party was at that period aware that entire or unopened
mummies are not unfrequently met. The brain it was
customary to withdraw through the nose ; the intestines
through an incision in the side ; the body was then shaved,
washed, and salted ; then laid aside for several weeks, when
the operation of embalming, properly so called, began.

As no trace of an opening could be found, Doctor Ponnonner was preparing his instruments for dissection, when I
observed that it was then past two o'clock. Hereupon it
was agreed to postpone the internal examination until the
next evening ; and we were about to separate for the
present, when some one suggested an experiment or two
with the Voltaic pile.

The application of electricity to a mummy three or four
thousand years old at the least, was an idea, if not very
sage, still sufficiently original, and we all caught it at once.
About one-tenth in earnest and nine-tenths in jest, we
arranged a battery in the doctor's study, and conveyed
thither the Egyptian.

It was only after much trouble that we succeeded in
laying bare some portions of the temporal muscle which
appeared of less stony rigidity than other parts of the frame,
but which, as we had anticipated, of course, gave no indication of galvanic susceptibility when brought in contact with
the wire. This, the first trial, indeed, seemed decisive,
and, with a hearty laugh at our own absurdity, we were
bidding each other good-night, when my eyes, happening

to fall upon those of the Mummy, were there immediatel riveted in amazement. My brief glance, in fact, ha sufficed to assure me that the orbs which we had all suppose to be glass, and which were originally noticeable for certain wild stare, were now so far covered by the lids, tha only a small portion of the *tunica albuginea* remaine visible.

With a shout I called attention to the fact, and it becam immediately obvious to all.

I cannot say that I was *alarmed* at the phenomenon because " alarmed " is, in my case, not exactly the word It is possible, however, that, but for the brown stout, might have been a little nervous. As for the rest of the company, they really made no attempt at concealing the downright fright which possessed them. Doctor Ponnonne. was a man to be pitied. Mr. Gliddon, by some peculia process, rendered himself invisible. Mr. Silk Buckingham I fancy, will scarcely be so bold as to deny that he made his way, upon all fours, under the table.

After the first shock of astonishment, however, we resolved, as a matter of course, upon further experiment forthwith. Our operations were now directed against the great toe of the right foot. We made an incision over the outside of the exterior *os sesamoideum pollicis pedis*, and thus got at the root of the *abductor* muscle Readjusting the battery, we now applied the fluid to the bisected nerves, when, with a movement of exceeding life-likeness, the Mummy first drew up its right knee so as to bring it nearly in contact with the abdomen, and then, straightening the limb with inconceivable force, bestowed a kick upon Doctor Ponnonner, which had the effect of discharging that gentleman, like an arrow from a catapult, through a window into the street below.

We rushed out *en masse* to bring in the mangled remains of the victim, but had the happiness to meet him upon the staircase, coming up in an unaccountable hurry, brimful of the most ardent philosophy, and more than ever impressed with the necessity of prosecuting our experiments with vigour and with zeal.

It was by his advice, accordingly, that we made, upon the spot, a profound incision into the tip of the subject's nose, while the doctor himself, laying violent hands upon it, pulled it into vehement contact with the wire.

Morally and physically—figuratively and literally—
was the effect electric. In the first place, the corpse
opened its eyes, and winked very rapidly for several
minutes, as does Mr. Barnes in the pantomime ; in the
second place, it sneezed ; in the third, it sat up on end ;
in the fourth, it shook its fist in Doctor Ponnonner's face ;
in the fifth, turning to Messieurs Gliddon and Buckingham,
it addressed them, in very capital Egyptian, thus—

"I must say, gentlemen, that I am as much surprised
as I am mortified, at your behaviour. Of Doctor
Ponnonner nothing better was to be expected. He is
a poor little fat fool who *knows* no better. I pity and
forgive him. But you, Mr. Gliddon—and you, Silk—
who have travelled and resided in Egypt until one might
imagine you to the manner born—you, I say, who have
been so much among us that you speak Egyptian fully
as well, I think, as you write your mother tongue—you,
whom I have always been led to regard as the firm friend
of the mummies—I really did anticipate more gentlemanly
conduct from *you*. What am I to think of your standing
quietly by and seeing me thus unhandsomely used ?
What am I to suppose by your permitting Tom, Dick,
and Harry to strip me of my coffins, and my clothes,
in this wretchedly cold climate ? In what light (to come
to the point) am I to regard your aiding and abetting
that miserable little villain, Doctor Ponnonner, in pulling
me by the nose ? "

It will be taken for granted, no doubt, that upon hearing
this speech under the circumstances, we all either made
for the door, or fell into violent hysterics, or went off
in a general swoon. One of these three things, was, I
say, to be expected. Indeed each and all of these lines
of conduct might have been very plausibly pursued.
And, upon my word, I am at a loss to know how or why it
was that we pursued neither the one nor the other.
But, perhaps, the true reason is to be sought in the spirit of
the age, which proceeds by the rule of contraries altogether,
and is now usually admitted as the solution of everything
in the way of paradox and impossibility. Or perhaps,
after all, it was only the Mummy's exceedingly natural
and matter-of-course air that divested his words of the
terrible. However this may be, the facts are clear, and
no member of our party betrayed any very particular

trepidation, or seemed to consider that anything had gone very especially wrong.

For my part I was convinced it was all right, and merely stepped aside, out of the range of the Egyptian's fist. Doctor Ponnonner thrust his hands into his breeches pockets, looked hard at the Mummy, and grew excessively red in the face. Mr. Gliddon stroked his whiskers and drew up the collar of his shirt. Mr. Buckingham hung down his head, and put his right thumb into the left corner of his mouth.

The Egyptian regarded him with a severe countenance for some minutes, and at length, with a sneer, said—

"Why don't you speak, Mr. Buckingham? Did you hear what I asked you, or not? *Do* take your thumb out of your mouth!"

Mr. Buckingham, hereupon, gave a slight start, took his right thumb out of the left corner of his mouth, and by way of indemnification, inserted his left thumb in the right corner of the aperture above mentioned.

Not being able to get an answer from Mr. B., the figure turned peevishly to Mr. Gliddon, and, in a peremptory tone, demanded in general terms what we all meant.

Mr. Gliddon replied at great length, in phonetics; and but for the deficiency of American printing-offices in hieroglyphical type, it would afford me much pleasure to record here, in the original, the whole of his very excellent speech.

I may as well take this occasion to remark, that all the subsequent conversation in which the Mummy took part, was carried on in primitive Egyptian, through the medium (so far as concerned myself and other untravelled members of the company)—through the medium, I say, of Messieurs Gliddon and Buckingham, as interpreters. These gentlemen spoke the mother-tongue of the Mummy with inimitable fluency and grace; but I could not help observing that (owing, no doubt, to the introduction of images entirely modern, and, of course, entirely novel to the stranger) the two travellers were reduced, occasionally, to the employment of sensible forms for the purpose of conveying a particular meaning. Mr. Gliddon, at one period, for example, could not make the Egyptian comprehend the term "politics," until he sketched upon the wall, with a bit of charcoal, a little carbuncle-nosed

tleman, out at elbows, standing upon a stump, with
left leg drawn back, his right arm thrown forward,
h his fist shut, the eyes rolled up toward heaven, and
mouth open at an angle of ninety degrees. Just in
same way Mr. Buckingham failed to convey the absol-
ely modern idea, " Whig," until (at Doctor Ponnonner's
ggestion) he grew very pale in the face, and consented to
ke off his own.

It will be readily understood that Mr. Gliddon's dis-
urse turned chiefly upon the vast benefits accruing to
ence from the unrolling and disembowelling of mummies ;
ologising, upon this score, for any disturbance that
ght have been occasioned him, in particular, the
lividual mummy called Allamistakeo ; and concluding
th a mere hint (for it could scarcely be considered more)
at, as these little matters were now explained, it might
as well to proceed with the investigation intended.
ere Doctor Ponnonner made ready his instruments.

In regard to the latter suggestions of the orator, it appears
at Allamistakeo had certain scruples of conscience, the
ature of which I did not distinctly learn ; but he ex-
essed himself satisfied with the apologies tendered,
d, getting down from the table, shook hands with the
mpany all round.

When this ceremony was at an end, we immediately
usied ourselves in repairing the damages which our
bject had sustained from the scalpel. We sewed up
e wound in his temple, bandaged his foot, and applied
square inch of black plaster to the tip of his nose.

It was now observed that the Count (this was the title,
seems, of Allamistakeo) had a slight fit of shivering
-no doubt from the cold. The doctor immediately
paired to his wardrobe, and soon returned with a black
ress coat, made in Jennings' best manner, a pair of sky-
lue plaid pantaloons, with straps, a pink gingham chemise,
flapped vest of brocade, a white sack overcoat, a walking
ane with a hook, a hat with no brim, patent-leather boots,
raw-coloured kid gloves, an eye-glass, a pair of whiskers,
nd a waterfall cravat. Owing to the disparity of size
etween the Count and the doctor (the proportion being
s two to one), there was some little difficulty in adjusting
hese habiliments upon the person of the Egyptian ;
ut when all was arranged, he might have been said

to be dressed. Mr. Gliddon, therefore, gave him his ar
and led him to a comfortable chair by the fire, while t
doctor rang the bell upon the spot and ordered a supply
cigars and wine.

The conversation soon grew animated. Much curiosi
was, of course, expressed in regard to the somewh
remarkable fact of Allamistakeo's still remaining alive.

" I should have thought," observed Mr. Buckingha.
" that it is high time you were dead."

" Why," replied the Count, very much astonishe
" I am little more than seven hundred years old ! My fath
lived a thousand, and was by no means in his dota
when he died."

Here ensued a brisk series of questions and computatior
by means of which it became evident that the antiqui
of the Mummy had been grossly misjudged. It h
been five thousand and fifty years, and some montl
since he had been consigned to the catacombs
Eleithias.

" But my remark," resumed Mr. Buckingham, " h
no reference to your age at the period of interment
am willing to grant, in fact, that you are still a you
man) ; and my allusion was to the immensity of tin
during which, by your own showing, you must have bee
done up in asphaltum."

" In what ? " said the Count.

" In asphaltum," persisted Mr. B.

" Ah, yes ; I have some faint notion of what you mean
it might be made to answer, no doubt—but in my tin
we employed scarcely anything else than the Bichlorid
of Mercury."

" But what we are especially at a loss to understand,
said Doctor Ponnonner, " is, how it happens that, havin
been dead and buried in Egypt five thousand years ag
you are here to-day all alive, and looking so delightfull
well."

" Had I been, as you say, *dead*," replied the Coun
" it is more than probable that dead I should still be
for I perceive you are yet in the infancy of galvanism
and cannot accomplish with it what was a common thin
among us in the old days. But the fact is, I fell int
catalepsy, and it was considered by my best friends tha
I was either dead or should be ; they accordingly embalmee

at once—I presume you are aware of the chief principle
the embalming process ? "

' Why, not altogether."

' Ah, I perceive—a deplorable condition of ignorance ¡
ell, I cannot enter into details just now ; but it is neces-
y to explain that to embalm (properly speaking) in
ypt, was to arrest indefinitely *all* the animal functions
ojected to the process. I use the word ' animal ' in
widest sense, as including the physical not more than
e moral and *vital* being. I repeat that the leading
inciple of embalmment consisted, with us, in the imme-
ately arresting, and holding in perpetual abeyance,
the animal functions subjected to the process. To
brief, in whatever condition the individual was, at
e period of embalmment, in that condition he remained.
w, as it is my good fortune to be of the blood of the
arabæus, I was embalmed *alive*, as you see me at
esent."

"The blood of the Scarabæus ! " exclaimed Doctor
onnonner.

" Yes. The Scarabæus was the *insignium*, or the
rms,' of a very distinguished and very rare patrician
mily. To be ' of the blood of the Scarabæus,' is merely
be one of that family of which the Scarabæus is the
signium. I speak figuratively."

" But what has this to do with your being alive ? "

" Why, it is the general custom in Egypt, to deprive
corpse, before embalmment, of its bowels and brains ;
e race of the Scarabæi alone did not coincide with the
stom. Had I not been a Scarabæus, therefore, I should
ve been without bowels and brains ; and without either
is inconvenient to live."

" I perceive that," said Mr. Buckingham ; " and I
esume that all the *entire* mummies that come to hand
e of the race of Scarabæi."

" Beyond doubt."

" I thought," said Mr. Gliddon, very meekly, " that the
carabæus was one of the Egyptian gods."

" One of the Egyptian *what* ? " exclaimed the Mummy,
arting to its feet.

" Gods ! " repeated the traveller.

" Mr. Gliddon, I really am astonished to hear you talk
this style," said the Count, resuming his seat. " No

nation upon the face of the earth has ever acknowled[
more than *one god*. The Scarabæus, the Ibis, etc., w
with us (as similar creatures have been with others)
symbols, or *media*, through which we offered worship
the Creator too august to be more directly approached.*

There was here a pause. At length the colloquy
renewed by Doctor Ponnonner.

"It is not improbable, then, from what you have
plained," said he, "that among the catacombs n
the Nile, there may exist other mummies of the Scaraba
tribe, in a condition of vitality."

"There can be no question of it," replied the Cou
"all the Scarabæi embalmed accidentally while ali
are alive. Even some of those *purposely* so embalm
may have been overlooked by their executors, and s
remain in the tombs."

"Will you be kind enough to explain," I said, "wl
you mean by 'purposely so embalmed'?"

"With great pleasure," answered the Mummy, af
surveying me leisurely through his eye-glass—for it w
the first time I had ventured to address him a dir
question.

"With great pleasure," he said. "The usual durati
of man's life, in my time, was about eight hundred yea
Few men died, unless by most extraordinary accide
before the age of six hundred; few lived longer than
decade of centuries; but eight were considered the natur
term. After the discovery of the embalming princip
as I have already described it to you, it occurred to o
philosophers that a laudable curiosity might be gratifie
and, at the same time, the interests of science much a
vanced, by living this natural term in instalments. In t
case of history, indeed, experience demonstrated th
something of this kind was indispensable. An historia
for example, having attained the age of five hundre
would write a book with great labour and then get himse
carefully embalmed; leaving instructions to his executo
pro tem., that they should cause him to be revivifie
after the lapse of a certain period—say five or six hundre
years. Resuming existence at the expiration of this tim
he would invariably find his great work converted into
species of hap-hazard note-book—that is to say, into
kind of literary arena for the conflicting guesses, riddle

1 personal squabbles of whole herds of exasperated
nmentators. These guesses, etc., which passed under
 name of annotations, or emendations, were found so
npletely to have enveloped, distorted, and overwhelmed
e text, that the author had to go about with a lantern
discover his own book. When discovered, it was never
rth the trouble of the search. After rewriting it through-
t, it was regarded as the bounden duty of the historian
set himself to work, immediately, in correcting, from
 own private knowledge and experience, the traditions
the day concerning the epoch at which he had originally
ed. Now this process of rescription and personal
ctification, pursued by various individual sages, from
ne to time, had the effect of preventing our history
m degenerating into absolute fable."

" I beg your pardon," said Doctor Ponnonner at this
int, laying his hand gently upon the arm of the Egyptian
" I beg your pardon, sir, but may I presume to interrupt
u for one moment ? "

" By all means, *sir*," replied the Count, drawing up.

" I merely wished to ask you a question," said the
ctor. " You mentioned the historian's personal correc-
n of *traditions* respecting his own epoch. Pray, sir,
on an average, what proportion of these Kabbala were
ually found to be right ? "

" The Kabbala, as you properly term them, sir, were
nerally discovered to be precisely on a par with the
cts recorded in the un-rewritten histories themselves ;
at is to say, not one individual iota of either was ever
nown, under any circumstances, to be not totally and
dically wrong."

" But since it is quite clear," resumed the doctor, " that
 least five thousand years have elapsed since your en-
mbment, I take it for granted that your histories at
at period, if not your traditions, were sufficiently explicit
a that one topic of universal interest, the Creation, which
ok place, as I presume you are aware, only about ten
nturies before."

" Sir ! " said the Count Allamistakeo.

The doctor repeated his remarks, but it was only after
uch additional explanation that the foreigner could be
ade to comprehend them. The latter at length said,
esitatingly—

"The ideas you have suggested are to me, I conf
utterly novel. During my time I never knew any
to entertain so singular a fancy as that the universe
this world, if you will have it so) ever had a beginning
all. I remember once, and once only, hearing someth
remotely hinted by a man of many speculations c
cerning the origin *of the human race* ; and by this individ
the very word *Adam* (or Red Earth), which you make use
was employed. He employed it, however, in a generi
sense, with reference to the spontaneous germinat:
from rank soil (just as a thousand of the lower *gen*
of creatures are germinated)—the spontaneous germinatic
I say, of five vast hordes of men, simultaneously upspringi
in five distinct and nearly equal divisions of the globe."

Here, in general, the company shrugged their shoulde
and one or two of us touched our foreheads with a ve
significant air. Mr. Silk Buckingham, first glanci
slightly at the occiput and then at the siniciput of Al
mistakeo, spoke as follows—

"The long duration of human life in your time, togetl
with the occasional practice of passing it, as you ha
explained, in instalments, must have had, indeed, a stro
tendency to the general development and conglomeratic
of knowledge. I presume, therefore, that we are to att
bute the marked inferiority of the old Egyptians in ;
particulars of science, when compared with the moderr
and more especially with the Yankees, altogether
the superior solidity of the Egyptian skull."

"I confess again," replied the Count, with much suavit
"that I am somewhat at a loss to comprehend you ; pra
to what particulars of science do you allude ? "

Here our whole party, joining voices, detailed, at gre;
length, the assumptions of phrenology and the marve
of animal magnetism.

Having heard us to an end, the Count proceeded t
relate a few anecdotes, which rendered it evident th;
prototypes of Gall and Spurzheim had flourished ar
faded in Egypt so long ago as to have been nearly forgotter
and that the manœuvres of Mesmer were really very co
temptible tricks when put in collation with the positiv
miracles of the Theban *savans*, who created lice, and a gre;
many other similar things.

I here asked the Count if his people were able to ca

ate eclipses. He smiled rather contemptuously, and
 they were.

This put me a little out ; but I began to make other
uiries in regard to his astronomical knowledge, when a
mber of the company, who had never as yet opened
 mouth, whispered in my ear, that for information
 this head I had better consult Ptolemy (whoever
lemy is), as well as one Plutarch *de facie lunæ.*

then questioned the Mummy about burning-glasses
 lenses, and, in general, about the manufacture of
ss ; but I had not made an end of my queries before
 silent member again touched me quietly on the elbow,
 begged me, for God's sake, to take a peep at Diodorus
ulus. As for the Count, he merely asked me, in the
y of reply, if we moderns possessed any such micros-
pes as would enable us to cut cameos in the style of
 Egyptians. While I was thinking how I should
swer this question, little Doctor Ponnonner committed
self in a very extraordinary way.

' Look at our architecture ! " he exclaimed, greatly
 the indignation of both the travellers, who pinched
 black and blue to no purpose.

' Look ! " he cried, with enthusiasm, " at the Bowling-
en Fountain in New York ! or, if this be too vast a
templation, regard for a moment the Capitol at
ashington, D.C. ! "—and the good little medical man
nt on to detail, very minutely, the proportions of the
ric to which he referred. He explained that the portico
ne was adorned with no less than four and twenty
umns, five feet in diameter, and ten feet apart.

The Count said that he regretted not being able to re-
ember, just at that moment, the precise dimensions
 any one of the principal buildings of the City of Aznac,
ose foundations were laid in the night of Time, but the
ins of which were still standing, at the epoch of his
tombment, in a vast plain of sand to the westward
 Thebes. He recollected, however (talking of porticoes),
at one affixed to an inferior palace in a kind of suburb
lled Carnac, consisted of a hundred and forty-four
umns, thirty-seven feet each in circumference, and
venty-five feet apart. The approach of this portico,
om the Nile, was through an avenue two miles long,
mposed of sphynxes, statues, and obelisks, twenty,

sixty, and a hundred feet in height. The palace it
(as well as he could remember) was, in one directi
two miles long, and might have been, altogether, ab
seven in circuit. Its walls were richly painted all ov
within and without, with hieroglyphics. He would
pretend to *assert* that even fifty or sixty of the docte
Capitols might have been built within these walls, but
was by no means sure that two or three hundred of th
might not have been squeezed in with some trou
That palace at Carnac was an insignificant little build
after all. He (the Count), however, could not conscier
ously refuse to admit the ingenuity, magnificence, a
superiority of the fountain at the Bowling-green, as
scribed by the doctor. Nothing like it, he was fore
to allow, had ever been seen in Egypt or elsewhere.

I here asked the Count what he had to say to
railroads.

"Nothing," he replied, "in particular." They w
rather slight, rather ill-conceived, and clumsily put togeth
They could not be compared, of course, with the va
level, direct, iron-grooved causeways, upon which t
Egyptians conveyed entire temples and solid obelis
of a hundred and fifty feet in altitude.

I spoke of our gigantic mechanical forces.

He agreed that we knew something in that way, l
inquired how I should have gone to work in getting up t
imposts on the lintels of even the little palace at Carnac.

This question I concluded not to hear, and demand
if he had any idea of Artesian wells; but he simply rais
his eyebrows; while Mr. Gliddon winked at me ve
hard and said, in a low tone, that one had been recent
discovered by the engineers employed to bore for wat
in the Great Oasis.

I then mentioned our steel; but the foreigner elevat
his nose, and asked me if our steel could have execut
the sharp carved work seen on the obelisks, and whi
was wrought altogether by edge-tools of copper.

This disconcerted us so greatly that we thought
advisable to vary the attack to Metaphysics. We sent f
a copy of a book called the *Dial*, and read out of it
chapter or two about something which is not very clea
but which the Bostonians call the Great Movement
Progress.

he Count merely said that Great Movements were ully common things in his day, and as for Progress, it at one time quite a nuisance, but it never progressed. Ve then spoke of the great beauty and importance of nocracy, and were at much trouble in impressing the int with a due sense of the advantages we enjoyed in ng where there was suffrage *ad libitum* and no king.

Ie listened with marked interest, and in fact seemed a little amused. When we had done he said that, reat while ago, there had occurred something of a very iilar sort. Thirteen Egyptian provinces determined at once to be free, and so set a magnificent example to e rest of mankind. They assembled their wise men, and icocted the most ingenious constitution it is possible to iceive. For a while they managed remarkably well; iy their habit of bragging was prodigious. The thing ided, however, in the consolidation of the thirteen tes, with some fifteen or twenty others, in the most ious and insupportable despotism that ever was heard upon the face of the Earth.

I asked what was the name of the usurping tyrant. As well as the Count could recollect, it was *Mob*.

Not knowing what to say to this, I raised my voice, d deplored the Egyptian ignorance of steam.

The Count looked at me with much astonishment, but ade no answer. The silent gentleman, however, gave e a violent nudge in the ribs with his elbows—told me had sufficiently exposed myself for once—and demanded I was really such a fool as not to know that the modern eam-engine is derived from the invention of Hero, rough Solomon de Caus.

We were now in imminent danger of being discomfited; it, as good luck would have it, Doctor Ponnonner, having llied, returned to our rescue, and inquired if the people Egypt would seriously pretend to rival the moderns the all-important particular of dress.

The Count, at this, glanced downwards to the straps f his pantaloons, and then taking hold of the end of ne of his coat-tails, held it up close to his eyes for some iinutes. Letting it fall, at last, his mouth extended itself ery gradually from ear to ear; but I do not remember iat he said anything in the way of reply.

Hereupon we recovered our spirits, and the doctor,

approaching the Mummy with great dignity, desired i
say candidly, upon its honour as a gentleman, if
Egyptians had comprehended at *any* period the ma
facture of either Ponnonner's lozenges, or Brandre
pills.

We looked, with profound anxiety, for an answer—
in vain. It was not forthcoming. The Egyptian blus
and hung down his head. Never was triumph more c
summate; never was defeat borne with so ill a gra
Indeed, I could not endure the spectacle of the p
Mummy's mortification. I reached my hat, bowed
him stiffly, and took leave.

Upon getting home I found it past four o'clock, a
went immediately to bed. It is now ten A.M. I ha
been up since seven, penning these memoranda for
benefit of my family and of mankind. The former I sh
behold no more. My wife is a shrew. The truth is
am heartily sick of this life, and of the nineteenth centu
in general. I am convinced that everything is goi
wrong. Besides, I am anxious to know who will
President in 2045. As soon, therefore, as I shave a
swallow a cup of coffee, I shall just step over to Ponnonne
and get embalmed for a couple of hundred years.

THE DEVIL IN THE BELFRY

"What o'clock is it?"—*Old Saying*.

EVERYBODY knows, in a general way, that the fine
place in the world is—or, alas, *was*—the Dutch boroug
of Vondervotteimittiss. Yet, as it lies some distance fro
any of the main roads, being in a somewhat out-of-the-wa
situation, there are, perhaps, very few of my readers wh
have ever paid it a visit. For the benefit of those wh
have *not*, therefore, it will be only proper that I shoul
enter into some account of it. And this is, indeed, the mo
necessary, as with the hope of enlisting public sympath
in behalf of the inhabitants, I design here to give a histor
of the calamitous events which have so lately occurre

thin its limits. No one who knows me will doubt
at the duty thus self-imposed will be executed to the
st of my ability, with all that rigid impartiality, all
at cautious examination into facts, and diligent collation
authorities, which should ever distinguish him who
pires to the title of historian.

By the united aid of medals, manuscripts, and inscrip-
ns, I am enabled to say, positively, that the borough
Vondervotteimittiss has existed, from its origin, in
ecisely the same condition which it at present preserves.
f the date of this origin, however, I grieve that I can only
eak with that species of indefinite definiteness which
athematicians are, at times, forced to put up with
certain algebraic formulæ. The date, I may thus
y, in regard to the remoteness of its antiquity, cannot
less than any assignable quantity whatsoever.

Touching the derivation of the name Vondervot-
imittiss, I confess myself, with sorrow, equally at fault.
mong a multitude of opinions upon this delicate point—
me acute, some learned, some sufficiently the reverse—
am able to select nothing which ought to be considered
tisfactory. Perhaps the idea of Grogswigg—nearly
incident with that of Kroutaplenttey—is to be cautiously
referred :—

It runs :—*Vondervotteimittiss—Vonder, lege Donder—
otteimittiss, quasi und Bleitziz—Bleitziz obsol : pro
litzen.* This derivation, to say the truth, is still coun-
enanced by some traces of the electric fluid evident on
he summit of the steeple of the House of the Town-
ouncil. I do not choose, however, to commit myself
n a theme of such importance, and must refer the reader
esirous of information, to the *Oratiunculæ de Rebus Præter-
eteris* of Dundergutz. See, also, Blunderbuzzard *De
Derivationibus,* pp. 27 to 5010, Folio, Gothic edit., Red
nd Black character, Catchword and No Cypher ; wherein
onsult, also, marginal notes in the autograph of Stuffund-
uff, with the Sub-Commentaries of Gruntundguzzell.

Notwithstanding the obscurity which thus envelops
he date of the foundation of Vondervotteimittiss, and
he derivation of its name, there can be no doubt, as I
aid before, that it has always existed as we find it at
his epoch. The oldest man in the borough can remember
ot the slightest difference in the appearance of any portion

of it ; and, indeed, the very suggestion of such a possibi
is considered an insult. The site of the village is i
perfectly circular valley, about a quarter of a mile
circumference, and entirely surrounded by gentle h
over whose summit the people have never yet ventu
to pass. For this they assign the very good reason tl
they do not believe there is anything at all on the otl
side.

Round the skirts of the valley (which is quite level, a
paved throughout with flat tiles) extends a continuc
row of sixty little houses. These, having their backs
the hills, must look, of course, to the centre of the pla
which is just sixty yards from the front door of ea
dwelling. Every house has a small garden before it, w
a circular path, a sun-dial, and twenty-four cabbag
The buildings themselves are so precisely alike, that o
can in no manner be distinguished from the other. Ow
to the vast antiquity, the style of architecture is somewl
odd, but it is not for that reason the less strikingly pict
esque. They are fashioned of hard-burned little bricl
red, with black ends, so that the walls look like a che
board upon a great scale. The gables are turned to t
front, and there are cornices, as big as all the rest
the house, over the eaves and over the main doors. T
windows are narrow and deep, with very tiny panes ar
a great deal of sash. On the roof is a vast quantity
tiles with long curly ears. The woodwork, throughou
is of a dark hue, and there is much carving about it, wi
but a trifling variety of pattern ; for, time out of min
the carvers of Vondervotteimittiss have never been ab
to carve more than two objects—a time-piece and
cabbage. But these they do exceedingly well, and inte
sperse them, with singular ingenuity, wherever they fir
room for the chisel.

The dwellings are as much alike inside as out, and tl
furniture is all upon one plan. The floors are of squa
tiles, the chairs and tables of black-looking wood with th
crooked legs and puppy feet. The mantel-pieces are wi
and high, and have not only time-pieces and cabbag
sculptured over the front, but a real time-piece, whic
makes a prodigious ticking, on the top in the middl
with a flower-pot containing a cabbage standing on eac
extremity by way of outrider. Between each cabba

ad the time-piece again, is a little china man having a
rge stomach with a great round hole in it, through
hich is seen the dial-plate of a watch.

The fire-places are large and deep, with fierce crooked-
oking fire-dogs. There is constantly a rousing fire, and
huge pot over it full of sauer-kraut and pork, to which
he good woman of the house is always busy in attending.
he is a little fat old lady, with blue eyes and a red face,
nd wears a huge cap like a sugar-loaf, ornamented with
urple and yellow ribbons. Her dress is of orange-coloured
nsey-woolsey made very full behind and very short in the
aist—and indeed very short in other respects, not reaching
elow the middle of her leg. This is somewhat thick, and
o are her ankles, but she has a fine pair of green stockings
o cover them. Her shoes, of pink leather, are fastened
ach with a bunch of yellow ribbons puckered up in the
hape of a cabbage. In her left hand she has a little heavy
Dutch watch; in her right she wields a ladle for the
auer-kraut and pork. By her side there stands a fat
abby cat, with a gilt toy repeater tied to its tail, which
' the boys " have there fastened by way of a quiz.

The boys themselves are, all three of them, in the garden
attending the pig. They are each two feet in height.
They have three-cornered cocked hats, purple waistcoats
reaching down to their thighs, buckskin knee-breeches,
ed woollen stockings, heavy shoes with big silver buckles,
nd long surtout coats with large buttons of mother-of-
pearl. Each, too, has a pipe in his mouth, and a little
lumpy watch in his right hand. He takes a puff and a
ook, and then a look and a puff. The pig, which is corpulent and lazy, is occupied now in picking up the stray
leaves that fall from the cabbages, and now in giving a
kick behind at the gilt repeater, which the urchins have
also tied to *his* tail, in order to make him look as handsome
as the cat.

Right at the front door, in a high-backed leather
bottomed armed chair, with crooked legs and puppy feet
like the tables, is seated the old man of the house himself.—
He is an exceedingly puffy little old gentleman, with big
circular eyes and a huge double chin. His dress resembles
that of the boys, and I need say nothing farther about it.
All the difference is that his pipe is somewhat bigger than
theirs, and he can make a greater smoke.—Like them, he

has a watch, but he carries his watch in his pocket. T
say the truth, he has something of more importance tha
a watch to attend to, and what that is I shall presentl
explain. He sits with his right leg upon his left knee
wears a grave countenance, and always keeps one of hi
eyes, at least, resolutely bent upon a certain remarkabl
object in the centre of the plain.

This object is situated in the steeple of the House of th
Town-Council. The Town-Council are all very little,
round, oily, intelligent men, with big saucer eyes and fat
double chins, and have their coats much longer and their
shoe-buckles much bigger than the ordinary inhabitants
of Vondervotteimittiss. Since my sojourn in the borough
they have had several special meetings, and have adopted
these three important resolutions :

"That it is wrong to alter the good old course of
things—"

"That there is nothing tolerable out of Vondervotteimittiss—" and

"That we will stick by our clocks and our cabbages."

· Above the session room of the Council is the steeple,
and in the steeple is the belfry, where exists, and has
existed time out of mind, the pride and wonder of the
village—the great clock of the borough of Vondervotteimittiss. And this is the object to which the eyes of the
old gentlemen are turned who sit in the leather-bottomed
arm-chairs.

The great clock has seven faces—one in each of the seven
sides of the steeple—so that it can be readily seen from all
quarters. Its faces are large and white, and its hands
heavy and black. There is a belfry-man whose sole duty
is to attend to it ; but this duty is the most perfect of
sinecures—for the clock of Vondervotteimittiss was never
yet known to have anything the matter with it. Until
lately, the bare supposition of such a thing was considered
heretical. From the remotest period of antiquity to which
the archives have reference, the hours have been regularly
struck by the big bell. And, indeed, the case was just
the same with all the other clocks and watches in the
borough. Never was such a place for keeping the true
time. When the large clapper thought proper to say
"Twelve o'clock !" all its obedient followers opened their
throats simultaneously, and responded like a very echo.

n short, the good burghers were fond of their sauer-kraut,
ut then they were proud of their clocks.

All people who hold sinecure offices are held in more or
·ss respect, and as the belfry-man of Vondervotteimittiss
as the most perfect of sinecures, he is the most perfectly
espected of any man in the world. He is the chief
ignitary of the borough, and the very pigs look up to
im with a sentiment of reverence. His coat-tail is *very*
ar longer—his pipe, his shoe-buckles, his eyes, and his
tomach, *very* far bigger—than those of any other old
entleman in the village ; and as to his chin, it is not only
ouble, but triple.

I have just painted the happy estate of Vondervotteimit-
iss : alas, that so fair a picture should ever experience a
everse !

There has been long a saying among the wisest inhabi-
ants, that " no good can come from over the hills " ; and
t really seemed that the words had in them something of
he spirit of prophecy. It wanted five minutes of noon,
·n the day before yesterday, when there appeared a very
·dd-looking object on the summit of the ridge to the
astward. Such an occurrence, of course, attracted uni-
·ersal attention, and every little old gentleman who sat
n a leather-bottomed arm-chair turned one of his eyes
vith a stare of dismay upon the phenomenon, still keeping
he other upon the clock in the steeple.

By the time that it wanted only three minutes to noon,
he droll object in question was perceived to be a very
liminutive foreign-looking young man. He descended the
·ills at a great rate, so that everybody had soon a good
ook at him. He was really the most finicky little personage
hat had ever been seen in ·Vondervotteimittiss. His
ountenance was of a dark snuff-colour, and he had a long
·ooked nose, pea eyes, a wide mouth, and an excellent set
·f teeth, which latter he seemed anxious of displaying, as
·e was grinning from ear to ear. What with mostachios
·nd whiskers, there was none of the rest of his face to be
·een. His head was uncovered, and his hair neatly done
·p in *papillotes*. His dress was a tight-fitting swallow-
·ailed black coat (from one of whose pockets dangled a vast
·ength of white handkerchief), black kerseymere knee-
·reeches, black stockings, and stumpy-looking pumps,
vith huge bunches of black satin ribbon for bows.· Under

R

one arm he carried a huge *chapeau-de-bras*, and under th
other a fiddle nearly five times as big as himself. In hi
left hand was a gold snuff-box, from which, as he capere
down the hill, cutting all manner of fantastic steps, h
took snuff incessantly with an air of the greatest possibl
self-satisfaction. God bless me !—here was a sight for th
honest burghers of Vondervotteimittiss !

To speak plainly, the fellow had, in spite of his grinning
an audacious and sinister kind of face ; and as he curvete
right into the village, the old stumpy appearance of hi
pumps excited no little suspicion ; and many a burghe
who beheld him that day would have given a trifle for
peep beneath the white cambric handkerchief which hun
so obtrusively from the pocket of his swallow-tailed coat
But what mainly occasioned a righteous indignation was
that the scoundrelly popinjay, while he cut a fandang
here, and a whirligig there, did not seem to have the re
motest idea in the world of such a thing as *keeping tim*
in his steps.

The good people of the borough had scarcely a chance
however, to get their eyes thoroughly open, when, just a
it wanted half a minute of noon, the rascal bounced, as
say, right into the midst of them ; gave a *chassez* here, an
a *balancez* there ; and then, after a *pirouette* and a *pas-de*
zephyr, pigeon-winged himself right up into the belfry o
the House of the Town-Council, where the wonder-stricke
belfry-man sat smoking in a state of dignity and dismay
But the little chap seized him at once by the nose ; gav
it a swing and a pull ; clapped the big *chapeau-de-bra*
upon his head ; knocked it down over his eyes and mouth
and then, lifting up the big fiddle, beat him with it so lon
and so soundly, that what with the belfry-man being s
fat, and the fiddle being so hollow, you would have swor
that there was a regiment of double-bass drummers a
beating the devil's tattoo up in the belfry of the steeple o
Vondervotteimittiss.

There is no knowing to what desperate act of vengeanc
this unprincipled attack might have aroused the inhabitant:
but for the important fact that it now wanted only half
second of noon. The bell was about to strike, and it wa
a matter of absolute and pre-eminent necessity tha
everybody should look well at his watch. It was evident
however, that just at this moment the fellow in the steepl

was doing something that he had no business to do with
the clock. But as it now began to strike, nobody had any
time to attend to his manœuvres, for they had all to count
the strokes of the bell as it sounded.

" One ! " said the clock.

" Von ! " echoed every little old gentleman in
every leather-bottomed arm-chair in Vondervotteimittiss.
" Von ! " said his watch also ; " von ! " said the watch
of his vrow ; and " von ! " said the watches of the boys,
and the little gilt repeaters on the tails of the cat and pig.

" Two ! " continued the big bell ; and

" Doo ! " repeated all the repeaters.

" Three ! Four ! Five ! Six ! Seven ! Eight ! Nine !
Ten ! " said the bell.

" Dree ! Vour ! Fibe ! Sax ! Seben ! Aight ! Noin !
Den ! " answered the others.

" Eleven ! " said the big one.

" Eleben ! " assented the little ones.

" Twelve ! " said the bell.

" Dvelf ! " they replied, perfectly satisfied, and dropping
their voices.

" Und dvelf it iss ! " said all the little old gentlemen,
putting up their watches. But the big bell had not done
with them yet.

" Thirteen ! " said he.

" Der Teufel ! " gasped the little old gentlemen, turning
pale, dropping their pipes, and putting down all their
right legs from over their left knees.

" Der Teufel ! " groaned they, " Dirteen ! Dirteen ! !—
Mein Gott, it is Dirteen o'clock ! ! "

Why attempt to describe the terrible scene which
ensued ? All Vondervotteimittiss flew at once into a
lamentable state of uproar.

" Vot is cum'd to mein pelly ? " roared all the boys,—
" I've been ongry for dis hour ! "

" Vot is cum'd to mein kraut ? " screamed all the vrows.
" It has been done to rags for dis hour ! "

" Vot is cum'd to mein pipe ? " swore all the little old
gentlemen. " Donder and Blitzen ! it has been smoked
out for dis hour ! "—and they filled them up again in a
great rage, and, sinking back in their arm-chairs, puffed
away so fast and so fiercely that the whole valley was
immediately filled with impenetrable smoke.

Meantime the cabbages all turned very red in the fac
and it seemed as if old Nick himself had taken possessi
of everything in the shape of a time-piece. The cloc
carved upon the furniture took to dancing as if bewitche
while those upon the mantel-pieces could scarcely conta
themselves for fury, and kept such a continual striking
thirteen, and such a frisking and wriggling of their pe
dulums as was really horrible to see. But worse than a
neither the cats nor the pigs could put up any longer wi
the behaviour of the little repeaters tied to their tails, an
resented it by scampering all over the place, scratchin
and poking, and squeaking and screeching, and caterwau
ing and squalling, and flying into the faces, and runnir
under the petticoats of the people, and creating altogeth
the most abominable din and confusion which it is possib
for a reasonable person to conceive. And to make matte
still more distressing, the rascally little scapegrace in tl
steeple was evidently exerting himself to the utmos
Every now and then one might catch a glimpse of tl
scoundrel through the smoke. There he sat in the belfr
upon the belfry-man, who was lying flat upon his bacl
In his teeth the villain held the bell-rope, which he kej
jerking about with his head, raising such a clatter tha
my ears ring again even to think of it. On his lap lay tl
big fiddle, at which he was scraping, out of all time an
tune, with both hands, making a great show, the nir
compoop! of playing " Judy O'Flannagan and Padd
O'Rafferty."

Affairs being thus miserably situated, I left the place i
disgust, and now appeal for aid to all lovers of correc
time and fine kraut. Let us proceed in a body to th
borough, and restore the ancient order of things in Vonder
votteimittiss by ejecting that little fellow from the steepl

THE BALLOON HOAX

[Astounding News by Express, *viâ* Norfolk !—The Atlantic Crossed in Three Days ! Signal Triumph of Mr. Monck Mason's Flying Machine !—Arrival at Sullivan's Island, near Charleston, S.C., of Mr. Mason, Mr. Robert Holland, Mr. Henson, Mr. Harrison Ainsworth, and four others, in the Steering Balloon, *Victoria*, after a passage of Seventy-five hours from Land to Land ! Full Particulars of the Voyage !

The subjoined *jeu d'esprit*, with the preceding heading in magnificent capitals, well interspersed with notes of admiration, was originally published, as matter of fact, in the *New York Sun*, a daily newspaper, and therein fully subserved the purpose of creating indigestible aliment for the *quidnuncs* during the few hours intervening between a couple of the Charleston mails. The rush for the " sole paper which had the news," was something beyond even the prodigious ; and, in fact, if (as some assert) the *Victoria did* not absolutely accomplish the voyage recorded, it will be difficult to assign a reason why she *should* not have accomplished it.]

THE great problem is at length solved ! The air, as well as the earth and the ocean, has been subdued by science, and will become a common and convenient highway for mankind. *The Atlantic has been actually crossed in a Balloon !* and this too without difficulty—without any great apparent danger—with thorough control of the machine—and in the inconceivably brief period of seventy-five hours from shore to shore ! By the energy of an agent at Charleston, S.C., we are enabled to be the first to furnish the public with a detailed account of this most extraordinary voyage, which was performed between Saturday, the 6th instant, at 11 A.M., and 2 P.M., on Tuesday, the 9th instant, by Sir Everard Bringhurst ; Mr. Osborne, a nephew of Lord Bentinck's ; Mr. Monck Mason and Mr. Robert Holland, the well-known aëronauts ; Mr. Harrison Ainsworth, author of *Jack Sheppard*, etc. ; and Mr. Henson, the projector of the late unsuccessful flying machine—with two seamen from Woolwich—in all, eight persons. The particulars furnished below may be relied on as authentic and accurate in every respect, as, with a slight exception, they are copied *verbatim* from the joint diaries of Mr. Monck Mason and Mr. Harrison Ainsworth, to whose politeness our agent is indebted for much verbal information respecting the balloon itself, its construction, and

other matters of interest. The only alteration in the MS
received, has been made for the purpose of throwing the
hurried account of our agent, Mr. Forsyth, into a con
nected and intelligible form.

" THE BALLOON

" Two very decided failures, of late,—those of Mr
Henson and Sir George Cayley,—had much weakened the
public interest in the subject of aërial navigation. Mr
Henson's scheme (which at first was considered very feasible
even by men of science) was founded upon the principle of
an inclined plane, started from an eminence by an extrinsic
force applied and continued by the revolution of impinging
vanes in form and number resembling the vanes of a wind
mill. But, in all the experiments made with models at
the Adelaide Gallery, it was found that the operation of
these fans not only did not propel the machine, but actually
impeded its flight. The only propelling force it ever
exhibited, was the mere *impetus* acquired from the descent
of the inclined plane ; and this *impetus* carried the machine
further when the vanes were at rest, than when they were
in motion—a fact which sufficiently demonstrates their
inutility ; and in the absence of the propelling, which was
also the *sustaining*, power, the whole fabric would neces
sarily descend. This consideration led Sir George Cayley
to think only of adapting a propeller to some machine
having of itself an independent power of support—in a word
to a balloon ; the idea however, being novel, or original
with Sir George, only so far as regards the mode of its
application to practice. He exhibited a model of his
invention at the Polytechnic Institution. The propelling
principle, or power, was here, also, applied to interrupted
surfaces, or vanes, put in revolution. These vanes were
four in number, but were found entirely ineffectual in
moving the balloon, or in aiding its ascending power
The whole project was thus a complete failure.

" It was at this juncture that Mr. Monck Mason (whose
voyage from Dover to Weilburg in the balloon, *Nassau*
occasioned so much excitement in 1837) conceived the
idea of employing the principle of the Archimedean screw
for the purpose of propulsion through the air—rightly
attributing the failure of Mr. Henson's scheme, and of Sir

orge Cayley's to the interruption of surface in the
lependent vanes. He made the first public experiment
Willis's Rooms, but afterward removed his model to the
elaide Gallery.

" Like Sir George Cayley's balloon, his own was an
ipsoid. Its length was thirteen feet six inches—height,
: feet eight inches. It contained about three hundred
d twenty cubic feet of gas, which, if pure hydrogen,
•uld support twenty-one pounds upon its first inflation,
fore the gas has time to deteriorate or escape. The
•ight of the whole machine and apparatus was seventeen
unds—leaving about four pounds to spare. Beneath
e centre of the balloon, was a frame of light wood, about
ne feet long, and rigged on to the balloon itself with a
twork in the customary manner. From this framework
is suspended a wicker basket or car.

" The screw consists of an axis of hollow brass tube,
ghteen inches in length, through which, upon a semispiral
clined at fifteen degrees, pass a series of steel-wire radii,
o feet long, and thus projecting a foot on either side.
ese radii are connected at the outer extremities by two
_nds of flattened wire—the whole in this manner forming
e framework of the screw, which is completed by a
vering of oiled silk cut into gores, and tightened so as to
esent a tolerably uniform surface. At each end of its
is this screw is supported by pillars of hollow brass tube
scending from the hoop. In the lower ends of these
bes are holes in which the pivots of the axis revolve.
om the end of the axis which is next the car, proceeds
shaft of steel, connecting the screw with the pinion of a
ece of spring machinery fixed in the car. By the opera-
•n of this spring, the screw is made to revolve with great
pidity, communicating a progressive motion to the
iole. By means of the rudder, the machine was readily
rned in any direction. The spring was of great power,
mpared with its dimensions, being capable of raising
rty-five pounds upon a barrel of four inches diameter
ter the first turn, and gradually increasing as it was
und up. It weighed, altogether, eight pounds six ounces.
ie rudder was a light frame of cane covered with silk,
aped somewhat like a battledore, and was about three
et long, and at the widest, one foot. Its weight was
•out two ounces. It could be turned *flat*, and directed

upward or downward, as well as to the right or left ; a
thus enabled the aëronaut to transfer the resistance of t
air which in an inclined position it must generate in
passage, to any side upon which he might desire to ac
thus determining the balloon in the opposite direction.

" This model (which, through want of time, we ha
necessarily described in an imperfect manner) was put
action at the Adelaide Gallery, where it accomplished
velocity of five miles per hour ; although, strange to sa
it excited very little interest in comparison with the previo
complex machine of Mr. Henson—so resolute is the wor
to despise anything which carries with it an air of simplici̇
To accomplish the great desideratum of aërial navigatic
it was very generally supposed that some exceeding
complicated application must be made of some unusual
profound principle in dynamics.

" So well satisfied, however, was Mr. Mason of t
ultimate success of his invention, that he determined
construct immediately, if possible, a balloon of sufficie
capacity to test the question by a voyage of some extent
the original design being to cross the British Chann
as before, in the *Nassau* balloon. To carry out his vie
he solicited and obtained the patronage of Sir Evera
Bringhurst and Mr. Osborne, two gentlemen well kno\
for scientific acquirement, and especially for the intere
they have exhibited in the progress of aërostation. T
project, at the desire of Mr. Osborne, was kept a profou
secret from the public—the only persons entrusted with t
design being those actually engaged in the constructi
of the machine, which was built (under the superintenden
of Mr. Mason, Mr. Holland, Sir Everard Bringhurst, a
Mr. Osborne) at the seat of the latter gentleman ne
Penstruthal, in Wales. Mr. Henson, accompanied by l
friend Mr. Ainsworth, was admitted to a private view
the balloon, on Saturday last—when the two gentlem
made final arrangements to be included in the adventu
We are not informed for what reason the two seamen we
also included in the party—but, in the course of a day
two, we shall put our readers in possession of the minute
particulars respecting this extraordinary voyage.

" The balloon is composed of silk, varnished with t
liquid gum caoutchouc. It is of vast dimensions, containi
more than 40,000 cubic feet of gas ; but as coal-gas w

ployed in place of the more expensive and inconvenient
drogen, the supporting power of the machine, when
ly inflated, and immediately after inflation, is not more
an about 2500 pounds. The coal-gas is not only much
s costly, but is easily procured and managed.

" For its introduction into common use for purposes of
rostation, we are indebted to Mr. Charles Green. Up to
s discovery, the process of inflation was not only exceed-
gly expensive, but uncertain. Two and even three days
ve frequently been wasted in futile attempts to procure
sufficiency of hydrogen to fill a balloon, from which it
d great tendency to escape, owing to its extreme subtlety,
d its affinity for the surrounding atmosphere. In a
lloon sufficiently perfect to retain its contents of coal-
s unaltered, in quality or amount, for six months, an
ual quantity of hydrogen could not be maintained in
ual purity for six weeks.

" The supporting power being estimated at 2500 pounds,
d the united weights of the party amounting only to
out 1200, there was left a surplus of 1300, of which again
00 was exhausted by ballast, arranged in bags of different
es, with their respective weights marked upon them—
cordage, barometers, telescopes, barrels containing
ovision for a fortnight, water-casks, cloaks, carpet-bags,
d various other indispensable matters, including a coffee-
rmer, contrived for warming coffee by means of slack-
ne, so as to dispense altogether with fire, if it should be
dged prudent to do so. All these articles, with the
ception of the ballast, and a few trifles, were suspended
om the hoop overhead. The car is much smaller and
hter, in proportion, than the one appended to the model.
is formed of a light wicker, and is wonderfully strong,
so frail-looking a machine. Its rim is about four feet
ep. The rudder is also very much larger, in proportion,
an that of the model; and the screw is considerably
aller. The balloon is furnished besides with a grapnel,
d a guide-rope; which latter is of the most indispensable
portance. A few words, in explanation, will here be
cessary for such of our readers as are not conversant
th the details of aërostation.

" As soon as the balloon quits the earth, it is subjected
the influence of many circumstances tending to create a
ference in its weight; augmenting or diminishing its

ascending power. For example, there may be a deposit
of dew upon the silk, to the extent even of several hundr
pounds ; ballast has then to be thrown out, or the mach
may descend. This ballast being discarded, and a cl
sunshine evaporating the dew, and at the same ti
expanding the gas in the silk, the whole will again rapi
ascend. To check this ascent, the only resource is
rather *was*, until Mr. Green's invention of the guide-ro
the permission of the escape of gas from the valve ; b
in the loss of gas, is a proportionate general loss of ascendi
power ; so that, in a comparatively brief period, the be
constructed balloon must necessarily exhaust all
resources, and come to the earth. This was the gr
obstacle to voyages of length.

" The guide-rope remedies the difficulty in the simpl
manner conceivable. It is merely a very long rope wh
is suffered to trail from the car, and the effect of which
to prevent the balloon from changing its level in a
material degree. If, for example, there should be a depc
tion of moisture upon the silk, and the machine begins
descend in consequence, there will be no necessity
discharging ballast to remedy the increase of weight,
it is remedied, or counteracted, in an exactly just prop
tion, by the deposit on the ground of just so much of t
end of the rope as is necessary. If, on the other hand, a
circumstances should cause undue levity, and conseque
ascent, this levity is immediately counteracted by t
additional weight of rope upraised from the earth. Th
the balloon can neither ascend nor descend, except witl
very narrow limits, and its resources, either in gas or balla
remain comparatively unimpaired. When passing ov
an expanse of water, it becomes necessary to employ ke
of copper or wood, filled with liquid ballast of a ligh
nature than water. These float, and serve all the purpo
of a mere rope on land. Another most important office
the guide-rope, is to point out the *direction* of the balloc
The rope *drags*, either on land or sea, while the balloon
free ; the latter, consequently, is always in advance, wh
any progress whatever is made : a comparison, therefo
by means of the compass, of the relative positions of t
two objects, will always indicate the *course*. In the sar
way, the angle formed by the rope with the verticle a:
of the machine, indicates the *velocity*. When there is

ngle—in other words, when the rope hangs perpendicularly, he whole apparatus is stationary ; but the larger the ngle, that is to say, the farther the balloon precedes the nd of the rope, the greater the velocity ; and the converse.

" As the original design was to cross the British Channel, nd alight as near Paris as possible, the voyagers had taken he precaution to prepare themselves with passports lirected to all parts of the Continent, specifying the nature f the expedition, as in the case of the *Nassau* voyage, nd entitling the adventurers to exemption from the usual ormalities of office ; unexpected events, however, rendered hese passports superfluous.

" The inflation was commenced very quietly at daybreak, n Saturday morning, the 6th instant, in the courtyard of Veal-Vor House, Mr. Osborne's seat, about a mile from Penstruthal, in North Wales ; and at seven minutes past leven, everything being ready for departure, the balloon vas set free, rising gently but steadily, in a direction iearly south ; no use being made, for the first half-hour, f either the screw or the rudder. We proceed now with he journal, as transcribed by Mr. Forsyth from the joint MSS. of Mr. Monck Mason and Mr. Ainsworth. The ody of the journal, as given, is in the handwriting of Mr. Mason, and a P.S. is appended, each day, by Mr. Ainsworth, vho has in preparation, and will shortly give the public a more minute and, no doubt, a thrillingly interesting iccount of the voyage.

"THE JOURNAL

" *Saturday, April the 6th.*—Every preparation likely to embarrass us having been made overnight, we commenced he inflation this morning at daybreak ; but owing to a hick fog, which encumbered the folds of the silk and rendered it unmanageable, we did not get through before iearly eleven o'clock. Cut loose, then, in high spirits, and rose gently but steadily, with a light breeze at north, which bore us in the direction of the British Channel. Found the ascending force greater than we had expected ; and as we arose higher and so got clear of the cliffs, and more in the sun's rays, our ascent became very rapid. I did not wish, however, to lose gas at so early a period of the adventure, and so concluded to ascend for the present.

We soon ran out our guide-rope ; but even when we had
raised it clear of the earth, we still went up very rapidly
The balloon was unusually steady, and looked beautifully
In about ten minutes after starting, the barometer indicated
an altitude of 15,000 feet. The weather was remarkably
fine, and the view of the subjacent country—a most
romantic one when seen from any point—was now especi
ally sublime. The numerous deep gorges presented the
appearance of lakes, on account of the dense vapour
with which they were filled, and the pinnacles and crags
to the south-east, piled in inextricable confusion resembling
nothing so much as the giant cities of Eastern fable. We
were rapidly approaching the mountains in the south, but
our elevation was more than sufficient to enable us to pass
them in safety. In a few minutes we soared over them in
fine style ; and Mr. Ainsworth, with the seamen, was
surprised at their apparent want of altitude when viewed
from the car, the tendency of great elevation in a balloon
being to reduce inequalities of the surface below, to nearly
a dead level. At half-past eleven, still proceeding nearly
south, we obtained our first view of the Bristol Channel
and, in fifteen minutes afterward, the line of breakers
on the coast appeared immediately beneath us, and we were
fairly out at sea. We now resolved to let off enough gas
to bring our guide-rope, with the buoys affixed, into the
water. This was immediately done, and we commenced
a gradual descent. In about twenty minutes our first
buoy dipped, and at the touch of the second soon afterward
we remained stationary as to elevation. We were all now
anxious to test the efficiency of the rudder and screw, and
we put them both into requisition forthwith, for the purpose
of altering our direction more to the eastward, and in a
line for Paris. By means of the rudder we instantly
effected the necessary change of direction, and our course
was brought nearly at right angles to that of the wind
when we set in motion the spring of the screw, and were
rejoiced to find it propel as readily as desired. Upon this
we gave nine hearty cheers, and dropped in the sea a bottle
enclosing a slip of parchment with a brief account of the
principle of the invention. Hardly, however, had we done
with our rejoicings, when an unforeseen accident occurred
which discouraged us in no little degree. The steel rod
connecting the spring with the propeller was suddenly

erked out of place, at the car end (by a swaying of the
car through some movement of one of the two seamen we
had taken up), and in an instant hung dangling out of reach,
from the pivot of the axis of the screw.   While we were
endeavouring to regain it, our attention being completely
absorbed, we became involved in a strong current of wind
from the east, which bore us, with rapidly increasing force,
toward the Atlantic.   We soon found ourselves driving
out to sea at the rate of not less, certainly, than fifty or
sixty miles an hour, so that we came up with Cape Clear,
at some forty miles to our north, before we had secured
the rod, and had time to think what we were about.   It
was now that Mr. Ainsworth made an extraordinary but,
to my fancy, a by no means unreasonable or chimerical
proposition, in which he was instantly seconded by Mr.
Holland—viz. : that we should take advantage of the
strong gale which bore us on, and in place of beating back
to Paris, make an attempt to reach the coast of North
America.   After slight reflection I gave a willing assent
to this bold proposition, which (strange to say) met with
objection from the two seamen only.   As the stronger
party, however, we overruled their fears, and kept resolutely upon our course.   We steered due west ; but as
the trailing of the buoys materially impeded our progress,
and we had the balloon abundantly at command, either
for ascent or descent, we first threw out fifty pounds of
ballast, and then wound up (by means of the windlass)
so much of the rope as brought it quite clear of the sea.
We perceived the effect of this manœuvre immediately,
in a vastly increased rate of progress ; and, as the gale
freshened, we flew with a velocity nearly inconceivable ;
the guide-rope flying out behind the car, like a streamer
from a vessel.   It is needless to say that a very short time
sufficed us to lose sight of the coast.   We passed over
innumerable vessels of all kinds, a few of which were endeavouring to beat up, but the most of them lying to.   We
occasioned the greatest excitement on board all—an
excitement greatly relished by ourselves, and especially
by our two men, who, now under the influence of a dram
of Geneva, seemed resolved to give all scruple. or fear, to
the wind.   Many of the vessels fired signal guns ; and in
all we were saluted with loud cheers (which we heard with
surprising distinctness) and the waving of caps and hand-

kerchiefs. We kept on in this manner throughout the
day with no material incident, and, as the shades of night
closed around us, we made a rough estimate of the distance
traversed. It could not have been less than five hundred
miles, and was probably much more. The propeller was
kept in constant operation, and, no doubt, aided our
progress materially. As the sun went down, the gale
freshened into an absolute hurricane, and the ocean beneath
was clearly visible on account of its phosphorescence.
The wind was from the east all night, and gave us the
brightest omen of success. We suffered no little from cold,
and the dampness of the atmosphere was most unpleasant;
but the ample space in the car enabled us to lie down,
and by means of cloaks and a few blankets we did
sufficiently well.

" P.S. [by Mr. Ainsworth.] The last nine hours have
been unquestionably the most exciting of my life. I can
conceive nothing more sublimating than the strange peril
and novelty of an adventure such as this. May God grant
that we succeed ! I ask not success for mere safety to my
insignificant person, but for the sake of human knowledge
and—for the vastness of the triumph. And yet the feat
is only so evidently feasible that the sole wonder is why
men have scrupled to attempt it before. One single gale
such as now befriends us—let such a tempest whirl forward
a balloon for four or five days (these gales often last longer)
and the voyager will be easily borne, in that period, from
coast to coast. In view of such a gale the broad Atlantic
becomes a mere lake. I am more struck, just now, with the
supreme silence which reigns in the sea beneath us, notwithstanding its agitation, than with any other phenomenon
presenting itself. The waters give up no voice to the
heavens. The immense flaming ocean writhes and is
tortured uncomplainingly. The mountainous surges
suggest the idea of innumerable dumb gigantic fiends
struggling in impotent agony. In a night such as is this
to me, a man *lives*—lives a whole century of ordinary life
—nor would I forego this rapturous delight for that of a
whole century of ordinary existence.

" *Sunday, the 7th.* [Mr. Mason's MS.] This morning
the gale, by ten, had subsided to an eight or nine-knot
breeze (for a vessel at sea), and bears us, perhaps, thirty
miles per hour, or more. It has veered, however, very

considerably to the north ; and now, at sundown, we are holding our course due west, principally by the screw and rudder, which answer their purposes to admiration. I regard the project as thoroughly successful, and the easy navigation of the air in any direction (not exactly in the teeth of a gale) as no longer problematical. We could not have made head against the strong wind of yesterday ; but, by ascending, we might have got out of its influence, if requisite. Against a pretty stiff breeze, I feel convinced, we can make our way with the propeller. At noon, to-day, ascended to an elevation of nearly 25,000 feet, by discharging ballast. Did this to search for a more direct current, but found none so favourable as the one we are now in. We have an abundance of gas to take us across this small pond, even should the voyage last three weeks. I have not the slightest fear for the result. The difficulty has been strangely exaggerated and misapprehended. I can choose my current, and should I find *all* currents against me, I can make very tolerable headway with the propeller. We have had no incidents worth recording. The night promises fair.

" P.S. [By Mr. Ainsworth.] I have little to record, except the fact (to me quite a surprising one) that, at an elevation equal to that of Cotopaxi, I experienced neither very intense cold, nor headache, nor difficulty of breathing ; neither, I find, did Mr. Mason, nor Mr. Holland, nor Sir Everard. Mr. Osborne complained of constriction of the chest—but this soon wore off. We have flown at a great rate during the day, and we must be more than half way across the Atlantic. We have passed over some twenty or thirty vessels of various kinds, and all seem to be delightfully astonished. Crossing the ocean in a balloon is not so difficult a feat after all. *Omne ignotum pro magnifico.* *Mem. :* at 25,000 feet elevation the sky appears nearly black, and the stars are distinctly visible ; while the sea does not seem convex (as one might suppose) but absolutely and most unequivocally *concave.**

* *Note.*—Mr. Ainsworth has not attempted to account for this phenomenon, which, however, is quite susceptible of explanation. A line dropped from an elevation of 25,000 feet, perpendicularly to the surface of the earth (or sea), would form the perpendicular of a right-angled triangle, of which the base would extend from the right angle to the horizon, and the hypothenuse from the horizon to the balloon. But the 25,000 feet of altitude is little or nothing,

" *Monday, the 8th.* [Mr. Mason's MS.] This morning
we had again some little trouble with the rod of the pro
peller, which must be entirely remodelled, for fear of seriou
accident—I mean the steel rod, not the vanes. The latte
could not be improved. The wind has been blowing
steadily and strongly from the north-east all day ; and s
far fortune seems bent upon favouring us. Just before
day, we were all somewhat alarmed at some odd noises and
concussions in the balloon, accompanied with the apparen
rapid subsidence of the whole machine. These phenomena
were occasioned by the expansion of the gas, through
increase of heat in the atmosphere, and the consequen
disruption of the minute particles of ice with which the
network had become encrusted during the night. Threw
down several bottles to the vessels below. See one of them
picked up by a large ship—seemingly one of the New York
line packets. Endeavoured to make out her name, but
could not be sure of it. Mr. Osborne's telescope made it out
something like *Atalanta*. It is now twelve at night, and we
are still going nearly west, at a rapid pace. The sea is
peculiarly phosphorescent.

" P.S. [By Mr. Ainsworth.] It is now two A.M., and
nearly calm, as well as I can judge—but it is very difficult
to determine this point, since we move *with* the air so completely. I have not slept since quitting Weal-Vor, but
can stand it no longer, and must take a nap. We cannot
be far from the American coast.

" *Tuesday, the 9th.* [Mr. Ainsworth's MS.] *One* P.M.
We are in full view of the low coast of South Carolina. The
great problem is accomplished. We have crossed the
Atlantic—fairly and *easily* crossed it in a balloon ! God
be praised ! Who shall say that anything is impossible
hereafter ? "

in comparison with the extent of the prospect. In other words, the
base and hypothenuse of the supposed triangle would be so long,
when compared with the perpendicular, that the two former may
be regarded as nearly parallel. In this manner the horizon of
the aëronaut would appear to be *on a level* with the car. But, as
the point immediately beneath him seems, and is, at a great distance below him, it seems, of course, also, at a great distance below
the horizon. Hence the impression of *concavity* ; and this impression
must remain, until the elevation shall bear so great a proportion to
the extent of prospect, that the apparent parallelism of the base
and hypothenuse disappears—when the earth's real convexity must
become apparent.

The Journal here ceases. Some particulars of the
descent were communicated, however, by Mr. Ainsworth
to Mr. Forsyth. It was nearly dead calm when the voyagers
first came in view of the coast, which was immediately
recognised by both the seamen, and by Mr. Osborne. The
latter gentleman having acquaintances at Fort Moultrie,
it was immediately resolved to descend in its vicinity. The
balloon was brought over the beach (the tide being out
and the sand hard, smooth, and admirably adapted for a
descent), and the grapnel let go, which took firm hold at
once. The inhabitants of the island, and of the fort,
thronged out, of course, to see the balloon ; but it was with
the greatest difficulty that any one could be made to credit
the actual voyage—*the crossing of the Atlantic.* The grapnel
caught at two P.M. precisely ; and thus the whole voyage
was completed in seventy-five hours ; or rather less, counting from shore to shore. No serious accident occurred.
No real danger was at any time apprehended. The balloon
was exhausted and secured without trouble ; and when
the MS. from which this narrative is compiled was despatched from Charleston, the party were still at Fort
Moultrie. Their further intentions were not ascertained ;
but we can safely promise our readers some additional
information either on Monday or in the course of the next
day, at furthest.

This is unquestionably the most stupendous, the most
interesting, and the most important undertaking ever
accomplished or even attempted by man. What magnificent events may ensue, it would be useless now to think
of determining.

"THOU ART THE MAN"

I WILL now play the Œdipus to the Rattleborough enigma
I will expound to you—as I alone can—the secret of th
enginery that effected the Rattleborough miracle—th
one, the true, the admitted, the undisputed, the indisput
able miracle, which put a definite end to infidelity amon
the Rattleburghers, and converted to the orthodoxy o
the grandames all the carnal-minded who had venture
to be sceptical before.

This event—which I should be very sorry to discuss in
tone of unsuitable levity—occurred in the summer of 18—
Mr. Barnabas Shuttleworthy—one of the wealthiest an
most respectable citizens of the borough—had been missin
for several days under circumstances which gave rise t
suspicion of foul play.   Mr. Shuttleworthy had set out fron
Rattleborough very early one Saturday morning, on horse
back, with the avowed intention of proceeding to the cit
of——, about fifteen miles distant, and of returning th
night of the same day.   Two hours after his departure
however, his horse returned without him, and withou
the saddle-bags which had been strapped on his back a
starting.   The animal was wounded, too, and covered wit
mud.   These circumstances naturally gave rise to muc
alarm among the friends of the missing man ; and when i
was found, on Sunday morning, that he had not yet mad
his appearance, the whole borough arose *en masse* to go an
look for his body.

The foremost and most energetic in instituting this searc
was the bosom friend of Mr. Shuttleworthy—a Mr. Charle
Goodfellow, or, as he was universally called, " Charle
Goodfellow," or " Old Charley Goodfellow."   Now, whethe
it is a marvellous coincidence, or whether it is that th
name itself has an imperceptible effect upon the character
I have never yet been able to ascertain ; but the fact i
unquestionable, that there never yet was any person name
Charles who was not an open, manly, honest, good-natured
and frank-hearted fellow, with a rich, clear voice, that di
you good to hear it, and an eye that looked you alway
straight in the face, as much as to say : " I have a clea

onscience myself, am afraid of no man, and am altogether
above doing a mean action." And thus all the hearty, care-
ess, " walking gentlemen " of the stage are very certain
o be called Charles.

Now, " Old Charley Goodfellow," although he had been
n Rattleborough not longer than six months or thereabouts,
and although nobody knew anything about him before he
came to settle in the neighbourhood, had experienced no
difficulty in the world in making the acquaintance of all
the respectable people in the borough. Not a man of them
out would have taken his bare word for a thousand at any
moment ; and, as for the women, there is no saying what
they would not have done to oblige him. And all this came
of his having been christened Charles, and of his possessing,
in consequence, that ingenuous face which is proverbially
the very " best letter of recommendation."

I have already said that Mr. Shuttleworthy was one of the
most respectable, and, undoubtedly, he was the most
wealthy man in Rattleborough, while " Old Charley Goodfellow " was upon as intimate terms with him as if he had
been his own brother. The two old gentlemen were next-
door neighbours, and, although Mr. Shuttleworthy seldom,
if ever, visited " Old Charley," and never was known to
take a meal in his house, still this did not prevent the two
friends from being exceedingly intimate, as I have just
observed ; for " Old Charley " never let a day pass without
stepping in three or four times to see how his neighbour
came on, and very often he would stay to breakfast or tea,
and almost always to dinner ; and then the amount of wine
that was made way with by the two cronies at a sitting,
it would really be a difficult thing to ascertain. " Old
Charley's " favourite beverage was *Chateau-Margaux*, and
it appeared to do Mr. Shuttleworthy's heart good to see
the old fellow swallow it, as he did, quart after quart ;
so that, one day, when the wine was *in* and the wit, as a
natural consequence, somewhat *out*, he said to his crony,
as he slapped him upon the back : " I tell you what it is,
' Old Charley,' you are, by all odds, the heartiest old fellow
I ever came across in all my born days ; and, since you
love to guzzle the wine at that fashion, I'll be darned if
I don't have to make thee a present of a big box of the
Chateau-Margaux. Od rot me,"—(Mr. Shuttleworthy had
a sad habit of swearing, although he seldom went beyond

" Od rot me," or " By gosh," or " By the jolly golly,")—
" Od rot me," says he, " if I don't send an order to town this
very afternoon for a double box of the best that can be got,
and I'll make ye a present of it, I will !—ye needn't say a
word now—I *will*, I tell ye, and there's an end of it ; so look
out for it—it will come to hand some of these fine days
precisely when ye are looking for it the least ! "   I mention
this little bit of liberality on the part of Mr. Shuttleworthy,
just by way of showing you how *very* intimate an understanding existed between the two friends.

Well, on the Sunday morning in question, when it came
to be fairly understood that Mr. Shuttleworthy had met
with foul play, I never saw any one so profoundly affected
as " Old Charley Goodfellow."   When he first heard that
the horse had come home without his master, and without
his master's saddle-bags, and all bloody from a pistol-shot,
that had gone clean through and through the poor animal's
chest without quite killing him—when he heard all this,
he turned as pale as if the missing man had been his own
dear brother or father, and shivered and shook all over
as if he had had a fit of the ague.

At first he was too much overpowered with grief to be able
to do anything at all, or to decide upon any plan of action ;
so that for a long time he endeavoured to dissuade Mr.
Shuttleworthy's other friends from making a stir about
the matter, thinking it best to wait a while—say for a week
or two, or a month or two—to see if something wouldn't
turn up, or if Mr. Shuttleworthy wouldn't come in the
natural way, and explain his reasons for sending his horse
on before.   I dare say you have often observed this disposition to temporise, or to procrastinate, in people who
are labouring under any very poignant sorrow.   Their
powers of mind seem to be rendered torpid, so that they
have a horror of anything like action, and like nothing
in the world so well as to lie quietly in bed and " nurse their
grief," as the old ladies express it—that is to say, ruminate
over their trouble.

The people of Rattleborough had, indeed, so high an
opinion of the wisdom and discretion of " Old Charley," that
the greater part of them felt disposed to agree with him,
and not make a stir in the business " until something should
turn up," as the honest old gentleman worded it ; and I
believe that, after all, this would have been the general

etermination, but for the very suspicious interference
f Mr. Shuttleworthy's nephew, a young man of very dis-
ipated habits, and otherwise of rather bad character.
'his nephew, whose name was Pennifeather, would listen
o nothing like reason in the matter of " lying quiet," but
nsisted upon making immediate search for the " corpse
f the murdered man." This was the expression he em-
•loyed ; and Mr. Goodfellow acutely remarked at the time,
hat it was " a *singular* expression, to say no more." This
emark of " Old Charley's," too, had great effect upon
he crowd ; and one of the party was heard to ask, very
mpressively ; " how it happened that young Mr. Penni-
eather was so intimately cognisant of all the circumstances
onnected with his wealthy uncle's disappearance, as to
eel authorised to assert, distinctly and unequivocally, that
•is uncle *was* ' a murdered man.' " Hereupon some little
quibbling and bickering occurred among various members
•f the crowd, and especially between " Old Charley " and
Mr. Pennifeather—although this latter occurrence was,
ndeed, by no means a novelty, for little good-will had sub-
.isted between the parties for the last three or four months ;
nd matters had even gone so far that Mr. Pennifeather
aad actually knocked down his uncle's friend for some
alleged excess of liberty that the latter had taken in the
incle's house, of which the nephew was an inmate. Upon
his occasion " Old Charley " is said to have behaved
vith exemplary moderation and Christian charity. He
arose from the blow, adjusted his clothes, and made no
attempt at retaliation at all—merely muttering a few words
about " taking summary vengeance at the first convenient
•pportunity,"—a natural and very justifiable ebullition of
anger, which meant nothing, however, and, beyond doubt,
vas no sooner given vent to than forgotten.

However these matters may be (which have no reference
to the point now at issue), it is quite certain that the people
of Rattleborough, principally through the persuasion of
Mr. Pennifeather, came at length to the determination of
dispersing over the adjacent country in search of the missing
Mr. Shuttleworthy. I say they came to this determination
in the first instance. After it had been fully resolved
that a search should be made, it was considered almost
a matter of course that the seekers should disperse—that
is to say, distribute themselves in parties—for the more

thorough examination of the region round about. I forget
however, by what ingenious train of reasoning it was tha
" Old Charley " finally convinced the assembly that thi
was the most injudicious plan that could be pursued. Con
vince them, however, he did—all except Mr. Pennifeather
and, in the end, it was arranged that a search should b
instituted, carefully and very thoroughly, by the burgher
en masse, " Old Charley " himself leading the way.

As for the matter of that, there could have been n
better pioneer than " Old Charley," whom everybody knew
to have the eye of a lynx ; but, although he led them int
all manner of out-of-the-way holes and corners, by route
that nobody had ever suspected of existing in the neigh
bourhood, and although the search was incessantly kep
up day and night for nearly a week, still no trace of Mr
Shuttleworthy could be discovered. When I say no trace
however, I must not be understood to speak literally
for trace, to some extent, there certainly was. The poo
gentleman had been tracked, by his horse's shoes (which
were peculiar), to a spot about three miles to the east o
the borough, on the main road leading to the city. Her
the track made off into a by-path through a piece of wood
land—the path coming out again into the main road, and
cutting off about half a mile of the regular distance. Follow
ing the shoemarks down this lane, the party came at lengt!
to a pool of stagnant water, half-hidden by the brambles, t
the right of the lane, and opposite this pool all vestige o
the track was lost sight of. It appeared, however, that a
struggle of some nature had here taken place, and it seemec
as if some large and heavy body, much larger and heavie
than a man, had been drawn from the by-path to the pool
This latter was carefully dragged twice, but nothing wa
found ; and the party were upon the point of going away
in despair of coming to any result, when Providence sug
gested to Mr. Goodfellow the expediency of draining the
water off altogether. This project was received with
cheers, and many high compliments to " Old Charley '
upon his sagacity and consideration. As many of the
burghers had brought spades with them, supposing that
they might possibly be called upon to disinter a corpse
the drain was easily and speedily effected ; and no sooner
was the bottom visible, than right in the middle of the
mud that remained was discovered a black silk velvet

waistcoat, which nearly every one present immediately
recognised as the property of Mr. Pennifeather. This
waistcoat was much torn and stained with blood, and there
were several persons among the party who had a distinct
remembrance of its having been worn by its owner on the
very morning of Mr. Shuttleworthy's departure for the
city ; while there were others again, ready to testify upon
oath, if required, that Mr. P. did *not* wear the garment in
question at any period during the *remainder* of that memorable day ; nor could any one be found to say that he had
seen it upon Mr. P.'s person at any period at all subsequent
to Mr. Shuttleworthy's disappearance.

Matters now wore a very serious aspect for Mr. Pennifeather, and it was observed, as an indubitable confirmation
of the suspicions which were excited against him, that he
grew exceedingly pale, and when asked what he had to
say for himself, was utterly incapable of saying a word.
Hereupon, the few friends his riotous mode of living had
left him deserted him at once to a man, and were even
more clamorous than his ancient and avowed enemies for
his instantaneous arrest. But, on the other hand, the
magnanimity of Mr. Goodfellow shone forth with only the
more brilliant lustre through contrast. He made a warm
and intensely eloquent defence of Mr. Pennifeather, in
which he alluded more than once to his own sincere for-
giveness of that wild young gentleman—" the heir of the
worthy Mr. Shuttleworthy,"—for the insult which he
(the young gentleman) had, no doubt in the heat of passion,
thought proper to put upon him (Mr. Goodfellow). " He
forgave him for it," he said, " from the very bottom of his
heart ; and for himself (Mr. Goodfellow), so far from
pushing the suspicious circumstances to extremity, which,
he was sorry to say, really *had* arisen against Mr. Pennifeather, he (Mr. Goodfellow) would make every exertion
in his power, would employ all the little eloquence in his
possession to—to—to—soften down, as much as he could
conscientiously do so, the worst features of this really
exceedingly perplexing piece of business."

Mr. Goodfellow went on for some half-hour longer in
this strain, very much to the credit both of his head and
of his heart ; but your warm-hearted people are seldom
apposite in their observations—they run into all sorts of
blunders, *contre-temps* and *mal àpropos-isms*, in the hot-

headedness of their zeal to serve a friend—thus, often with the kindest intentions in the world, doing infinitely more to prejudice his cause than to advance it.

So, in the present instance, it turned out with all the eloquence of " Old Charley " ; for, although he laboured earnestly in behalf of the suspected, yet it so happened somehow or other, that every syllable he uttered of which the direct but unwitting tendency was not to exalt the speaker in the good opinion of his audience, had the effect of deepening the suspicion already attached to the individual whose cause he pled, and of arousing against him the fury of the mob.

One of the most unaccountable errors committed by the orator was his allusion to the suspected as " the heir of the worthy old gentleman, Mr. Shuttleworthy." The people had really never thought of this before. They had only remembered certain threats of disinheritance uttered a year or two previously by the uncle (who had no living relative except the nephew), and they had, therefore, always looked upon this disinheritance as a matter that was settled—so single-minded a race of beings were the Rattleburghers ; but the remark of " Old Charley " brought them at once to a consideration of this point, and thus gave them to see the possibility of the threats having been nothing *more* than a threat. And straightway, hereupon, arose the natural question of *cui bono ?*—a question that tended even more than the waistcoat to fasten the terrible crime upon the young man. And here, lest I be misunderstood, permit me to digress for one moment merely to observe that the exceedingly brief and simple Latin phrase which I have employed, is invariably mistranslated and misconceived. " *Cui bono ?* " in all the crack novels and elsewhere,—in those of Mrs. Gore, for example (the author of *Cecil*), a lady who quotes all tongues from the Chaldæan to Chickasaw, and is helped to her learning, " as needed," upon a systematic plan, by Mr. Beckford,—in *all* the crack novels, I say, from those of Bulwer and Dickens to those of Turnapenny and Ainsworth, the two little Latin words *cui bono* are rendered " to what purpose ? " or (as if *quo bono*) " to what good ? " Their true meaning, nevertheless, is " for whose advantage." *Cui*, to whom ; *bono*, is it for a benefit ? It is a purely legal phrase, and applicable precisely in cases such as we have now under consideration, where the probability of the doer of a deed hinges upon the probability of the benefit accruing to this individual or to that from the deed's accomplishment. Now, in the present instance, the question *cui bono?* very pointedly implicated Mr. Pennifeather. His uncle had threatened him, after making a will in his favour, with disinheritance. But the threat had not been actually kept; the original will, it appeared, had not been altered. *Had* it been altered, the only supposable motive for murder on the part of the suspected would have been the ordinary one of revenge; and even this would have been counteracted by the hope of reinstation into the good graces of the uncle. But the will being unaltered, while the threat to alter remained suspended over the nephew's head, there appears at once the very strongest possible inducement for the atrocity; and so concluded, very sagaciously, the worthy citizens of the borough of Rattle.

Mr. Pennifeather was, accordingly, arrested upon the spot, and the crowd, after some further search, proceeded homeward, having him in custody. On the route, however, another circumstance occurred tending to confirm the suspicion entertained. Mr. Goodfellow, whose zeal led him to be always a little in advance of the party, was seen suddenly to run forward a few paces, stoop, and then apparently to pick up some small object from the grass. Having quickly examined it, he was observed, too, to make a sort of half attempt at concealing it in his coat pocket; but this action was noticed, as I say, and consequently prevented, when the object picked up was found to be a Spanish knife which a dozen persons at once recognised as belonging to Mr. Pennifeather. Moreover, his initials were engraved upon the handle. The blade of this knife was open and bloody.

No doubt now remained of the guilt of the nephew, and immediately upon reaching Rattleborough he was taken before a magistrate for examination.

Here matters again took a most unfavourable turn. The prisoner being questioned as to his whereabouts on the morning of Mr. Shuttleworthy's disappearance, had absolutely the audacity to acknowledge that on that very morning he had been out with his rifle deer-stalking, in the immediate neighbourhood of the pool where the blood-

stained waistcoat had been discovered through the sagacit
of Mr. Goodfellow.

This latter now came forward, and, with tears in his eyes
asked permission to be examined. He said that a ster
sense of the duty he owed his Maker, not less than hi
fellow-men, would permit him no longer to remain silen
Hitherto, the sincerest affection for the young man (not
withstanding the latter's ill treatment of himself, Mr
Goodfellow) had induced him to make every hypothesi
which imagination could suggest, by way of endeavourin
to account for what appeared suspicious in the circum
stances that told so seriously against Mr. Pennifeather
but these circumstances were now altogether *too* con
vincing—*too* damning ; he would hesitate no longer—h
would tell all he knew, although his heart (Mr. Goodfellow's
should absolutely burst asunder in the effort. He the
went on to state that, on the afternoon of the day previou
to Mr. Shuttleworthy's departure for the city, that worth
old gentleman had mentioned to his nephew, in *his* hearin
(Mr. Goodfellow's), that his object in going to town on th
morrow was to make a deposit of an unusually large sum
of money in the " Farmers' and Mechanics' Bank," and
that, then and there, the said Mr. Shuttleworthy ha
distinctly avowed to the said nephew his irrevocable de
termination of rescinding the will originally made, and o
cutting him off with a shilling. He (the witness) nov
solemnly called upon the accused to state whether wha
he (the witness) had just stated was or was not the trut
in every substantial particular. Much to the astonishmen
of every one present Mr. Pennifeather frankly admitted
that *it was*.

The magistrate now considered it his duty to send
couple of constables to search the chamber of the accused
in the house of his uncle. From this search they almos
immediately returned with the well-known steel-bound
russet leather pocket-book which the old gentleman ha
been in the habit of carrying for years. Its valuabl
contents, however, had been abstracted, and the magistrat
in vain endeavoured to extort from the prisoner the us
which had been made of them, or the place of their con
cealment. Indeed, he obstinately denied all knowledg
of the matter. The constables, also, discovered betweer
the bed and sacking of the unhappy man, a shirt and neck

handkerchief both marked with the initials of his name, and both hideously besmeared with the blood of the victim.

At this juncture, it was announced that the horse of the murdered man had just expired in the stable from the effects of the wound he had received, and it was proposed by Mr. Goodfellow that a *post-mortem* examination of the beast should be immediately made, with the view, if possible, of discovering the ball. This was accordingly done ; and, as if to demonstrate beyond a question the guilt of the accused, Mr. Goodfellow, after considerable searching in the cavity of the chest, was enabled to detect and to pull forth a bullet of very extraordinary size, which, upon trial, was found to be exactly adapted to the bore of Mr. Pennifeather's rifle, while it was far too large for that of any other person in the borough or its vicinity. To render the matter even surer yet, however, this bullet was discovered to have a flaw or seam at right angles to the usual suture ; and upon examination, this seam corresponded precisely with an accidental ridge or elevation in a pair of moulds acknowledged by the accused himself to be his own property. Upon the finding of this bullet, the examining magistrate refused to listen to any further testimony, and immediately committed the prisoner for trial—declining resolutely to take any bail in the case, although against this severity Mr. Goodfellow very warmly remonstrated, and offered to become surety in whatever amount might be required. This generosity on the part of " Old Charley " was only in accordance with the whole tenor of his amiable and chivalrous conduct during the entire period of his sojourn in the borough of Rattle. In the present instance, the worthy man was so entirely carried away by the excessive warmth of his sympathy, that he seemed to have quite forgotten, when he offered to go bail for his young friend, that he himself (Mr. Goodfellow) did not possess a single dollar's worth of property upon the face of the earth.

The result of the committal may be readily foreseen. Mr. Pennifeather, amid the loud execrations of all Rattleborough, was brought to trial at the next criminal sessions, when the chain of circumstantial evidence (strengthened as it was by some additional damning facts, which Mr. Goodfellow's sensitive conscientiousness forbade him to

withhold from the court) was considered so unbroken and
so thoroughly conclusive, that the jury, without leaving
their seats, returned an immediate verdict of " Guilty
of murder in the first degree." Soon afterward the unhappy wretch received sentence of death, and was remanded to the county jail to await the inexorable vengeance
of the law.

In the meantime, the noble behaviour of " Old Charley
Goodfellow " had doubly endeared him to the honest
citizens of the borough. He became ten times a greater
favourite than ever ; and, as a natural result of the hos-
pitality with which he was treated, he relaxed, as it were,
perforce, the extremely parsimonious habits which his
poverty had hitherto impelled him to observe, and very
frequently had little *réunions* at his own house, when wit
and jollity reigned supreme—dampened a little, *of course*,
by the occasional remembrance of the untoward and
melancholy fate which impended over the nephew of the
late lamented bosom friend of the generous host.

One fine day, this magnanimous old gentleman was
agreeably surprised at the receipt of the following letter :—

Charles Goodfellow, Esq., Rattleborough. From H., F., B., & Co. Chat.-Mar. A—No. 1.—6 doz. bts. (½ Gross).

" *Charles Goodfellow, Esquire ;*
  " *Dear Sir*—*In conformity with an order transmitted
to our firm about two months since, by our esteemed
correspondent, Mr. Barnabas Shuttleworthy, we have
the honour of forwarding this morning, to your address,
a double box of Chateau-Margaux, of the antelope brand,
violet seal. Box numbered and marked as per margin.*
         " *We remain, sir,*
               " *Your most ob'nt ser'ts,*
                     " Hoggs, Frogs, Bogs, & Co.
  " *City of*——, *June* 21, 18—.

    " P.S.—*The box will reach you, by wagon, on the day
after your receipt of this letter. Our respects to Mr.
Shuttleworthy.*   H., F., B., & Co."

The fact is, that Mr. Goodfellow had, since the death of
Mr. Shuttleworthy, given over all expectation of ever
receiving the promised Chateau-Margaux ; and he therefore looked upon it *now* as a sort of especial dispensation
of Providence in his behalf. He was highly delighted, of
course, and in the exuberance of his joy invited a large
party of friends to a *petit souper* on the morrow, for the
purpose of broaching the good old Mr. Shuttleworthy's

resent. **Not** that he *said* anything about " the good old
Mr. Shuttleworthy " when he issued the invitations. The
act is, he thought much and concluded to say nothing at
all. He did *not* mention to any one—if I remember aright
—that he had received a *present* of Chateau-Margaux.
He merely asked his friends to come and help him drink
some of a remarkably fine quality and rich flavour that
he had ordered up from the city a couple of months ago,
and of which he would be in the receipt upon the morrow.
I have often puzzled myself to imagine *why* it was that
" Old Charley " came to the conclusion to say nothing
about having received the wine from his old friend, but I
could never precisely understand his reason for the silence,
although he had *some* excellent and very magnanimous
reason, no doubt.

The morrow at length arrived, and with it a very large
and highly respectable company at Mr. Goodfellow's house.
Indeed, half the borough was there—I myself among the
number—but, much to the vexation of the host, the
Chateau-Margaux did not arrive until a late hour, and
when the sumptuous supper supplied by " Old Charley "
had been done very ample justice by the guests. It came
at length, however, a monstrously big box of it there was,
too,—and as the whole party were in excessively good
humour, it was decided, *nem. con.*, that it should be lifted
upon the table and its contents disembowelled forthwith.

No sooner said than done. I lent a helping hand ; and,
in a trice, we had the box upon the table, in the midst of
all the bottles and glasses, not a few of which were de-
molished in the scuffle. " Old Charley," who was pretty
much intoxicated, and excessively red in the face, now took
a seat, with an air of mock dignity, at the head of the
board, and thumped furiously upon it with a decanter,
calling the company to keep order " during the ceremony
of disinterring the treasure."

After some vociferation, quiet was at length fully
restored, and, as very often happens in similar cases, a
profound and remarkable silence ensued. Being then
requested to force open the lid, I complied, of course,
" with an infinite deal of pleasure." I inserted a chisel,
and giving it a few slight taps with a hammer, the top of
the box flew suddenly off, and, at the same instant, there
sprang up into a sitting position, directly facing the host,

the bruised, bloody, and nearly putrid corpse of th
murdered Mr. Shuttleworthy himself. It gazed for a fev
moments, fixedly and sorrowfully, with its decaying an
lack-lustre eyes, full into the countenance of Mr. Good
fellow ; uttered slowly, but clearly and impressively, th
words—" Thou art the man ! " and then, falling over th
side of the chest as if thoroughly satisfied, stretched ou
its limbs quiveringly upon the table.

The scene that ensued is altogether beyond description
The rush for the doors and windows was terrific, and many
of the most robust men in the room fainted outrigh
through sheer horror. But after the first wild, shrieking
burst of affright, all eyes were directed to Mr. Goodfellow
I I live a thousand years, I can never forget the mor
than mortal agony which was depicted in that ghastly
face of his, so lately rubicund with triumph and wine.
For several minutes he sat rigidly as a statue of marble ;
his eyes seeming, in the intense vacancy of their gaze, to
be turned inward and absorbed in the contemplation of his
own miserable murderous soul. At length their expression
appeared to flash suddenly out into the external world,
when, with a quick leap, he sprang from his chair, and
falling heavily with his head and shoulders upon the table,
and in contact with the corpse, poured out rapidly and
vehemently a detailed confession of the hideous crime for
which Mr. Pennifeather was then imprisoned and doomed
to die.

What he recounted was in substance this :—He followed
his victim to the vicinity of the pool ; there shot his horse
with a pistol ; despatched its rider with the butt end ;
possessed himself of the pocket-book ; and, supposing the
horse dead, dragged it with great labour to the brambles
by the pond. Upon his own beast he slung the corpse
of Mr. Shuttleworthy, and thus bore it to a secure place
of concealment a long distance off through the woods.

The waistcoat, the knife, the pocket-book, and bullet,
had been placed by himself where found, with the view of
avenging himself upon Mr. Pennifeather. He had also contrived the discovery of the stained handkerchief and shirt.

Toward the end of the blood-chilling recital, the words
of the guilty wretch faltered and grew hollow. When the
record was finally exhausted, he arose, staggered backward from the table, and fell—*dead*.

The means by which this happily-timed confession was
xtorted, although efficient, were simple indeed. Mr.
Goodfellow's excess of frankness had disgusted me, and
xcited my suspicions from the first. I was present when
Mr. Pennifeather had struck him, and the fiendish expres-
ion which then arose upon his countenance, although
momentary, assured me that his threat of vengeance
would, if possible, be rigidly fulfilled. I was thus prepared
to view the *manœuvring* of " Old Charley " in a very
different light from that in which it was regarded by
he good citizens of Rattleborough. I saw at once that all
he criminating discoveries arose, either directly or in-
directly, from himself. But the fact which clearly opened
my eyes to the true state of the case, was the affair of the
bullet, *found* by Mr. G. in the carcass of the horse. *I* had
not forgotten, although the Rattleburghers *had*, that there
was a hole where the ball had entered the horse, and another
where it *went out.* If it were found in the animal then,
after having made its exit, I saw clearly that it must have
been deposited by the person who found it. The bloody
shirt and handkerchief confirmed the idea suggested by
the bullet ; for the blood on examination proved to be
capital claret, and no more. When I came to think of
these things, and also of the late increase of liberality
and expenditure on the part of Mr. Goodfellow, I entertained a suspicion which was none the less strong because
I kept it altogether to myself.

In the meantime, I instituted a rigorous private search
for the corpse of Mr. Shuttleworthy, and, for good reasons,
searched in quarters as divergent as possible from those to
which Mr. Goodfellow conducted his party. The result
was that, after some days, I came across an old dry well,
the mouth of which was nearly hidden by brambles ;
and here, at the bottom, I discovered what I sought.

Now it so happened that I had overheard the colloquy
between the two cronies, when Mr. Goodfellow had contrived to cajole his host into the promise of a box of Chateau-
Margaux. Upon this hint I acted. I procured a stiff piece
of whalebone, thrust it down the throat of the corpse, and
deposited the latter in an old wine box—taking care so to
double the body up as to double the whalebone with it. In
this manner I had to press forcibly upon the lid to keep it
down while I secured it with nails ; and I anticipated, of

course, that as soon as these latter were removed, the top would fly *off* and the body *up*.

Having thus arranged the box, I marked, numbered and addressed it as already told ; and then writing a letter in the name of the wine-merchants with whom Mr. Shuttleworthy dealt, I gave instructions to my servant to wheel the box to Mr. Goodfellow's door, in a barrow, at a given signal from myself. For the words which I intended the corpse to speak, I confidently depended upon my ventriloquial abilities ; for their effect, I counted upon the conscience of the murderous wretch.

I believe there is nothing more to be explained. Mr Pennifeather was released upon the spot, inherited the fortune of his uncle, profited by the lessons of experience, turned over a new leaf, and led happily ever afterward a new life.

THE COLLOQUY OF MONOS AND UNA

Μέλλοντα ταῦτα.

SOPHOCLES—*Antigone.*

" These things are in the near future."

UNA.   " Born again ? "

MONOS.   Yes, fairest and best beloved Una, " born again." These were the words upon whose mystical meaning I had so long pondered, rejecting the explanations of the priesthood, until Death itself resolved for me the secret.

UNA.   Death !

MONOS.   How strangely, sweet Una, you echo my words ! I observe, too, a vacillation in your step, a joyous inquietude in your eyes. You are confused and oppressed by the majestic novelty of the Life Eternal. Yes, it was of Death I spoke. And here how singularly sounds that word which of old was wont to bring terror to all hearts, throwing a mildew upon all pleasures !

UNA.   Ah, Death, the spectre which sat at all feasts ! How often, Monos, did we lose ourselves in speculations upon its nature ! How mysteriously did it act as a check

to human bliss, saying unto it, " thus far, and no farther ! "
That earnest, mutual love, my own Monos, which burned
within our bosoms, how vainly did we flatter ourselves,
feeling happy in its first upspringing that our happiness
would strengthen with its strength ! Alas ! as it grew,
so grew in our hearts the dread of that evil hour which was
hurrying to separate us for ever ! Thus in time it became
painful to love. Hate would have been mercy then.

Monos. Speak not here of these griefs, dear Una—mine,
mine for ever now !

Una. But the memory of past sorrow, is it not present
joy ? I have much to say yet of the things which have
been. Above all, I burn to know the incidents of your
own passage through the dark Valley and Shadow.

Monos. And when did the radiant Una ask anything
of her Monos in vain ? I will be minute in relating all,
but at what point shall the weird narrative begin ?

Una. At what point ?

Monos. You have said.

Una. Monos, I comprehend you. In Death we have
both learned the propensity of man to define the indefinable.
I will not say, then, commence with the moment of life's
cessation—but commence with that sad, sad instant when,
the fever having abandoned you, you sank into a breathless
and motionless torpor, and I pressed down your pallid
eyelids with the passionate fingers of love.

Monos. One word first, my Una, in regard to man's
general condition at this epoch. You will remember that
one or two of the wise among our forefathers—wise in fact,
although not in the world's esteem—had ventured to
doubt the propriety of the term " improvement," as
applied to the progress of our civilisation. There were
periods in each of the five or six centuries immediately preceding our dissolution when arose some vigorous intellect,
boldly contending for those principles whose truth appears
now, to our disenfranchised reason, so utterly obvious—
principles which should have taught our race to submit to
the guidance of the natural laws rather than attempt their
control. At long intervals some master-minds appeared,
looking upon each advance in practical science as a retro-
gradation in the true utility. Occasionally the poetic
intellect—that intellect which we now feel to have been
the most exalted of all—since those truths which to us

s

were of the most enduring importance could only be reached
by that *analogy* which speaks in proof-tones to the imagination alone, and to the unaided reason bears no weight
—occasionally did this poetic intellect proceed a step
farther in the evolving of the vague idea of the philosophic,
and find in the mystic parable that tells of the tree of
knowledge, and of its forbidden fruit, death-producing, a
distinct intimation that knowledge was not meet for man
in the infant condition of his soul. And these men—
the poets—living and perishing amid the scorn of the
" utilitarians "—of rough pedants, who arrogated to themselves a title which could have been properly applied only
to the scorned—these men, the poets, pondered piningly
yet not unwisely, upon the ancient days when our wants
were not more simple than our enjoyments were keen—
days when *mirth* was a word unknown, so solemnly deep
toned was happiness—holy, august, and blissful days
when blue rivers ran undammed, between hills unhewn
into far forest solitudes, primæval, odorous, and unexplored
Yet these noble exceptions from the general misrule served
but to strengthen it by opposition. Alas ! we had fallen
upon the most evil of all our evil days. The great " move
ment "—that was the cant term—went on : a diseased
commotion, moral and physical. Art—the Arts—arose
supreme, and once enthroned, cast chains upon the intellec
which had elevated them to power. Man, because he coul
not but acknowledge the majesty of Nature, fell into childish
exultation at his acquired and still-increasing dominio
over her elements. Even while he stalked a God in hi
own fancy, an infantine imbecility came over him. A
might be supposed from the origin of his disorder, he gre
infected with system, and with abstraction. He enwrappe
himself in generalities. Among other odd ideas, that o
universal equality gained ground : and in the face of analog
and of God—in despite of the loud warning voice of th
laws of *gradation* so visibly pervading all things in Eart
and Heaven—wild attempts at an omni-prevalent Demo
cracy were made. Yet this evil sprang necessarily fro
the leading evil, Knowledge. Man could not both kno
and succumb. Meantime huge smoking cities aros
innumerable. Green leaves shrank before the hot breat
of furnaces. The fair face of Nature was deformed as wit
the ravages of some loathsome disease. And methink

sweet Una, even our slumbering sense of the forced and of the far-fetched might have arrested us here. But now it appears that we had worked out our own destruction in the perversion of our *taste*, or rather in the blind neglect of its culture in the schools. For, in truth, it was at this crisis that taste alone—that faculty which, holding a middle position between the pure intellect and the moral sense, could never safely have been disregarded—it was now that taste alone could have led us gently back to Beauty, to Nature, and to Life. But alas for the pure contemplative spirit and majestic intuition of Plato! Alas for the μουσική which he justly regarded as an all-sufficient education for the soul! Alas for him and for it! —since both were most desperately needed when both were most entirely forgotten or despised.*

Pascal, a philosopher whom we both love, has said, how truly!—" *que tout notre raisonnement se réduit à céder au sentiment;* " and it is not impossible that the sentiment of the natural, had time permitted it, would have regained its old ascendency over the harsh mathematical reason of the schools. But this thing was not to be. Prematurely induced by intemperance of knowledge, the old age of the world drew on. This the mass of mankind saw not, or, living lustily although unhappily, affected not to see. But, for myself, the Earth's records had taught me to look for widest ruin as the price of highest civilisation. I had imbibed a prescience of our Fate from comparison of China, the simple and enduring, with Assyria, the architect, with Egypt, the astrologer, with Nubia, more crafty than

* " It will be hard to discover a better [method of education] than that which the experience of so many ages has already discovered; and this may be summed up as consisting in gymnastics for the body, and *music* for the soul."—*Repub.* lib. 2. " For this reason is a musical education most essential; since it causes Rhythm and Harmony to penetrate most intimately into the soul, taking the strongest hold upon it, filling it with *beauty*, and making the man *beautiful-minded.* . . . He will praise and admire *the beautiful*; will receive it with joy into his soul, will feed upon it, and *assimilate his own condition with it.*"—*Ibid.* lib. 3. Music (μουσική) had, however, among the Athenians, a far more comprehensive signification than with us. It included not only the harmonies of time and of tune, but the poetic diction, sentiment, and creation, each in its widest sense. The study of *music* was with them, in fact, the general cultivation of the taste—of that which recognises the beautiful—in contradistinction from reason, which deals only with the true.

either, the turbulent mother of all Arts.   In the history *
of these regions I met with a ray from the Future.   The
individual artificialities of the three latter were local
diseases of the Earth, and in their individual overthrows
we had seen local remedies applied ; but for the infected
world at large I could anticipate no regeneration save
in death.   That man, as a race, should not become extinct,
I saw that he must be " *born again.*"

And now it was, fairest and dearest, that we wrapped
our spirits daily in dreams.   Now it was that, in twilight,
we discoursed of the days to come, when the Art-scarred
surface of the Earth, having undergone that purification †
which alone could efface its rectangular obscenities, should
clothe itself anew in the verdure and the mountain-slopes
and the smiling waters of Paradise, and be rendered at
length a fit dwelling-place for man :—for man the Death-
purged—for man to whose now exalted intellect there
should be poison in knowledge no more—for the redeemed,
regenerated, blissful, and now immortal, but still for the
material, man.

UNA.   Well do I remember these conversations, dear
Monos ; but the epoch of the fiery overthrow was not so
near at hand as we believed, and as the corruption you
indicate did surely warrant us in believing.   Men lived and
died individually.   You yourself sickened, and passed
into the grave ; and thither your constant Una speedily
followed you.   And though the century which has since
elapsed, and whose conclusion brings us thus together
once more, tortured our slumbering senses with no
impatience of duration, yet, my Monos, it was a century
still.

MONOS.   Say, rather, a point in the vague infinity.
Unquestionably, it was in the Earth's dotage that I died.
Wearied at heart with anxieties which had their origin
in the general turmoil and decay, I succumbed to the
fierce fever.   After some few days of pain, and many of
dreamy delirium replete with ecstasy, the manifestations
of which you mistook for pain, while I longed but was
impotent to undeceive you—after some days there came
upon me, as you have said, a breathless and motionless

* " History," from ἱστορεῖν, to inquire.
† The word " *purification* " seems here to be used with reference
to its root in the Greek πῦρ, fire.

torpor; and this was termed *Death* by those who stood around me.

Words are vague things. My condition did not deprive me of sentience. It appeared to me not greatly dissimilar to the extreme quiescence of him, who, having slumbered long and profoundly, lying motionless and fully prostrate in a midsummer noon, begins to steal slowly back into consciousness, through the mere sufficiency of his sleep, and without being awakened by external disturbances.

I breathed no longer. The pulses were still. The heart had ceased to beat. Volition had not departed, but was powerless. The senses were unusually active, although eccentrically so—assuming often each other's functions at random. The taste and the smell were inextricably confounded, and became one sentiment, abnormal and intense. The rose-water with which your tenderness had moistened my lips to the last, affected me with sweet fancies of flowers—fantastic flowers, far more lovely than any of the old Earth, but whose prototypes we have here blooming around us. The eyelids, transparent and bloodless, offered no complete impediment to vision. As volition was in abeyance, the balls could not roll in their sockets—but all objects within the range of the visual hemisphere were seen with more or less distinctness; the rays which fell upon the external retina, or into the corner of the eye, producing a more vivid effect than those which struck the front or interior surface. Yet, in the former instance, this effect was so far anomalous that I appreciated it only as *sound*—sound sweet or discordant as the matters presenting themselves at my side were light or dark in shade—curved or angular in outline. The hearing, at the same time, although excited in degree, was not irregular in action—estimating real sounds with an extravagance of precision, not less than of sensibility. Touch had undergone a modification more peculiar. Its impressions were tardily received, but pertinaciously retained, and resulted always in the highest physical pleasure. Thus the pressure of your sweet fingers upon my eyelids, at first only recognised through vision, at length, long after their removal, filled my whole being with a sensuous delight immeasurable. I say with a sensuous delight. *All* my perceptions were purely sensuous. The materials furnished the passive brain by the senses were not in the least degree wrought into shape by the deceased understanding. Of pain there was some little ; of pleasure there was much ; but of moral pain or pleasure none at all. Thus your wild sobs floated into my ear with all their mournful cadences, and were appreciated in their every variation of sad tone ; but they were soft musical sounds and no more ; they conveyed to the extinct reason no intimation of the sorrows which gave them birth ; while the large and constant tears which fell upon my face, telling the bystanders of a heart which broke, thrilled every fibre of my frame with ecstasy alone. And this was in truth the *Death* of which these bystanders spoke reverently, in low whispers—you, sweet Una, gaspingly, with loud cries.

They attired me for the coffin—three or four dark figures which flitted busily to and fro. As these crossed the direct line of my vision they affected me as *forms* ; but upon passing to my side their images impressed me with the idea of shrieks, groans, and other dismal expressions of terror, of horror, or of woe. You alone, habited in a white robe, passed in all directions musically about me.

The day waned ; and, as its light faded away, I became possessed by a vague uneasiness—an anxiety such as the sleeper feels when sad real sounds fall continuously within his ear—low distant bell-tones, solemn, at long but equal intervals, and commingling with melancholy dreams. Night arrived, and with its shadows a heavy discomfort. It oppressed my limbs with the oppression of some dull weight, and was palpable. There was also a moaning sound, not unlike the distant reverberation of surf, but more continuous, which, beginning with the first twilight, had grown in strength with the darkness. Suddenly lights were brought into the room, and this reverberation became forthwith interrupted into frequent unequal bursts of the same sound, but less dreary and less distinct. The ponderous oppression was in a great measure relieved ; and, issuing from the flame of each lamp (for there were many) there flowed unbrokenly into my ears a strain of melodious monotone. And when now, dear Una, approaching the bed upon which I lay outstretched, you sat gently by my side, breathing odour from your sweet lips, and pressing them upon my brow, there arose tremulously within my bosom, and mingling with the merely physical sensations which circumstances had called forth, a something akin to sentiment itself—a feeling that, half appreciating, half responded to your earnest love and sorrow ; but this feeling took no root in the pulseless heart, and seemed indeed rather a shadow than a reality, and faded quickly away, first into extreme quiescence, and then into a purely sensuous pleasure as before.

And now, from the wreck and the chaos of the usual senses, there appeared to have arisen within me a sixth, all perfect. In its exercise I found a wild delight—yet a delight still physical, inasmuch as the understanding had in it no part. Motion in the animal frame had fully ceased. No muscle quivered ; no nerve thrilled ; no artery throbbed. But there seemed to have sprung up in the brain *that* of which no words could convey to the merely human intelligence even an indistinct conception. Let me term it a mental pendulous pulsation. It was the moral embodiment of man's abstract idea of *Time*. By the absolute equalisation of this movement—or of such as this—had the cycles of the firmamental orbs themselves been adjusted. By its aid I measured the irregularities of the clock upon the mantel, and of the watches of the attendants. Their tickings came sonorously to my ears. The slightest deviations from the true proportion—and these deviations were omniprevalent—affected me just as violations of abstract truth were wont on earth to affect the moral sense. Although no two of the time-pieces in the chamber struck the individual seconds accurately together, yet I had no difficulty in holding steadily in mind the tones, and the respective momentary errors of each. And this—this keen, perfect, self-existing sentiment of *duration*—this sentiment existing (as man could not possibly have conceived it to exist) independently of any succession of events—this idea—this sixth sense, upspringing from the ashes of the rest, was the first obvious and certain step of the intemporal soul upon the threshold of the temporal Eternity.

It was midnight ; and you still sat by my side. All others had departed from the chamber of Death. They had deposited me in the coffin. The lamps burned flickeringly ; for this I knew by the tremulousness of the monotonous strains. But suddenly these strains diminished in distinctness and in volume. Finally they ceased. The perfume in my nostrils died away. Forms affected my vision no longer. The oppression of the Darkness uplifted itself from my bosom. A dull shot like that of electricity pervaded my frame, and was followed by total loss of the idea of contact. All of what man has termed sense was merged in the sole consciousness of entity, and in the one abiding sentiment of duration. The mortal body had been at length stricken with the hand of the deadly *Decay*.

Yet had not all sentience departed ; for the consciousness and the sentiment remaining supplied some of its functions by a lethargic intuition. I appreciated the direful change now in operation upon the flesh, and, as the dreamer is sometimes aware of the bodily presence of one who leans over him, so, sweet Una, I still dully felt that you sat by my side. So, too, when the noon of the second day came, I was not unconscious of those movements which displaced you from my side, which confined me within the coffin, which deposited me within the hearse, which bore me to the grave, which lowered me within it, which heaped heavily the mould upon me, and which thus left me, in blackness and corruption, to my sad and solemn slumbers with the worm.

And here, in the prison-house which has few secrets to disclose, there rolled away days and weeks and months ; and the soul watched narrowly each second as it flew, and, without effort, took record of its flight—without effort and without object.

A year passed. The consciousness of *being* had grown hourly more indistinct, and that of mere *locality* had, in great measure, usurped its position. The idea of entity was becoming merged in that of *place*. The narrow space immediately surrounding what had been the body was now growing to be the body itself. At length, as often happens to the sleeper (by sleep and its world alone is *Death* imaged)—at length, as sometimes happened on Earth to the deep slumberer, when some flitting light half startled him into awaking, yet left him half enveloped in dreams—so to me, in the strict embrace of the *Shadow*, came *that* light which alone might have had power to startle—the light of enduring *Love*. Men toiled at the grave in which I lay darkling. They upthrew the damp earth.

Upon my mouldering bones there descended the coffin of Una.

And now again all was void. That nebulous light had been extinguished. That feeble thrill had vibrated self into quiescence. Many *lustra* had supervened. Dust had returned to dust. The worm had food no more. The sense of being had at length utterly departed, and there reigned in its stead—instead of all things, dominant and perpetual—the autocrats *Place* and *Time*. For *that* which *was not*—for that which had no form—for that which had no thought—for that which had no sentience—for that which was soundless, yet of which matter formed no portion—for all this nothingness, yet for all this immortality, the grave was still a home, and the corrosive hours, co-mates.

THE END

MADE AND PRINTED BY THE GREYCAINE BOOK MANU-
FACTURING COMPANY LIMITED, WATFORD, HERTS.